Maggie Ford was born in the East End of London but at the age of six she moved to Essex, where she has lived ever since. After the death of her first husband, when she was only twenty-six, she went to work as a legal secretary until she remarried in 1968. She has a son and two daughters, all married; her second husband died in 1984.

She has been writing short stories since the early 1970s.

Also by Maggie Ford:

The Soldier's Bride
A Mother's Love

Maggie
FORD

Call
Nurse
Jenny

EBURY
PRESS

1 3 5 7 9 10 8 6 4 2

First published as *For All the Bright Promise* in 1998 by
Judy Piatkus (Publishers) Ltd

This edition published in 2014 by Ebury Press, an imprint of Ebury Publishing
A Random House Group Company

Copyright © 1998 Maggie Ford

Maggie Ford has asserted her right to be identified as the author of
this Work in accordance with the Copyright, Designs and Patents Act 1988

The Random House Group Limited Reg. No. 954009

Addresses for companies within the Random House Group can be found at
www.randomhouse.co.uk

A CIP catalogue record for this book
is available from the British Library

The Random House Group Limited supports the Forest Stewardship Council®
(FSC®), the leading international forest-certification organisation.
Our books carrying the FSC label are printed on FSC®-certified paper.
FSC is the only forest-certification scheme supported by the leading
environmental organisations, including Greenpeace.
Our paper procurement policy can be found at:
www.randomhouse.co.uk/environment

Printed in Great Britain by Clays Ltd, St Ives plc

ISBN 9781785032189

To buy books by your favourite authors and register for offers visit:
www.randomhouse.co.uk

Chapter 1

From her bedroom window Jenny Ross could look down into Victoria Park Road, where she lived. Her mother preferred the back bedroom, which was far quieter.

The houses at this end, coming off from the busy Cambridge Heath Road, one of the many arteries serving East London, were modest two-up two-down homes with tiny gardens at the back but none in the front. They weren't exactly poor or slummy – being in the better part of Hackney – but they couldn't match the fine houses further along, those that faced or backed on to Victoria Park itself.

Some were double-fronted, some three-storied. All had long if narrow back gardens. They had front gardens with low brick walls and shrubbery to shield them from the noise of poorer East End children who trooped to the park in hordes for a bit of fresh air with packets of sandwiches and bottles of lemonade, or to swim at the lido, costumes tucked under their arms, or to feed the ducks with stale bread or just to hang around the ornate drinking fountain and clink the dented metal cups on chains against its granite sides as loudly as they could. The sound could sometimes be heard clear across the park's lawns and flower beds and playing fields.

At her dressing table Jenny leaned nearer her window to see better the large houses once occupied by the middle class in a previous era: small business people, shop owners, bank clerks, all waited on by armies of domestic staff as their basements still bore witness. Now, in 1939, domestic staff were a thing of the past except for the occasional charlady who lived out and came and went at set times. Vacuum cleaners had taken over, and white vans that collected laundry once a week, returning everything clean and pressed the same day, and dry cleaners for finer clothes.

Lipstick poised, Jenny wasn't thinking much about these things. She was thinking more about one particular house, the first one in that row of houses which she could see well, almost opposite. It too was large, not as large as some of those further along, though fine enough, but in that house lived Matthew Ward with his mother and father and sister Louise.

Jenny had met him through becoming friends with his sister four years ago when she and her mother had first come to live in this area after her father had died. Mumsy, who had leaned on her husband all her life, had been inconsolable. After his death, unable to face living in their house in Approach Road on the other side of the park, it had been decided she and Jenny leave all their painful memories there and move. They hadn't moved far, but it was smaller, more manageable; it was comfortable and held no sad memories though Jenny suspected Mumsy still carried each and every one of them in her heart like little fetters. But had they not come here she'd never have met

Matthew. He had been sixteen then, and she fifteen.

She thought of Matthew now; how her heart raced every time she saw him. She thought of the looming threat of war, as most people were doing. Barrage balloons were already floating in the breeze on the end of their cables like fat floppy silvery fish, soldiers were digging trenches in the parks and anyone with a garden was sinking an Anderson shelter into it. And already children were being evacuated to the country to escape possible air raids. But mostly she thought of Matthew, whether he'd be sent away to fight – if there was a war.

For a moment, she took her eyes off his house, bathed in the golden light of an August evening, the sun still well above the horizon so as to make it still seem afternoon. It was no good watching the house forever. No sign of life from there. He must already have gone while she had been helping Mumsy to clear away the dinner things. Lingering dismay hung heavy inside her but she doggedly applied her lipstick in the dressing-table mirror all the same. Perhaps she could still make it in time.

Her bedside clock stated ten past seven and she was not yet ready. It was a good ten minutes' walk along Cambridge Heath Road to St John's hall. No good getting a bus, she might have to wait ten minutes for that. St John's Friday night dance started at seven thirty, but there was no guarantee that Matthew would even be there, though he'd said he would be.

She had met him closing up his father's electrical shop as she got off the bus from Leadenhall Street where she worked in an accountant's office. He had grinned at her as she passed, totally unaware how her heart had flipped at the sight of him.

'You look a bit hot and bothered, Jenny.'

She hated his shortening of her name. He was the only one among her friends who did. But she smiled. 'So would you be, working in the City. You're lucky. It's been a real baker there today.' She had hastily changed the subject to what had been uppermost in her mind, posing her question as casually as she could. 'Are you going to the hall tonight?'

Most of the young people she knew frequented the events St John's church put on. Matthew was a helper with the Boys' Brigade, she a Girl Guide lieutenant, and both of them, like most of their friends, would help out at bazaars and church fetes and Sunday school. And there was the Friday dance.

Matthew had lifted his broad shoulders in a gesture of doubt. 'I'll see how I feel come seven o'clock. Bit too hot for dancing. Might think of going to the lido for a swim. Did have a date for tonight. Mare Street Regent, but it was only casual. It's too hot to sit in the pictures.'

So that had been that. She had laughed lightly, nodded and moved off, feeling vaguely sad for the casual date waiting about outside the Regent cinema, golden hopes dying as frustration set in. That was how he was, quite unaware of the hearts he broke, hers included. But then, she'd never registered in his book. She was more certain than ever that he wouldn't be at the dance tonight, since his front door remained firmly closed when she glanced yet again towards his house. But just in case . . .

Hardly had the thought touched her than she saw the

door open. And there he was. Her heart that a second before had sunk into her very slippers now rose like a bird leaving a tree's topmost branch.

Mesmerised, she watched the tall, lithe figure stride with an easy grace along the road, crossing it diagonally to pass beneath her window. Gaining Cambridge Heath Road, he turned – and Jenny's heart leaped again for joy – in the direction of St John's.

The second he was out of sight, she jumped into action. Reaching blindly for the pillbox hat that went with her blue flowered summer dress, her unguided fingers caught the small froth of blue net and sent it tumbling to the lino from its already precarious perch on the edge of her dressing table.

'Damn! Bloody, bloody damn!' she burst out. Why was it that the mere sight of him sent her into paroxysms of clumsiness, she who at work was always known for being so calm and collected? One can always rely on Jenny Ross to cope in a crisis – she'd heard it said more than once and even derived a certain modest pride from it. Yet coming anywhere near or even seeing Matthew Ward was enough to make her no longer mistress of her own actions. And now, the mere thought of arriving late for the Friday dance perhaps to find him gone off elsewhere by the time she arrived, perhaps taking most of her friends with him, sent her into a panic she'd rather no one witnessed.

It seemed all the more precious to be near him these days what with the threat of war and young men talking of joining the Territorials, keen as mustard to have a go if the balloon did go up. Nothing their parents said of the

Great War seemed to be making any difference to some of them. And if Matthew joined up, it would be goodbye to her secret joy of being near him.

She had no illusions about herself. Even as she crammed the stylish little hat on her head, she tried not to acknowledge the ginger hair, which some called auburn but which to her could be nothing other than ginger, nor the milky complexion that went with it, typical of those of her colouring. She was well aware of Matthew's preference for dark-haired, petite types.

As far as she could see the hat did nothing for her. She smiled grimly at her reflection in the dressing-table mirror, the raging curls swept severely back from a high forehead into a comb at the nape of her neck; her mouth wide, her nose, in keeping with her firm narrow face, very straight. How she would have preferred to have a short retroussé nose like that of Jean Summerfield, Matthew's current girl, even though such a one would have looked incongruous on the face her critical green eyes now studied. A strong reliable face to match a strong reliable body.

Jenny gave a huge sigh. Well, make the best of a bad job. Mirror, mirror on the wall . . .

'I wish I was dark-haired and petite,' she'd remarked to Matthew's sister only a few weeks ago, her thoughts still centred on Jean Summerfield.

'Why?' Louise had said in her blunt, straightforward way. Louise was the type who offended quite a lot of people by her almost epic frankness, rather like her mother, never seeing it as offensive, though people knew where they were with her. Not one to falsely flatter, also like her mother, one could always rely on the truth with Louise Ward. The way she had said 'why' had given Jenny a certain encouragement to open her heart to her.

'It's the sort Matthew usually falls for,' she'd admitted.

'And you'd like my brother to fall for you?'

That had been just a little too candid and Jenny remembered cringing inwardly, wishing she'd bitten off her tongue. 'Of course not. It's just that I hate being ginger and tall. I hate my face and my frame. I'm so ungainly.'

'You're not ungainly,' Louise had said without glancing up from the dusty old church hall bunting they'd been sorting out ready for yet another church fete to raise funds.

When she hadn't answered, Louise, still busy unravelling strings of faded triangular pennants, had gone on: 'I suppose you are tall. What, five foot eight? But you've got a nice figure, and there's nothing wrong with your looks as I can see.' Louise had stopped what she was doing to search her mind for a comparison, 'A bit like Katharine Hepburn . . .'

'For heaven's sake, Louise!' Jenny had broken in with a self-critical laugh. If the girl had been a natural flatterer she could have been forgiven, but this sweeping statement set Jenny, crouching beside her, back on her heels. 'I can't compare with a *film star*.' Hepburn of Hollywood with her high cheekbones and dancing eyes was one thing, Jenny Ross from across the road with her too-curly hair and her wide shoulders was quite another. 'For heaven's sake, Louise, don't be so silly.'

But Louise had looked up from sorting bunting to

regard her closely, comparison to screen idols forgotten. 'You haven't got a *thing* about my brother, have you?'

'No.' Jenny had also put aside Katharine Hepburn, her face warm before the younger girl's shrewd smile. Louise never smirked or grinned. She smiled, as she had then, in a lofty way, the way her mother did, making the recipient want to crawl under a stone.

'I think you have. I think you fancy him.'

'No, I don't.'

One couldn't go on denying hotly. She could only appeal to Louise to say nothing to Matthew of what she'd after all merely surmised.

Now she stared in the mirror, wanting so much to believe Louise's unintentional flattery, but the green eyes beneath the flaming hair merely gazed back in disparagement. Beautiful? Striking? What man, and by what man she knew she meant Matthew, would ever throw himself at *her* feet?

Jenny smiled grimly at her reflection, and turning from its cruelty, she snatched up her handbag from the bed and hurried downstairs to kiss her mother before leaving the house.

She found her on hands and knees in the kitchen, sleeves rolled to the elbows, one plump arm wearily describing soapy circles on the linoleum with a scrubbing brush. Disbelief sharpened Jenny's tone.

'Good God, Mumsy, what on earth are you doing?'

The soft rounded face looked up, downy cheeks flushed from her task, apologetic hazel eyes meeting her daughter's. To Jenny, gazing in horror, she looked much older than her fifty-two years as with a tremulous sigh she sank back on to her ankles. 'The floor looked a bit smeary, dear. I . . .'

'But I washed it all over this morning, Mumsy, before I left for work.'

Whatever possessed her mother? She was forever pottering around the house, doing things that never needed to be done, often after Jenny herself had done them. It made a mockery of all the help she gave.

'I just thought a small wipe-over.'

'With soap and scrubbing brush?' It was hard to mask irritation, only too aware of what lay behind all this. 'How can I go out while you're tiring yourself out completely, doing things like this?' It was a way to keep her here, and if she wasn't careful, it would.

'Leave it, Mumsy. Go and rest.'

Mrs Ross drew the back of a wet hand limply across her brow. 'I do really feel I must. I'm so hot.'

'I don't wonder.' Jenny moderated her tone, understanding replacing annoyance. Two years was far too short a span to expect her mother to get over losing Daddy. She herself hadn't yet quite got over it. But she had a job to go to, lots of diversion, friends in the evenings. Mummy had nothing. The woman next door was as deaf as a post. The young couple on the other side had their parents, brothers and sisters, a host of friends, all of them visiting and in turn to be visited, too absorbed in their own pursuits to bother with a woman who tended to wrap herself in her self-imposed shroud of isolation. As for those in their big new houses lining the park, they

with their bridge parties and their bowling and tennis and
their theatres, to them those in the smaller houses were
a world away, seldom encountered for long enough to
exchange a word or two. Mumsy was a lonely woman. It
was cruel to go off and desert her right now, and Jenny
would quite readily have given up her evening to keep her
company in normal circumstances, but tonight Matthew
was drawing her as a lodestone attracts iron.

Relieving her mother of the scrubbing brush, Jenny
tipped the pail of suds down the sink. 'Go and sit in the
back garden, Mumsy. Take a book with you,' she ordered,
feeling a pang of sorrow at the feeble ploy to keep her
here. 'It's still lovely and sunny by the back door.'

Installed in a deckchair in front of the small border of
bright annuals which Jenny herself had planted, Mrs Ross
gazed up at her. 'You won't be too late home, will you,
dear?'

'No, Mumsy, I won't.'

She was rarely late home – usually eleven at the latest,
knowing her mother's dread of being alone, but the
regularity of the query irked a little.

'I wish you didn't have to go out, dear.'

'I always go out on Friday night.'

'I suppose you'll be out tomorrow as well.'

'Just swimming, that's all. I'll have the rest of the
weekend with you.'

Mrs Ross heaved a sigh that said how quickly the
weekend would go before she must spend the coming
week on her own until Jenny came home of an evening.
But before the matter could develop further, Jenny dropped

a hasty kiss on the flaccid cheek and went back into the kitchen to mop up the suds on the floor.

It hardly seemed worth going out now. Matthew would already be there. What if he'd taken it into his head to go off somewhere else? She'd have no idea where, and without him, the dance would go down for her like a soggy bun.

She had to at least try. Fraught with anxiety she called goodbye to her mother and hurried off. Turning into Cambridge Heath Road, she caught her breath in a huge gulp of relief. Jean Summerfield was just in front of her, sauntering along as though she had all the time in the world to spare. Breaking into a run, Jenny caught her up.

'Gosh, am I glad to see you,' she burst out, falling into step, already flushed from her short spurt on this hot evening. 'I did think I was going to be late. Matthew's already left. You know what he's like. He could go off anywhere without waiting for us.'

'Oh, he'll wait for me.'

Jean was a willowy brunette. Looking cool as a cucumber, she turned an extremely pretty oval face to Jenny, her voice a purr of self-assurance. She'd been going out with Matthew for nearly two months, a long time for any girl where he was concerned.

Jenny wasn't so sure he'd wait. He might be going out with Jean but he'd been seen on two occasions with that blonde Middleton girl from St Anne's Close, a fact Jean shrugged off with affected nonchalance. Jenny reflected that had she been treated like that, she would have given Matthew his marching orders long ago no matter how it

broke her heart. Trouble was, Matthew's dreamy brown
eyes hardly ever strayed in her direction, not in *that way*,
so there'd never be a chance of her putting that valiant
promise to the test.

'Marie Middleton told me yesterday she'd be there,' she
remarked, more from the need to move Jean along faster
than from any sort of spite, but Jean flicked her a look
saturated with venom.

'For your information, she's not his sort. He doesn't
care for blondes. Or *redheads* for that matter, if you want
to know.'

The dig wasn't lost on Jenny and she felt ruffled. She
was no competition. 'I just happened to see him eyeing her
at the dance last week, that's all.'

She found herself rewarded by another glare, the small
pretty face with its retroussé nose and bright red lips
waspish. 'You keep your eyes to yourself. Dennis Cox is
your partner. Anyway, Matthew told me he thinks I'm the
tops. So there!'

Even so, her stride had quickened, past the Council
offices, past the Bethnal Green Children's Museum set
back from the road, on their right a train travelling the
viaduct above the small shabby shops, filling the air with
smoke and a sooty smell. They covered the half-mile to
their destination far more quickly than Jenny ever guessed
a small-built girl could, and she had to hurry to keep up
with Jean, who was rattled.

Finally reaching St John's church at the Salmon and
Ball crossroads, they were both hot, Jean's cheeks glowing
prettily, Jenny's a fiery flush. In the hall, the pianist,

drummer and saxophonist on the tiny stage, with its brown curtains hanging limp and dusty with East End smoke, were still sorting out their arrangements. The hall, with its faded religious prints around the walls and its small grimy windows, echoed with the garbled conversation of young people perched on splintery bentwood chairs waiting for the dance to start, girls in bright dresses, boys with hair slicked back with Brylcreem, their suits well pressed, jackets already hanging on chairbacks to reveal well-ironed white shirts.

Early arrivals had already commandeered the few folding tables on which to put their soft drinks and crisps. Jenny's gaze flicked anxiously to each one, knowing that if Matthew was still here, he would certainly have got himself a table. He had, of course – one of the better tables at the far end of the hall, near the band.

Sharing the table were Freddy Perry and Eileen Wilcox, who only had eyes for each other these days, and Dennis Cox. The latecomers were immediately spotted by Matthew who was instantly up from his seat, beckoning, his handsome face alive with welcome as they came over, his lips parting in a wide smile that revealed even white teeth.

'Thought you two would never arrive.' It was a full-toned voice that reflected a zest for life and the natural impatience of a soul seldom in need of rest. 'We got our drinks before it got busy.' He eyed the bar at the far end with its two ladies serving a growing queue. 'What would you like?'

Jean dropped into the seat he'd vacated, very sure of

herself. 'God, it's hot! A nice long cool lemonade, darling, large as they can make it.'

Jenny hesitated, wondering if she should offer to pay for herself or not. She heard him chuckle wickedly.

'Come on, Jenny, make up your mind.'

His well-spoken accent made the playful quip sound flippant. Those living in such as Victoria Park Road tended not to have the accents of the East End. Matthew had once said that his mother had been a lady's maid before she'd married. Jenny supposed that the mannerisms of her then upper-class employers must have rubbed off on her, though to her mind Mrs Ward boasted just too many airs and graces. Not that it bothered Jenny. She was well spoken too, her family as good as any. And all her friends spoke very much the same, so there was really nothing for his mother to be snobbish about. Thank God Matthew wasn't. He even joked about it, apparently to his mother's face as well as behind her back. Still, the quip took Jenny a little off guard.

Her already bright flush deepened. 'Can I have lemonade too?' Her thin enquiry annoyed her. His ringing laugh made her wince.

'What makes you think you can't?'

It wasn't his fault. She was an idiot. It was being so close to those velvet-brown eyes. Flustered, she hurriedly sat down next to Dennis Cox.

Dennis immediately began to monopolise her with an account of his new job. Coming straight from college armed with diplomas and bags of hope, he had landed himself a position in a firm of London solicitors. Listening to him, Jenny could well imagine him in years to come, bustling from court to court, bundles of legal briefs under his arm, probably having grown much plumper than he was now.

He was still expounding on his future when Matthew returned with two glasses of lemonade for the girls and two of ginger beer for himself and Dennis. Jenny smirked covertly. She'd seen the drill before. He probably had a tiny flask of whisky in the inside pocket of his jacket now hanging over the chairback. The moment the ginger beer was gone, empty glasses would be surreptitiously replenished by the contents of that flask, the same colour as the soft drink. Lots of the boys did it, not enough to get drunk on, but enough to be lively. If St John's vicar were to know, he would have a fit.

Matthew was lifting a mocking eyebrow at Dennis. 'Why don't you give the mouth a rest, Cox, and do some work for your living? There's two more drinks on the counter, and some crisps. Go and get them for us, eh?'

Dennis looked affronted. 'See here – I've been sweltering all day in the City.' The amiable laugh at his protest provoked even more indignation from him. 'All right for some. All you do is drive about in your dad's van all day. So what happened to that smashing job you were offered by Marconi's when you left college last year? I thought you were going to be big in radio communications or something.'

If he had hoped to rattle his opponent, he was disappointed. 'Turned it down in the end, old man. Dad's shop takes priority. His chest plays him up sometimes and there's only him to run it. He's not getting any younger.'

'And of course it'll be yours one day, won't it?'

The remark had an insinuating ring to it and although Matthew's easy grin did not alter, the dark eyes adopted a fractionally harsher glow. 'I don't need to prove I've more brains than you by sweating in some office.'

'You're just plain lazy,' Dennis sneered.

'I probably am.' The good humour had returned. 'Come on, Cox, get cracking. It's on the counter, all paid for.'

Slipping into a spare seat beside Jean, he left the peevish Dennis no option but to do as ordered. Eileen and Freddy, lost in each other, hadn't caught the small note of dissension, their hands hidden under the table.

Matthew grinned. 'Now then, you two. You're in company, remember? There's a time and place for everything, you know.' As their hands came back into sight, the pair looking sheepish, he turned his gaze on Jenny.

'You look nice tonight, Jenny. Blue suits that hair of yours.' The impish grin seemed to her to belie the compliment.

'You mean ginger?' she corrected, but was halted by the unexpected change in his expression.

'Some girls would give their eye teeth for that colour,' he said slowly, his scrutiny of her so deep and personal that she felt her cheeks flush and her heart give a leap. But Jean's brittle voice cut in.

'Matthew, I'm still waiting for my lemonade.'

The glass was within arm's reach, but he must have realised it was the only way she could get his attention at this moment for as he pushed the glass towards her, he treated her to a low 'mee-ow'. Jenny wanted to laugh out loud as Jean tossed her short dark curls in pique, a pout spoiling her pretty face. It was good to know she wasn't alone in getting the raw edge of Matthew's sometimes far too caustic wit.

When Dennis returned with the remaining refreshments, vague hostilities faded. The hall was growing uncomfortably hotter by the minute with so few windows capable of being opened. The band was still warming up, sheet music was being turned, scales on the sax being tentatively tested, the drums tapped at intervals. Dennis turned his attention to studying his already half-drunk ginger beer, eager for the small tot of whisky to liven it up.

'What do you think of this Hitler lark then? Me, I think he'll go into Poland, whatever Chamberlain says. If you ask me, we're being cocked a snook at. I don't relish giving up a brand-new job, but I'd be willing to go and fight him. The RAF for me. What about you, Matthew?'

'Haven't given it much thought.' Matthew's tone was airy.

'You should, old man. Don't want to sit by too long and get roped into any old thing when they start conscripting. Get in quick, I say. We're all officer material, you know, with our education.'

Jean gave a little giggle, pique forgotten, and squeezed her partner's arm. 'You'd make a spiffing officer, darling.'

'Will it be the RAF for you too?' Dennis was looking at him, waiting for a reply. 'It's the only service to be in. Great uniforms.'

His quarry leaned back in his chair, squinting through the shafts of dust-laden sunlight at the yellowed windows. It was as though he hadn't heard a word of anything that had been said.

'Ye gods,' he sighed, his favourite expression. 'It's bloody hot in here.'

'It's been a hot summer all round,' Jenny offered quickly, all she could think to say with an uncomfortable sense of embarrassment at the way he seemed to have neatly evaded Dennis's question.

But Dennis appeared to have forgotten his own question. 'Where's that flask then? You did bring it?'

'Does it matter?' Matthew grimaced as the band at last sprang into action with a ragged tempo that echoed tinnily around the hall. 'Who wants to bother with this rubbish anyway?'

'I do, Matthew,' Jean protested. 'Listen, darling, it's a waltz.'

He was an excellent dancer, as he was excellent at most things, and Jean was aching to show off in his arms. But he continued to frown at the tempo that would fail to allow him full enjoyment of his skill.

'I know.' His face brightened on a flash of inspiration. 'Why don't we go swimming?'

'Swimming?' There was an echo of disbelief from everyone except the couple still locked in each other's gaze.

'Victoria Park Lido. This time of year it's open till late. We could pop home, pick up our togs and be there inside fifteen minutes. Who's game?'

'Me.' If there was a sport Jenny felt happy with, it was swimming. But Jean was pouting again. Water would spoil those tramline Marcel waves of hers, even under a swimming cap. But rather than lose him this evening as she might well do, she grudgingly agreed. Dennis too had little love of water, but he agreed, not wanting to appear soft.

Matthew regarded the two lovers. 'A dash of cold water wouldn't do you two any harm. Fancy going for a swim?'

'What?' They looked blank.

'We're going to the lido. You two want to come?'

For a moment they regarded each other, coming to a silent mutual agreement. 'No . . . Not really.'

Matthew's laugh dismissed them. 'Right then, it's us four.'

It was a dash to get swimming costumes and towels, then back to meet at the park gates. Matthew, with one arm around Jean's shoulders, led the way, Jenny and Dennis following behind.

The evening belonged to Jenny, with Jean, eager to preserve her Marcel waves, sitting on the side of the pool, just her feet stirring the water as she posed hopefully for Matthew's attention.

Dennis, after lowering himself tentatively to his well-fleshed waist in the shallow end, pulled himself out again, shivering with the shock of cold water after the heat outside, then went and sat beside Jean. Matthew was unsympathetic.

'Come on, Cox, shut your eyes and jump. There's enough flesh on you to keep you warm on an iceberg!'

He himself had taken a flying header into the deep end, surfacing among the other swimmers to flick water from his dark hair with a brisk toss of his head before making it the length of the baths with a fast crawl to confront the shivering Dennis, his taunting laugh echoing over the surrounding tree tops above the cries and shouts of the other bathers.

Dennis declined to join him so he swam off again, deftly avoiding those around him, Jenny close behind matching stroke for stroke, until he hoisted himself out at the far end and made for the diving boards. Treading water, she watched the lean figure appear on the top board, poised, waiting for a clear space below before launching itself off, piercing the surface like an arrow. The skill and grace took her breath away. At the same time she felt a small sense of foreboding take hold. He took his physical assets so much for granted, that slim tireless body fashioned to perfection, that abundance of health, that quick alert brain. War was coming, unavoidable. Young men like him would be taken to fight for their country. She had heard her own father's account of the last war, the trenches, the mud, death from disease, bullets, shells, gas; men blinded, maimed, the rest of their lives ruined.

As a child she had shuddered from her own imaginings after listening to such talk. Now she shuddered again, seeing perfect bodies reduced to utter wrecks, bodies like Matthew's. She swam slowly now, trying to push away such visions, but they persisted. Men with such bright promise to their lives, so many blessings to look forward to, plucked off the fair tree like ripe fruit. True, there were those who had, and those who had not. Matthew was one to whom everything had been given; it seemed almost unfair that so many blessings should be heaped on one person while another knew little but ill health and hard luck. Yet how much worse would it be for someone like Matthew, with everything, if his happy world should crumble than for another already equipped for adversity? With no experience of how cruel this world could be, couldn't Matthew be more stricken than the already ill-fated should he come face to face with the worst aspects of this world?

Jenny pulled her thoughts up sharply. It was this threat of war. It might even yet be averted and there'd be no more need for morbid reflection. Matthew was climbing the diving board again. This time she turned away, again plunging into her own pool of dejection. War was no respecter of the beautiful and Matthew was indeed . . .

Her feet were suddenly tugged from below and she instinctively gulped air before going under, surfacing again to see him grinning into her face.

'You . . . you . . .' she spluttered at him.

Dejection swept away, she grabbed for his hair, a move he easily evaded. Together they wrestled, spluttered, yelled, laughed. His hands were cool on her body, his arms strong, hoisting her from the water as the whistle sounded for the lido to close. Jean was jealous, purposefully ignoring her. No doubt Matthew would kiss her into a better frame of mind when he took her to her door to caress her in a way Jenny could only dream of. But this evening had been hers. She was content, even to the point of allowing Dennis to drop a kiss on her cheek without shrugging him off, but no more than that.

They dawdled across the park, taking their time with the air still warm, lounging on a bench talking, giggling, Matthew bent on petting Jean into a forgiving mood. Then they went on in the last crimson glow of this midsummer evening which promised another fine day tomorrow. Matthew cocked a weather eye at the darkening red streaks, remarking, 'Red sky at night, shepherds alight!' His humour was whimsical as always, his mind on the rewards Jean would bestow on him for all the attention he intended to shower on her at her door.

When the friends parted company, Jenny glanced at the purpling sky promising its fine tomorrow. How many tomorrows before the sky darkened forever with Matthew far away? She firmed her lips and shrugged away the thought.

Chapter 2

With the metallic voice of Prime Minister Neville Chamberlain fading away, followed by a defiant rendering of 'God Save the King,' Jenny turned her gaze to her mother's face. It was chalk-white.

'What are we going to do?' For some reason the futile question got under Jenny's skin. She got up from the armchair where she had been sitting taking in what the sad, disillusioned, somewhat quavering voice had to say, hardly able to believe its message no matter that they'd seen it coming for weeks and especially these last few days, and switched off the radio.

'Not much we can do, is there? Sit tight, I suppose.'

'It won't be like the last war.' Mrs Ross, still huddled in her armchair, looked like a plump little elf amid the silence that seemed to have closed in around them now the wireless had been turned off. 'That was the first time ordinary English civilians had ever been bombed. We can expect them to do it again. And this time they'll use gas on us. Why were we issued with those horrible gas masks last year if they didn't think it would be used against ordinary people? Evil-smelling rubber thing, it smells like gas itself.'

'For goodness' sake, Mumsy.' She tried to be flippant. 'How would you know how gas smells? Except what comes out of the stove. It's all a storm in a teacup. Everyone says that once England has shown her teeth and stopped appeasing him, Hitler will back down. It's a show of strength, that's all. In a month this will all be behind us. Now I'm going to make a cup of tea. I think we both need it.'

Wishing she felt as certain as she hoped she sounded, Jenny went into the kitchen to put the kettle on, followed by her mother who had herself into gear at last. She was sure there'd be more alarmist sounds from her, but thankfully she said nothing, going about the task of setting out the teacups and saucers, the clink of china unreal in the odd sort of silence that lay over them. It was far too beautiful a sunny Sunday morning for such news.

She was on the point of emptying the teapot of its dregs from the last brew made just before Chamberlain's awaited announcement when there came a strange sound, a distant wailing, followed by another, much closer. For a second it was unidentifiable. Then Jenny realised.

'Oh, God, Mumsy, it's an air-raid siren.'

They stared at each other, her mother with fingertips bent against her lips as though to stop their sudden trembling, Jenny with the teapot hanging loose by its handle from her momentarily paralysed fingers.

Her flesh had gone cold, the rising goose pimples conveyed an actual sensation, the fear that clutched at Jenny's heart was like cold fingers attempting to restrict its pumping, pumping so heavy that it felt as though it were in her throat.

It was her mother who first came to life, swinging away from her with a cry, making for the hallway and the front door. She had flung it open before Jenny could collect herself enough to chase after her, catching her halfway down the few stone steps to the street.

'No, not that way. We must go down into the Anderson shelter.'

A man's voice was calling to them from across the road. 'Over here – into our shelter.'

It was Mr Ward standing at his gate beckoning to them. After a brief hesitation, Jenny took her mother's arm, hurrying her diagonally across the road. It would be far more comforting and, even though erroneously, it felt safer to be with others than the two of them all alone in the darkness of the newly built shelter put in for them by a paid man, having to sit by candlelight with the dank shelter's earthy smell all around them. Mr Ward would never know the relief with which she hurried towards him.

He was a tall man, in his early fifties she reckoned, who must have been an extremely handsome man in his youth – still was, she supposed. He looked very much like Matthew except that he was very thin and looked drawn. Matthew said his father had received a touch of mustard gas in the last war, leaving him with a slightly weak chest. He seemed a kindly man, and always nodded to her or her mother when passing them in the street, not like his wife who, though she would always nod too, left one with a feeling of inferiority. However, Jenny was sure she had no idea of the effect she had on others. She struck Jenny as somehow being older than her husband though she probably wasn't: it was just her attitude that made her seem so. Thirty years ago one might have called her a handsome woman and she still carried herself like a duchess. Jenny was sure she had a kind heart for all that but she had never felt at ease meeting her in the street. And now she was being asked to enter her home – or at least her Anderson shelter.

'We do have our own,' she explained as she came up to Mr Ward. 'We had it put in for us last week.'

He held an arm out as though shepherding them. 'Even so, we can't see two women alone down one of them. This is a time for us all to help each other. Come along.'

They followed him nervously through a narrow side gate into a small, neatly laid out town garden surrounded by trees and bushes whose dusty leaves screened it from neighbours' eyes. Mrs Ward liked privacy.

'Will Mrs Ward mind?' Jenny queried behind him.

'Why should she mind? We should all stick together in these times.' He sounded so like Matthew. Jenny fell silent as she followed him to the mound at the end of the garden that now covered the raw corrugated iron structure half sunk into the ground, its straight sides and curved top precisely fitted together, the soil already made a little less unsightly by a transplantation of geraniums and Michaelmas daisies. Her own, so far covered only by bare earth, had more the appearance of a wallowing elephant as it awaited a few plants to disguise its grimly utilitarian purpose.

She watched as he handed her mother down the four wooden steps to below ground, then herself. There was a curtain across the square entrance covering a small door already fitted. Hers so far had just a curtain. The door stood open and as she entered Mr Ward let the curtain fall back to its proper position, to shut out any light that might be seen at night by enemy bombers looking for a target. She was amazed at the light there actually was. An electric bulb in the centre of the curved roof, shaded by a small but beautiful orange lampshade, cast a cosy glow. But then, Mr Ward knew all about electricity, didn't he? The interior, measuring six foot by eight, was made to seem much narrower by double bunks lining either side to accommodate this family of four. At the far end a small table with a red chequered cloth held a decorative oil lamp; a square mirror propped against the back wall reflected everything back to give the illusion of a less cramped space. Above it a shelf bolted to the corrugated iron held provisions for a night's stay. The cold iron was painted pink, and a pink brocade curtain partly shielded the back wall for an extra sense of snugness. Thus a cosy retreat had been fashioned from what could have been an uncomfortable hole in the ground. Even the pervading mustiness of damp earth was allayed somewhat by a large bowl of home-made pot-pourri beside the lamp.

Mrs Ward was standing by the table, her posture very upright, her expression stiff, the unwilling hostess compelled to receive uninvited guests, which Jenny felt she and her mother must be. They were intruders into this extension of her home, which this musty-smelling underground shelter with its effort to appear cosy indeed was. Yet behind the stiffness lay an attempt to hide her fear for the moment, the air-raid warning having now faded away to leave an eerie silence outside.

'Thank you so much for having us,' Mrs Ross began in a small voice, she too feeling the tension, not just because of this impending air raid. In return she received a wintry smile but no word of welcome.

Jenny stood uncertain, wishing they hadn't accepted Mr Ward's invitation. In their own damp, half-finished shelter they'd at least have felt at ease, if isolated. She was glad Louise was also there.

Crouched forward on a lower bunk so that her head wouldn't knock against the one above her, her arms clasped about her chest in foreboding, Louise looked as though she were making some sort of obeisance at her mother's feet. But there the impression of humility ended. A younger version of her mother in many ways, Louise at seventeen bore all the hallmarks of becoming a staid, strait-laced woman by her forties. Already she had a tendency to bossiness and certainly a way of managing people whether they liked it or not. She was nevertheless a generous-hearted person, which Jenny imagined she owed to her father, and she had found herself liking Louise from the very start. Mumsy said once, when she had mentioned it, that Louise was rather like a black widow spider! But Jenny considered Louise's way of calling a spade a spade very commendable and people could not be held responsible for who they took after at birth. She was heartily glad, though, that Matthew took after his father rather than his mother.

'Not made a bad job of it, have we?' Mr Ward was

saying with pride in his voice. 'Me and Matthew put it up between us, but the titivating bits his mother did, and a great job she's made of it too. Never know how long we might have to stay down here if things get really bad.'

He gestured to the other lower bunk. 'Well, sit down then, both of you. Make yourselves at home.'

'Where is Matthew?' Jenny asked as she sat.

'Out with a friend, apparently.' Mrs Ward's reply was chilly, sharp, it seemed to Jenny, disapproving of her son's absence at such a perilous time. Jenny fell quiet. She might feel safe here, yet in the chill that had descended she wished she could be anywhere but here.

Her mother ventured, 'Young people seldom understand,' only to be met with more bleak silence, and in this vein the five sat facing each other, the Wards on one side, Miss and Mrs Ross on the other, each with their own thoughts, waiting for the first distant roar from swarms of enemy bombers they were sure were coming to annihilate them all.

Every now and again, her mother sighed, 'Oh, dear.' Mr Ward cleared his throat quite a lot, now and again smiling encouragement at them as they waited. Mrs Ward's face remained stony, but Jenny noticed how she twisted her hands together at one or two unguarded moments, and despite her own fear that persisted in clutching at her stomach, she found herself looking on the woman as being capable of human emotions after all. She knew so little about her, wondered how Matthew and his sister could live with such an unapproachable woman, except that she was their mother and they were used to her, she supposed.

But over and above her fear of the unknown beyond this shelter, she counted the minutes when she could be away from here.

Relief was a surge of joy in more ways than one when after only ten minutes – though it had seemed like an hour – the sweet single note of the all clear sounded. Everything that a moment before had seemed suspended in a sort of bubble of waiting, sprang back into life. Voices could be heard beyond the shelter. The whole street seemed to be alive with people as Jenny and her mother emerged to go back home.

She had never seen Victoria Park Road like this before, neighbours standing about in groups discussing where they'd been and what they had been doing at the moment of the siren sounding, speculating if it had been just a false alarm or not.

For Jenny it was an event she felt she'd never forget, not so much because of the fright as the camaraderie that appeared after it. Also it had been her first-ever glimpse into Matthew's home, at least as near as she imagined she'd ever be to it. A little like an eavesdropper, she had watched those twisting hands of Mrs Ward as she'd sat on the edge of one of the lower bunks, had been given an ever-so-brief peep behind the barrier she appeared to put up between herself and everyone else. Although Matthew hadn't been there, just being in the Wards' Anderson shelter had made Jenny feel closer to him than she had ever felt before.

*

Everyone had grown closer that Sunday. Men who would hardly have nodded the time of day to each other on their way to business, their privacy a virtual barbed wire fence, now passed on their observations of what the next few months might have in store for everyone. Women from the larger houses were even nodding more often to those in the smaller ones, snobbery magically put aside. Only on the bus going each day into the City were people still reserved, minding their own business, reading their paper, staring out of the window, perhaps smoking their pipes and cigarettes a little more reflectively, isolated from each other, apart from those riding together, Cockney vowels ringing loud, and of course the cheery voice of the bus or tram conductor calling for fares and pinging his ticket machine.

Everything was changing. The instant blackout extinguished all light but for the dimmest of blueish light in buses and trains. London's main railway stations were alive with men and women in uniform, with loved ones saying goodbye, husbands embracing wives, fathers kissing their children, mothers clinging to their sons, sweethearts interlocked. For some reason public transport became erratic; no one could be sure of getting to their destination on time any more. Not that civilians had many destinations to go to other than to work, since access to the coast just for pleasure was now forbidden unless one had a relation living there or specific reason to go. Seaside holidays stopped.

Everything stopped. On the wireless the BBC closed down its regional services, sticking to just one, the Home Service; schools closed, places of entertainment shut down to dissuade people from gathering in any one place for fear of hundreds being killed at once in an air raid.

St John's Girl Guide and Brownie troop and its Boys' Brigade ceased to meet, most of the children evacuated anyway from the East End to the country, away from bombs expected to fall on the population in a matter of days or weeks. The second wave of children to go since the Munich scare of 1938, they toddled off with their gas masks and their packets of sandwiches for their journey into the safe heart of the countryside, labels fastened to coat collars, mothers anxiously watching them go and wondering if they would ever see them again. Witnessing the scenes at Liverpool Street Station, and the looks on those mothers' faces as she passed on her way to work, Jenny could almost feel the heaviness of their hearts.

'It all seems so strange. I still can't get used to all this.'

Mrs Ross was helping paste strips of gummed brown paper tape in the recommended criss-cross pattern on the window panes, supposedly to help stop flying glass from the effect of a bomb blast.

'It makes the windows look so horrible. I don't like it at all.'

'It doesn't matter if we like it or not.' The gum tasted awful; Jenny pulled a face as she licked. She had tried resorting to a saucer of water to dip the gummed side in, but it was awkward, far quicker to steel herself to licking. 'They say it's safer. They say just one shard of flying glass can kill. I don't fancy being slashed by something like that, not even in a small way.'

Not that there had been any air raids since that first false alarm, a stray French plane at the time unidentified over the Channel, they had been told. But it was better to be safe than sorry.

Mumsy had already complained about the blackout regulations. Their own efforts were still temporary, made with flimsy frames of batten wood and cardboard with black paper pinned to them, and they had draped their shades with thick material for the time being to lessen any light that might escape. The result was having to sit in a dingy room and that in itself lowered the spirits. In time they would get proper heavy material instead of the present light curtains that let out a little too much light.

Of all the deprivations and inconveniences that had arisen, blackout was the worst. Air-raid wardens already knocked on doors ordering erring occupants in superior tones to 'Put out that light!' A lot of things irked, not the least of them, Jenny calculated, the total change in her social life.

With the departure of London's East End children the young men went off too. Of Jenny's little set Dennis Cox said goodbye and joined the RAF. He asked if he could write to her and Jenny had half nodded, rather hoping he might forget once he got out into the wide world and met other girls. She couldn't tell him she felt somewhat relieved to see him go. She had never really fancied him, but had just been naturally thrown together with him, and consequently was sometimes thought of as his partner.

Jean Summerfield's parents, deciding that London was

a dangerous place, went to relatives in Devon, to fulfil a longstanding dream of a cottage by the sea.

Jean's going was rather heartening. Although Jenny had never presented any competition for Jean where Matthew was concerned, Jean would nevertheless no longer be around to disconcert her.

Freddy, who'd enlisted as a part-time soldier during the Munich crisis before he had begun going seriously with Eileen, was called up immediately. Hastily, he and Eileen planned a registry office wedding, and leaving her pregnant, though neither knew that, he went off into the Pay Corps.

Of the group only she and Matthew remained. Obviously he was perfect for conscription under the new National Service Act, but unlike the other two he made no move to volunteer, much to Jenny's confusion. She had expected him to be the very first to do so but now she remembered the day when he had hurriedly and so noticeably – at least to her – changed the subject when Dennis had asked what service he had chosen to go into.

Already three weeks into this war, August and that particular Friday dance seemed years away. Yet every time she saw Matthew, that incident became like yesterday and the embarrassment she had felt then burned as acutely as ever, now also coupled with bewilderment. It was her mother, who like most meek souls always managed to extract a confidence from the most private of people, who treated Jenny to Mrs Ward's admission of dismay at her son's odd reluctance to join up.

'She really expected him to apply for a commission

by now,' Mrs Ross related to her daughter as she treadled away on her sewing machine, making blackout curtains to replace the black paper they'd had to use as an emergency measure.

'I don't actually expect it's cowardice, but I'm sure she feels a certain embarrassment about it. She's a person who needs to hold her head up in front of others but how can she while young Matthew is still hanging round? He *must* know he'll be called up sooner or later. I imagine he's thinking right now what a pity it was he didn't take that Marconi job as she wanted him to – he would have had a reserved occupation by now and no one to query his remaining at home.'

Jenny was threading tape through a finished curtain. She let it drop on to her lap. 'That's unfair, Mumsy.'

'I don't think so, dear.' Mrs Ross gave an extra push down on the foot treadle and with a final spurt pulled the fabric free of the machine needle, snipping off the cotton. 'If you ask me, I think he's quaking in his shoes in case he's called up.'

'That's not true, Mumsy!'

'True or not, I think he's being rather silly. He'll end up being pushed into any old thing – something quite unsavoury, with all the riffraff. All that education gone to waste. Unless of course he *is* hoping he'll be deferred. He could be, with his father not in good health and needing help with his business. But I think it unlikely. I hear there are some who are applying for deferment *and* getting away with it. Perhaps that is what's on his mind.'

Extracting the last curtain from the machine, she stood

up, stretching her back painfully. After she had laid the curtain across the chair she lifted the domed cover of the sewing machine back into place. 'There – that's done.'

'Matthew wouldn't do a thing like that,' Jenny said, even though her mother seemed no longer to be listening, apparently more anxious to measure her finished work against the upstairs windows. But her taciturn departure left behind waves of doubt pounding in Jenny's breast. What if her mother was right? Meek she might be. Indecisive and dependent she might be. Silly she wasn't.

Angrily, Jenny fought to push away the doubts her mother had sown. The curtain destined for this room idle in her lap, she gazed out of the living-room window at the warm blue of a late September sky. Each pane was criss-crossed by gummed strips of brown paper but she hardly noticed.

'He must have his reasons,' she said aloud several times to the blue sky beyond. 'He must have.' But it wasn't enough.

When the doubts her mother had voiced, innocently she was sure, began to bear down on her like a ton weight, she approached Louise. As his sister she must know more of the inner workings of Matthew's mind than anyone. Approaching his mother was unthinkable. His father would probably be very hurt by any reference to his son even being thought suspect; the last thing Jenny wanted to do was to hurt anyone with her prying. But she had to unburden her doubts on someone. Louise was the most likely candidate.

She caught her on Thursday evening in the church hall,

sorting out old Brownie uniforms for storing away for the duration. Louise looked up at her approach and smiled, a smile closely resembling that of Mrs Ward. 'Can I help you, Jenny?' Not 'Hello, what are you doing here?'

She smiled – there was no harm in Louise – and launched into her question. 'I was wondering about Matthew. Is he thinking of joining up yet?'

Louise's face went suddenly frosty. She seemed to age ten years, become Jenny's senior. 'Why don't you ask him? It's his business.'

That was all. Incapable of pursuing it, all she could do was say brightly, 'I suppose so – see you then, Louise,' and depart hurriedly, aware of Louise looking after her as she went.

Chapter 3

September twenty-ninth, Friday; Matthew's twenty-first birthday was two days off. He was to have thrown a party on the Saturday in Dennis Cox's home, his own mother declining to open hers to a troop of heavy-footed young people. But Dennis had joined up and so had most of Matthew's friends. So Jenny saw herself as a poor substitute when she accepted his invitation to help him celebrate his majority with a meal at a tiny restaurant by the Salmon and Ball pub in the Bethnal Green Road.

'Why me?' she'd asked, aware that had Jean still been around or the Middleton girl, now engaged to a young soldier, and had not declined, she would not have been so honoured.

'Why not?' he'd countered with a flippancy that didn't quite manage to hide a certain despondency in his voice.

He was missing everyone, that was certain, and again that insidious suspicion her mother had innocently planted plucked at her. Was he really scared behind that facade he'd put up? She kept telling herself that he must have some honourable reason for rejecting his mother's intentions for him to get himself a commission, but the more she tried to convince herself, the harder it was to believe it. What young man would scorn the chance of an officer's uniform? With his education he would certainly become an officer.

Sitting opposite him at a small table in the restaurant, gas masks in their square boxes hanging on the backs of their chairs, she forced herself to smile at him whenever his brown eyes met hers, knowing he was only using her as a bolster against his own loneliness.

It had been a wonderful meal, yet she had felt that every mouthful had to be forced down; Matthew too just picked at his food, although he had done a great job on the wine, even ordering a second bottle only to consume most of it himself.

Jenny fingered her liqueur glass of Tia Maria, gazing at the thick dark liquid in its narrow vessel. 'You're not enjoying this evening one scrap, are you?' she finally burst out.

He glanced up from the brandy he had ordered. 'Are you?'

'I was asking you, Matthew.'

'Me? I'm having a whale of a time.'

The remark, to her ear loaded with sarcasm, full of the implication that in normal circumstances she'd be his very last idea of a companion, struck at the very core of her being. She could find no reply to give him, and felt starkly aware how easily and suddenly adoration can be changed to vague hostility, no matter how temporary, for her heart told her that it could only be a short while before her secret feelings of love returned.

In silence she watched him lift the brandy glass, study

the amber liquid, swirling it thickly around the bowl. Bringing it to his lips he threw back his head, draining it in one gulp and coughing a little against its fiery taste. He signalled to the wine waiter for another.

'You'll get yourself plastered,' she warned, finding her voice again as the drink arrived moments later.

'Wouldn't be such a bad idea.'

'It would be a silly idea. You'll spoil your birthday.'

'Some birthday,' he muttered ruefully, taking a long swig.

Ignoring the connotation of her being poor company, Jenny opened her handbag and brought out a small oblong package wrapped in coloured paper. She laid it on the table in front of him.

'It's not much I'm afraid, but – happy birthday, Matthew.'

For a moment he stared at it, then his face lit up. 'You didn't have to do that, Jenny.'

He sounded suddenly like an excited schoolboy and she forgave him his shortened use of her name, her heart lifting as he began tearing off the wrapping with genuine pleasure as though this was the most important gift he had ever received. It was especially flattering as she knew of the presents he'd been given by his family. He had already shown her a monogrammed silver cigarette case from his sister. In fact Louise had asked Jenny's advice on what to get him.

'Matthew smokes,' she had told Louise. 'Why not get him a cigarette case? He hasn't got one.' So apparently that was what she had done.

He'd also mentioned getting a couple of hundred pounds in bonds from his grandparents, his father's people who lived in Finchley in north London – there were apparently no grandparents on his mother's side. Then there had been the main present, a Ford Eight from his parents, in which he had proudly driven her the half-mile or so to the Salmon and Ball.

'Well, open it then,' Jenny urged as he paused over the slim blue box she had given him, now stripped of its colourful wrapping. Carefully he lifted the lid to gaze down at the humble pen and pencil set.

'Jenny . . . that's really nice.'

She shrugged. 'It's just ordinary. I mean, it looks silver but it isn't really. I expect you already have a set.'

'No, I haven't.' He glanced up, giving her a long look. 'Thanks Jenny – it's the best present anyone could give me. I'll probably need something like this when . . .' Breaking off mid-sentence, leaving her to wonder what it was he had been about to say, he placed the box in his breast pocket with almost reverent care.

'What about your other presents?' she reminded him.

He gave a sardonic chuckle. 'Beware Greeks bearing gifts.'

'How do you mean?'

'I mean I feel I've been put under obligation by some people.'

'What obligation?'

'Oh . . .' He heaved a sigh, playing absently with a box of matches put on the table for smokers' convenience. 'Doesn't matter. Family business. But thanks, Jenny, for the gift.' He reached for his glass. 'Anyway, happy birthday, Matthew! May you have many more – God willing.'

Not waiting for her to lift her own slender glass, he drained his at a gulp, blinked, then grinned across at her. 'I think I'll have another.'

Jenny gnawed at her lip. 'No, don't, Matthew.'

'It's my birthday,' he stated truculently, then grinned again. 'Good old Libra, that's me. Stuck in the balance. Death of summer, birth of darker days. God! I wish I'd been born in spring, years from now.'

He was talking nonsense. He'd definitely had enough. But apparently he wasn't of the same opinion as her. 'I'm going to have another.'

Frowning, he clicked a finger and thumb rudely at a passing waiter. 'I want another brandy.'

'Please, Matthew,' Jenny hissed, embarrassed. 'You mustn't.'

His frown deepened. 'Christ! Not you as well.'

'Me?'

'Telling me what to do. Making decisions for me. Jus' like my mother. She does that, all the time. Louise and I, we jus' laugh, but sometimes . . . Time I was allowed to make decisions for m'self. Where's that waiter? Ah.'

The man stood beside him, polite yet superior, his elderly face lined and wise, his tone conveying the faintest hint of disapproval. 'You ordered another brandy, sir.'

'I did,' snapped Matthew, but the wind had gone out of his sails. He sat slumped a little as the drink was placed before him. Listlessly he pulled out the new cigarette case, offered one to Jenny which she declined, took one himself, lit it from a gold lighter, a present from an uncle, and drew in a deep lungful of smoke.

She had never seen him like this. It was as though she was looking at a totally different person to the buoyant carefree spirit of only a few weeks earlier. It made her heart ache.

'It's getting late,' she urged, and when he shrugged, continuing to smoke, his brandy untouched, she added, 'My mother doesn't like me to be out too late. She gets lonely. She'll be anxious.'

At last he spoke. 'You too?'

'What do you mean, me too?'

'Parent trouble.'

'No, not really. It's just that now there's a war on, she worries.' But a glimmer of his problem had begun to show itself. She leaned towards him. 'Matthew. What's the matter?'

'Who says anything's the matter? I'm fine. Couldn't be better. I've got my future nicely cut and dried, no worries, nothing. Life's grand. Just sit back and let my dear mother do the worrying for me, the arranging, the thinking. Who cares?'

He cut off abruptly, stared down at his untouched drink as though unsure how it came to be there, then he grimaced and sucked in his breath, pushing the glass from him and stubbing out his cigarette.

'Ye gods! Jenny – let's get out of here.'

Gathering up her coat, her handbag, the unsightly square box on its cord, while he paid the bill, she hurried after him, thankful that he seemed to be walking from the restaurant more steadily than she had dared to hope. But once outside on the pavement the air hit him and he swayed.

She took his arm firmly. 'You can't drive back in this state.'

'It's only a mile.'

'It's so dark. You'll have us hitting a lamppost. We could walk. I've got my torch. So long as we don't collide with a wall of sandbags.' She tried to make a joke of the sandbags surrounding the council offices. 'You can get your car tomorrow. And you must clear your head before you get home.'

'*Must*?'

She realised she had probably sounded slightly domineering. His earlier words spoken against his mother's efforts to sort out his future ought to have warned her. She hurried to repair the damage, giving a light laugh.

'Your mother will hit the roof if she sees you. You'll never hear the last of it.'

'You can say that again.' He chuckled too, his tenseness easing a little as, falling silent, he leaned on her, letting her guide him. Neither spoke as they negotiated the quiet crossroads under the railway bridge.

It was darker than they had anticipated after the restaurant lights, dim as they had been. Not a chink of light shone anywhere. Jenny's small torch, itself covered by black sticky paper with just two tiny holes cut in it, gave hardly a beam and they needed to walk slowly, cautiously, in case they bumped into something hard like a pillar box or a lamppost, none of them lit, all of them obsolete. The bowl of the sky these days was dead-black from horizon to horizon as no one in town had ever seen it; stars looked as large and bright as sequins and the Milky Way stood out like a solid path of frozen mist in the enveloping silence up there.

'Isn't it beautiful?' Jenny breathed, glancing upwards in wonder at it as they felt their way along. Time stretched out in silence between them; she judged that soon they would come upon that unevenly built wall of sandbags round the council chambers, so she moved even slower. Suddenly Matthew came to an abrupt halt, dragging on her arm.

'What is it?'

She heard his sigh. 'It's . . . not been a very successful evening, has it?'

There was a slur to his words which she tried to ignore and she attempted to make yet another joke. 'My fault, or yours?'

'Mine.'

'You've not been the jolliest of people tonight,' she admitted candidly.

'And of course, you know why.' Again that sarcastic ring, but at whom she did not know.

'I don't think I do.'

'Yes you do. It's what's been hanging over my head these last few weeks. I know my mother means well, but she rather jumped the gun telling people her son was going to be an officer. Let her down, didn't I? And now everyone thinks I'm scared to join up, yellow, because I've not made any move to do anything. I can see it in their faces. I can see it in yours.'

'Not mine, Matthew! I don't think that.' But she did think that, had battled with her conscience, tried to ignore the thoughts that assailed her. It had to show in her face, in her voice, no matter how she tried to disguise it, even from herself, as she told herself that Matthew was no coward.

She heard his explosive laugh. 'There's blind faith for you! Real true loyalty. No doubts at all.'

He shrugged away from her, supporting himself with one hand against a lamppost. 'Don't you have jus' one small doubt, Jenny, in that great big heart of yours? Aren't you just a little curious to know why I . . . why I didn't volunteer, like Dennis and Freddy and half the country?'

His attitude confused her, put her at odds with herself. Her entire evening with him had been spent struggling with that malignant tumour of doubt, not knowing for a moment that he'd perceived the cracks in her armour. Now he was accusing her and she had no defence. She reached out and took his arm. 'I don't know why, Matthew. You're making me feel very unhappy.'

'I'm sorry.' She wasn't sure if the apology was genuine or spoken in anger. 'Seems it's the fashion t'be unhappy.' His body seemed to sag a little against the lamppost.

'All I know is I've got to tell *someone*.' For a moment he fell silent while Jenny waited, then quietly, as though ashamed of himself, he said, 'Someone I can trust. I trust you, Jenny. Above anyone else I know, I trust you. I wish . . . I jus' wish . . . God, I feel a bit sick.'

She waited while he rested his head against the iron

post. In the utter darkness, but for the pinprick of light from her torch, she could hardly see him. Standing there, she stared into the black night, the chill of autumn creeping about her shoulders all the more chill for there being no light anywhere. It felt as though they were the only two people in the whole world; East London was preparing for sleep, no buses, no vehicles of any kind drove past them, just a low hum of which she was only just aware could be heard, so low it was, of some distant flicker of life in this darkened city. Silence, the silence of a metropolis waiting for that something it knew would happen eventually.

She shivered, not from cold, but from foreboding, thankful for the presence of Matthew, even if a little the worse for wine and brandy. Yet if she hadn't gone out with him this evening, she wouldn't be here now to feel this fear of the dark, this ominous dark with its low distant rumbling like the warning of a storm yet to break but still unseen. And again she shivered.

Matthew's voice made her jump, even though it was so low that had a breeze ruffled the still air, she would have missed his words.

'All my life . . .' He paused as though thinking it out, then began again. 'All my life Louise and I have been nursed along, protected, pampered. Our parents have always been there to fight our fights, solve our problems, especially my mother. I know she always meant well so I let her get on with it. I even thought it funny. But I took it all for granted. My fault. But there comes a time . . . I've just begun to realise the harm it's done. It's like being smothered by a blanket, warm and safe, but – well, suffocating if it's pulled too close. Throw it off and you realise just how fresh the air can be. D'you know what I'm trying to say, Jenny?'

He didn't wait for her reply. 'I've got to break away. Make my own life. But how the hell do you say to someone you love, someone who loves you: "Thanks for everything, but I'm off"'? She does love me, but so, I don't know, so selfishly, and she doesn't even realise it.'

His words trailed off as he became lost in his thoughts while Jenny stood by not knowing what to say.

He began to talk again. 'This war. It seemed my chance to get away without hurting her feelings. But she's cheated me even out of that. And she can't see it. Had it all worked out for me, trying to help, holding my hand yet again, making enquiries to get me into some officer cadet training unit or other. I don't know what she had in mind or thought she could do – I've not been listening that much. All I know is that this time I want to do things for myself. I'm twenty-one. I don't want her to keep holding my hand.'

Jenny found her voice. 'Can't you explain to her how you feel?'

'Explain!' His voice was still slurred. 'Don't think she'd understand. Only hears what she wants to hear. Diff'rent for Louise. She's a girl. She's nat'rally happy to cling to her mother. But me. Got to let go. Let it go on too long. Should've volunteered for the Territorials last year, but she talked me out of it. Scared then at me going off and getting m'self killed. Everyone was panicking a bit at that time. But now she can see it's inev . . . inevitable she's doing her damnedest to see me in the best possible situation, going into an officer cadet training college, getting a safe job. But I don't want a safe job. I'd have liked to become an officer, but *I* wanted to sort it out. *I* wanted to. She's spoiled that for me. Now, Freddy's got married and joined up. Dennis – that soft idiot – is having a go. Suddenly I'm still a boy in a world of men, and it's shaken me. I decided I wouldn't sign on under her rules – thinking she can sort it all out for me. I'm going to wait 'til I'm called up, take my chances.'

'That could be rough on you,' Jenny said. 'You'd just be in the ranks.'

'Exactly. I want to rough it, start from the first rung for a change, on my own. If I get a couple of stripes, it'll be on my own merit. If I get as far as a commission, it'll be my own doing. I probably will get a commission – my education – but it won't be my mother getting me there. I want to do it all on my own, and if . . . if . . .'

He broke off. 'Oh, God, I feel sick.'

In sudden urgency, he leaned towards the kerb and retched quietly.

'You see, Mumsy?' Jenny cried first thing next morning at breakfast after relating Matthew's explanation for not apparently leaping headlong into the forces, her faith in his intentions now unshakeable. 'He isn't a coward. He simply wants to do things his way.'

Mrs Ross's smile was one of sad experience. 'Doing things his way could be biting off more than he can chew. He's always been used to the soft life by all accounts. He'll be in for a shock, I should imagine.'

'So will a lot of men,' Jenny said firmly. 'They'll have to get used to it. I can't see why he should be any different. He'll learn to adapt, like most people do when there's no going back. I'm sure we'll be seeing a side of Matthew no one ever saw before.'

'Well, we shall see, I suppose.'

'Yes, we shall,' Jenny stated with conviction, rising from the breakfast table to start clearing away, confident in the eventual fulfilment of her conviction. She didn't have to wait for long.

Two weeks prior to Christmas, the autumn having been so uneventful it hardly seemed they were having a war at all – people were calling it the phoney war, the funny war, even the bore war, and some evacuees were even returning home – Jenny opened the door to a knock. There he stood, one leather-gloved hand clutching a small suitcase, his overcoat collar turned up against the chill wind, the well-cut suit beneath soon to be exchanged for the rough khaki of a private in the Royal Corps of Signals. His smile was wide, his long narrow eyes bright. He looked as though he had been given a birthday present.

'Thought I'd pop over to say cheerio.'

Not knowing what to say, all she said was, 'Come in out of the cold for a second,' and all but dragged him across the doorstep as her mother came from the living room to wish him well and invite him to come and sit by the fire for a moment.

'It's warm in there, Matthew. There's such a draught from the door.'

'No thanks, Mrs Ross,' he said as Jenny dutifully closed the door a little. 'Got a train to catch. Just thought I'd say a quick goodbye to Jen . . . Jenny.'

Despite the miserable feeling inside her at Matthew's going, Jenny couldn't help but smile at the hasty correction before her mother as the woman melted discreetly back into the living room, leaving the pair of them to say their goodbyes. She wondered if her mother suspected the feelings she had for Matthew. If she did, she had never betrayed it.

Alone with him, she still couldn't come up with anything wise or clever to say.

'So you're off then.' It was the only thing she could find, obvious, inane, feeble, betraying nothing of the desolation churning in the pit of her stomach.

'Yes.'

'I hope you get by all right.'

'I hope so too.'

'Nice of you to come over to say goodbye.'

At this he gave her one of those searching looks that never failed to set her heart racing with useless hope. 'Well, I would, wouldn't I?'

'Why?'

'Because . . . it's you. My best friend.'

It wrung her heart. She would always be his best friend, no more than that. That was obvious now.

'I'll miss you, Matthew,' was all she could find to say, a catch in her throat that she hadn't wanted to be there, to her annoyance quite audible.

On impulse she reached up and touched his smooth

cheek, then with the same spontaneity, leaned forward and planted a kiss where her hand had momentarily touched. The flesh felt cold from the biting wind outside but the spicy fragrance of his skin warmly filled her nostrils. She stood back, alarmed by her own temerity. For fear of ridicule she had never before dared kiss him. What would he think now?

'Take care of yourself, won't you?' she heard herself say.

His smile was not at all taunting. 'Don't worry, I will.'

Some of her composure returned. 'I'm glad you got your own way in the end.'

'Don't know about that,' he laughed, the laugh light and confident in a way she'd never heard before; before it had always been touched by a tinge of defiance. 'It's up to me now to prove myself right. Anyway, if I don't swim, I can only sink.'

The old defiance coming back, the caustic quip.

'Don't say that.' She experienced a shudder of sudden apprehension, a premonition, dread, so light that it went as quickly as it had come. His was a charmed life, bright with promise. He'd be all right. People like him always were. He had to be.

The easy expression had faded to be replaced by a thoughtful, almost affectionate regard. 'I'd like to thank you, Jenny, for making up my mind for me – the night we had that dinner together.'

Her face grew hot. 'I did nothing . . .'

'You listened. It was enough.'

She was startled by his arm coming around her waist,

pulling her gently towards him; then he kissed her full on the mouth. It was a long lingering kiss, revealing the passionate core of him that she had always imagined yet thought she would never be invited to probe. Even now she knew it came purely from regret at leaving a dear friend, or perhaps from his trepidation at the unknown into which he was about to step, but no more than that.

Curiously dizzy, she felt herself put gently from him. When she spoke she was annoyed to find that her voice shook. 'Lots of luck, Matthew.'

'You too, Jenny. I'll write, let you know where I am. Although God knows where I . . . where any of us will end up. But things will never be the same again.'

'I suppose not,' she replied lamely, her shaken nerves calming at last.

For a moment he looked searchingly at her. Then he held out his hand, unaware of anything behind her candid grey-green eyes but what she knew she dared convey – a friendly regret of his going. Yet, oh, how she wished it possible to show him how she truly felt as she took the offered hand, the cool slim fingers closing over hers in a firm and steady grip that had the essence of real friendship in it. How she wished it was love rather than friendship, but she wasn't prepared to fool herself.

'I don't know when our paths will cross again,' he said, his tone low and full, 'if they ever do. But whatever happens, Jenny, I want you to know that you'll always be one of my nicer memories.'

'Perhaps we could keep in touch,' she said quickly and he smiled, almost gratefully.

'Perhaps we will. I'll try and write to you, Jenny. Look after yourself.'

Then he was gone, out of the door and down the steps to the street, turning towards Cambridge Heath Road and the nearest bus stop, moving on swiftly with that fast springy step of his.

The fierce wind battered at his trilby on which one hand was keeping a tight hold. Perhaps that was why he didn't turn and wave, she thought as she stood watching him going out of her life.

Whether his own family had stood at their door to see him go on his way, she had no idea. Her eyes had become too misted to see that far, which she blamed on tears caused by the bitter wind. She couldn't recall when she had cried last, apart from when her father had died, of course. She wasn't really crying now, except that the wind touched a little colder against a small part of her cheek where a rivulet had begun to trickle down as finally she turned and came back into the house.

Chapter 4

A few weeks later, as promised, came a letter from Matthew, from Catterick in Yorkshire, full of his traumatic introduction to the regimental sergeant major, to his platoon sergeant, to square bashing and to evil food and hard beds.

Slowly getting to be a proper soldier – in hot water all the time. Uniform fits where it touches. The chaps in my hut took the mickey out of my accent at first. I never knew I had one. Said I sounded a bloody snob (their words) and damned arrogant, which I didn't like that much. They started to call me College Boy, but after I had a set-to with one of them and duffed him up, and got seven days C.B. – not College Boy, but Confined to Barracks, they have started calling me Matt and sometimes Wardy after my surname because there's another Matthew in the platoon. So I suppose being called that must stand for something. They're not a bad bunch once you get to know them. I still can't get used to being bawled at . . .

There were two pages of cheerful grousing. He seemed quite genuinely happy, a vastly different man to the one who had said goodbye to her that day. If anything, he seemed happier than he had been in his carefree days before war had broken out, despite the restrictions of army life. Jenny could only think poetically of a bird released.

He had concluded his letter by writing that he was off down the local with a few mates for a couple of jars.

Jenny wrote back, heartened by his writing to her, but he did not reply. In his usual careless fashion he had written as promised and had already forgotten her. She could imagine him skipping through her reply, thinking he'd answer it when he had the time, but with his thoughts on other things he had probably put it away and lost track of it, his promise pushed further back into the corner of his mind, eventually to die altogether.

Taking what struck her as an obvious hint, she didn't write again, so that the only news she gleaned of him was what filtered through from his mother to others and thence now and again to her mother.

The only one left at home out of the old crowd she'd once gone about with, Jenny began to experience a very real dread of being tied to her home forever, staying in night after night after work, keeping her mother company through the long dreary winter days stretching ahead.

Her whole life had become dreary. Coming home on slow buses in the blue glow that enabled the conductor to see the coins he was given, masked headlamps just penetrating a stygian winter evening although street lamps gave out a tiny downward pinprick of light with the slight relaxing of blackout regulations now that no air raids seemed forthcoming, all made for a miserable existence. There was no point her going out for an evening. The West End was no longer lit up like a Christmas tree. And although cinemas, theatres, dance halls and restaurants had all reopened, football stadiums following suit, what fun could be had going anywhere alone?

Even Matthew's sister had gone away to stay with relatives in Surrey. True, Jenny was again helping run the Girl Guides, the vicar of St John's having restarted all its groups, but it wasn't the same any more. There now seemed just her and Mumsy, the two of them even spending their Christmas alone.

She nurtured wild thoughts of joining one of the women's services – anything to escape this purposeless role of companion to a parent who was prone to seeing herself as already approaching old age. Sympathise with her as she did, Jenny longed for something to give her life meaning, to be somewhere where she didn't have to make understanding noises or give her mother comforting pats on the hand. It was unkind to think like that but she couldn't help it. Everyone was off somewhere. She alone was stuck at home. But when it came down to brass tacks, how could she be so cruel as to desert Mumsy who'd always had a need to lean on her as she had leaned on her husband? Yet were circumstances to call on her to stand on her own two feet Mumsy might surprise everyone by coping admirably, as people often do when forced to battle on alone.

She was slowly coming to know the dilemma that had

faced Matthew, but it was her mother who solved her problem, quite by chance.

'I wish you didn't have to work in the City,' she said towards the end of May. 'What if they do start bombing London?'

The papers had reported an air raid on industrial Middlesborough and earlier that month bombs had been dropped near Canterbury, without casualties, but too near for comfort; she was alarmed for her daughter's safety.

'Perhaps you could find yourself something local, away from the City.'

Something local? And be even more at her mother's beck and call? Again came that desire to escape.

'I really should be thinking of doing something towards helping the war effort,' she ventured, immediately crushed by the alarm on her mother's face.

'You mean war work? Oh, no, dear, you couldn't go working in a *factory*. Not a nicely brought up young girl like you.'

'Lots of *nicely* brought up young girls are doing heavy, dirty jobs. I don't see why I should be any different.'

She thought again of Matthew, her heart going out to him for that time of his dilemma. But again it was her mother, mind working on possible ways to have her daughter closer to home, who came to the rescue.

'I was wondering, dear. Perhaps you're right about helping with the war effort. What if you applied for a job in some local hospital? They are crying out for help. There's the chest hospital just the other side of the park. All in the open air. You could go along there and make enquiries.'

With mixed feelings, just to appease her mother, Jenny went along to 'make enquiries'. It was even nearer home but at least she'd be meeting people, new people, instead of the same old faces in the same old stuffy Leadenhall Street office. It would be nice to get out of it and into someone else's world for a while. She had little idea how one went about applying for jobs in hospitals but assumed it to be much the same as anywhere else. The middle-aged, prim-faced woman who had probably never seen any other application to her shiny well-scrubbed cheeks than soap, looked up at Jenny from her desk, her gaze full of disparagement.

'I am afraid there are no places at the moment for untrained girls. If you care to register in the proper manner you can go to a training hospital if you seriously wish to become a nurse.'

She hadn't for a second thought of becoming a nurse. All she'd come for was a job nearer home. The woman seemed to glare at her.

'If you are looking for romance and excitement, young lady, you will be sadly disillusioned. This is a *demanding* profession, physically, mentally, suited only for the most dedicated women and entailing sheer hard slog and long hours for precious little reward other than the satisfaction of seeing a patient recover under quiet, efficient, selfless nursing.'

'That's all the reward one needs,' Jenny said without thinking, carried along on the woman's zeal. She saw the thin lips compress at her audacity in adding her opinion.

'All too often it is not. After giving oneself until one is

drained utterly, and then to be required to do extra duty, one begins to wonder. Such doubts can often form in the mind of a nurse pushed beyond endurance when she grows weary. It is those who find that little extra strength to push aside such doubts who make true nurses. I regret they are all too few.'

Rather than risk another comment that would most certainly be ripe for criticism by the look of this woman, Jenny held her tongue, not sure if she actually wanted all this. Yet she felt herself already being absorbed, the idea of hard unrewarding work an answer, even preferable to the boring, barren futility that had lately become her life.

Refusing to give herself time to think, she filled in the application form under the stern, sceptical eye of her interviewer, if only to show her that she wasn't afraid of hard work.

It was not long after, wondering just what she had got herself into, that she was bidding goodbye to a tearful parent to commence training at a hospital in the heart of Hampshire. She had escaped.

'I don't think I'm cut out for this.'

The fair-haired girl's plaintive sigh reached Jenny from the other side of the bed as they removed the soiled bottom sheet from underneath an incontinent elderly patient.

Trying to ignore the smell wafting up from the stained sheet, Jenny smiled across at her fellow student nurse. 'We were told to expect this, you know.'

'One thing bein' told what to expect, another 'aving

it right up your nose. I think I'd sooner 'ave joined the WAACs than this.'

'What, with bombs dropping all over the place around London?' The girl was a Londoner and had been glad to be here in Hampshire. 'Sooner or later London will become a target and you could be stuck with a searchlight unit. That's what they go for first, you know, searchlights. I would sooner be here and safe, with all the slops and bedpans, for all the hard work we have to do.'

All too soon after being sent to Hampshire, Jenny had discovered what real mental exhaustion was as she strove to absorb what the demonstrators and lecturers were telling her. Her ankles had ached from endless bed-making, scrubbing miles of floors, interminable polishing of bed springs and scouring what seemed like millions of metal bedpans until they shone again after being emptied down the sluice.

But for all the headaches: trying to cram six months' training into six weeks, a wartime necessity; the drudgery, being saddled with the distasteful chores second-year nurses passed on to student nurses; all the cleaning up of incontinent patients, emptying slops and bedpans, mopping soiled floors, she had discovered that caring for those unable to care for themselves had its rewards. She really did feel she was doing something worthwhile at last. Often Jenny could hardly believe it was really she who now trod the wards in the uniform of a nurse – not that the uniform enhanced her appearance.

In lisle stockings and flat leather lace-ups, a white apron so starched that it practically stood up by itself, and indeed stood out from the blue striped dress like a bell-tent, she spent hours before a mirror battling with the piece of snow-white material that would eventually form her cap – at least once she had mastered the technique of folding it correctly so that the pinched pleats lay flat enough not to flap about over the crown of her head like some wayward seagull.

Like a true nurse she worked hard to aspire to the art of moving swiftly yet quietly, but with all that quantity of starch, quietly was virtually an impossibility. Her starched uniform heralded her approach with all the subtlety of an oncoming express train.

There was scant opportunity for going home. In this she felt a little guilty. Poor Mumsy, all alone because she had been selfish enough to want to get away. Well she *had* got away, and she *would* have gone home, but a train packed to suffocation with servicemen and women could take three times as long as in peacetime, incessantly stopping and starting and then crawling along between times. Too much of a chunk out of one's day off. Such a thing as a whole weekend off hardly existed. And after working twelve hours at a stretch, she was only too glad to 'live in', falling into bed utterly exhausted to sleep away her day off.

With the beautiful early summer of 1940 she spent many a free day in the corner of some field with a friend or two, dozing in the hot sunshine pouring from a cloudless sky, only too glad to think about absolutely nothing, least of all guilt at not going to see Mumsy.

That year she got home twice, the first occasion in August, the second occasion in the autumn when she ran into Matthew Ward on his way back to his unit after a week's leave. She was amazed at the change in him. In one short year he had become more broad-shouldered, more steady-eyed. He looked taller, older, yet the ring of devilment still echoed in his voice as he greeted her.

'Ye gods! Jenny! And every inch a nurse. You look a picture.'

'So do you,' she returned lightly. She wasn't about to upbraid him for not ever writing to her again. The feeling she'd long thought dead now rose again like a bird as she regarded him.

His uniform, although still the rough khaki of rank-and-file, gave him a debonair appearance, and on his sleeve he bore the twin stripes of a corporal. He was making it there, Jenny thought with a small leap of pride in her heart for him, his own way.

'Not yet an officer, I see,' she said with a brave attempt at flippancy and he gave her a grin, crooked and rueful.

'My CO suggested I put in for it. Went up before the Selection Board but got cheesed off with the stupid questions they asked. Afraid I got a bit bolshie with some silly arse of a psychiatrist there and they chucked me out. Not literally, but well, turned me down – at least for the time being.'

As he chatted, Jenny couldn't help but notice how some of the edges of that 'college-boy' accent had blunted. Listening to him now, each word had a rough-and-ready tinge to it. Oddly enough, it rounded off this new Matthew to perfection – a man of action, certain of himself, a man able to fight his own fights without help from anyone. She wondered as he went on talking how his mother viewed this new person. Did it pull at her heartstrings for the boy he had once been? It didn't pull at her own, that was certain, except to make her heart swell with pride and love for this man who stood chatting lightly, without a care in the world because he had been able to surmount each obstacle as it had come his way.

'I expect the Selection Board will have another bash at me before long,' he was saying. 'The CO was damned disappointed, though God knows why. Me – I'm not sure I want to bother now. I've got a great crowd of mates and just now we're too busy playing soldiers on some godforsaken Yorkshire moor for me to worry just yet about trying to become an officer.'

'What do you do?' she asked.

For an answer he placed a finger against his lips in a playful gesture. 'Careless talk costs lives. Really, we just muck about out in the field with walkie-talkies, practise radio relay, get wet and tired and lost. Usually end up in the right place, eventually, then all go back to the schoolroom to learn where we went wrong. Then we all go off to the pub and forget it. It really is a load of old bull. I don't think any of us bother to take it in except enough to keep our sergeant happy. Don't know as I want to start seriously studying again just to be an officer. Had enough of that at college.'

He paused to regard her closely. 'But what about you? I bet you do enough of it. A nurse, eh? Always thought you were cut out to be something like that. I think that's why I admired you so much, Jenny. Got anyone in tow yet?

Some handsome young doctor?' There was a look in his eye that made a spark of hope leap inside her.

'No one at the moment,' she said, smiling, then she said something utterly stupid before she could stop herself. 'I don't have the time.'

'Me too.' He gave a low chuckle. Had she disappointed him? 'Having too good a war to get roped in. Women tell you too much what and what not to do. I'm free for the time being. But you never know, do you?'

He broke off and on a sudden thought crooked his arm and tugged back the sleeve of his overcoat to glance down at his wristwatch, the gold one which he had told her last year had been given him by his father's sister for his twenty-first. 'Ye gods! Got to go, Jenny. If I miss my connection I'll get put on a charge for being late. Cheerio then. And take care of yourself.'

'You too.' Dismally, she was aware she had blown the one chance she might have had of his asking her for a date, or even if he could write to her. On sheer impulse born out of desperation she leaned forward and laid a kiss full on his lips. Expecting him to pull away she was surprised by his arm coming around her, the kiss being held, and it was she who broke away in a fluster, taken off guard by the strength of his lips on hers, there in the street.

'Like you said,' she burst out idiotically, 'you'll be late.'

He nodded, seeming to gather his wits. 'Yes, I will. I'll write to you, Jenny.'

He seemed so tremendously happy as he went on his way. Rosy from his promise, the pressure of his lips still felt on hers while her own foolish confusion mocked her, she watched him go, shouldering his small pack, his step jaunty. War hadn't touched him at all. The terrible events of Dunkirk, of desperate men with their backs to the sea until the armada of small boats had come to their rescue, had passed him by. If anything, she had seen more of conflict than he.

A fleeting vision of her part in it passed through her mind, days and weeks compressed into seconds as she watched Matthew's departing figure. A once-quiet, smoothly running hospital suddenly filled with a consignment of casualties from those beaches. A first-year student nurse thrown into the deep end trying to cope with a picture of defeat, the exhausted, the filthy, the torn bodies, her first-ever experience of war at its most vicious, all the worse because her life as a student nurse only the previous day had been so sedate.

Surrounded by that upheaval, she had cooked porridge, cut mounds of bread and butter, helped undress those who passed out into sleep the moment they were left alone, sometimes just where they stood. She had washed the wounded, tried not to weep over the dying or turn away as gangrenous or maggot-infested wounds were uncovered, and had wished to God she had been qualified to do more than just assist and cut bread while those skilled medical teams operated on the suffering. And the June sun had shone on.

She saw Matthew turn, throw her a careless wave. She waved back, smiled. No ghosts of dead and dying comrades, no splattered bodies and shattered limbs haunted his vision. He had continued, as he'd said, to play at soldiers in the safe environs of a Yorkshire moor. Pray God, Jenny thought as she waved, heartened by his promise to write to her, there would never be need for it to be otherwise.

For a week as he took orders, drilled, cleaned his equipment and uniform free of moorland mud and grass knowing that next day they'd need cleaning all over again, Matthew thought of Jenny Ross and the kiss she had given him. No mere friendly one. He'd always had a sneaking suspicion that underneath that touch-me-not exterior she'd always presented, she had been in love with him. That kiss had proved it, but even then she had broken away before it had had a chance to develop, becoming all formal again, telling him he'd be late back.

Each time he thought about it, he found himself shaking his head in disbelief, found himself wondering about the feeling it had promoted, musing about the girl herself.

Her nurse's navy-blue coat had suited her colouring. Hair, burnished to old gold by August sunshine, still flared despite being drawn into a neat roll behind her ears; it made her look pretty really. He'd never noticed before. Probably the uniform? Not as leggy as he'd once thought her, not so overwhelming and always ready to help everyone. That had always been her trouble. She'd seemed more at ease. She'd make someone a wonderful wife one day.

The thought brought an unexpected pang deep inside him, rather like a longing. He'd write to her again, definitely. In the past she'd always been too much of a managing person to be thought of in any other way than as a friend. Back in those careless days he had much preferred girls who liked to lean on a man rather than have a man lean on them. Jenny had never leaned on anyone. Perhaps she'd changed, had grown less independent. Perhaps it would be nice to find out. At the thought a small ripple of excitement made itself felt in the pit of his stomach.

Sitting on his bed cleaning his equipment after a day on some muddy moor, he found himself wanting to find out, thinking about her, her life. Yes, when this bloody training allowed him a moment to himself, he would write. Good to have a girl to write to. He hadn't got her hospital address but her mother could forward it on. And when he next came home on leave . . .

Chapter 5

He had meant to write. But that weekend, with the Army's usual lack of forewarning, his whole unit found itself transferred to a camp just outside Birmingham. With all the excitement that went with it, writing to Jenny had to be put to one side. That week he had a lot to do, settling in, and the following Saturday when he and a few mates wangled an evening pass into Birmingham, it was shelved again. But he would write, he told himself as he picked up his pass. He still felt good about her.

Cadging a lift in the back of an Army truck to save a bus fare, the group split up to find their own way to whatever part of the city they sought for a few hours' pleasure. Matthew found a dance hall near the town centre. Obviously popular, it was packed, the floor crammed with couples, girls in bright dresses, men in uniform, a tight kaleidoscopic mass gyrating slowly to a strict-tempo waltz by a top-quality band.

'We'll slope off then, see what talent there is.' Once the last two mates with him moved away, Matthew found himself alone, already losing interest.

'See you later,' he muttered to himself, for they had already melted into the crowd. He didn't know why he felt so despondent. Jenny crossed his mind briefly, though why, he couldn't say. She had never excelled as a ballroom dancer. She knew how to dance, but she was better at sports like swimming and badminton and tennis. So why this odd pang thinking of her here in this unfamiliar dance hall? Yes, he was feeling at a loose end at this moment. He would write to her when he got back to camp.

What he needed now was someone to take away this unaccustomed loneliness he was experiencing. With an effort he perked himself up and surveyed the crowd, as his mates were doing a little way off.

Not much was here except for one petite dark-haired girl at one of the far tables, visible now that the floor was clearing from the waltz just ended and the lights were coming back up. She was with a Marine. Yet the way they were leaning away from each other, not talking, conveyed that she might not be with the Marine for much longer. Matthew took heart, began to feel better. She'd do.

'Found anyone yet, Matt?' Dave, one of his mates, was back, himself still looking for a likely partner.

Matthew nodded towards the girl and drew a knowing chuckle from Dave as he followed the direction of the nod. With the remark, 'Didn't take you long, then,' the stockily built Dave prowled off on another search.

Alone again, but this time feeling somewhat better, he fished into the breast pocket of his khaki battle blouse and pulled out the silver cigarette case his sister had given him; he had almost forgotten his twenty-first, it seemed so far away. Lighting a cigarette, he leaned against one of the pillars at the entrance to the large hall and inhaled slowly.

He needed to summon up some sense of nonchalance, and, surrounded by a protective cloud of smoke which he was exhaling, he found it.

He seldom needed courage to approach any girl, even when she was with a partner. One could soon calculate whether the partner was steady or merely casual and act accordingly. But that pale oval face set in a mass of luxurious dark hair, hair that even from here contrasted startlingly against the simple yellow dress she wore, brought an odd trepidation that he could not shake off. Suddenly it seemed very important that he should. Jenny, with her fiery hair and her straightforward manner, faded a little as he began his slow walk towards the girl with the Marine.

As if sensing his approach, hardly had he taken half a dozen steps than the girl turned her head towards him. Her lips broadened into a tiny smile, its message unmistakable. She had been looking thoroughly bored, but already the bored look had fled, leaving hope in its place. Matthew's heart lifted. It might not be such a bad evening after all. He threw a glance at her partner as he drew nearer. No wonder she was bored. The guy's face sported a mass of ripening acne. Other than that he could probably be classed good-looking, but in his present condition he couldn't be very savoury to her.

Matthew stubbed out his cigarette in an ashtray on one of the tables he passed, bringing a surge of interest from the hopeful ring of girls around it, each young eager face looking up in brief anticipation of being asked for the quickstep now being struck up by the band.

The dark-haired girl had turned away from him, seeing him bend forward towards the table, assuming she hadn't been the object of his desire after all. He saw a small upward-tilted nose and lips carrying just a little too much bright red lipstick but which now possessed a most becoming little pout. Why did he suddenly feel so shaky?

Matthew took a deep breath and walked the last few paces as nonchalantly as he could. It was the fate of all faced with the prospect of asking the girl of their choice for a dance, especially if she struck them as ravishing, to feel at least a fraction nervous, alive to the possibility of an abrupt turndown, having to walk away as though it hadn't mattered to them in the least. He had hardly ever suffered from that, but this time, inexplicably, he had joined the ranks of the nervous, at the last minute losing his nerve.

Pausing in front of a wide-eyed blonde, her hair dragged into what was currently called a victory roll, he offered her his hand, at the same time executing a casual tilt of his head towards the rapidly filling dance floor. In a trice the blonde was on her feet, almost knocking over her port and lemon in her haste. Seconds later he was winging her away across the floor, choosing one of the gaps that still remained between the fast-moving couples. To his relief the blonde danced well. Conscious of the eyes of the dark-haired girl following his progress, he couldn't have borne someone who might have hampered his steps.

'You're ever such a good dancer,' came the light words whispered into his ear, to which he nodded absently.

He had no need to be told he was a good dancer. He'd

always gained pleasure from it, from being watched, stretching his talents to the full. Yet it had become imperative to put his present partner through every intricate movement of the quickstep he knew, so that those dark eyes watching him would know he was good. Though God knows why that should matter.

A disconcerting thought came. What if she were only mediocre? All this weaving and twirling could frighten her off. Immediately he moderated his steps – the floor was becoming too crowded for showing off anyway – and fell to making occasional light-hearted smalltalk with his partner.

The ending of the quickstep came as something of a relief. Escorting the blonde back to her seat, he made for the bar and the safety of those hovering males who, despite the romance of their various uniforms, hadn't yet felt inclined to leave their kind and ask for dances, and couples having already found a partner for the evening – perhaps, he grinned, for life.

Yet for all the press of people, he could still sense the dark-haired girl's eyes watching him, and he found his need to know more about her pushing away that last-minute reluctance he had felt.

For the past half-hour the dark-haired girl had sat out through dance after dance, feet tapping under the table as she watched the couples, uniforms and dresses melting together as one, moving around the floor.

Susan Hopkins cast her escort a contemptuous glance. Apart from one visit to the bar for a pint of black-and-tan for himself and a small port and lemon for her, he hadn't moved out of his seat the entire evening.

He had cut such a dashing figure in his dark blue Marines uniform when she'd first met him last week: tall, broad, the briefest scarring on his face from an old outbreak of acne giving it a certain rugged look. She had felt proud to be on his arm. They had gone to the pictures, the cheapest seats, but he'd explained he hadn't drawn his pay yet and she was ready to forgive him. He had asked to see her again, but this evening instead of his gorgeous dress uniform, he had turned up in this horrid khaki thing. It diminished the aura of romance, of the debonair. Not only that, but the dormant acne had run riot during the past week she hadn't seen him.

She'd never been endowed with a strong stomach for unsightly things like suppurating pimples or nasty-looking cuts and bruises. Any physical defect aroused squeamish sensations. It was just as well, she thought watching the dancers, that he hadn't taken her on to that floor – being so close to those yellow-headed pimples would have made her positively sick. Most certainly there'd be no goodnight kiss, that's if she could get out of his taking her home at all. Already she was rehearsing a polite farewell, this date definitely their last.

The previous waltz had been in full swing, the lights dimmed, the faceted crystal orb in the centre of the ceiling flicking sensuous rainbow flecks over the dancers. Suddenly, she had felt an explicable compulsion to turn her eyes towards the hall entrance.

Among the slick RAF uniforms, the rakish body-hugging

navy blue, the officers' smooth attire, the soldier's khaki battle dress was unspectacular. The man it clothed, however, made it look as superior as any officer's as he leaned with casual grace against one of the dance hall's pillars. She saw him reach into his breast pocket, extract a cigarette case; with growing interest watched him light a cigarette, his head bent for a moment over the flame. It was then he looked at her, directly, just as she was sure he'd done earlier, which had caused in her that odd need to turn. It was as though he had actually spoken to her. When their gaze met across the clearing dance floor, she had looked quickly away, filled with embarrassment.

The band had struck up with a quickstep. The man by the entrance stubbed out his cigarette and began walking towards her, making her heart start to pound against her ribs with excited anticipation. But as she composed herself to rise casually at his invitation to dance, ignoring her Marine, the soldier had paused just a few steps away, bending towards a common blonde in a red dress sitting nearby. Seconds later he had whisked her away.

Pique had replaced embarrassment. How dare he? Susan watched him move with supple grace across the filling dance floor with the girl, looking quickly away every time he glanced briefly in her direction. But she didn't miss his expression. What was it? Appraisal? Amusement? Taunting, perhaps. When the quickstep ended with a final flourishing crash of cymbals and a flamboyant twirl of female partners, she pretended not to look as he conducted the blonde back to her friends. But at least, instead of lingering, the soldier turned and sauntered away to the bar.

In that instant, Susan Hopkins made her decision. 'Oh, look!' she burst out to the practically lifeless Jack, 'I've just seen a friend of mine. Must pop over and have a word. Won't be a tick.'

Giving him no time to reply, she was off, skirting the vacated dance floor, timing it perfectly so as to collide with her quarry as if by accident. It worked, even if in the process she trod on his foot, something she had not planned, almost taking herself off balance. Instinctively he caught her, held her steady with firm hands on her shoulders. 'Careful there!'

Deep brown eyes fringed by thick lashes gazed down at her in open amusement. Her embarrassment was more real than she had intended.

'Oh, golly! I'm sorry. I didn't mean to . . . Did I hurt you, like?'

'You?' He laughed, taking stock of her diminutive figure. 'I don't think you've broken any toes.'

'Oh I'm ever so glad.'

She was instantly conscious of her Birmingham accent against the refined tones of this man. Yes, he was a corporal, but his speech sounded so incongruous with the mere two stripes on his arm. His smile gently mocked her.

'What, that you didn't hurt me, or that you stepped on my foot?'

Susan fell silent. He must have seen through her ruse. Her face felt hot. Whatever possessed her to embark on this silly idea in the first place?

'You came at me like an express train,' he was chuckling. 'A fraction more weight on you and you could really have done me an injury. There have to be subtler ways to start up a conversation.'

Indignation finally rescued her from embarrassment. 'Fancy yourself, don't you?'

The grin diminished a little. A momentary look of sadness, loneliness perhaps, crossed his face, and she had a strong feeling he was about to play it down as if she almost heard his words form in her head: I'd be the only one that does. But instantly he brightened, his tone teasing. 'Don't tell me you've not been watching me right from the moment I came in. Actually, I'm flattered.'

Now she was embarrassed again – that look that had passed so briefly across his eyes had gone. 'Well, I might've looked at you. You're a good dancer. Everybody looks at good dancers, don't they?' She wriggled a little in the grasp he still had on her. 'I've got to go back to my friend.'

He released his grip. 'The chap you were sitting with? Is that all he is – a friend? And there was I thinking, the prettiest girl in the hall and she's already spoken for.'

That was why he hadn't asked her to dance. She felt a surge of anger towards her innocent escort for spoiling her chances.

'I'm not *spoken for*, if that's what you call it. I just came in with him. Just a date, like, for this evening, that's all.'

'So you're free to dance with whoever you please?'

Why did she feel he was mocking her? If it hadn't been for that look that had flicked past his eyes, she'd have walked away by now. She had to put up some resistance so as not to look cheap. He mustn't think she had engineered this meeting. 'Not with you,' she said, trying to appear in control.

'Remember it was you who got in touch with me first, to coin a phrase,' he laughed. He *did* think she'd engineered it all. 'Well, you win. Would you care to dance?' He gave an explosive laugh as she tossed her head in sulky refusal. 'Ye gods! How kaleidoscopic can you get?'

She wasn't sure what that meant but it didn't sound very flattering, and in a huff she swung away. He caught her arm lightly.

'I'm sorry. Don't go.' There was genuine contrition in his dark eyes as she turned to look at him, immediately replaced by a look of enthusiasm as the band struck up. 'Listen. It's a foxtrot, the best dance there is, even better than a tango. You foxtrot?'

She loved nothing more. Moreover he seemed to her so like a young boy in his own delight at it that she nodded despite herself; instantly he caught her up and whisked her away on to the dance floor to the delightful slow and regular beat of a rendering of Glenn Miller's 'Moonlight Serenade'.

It was like gliding on clouds. Guided with swaying grace through each intricate movement, she floated. Small though her limbs were, she followed his long steps without faltering, each change of direction, each smooth turn, each measured pause. He was so easy to dance with it was as though they were one person. He didn't speak, seemed conscious only of the variety of moves, practically turning them into an exhibition with not too many on the floor for this rather specialised number, unlike the popular easy-to-do waltz that always filled the floor to crush proportions.

At first she felt uncomfortably conscious of being seen so on display, especially by her former companion. But there was no need to worry. A glance towards where she had left him revealed him looking as though he'd fallen asleep. She was sure that had her handbag not been in his keeping he'd have left. Well, as soon as the number finished she'd retrieve her bag and leave him to it. If the man she was now with chose not to see her home after the dance, she'd see herself home, though she hoped it would not be that way. But either way, at least she would escape those horrid pimples.

The music ending, a ragged clap came from those who'd attempted the dance. Susan smiled up at her partner, awaiting his next move.

It came as she had hoped. 'Do you fancy a drink?'

Susan thought quickly. 'Have to get me handbag first. I left it on the table. I could see you at the bar if that's okay. Won't be a tick.' Somehow her accent no longer mattered. He smiled.

'I'll see you there, then.'

She was off. 'My friend's asked me to see her home afterwards,' she told her Marine with a play at urgency as he looked up with an apathetic grin. 'She's frightened of going home on her own. Hope you don't mind. I am sorry about that.'

There was little he could do as she whisked up her handbag. After all, he was only a casual date. A one-evening date. No doubt he'd slide off and find himself someone else and no harm done. It happened all the time, had once happened to her, annoyingly. But not tonight, she prayed as she made her way back to the bar.

She found her corporal, slim, tanned fingers curled around a pint of bitter, the other hand holding a small glass which he offered her with a grin. 'Thought you'd be a gin and orange person. Am I right?'

'Ooh, loverly. Thanks.' She smiled up at him, taking the glass and sipping at it carefully. 'I hadn't better get myself sozzled, had I?'

'You've probably never been sozzled in your life,' he said solemnly.

'I've bin a bit woozy, like. A couple of times.'

He produced his cigarette case and flipped it open towards her.

She regarded it with admiration as she shook her head. 'I don't smoke. Real silver, in'it?'

He shrugged as though her comment had touched a raw spot, but she didn't interest herself beyond that. The orchestra had reached an interval after a jive that had jammed the floor to suffocation; it was the bar that was now crowded, the babble deafening. But between her and her new partner an awkward silence had fallen, threatening to drag on if she didn't find something to say soon. She gazed about, racking her brain and sipping her drink far too quickly. It was he who broke the hiatus. She saw his lips move but couldn't make out what he said above the noise.

'What?'

He raised his voice. 'I said I still don't know your name.'

'Sue Hopkins,' she yelled back.

'Sorry?'

'Sue . . . Susan Hopkins.' No one ever called her Susan, but announcing her name in full above the din helped make it clearer.

Quite audibly, in one of those odd pauses that can occur in the midst of a dozen conversations, she heard him repeat her name, savouring it as though he thought it the finest in the world. Had it been Cleopatra it could not have sounded more romantic to her ears, the way he pronounced it.

She looked up at him, shouting over a new wave of babble. 'What's yours?' For a moment she thought he hadn't heard; his head tilted slightly as though considering her, then with a glance around the crush of people he grimaced.

'I've had enough of this. Shall we get out of here – go for a walk?'

Just catching the words, not knowing what to say, she nodded. He shouldered his way through the crowd to place her glass together with his own on the bar. Then he was back, tilting his head at her, and she could only follow him, an odd excitement taking hold somewhere deep inside her. The dance didn't matter any more.

Outside, enveloped in the pitch dark of blackout regulations, it was like entering another world. People moving cautiously, heralded by the merest pinprick of torchlight, came at them out of total darkness, to disappear just as totally. Vehicles, few and far between, lights all but obscured by black paint, faintly showed the kerb for a moment to leave it even more dark and dangerous to the pedestrian after they had driven by. Susan huddled close to her companion.

'You've not yet told me your name,' she reminded him as they took their first few steps, slow and measured in the fitful light of the tiny hand torch she'd produced from her handbag. The reminder was whispered, for their surroundings seemed to demand muted voices, muted sounds.

'Do you want all my name?' she heard him chuckle.

'Why not?' she challenged.

There was a pause, then he said, 'Matthew Leonard Ward.'

'Sounds posh,' she breathed, awed, and tucked her arm more firmly through his.

'Not really. Leonard's my father's name. My mates in my unit call me Matt. My mother would have a fit if she heard. She's always insisted on me being called Matthew. She's a stickler for respectability and . . .'

The tale, bordering upon tongue in cheek, was interrupted by a body colliding softly with them and a mumbled apology as it continued on its way through the blackout. But Susan was wondering about this mother – she sounded a right dragon.

'Damned stupid blackout,' Matthew was saying. 'Nothing happening and they black everything out. When there's a raid, they light everything up, switch on all the searchlights. That's what I'm on at present – searchlights. I'm in the Signals and they stick us on searchlights. Now that's what I call great thinking.'

'Got any brothers or sisters?' she asked, changing the subject from what he did in the Army. He was a corporal and that was all that mattered. She wished he'd been an officer but officers didn't look at girls like her. They went to better places than the Troc.

'One sister, Louise. Reminds me of our mother.'

It seemed he said it a little too tersely for comfort and she hurried to put some lightness back in their conversation. Nasty moments, like nasty cuts, even small ones, unnerved her, made her shudder. There were plenty of arguments in her house but she was used to them. Quickly healed, easily got over. It was with strangers that she cringed at moments like this.

'I've got lots,' she said in an effort to sound bright. 'Two sisters and three brothers. It must be funny having a whole bedroom to yourself. Sort of lonely, like.' This she said with a small pang of sadness for him. Perhaps it was the way he had said 'one sister', as though he regretted not having a brother or something. She'd always been told that only children were lonely children, and two wasn't much more than one. He and his sister were probably spoiled, where she'd never been, and it was still probably lonely and quiet. She hated quiet in a house, never having known it.

He didn't reply. They walked on in silence, uncomfortable silence it now seemed to her.

'It's getting late, I think I'm going to have to be going 'ome soon,' she burst out in a fast gabble, far too loudly, her voice sounding high and thin, lacking sophistication. He, the soft-spoken, refined man-of-the-world from down south would be jolted to his senses, seeing her as just a local girl from Birmingham, without education, the product of a crowded family. The spell had been broken.

'It must be nearly eleven,' she ploughed on, hating herself, the way she spoke, the way she acted. She had ruined the evening for herself. 'It's the air raids we've bin havin-g . . .' The accent fell on the 'g'. He didn't sound his at all, the 'ing' soft and alluring. She should have tried to copy it. Too late now. 'Me mum and dad like me home before anything starts. They worry about me, y'see. And I do have to think of them, don't I? It's only right.'

'Yes, it is only right,' he agreed with a deep sigh which dispirited her even more though she didn't know why. 'Do you live far from here?'

'Not far.' She could in fact walk home from here, which appeared now to be what she was going to do. 'Only walking distance.'

That damned 'g' again. *Walking,* she said in her head, walking. 'I sometimes catch a bus if it's raining,' she finished aloud, forgetting again.

'Well, it's not raining, so may I walk you home?'

Susan held back the gasp of joy. He wasn't disapproving of her after all. But she mustn't sound too eager. 'I suppose you could, if y'like. To the top of my road? I can go on from there. But you don't have to.' She had suddenly remembered what her turning would present to him. No doubt he came from a posh part of the south. 'Don't you have to be getting back to where you're stationed?'

'I've enough time to see you home, I'm sure.' How

beautifully he spoke, his tone soft, seductive. He took her arm. 'I'll let you show me the way.'

And, she hoped, the picture of the road where she lived fading into obscurity, he'd kiss her goodnight, and ask to see her again. Oh, please, God, let him.

Chapter 6

It took ages to get to sleep for thinking about her evening's success. Lying in bed in the cramped little bedroom she shared with her two younger sisters at the top of the house, she tried to imagine the world Matthew had described to her as he walked her home. How different it was. The bedroom he had all to himself sounded as though it could swallow this one twice over and still have space to spare.

Hers, measuring four long paces each way, held her single bed and one, three and a half foot wide, for Beryl and June. Hers stood tight against the window wall, theirs against the opposite one, with just space enough between the two to shuffle into bed, going sideways. The wall where the door was had a single wardrobe and a three-drawer chest. Not one drawer or the door to the wardrobe could be opened fully because the beds got in the way. What couldn't be got into drawers or wardrobe went under the bed; every morning in this room resembled a public jumble sale, all three girls squeezing past each other to dress.

The only wash basin was downstairs by the back door in a tiny recess. It meant moving aside to let pass anyone wanting the toilet which stood in a block of six in the communal back yard. It all made for hot tempers when three boys, three girls and two adults were trying to manoeuvre around each other to go their separate ways for the day. Their father moreover did not look kindly on a girl trying to put on her make-up when he wanted to get to the mirror to shave.

Across from her bedroom was the room, even smaller, of her three young brothers, still just boys. Below theirs was her parents' bedroom, below that the living room with an area at one end for cooking. This, their only family room, had five doors: one for the recess where they washed, one to the cellar, one to the yard; a fourth to the street was never used because of a settee in the way – the back door served as the only exit in this place – the last leading to the stairs winding up to the upper rooms.

This was her home, each room atop the other. But for the block of exactly similarly designed houses on either side, each propping the other up like something built from a pack of playing cards, Susan was sure it would have fallen over. Built at the turn of the century for factory workers, the houses were dark, dingy, featureless, all looking as if they had been accidentally leaned on at some time by a careless giant who had concertinaed them, squeezing them upwards like toothpaste from a tube.

She had never considered her home this way before. She'd been born here. All her friends lived in similar places. Some day when she married she had expected to move in to something much like them. But tonight she had peeped into an environment Matthew Ward had described as they walked home, and now she saw these surroundings through a veil of angry discontent, for the first time in her life feeling ashamed of where she lived.

His home might be in London but it sat in a tree-lined road. There were no trees in her street. His overlooked a park. Birmingham had its share of parks and open spaces but not where she lived. His house had hot water, and a bathroom. Her bath hung on the back door, her lav was one of a block of six in the communal yard, with doors so warped anyone emptying rubbish in the dustbins alongside could peep through if they felt that nosy.

Filled with resentment, Susan found herself listening for sounds she had never really noticed before: Beryl, sixteen, eighteen months younger than her, sighing in slumber, probably dreaming; June, fourteen and just left school, a restless girl even in her sleep; her father coughing – too many cigarettes made him bronchial. The back door opening then closing gave a little shake to the house – her mother was coming in from the Red Lion at the end of the street where she was barmaid five evenings a week. Soon came the whistling of the kettle, rising rapidly to a thin scream, fading away, like a soul dying, as it was lifted from the gas stove to make her mother's cocoa.

Susan was still awake when the house vibrated to her mother wearily mounting the stairs. The bedroom door below scraped over the lino, then scraped again as it closed. Complaining bedsprings. The intermittent cough ceased. The springs squeaked afresh as Jack Hopkins humped himself over his wife. After urgent whisperings and a giggle, the springs were soon going like a park seesaw, her mother's mounting joy evident. Then, after a while, silence. Later came heavy snoring – there were no secrets in this house.

Outside sounded the small noises of the night: the mewling cat near at hand, a dog barking further off; an urgent click of high heels on the pavement below, the clink of a milk bottle being put out for the morning; a low distant growl of a solitary lorry, perhaps an army truck, passing a few streets away on its way through the city towards some barracks or other. She thought of Matthew, probably asleep in his. Dreaming of her? Or was she forgotten? She didn't think so. He had asked her for a kiss on the corner of her street, hadn't taken it as his right but had asked permission. He'd asked to see her again. He would write to her when he next got a pass. He had even stood watching her go on along her road, given a brief wave as she turned reaching her door, and gone on his way.

At the recollection a tingle passed through her and in a sudden bout of ecstasy, Susan drummed her heels up and down beneath the bedcover and, taking the sheet between her small teeth, bit hard to relieve the pent-up joy. What did he look like in his sleep? Trying to imagine him, the sounds of the sleeping world went unheeded.

From far away came another sound, faint, but its message already understood, tensing the muscles, plucking at nerves. Rigid, Susan lay listening, waiting though instinct told her to get up and run, though where she was not sure.

The thin lone voice was joined by another, slightly nearer, then another, nearer still, each rising and falling in its own time. The first, hardly discernible now with those nearer wails taking up the cry. That first and the second and the third had died away, their message complete, but their relay was still advancing like a relentless tide.

Her parents' door opened. Her mother called up, 'Sue! Get the gals up. Robert! Les! John! Come on!' Her tone was one of piercing urgency. But Susan was already up, shaking the girls awake.

'Warning's gone. Come on – hurry up.' She dared not put on a light. The blackout curtains were a flimsy affair that needed time to check before one could be sure no chink gleamed out into the night. There was no time to check.

Transition from deep sleep to alert wakefulness was immediate, a gift given only to animals and those in peril. They were on their feet feeling for top clothes – like herself, these times they went to bed in their undies, the easier to dress in an air raid.

Beryl was shivering. 'Brr! I'm cold.'

In the darkness, June's voice: 'I think I've got Beryl's dress on.'

'It don't matter – just hurry up.'

'It does. She'll tear the seams.'

'Then hurry up and change over. We've got to get down the cellar.'

The boys were already racing past the door, boots clumping down the stairs. Grabbing handbag and warm coat, Susan pushed the girls ahead of her, hearing the first crump of anti-aircraft guns.

'Where's the gals?' came her mother's anxious call.

'Sod the gals!' came her father's grating voice. 'Where's my fags?'

'Blow your soppy fags – there's some in the cellar.'

'Tailor-made make me cough. I don't like 'em.'

'You'll have to lump 'em! Where're you gals?'

'Coming, Mum.'

The siren on the roof of the police station in the next street broke into its frantic exchange with an ear-splitting wailing. At the same time the ack-ack gun situated on a piece of waste ground at the far end of the road began cracking. The Hopkins family, like every family around them, all but fell down the four concrete steps into the cellar to be cocooned in comparative safety for the next several hours among the junk of a lifetime spent living in one house. The junk was now pushed to one end to accommodate an ancient double bed, a sagging put-u-up, two camp beds, an oil stove for warmth and a portable electric ring to brew tea, the concrete floor sporting a tattered rug to give a semblance of comfort while age-old cobwebs made grey curtains against the walls.

In this underground environment they sorted themselves out a little more calmly but no less tensely beneath the cold glare of a single electric bulb while above them the night began to rage.

As anti-aircraft guns began whacking away at laden German bombers droning above with their deep-throated, throbbing engine note, most likely caught in a web of searchlights, Susan sat thinking of Matthew. He had said he was in a searchlight unit. Was he on duty tonight? Searchlights were always vulnerable to attack. What if . . .

A noise, like the tearing of canvas, made the family

start. It seemed to be in the very cellar. The explosion sent them cowering to the floor as the light bulb swung madly on its flex to send the shadows of the camp beds flying wildly across the bare brick walls.

When nothing more happened they got to their feet, their hearts still racing, to sit back on the edge of the beds or on one of the old kitchen chairs long since consigned to the cellar.

'Sounded like it fell right in this street,' Vi Hopkins said. 'Jack, you ought to go and look. They might need some help.'

Shakily Jack reached for a tailor-made cigarette. 'There'll be others helping, I expect. Better not get in the way, like.'

'Long as it wasn't our house.'

'We'd know if it was, with dust and stuff. And the roof would've come in on us.'

'So much for being safe,' Vi remarked, looking up at the still-intact basement ceiling. But even if the house suffered, cellars would stand up to anything so long as it wasn't a direct hit. 'Someone in this street must have got it though,' she mused sadly. 'Hope no one was hurt.'

'We'll know in the morning,' Jack said as the worst of the raid drifted off. The bombers might come back, or they might not. It all depended. But while there was a lull, it was best to sleep. He climbed into the ancient double bed, fully dressed, pulling the blanket over his head.

Susan looked at him, contempt a dull, wordless emotion inside her, and thought of Matthew out there amid falling, jagged-edged, razor-sharp shrapnel from anti-aircraft guns, a tin helmet his only protection as he did whatever people did with searchlights.

With morning and the all clear, the sun shining as though in mockery of last night's devastation, her father returned from his reconnoitre to say the near-miss had flattened two houses at the end of the road opposite the Red Lion.

'Hope it's not put paid to my job,' Vi sighed. 'I need that money.'

'They said one landed in Lile Street.' He worked in Lile Street in a small factory making the springs that went inside the chin straps of steel helmets. War work and his bronchitis had kept him out of the forces.

'Anyone hurt on our street?' Susan asked.

'One of the families was in someone else's basement. But they can't find the woman as lives in the other one. You know, that one with the frizzy hair. Husband's in the Merchant Navy.'

'Mrs Norton. She often comes into the Red Lion for half a pint. Oh, not her.'

'Old Hardwick said he asked her into his basement, but she wanted to stay in her own place, like. She must be under all the rubble. They're digging now.'

'Oh, that's terrible.' Susan rather liked the plump little woman who always smiled at her when they passed each other. To think of her dead, bleeding limbs all broken and crooked . . . Shuddering violently, Susan thrust away the horrific injuries her imaginative brain conjured up. She was going to have to pass that house this morning on her way to Cotterels, just off Broad Street where she worked behind the counter selling underwear. What if the broken bleeding body was brought out just as she was passing? She'd be sick there on the spot.

The gap where the two houses had stood towards the end of the long row just like hers struck Susan as she passed as being like two missing teeth in a previously unbroken set, albeit that the set was full of decay, their stumps a pile of rubble. The roofs of the houses on either side were gone, and the windows in all the others were gone too. So were several windows in Susan's own home. She had left her parents clearing up the glass and her father re-hanging the front door, blown off in the blast, leaving the back of the settee and the living room beyond open to the street.

The Red Lion was minus all its windows, doors and most of its tiles. Already men were spreading a tarpaulin over the roof, the publican having erected a hastily painted sign: 'More Open than Usual.'

Susan tried not to look as she passed the ARP and Auxiliary Fire Service men working among the rubble, faces white with dust, their sweat for all the chill of the bright March morning tracing sepia rivulets down their cheeks.

'Watch that wall!' The warning made Susan stop, but the caller was talking to a comrade. 'Looks dodgy. There's a gap down here. Hang on a minute. Listen.'

She wanted to walk on, but found herself standing mesmerised as the man shone a torch into a hole for another to peer in. 'See anything?' He shouted into the hole. 'Anyone there? Are – you – all – right?' Then to the other man, 'What's the old girl's name?' The name supplied, he called, 'Mrs NORTON!'

'There,' he broke off. 'Is that a leg? Can you see?'

'Only a bit of wood.'

'MRS NORTON! It's no good – someone'll have to get down there.'

It was impossible to tear herself away as a slim man began to squeeze himself through the aperture, careful not to dislodge loose bricks, splintered beams, and broken furniture balanced so delicately. What would they bring out? Susan wanted to run but couldn't. It was like being a rabbit hypnotised by a snake's stare. Her stomach churned with a sick feeling.

The AFS man was halfway in when a shout came. 'There she is!'

Heads swivelled. Turning into Calvert Street, the small round figure, seeing her home in ruins, had broken into a run. Old Mr Hardwick caught her in his arms as she came abreast of him. 'Where've you been, love? We thought you were . . .'

Over his shoulder her eyes surveyed the destruction. 'It's all gone. All my nice furniture . . .'

'Never mind your furniture. 'S long as you're safe.'

'All my John's stamp collection. What's he gonna say?'

'He'll be only too glad to know you're safe when you write to him. You come into my house now and I'll make a cup of tea. You probably need it.'

Being guided across the road towards his own window-less home with its patches of missing tiles, ('Thank God it fell at the back of them places, or I'd of had nothing left either,' he'd said earlier) her gaze still clung to the wreckage.

'Sorry I didn't take up your offer,' she was apologising, as though that mattered now. 'I ran round to my daughter's place as soon as the siren went off round here. I had to be with her. She's on her own too – him in the Navy. I didn't want her to be alone. I shouldn't of gone.'

'If you hadn't of, you'd of been down there,' soothed Mr Hardwick as they passed Susan without seeing her.

The diggers were brushing themselves down. Neighbours waiting in the wings had come out with cups of tea for them as Susan went on her way, leaving them standing in groups, sipping gratefully. She had much happier thoughts now, eager to tell Marie who worked with her behind the counter on ladies' and men's underwear all about the new chap she had found.

A week went by. A fortnight. Disappointed, Susan had given up expecting to hear from him. Then came a letter. There was a Hollywood musical on at the Odeon. Would she care to meet him outside at six thirty?

Would she *care*? She took so long with her make-up, getting her long dark hair just right, choosing what dress to wear, that she made herself late, finally arriving to find him pacing up and down outside. But his face brightened as he saw her; taking her arm, he conducted her inside.

It was wonderful walking into the cinema on his arm, her small figure making him seem taller than he was. Wonderful standing in the foyer, its dull blue lights, in recognition of blackout regulations despite the two lots of dense velvet curtains shielding the line of doors, giving the sumptuous decor a strange wan look as she stood aside for him to pay at the kiosk – tickets to the balcony, of all things. Wonderful going up the wide, carpeted stairs that muffled their footsteps and then sitting with his arm about her shoulders in the comfortable plush seats as they watched Eleanor Powell dance across the screen in typical Hollywood splendour. Afterwards they had taken a long saunter while he told her more about himself and she in turn told him something, not too much, of her life. His arm had been about her the whole time and the warm September night had wrapped itself about them both, a light warm breeze playing with her hair and the hem of her summer frock, and they might have been somewhere on a high mountain top rather than a crowded, dirty, smelly, bombed city.

In a quiet dark corner away from homeward-bound cinema and theatre crowds, he had drawn her to him and kissed her, a long lingering kiss that had set her blood tingling. He had asked no more of her than that, but she knew that they would meet again, and again, and she couldn't wait to get to work on the Monday to tell her two workmates there all about it. She was his girl. It was almost too good to be true, unbelievable. Susan prayed that night for this thing to last forever.

Chapter 7

His back against the unlit mobile searchlight, Matthew stood beside the as-yet mute field telephone, his companions waiting, watching. Nothing doing yet but there soon would be. Thin clouds scudding across a full moon would soon disperse, leaving sky and earth bright from what had become known as a bomber's moon – ideal for Jerry who had already checked the weather and knew he could enjoy good hunting tonight.

Which city would Jerry go for? Birmingham? Coventry? Callous to hope it would be Coventry, but Susan lived in Birmingham. What if she suffered a direct hit? It didn't bear thinking about.

They had been writing to each other for two months now. Each time he thought of her, which seemed to him to be every other second, a flood of warmth swept through his insides followed by cold fear for her safety. He'd never felt like this before. If he were to lose her now . . .

The man beside him chuckled. 'What's that great big sigh for, Matt? Not that girl you go to see every time you get a pass?'

Bob Howlett was a close mate, of a similar background to his own. Their accents often drew smirks from the mix of Welsh, Scots, Midlanders and Cockneys, especially their rough-tongued sergeant, Pegg, constantly and vociferously cursing his luck in being saddled with a couple of junior NCOs whose education put them far above him, except for his military dedication, though theirs, according to him, was nil. Both had been before the selection board. Both had been rejected, one for his flippancy, the other for his apathy. Bob possessed no ambition whatsoever. Six feet tall and thin as a pole, propped at the moment against the sandbagged parapet he looked like a loose bag of bones with a stoop that resisted all the Army's attempts to straighten him up. Nose aquiline, chin long and narrow, physically he was the most unprepossessing man Matthew had ever known, yet he displayed the sweetest disposition and an agonisingly mild temper. People didn't come any better than Bob Howlett. Too good ever to become an officer.

Matthew grinned at him, laying aside thoughts of Susan for a little moment to follow this second train of thought. 'I wonder what old Peggy would do if either of us ever did get a commission?'

'Follow us to the ends of the earth probably,' Bob said with lethargic sagacity. 'It won't be me though. I'm no leader of men. Don't want to be. All I want is this war to end and me to be back with Phyllis and the kids.'

'Amen,' Matthew echoed fervently, at the same time hoping that Bob wouldn't suddenly bring out his latest photos of his blonde-haired wife and three children as he was wont to do.

From far away came an almost inaudible eerie wail of

a civilian air-raid siren. But for the stillness of the country around, it would not have been detected at all. Their own klaxon had sounded a short while before, sending men running to their stations. As though in obedience to that faint wail, the moonlight poured out from its shielding of cloud to throw every object on the earth beneath into stark relief. From the direction of distant Coventry tiny dull flashes silhouetted the black horizon. Thin cones of light, made squat by distance, began to play back and forth, crossing and re-crossing the sky in slow motion, low down, like flat furtive ghosts. Hardly discernibly came a low and ominous crump-crump, crump-crump-crump of a far-off barrage. Coventry was getting it. Matthew found himself offering up silent prayers of thanks, his radio set still quiet, their own searchlight still in darkness. Not Birmingham tonight, thank God.

The field radio crackled. Suddenly sick at heart, Matthew unhooked the earphones and put them on to note the coordinates they conveyed. A shape materialised from the darkness of the field around to stand beside him.

'Why are we still in darkness, sonny?' Sergeant Pegg's voice filled the night air, making the nearby mobile parabaloid sound indicators tremble.

Matthew sprang to his job. 'They're going on now, Serg.'

To his barked command, the huge disc clonked. A shaft of blinding light pierced the sky, here picking out remnants of fagged cloud in fleeting, flat and fuzzy patches, moving hastily on, there the cone's vortex swallowed up eerily by the immensity of space. But Sergeant Pegg was not happy.

Stepping close, he put his lips close to his quarry's ear to be heard over its messages.

''Alf asleep was we, Corp'ral?'

'No, sir.'

'Well, I suggest yer get yer finger out a bit more sharpish, next time, an' stop bloody daydreamin'. Fine example you are. Whatever'd 'appen to us if you ever got a commission? The day you do, my arse'll turn into a bleedin' pumpkin, that's wot. Now keep yer mind on yer job or I'll 'ave them stripes orf yer before yer can say, "Oh bloody my!"'

For twenty minutes Matthew kept his mind on his job, the sound indicator booming and roaring, amplifying every sound of any plane overhead, pinpointing its direction. On one occasion his searchlight trapped a plane, prompting others to sweep over and join it in a perfect star of beams, the ack-ack guns in a nearby sandbagged pit consequently opening up in an energetic earsplitting barrage. The plane swopped east, then north, finally managing to evade the deadly nucleus of light by slipping behind a low cloud and no doubt veering off to rejoin its fellows over Coventry.

One by one the searchlights were doused. Matthew's radio went quiet. Bob and the rest of the crew fell to rolling cigarettes.

'Tell you what,' he said, his tone low and confidential, recalling the sigh Matthew had given earlier and interpreting it correctly as only a gentle, perceptive soul could. 'Why don't you propose to this girl of yours? In a letter. See what she says.'

Matthew looked up with a frown from the cigarette

he too was rolling. On a corporal's pay, packet cigarettes ran away with money and he did his best to discourage his parents sending cheques; telling them in no uncertain terms that it made him look bad before his hut-mates and that he was managing adequately enough.

'I've only known her two or three months. I can't go mad.'

'If you feel about her the way you appear to me to, I would say you wouldn't want to lose her to someone else. Better now than never.'

That was true. But marriage. Matthew gave Bob a nod to placate him and told himself he'd have to think about that one. The more he thought about it, the more it seemed it was what he wanted. He remembered having the same feeling about Jenny, strange little twinges of excitement in the pit of his stomach when he thought of her, but Susan had come along and the sensation had transferred itself to her, fourfold. He knew now who he wanted, that it was Susan for whom he would further his career, making her proud of him. Perhaps he'd take Bob's advice, re-apply to the selection board. A man should do all he could to support his intended.

Sitting on his bed, a book on his knee for support, he absorbed himself in putting down on paper all he wanted to say. But reading it back, he cringed. The worst drivel he'd ever read – she'd laugh her head off. Better to tear it up before he did any damage and made a complete fool of himself.

But he didn't tear it up. Instead he folded the flimsy wartime paper and laid it carefully inside his pay book.

Finding a fresh sheet of paper he penned another letter, full of the things he normally wrote to her, his hut-mates, their doings, the smelly Eddie Nutt whose socks stank the place out every time he opened his locker, the lecherous clown Taffy Thomas, the foul-mouthed Bert Farrell, Bob and his family, Sergeant Pegg, the rotten food, the hard beds, how much he looked forward to seeing her again and hoped it would be soon, and how was she, and what had she been doing?

'Ward, M.L.C. 092.' Matthew shouldered through the waiting men to receive two letters. Perched on a wall in the weak sunlight of the November morning that threatened rain, he put aside the one from his parents and opened the other with its large childish handwriting.

The letter was short, two small ruled pages, laboriously written, with several words misspelt, which evoked a surge of compassion . . . no, more one of tenderness. It was little more than an outline of her activities since he'd last seen her – pictures with a girlfriend, a dance or two. A twinge of panic smote him that she could so easily meet someone else during one of those dances, someone more conveniently to hand than he.

'Damn this bloody war!' he uttered so vehemently that Bob looked up and grinned.

Hastily scanning the second page of writing which didn't quite reach to its foot, it was the last line that brought relief flooding through his chest in a hot glow: 'I've been worried you might get fed up of riting to me. I cant wait to here from you.' A thousand words penned by the world's greatest poet could not have conveyed as much meaning as he read into that one artless sentence.

Life took on new meaning; time was a most precious commodity. But it was one the Army seemed perversely set on spinning out into an eternity of misery, for just as he was settling down after his day's duty to write to her the beefy bulk of Sergeant Pegg appeared to announce that the whole unit was on the morrow being sent to the wilds of Wales on an exercise, duration not divulged, all passes cancelled. Matthew, who had planned on wheedling a few hours' pass for himself, suffered an intense sense of loss hardly to be borne.

'Damn this bloody war!' he uttered for the second time that day as he fought to rush off a letter to Susan.

The Blitz was a tyrant. Begun in September and still going strong, there was no chance for Jenny to be at home for Christmas or New Year. Her mother had either to spend both on her own or go to her sister in Leicester. That she wouldn't do, fearing to travel alone. Daddy had always done everything and she, used to following him around like a small puppy, had still not learned independence.

'Can't you *try* to get away, dear,' she asked when after the sixth or seventh attempt Jenny got through on the telephone to the couple next door – well, the girl next door now that her husband had been called up.

Her mother sounded out of breath from hurrying into the other house, shouting down the mouthpiece as though distance made this obligatory although there'd not been a lot of static crackling over the wires.

'I'm on duty, Mumsy. I can't just get time off. It's terrible here. So many people being brought in injured.'

'I don't like us being apart.' The voice filled with consternation. 'I'll have to spend all night Christmas down the shelter all on my own. We've had a bomb come down near here. Some of the tiles are off. It's only a matter of time before this place is hit. I wish you were here. I feel so . . . so . . . isolated. Can't you come home?'

'They need every nurse they can get here at the moment, Mumsy.'

'Well, it's terrible. They should allow you home for New Year at least.'

'German bombers don't worry about holidays, Mumsy. They'll drop them whatever day it is.'

'I don't think I can stand being here all on my own.'

'Can't Joan next door come into our shelter with you?'

'I couldn't ask her that, dear.' Her mother's voice had dropped to a whisper lest the girl overhear. 'I couldn't open my house to *strangers*.'

'She's not a stranger. You're in her house right now. Now she's on her own too, you could both become quite good friends and help each other. We need to help each other these days.' The Blitz had made everyone conscious of the need for people to help each other.

'She won't be here at Christmas or New Year. She's spending the holiday with her family or her husband's family.'

Jenny tried not to let her sigh echo down the line. 'Well, I can't come home. The hospital's bulging. There are even beds in the corridors. And during an air raid we have to get as many as we can under the beds or down into the basement. It's like another hospital down there.'

'If you asked them nicely, they'd let you have just *one* day?'

'I can't, Mum.' She'd not been listening. 'This line's going funny. I'll have to ring off.'

'But Jenny . . .'

'I'll try to get home for a few nights after New Year, but it's impossible at the moment. You'll be all right, Mumsy.' She wanted to say that her being at home wouldn't stop a bomb dropping on it. 'I'll get time off eventually. I shall need it to get over all that we're going through here.'

'What, dear? What?' The crackling was growing noisier; impossible to hear anything now. And her time was almost up, her money running out. Moreover, she knew she was taking liberties during work time.

'I've got to ring off, Mumsy. Love you.'

'What?'

'Love you, Mumsy. I must go.' A sturdy, starched blue figure was approaching. 'I'm on duty. I'm wanted. Try to get home as soon as I can.'

She replaced the receiver on its hook, goodbyes cut short by the glare from the stone-grey eyes of Miss Grenville, approaching with a few attendant senior staff.

'Have you not enough to do, nurse?' The question was quietly authoritative. Jenny's reply was hasty, unrehearsed.

'My mother, Matron, asking if I'd be spending Christmas with her.'

In truth she had no real wish to go home. Christmas here would be far more exciting if she could believe what

the nurses who'd been here last Christmas told her: wards
decorated with paperchains fashioned from whatever
coloured paper they could get hold of, spending any off-
duty hours in each other's rooms to make them; going
round the wards on Christmas Eve, their blue capes drawn
close around them as they sang carols in muted voices,
each nurse holding a lit candle; later sitting in the nurses'
quarters all cosy and warm by a fire while others piled in to
roast chestnuts and eat the mince pies someone's mother
had sent, swapping jokes and stories of latest conquests
with junior doctors.

That had been last year's. Jenny looked forward to
this year's but wondered if it would have changed since
the Blitz started. But anything was better than just sitting
at home with Mumsy, even if there was an air raid on
Christmas Day itself. She wouldn't even put that past the
enemy.

She had been transferred to the London Hospital from
her teaching hospital in October, a month after the Blitz
had started. Eight weeks on and night bombing was
still going on, not a single night free of it, remorseless,
dominating all else. As darkness fell, she, like everyone
else, merely prepared herself for the wail of sirens, the
drone of bombers, and the horrible tearing sound and
crash of falling bombs when the very air shook and
dust drifted in from everywhere. The sky turned lurid to
the mad clanging of fire engines, ambulance bells that
heralded another stream of casualties. She and everyone
felt it would go on until the war was finally won, all
steadfastly refusing to imagine it could be Britain who

might lose. Such a prospect remained so preposterous it was unthinkable.

Jenny stood aside for Matron's entourage to pass, waiting to make her escape back to her ward, but the woman halted, eyes fixed on her. 'If you are on duty, nurse, then you should know that telephone calls are not permissible. If you are not on duty, then you are off limits. I shall see you in my office at six thirty.'

'Yes, Matron.' Jenny watched miserably as she and her staff moved on. Six thirty. Well planned. Two days remained before Christmas and the evening had only just grown dark because of the introduction of British Summer Time. Clocks were now kept one hour forward the whole year round to confuse an enemy whose own time remained as it had been prior to hostilities. The bombers would not arrive for a couple of hours yet. Plenty of time was left for civilians to get home from work, eat and get into shelters, and for her to endure a formal and uncomfortable dressing-down from Matron.

She had been through the drill before, standing in the centre of Miss Grenville's office, Miss Grenville walking around her with measured steps, quoting hospital rules to her in quiet tones as measured as her walk. No punishment had been meted out: humiliation constituted punishment enough. Jenny found herself almost wishing the bombers would come early, requiring her duties to take precedence over any visit to Matron. But that would come sooner or later.

The all clear sounded just before dawn; while the people of the East End sank back to pick over lost homes, grieve lost loved ones, or just feel glad that they had escaped unscathed, the doctors and nurses of the hospitals all around toiled on, endeavouring to repair often irreparable injuries. For Jenny, exhausted by morning, her talking-to from Matron was just added torture. She fell thankfully into her bed in the nurses' quarters to forget about everything for a few hours until night came again. A week of that and then it would be days, spent mopping up the dregs from the previous night.

By February, freezing and cheerless, it was a wonder there were any buildings left to be bombed. Even some already flattened received a second direct hit. Yet, emerging for a breather in the cold light of dawn, she was always amazed so many still stood, windowless, battered sentinels. How this hospital had got away with just glancing blows so far seemed a miracle. How those who worked within it kept going was a miracle. Exhausted nerves stretched like rubber bands, they remained professional amid unbelievable chaos. As for herself, she was just an efficient puppet in a starched apron; obedient, mechanical, quietening some hysterical parent while nearby a terribly injured child seemed far more in need of her help; a mind trained at last to say, 'Walk, nurse,' when the sight of a woman with broken legs going into labour screamed for her to run, maybe knocking someone over in the process. It was frustrating, while the injured poured in still, covered in dust and blood, to be required to make tea for overstrained doctors. Though often essential, keeping them going, more often than not the tea remained untouched. It was hard at times to be obedient.

She recalled resentment when, wanting to stand by for the injured to arrive, she'd be required instead to help transfer geriatric patients to the basement. Coaxing the frail and sometimes perverse elderly into wheelchairs to be trundled to safety could test obedience to breaking point and struck a poor second to the business of tending victims of bomb-blast and fire.

'I feel more like a maid-of-all-work than a nurse,' she complained in early March, the night bombing still going full blast, as they carried a dear old soul back up a flight of stone stairs after the all clear had sounded. The lift was again out of order. O'Brien gave a tinkling laugh.

'Dear Mother o' God, isn't that what we're here for?'

O'Brien was small, dark and Irish, a bundle of smiles and dedication whose upbringing had endowed her with the unquestioning obedience of a nun. At times Jenny envied as well as admired her. When it seemed impossible the hospital could continue after broken gas mains cut off the cooking facilities and all they had to cope with was a portable paraffin stove, O'Brien's tranquillity as they fought with the thing reduced Jenny to a state of humility. With no running water for days on end, O'Brien took it all in her stride, emptying bottles of disinfectant into basins of cold water for washing hands after each dressing until the liquid turned cloudy grey, all the while praising God for the blessings of disinfectant.

At these times, Jenny yearned for the smooth routine of that teaching hospital in Basingstoke. She had learned her skills there, but East London was the acid test of a nurse's stamina. Here, controlling fatigue meant overcoming not the simple weariness of a few nights' lost sleep but the perfidious wearing down of her mental faculties, creeping up on her like a hooded assassin. The only hint of anything amiss would be a second or two of apparent sleep, yet coming back to herself to find she had accomplished her task as though she had been wide awake all the time.

More alarming were those longer moments of forgetfulness, as when she had taken a pile of bedpans, not to the sluice, but straight through the doors of an operating theatre without any recollection of how she had got there. Beating a hasty retreat, she had felt flustered and very much awake.

Much more recent had been that strange hallucination when she had looked up from taking a blood pressure to see a haggard and terribly emaciated young man standing at her elbow.

She remembered saying, quite loudly, 'I'll be with you in just one minute,' and wondering vaguely at the astonished look from her female patient. She had turned again to find the young man was not there. He never had been. Recognising her mistake for what it was, a figment of total exhaustion, it had taken a while to shake off a belief that it had been a premonition of some sort, for what really alarmed her was that every time she thought of it, the young face hovering before her seemed to be that of Matthew Ward.

It left her wondering for days how he was, where he was. In fact she could hardly wait for her next time off duty and she sacrificed a night out with the girls to pop home instead. The air-raid sirens hadn't yet sounded and after sitting for a while in the back garden with Mumsy in the improving April weather, she wandered down to the shops in Mare Street where Mr Ward had his electrical shop, with the precise aim of casually asking how his son was doing.

'Stationed in Wales at the moment,' she was informed as he handed a customer a repaired radio. Such things these days were either repaired or second-hand, most things not on ration having vanished from sight.

'He was near Birmingham,' Mr Ward went on. 'But like always, being trooped all around the country.'

'He's okay then?' she pressed, still unable to get her hallucination out of her mind. At least he hadn't been sent overseas.

'Fine. Had a letter from him a few days back.' How like Matthew he spoke. 'Found himself a girl. Don't know how serious it is, but he seems smitten by her. That's how it goes. In the forces, you meet all sorts. His mother's not pleased. Says it probably won't last as she's in Birmingham and he's in Wales.'

And Jenny's heart had sunk as she smiled and left, although it had been inevitable he would meet someone. She thought of herself, out of sight and out of mind. She should stop thinking about him and get on with her own life. But at least he was safe.

In no mood to go home just yet to have Mumsy defining the bleakness she knew must show on her face, she wandered down to St John's church. She needed time to think. Of what, she had no real notion, but she had to sort out her thoughts of the future. It was imperative to stop dreaming of Matthew and get on with her own life.

St John's stood closed on this early Saturday evening but did not look quite so isolated and remote as it once had behind its tall iron railings. They had gone now, as had all iron railings, to be melted down into guns and tanks in the fight for victory over the enemy. It now stood amid the open space looking slightly vulnerable, its sooty brick bathed a dirty gold from the slanting sun, its once-proud stained glass windows now war damaged and mostly boarded up, no longer reflecting back the golden glow.

For a while Jenny stood there, contemplating whether she should go back home now, but she let her feet carry her towards the church itself and into the neatly laid out gardens behind it, still known locally as Barmy Park from the asylum for the insane that had once stood there. Sinking down on a bench with the low sun full on her, she watched people wander past, their thoughts most likely on enjoying a little fresh air before consigning themselves to the communal shelters and Bethnal Green Underground to await the arrival of the night bombers. All these people were passing yet she saw herself as quite alone, not because they ignored her but because she wanted it, so that she could think in peace of Matthew, of herself, of how she stood with him and he with her. Once again she decided to stop thinking about him and get on with her own life.

With that in mind, she got up and resolutely turned her face towards home. A voice hailed her as she passed the church again. Louise Ward ran up to her, slightly out of breath, cheeks flushed, her mousy hair rolled up primly in a style known as a victory roll, unflattering for anyone with the broad jaw line which she had inherited from her mother.

She looked excited. 'What're you doing here, Jenny? I thought you were nursing.'

'I've got a day off,' Jenny supplied but Louise could hardly contain herself.

'I'm only home for the weekend. Guess what, Jenny, I've gone and joined the Wrens.'

'You've what?' Jenny stopped walking.

But nothing could diminish the enthusiasm shining on Louise's face. She looked transformed. Gone was the prudish strait-laced mien. This girl glowed, and Jenny recalled the exact look on her brother's face when he'd come to say goodbye that cold winter day. It was like looking at a bird newly released from a cage and she realised that Louise, for all she would never have admitted it, had been as trapped as he had been once she blossomed into her teens. Without warning she had broken loose from all the old ties that had bound her. Because of the war she was suddenly her own person. 'I'm eighteen now, eligible to join up. I signed on and they took me. I had a medical and I passed A-one. I want to see the world.'

See the world. Perhaps dangerously so. Jenny eyed her dubiously. 'Did you tell your parents what you intended to do? What do they think?'

Louise gave a giddy laugh. 'Mother was shocked rigid. Dad hasn't said much. I sprang it on them. If I had told them what I was going to do Mother would have stopped me, I know. It took me being evacuated . . . well, not exactly evacuated but more or less . . . to give me a taste of what could be had. So I signed on for the WRNS. I'm leaving next week for Portsmouth.'

Walking home with Louise chatting incessantly at her side about her medical, how girls were needed to relieve Royal Navy personnel from office duties, how she had been told that they could be sent anywhere in the world and all the countries she might see, Jenny found it impossible to broach the subject of her brother's involvement with the anonymous Birmingham girl and if she thought it could be serious. Yet again she told herself to put it out of her mind, that their lives had gone their separate ways. But how nice it would be had it been otherwise.

Chapter 8

The coming of spring found Matthew still crouching in ditches in the wet wilderness of Fforest Fawr in the heart of Wales, trying to keep a crackling field radio dry under a gas cape.

'One thing's obvious,' he muttered to Bob Howlett beside him. 'She's no letter writer.'

In four months he had written Susan one letter a week as regularly as clockwork, each one several pages long. In return he had received just five letters from her, each hardly more than two sides of a piece of Woolworth's notepaper. Her bad spelling, he understood, perhaps made her slow to reply, but if she had any feelings for him, surely she'd write more frequently.

'She's lost all interest in me,' he said miserably. 'Bound to happen, she there and me here, and Birmingham full of uniforms.'

'Is that what you think?' Bob asked, scanning the rain-soaked peaty moorland. 'That she's just uniform crazy and nothing else?'

'No, of course I don't. But no girl is going to wait for months.'

'Lots do, in wartime. They'll wait for years.'

'Yes, if they've been going steady long enough. We hardly met above a couple of times. I wouldn't blame her.'

Beside them, Taffy Thomas shifted his uncomfortable position on his haunches. A Welshman he was, but from sunny, civilised Aberystwyth on the coast. This part of the country with its sopping heather wasn't his cup of tea at all.

'What you need is to get it out of your system, boyo. A bit of diversion. Two sisters I know of. Real beauties, the pair of 'em. Met 'em a week or two ago. One for me, one for you, eh? Make you forget your poor broken heart, that will.'

'No thanks, Taff,' Matthew murmured. Taffy looked mildly spurned.

'There's a terrible waste. Just have to do the best I can with both of 'em, then, won't I?' Grinning, he went back to scanning the horizon and misty forms of men scurrying about on manoeuvres, what could be seen of them through fine rain and the smoke of the thunder flashes going off.

Returning to camp, Taffy was off to the farmhouse where the sisters apparently lived; their father was in the Army, their mother working late in some nearby town. He returned later that evening, a little the worse for wear and very triumphant.

'Missed a treat, you did,' he stated, flinging himself on his camp bed in the tent he shared with Matthew and Bob. 'Damned stupid, you, mooning after a girl that don't want to know, as far as I can see.'

Having spent the entire day trying to put Susan out of his mind and annoyed that she refused to go, Matthew allowed his curiosity to arouse itself, if only moderately. 'What's she like then, this sister?'

Taffy let out an odd sound that passed for a knowing laugh, rather like a lion grunting. 'Big. Would eat you for breakfast, boyo. Put the blood back in your veins for you though. I could take you next time, if there is a next time. And if you was to get a letter from your girl, then no need to tell her, is there?'

'Might take you up on that, Taff.' Defiance held him in a vice. Two weeks waiting for a response to his last letter to her, and still nothing.

'You're on then,' said Taffy, and Matthew's mood loosened enough for him to give way to a terse chuckle.

'You're a lecherous swine, Taff.' But at this moment Taffy was a tonic to an aching heart.

A few days later he was glad he hadn't been led into temptation, with fatigues preventing him sneaking out of camp with Taffy to the infamous farmhouse. Handed a letter from Susan, he read what seemed to be the usual dutiful scribble, except for one short badly spelt paragraph:

> I hope you don't think I'm not intrested, Matthew. I don't know how to put my feelings down on paper because when I read it it sounds so silly so I just tare it up. But I do need to tell you that I reelly do . . .

The next two words had been crossed out, obliterated so completely that a diviner couldn't have read them, after which she had continued:

I won't half be glad to see you again so I can tell you
how I reelly feel.

All at once it seemed his luck changed. Before he had a
chance to reply, the whole unit was returned to Northwood
and with a forty-eight-hour pass to boot. On wings of
joy he rushed to the phone box on his arrival, finding a
lengthening queue of Army personnel eager to tell families
of the chance to be with them for the weekend.

In a fever of impatience he tagged on to the end of
it, cursing the time the one already in the phone box
was taking. At last, the receiver in his grasp, he gave the
exchange the telephone number of the shop where Susan
worked, having long ago looked it up after she had told
him where she was employed.

'Hello?' A high, piercing voice spoke loudly in his ear
as he asked for Susan. And then, querulously, 'Who is
this?'

'Can I speak to Miss Susan Hopkins?' he repeated.

'I'm sorry,' came the voice, quite tersely. 'Staff aren't
allowed to take private calls.'

'But this is urgent.'

'I'm very sorry, sir. This telephone is for customer
enquiries only.' She wasn't a bit sorry, in fact she sounded
highly pleased to refuse his request. 'Only if the call is
from the family of one of our staff with dire news do we
allow them to take a call.'

'Then could you give her a message?' he intercepted.
'Could you tell her I'll see her tonight – on the corner of
her road – at six-thirty?'

The voice had become filled with exasperation. 'Really, sir, I am far too busy to relay messages from every Tom, Dick and Harry arranging dates with members of my staff.'

'Please – just this once. We're – we're . . .' He thought quickly. 'We're engaged, and . . .'

He broke off as the phone-box door was yanked open. The voices outside came instantly loud, the speaker even louder.

'Git a bleedin' move on, mate. There're others out 'ere, y'know.'

Matthew shot out a hand and jerked the phone-box door shut again. 'Please . . . I've been away on a training course.'

'Engaged, you say?' There was now lively curiosity in the voice on the other end of the phone, and for an instant he hesitated. What had he said? Then he came to an instant decision. 'That's right. And I need to speak to Miss Hopkins. It is very important.'

He waited while the faceless one ruminated on this piece of news.

'Well,' it deliberated at length, 'I really cannot alter our rules, but on this occasion I will pass on your message. What name?'

'Matthew Ward.'

'Very well. But I sincerely hope you are not making a fool of me, Mr Ward. And please keep in mind that my staff are *not* allowed to make use of this telephone for private purposes unless in an emergency.'

'I'll remember. And thank you.'

Thoughtfully he replaced the receiver. Engaged, he'd said, in fear of being cut off. Engaged. Well, why not? All that fretting, all that longing, the tone of her last letter – he was sure now that those obliterated words had been 'love you'. And didn't he want this relationship to last? And hadn't he spent these past four months pining, if he really admitted to it? Well then . . .

The prospect of being engaged sent a thrill of excitement through his veins he hadn't expected. Lost in thought, he opened the door of the phone box to be almost pushed against the edge of it by a soldier squeezing by to get in, throwing Matthew a baleful glance as he did so.

''Bout bloody time too, mate! Got *my* missus ter phone too, y'know.'

The stress lay on 'my'. The man assumed he was married. He would be, soon. And again a thrill coursed through his veins.

He hadn't expected Susan to be there on the stroke of six thirty, but not finding her there on the dot, irrational anxieties began instantly to manifest themselves. Had the manageress not passed on his message? Had he in fact frightened her off with his damned silly proposal? Wouldn't any girl be? She'd never said she loved him, apart from that crossed-out bit in her latest letter which could have been anything, just a spelling mistake too bad to let by. That bit in her letter about wanting to tell him how she really felt, one could read all sorts of meaning into such a line. In retrospect he had kidded himself. He was a fool.

It occurred to him as he waited in the damp warmth of this still-light mid-April evening that he didn't really know anything about her. He *felt* that he knew her, but it wasn't the same thing.

Staring along her street that teemed with grubby children at play, their shouts echoing from the flat, scabrous walls on either side set with endless doors and windows, not a tree, a plant, a blade of grass to be seen, he realised how unlike was her life to his. He had to be honest with himself. Because he thought himself in love was he seeing all this and her too through rose-tinted glass? Perhaps, as well as love, did he feel some sadness and pity for her too? Without that he would be viewing these slums with utter distaste, eager only to get away.

Where he stood was a pub, its blown-out windows and frames covered by sheets of waterproof-painted cardboard, its walls, door and sign pockmarked from flying shrapnel. Across the road, a little way down, a gash in the previously unbroken row of terraced houses held a pile of rubble, a result of the bomb Susan had told him about. The slanting evening sun picking out the interior walls that had once been private pitilessly exposed the wallpaper, the poor fireplaces, the smallness of the rooms that had once been, and almost touching the rubble, the houses of the next street, hitherto unseen from here, now peeped through like people surprised at being caught in the open.

He glanced at his watch. Six thirty-five. Was that all? A breathless voice called his name, light footsteps from behind him came running, and there she was, almost falling into his arms as he turned, her tone gabbling with panic.

'Oh, Matthew. I had to stay behind at work. Stock-taking.

I got your message but I only just got away and nearly missed the bus. I was so scared you wouldn't wait. I thought you might think I didn't care and give up and go away . . .'

She was reaching up, kissing him, here in the street for everyone passing by to see. 'Oh, Matthew, did you mean what you said? On the phone? You did mean it, didn't you?'

He nodded, gently stopping her frantic embrace, aware people were grinning as they went past. 'It wasn't a very romantic way to propose . . .'

'Oh, it was!' she broke in, still holding tightly to him. 'I never dreamed I'd get such a romantic proposal. And to think that bitch didn't tell me until it was time to close and then said we had to do stock-taking. She let me go a bit earlier, but I hate her.'

'Doesn't matter. You're here.' She'd never know how relieved he felt. 'I want to take you out, Susan, to celebrate. I can't afford much in the way of a posh restaurant, but . . .'

'I couldn't eat. I'm too excited,' she burst in. 'I want to go somewhere quiet with you, darling. Just us two, and we can talk all about *things*. We've got to discuss things.'

'Yes.' Her closeness was making him feel worked up inside, a sort of churning making it hard to breathe properly. They had to get away from here. 'Where do you want to go?'

At last she broke away, thought for a moment. 'It's still light. It'll stay light for ages yet. Let's get some sandwiches and take them up on Beacon Hill. We can watch the sunset and be all romantic – just you and me. It only takes half an hour to get there.'

On the rounded promontory called Beacon Hill, more or less deserted but for one or two people walking dogs, they reclined on Matthew's greatcoat on the rabbit-nibbled turf to eat a couple of meagrely filled off-ration chicken sandwiches as the sun sank lower.

'On a clear day you can see ten counties from here,' Susan said, huddled inside her coat against the rapidly cooling air. The sun had become a red ball in the smoky haze of the city, outlining the rim of their world. She pointed southwest. 'That's the Malvern Hills.'

Matthew looked, then laughed. 'Clouds.'

'They're hills, Matthew.'

'All right, hills,' he laughed and she turned a petulant face towards him.

'Don't make fun of me.' Her lips were so close that he leaned forward and kissed them, tasting the sweetness that was her lipstick but which he was sure must also be her lips. Forgetting her pique she returned the kiss, nestled against him, lying quiet now and watching the rim of the sun finally sink out of sight, leaving its reflection to tint the clouds orange and pink, that in turn bathed the earth in ruddy glow.

'Matthew,' she said quietly, slowly, relaxing against him. 'You did mean it, about us being engaged? Only it was so casual. It was romantic, being said over the phone, but . . . well, you know, if you said it again now.'

He tightened his arm around her. 'Darling, I'm saying it now. Shall we get engaged?' Yes, this was what he wanted.

Couldn't imagine life now without her. She would be his wife. He felt his insides leap with the joy the thought brought. 'Susan, I want to marry you.'

He heard her deep intake of breath, her reply exhaled in a series of long sighs. 'Oh . . . Oh, Matthew. Oh . . .' She seemed incapable of saying anything else. It meant yes, he knew. But there were material things to think about too, unwanted material things. 'I'll have to tell my mam and dad.'

'Will they object?' She was still not twenty-one. She must have their consent. His heart fell a little. But he needn't have been anxious.

'No. They'll be glad to see me go and make a bit more room. I've got three brothers and two sisters and we've only got three bedrooms. They'll be thrilled, especially as you're someone really nice with enough money . . .'

'Hold on,' he curbed her, laughing. 'I'm not Rockefeller, you know. I'm existing on a corporal's pay.'

'But your family's well off, aren't they?'

'They're nothing to do with me.' He hoped he hadn't sounded a bit grim but he didn't want to think about them at this moment. 'You'll be marrying me, not them.'

'I know. Oh, Matthew, of course I know. Married. I'm going to have to pinch myself to make sure this is me.' She had turned, lifting her face to his. 'I shall love you always, Matthew. Always and always.'

And on her cue he kissed her with a pressing need for her bursting inside him like a radiant explosion. Consumed by its heat he let his weight bear her down beneath him and on the warmth of his greatcoat they made love, she in trusting joy of his promise and he in the knowledge that they would be together till all eternity. And it was beautiful.

He wrote home, cramming his letter with Susan's charms, and defiantly told them that he was engaged.

That Sunday he went dutifully to see Susan's family. Susan had already broken the news and her mother, fair, full-bosomed and not a bit like her trim daughter, planted a kiss on his cheek in a cloud of Evening in Paris perfume.

'She's right about you being so good-looking, love, ain't she, Dad?'

'She's right, yeah,' echoed Mr Hopkins.

Susan's two sisters sat on the arms of the settee, the air around them redolent of peardrops from nail varnish being applied as they both regarded Matthew with mute envy of their sister.

Two of her brothers were in the street, the youngest sprawled on a mat in front of an empty firegrate torturing a clockwork train with a screwdriver.

The place smelled of Sunday midday dinner and Matthew was glad he hadn't been invited to eat with them; the lingering odour of overboiled cabbage almost overwhelmed him so that it was difficult to draw a breath without feeling nauseated. Susan, sweet and fastidious Susan, deserved better than this. He would give it to her as soon as this war was over and they could find a place together. Meantime, as soon as they were married she might go to his parents and live in a far more wholesome atmosphere.

Mr Hopkins, a small man who looked as if he had once

been handsome, lounged in an armchair rolling a cigarette which he lit. The match was dropped in the empty grate, the matchbox replaced on an already cluttered mantelpiece. 'Wondered who she'd end up with,' he muttered.

'I'm very glad she's found herself a nice lad,' said Mrs Hopkins, handing Matthew a cup of tea while Susan, sitting beside him on the edge of the settee, smiled with satisfaction and cuddled nearer to him. Her teacup was on the floor at her feet, the liquid in it strong and muddy, as was his. He took a sip, tried not to grimace and put it down beside hers. Behind him a mound of well-thumbed magazines kept sliding forward, making his seat uncomfortable.

'When you planning to marry then?' Mr Hopkins asked.

Matthew glanced at Susan, saw her eyes, those deep blue eyes, full of trust. 'As soon as possible,' he answered.

Mr Hopkins coughed, a moist rumbling cough, and flicked the wet butt of his cigarette into the grate. 'Up the spout is she, then?'

'I'm sorry?' Matthew queried at once, hardly believing what he heard and appalled.

'Pregnant is she?'

Susan's two sisters giggled. The boy on the mat looked up, mildly interested. Mrs Hopkins gave a small embarrassed tut.

'No, Mr Hopkins, she isn't,' Matthew said tersely, wanting to be out of here as soon as he possibly could. Love Susan as he now did, beyond measure, he did not want to set foot in her parents' house ever again. This man repelled him. But that Susan was small like her father, it seemed incredible that he was indeed her father. With no way to explain to him, a man who confused love with lust, his feelings for his daughter, he said instead, 'If I'm posted before we can be married, there might not be another chance for a long time.'

Mrs Hopkins was giving him a scrutinising look. She had quite large breasts. They strained at her sturdy white brassiere, the top of which was visible above a blue organdie blouse. Matthew looked quickly away, thinking of Susan's small firm breasts. He longed to be out of here, to be alone with her.

Mrs Hopkins was appraising him slowly. 'I must say, though, it fair took us all by surprise, our Sue telling us last night as you'd asked her to marry you. Came as a bit of a shock, like. No wonder we thought you and her had been up to a few tricks.' She gave a tinkling laugh at his look. 'Come on, love. We've all done it. But whether she is or she ain't, I'm glad you're serious about her. And if it's all right with her, then it's all right with us.'

The china-blue eyes followed him slowly as somehow he got to his feet, his hand seeking Susan's and holding it firmly. 'I'll have to be going now, Mrs Hopkins.'

She looked surprised. 'You ain't drunk your tea yet.'

'No, I've got to get back to camp. And Susan and I, well we . . .'

She giggled at his awkward pause, her tone full of feminine wisdom. 'Of course. You two want a bit of time alone – to say goodbye, proper like.' She came over and took his hand in her soft one. 'Now you come and see us again as soon as you can. You're always welcome. I'm glad for you both. I know how hard it is for people in love to wait, but meeting you, I know you'll take care of her no matter what you two get up to. I reckon our Sue's a lucky girl and at least you've asked to marry her. So we can look forward to you both setting a proper date, eh? And soon, eh?'

'Well, as soon as the Army lets us.' He looked at Susan and saw her eyes shining. 'I don't know when that will be, but I'll try to get something sorted out. It will probably have to be at short notice, knowing the way they work – probably end up in a registry office. The Army doesn't give weddings top priority for leave.'

Again he looked at Susan, expecting to see disappointment in her face at the possible lack of a wedding without the trimmings, but her eyes were still glowing.

Chapter 9

The Blitz was over. The evening following that Saturday the tenth of May, the worst night of any that the enemy had dished out, people went to their places of safety as usual, nurses stood on alert to receive yet another influx of casualties as usual, but the bombers didn't come.

'I wonder what's wrong?' Jenny's question echoed that of many, almost as though they had been robbed of something. Quite silly really. But O'Brien, jolly as always, had an answer.

'Ah well, isn't it Sunday, an' all? And isn't it about time they'd be thinkin' of havin' a day of rest? Holy Mother o' God, I expect they need it.'

'If they don't, then we do,' Jenny said with just a twitch of a smile. 'But I don't think Hitler believes in Sundays or God.'

Like everyone else she was holding her breath. Come Monday, after lulling poor battered Londoners into a false sense of security, they'd be back again – part of Hitler's plan to demoralise them further, it had to be – and she would again form part of a team trying to patch up a new intake of victims. But after a fortnight and everything still quiet, Jenny felt she could at last let out her breath.

She was also given her first full weekend off in months.

'Now you'll have the whole weekend with your mother,' O'Brien said, a wistful lilt in her tone that there was no chance of her getting home to see her family, way off in Northern Ireland. She'd have been appalled to know that the prospect of spending the weekend with her own mother didn't fill Jenny with as much joy as she supposed.

All she wanted was to relax a little. Being with her mother, telling her how lonely she felt, was only swapping one tension for another. Of course it was uncharitable to think like that, but now that the worst of the air raids seemed to be over she felt she would have liked to spend this first weekend off in the company of the friends she had made. She needed a bit of fun, a bit of freedom, for who knew what lay around the corner?

The city's ruins had still continued to smoke ten days after the Blitz ended. Victims were still being dug out of the rubble, domestic services were still not working properly, thousands of families remained without homes, and streets still stayed blocked; sometimes a street had to be cordoned off where an unexploded bomb was being defused.

But slowly the intake of casualties was diminishing and this past fortnight had given Jenny a taste for a new freedom that had begun to be felt by her and her colleagues, a sense of adventure as after a night out she and a few others would clamber back into the nurses' home via a window surreptitiously left unlocked. The hospital's notion of keeping an eye on its vulnerable young nurses meant proper curfew being kept, with doors locked at ten thirty prompt. Anyone returning later than that must get past the superintendent's office, and if she didn't have an official pass, issued to very few for special circumstances only, a visit to Matron the next morning would ensue – a fate usually worse than death. But rules were made to be flouted. After months of air raids with hardly a moment for herself except to flop down exhausted on a makeshift bed in the safer basement after duty, Jenny felt happy to flout them with the rest.

'No, not this weekend,' she told O'Brien as they ate after-duty Bovril sandwiches in O'Brien's room. 'My mother's not expecting me. A few of us are going to a dance at the Palais in Hammersmith. I don't want to miss it.'

O'Brien stopped halfway to taking a bite from her sandwich. 'But I heard you once say you were not much of a dancer, did I not?'

'I'm not. But I'd still like to go. Be nice to let my hair down for once. Why don't you come too?'

'Me? Bejesus, I'd be no good. I've two left feet, so I have.'

'Me too. But it'll get us out of ourselves for a while. We'll keep each other company.' She wouldn't feel so out of it with O'Brien as her life raft, someone to talk to while the others were whirled off in the arms of those who picked them for partners.

It was with amazement that Jenny found herself among the chosen at the very first dance, a waltz, something she could do fairly well without falling over her or her partner's feet. She was in fact asked to dance several times and discovered she wasn't half as left-footed as she had once thought herself, so long as she concentrated on what her partner was doing, and so long as it was a waltz or a not-too-fast quickstep. She felt guilty leaving O'Brien, glad to sit out the more difficult dances, the foxtrots, the tangos and the seductive rumbas. O'Brien seemed quite content just to sit and watch, even pushing Jenny to dance with anyone who came up to them.

'I was niver a one for this,' she said brightly, her ready smile hardly leaving her round face. 'Now a good jig is more in my line, so it is.'

But as the evening wore on, she began to fidget and look at the clock high on the white and gold wall above the band.

'If we don't leave soon, Ross, we'll be back too late to get in properly and have to creep past the superintendent's office, so we will, and if we're caught it will be Matron's office in the morning.'

Jenny laughed. 'That's all solved. Bennett left a lavatory window open and a dustbin underneath.'

'And what if someone closes it?'

'They won't. She's given instruction to one of the night staff to keep an eye on it. But it's still early yet.'

Someone coming towards her with a purposeful expression which she was coming to recognise as an invitation – and the dance was a waltz, thank God – stopped her from saying any more. Not only that but she thought she recognised him as one of the young junior doctors from the London. He held his hand out to her and nodded enquiringly.

Whisked away, her feet by now adjusting to one or two

of the more intricate waltz steps, she was unsurprised but highly delighted when he said, 'I know your face.'

She leaned back from him to study him. 'I'm a nurse.' The floral dress she wore would not have betrayed her. 'I work at the London.'

'I thought I'd seen you somewhere. That's where I work.'

'Oh.' She felt him swing her and concentrated on matching the step and not squashing his toe in the process.

'I'm on Dr Farnborough's team. A junior doctor so far. But I hope to qualify next year. My father's a GP. In Bristol. I'm Ronald Whittaker.'

'Jenny Ross,' she reciprocated. 'I'm just a nurse. Studying hard.'

He chuckled as he swung her into a turn. 'Don't ever say just a nurse. You lot have been worth your weight in gold these last months of the Blitz. Couldn't have managed without a single one of you.'

'Not the mess I've been getting into during the worst of it,' she said with a small self-deprecating laugh. 'Dropping basins of water all over the place . . . Oops! Sorry.' She'd caught his toe, breaking his turn but he hardly noted it. He was staring at her, slowing his steps down more to a walk.

'I know you,' he burst out in revelation. 'Yes. During an air raid. In the basement.'

The basements had doubled as operating theatres and casualty. And now she definitely recognised him too, and the recollection made her blush. He had been assisting in stemming a haemorrhage. She had knocked into him as she hurried past with a basin of disinfection solution.

The liquid had tipped all over the floor so that she had been obliged to mop it all up, getting in the way while all around people cried out for relief from their pain. Later he had come over to ask how she was. All that had been going on around them and he had asked how *she* was.

By the end of the waltz, to her astonishment, he was asking her if he could see her again. 'I know we work in the same hospital, but I would like to see you on a social basis. Perhaps we could go across the road to the pub for a drink, when we're both off duty.'

Before she could stop herself, she said, 'I'd like that.' Seconds later that last kiss Matthew had given her flashed through her mind, a kiss that meant so much at the time. But that was it – *at the time.* Time had gone on. Their ways, which she'd thought might hold promise, had taken their own turnings and she'd vowed to get on with her own life. Maybe this man was her new life, her future. Matthew certainly wasn't. He was the past.

She found she and Ronald had something in common. He knew the Basingstoke teaching hospital where she had been. He had left just before her arrival. It seemed such a coincidence and only natural they should make a second date as soon as their off duty hours again matched. And when on their third date he told her he thought she was quite lovely, the understatement carrying a depth of honesty, she felt uplifted and indeed felt lovely for the first time ever. Even so, old habits tended to die hard; his admiration of her made her scoff.

'Don't be silly, of course I'm not. I wish I'd been born dark-haired.'

'You've got gorgeous hair, Jenny.'

They sat in darkness on one of the few market stalls operating in wartime, manned by older men and some women holding the fort for their own menfolk away at the war. Whitechapel's street market, a thriving place before the war, had become sparse, the variety of goods narrowed down to vegetables, second-hand clothing, bike parts, and so on. Perched on the empty stall between a skeleton of rusting tubular uprights, breathing in the dank odour of cabbage leaves trodden underfoot earlier and the sweet waft of beer from the pub they'd just left, he couldn't see her in the blackout, nor she him, but his hand moved up and in the inky blackness felt its way across her short curls. 'I do so love touching your hair, Jenny.' He leaned forward, gave her a kiss. 'I know this sounds sudden, but, Jenny, I love you.'

For a moment she was quiet, then she said softly, 'We've only seen each other three times. You can't. It's too early.'

'It's never too early, darling. I am, I'm in love with you.' He kissed her again, gently, and all she could do was kiss him back, telling herself that Matthew was another world, a closed chapter. She felt a little sad, but this was *her* life. And she had to take it with both hands.

Sitting in the sunshine of her tiny back garden, overlooked by all the other houses around that were beginning to cast lengthening shadows across it, Jenny let her mind move gently over that third date. It had been far too early for him to start professing love. Had she felt the same it would have been fine, but she hadn't. Nice as he was, she became angry with herself that even as he kissed her, Matthew with his quirky smile had floated into her head, making her merely suffer the kiss, thus allowing some past infatuation to spoil what could become something worthwhile.

She found herself telling Ronald that this weekend she had to spend some time with her mother. After all, duty came first. But was it really that there might be a slim chance of bumping into Matthew or at least finding out how he was? She needed time to think – about Ronald, about her life, to shake off this silly longing and grow up. Ronald was a nice person but it was early days yet. A day or two away from him might clear her head and let her see things as they stood. Too easy to end up an old maid in crying after something that couldn't be had when what could be had was maybe staring her right in the face.

'Jenny, dear, come in and have your tea.' Her mother, calling to her, interrupted her reverie.

'I thought we could take a little stroll in the park afterwards,' Mrs Ross continued as they sat together in the small dining room with the sun pouring in through the window. 'It's a lovely afternoon and I don't usually care for going for walks on my own. But now you're here it would be nice for us. They don't give you half enough time off at that hospital.'

Jenny held back a sigh of protest. She didn't want to stroll anywhere. It had been peaceful just sitting in the back garden relaxing in the gentle curve of the deckchair. So long since she'd been able to relax. Resigned, she went to gather up a cardigan.

'No one would dream there was a war on,' her mother

murmured as they passed the noisy Victorian drinking fountain with its usual cluster of children around it denying visitors a chance of peace or a sip of water.

'Let's take a walk over to the other end,' Mrs Ross suggested with a grimace towards the raucous, scruffy children. 'It's quieter over there. I like the grottos and rockeries with all the rhododendrons. They should be in bloom.'

It was a long walk; the park was vast. Jenny let her mother chatter on as they wandered past the wide lake with its twin islands designed as sanctuary for water fowl. There was another lake, an ornamental pond near the main entrance with fish and water lilies. But it was all beginning to look a little sad. Parts of the park had been turned over to allotments rented by local men too old to be called up. Jenny could see some of them hoeing around their spring cabbage, lettuce, onions, carrots, stringing up runner beans, all bent on their work, everything else around them going unnoticed. Men who no doubt had once only ever got their hands in the soil for a hobby, now dug like navvies. Tomorrow, Sunday, they would be at it again, bending their backs and trundling their wheelbarrows home laden with tools or green produce to help supplement the family rations for another week. People who had any sort of garden or back yard now kept chickens for their eggs and flesh – another boost to a larder slimmed by rationing.

The cricket field now had guns on it, multi-barrelled cannons that had made a terrible row during the Blitz. 'I'll be so glad to see the end of this terrible war,' her mother was saying. 'It would be so nice for you to go back to a nine to five thirty job and come home every night like you used to.'

'It can't last forever.' She didn't want to go back to some nine to five thirty job. Nursing, for all its restrictions, its rules and regulations, had given her in its own way a taste for freedom. She wanted more and by the time this war came to an end she hoped she would have moved on, living a life of her own. That could be a long way off; the war, the way it was going, seemed to have no end to it at all. Night bombing had ceased for the time being but that was no guarantee it wouldn't start up again. Everyone, for all they had breathed a sigh of relief, was still on edge. The Germans had all of Europe; only this island was left, with just a strip of water between it and the enemy. German invasion was all the talk. Meanwhile British merchant ships were being sunk, every day another one, tightening rationing still more. Even clothing had now gone on ration. The loss of seamen's lives meant it broke the heart to listen to the news. War in North Africa was now going badly, troops had been pulled out from Crete. No one knew what would come next. She could be thirty by the time it all ended.

'I know it won't last forever, dear,' her mother was saying, clinging to her arm as though needing support. 'It's just becoming too much for me, for all of us. Look at the bread we eat. Grainy, grey stuff, going stale almost as soon as it's cooled. Real white bread's a thing of the past. By the way, the tiles on our roof have been mended, by quite an elderly man who came. The bombing did such a lot of damage.'

'We're lucky. People have had it really bad elsewhere.' She thought of the injured brought into casualty, smothered in dust and grime and bits of brick, operated on hardly cleaned up. She thought of the gaping spaces left in blocks of tenements, just rubble now, still uncleared and beginning to settle and weather, greening with fast-growing weeds; places where people had once lived. All their possessions were now gone, perhaps they themselves were gone.

'Yes,' her mother agreed, sobered by much the same thoughts. 'We have been lucky. The times I've put my hands together and . . .'

A voice calling Jenny's name cut her short. They turned to see a fair-haired girl pushing a pram in which a child around a year old sat. At her side was a fresh-faced young man sporting a pencil moustache and wearing an officer's uniform. Instantly Jenny recognised them.

'Eileen! Freddy!' She grasped each in greeting as they came up to her. 'How are you?'

Eileen's voice hadn't changed, the same dreamy one she remembered. 'I thought it was you, Jenny. I said to Freddy, "I'm sure that's Jenny Ross," didn't I, Fred? How are you, Jenny. Are you still nursing?'

'I'm fine,' Jenny returned, formally now the surprise of seeing them had passed. 'Yes. In London now. I'm home for the weekend.'

They nodded without interest. 'Freddy's home on leave,' Eileen said while he smiled rather superciliously. If Eileen hadn't altered, he had, from the soft lovesick youth to a man with a bearing that suggested arrogant confidence.

Jenny turned her attention to the little boy in the pram. 'What's his name?'

'Simon. He'll be a year old in three weeks' time.'

'He's a handsome lad, Eileen.' She cooed at him but the boy merely stared back, solemn round eyes regarding her with that peculiar stare most one-year-olds adopt, their trusting baby smiles long since used up. 'You must be very proud of him.'

Freddy nodded and looked pleased while Eileen bent forward over the top of the pram and touched her offspring's fair head with a fond and possessive hand. But her face had clouded.

'I wonder sometimes if this is a world we should be bringing children into, what with our boys bombing Germany, and the Italians on their side, and the fighting in North Africa, and with all this bombing. My mum and dad's house got a direct hit you know. But they weren't in it at the time.'

'Oh, dear.' She didn't fancy conversing about the Blitz. It was past.

'And after all our RAF boys did last summer, fighting up there all alone in the air. You heard about poor Dennis Cox? Killed in his Spitfire.'

Jenny had heard. She nodded solemnly.

'Damned waste,' Freddy said abruptly.

'You used to be his girl at one time,' Eileen said, looking pityingly at her. 'It must have come as a terrible shock to you especially.'

'It was never serious between us,' Jenny said while her mother gave a sad sigh and murmured something about

Dennis Cox being such a nice boy too. 'We were just friends really.'

'Even so . . .' Eileen persisted lugubriously, making Jenny want to laugh. Like many who lead uneventful lives, which was how Eileen struck her, she seemed to need to feed, like a carrion crow, on the tragedy of others. 'It doesn't seem possible, though. Poor Dennis Cox – dead. It's terrible.'

'Yes, terrible,' Jenny echoed. So many people dead. So many lives spoiled by loss, by permanent injury, by sights they should never have seen. Men in battle, civilians who should never have been anywhere near a battle, children too young to be thrown into war, young people just leaving school with all their lives ahead of them, their eager lives consisting of but a few short years after all. They shall not grow old as we who are left grow old . . . Jenny felt tears prickle her nose and sniffed them back, probably sounding as though she was making light of Eileen's pet word, terrible, for the tragedy that hung about so many people. But it was true: having seen so much, tended so many dying and torn bodies, she couldn't find it in her to reserve sorrow for Dennis Cox alone.

'But have you heard about Matthew Ward?' Eileen had perked up.

Jenny's heart gave a sickening leap, fear for him pounding like a hammer in her throat. 'What about him?' It was all she could manage.

'Got himself engaged. To a Birmingham girl. They're getting married soon apparently. Now, he's the last person I'd ever have imagined would settle down. I said to you,

Fred, didn't I? "He'll end up a bachelor," I said, didn't I? And you said, "He'll still be chasing skirts at forty." You said, "Men like that who can get their pick of girls usually end up with no one. Far too choosy for their own good." Do you remember saying that, Fred?' And as he nodded, 'So you could have knocked me over with a feather when his father told me in his shop the other day. I don't think his parents are very keen. A girl from Birmingham. So far away, isn't it? He sounded as though Matthew was really in earnest about her.'

Jenny's heart, still reeling from her initial fear, now felt as though it was plummeting slowly, a broken-winged bird, spiralling down and down. 'I didn't know,' she said, trying to sound unconcerned, but her voice trembled.

'And so sudden,' Eileen was saying blithely. 'I wonder if he's had to. I wouldn't be a bit surprised, you know. I bet his parents feel terrible.'

In the lounge Lilian Ward glared at the letter which had arrived only moments ago.

'How could he? He hardly knows the girl. He's only just met her. And bringing her here this weekend. It gives me no time whatsoever to prepare and get some food in. I hope she'll be bringing her ration book. I'm not in the mood to feed strangers. He has no consideration at all. Doesn't even ask if I *want* to see this . . . whoever she is.'

Leonard Ward watched her stalking back and forth between the leather three-piece suite and the coffee table where he sat with his breakfast cup of tea by the open bay

window of the front lounge before leaving to open up his
shop.

In summer it was nice to sit a while here with the morning
sunshine slanting in, warming his chest that played him up
so in winter, the curtains moving gently in a breeze off the
park that brought the sharp scent of cut grass. From here
he had a fine vista of the park peeping between the large
houses opposite. Even so he looked forward to being in the
shop to smoke his pipe. No Lilian there to frown and order
him into the back garden. He'd have liked his pipe now,
but he could hardly get up and walk out with her so furious
about Matthew's letter.

'He's already told us about her,' he reminded gently.

'Yes, absolute volumes in his last letter. Not one word
asking how we are. Nothing but this . . . what's her name?'
She consulted the letter again, then refrained from using
it. 'This . . . girl. Now he wants *us* to meet her. Says he's
serious about wanting to marry her. We'll see about that.'

'He's over twenty-one, Lilian. Not much you can do
about it.'

She was not to be mollified. It would take quite a bit
of patience and understanding, perhaps even firmness, to
calm her down. She had always been a dominant person.
Perhaps that was why he had married her, a woman who
had known her own mind and stuck to it in an age when
most women were mostly pliable, soft creatures looking
to marriage and security. All that despite being in service
when servants were expected to be servile.

Leonard smiled. He could forgive her domineering
nature, which concealed a good and caring heart. And at

the moment that good and caring heart was being tested to the limit. When all was said and done, Matthew was at fault.

'After all we have done for him,' she continued, still pacing, her back stiff, her indignation solid enough to be cut with a knife. 'This is how he rewards us, telling us he intends marrying some common thing from Birmingham, someone we don't even know, and actually bringing her here for us to meet. No warning whatsoever.'

Leonard allowed a little longer for effrontery to cool before getting up and saying he must be off before his customers began to wonder what had happened to him.

Opening up, his first customer had been Eileen Perry who used to be giggly Eileen Wilcox. In just two years she had now become a plain, staid, contented housewife and mother. Her husband was in the forces, but a quartermaster or something that didn't see combat, so she didn't bear that strained expression many wives had with husbands fighting somewhere far away.

Eileen had asked after Matthew and, glad of someone to talk to about it, he told her perhaps more than he should. Later he wondered if it had not been better kept to himself, for Eileen Perry loved a gossip and nothing displeased Lilian more than her private concerns being aired in public.

Ah, well, the deed was done now, he thought as he served customers with torches and fuse wire and round two-pin plugs and took in the odd wireless for repair, and wondered what this girl, this Susan from Birmingham, would be like. Utterly beautiful, stunning, marvellous,

Matthew's earlier letter had gone on among many other things, all of which his mother had dismissed with several sharp and disparaging snorts of disgust.

Chapter 10

Susan stared at the large bay-windowed house as Matthew held open the gate for her. She'd seen such houses in the better parts of Birmingham but had never been in one.

Ahead of her lay a wide gravel area bordered by small flower beds in full bloom, and shrubbery. The bay windows displayed white lace curtains, each so perfectly pleated that they resembled a regiment of soldiers. Susan saw a downstairs curtain twitch slightly and felt observed, rather like a fish in a glass tank. She shivered, hesitating in the gateway.

'Oh Matthew, I hope they'll like me.'

She strove hard to say like, rather than loik; strove to keep her voice from shaking. She'd been practising for this day ever since he had said he was taking her to meet his parents, but it was no less harrowing for all that. But Matthew had told her time and time again that he adored what he called her singsong accent, so surely they would like it as well and thus her.

'Of course they'll like you,' he laughed, taking her arm supportively as they went towards the door, a gesture for which she felt grateful. 'They'll fall in love with you at first sight, just as I did.'

Reaching the porch he planted a small encouraging kiss on her cheek, but in the state she was beginning to get herself into at the daunting prospect ahead, its message was lost on her, for as though by a given signal she saw an indistinct wavering shape distorted by the fluted glass of the door appear behind it, the door opening almost immediately. A slim, tall, upright woman with vivid blue eyes stood there looking at the two of them. An angular face, still with traces of beauty, topped by short greying hair whose stiff waves looked as regimental as the pleated curtains that had twitched earlier turned now to her, its smile of welcome seemingly chiselled from granite.

Matthew pushed Susan forward a fraction. 'Mum, this is Susan.'

Even in the midst of her fear of the brittle blue eyes, so different to Matthew's soft brown ones, Susan wondered at his use of Mum rather than Mother. Mrs Ward looked as though she should be called 'Mother' or even Mater; certainly not Mum.

The woman extended a hand in formal greeting rather in the manner of a pontiff suffering the touch of some unwashed layman. Obediently Susan took it, finding it stiff and cold. But with etiquette observed, Mrs Ward withdrew her hand and stepped back for them to enter.

'Was it a decent journey, Matthew, dear?' The voice was warm and took Susan completely by surprise. The woman was human after all. 'I did begin to think you were just a little late.'

'You know what travelling's like these days, Mum,' Matthew laughed easily and kissed her offered cheek.

'I never travel far these days,' she said as he put down his kit and Susan's small, slightly battered weekend suitcase in the wood-floored hall, a hall of such width that Susan felt her whole family could have almost lived in it. She thought briefly of her own cluttered living room with its old furniture and with its everlasting noise of argument and laughter. About this place there was a silence that seemed almost tangible, as if a cold ghost lived there.

'Dad home?' Matthew queried easily as he and Susan followed his mother into the lounge. Susan wished she could feel as easy, but then, he would feel easy, wouldn't he? This was his home.

The lounge was huge. The furniture looked lost in it, sparsely and tastefully laid out; a parquet floor bordered a large beautifully patterned carpet that looked sort of Turkish. Through the bay window, the high summer sun cast a minimal vertical strip of gold on to one tiny area of the wood floor, missing the carpet completely, which Susan imagined would never be allowed to be touched and consequently faded by any lengthening shaft of autumn sunshine. Mrs Ward probably had one of those posh blinds that well-off people used to keep damaging sunlight out.

'He'll be home for lunch,' his mother answered. 'As usual. But of course he must go back afterwards to open up for the afternoon, Matthew, whether you're here or not.'

'So you're the Susan we've heard so much about in Matthew's letters. He certainly didn't lie about you.'

Mr Ward's appearance prompted a surge of relief after an hour stiff and fraught with tension. She took to him the

moment he came in at the back door to immediately shake
her hand and utter his hearty comment before turning to
his son to ask how long he would be home.

'We go back Sunday night,' Matthew supplied with a
chuckle at the innocent, stock question asked nowadays of
every serviceman home on leave.

Mr Ward too gave a low chuckle not unlike his son's,
with a touch of mockery in it that could be taken the wrong
way if one missed the whimsical gleam in his eyes. They
were slightly lighter than his son's, more hazel than brown;
she could see who Matthew took after, glad that it wasn't
his mother. But if he'd taken after his mother, she knew
she wouldn't be here with him now.

'Don't give you long, do they? Well, we've got you for
the weekend at least. We promise to send you back all nice
and clean.'

She had a feeling that as a young man Mr Ward might
have possessed the same caustic humour as Matthew, but
that it had mellowed or been mellowed by life. She wasn't
usually clever enough to see inside people, but he was so
much like Matthew in looks and manner, she felt she could
guess at the person he'd once been because Matthew had
been a bit like that when she'd first met him.

It came to her that she still knew very little about
Matthew as they sat down to a small but beautifully set-out
cold lunch of salad and luncheon meat, all she supposed
the Wards' food ration would stretch to (dutifully she
had handed over her ration book which Mrs Ward had
not waved away). They were making conversation from
which she began to feel excluded. At ease with his family,

he was a stranger to her. Why had she consented to come here, when his way of life was so removed from hers? There came a dull feeling that once back in Birmingham, it would be the end of her and Matthew. She didn't fit in here. She was yet to meet his sister. If she was anything like Mrs Ward . . .

Susan felt most uncomfortable, smiling when she thought she ought to, answering the odd question put to her mostly by the friendly Mr Ward. The afternoon when he would disappear back to his shop loomed before her like a prison sentence. To sit looking at Mrs Ward's chilly expression all afternoon was not to be contemplated. She dreaded the moments when Matthew, quite at home among his own, would blithely wander off on some pursuit and leave her alone with this woman.

Mr Ward left, saying he would see her later that evening. Mrs Ward led them upstairs for Susan to put her case in the room allotted to her and freshen up. Freshen up sounded so posh.

'The bathroom is there.' She indicated a door at the end of a long landing which curved slightly at the end.

Susan nodded wordlessly. She had never seen a bathroom. The sort of people she knew in Birmingham did not have them. At least this would be a small refuge for her where she could escape this woman's penetrating eyes.

The landing had six other doors. Six. Susan had never seen such a thing. Surely, other than the bathroom, the rest couldn't be all bedrooms. Matthew said his was a four-bedroom house, so the one at the opposite end to the bathroom might be a cupboard.

'And this is your room.'

The door she had assumed to be to a cupboard was opened for her to inspect her quarters. And what quarters. Everything became a pink and white blur as, blindly, Susan stepped within as she had been bidden, a faint smell of lavender greeting her. It was neat and modest in size, though not what Susan would have called small by any means, with a single bed, a dressing table with delicate white and pink jars on it, and a mirror, a cupboard and a chair. The walls, curtains, bedspread and a fluffy rug by the bed were pink, all the furniture white, and the linoleum brown, the only contrast. Susan stifled a gasp of awe; tried to behave as though she were used to this sort of room.

'Thank you very much, Mrs Ward,' she managed in a whisper, while Matthew grinned and said loudly:

'My room, of course, is that end, by the bathroom.' In other words he and she would be separated by two doors, but only she was meant to detect the amused connotation he was conveying, his mother quite oblivious as she left them to go into their separate rooms to unpack what they'd brought with them.

He did indeed go to his door and open it, but as his mother went on out of sight down the stairs, he stepped back and came towards Susan, moving silently.

'I'll help you unpack,' he whispered purposefully and instantly she knew what he meant.

A knot of excitement formed deep in her stomach as she went into her room. Matthew followed quietly, no longer the stranger he had seemed during lunch.

For the sake of propriety as he pressed her down on the

bed with the sun shining bright through the window, she whispered, 'What if your mother comes up and catches us?'

He was bending over her, his mouth ready to close upon hers. 'She won't. As far as she's aware, you'll be unpacking in your room and I in mine and good manners will prevent her intruding into either.'

'But if she hears . . .' But Matthew's lips closing over hers smothered any further protest as, his weight upon her, her body responded with waves of longing surging through it.

'She doesn't like Susan, does she?'

Matthew leaned with his back against the bench in the work room behind his father's shop. The question was a foregone conclusion, but he had to ask it. Now was the time.

The shop was quiet for the moment. Saturday afternoon shopping took many people up west now that they felt safer with the Blitz failing to return. Not that there was much to buy; coupons, ration books, points, had put paid to casual spending. People were forced to save up a certain amount of points to buy a dress or a pair of shoes, so all the joy had long gone out of buying. But it was an excuse to get out, wander around the main shops, perhaps take in a cinema or theatre afterwards to forget shortages, loved ones overseas, the war itself.

With the shop quiet, the opportunity for a heart to heart with his father presented itself nicely. Susan had popped out to get some sweets with the coupons she had been saving for this weekend. She'd be back within a short while and in that time Matthew intended to tax his father on his mother's reaction to Susan. No good asking her how she felt. She'd merely have given him a blank stare and remarked that it was his business at whom he threw his hat, the remark full of disapproval. And he already knew by her attitude that she disapproved, so why ask? Yet he needed to ask, and now his father leaned back in his creaking swivel chair and, pressing dark, pungent tobacco into the bowl of his pipe with his thumbs, frowned in deep thought.

'You know your mother,' he said after a while, effectively avoiding a direct reply. 'Never been one to show her feelings.'

'That's what I told Susan. She's dead scared of her.' He saw the knowing half-smile his father gave and anger rose up inside him. 'Why the hell can't she be normal, like other people?'

'You mean she doesn't conform to your idea of normal, all sugar and spice.' There was reprimand in the quiet tone. 'Does that mean she should be discredited? She is honest and upright and has always done her best for you and Louise – in her own way, the only way she knows.'

'Yes, I know. I'm sorry.' He felt chastened. No one could accuse his mother of under-handedness or paying lip service to anyone. If she called a spade a spade, everyone could be certain it was nothing else. But if only she had one gentle streak in her, let the rules be bent ever so slightly; if only she was capable of letting people down lightly with a little white lie now and again. Timid people like Susan needed a little gentle understanding.

His intention had been to come out this afternoon to see his father, leaving Susan and his mother together to get to know each other without his having to hold Susan's hand, but she had begged to be allowed to come with him. Looking into the pleading in those blue eyes, he knew that to refuse her would have been like leaving a lamb in a lion's den.

His father lit his pipe, its acrid smell mixing with that of solder and flux and dust. It brought a sense of nostalgia, of belonging, that Matthew had once taken for granted, had thought would last forever, but now made his thoughts keen-edged with the knowledge that at any time he could be sent away to God-knows-where, perhaps never to come back. He felt his heart grow pinched and small with the fear of all this being taken from him.

'Your mother,' Leonard was saying, puffing a cloud of blue smoke into the air. 'She has always had high principles, from the day I first saw her. She frightened the life out of me, you know. Me, who always saw girls as soft, pretty creatures with no brains, whom men could command, to see a young woman come striding into my father's draper's shop as though she owned it, really got up my nose at the time. But I couldn't get my mind off her. She fascinated me. She was a beautiful woman, your mother, beautiful and straight-backed, and she held her head high. I used to look for her coming in. But I couldn't get up the courage to tell her how I felt about her. When I did, she turned me down flat.'

Leonard gave a small quirky grin at the recollection, his pipe gripped firmly between his teeth. 'You could never know what that's like, to open up your heart to a woman when it's not in your nature to do so and be turned down the way she turned me down. But finally we did start walking out together. She's a woman in a million, Matthew, believe me.'

'I didn't mean to discredit her,' Matthew said, shame-faced. 'But she's got to understand that I intend to marry Susan. I don't want her resenting Susan. I know she does already and I don't know why she should. She's only just met her, and Susan's the most likeable person I know. She's sweet-natured and loving. She's not pushy and loud. So why?'

The old chair creaked as Leonard leaned back into it again. 'Maybe she considers you both a little young and hasty. You and Susan have known each other only a few months. You've hardly had much chance to see each other regularly. Perhaps if you both waited a while longer.'

'What's there to wait for?' This was his life. They had theirs to look back on, had been fortunate, but what had he got to look back on so far, and how much future would be allowed to him? 'This isn't peacetime with long, well-arranged white weddings and strings of bridesmaids and a fine honeymoon afterwards. We might not have tomorrow and forever. I could be sent overseas at any time. I might not see her for years. I might even be . . .' He checked the words quickly, then reverted to the hackneyed idiom of defiance: 'We have to have something to cling to in this war.'

'Yes.' The pipe stem clicked audibly against Leonard's teeth. 'This bloody war.'

The shop bell tinkled. To its peremptory summons, he hoisted himself out of the chair, knocking the pipe out on the bench.

Matthew listened to the murmur of voices beyond the opaque glass of the dividing door, the conclusive note of a customer departing. The bell tinkled again, fell silent. Leonard came back into the back room bearing a domed, fretwork-fronted wireless set which he set down on the bench. He chuckled, making a joke against himself.

'Look what I've come down to. My father loved his little drapery shop and said I would inherit, but he died in debt and lost nearly all of it. It was your mother who was my widowed mother's mainstay. She made her sink what little was left into another shop after the last war, saying that electrical goods would be the coming thing. She was right. We did well. That's how we came to live in a nice area like Victoria Park Road. I'm no snob and I know where I came from, but your mother wanted better things for you and your sister. That and her love of the old order of things makes her seem to act above herself, but her heart's in the right place where you and Louise are concerned. I've got a lot to thank your mother for.'

The last words had a ring of finality about them. There was no more to be said on that score. Besides, any minute Susan would come running in, waving her few ounces of sweets in triumph. Matthew changed the subject, nodding towards the wireless come in for repair.

'Bloody ancient thing, that one. Looks a bit beyond it to me.'

Leonard grinned compassionately. 'She's a widow.

Can't afford much. Asked if I could do anything with it before Tuesday. Doesn't want to miss ITMA. Tommy Handley's her only bit of pleasure these days. God knows, she needs someone to cheer her up, if only on the wireless. There's little to cheer anyone up lately. Every time you tune in there's another setback – what with Rommel and Tobruk. And Crete, us having to pull out, five thousand killed . . .'

'I heard,' Matthew said tersely.

'Enough to make anyone lose heart. But it comes to something when you hear people say we might have to negotiate peace terms with Germany.'

'Rumours,' Matthew snorted. 'Like the bomb that chases people around corners – the German secret weapon. Some are actually believing it.'

'Everyone's on edge, that's why.' Leonard began unscrewing the casing of the wireless cabinet, lifting it up to reveal coloured wires and oblong valves. 'London blitzed to buggery, Coventry too, then suddenly, silence, everyone wondering what Hitler has up his sleeve next. Invasion probably. I don't know.'

Matthew nodded glumly. He'd seen the scenes of devastation as he and Susan took a bus from Euston railway station to home. He had rejected taking the underground, not wishing to subject Susan to the wretched bits and pieces of the thousands who had used the platforms as shelters during the nightly air raids and who still stubbornly went down there at nightfall, refusing to believe the Blitz would not return.

Above ground had looked just as dismal, pitiful.

Through the bus windows they had gazed at acres of blackened ruin still uncleared, walls precariously hanging, charred timbers, twisted girders pointing skyward with accusing fingers, the air still heavy with an acrid effluvium of burning that remained in their nostrils long afterwards, a memento of all London had suffered. And even in his own long road fronting an open park some houses had gone. After those guns and searchlights sited in the park itself, he supposed.

He watched his father extract a valve from the set. Testing it, he shook his head with tacit sympathy, then replaced it with one salvaged from another old set already beyond repair. Plugged in, the set crackled into life with tinny music.

'Ah, she'll be pleased,' he breathed. 'Defeated by a dud valve. I won't charge her for that. Husband died two years ago and she hasn't a soul to turn to. Though she keeps telling me her son is serving on the *Royal Oak*.'

'*Is?*' Matthew queried. 'The *Royal Oak* was sunk at Scapa Flow at the beginning of the war. All hands lost.'

'Exactly.' Leonard nodded, replacing the casing. 'Not a soul to turn to. I'll get this back to her this evening. She'll be pleased.'

The shop bell tinkled again. This time the back-room door burst open and there stood Susan, her small oval face brighter and happier than he'd seen it all day, his mother forgotten.

'I bought some toffees,' she announced. 'Do you want one, Mr Ward?'

As his father shook his head congenially, Matthew

came over and put an arm around her, his mind on her alone, the poor bereaved woman still living in the past put aside. Her empty life wasn't his problem. Everyone had problems these days.

'So you're really going to get married?'

Louise had come home on a weekend leave, declaring it fortunate to have fallen the same time as her brother's. She, as yet still in her WRNS uniform, sat opposite him and Susan in the front lounge regarding him with the steady critical gaze of a nineteen-year-old who felt she knew the world. Two weeks ago she had just seen one of her comrades break down after hearing the news that her fiancé's ship had been torpedoed; he had gone down with it. Her gaze was now fraught with concern as well.

'Not much joy being in love in wartime, that's my opinion. But I wish you both all the luck in the world. I don't suppose it'll be a white wedding, but the result's just the same I reckon.'

Susan simpered and sat close to Matthew, looking up at him for guidance. He gave his sister a rueful grin. 'I hope to get a twenty-four-hour pass for it if I'm lucky. We'll have to make do with that. It'll have to be in a registry office, I expect.'

'Well, perhaps I might wangle some leave. When's it to be?'

Matthew's smile hovered. 'We're not quite certain yet. Whenever we can. Probably at short notice. You should know what the forces are like. It'll have to be in Birmingham, near where I'm stationed. And with Mum and Dad down here, and Susan's people up there, I don't suppose there'll be many of our side there at all. It's going to be a rush in the end.'

Louise looked distinctly put out. 'You don't want me there, that it?'

'No, that's not it, Sis.' He was looking dark. 'I want you there. I want all our people there. I'd have liked to have a big white wedding, for Susan's sake. I wish we could.'

At which Susan clung closer to him, his arm tightening reassuringly about her. Louise, Susan thought, for all she was only a year older than herself, had a lot of her mother in her. And as Mr and Mrs Ward came in from the dining room where they had been lingering over a leisurely cup of tea Louise, it seemed, wasn't ready to pull her punches.

'Did you know they plan to get married in a registry office? It's going to have to be done on the quick, so he says. No time for me to arrange leave to be there to see him married. Him, my one and only brother.'

'That's unkind, Louise,' Matthew shot at her, but it was evident she was disappointed. 'Of course you're invited if you can make it. You'd be the first one to be invited. My one and only sister.'

That last sounded dangerously like sarcasm and probably was, and Leonard Ward looked at his son while Lilian stood aside, her face tight. But his was benign. 'Where do you plan to live afterwards, Matthew?'

It was a practical question, but one that betokened acceptance of his intentions, and Susan, feeling Matthew's body relax, realised it had become taut as Louise had railed on.

'We'll get ourselves a furnished flat for the time being, where I can get backwards and forwards from with a special pass.'

Leonard frowned. 'Not much of a start, a furnished flat. You'd need something unfurnished. Something to call your own. Your own furniture, not someone else's rubbish. Your mother and I aren't broke . . .'

'No thanks, Dad.' Matthew stopped him sharply. 'We can manage.'

'I want to say something else, son. It's that if you're posted away at any time or, God forbid, sent overseas, Susan will always be welcome to come here and stay with us.'

Susan's face went blank and Matthew hurried to her rescue. 'That's nice of you, Dad, but we'll get by. Lots of married women have to manage on their own these days when their men go away. And I expect her own family will be there to help.'

'Just a suggestion.' Leonard went to sit in one of the armchairs but Lilian remained standing, her hands clasped firmly in front of her.

'This is all very well. No one has any *idea* when this is to happen. All we know is that it is going to happen. We have merely been *told.* It would be nice if you discussed it more fully with us, your parents, Matthew?'

He matched her hard stare. 'I thought that was precisely what we were doing – discussing Susan and me getting married.'

'Would you be discussing it now if Louise hadn't blurted it out a few moments ago?'

'Probably,' he returned succinctly, at bay.

Susan cut in, amazed at her own boldness. 'We want to get married ever so much, Mr Ward.' It was far easier to appeal to him than his wife. 'I know we've not been together very long, but me and Matthew do love each other a lot. It don't have to take years just to know that. It can happen very quickly sometimes.' She paused for breath, anxious now at having said so much, uninvited.

He smiled at her. 'I know. So how soon would you *like* it to be?'

'Could be next month,' Matthew replied for her, his tone easier now. 'It'll have to be in Birmingham. I've exhausted all my leave so I'll only get a special day off, I suppose. I'll have to beg for that, I expect.'

'We'll try to make it up there if we can,' added his father. He gave a small apologetic chuckle. 'That sounds terrible, I know – try. But nothing's easy these days. Send us a telegram the second you know, and we'll be straight on a train. If I can get some extra petrol coupons . . .' again he gave a chuckle, a somewhat knowing one this time, 'we'll get the car out and use that. It's kept in good working order, you know, but we don't use it, at least very seldom these days. It's yours still, Matthew, sitting there, your twenty-first present. It's in a garage near the shop, waiting for the time you can use it again, Matthew. And talking of presents. Wedding presents of any good quality being hard to come by, would money be okay?'

'That'll be fine,' Matthew said a little tersely, making Susan look at him in surprise. 'But I still have that trust Grandfather left me. We won't go short.'

'Just a token wedding present.'

Susan felt sorry for Mr Ward, hearing the lame ring in his voice. She even felt faintly annoyed at Matthew. Why should he react so unthankfully to his father's generosity?

As Matthew travelled on the train back to Birmingham the following day to be in camp by Monday morning, Susan taxed him on it.

'You shouldn't have gone off at your dad like that, darling. He was only being kind. You acted as if you were bent on having a row with him.'

Matthew was staring out at the passing scenery beyond the carriage window. 'Did you see my mother's face?' he queried without turning. 'In my family we don't need to row. Never a raised voice, but the result's the same – no winners or losers. In a way, worse than any full blown row – no chance for anyone to release their pent up anger.'

He sounded so dark that Susan quickly changed to a lighter subject. 'Your dad said about some money left to you.'

He remained thoughtful for a moment. 'For when I was twenty-one. About five thousand, but I haven't touched it. Wanted to wait until the war was over and I came out of the Army. I expect many of us will come out without a bean, so it'll come in handy.'

'And it'll have made interest,' she added. At the mention of such an amount her eyes had widened. Five thousand pounds. A fortune. To think, being married to someone really well-off. She could hardly wait.

'Let's get married as soon as we can,' she entreated and

had him turn to her to put his arm about her shoulder and cuddle her close, prompting quiet smiles from the others in the carriage with them.

Chapter 11

Jenny gazed through one of the pub windows near which she sat, many of them still damaged by the Blitz and patched up as best as could be until shortages allowed for new windows to be put in. God knows when that would be.

Outside, Whitechapel Road was buzzing with stalls and people this Tuesday lunchtime. Whitechapel Road was exceptionally wide for London. It had apparently been made that way in the days of footpads so that they had no cover from which to spring out on passing horsedrawn mail and passenger coaches. Part of that wide road had, she'd been told, for this last hundred years been railed off for a market which still thrived and the noise of buying and selling came loud through every hole and crack in those of the pub's windows not yet completely repaired.

Despite the war, the market was in full swing; maybe now it evoked the days before the motor car. These days hardly any private cars were being used with petrol rationing the order of the day. Some lorries, though, still tried to make deliveries when they could. But there were a lot more handcarts than in peacetime, and the horsedrawn wagon could be seen in great numbers.

Across the still wide road beyond the hubbub and movement sat the London Hospital, a serene potentate, quieter now that the nightly air raids had passed. The injured were being seen to and sent home with no more being brought in to replace them; the hospital had started getting back now to the normal traffic of poorly children and the ailing elderly, those injured by accident instead of design, pregnant women needing treatment, and the ordinary sick; the outpatients department too had reverted to its normal routine rather than the unending stream of bloodied, bomb-torn bodies. Everyone now had time at last to let out a sigh of relief, Jenny included. She had gone back to work after her first weekend off in ages to find that even in the short time away things at the hospital had quietened still more.

'Penny for them.' Ronald's warm hand closed over her fingers and she quickly withdrew hers.

'Not worth a penny.'

'Ah, well, a ha'penny then.' His light brown eyes were searching her green ones as she looked briefly at him. They were full of adoration. 'No, on second thoughts, Jenny, the smallest thought of yours has to be worth more than a million to me.'

'Don't be silly.' She hated him behaving like this, specially when her inability to return his feelings made her seem hardhearted and his obvious love for her so pitiful. But one couldn't make love happen. 'I was thinking about the people out there, and the hospital. That's not worth a light.'

'Talking shop isn't. Let's talk about us instead.'

'Not just now, Ronald.' She didn't mean to sound so sharp.

Her thoughts as his hand closed over hers had been dwelling on the news she had received about Matthew while home, and then on the surprise glimpse she'd had of him from her bedroom window on the Sunday, his arm around the dainty dark-haired girl he was intending to marry. From her vantage point, Jenny had seen her lift a pretty face ardently to his as they passed underneath her window, and he had paused and kissed her lips. Jenny had felt the passion of that kiss writhe in her bones. It still did.

Gazing through the pub window she savoured a masochistic urge to retain the memory in a moment of self-torture, utterly futile for all it made her feel nearer to the man she knew she could never have. Matthew would marry his Birmingham girl and Jenny would never see him again.

Then Ronald laid his hand over hers, and instead of her private moment being gently suffered as it needed to be, those precious thoughts had raced through her head like a damned whirlwind, to be swept away.

They departed the Birmingham registry office in a thin shower of home-made confetti and a host of good wishes. The reception had been short, a modest gathering filling the little room with perfume, cigar smoke and perspiration.

'I just hope he knows what he is doing,' Lilian Ward said, watching the happy pair go off.

'Of course he knows what he's doing.' Leonard's

own gaze followed the taxi taking Matthew and his new wife off into the unknown; it softened reflectively at the recollection of his son's departing words to him. 'If anything happens to me, Dad, you two will look after Susan, won't you?'

'Nothing's going to happen to you, son,' he had told him sternly, but who could be that certain?

'But it's wartime,' Lilian's voice cut in. 'They don't know what lies ahead of them.'

'It was wartime when we married,' he reminded her gruffly.

Nothing had happened to him, had it, apart from a dose of mustard gas. Left his chest weak, but he'd survived. And so would Matthew.

The taxi going out of sight, he turned back to the registry office with the others to gather up the few belongings they had left behind when they'd gone to wave the happy pair on their way.

Lilian's lips had tightened. She had no wish to be reminded of that utterly mad escapade of hers when she had been young, leaving service to get married to a man going off to join up. She, who had always kept her emotions in check, doing such a headstrong thing! She hated being reminded of it. 'That was entirely different,' was all she could find to say.

'Absolutely.' Leonard gave a playful laugh. 'But we might not have married had I not swept you off your feet.'

'Fiddlesticks!' she shot at him, leaving him to smile after her as she marched ahead of him up the steps of the registry office to retrieve her hat that went with the smart suit she had bought with almost a year's worth of clothing coupons to see her silly, lovesick son married.

In the taxi, Matthew bent towards his wife and tenderly kissed her. He did it, not just because he was in love with her, but to reassure himself of their future together. He badly needed that reassurance.

In the registry office he had stood beside her, smiling, feeling hot and sticky in his khaki uniform as with one eye on the large round clock on the wall he received the felicitations of those gathered there.

Susan had been dewy-eyed the whole time, overcome by the joy of her new estate, the centre of attraction. Her sisters had wept obligingly, her mother copiously, as though her dear daughter were being whisked away to Devil's Island rather than wedded bliss. Friends and family on both sides had kissed Susan and shaken Matthew's hand before wandering off to try the tiny, practically fruitless wedding cake Susan's mother had made, rations not stretching to anything more. Its much larger, thinly iced cardboard cover was impressively decorated to emulate the fine wedding cakes of pre-war years.

Susan's mother had looked overdressed in fluffy pink beside his own mother in a tasteful beige suit, yet it was for his mother rather than Susan's that he felt somehow more embarrassed; the way she stayed aloof from Susan's mother as though she were a lesser being.

His father had been different again. He stood talking to Mr Hopkins, oblivious of the man's rusty best suit, his tobacco-stained teeth when he smiled, the rolled cigarette hanging wetly from his lips.

There had only been Matthew's parents on his side, and Bob Howlett as his best man, the rest Susan's, relatives, friends, workmates, all laughing and gabbling away in incomprehensible Birmingham accents, filling the tiny room with noise and tobacco smoke. It had been a relief to get away, to be alone with Susan at last, his kiss in the taxi a promise of that to come in the small one-bedroomed flat he had found for them, their own little love nest.

Susan returned his kiss, then broke away, pouting a little. 'I wish we weren't going to have to live in those two tiddly little rooms.'

'Why?' He grinned down at her. Pouting, she looked so pretty, her sweet red lips that he wanted to kiss again pushed out invitingly.

'I was just thinking, Matthew, you coming into that trust your dad was talking about, I mean, surely, couldn't we have got something better?'

'You liked them when we found them,' he told her, frowning. 'You called them adorable, cosy, our own little love nest.'

'Yes, but that was before . . .'

His frown deepened as she paused. 'Before what, darling?'

'Well, before . . .' She tutted, shrugging. 'Oh, nothing. But we will get something better in time, won't we?'

'Yes, of course.' Matthew's brow cleared. He was being stupid about the money coming to him, having for so long conditioned himself against the help his mother, almost selfishly, tried to give him. Even this trust seemed somehow tainted with her influence although he knew that too was stupid. And why should Susan be the loser because of his ridiculous obsession? Whatever he had was hers as well, and he shouldn't be selfish in his feelings about it.

'As soon as we get sorted out, I'll look for somewhere you really like,' he promised and was rewarded by her instantly snuggling against him, her surge of joy rippling through him as well.

The taxi began to slow to his directions at a row of small terraced houses behind spiked railings, with narrow patches of barren gardens in front. Worn steps led up to the sepia glass-panelled doors with names above each one: Rose Villa, Acacia Villa, Magnolia Villa, the taxi finally drawing up outside the one called Laburnum Villa.

The driver leapt out, opened the taxi door for them and, accepting Matthew's generous tip, called good luck before getting back into his vehicle and rattling away to his next fare.

In the bright sunshine they gazed at their new abode. The owner of the house, a Mrs Robertson, had recently lost her husband. It was the first time, she'd said when Matthew had gone there, that she had ever let rooms, and from her nervousness and the modest rent she'd quoted, he had almost been tempted to offer her more, but a corporal's pay didn't stretch to such gallantry. At the time he had been labouring under his ridiculous aversion to using any of the trust his grandfather had left him. He had kept his mouth shut and guiltily counted his good luck at the poor woman's expense.

Susan's hand tightened convulsively on his arm. He understood. It might be a modest start but she was still excited at the prospect of entering their first-ever home, closing their door on the world and being alone together.

He patted her hand encouragingly. 'We'll find something much better later. But today's our wedding day. Tomorrow I have to be back in camp, so let's make the best of today.'

This wasn't how it should have been. There should be a honeymoon, somewhere on the coast, somewhere really nice, Bournemouth or Torquay, a lovely hotel. There should have been a church wedding that had taken at least six months to prepare, and a good reception, with lots of money spent on it. There should have been a nice house awaiting them, the furniture bought and sitting inside to welcome them. Bloody war. Bloody Army. Bloody way of having to live . . .

Mrs Robertson was waiting for them. She had given him a key when he paid the deposit money, but motherly soul that she was, she had been waiting for them and now opened the door as they mounted the five shallow steps.

'Come in, dears. Do come in.' Her voice was high, a little weak, a little weepy; that of a woman in her late sixties still not yet adjusted to the loss of a husband after a long married life.

'Now you must treat this place like your own,' she continued, following them to the narrow flight of stairs, eager for conversation. Her main aim in letting her two upstairs rooms had been to secure a little company. 'Don't ever think you have to stand on ceremony now. Come and go whenever you want. It's nice to know there's someone else in the house besides me. There's a little gas ring and a portable stove upstairs, as you know, and there's a basin in the bedroom. My dear George had it put in when we had the bedroom. But of course, I sleep downstairs now. If you'd like a cup of tea now, my kettle is on the boil . . .'

'It's very nice of you, but no thank you,' Matthew cut in, trying not to sound rude. All he wanted was Susan to himself. They'd have so little time together as it was without sitting in their landlady's kitchen drinking tea and possibly listening to her life with her George, dear as he must have been to her.

He could feel the woman's gaze following them wistfully up the stairs, her thoughts no doubt on when she'd been their age with all her life before her. He felt a surge of bitterness shoot through him. All her life before her – did he and Susan have all theirs before them, say forty years of marriage as she'd had, or would theirs be cut short by war? A quick, easy calculation, done automatically, told him that the woman had been married before the last war, but her husband had been lucky and survived it. Would he be as lucky surviving this one? A shudder passed through him and was gone as, reaching the little landing, he shrugged it away and opened the door to the larger room that had once been a bedroom, now their living room.

Susan paused on the threshold looking in, not attempting to enter. 'It's smaller than I thought it'd be.'

'But it's ours. At least for a while.'

He made his voice sound light and jaunty, needing to brighten up. Flipping open the door next to it, he lifted her and bore her inside, kicking the door closed behind him,

with her clinging to him, any dejection she might have had
dispersing. In one easy movement he tossed her on to the
double bed that almost filled this even tinier room. The
bedsprings bounced madly under the impact of their light
burden.

'That's your place, Mrs Ward,' he announced firmly, and
while she lay breathless and laughing, he sat on the foot of
the bed, yanking off boots, then socks, battle blouse, shirt,
trousers, leaving the clothes draped untidily over the brass
bedrail, one or two items already falling on to the floor in
his haste as he flung himself down beside her. 'And this is
mine. Now – we'll start on you.'

'Matthew!' she squealed as he made to get her out of
her suit jacket. 'You'll rip the buttons off. It's a new suit.'

'Well, you do it.'

'No, I want you to do it. But mind the buttons.'

With her he romped and laughed. With her help he
rid her of one garment after another, she making a play
at struggling, he at Victorian mastery, until finally she
lay naked beneath him, his wife, ready for his demands,
but still laughing, the pair of them trying hard to keep the
sound down away from the woman below.

'I've one night with you, woman,' Matthew hissed.
'And I intend to make the most of it. So behave yourself
and do your duty. Now, lie back.'

After love stolen previously in secret, purported to be
all the sweeter for that, this love was the most wonderful
thing he had ever known. It must have been for her too,
for she complied without any of the earlier tension he
had always felt in her, the desperation of her acceptance

of him. Together, man and wife, it would be the first of a glorious uniting, quite beautiful and satisfying. What more could either of them, or anyone, want than this?

He opened his eyes. He must have dozed. Sunlight was touching one wall of the bedroom; the sun had moved round just a little, so it was still afternoon. He couldn't have slept long.

Turning his head leisurely to look at Susan, he studied her. She lay with eyes closed, vulnerable to his scrutiny so that he felt vaguely guilty in taking advantage of it. Deep in sleep, her breathing sounded gentle; her dark lashes lay against the pale cheeks, lips just slightly thinned as though in a smile of contentment. Matthew watched the quiet rise and fall of her breasts, small and firm with pale nipples, her flesh stretched taut as she lay full length, legs outstretched, the soft darkness rising between her thighs such that he wanted to bury his face there.

He felt his breath come shuddering with a longing to make love to her again. It wasn't purely a physical need, but it still seemed he hadn't been near enough to her even then – could never be near enough. No man is an island? Bloody hell! Of course he was. Trapped and isolated by thoughts impossible to explain, not even to this girl who had become his very life, whom he had this day married. He might try for a lifetime to describe to her how he felt, but she would never really know what it was he was trying to say. In turn could he ever really know her mind? He could bury himself inside her in a brief moment of love, tell himself they were one, yet he would still not know.

They were two people, each with their separate sensations. It was that, he guessed, which really disturbed him, that they couldn't truly ever be one in the sense he wanted – in a sense even he couldn't understand. Suddenly angry at what he could not define, he swore softly and closed his eyes, perhaps the easier to unravel this unsettling need.

Her hand brushing lightly against his thigh brought him suddenly awake. The sun had moved round, now playing on their naked bodies. He glanced at his watch. He had slept away another hour – another precious hour lost in this one day together, and again he felt angered by the thoughts that had plagued him, by fate, by the powers that would soon tear him away from Susan. If only this moment could last forever, the sun hang in its present position, its light remaining warm and luxurious on their bodies.

Susan's hand moved, caressing, not sensuously but possessively, claiming him as her own, reassuring herself of his nearness. The touch brought him back to reality. In the morning he must leave her, go back to the army that had first claim on him.

He stared up at the ceiling, an intense hatred seething inside him of those who could push him this way and that, a puppet manipulated by the strings pulled by some faceless power that had for this one day allowed the strings to dangle and leave him thinking himself free, only to pluck him up in the midst of his happiness to bend him again to obedience. One small jerk on a thread could tug him from this girl he had made his wife; another thread jerked would send him headlong into battle to fight not for his own life but for a continuance of a way of life. And if he should fall, the strings would be severed and he, like the toy he was, would be cast aside, the war going on without him, the peace when it came not for him to see.

Today he had been shown something so sweet, so wonderful; to have it all snatched away now came like a bitter taste in his mouth.

He sat up abruptly, went over and fumbled in the breast pocket of his battle blouse for a cigarette to calm his thoughts. At least moving about had dulled that sensation of panic he had felt. Susan had gone back to sleep. That was if she had woken at all: her hand on his thigh had likely been a purely instinctive gesture. He sat on the edge of the bed and watched her contented slumber. Susan lived for the day. She bent with the breeze, like a slender sapling and harboured no thoughts she couldn't understand. He envied her contentment.

Lethargically, he stubbed out the butt of his cigarette in the ashtray on the round cane table by the bed. The small stab of heat scorched his finger and thumb, making him draw in a hiss of breath. Susan stirred, rolled over on to her side and laid a loving hand on his arm.

'Happy, darling?'

'Uh-huh.'

His reply was purely automatic. He wasn't happy. Their marriage, hardly off the ground, could be cut short within hours.

Her hand began to travel, conveying its own message. Arresting its journey with his own, he held it in a firm grip for a moment, then casting away the dismal thoughts, fell back on the bed and turned until he lay over her.

'You're a little pig,' he told her, masking that earlier anger with a deep-throated chuckle. 'You're a greedy little pig.'

It made her giggle. She fought him as he took command, but only for a moment or two, and it was really she with her gentle resistance who commanded.

Loving her took away the last of his anger and yet this time he took her as a starving man might devour a morsel of bread lest it be snatched from him. And it was a terrified love that burned in his breast.

Chapter 12

'You're going through with it this time then.'

'I owe it to her.' Matthew stared blankly at the dartboard at which they were playing in one corner of the little hut where the NAAFI served refreshments to the ranks.

Bob Howlett grunted and launched his three darts at the board in quick succession, adding up his score as the last one embedded itself in the cork surface. 'Fifty-six. Leaves me double seven.' Retrieving his darts, he stood back, allowing Matthew to take his turn.

Matthew fixed his sight along the line of flight. 'How can I let her exist on a corporal's pay when I could see her more comfortable on an officer's?'

He sent the first dart on its way as though at an enemy. Twenty. All he needed now was a double six to finish, winning him the game and a free cup of coffee from Bob. But he was keyed up. This morning he'd had an interview with the CO, who promised to put his name forward. He'd hear in a couple of weeks, and depending on the selection board he would be sent off to OCTU for that pip on the shoulder that meant better pay and a lot more allowances for Susan. It meant leaving his best mate behind, but Susan's well-being took precedence over all else.

Ever since their marriage last month she had been worrying about that bloody trust that had come his way. Yes, he could have dipped into it, and yes, they could be living well, but there was after the war to think of. After the war he'd have to get himself a job, and if tales of the last war were anything to go on, getting a job with thousands piling out of the forces could take months, maybe years. That trust would be needed to stand them in good stead while he hunted. Oggle-eyed at the idea of five thousand pounds, Susan naturally hadn't been able to see beyond the end of her nose. It was up to him to think ahead for both of them, and a pip on his shoulder, perhaps two in time, would keep her better contented until the war was over.

Bringing his thoughts back to the game, he licked his lips and took aim for the double six, the narrow area between the twin wire rings looking narrow indeed on the right-hand side of the circular board. With a dull thud the dart landed squarely in the single six. Matthew swore while Bob grinned.

'Double three you want,' he blared in triumph. If the last dart landed in the single three section, one-double-one was the only place left to go, the most awkward of scores well named as being up in the madhouse. Bob would surely make his double seven first and the buying of the coffee would be down to Matthew instead, though it was the winning that mattered most.

Balancing his weight on the ball of his right foot, he took aim, let fly. The steel point landed neatly between the parallel wires of the double six as though put there by hand.

'Yes!' he exploded. Susan, his interview with his CO, his ambitions for a commission for the moment forgotten. 'A cuppa you owe me, Howlett.'

Gathering up their darts they made their way to the tea bar. Sipping hot camp coffee in a haze of cigarette smoke, Bob asked casually, 'Did your Susan ask you to put in for an interview then?'

'No, it was my idea.' To avoid Bob's eyes, he gazed around the white painted walls of the NAAFI hut, the corner with the dartboard now taken over by others. At a battered old piano, a group of RAOCs were trying hopelessly to harmonise. *I'll be with you in apple blossom time, I'll be with you to change your name to mine . . .* Mouths hung open, cigarettes burned away in tin ashtrays. *Some day in May, I'll come and say, happy the bride the sun shines on today . . .*

'I'll miss you, y'know, Matt.'

Matthew wrenched his attention back to Bob. 'No you won't.'

'Balls!'

'Well, I suppose I'll miss you too, but I don't think I'll miss any of the others.'

Bob was contemplating the sticky black sludge at the bottom of the thick, straight-sided cup he held as though expecting to see a gold nugget lying there. 'Them too, I expect.'

'Certainly not muck like Farrell.' The man with his coarse turn of phrase had always made a point of taunting Matthew and Bob as snot-nosed college boys, a jumped-up pair of pricks, fairies, a couple of queers, and had more than once referred to Susan, whom he had never seen, as an easy bit of skirt until Matthew once almost punched him. Bob had leapt in and pacified him with the assurance that Farrell wasn't worth wasting the skin of his knuckles for.

Bob gave a small, sagacious smile. 'You'll meet muck wherever you go, in all walks of life. Muck isn't reserved entirely for the ranks, old son.'

They fell silent while across the groups of square tables the singing floated. *Church bells will chime, you will be mine* . . .

'Anyway,' he said as they left the hut, 'Susan will be pleased if I get a commission.'

Monday morning, six thirty, October rain coming down in buckets marking the tag-end of summer. Matthew trudged from the bus stop to the main gate of the camp. 'Ye gods – what a morning.'

The collar of his greatcoat wet against his neck, he thought of the cosy flat he'd left behind as he displayed his pass for inspection. Last night he and Susan had snuggled up together, the curtains drawn while rain spattered unseen on the window panes. She would be getting up now, getting ready for work. Every morning until next Sunday when he, hopefully, would be back with her, granted a sleeping-out pass. He supposed he could count himself lucky. Most could only dream of their wives far away.

She'd been over the moon when he had told her about his name being put forward for a commission. She'd squealed in delight and clasped him to her and they had made ecstatic love. But the weeks had dragged on with nothing more heard. He'd seen his CO, Major Deeks, again, who had said that the wheels of Army protocol turned rather slowly sometimes but he would hear eventually and not to worry. Matthew had nodded and come away, visualising his name lying on some desk at the bottom of a pile of others.

Men were moving about the parade ground. The rain brought up the smell of wet tarmac. Matthew straightened and threw up a salute to a couple of officers as he passed them. They barely glanced at him, swagger sticks in gloved hands half lifted to their caps as they walked on in deep conversation. Elegant, relaxed, the rain seemed hardly to touch them whereas it pelted with malicious glee on other ranks. How long before he would saunter past some poor bloody corporal, hardly noticing him as he returned the stiff salute with a casual lift of a swagger stick? If he was accepted, that was. Depressed by the weather, he couldn't see it ever happening.

Bob was waiting for him inside the mess hall as Matthew pushed his way in. The place echoed to the bass babble of men's conversation, the rattle of crockery and scrape of cutlery across plates. His nostrils were assailed by the clogging odour of cooking grease and the sharp tang of burned bacon over which hung the faint reek of the fish from yesterday's dinner.

Soaked from his own dash to the hall, Bob looked like a very thin Great Dane that had been doused by a bucket of water, his long face drooping. Matthew immediately felt for him. He could only have received some bad news, perhaps from home. Had something evil happened to Bob's wife, his children, his parents? Matthew hurried up to him.

'Something wrong?'

Bob's expression didn't alter. 'Can you stand a shock this time of the morning?'

So it wasn't bad news – not that bad anyway. Matthew grinned with relief for his mate. 'Fire away.'

'We're moving out. The whole unit.'

Matthew gazed up at the pale grey eyes. Dismay had already begun to creep through his stomach. Uprooted after just three short, settled months of marriage. 'You sure? Where to? When?'

'No idea. But soon. Bet your boots on it. Peggy let it out last night.'

They had joined the queue being doled out breakfast. Matthew never had breakfast with Susan, needing to be back at camp on time. He looked with distaste at the congealed mounds of dried egg substitute in the trays, the frizzled bits of bacon, the sticky mass of baked beans, the half-burned slices of toast. A couple were being dumped on his plate with a sound like wooden discs, a dollop of dried egg and a portion of beans unceremoniously plopped on top of each blackened slice, a piece of bacon rattling beside them.

Bob surveyed his breakfast with equal distaste. 'Happy as a bloody sandboy, is our Sergeant Pegg. Said that's just what college queers like us need – a bit of action.'

'Action? What action?'

'It's only rumour so far,' Bob soothed. 'Even though

Peggy delighted in telling us it could be overseas. Silly arse! He should know about careless talk. Trouble is, old sweats like him seldom get things wrong. They develop a sixth sense about rumours after twenty-odd years' service.'

They found a table and put down their mugs of strong tea. Matthew sat staring at the cooling mess on his plate, his appetite gone, his earlier dismay at Bob's news already turned to premonitory fear. As Bob said, old sweats were seldom wrong about rumours.

Eddie Nutt, Taffy and Farrell joined them with their own food, Farrell's narrow face buried in his mug as soon as he sat down, his slurps carrying across the table. Matthew regarded him. How the man's wife put up with him beggared the imagination, unless she was similar. Birds of a feather.

'Heard our sergeant's bit of news, have you then?' Taffy asked, seeing Matthew's tight expression. 'Abroad, it looks like.'

'Fink we'll get embarkation leave?' Farrell spat bits of half-chewed bacon in every direction as he spoke.

Bob put down his hard-as-rock toast and sipped his tea. 'Peggy could still have it wrong, you know. Though he shouldn't be babbling on about it.'

Taffy grinned. 'Indeed no. That's all Adolf is waiting for, isn't it, to hear what's going on in B Troop. Turn the tide of the war, that will, knowing B Troop might be going overseas.'

Farrell belched loudly. 'They oughter give us leave. If they do, I'm gonna do my missus every night till I get back, give 'er somfink ter bleedin' fink about – anuvver kid. She's always goin' on abart bein' bleedin' bored.' He guffawed at his own joke.

Ronnie Clark, who had come to sit with them, leaned his heavy young chin on his fist. 'If anyone's bored, I am. A bit of action would be welcome.'

'Speak for yourself,' Bob said. 'All right for single chaps like you.'

Matthew pushed his plate away, untouched. 'I think I'll go and get into something dry.'

'I'll come with you,' said Bob, getting up and trailing after him.

The passing days saw rumours gaining momentum. Someone had seen tropical kit being sorted in the QM stores. Two words from a snippet of conversation had been overheard between two officers from their unit – North Africa.

Suddenly it was official: no destination divulged, for obvious reasons, but an issue of tropical kit; half a dozen painful jabs against those nastier diseases prevalent in hot climates that left every victim stiff and aching, and embarkation leave.

Matthew looked in vain for a summons from the selection board. There could be every chance if he were selected of getting out of being sent overseas, at least for the time being, but word from that direction remained stubbornly silent. He'd left things just that bit too late, had been far too bloody complacent, thinking his luck would last forever.

*

Susan stood in the passage, suitcases packed. She had tried to be brave, to keep her voice even and not break down in tears; had tried not to give way to that terrible panic that all but overwhelmed her when he had appeared on the doorstep explaining the reason for being laden down with full kit.

She still felt dazed; had spent much of her time weeping in secret in the bathroom they shared with their landlady, hoping Matthew would not hear her or notice her red and swollen eyes when she emerged; had kept her head averted from him as much as possible in case he did notice. If he did, he said nothing, but cuddled her a lot, assuring her it would be all right.

'Have you got everything you need?'

Susan nodded dismally as they stood in the passage saying goodbye to Mrs Robertson who also looked unnecessarily upset, probably because she must now look for new tenants, these having been with her for such a short while.

Receiving a peck on the cheek from Mrs Robertson Susan picked up the two suitcases and followed Matthew out to the waiting taxi. The rest of their bits and pieces, ornaments, the clock, the little square wireless set, wedding gifts, would be stored in her parents' attic. Susan would have liked to go to live there but her mother had looked askance.

'We got no room here now, love, not with your gran having to stay with us an' all. Her place was condemned after that bomb fell nearby. Matthew's people have got lots of room. You can stay with them, love, can't you?'

She loathed the thought of living for God knows

how long with the formidable Mrs Ward. The woman frightened her. But there was nothing for it except to go there. Matthew was so sure she'd be well looked after that she felt compelled to keep her thoughts to herself.

But in the taxi she couldn't help herself. Clinging to him, she buried her head in his shoulder. 'What am I going to do, Matthew, when you're gone? I'll be left all alone.'

'No you won't.' His voice shook. 'Mum will look after you as though you were her own daughter. And I'll come back. I'll come back.'

He heard the desperation in his words. Susan clinging to him made him ever more afraid of what lay ahead. Would he end up fighting in North Africa? The papers were full of Britain's new offensive against Rommel out there, but British soldiers were still being killed and who could say Rommel wouldn't turn and push them back again with even more men slaughtered, himself, Matthew Ward, perhaps one of them? Never to see Susan again. She would become a widow when she had scarcely become a wife.

The thought stayed with him throughout the interminable journey to London. Their train stopped and started, which seemed the normal thing these days; the delays got worse still as it hit fog just after Watford.

The thought persisted even as he smiled greeting at his parents, his mother taking Susan up to his old room which would now be hers until his return – if he returned. What would happen to Susan if he didn't? Where would she go? She'd marry again, in time . . . God, he had to stop thinking about it, think positive. Of course he'd come back. Yet a premonition that he might not haunted his troubled sleep that night, even though lovemaking helped him wipe it away for the while.

It wasn't that bad coming home, Jenny told herself firmly as, in scarves and warm coats, she and Mumsy walked down to the shops, her mother hanging on her arm in the jaundiced mist of this October Saturday morning. So long as she didn't have to do it every time she had a couple of hours off.

Mumsy, on the other hand, would have relished every second of her free time. But Jenny needed some time with her friends, and there was Ronald too, their off-duty hours coinciding so seldom. What chance they did have to go out together they usually spent going somewhere to eat. Hospital canteen food tasted disgusting and there was not much of it.

A forty-eight-hour week and sometimes eight weeks of night duty when all she wanted to do was go home to sleep, exhausted, until it was time to catch a bus back, took away any desire to go rushing off to see Ronald if he too was off duty. Time off came seldom enough and if he wasn't available it was fun spending it with friends now and again. While she made her way home, which was only a bus ride away, they, getting back after lights out, evaded the porter at the gate by climbing the railings; whispers and stifled giggles erupted as they clambered back into the nurses' residence through purposely unlocked windows before the night super began her rounds. She missed all that coming home.

If only her mother would make some attempt to join some women's group or other. There were plenty of them: wives whose husbands had been called up, elderly widows, spinsters, all knitting socks and scarves for 'the boys', or planning charity events, all an opportunity for socialising and filling in their lonely lives, but her mother had never been outgoing and that first approach towards a group of virtual strangers was always the hardest step for anyone to take.

'I couldn't go alone. I wouldn't mind if I had a friend to take me.'

'Then find a friend. Mrs Crompton next door. She lives alone. Or your other neighbour. I know she's younger than you, but she's on her own with her husband away.'

It was easy to say, but she wasn't the one having to do it. Her mother had gripped her arm hopefully. 'Perhaps you could come with me.'

'I'm a nurse, Mumsy. I can't have afternoons off whenever I please.'

She had hated the reluctance that made itself felt, wished she didn't feel so glad at having an excuse not to have to sit with those women with little else to do but discuss children, home life and the ever-tightening restrictions on food rationing as they knitted or planned their events.

Her mother would never understand. Hospital was another world, a little kingdom behind whose walls existed a strictly graded society of doctors and nurses, over which, next to the Matron's, the sister's authority was law. The outside world never penetrated that kingdom; even patients became changed creatures once they came in, lying in their beds in stiff rows, obedient to the ward sister. But Jenny loved it.

Soon to be a second-year nurse, at the moment on the men's medical ward, she was slowly climbing the ladder to the day when those magic letters SRN could be put after her name. Her feet had long ago stopped swelling like balloons and her back aching from long hours on her feet. She could take twelve hours on them almost, if not quite as lively as when she'd begun. She could fold counterpane corners to perfect angles; her mistakes were far fewer than they had once been, her intricate cap folded just right, the leg o' mutton sleeves of her uniform perfect. She'd be sitting for her second state examination early next year and after that her Preliminary. Still a long way to go, but she would get there in the end in spite of Mumsy looking towards the day when she'd leave nursing and go back to doing a nine to five job.

They were coming back home, turning into Victoria Park Road, when two young people came towards them out of the mist through which the sun was at last beginning to struggle. Jenny immediately recognised the figure of Matthew Ward and they halted simultaneously, she pulling her mother to a stop just as he did the girl on his arm. His face lit up.

'Ye gods, Jenny! Didn't expect to see you!'

'Home on leave then?' she asked, trying to control the joy that leapt inside her at seeing him, angering her in remaining as acute as ever, for all the girl with him.

There was a noticeable tightening of his features but he grinned, she was certain, with forced cheerfulness.

When he spoke it was in a similar vein, an effort at banter.
'You're not going to ask me when I'm due back, are you?
Everyone asks that, as though they'll be only too glad to
see me gone again. But, no, I've been given fourteen days'
leave – out of the blue.'

Adding that last on a more intense note, it needed no
lecture to know what it meant. The obvious effort he was
making to be cheerful helped bear out the message. Her
next question, 'Where are they sending you?' sounded
stupidly superfluous. How could he know that? He obliged
with a shrug, then collected himself and turned to the
small, neat girl beside him.

'By the way, this is Susan – my wife. Susan, this is Jen
. . . This is Jenny Ross, an old friend from the crowd I
used to go around with before the war. Jenny lives nearly
opposite my parents.'

His use of her full given name, the first time she could
ever recall, now spoken so formally, so neatly severed
her from him that she actually felt pain. They'd gone
their separate ways, yet even now her heart cried out to
be the one on his arm instead of the girl to whom she
now cordially smiled, saying it was nice to meet her and
politely introducing her mother.

'Me and Matthew's staying at his parents,' the girl
supplied in a broad Birmingham accent, her small oval
face quite beautiful and full of adoration as she glanced
up at him; Jenny could clearly see why he had married her.
'I'm going to live with them while he's away. You living so
near then, I might probably see something of you.'

'I expect so,' Jenny obliged, her eyes travelling to

Matthew. All she wanted now was to be away from here
to suppress the sick thumping in her breast. It wasn't fair.
'Well, I won't keep you. This damp weather is chilly.' On
an impulse she took off a glove and held out her hand to
him. 'Well, wherever it is they send you, Matthew, keep
safe, and . . .'

Words echoed inside her head, a sharp recollection of
what he had once said to her: 'And whatever happens,
you'll always be one of my nicer, memories.' She had once
had the audacity to think they might have been words of
affection, a prelude to something more. But they had not
presaged anything.

She had nearly begun to repeat them word for word.
Would he have recalled himself saying them? And if so,
would he have thought she was being just a little bitter?
No, he'd probably forgotten, had never really meant them
in the first place, flippant as he'd been those days. And yet,
her mind conjured up the look in his dark eyes at the time.
He had meant them when he said them, she was certain,
but much water had flowed under the bridge since then,
and now he was married and in love with his wife, his
Susan – that could be seen with half an eye.

'And come back soon,' she finished instead, hardly
realising that her voice had dropped to a whisper, almost
a prayer, a secret shared between herself and him. But he
hadn't noticed as he too removed his leather glove and
took her hand, his warmth on her chill flesh making her
senses leap. Was it her imagination or did his hand hold
hers just that bit longer than was necessary? Was there a
spark remaining of that which she thought she had seen

in his eyes that day? Silly fool, it had to be her foolish imagination, nothing more.

After they parted she repeated those last words to herself: 'Come back soon.' Now they had become truly a fervent prayer for his safekeeping as she fought the heavy lump in her heart.

Chapter 13

He had meant to make his last night with Susan memorable. Instead, beset by anxiety, he'd failed her, the first time ever. She had been wonderful about it, told him it didn't matter, but he knew she was tearful when she finally turned over to go to sleep, he with his arms about her, cuddling her close.

Mortified by his inability to fulfil her, and himself, Matthew lay awake listening to her occasional sighs as though she was grieving the loss of something precious, yet he knew she was asleep because when he asked if she felt all right there was no reply. Loath to disturb her he left unsaid the words he needed to say.

Awakening to grey light filtering through the curtains and immediately conscious of a deep anger at sleep itself having robbed him of those last few hours with her, he turned to gaze at her sweet face on the pillow beside him, the full lips in gentle repose. He was about to waken her and would have made perfect love to her but for the knock on the door and his father entering in response to his reluctant bidding with a cup of tea for them.

From then on things took on a sense of urgency, washing, dressing, packing his kit, forcing down the boiled egg and toast his mother insisted would 'keep him going', everyone's conversation stilted, shallow, tense.

It had been agreed they'd say their goodbyes here in the privacy of their own home, the severing made clean, but at the last moment Susan pleaded to be allowed to accompany him the whole way to Charing Cross where he was to board the train for Southampton. The prospect of seeing her standing there, a small isolated figure among the seething crowds in that vast station as his train took him from her, was more than he could bear to contemplate; shattering him as well as her. He took her in his arms.

'No, darling, I want you to stay here. It'll only be dragging things out if you come, and the end will be just the same. On top of that you'll have to come all the way home without me.'

She would not see it. In fact his final goodbyes turned into something like pandemonium. Having said farewell to his parents, his father gripping him firmly in a bear hug, telling him to watch himself, his mother kissing his cheek, assuring him she would look after Susan, charging him to look after himself in that cold, stiff manner which he knew hid emotions she had long ago taught herself never to show, Susan standing away from him with her back pressed against the wall of the hall, her naturally pale face now chalk-white, her small slender body as rigid as the wall that alone seemed to be holding her up, she flew at him as though unseen hands had suddenly propelled her forward.

'Matthew, don't leave me! Oh, don't . . . please don't leave me.'

He had to struggle to extricate himself, physically handing her to his mother who held her in a firm grip, her older face like granite. He'd wanted to crush Susan to him, but her demonstration threatened to undermine his own resolve not to give way to too much emotion, so while her tears flowed shamelessly unchecked, his had to remain unshed as he'd put her from him with futile words. 'It'll be all right, love. I have to go. You've got to be brave.' Though what order he said them in he did not know.

He could still hear her calling his name, her voice echoing down the street after him as he stood now on Southampton docks amid long, snaking, khaki queues waiting to board the ship that would take them to God knows where – no one knew as yet, except that they all carried tropical kit.

A fine drizzle sifted down upon the shoulders of the slowly moving queues, upon the loose piles of kitbags ready to be loaded on board, and on trucks and other equipment to be transported the several thousand miles to, where? North Africa? India? It might be India, Matthew prayed. Far away from any war zone. It could be that those in charge thought there was some need of men in that region or perhaps South or West Africa? There they could expect a life of relative luxury, and in time to come back safely. Matthew crossed his fingers as he took his turn to move up the gangway leading to the ship's dark innards.

As soon as permitted, he would write to reassure Susan how well he was and that there had been no need for her to worry about his safety – fair enough, only that he wished he was back with her instead of here. But one must not think of that. Every man here must have loved ones on his mind but knew better than to give too great a thought to it. Pushing that last sight of Susan's tear-ravaged face from his mind, he looked down at the oily green swell rising and sinking between the troopship and the quayside. It was like some slow-breathing animal waiting to engulf them all. From it rose a reek of decayed seaweed, engine oil and bilge water which he could see gushing in small spurts from an outlet below him amid a wreath of steam.

Gaining a position against the deck rail as he and his platoon made it into the ship, he leaned over to watch the water still heaving and sinking, heaving and sinking below the slow climbing of soldiers up the three sets of gangways.

'Get yer arse away from there,' Sergeant Pegg interrupted his reverie. 'All of yer – this way.'

Following him, Matthew found himself in the place where he and the others were to live out the next few weeks; a place with all its port holes well screwed down so no light could escape across a pitch-dark sea to lurking U-boats, their quarters thus promising to become hot and unbearable as they approached the tropics; a place where narrow wooden bunks had been built almost side by side, forcing men by lack of space to share with their fellows most of their personal functions, including seasickness. The all too few, once-elegant toilet facilities for paying passengers, now to be called latrines, had had all but their basic amenities torn out, even their doors, and were painted overall-grey. They needed to accommodate four times as many troops. A line of convenient buckets fixed nearby to make up for the lack of facilities would soon waft their stink to the quarters as they filled before being emptied by fatigue squads. It was a place where snoring, coughing, farting, scratching, conversation and talking in one's sleep would be no secret from anyone.

In this impending claustrophobic atmosphere, Bob dropped his kit down on to a so-far unclaimed area, once beautifully carpeted, now mere metal deck where he and the rest of them would be expected to share their lives in close harmony with all walks of life.

'Like a bloody cargo of meat,' he observed drily and everyone agreed, finding the quip unfunny.

Settled on a top bunk, Matthew wrote his first letters home, the first a brief one to his parents, the second to Susan pouring out all that he had been unable to say to her face. He'd have given the world to see her read it, see her smile with all the confidence he was instilling in her of his safe return.

He could hardly wait for the letter to be collected along with everyone else's and taken ashore for posting prior to moving off, yet it would go with his mixed feelings. In a couple of days it would reach Susan. By then he'd be nearly a thousand miles away. So he concentrated on visualising her beautiful oval face, her tremulous smile as she read, her expression glowing with love, with the certainty of his coming back to her. He worked on retaining that vision. It was one he must carry with him to whatever ends of the earth he was bound for as with the clanging of bells and the deep rumbling of engines vibrating through his whole body, diminishing, then building up again, the great ship began to slide away from the dockside.

His letters sent on their way, Matthew went up on deck – better than meditating below – to watch the huge one-time P&O liner do its majestic about-turn in the incredibly narrow channel, the deep heavy pulsating of engines finally dying away to a regular thumping that in a while would be hardly noticeable, a rhythm to which its cargo of troops would work, rest and think for weeks to come before again setting foot on terra firma.

Jenny sat on the cold park bench staring down at the ring, a band of three diamonds, sitting snugly in the box he had brought from his pocket. What on earth was she to say to him?

'You gave me no warning or what you intended, Ronald.'

It was almost an accusation. What was she supposed to say – this is so sudden – like in those Hollywood films they turned out, those love-scene dialogues so unreal? Don't ask for the moon, darling, when we have the stars . . . Was that it? It would seem laughable if this wasn't so serious.

She turned her eyes from the surprise engagement ring to the man who now held it up for her inspection, ready to be slipped on to her finger. But she had her gloves on. Was she supposed to take them off, or would he? It all threatened to become a clumsy business, stripping it of any romance there might have been. Romance? Really, she wasn't sure she loved him enough to accept his ring. The thing was, she'd let him make love to her. Well, not actually make love, although he'd seen more of her than she'd intended him to see, for every time they got into a clinch, something stopped her, almost as if she were saving herself for someone else. But what someone else? Well, she knew who that was. But it was silly. He was beyond any hope of hers. Married, overseas, his wife waiting for his return. And yet, to accept this ring, this contract for marriage, would be to finally accept the absurdity of that dream to which she had clung for so long.

'You must have known, Jenny,' he was saying, his eyes full of query, his good-looking face a picture.

She looked back at him. Yes, he was handsome. Any girl would have taken him immediately. He could have his pick, but he had chosen her. What did he see in her? What did he see that Matthew had never seen? Yet handsome as he was, there was something missing. What it was she couldn't say. Whatever it was, it wasn't right to hurt him. Ronald, I don't love you.

'I suppose I should have expected it,' she answered instead.

'Then put it on, my love.'

Grasping the fingertips of the woollen glove with her right hand, she pulled it off carefully, finger by finger, making a meal of it, the damp cold December air touching her exposed hand, and held out the hand for him. She watched him slip the ring over the knuckle of her engagement finger with a sort of ritual reverence. It went on so easily, she wondered how and when he had discovered her fit, pondering over it when she ought to have been gasping with pleasure at his wordless proposal.

Hardly giving her time, sitting there in Green Park, to admire what glitter the stars afforded the diamonds with no other lighting, not even a moon visible, he gathered her into his arms.

'Darling Jenny, you've made me the happiest man. The first moment I get, I'll take you to meet my parents. They'll be so surprised.'

Silently Jenny allowed herself to be held, leaning against him at an awkward angle. Seeing her ring glittering but faintly in the darkness over his shoulder she thought of what lay ahead. His parents lived in Bristol. All she could think of was having to go all that way to meet them, of being introduced into his life, quite expected to leave her own behind her. There was her mother to think of. She had no one else but her. Left behind and lonely. There were all the things she had known. Left behind. And there was Matthew, part of her past. Left behind. Panic seemed to take a great bite out of her heart.

'No!' She pushed him away, so hard and suddenly that he all but fell off the seat, regaining his balance with an effort. 'No, Ronald, I can't.'

He looked so taken aback, she could have cried. But there was no altering what she had said. 'I really can't, Ronald.'

'Why not?' For a moment he looked stupid, then he relaxed a little, even grinned. 'Come on, darling. It is a bit frightening I expect, saying yes. But it'll be all right. Let's just sit here quietly for a while. Let you get used to the idea. I shouldn't have sprung it on you like that. But we don't have to get married immediately. A few weeks, a couple of months perhaps.'

'But there's my mother. She doesn't know.'

'Neither do my parents. We'll tell them as soon as possible. I'll write to mine and you write to your mother, warn them . . . no, not warn them, tell them. Oh, Jenny, I've dreamed of this day – me giving you a ring and you accepting. We'll be . . .'

'I haven't accepted yet, Ronald.'

'What?'

'I haven't accepted. You put the ring on my finger, then you grabbed me and cuddled me.'

'You let me put it on. You let me cuddle you.'

'I wasn't thinking. You took me by surprise. It all happened too quickly for me to say anything.'

Comprehension was creeping not so much into his expression, which in the dark she could not properly see, but into his voice, the stiffening of his posture. 'You mean, you don't want me? You don't want to marry me?' His consternation mounted as Jenny remained silent, unable to trust her voice. 'But we get on so well.'

'I know.' She had to say something. 'I just don't . . . I don't know.'

'You don't love me enough to marry me.'

'Oh, Ronald.' What was she trying to appeal to? He got up, took her hand and gently pulled her to her feet.

'We should be getting back to the hospital. I'm on call tonight.'

'What about the ring?' It was as though they were discussing work.

'Keep it for now. See how you feel as time goes on. I suppose I did jump the gun a bit. But I do love you.'

'I know you do.' How could he stay so calm? Another

man would be ranting and raving at her now, for letting him down, making a fool of him.

'Don't you love me at all?' was all he said.

Her heart went out to him. How could she say to him, 'I like you'? How could she insult him like that? In a way she did love him. If only that other face didn't persist in floating before her eyes. Ronald made her feel good when he was around, feel wanted, feel important. His touch did excite. But when he wasn't there, she didn't think about him at all, had never found herself yearning for the time to come for them to meet. So did she love him or not? It seemed she didn't, yet when she saw him her heart leaped with the pleasure of seeing him. They got on well together, never quarrelled. They could chat until the cows came home. She felt easy with him in a way she had never done with Matthew Ward. But Matthew, though claimed, still haunted her.

'You took me by surprise,' she said miserably for an answer as they began making their way out of the darkened park whose gates stood open all night so people could gain access at a moment's notice to the air-raid shelters built there. 'Don't be annoyed.'

'I'm not annoyed.' No, he wasn't annoyed, just deeply hurt.

'I need time to get used to it. I will keep the ring for a while. And I will think about it, Ronald. I promise.'

After all, she must. Theirs would be a stable marriage, she knew that by just knowing him. She would be a fool not to say yes in the end.

'Good girl,' he breathed, his confidence returning, and

gave her a thank-you peck on the cheek as they walked on through the darkened streets.

Bombay had hit the troops newly arrived from the sedate, restrained British Isles, most never having set foot on any foreign soil before, not even France, like a bomb. It was an exotic disturbing place, full of disquiet and unheaval. Fine buildings rubbed shoulders with such squalor as Matthew could never have imagined and made him at first feel sickened. But slowly, confronted by its sights and sounds, its unfamiliar aromas and an atmosphere so indigenous that it seemed there could be no other city in the world like this, his eyes became blinded to all but the worst of sights, and all his prayers were those of gratitude that their final destination had been here and nowhere else.

Amid speculation they had pulled in to Gibraltar, spent a day on the Rock while U-boats reported to be lurking outside the Med were being dealt with by the Royal Navy. They hardly had time to see anything Gib had to offer before the ship sailed onward, not into the Mediterranean as had been expected but south, down the coast of Africa, pausing at Cape Town, then round into the Indian Ocean where they finally disembarked at Bombay.

In the pleasant warmth of an Indian November, Matthew sat on his bed writing letters home to say where he had landed up and thought of the chill sleet of England, and of the commission he'd narrowly missed by being too complacent and seeking it too late. Now he saw it as providential that he had not done so. Had he got a commission, who was to say he might not have ended up on some field of battle instead of here. It *was* providence. He should have known. He had always been pretty lucky in nearly everything.

Leaving her house, Jenny saw Matthew's wife emerge from hers. They caught sight of each other at the same time; she saw the girl hesitate and almost draw back as though about to hurry back indoors. But Jenny wasn't to be avoided. She turned in her direction, her steps rapid. 'Hi, there!'

She had been aching for weeks to have a chat with her, telling herself it was of no consequence to her if she didn't, yet feeling a compulsion to look over to the Wards' house every time she came home. She'd told herself she was only coming home at every opportunity for her mother's sake, yet a tiny voice inside her kept repeating the true reason for her visits. That tiny voice was telling her now of the truth behind the avid eagerness with which she called out, 'Hi, there!'

The girl smiled, nodded briefly, but the ice was broken.

In seconds Jenny was at her side. 'Haven't seen much of you since we were introduced.' She was talking like some schoolgirl, far too fast, far too exuberant.

Susan shook her head rather solemnly. 'I haven't been out a lot.'

'Well, I only get home at odd times. That's a nurse's life for you.' She laughed.

'You're a nurse?'

'Didn't Matthew mention it?'

'No, he didn't.'

They had begun to walk towards the main road, Jenny hiding her disappointment that Matthew hadn't thought of her even enough to mention her job to his wife. But then, he wouldn't, would he?

'Where are you off to, then?' she asked and saw the girl shrug.

'I don't know really. I just had to get out for a walk somewhere. I was going to the park, but it don't matter much where I go.'

She sounded so down. Jenny took a quick guess at what must have driven the girl out. She herself wouldn't relish being closeted with Mrs Ward for days on end. Her own mother with her constant small complaints of loneliness was enough to endure, but Jenny reckoned Mrs Ward could knock spots off Mumsy for driving a person away.

'It's a bit chilly for walking,' she observed as she fell in beside her. A thin fog was threatening to thicken. It clung with cold fingers around cheeks and lips and penetrated the shoulders of the heaviest coat. In mid November, elsewhere on the Continent, flurries of dry snow probably covered everything in glorious pristine white – she still felt a thrill at new fresh snow for all its inconvenience – but here it only got damp and any snow that might fall would soon melt on this seawashed island. Yet she'd rather have all the peasouper fogs unconquered England could dish out than the dazzling whiteness of an occupied Europe. Nineteen forty-two waited just six weeks away – how much longer would this war go on and when would Matthew come home again?

'Have you heard from Matthew?'

Susan appeared to brighten up. 'We had his first letters in the week. Airmail. One for me and one for his parents. From India, Bombay.'

A vast surge of relief poured over Jenny. Far far away from any fighting. Thank God, oh, thank God.

'That's good,' she said evenly. 'I bet you're glad.'

Susan nodded. 'I wish he was here instead. I wanted to tell him my news to his face, not in a letter. It won't be the same written in a letter. Oh, if only he'd been able to stay here a few weeks longer, I could've told him to his face and seen it all light up. I'm going to have a baby.'

'Oh, I'm so glad for you.' It was even more of an effort to keep her voice steady. Marriage, now cemented by a forthcoming baby. 'You must be very thrilled.'

Susan didn't look thrilled. 'I would be if it wasn't for her, his mother. She's really pleased of course. But she's started making plans for it already, telling me what I should do and what I shouldn't do. I really feel like I'm in a prison.'

The same as Matthew had felt; his mother's over-eagerness to guide and help had only been instrumental in sending him away from her. She felt suddenly sad for Mrs Ward, only able to express love by managing the lives of those around her, succeeding only in driving them away with their misguided conception of her actions. Even Louise, with that time she had secretly applied for the Wrens. She had confided in Jenny. 'I never told Mummy at that time until I was quite sure I would be accepted,' she'd said. 'But honestly, Jenny, she can be quite suffocating at times.' Exactly as Matthew had felt, and now Susan.

'I don't know how long I'll be able to stand it,' Susan was saying. She had begun to screw up beneath her winter coat, the damp cold eating into her small frame. 'She watches me all the time. Everything I eat, everything I do. I was sick first thing yesterday morning. That confirmed it but she carted me off to the doctor to be sure. I hate doctors. I hate the smell of their waiting rooms, and ill people all round the room.'

She seemed bent on unburdening herself to someone. 'I was sick again this morning and she said I should stay in bed. She kept coming in every half-hour to see how I was. I don't want to stay in bed. She said I wasn't to go out, I'd catch cold, but I came out just the same. I know it'll annoy her. She'll be all stiff and starched with me when I get back, like I was a kid, or something. I wish Matthew was here. He'd stick up for me.'

She was beginning to shiver. She seemed so small; a waif. 'Perhaps some evenings when I'm home,' Jenny offered readily, 'if you want to come over to us for a chat, you're welcome. It'll get you out of that house.'

She felt she had never seen anyone look so grateful. 'Could I?'

'Of course.' Also Susan would keep her abreast of news of Matthew, though Jenny didn't admit to it even to herself, for all the tiny voice inside did.

The following ten days saw Jenny on nights, taking over from a girl who had gone down sick. Sleeping most of the day, she was unable to honour the invitation to Susan. But she had managed to get Christmas off. Ronald, still waiting for her answer, had asked to take her home to see his parents, but it seemed only right to think of her mother first on this, the one special family holiday of the year. On top of that it was a time when Mumsy would be thinking of Daddy, who had died just one month before the festive season, for all the years were stretching on.

She hadn't told her mother about Ronald yet. The first thing she'd do would be to start fretting about the impending loss of her daughter, as if Jenny would forsake her entirely. Maybe all mothers felt that way but most wouldn't make a meal of it. Not that Mumsy meant to drag on her, but Jenny found herself dreading the day when she must tell her.

That she would marry Ronald was in no doubt. He was kind and considerate and steady, and she did love him – not in the silly way she'd felt for Matthew – still did, she was ashamed to realise, constantly telling herself off about this idiotic wishing for something that couldn't be – but in a comfortable way which common sense told her would last and last.

It did seem a shame to keep fobbing him off so. Perhaps she would tell him her decision when the spring came and the spirits rose with the climbing of the sun. These days she had no deep feeling for love or anything approaching it. The weather stayed too cold for strolling in parks, so they went to the Natural History Museum, had tea in its restaurant, talking of this and that. He held her hand and gazed at the ring she'd begun to wear when with him, capitulating at last. He spoke of marriage, their future together, again broached the subject of her coming home with him to see his parents, if not Christmas Day, then Boxing Day.

'I know it sounds churlish,' she told him. 'But my mother's all alone. I couldn't dream of leaving her as soon as Christmas is over. She's made a Christmas pudding too. Saved up her dried fruit coupons all year for the thing. She'd be left to eat the rest all by herself on Boxing Day. They don't keep, you know, not like they used to before the war.'

For some reason he thought that funny. His laughter annoyed her for yet some other unaccountable reason.

'I just couldn't leave her,' she stated huffily. The pudding had been just an excuse. It wasn't funny, at least not all that much. Even less, again for some unknown reason, when she remembered that there would come a time when he would insist on naming the wedding day. Why did her insides crawl with reluctance at that thought? Later as she melted into his arms, she wondered why she had felt so reluctant. This was what she wanted, or what common sense told her she must want. Security, friendship, someone to be with, all of those things. And of course love. She did love Ronald, she told herself severely.

Monday came again, one more week nearer to Christmas. Jenny was working, swotting for her second state examination as she had been doing these past months while Ronald worked and studied towards becoming a GP. She had been nearly two years doing practical work on the wards. A couple of years had to pass yet before she could add SRN after her name, though perhaps in wartime it might come quicker. But would she ever get it, now that she appeared to be Ronald's fiancée?

She was just going on the ward when a nurse came hurrying towards her. 'Telephone call for you, love. Better cut short whoever it is or you'll make yourself late.'

'Did they say who it is?' Jenny called as she made her way to the old-fashioned phone fastened to the wall down the passage. Her heart had begun to beat. It could only be bad news. Her mother? She had been all right when she'd left home an hour ago.

'Didn't say,' came back the answer, but Jenny was already there, her ear to the earpiece.

'Hello? Hello.'

A girl's frantic voice assailed her ears. 'Jenny – oh, thank God it's you. I tried to get you before you left. But you'd already gone. I had to talk to *someone*.'

'Who is it?' Jenny interrupted the tirade, not recognising the voice.

'Susan, across the road. I must speak to you. There's no one else.'

'Susan, what's the matter?' She felt just a little peeved being made late by Susan's trivial need to phone her. Nothing at all to do with her mother.

'Haven't you heard the news on the wireless?' The girl's voice still held a note of panic. 'Japan's just declared war on America, and us. They've bombed a base belonging to America, called Pearl Harbor, in the Pacific. Matthew's out there in India. I'm so worried.'

Jenny's mind flitted over past world atlases of her childhood, the Indian continent marked in pink, Siam and similar countries further east in yellow, then pink again for Malaya, Borneo, Australia. The Pacific, light blue, dwarfed all else. Where Pearl Harbor was she had no idea but it belonged to the USA and was probably somewhere in the Hawaiian islands. Far away from India. Matthew was safe.

'Susan, if war breaks out there, do you know how far away from it Matthew will be? A good couple of thousand miles at least. If he was still stationed here in England he'd be nearer to a war zone. So there's nothing to worry about. Nothing at all.'

The voice at the other end had calmed a little. 'I've sent off an airmail letter to him to tell him about the baby. He'll get it in a day or two. I know he'll be thrilled. You are sure about him being safe in India?'

'I couldn't be surer,' Jenny said, smiling into the mouthpiece. She was going to be late. 'I must go, Susan. I'm at work. See you soon.'

She replaced the receiver and hurried off. She wouldn't be able to listen to the wireless until she came off duty. Perhaps by then there might be a bit more about this new war so far away. But one thing was certain. Matthew, soon to be a father, was indeed safe and it was best not to let her mind keep dwelling on him.

Chapter 14

Among other things, some of the garrison were staging a panto for Christmas and requests had gone out for anyone with talent wanting to join the chorus to come forward. All the acting roles had of course long since gone to those who'd been stationed there some time.

'Go on, Matt,' Bob urged, hearing about it. 'You've not got a bad voice. How about giving your tonsils an airing?'

Matthew had his pencil poised over a blank air letter. Seventh of December already and he needed to write to Susan again. He was waiting for one from her. It should come any moment but in the meantime . . .

He looked up, gave a small explosive chuckle of self-derision. 'One sound from me and I'd be given the about-turn.'

'Don't be daft. It's not half bad, your voice. Now, me, I'd turn lemons sour. Go on, have a go.'

Again Matthew chuckled, but the idea was tempting. He was bored. Life here was one round of ticking over, being given jobs just to kill time and keep men occupied: in the soporific air of old colonial India they painted flagstaffs, whitewashed stones around brigade HQ, cleaned windows, swept paths, spit-and-polished equipment, attended parades and spent the hotter parts of the day in cool schoolrooms, the strong sunlight thwarted by fretted shutters, the still air stirred by squeaking, slowly revolving fans. With time to laze in the shade, seek somewhere to booze away an evening, what at first seemed delightful had quickly palled.

He was about to say he might think about having a crack at it when Ronnie Clark burst into the barrack room like a tornado. Unable to take in quite what he was blabbering about, those absorbed in reading tatty paperbacks, writing letters, darning socks, looked up.

'Who's bombed what?'

'The Japanese. They've gone and bombed Pearl Harbor.'

'Where the bloody 'ell's Pearl 'Arbor?'

'It's an American naval base in Hawaii,' Matthew supplied, which had Farrell sneering across at him.

''Ark at bleedin' know-all.' But Matthew ignored him. His heart was already filling with a kind of animal fear, nameless and undefined, having nothing yet to draw on, just an instinct of some threat looming from a totally unexpected direction.

'Where did you hear this?' Bob was demanding.

'Over the radio.' Ronnie Clark had been on duty all morning in the communications room. 'A few minutes ago. They've bombed Singapore too.' He looked significantly towards Jeff Downey whose thick lips had dropped open in awe. 'Bet you're glad we didn't go there as you wanted to.'

'The Yanks'll come inter the war now, won't they?' Eddie Nutt said.

'Bugger the Yanks!' someone snapped. 'What about us? Us fighting bloody Jerries, bloody Ities, and now bloody Nips. It ain't fair! Just as we're getting the best of the Jerries in North Africa an' the battle of the Atlantic's goin' our way and everyone's goin' on about us openin' up a second front, now we're inter another bloody war. Ain't it just fair!'

It was Sergeant Pegg who put it all into perspective for them. 'What you lot worrying about them short-arse little monkeys for? Most of 'em wear glasses. Planes tied up with string, like them bloody toys they export to us. I'd sooner fight an 'undred of them than a dozen of Rommel's lot. The Yanks comin' in, all we'll see of them boss-eyed, bow-legged little yeller bleeders'll be their backsides. The Yanks comin' in'll shorten the war in Germany too.'

It all seemed logical and heartening even when days later they were moved on to the transit camp at Deolali; from Deolali station a horrendous three-day train journey across the Indian continent began, to Calcutta, Assam, and on to Rangoon in Burma to join Burmese and Indian brigades there.

Matthew's letters home had been written in fits and starts. Susan's had been delayed because those to her were always precious and needed thinking about, dreaming over. Now there was no time for dreaming. What he had written would have to be sent off as it was. He hadn't heard from her yet, but with all this sudden moving out, hers must still be catching him up. He would get it sooner or later, but it was hell not hearing.

'Knowing the Army,' Bob said as they strolled through

the paved courts of the ancient Shwe Dagon pagoda on their first off-duty sightseeing trip, the hot spicy smells of India now replaced by the milder flowery ones of Burma, 'our mail will all come in one batch.'

'And wait another couple of months for the next lot,' Matthew agreed. Pensively he gazed up at the scores of lesser pagodas that surrounded the great *stupa,* of the Shwe Dagon, its graceful curves clad in pure beaten gold.

His ears filled by the soft slap of bare feet on warm tiles, the low murmur of devotees at prayer, the droning intonation of Buddhist monks, the twitter of birds and the gentle tinkle of tiny bells, he watched a group of Burmese women at their labour of devotion, sweeping the smooth paving with flat, fan-shaped brooms. In crisp, straight blouses over colourful skirts, *longyis*, that wrapped tightly around their legs, their shining black hair pulled into a bun at the back of the head and secured by a gaudy flower, they looked sleek and clean, a far cry from the ragged denizens of Bombay.

'I wish my Susan could see all this,' he murmured.

'Yes, a regular Cook's tour, and not costing us a penny,' said Bob appreciatively. 'Just look where we've been at the expense of the Army. We've stopped off at Gib, West Africa, Cape Town, Bombay, Deolali and now Rangoon. Wonder where we'll end up next?'

'This is as far east as I ever want to go,' Matthew said, his mind on their newest enemy. Short, bow-legged, short-sighted they might be, but they still had guns and shells and mortars, and could kill. He didn't fancy Susan becoming a widow just yet.

Taffy had joined them, coming from a side street with a wide grin of self-satisfaction. Matthew gave him a disparaging look. 'Not in the middle of a Sunday afternoon.'

Taffy's grin widened even more. 'Best time for it, isn't it? Make you pretty thirsty, mind.' He eyed one of the many water-sellers squatting on a corner beneath the shade of a tree, clinking a metal cup against a container with a loud urgent rhythmical clatter.

'Wouldn't risk it,' Matthew warned. 'Wait till you get a beer from the mess instead.'

He paused by an ancient crone squatting under a large spreading tree near some open-fronted shops. Surrounded by several of her family and a few onlookers, she leered up at Matthew, her few remaining teeth stained red by betel-nut juice.

'Tell fortune, soldiya?' she croaked in English. There had been a British garrison here long enough for those like her to have a passing knowledge of their language. Dusty feet splayed from beneath a rusty longyi, the old fortune-teller beckoned with clawed hands. 'You want know of long life, soldiya, love, ha?'

'Go on, give it a go,' Bob urged.

'What about you, Taff?' Matthew asked. 'Might find out you're going to turn over a new leaf and find yourself a decent wife. Put a stop to all that whoring of yours.'

Taffy's handsome face was full of injured pride. 'There's nice! You just leave me be to find me own wife when I'm good and ready.'

Matthew laughed and glanced again at the crone with

her vermilion grimace. On impulse he squatted in front
of her, extending his hand, but the woman waved it away.
'You pay. You pay.'

A couple of coins dropped in her palm quickly appeased
her and the old witch grabbed his hand to scrutinise it.
Tracing the lines of his palm with a piece of indelible
pencil until most of them were linked in mystical triangles
and trapeziums, she studied the results, her voice a cracked
sing-song.

'See baby. See lady. Lady has your heart, soldiya.'

'I bet she says that to everyone,' Taffy interrupted with
a chortle.

Matthew was about to ask, what baby? But the woman
went on: 'One more lady has heart for you.'

'Two?' Taffy gave another chortle. 'And you talk about
me, boyo?'

'Lady with bright hair,' went on the crone.

'No, dark,'Matthew corrected.

The black eyes like polished jet glittered angrily. She
glanced round and pointed at the distant Shwe Dagon
pagoda glinting like a gold nugget in the sunshine behind
the low buildings.

'Bright.' She waggled her old head lest her prediction
be contradicted again. 'Like Shwe Dagon.'

He let her have her way. After all it was only a bit of fun.
But the old woman's eyes had gone dark. She regarded him
narrowly. 'See bad thing here. Binding rope. Bad thing.'

'The ball and chain, that is,' laughed Taffy. 'Don't need
your hand read to know that, do you?'

Matthew resolutely kept his palm upwards. 'What do

you mean, bad thing?' Was she referring to Susan? Was everything all right with her? The questions came even as he derided this odd belief in the woman's words.

But the crone had dismissed him, already casting about for other clients. Nor, strangely enough, would she take his offer of any more money.

'A baby! Ye gods, she was right.' Matthew stared at the letter that had at last caught him up. He waved it in Bob's face. 'That old bird who told me my fortune said she saw a baby and Susan says here that she's pregnant.'

For hours last night he had lain beneath his mosquito net studying his palm in the glow of a pale shaft of moonlight through the high barrack-room window, trying to make sense of the marks of the indelible pencil. Now had come Susan's letter. It was uncanny. 'I'm going to be a father.'

Bob, a father of three, regarded him as an old dog might a boisterous puppy. 'Well, if she's pregnant, obviously you will be. You're not unique.'

'I feel unique. God, I feel . . .' There was no way to describe how he felt. Susan, his sweet timid Susan, to be a mother. He thought again of that old crone. Binding ropes she had said. Of course, a baby was binding, tying him and Susan together. Of course. Last night that prediction had worried him, he had been unable to pinpoint any of it. Now it all came plain. 'I'll never doubt a fortune-teller again,' he announced. Bob grinned.

'A shot in the dark. Their stock in trade – make it enigmatic enough and you can read anything you want into what they tell you.'

'Two shots in the dark? No, there is something in it, Bob.'

While Bob chortled, Matthew returned to reading the rest of his letter. It said she was two months pregnant. The letter was nearly three weeks old, so it had happened on his embarkation leave. She would be having the baby around June or July time.

'We might all be home by then,' he said to Bob, roughly calculating the date. 'With the Yanks in the war now it could shorten it considerably.'

Bob's unprepossessing features were wreathed in smiles of joy for him. 'Could be. One never knows. I tell you what, we'll have a drink tonight to celebrate you being a prospective father, wet the baby's head. Drinks on you of course.'

'Thanks very much!' Matthew chuckled, but Bob corroborating his own certainty of being home by next summer heartened him even more.

In this frame of mind he began on his reply to Susan. But it wasn't easy to put into it all he felt. He was in danger of writing a load of drivel and finally had to put it away until the next morning when he might be able to collect his thoughts better. It was the twenty-second of December, with Christmas and its panto, in which he'd got himself into the chorus, not sure if he even wanted to bother, three days away. The next morning the bombers came.

Throughout Christmas and into the early days of 1942, Rangoon continued to be bombed. Detailed to help supervise hordes of terrified refugees pouring out of the city, helping to fill in at the docks now forsaken by hundreds of Indian dock workers who'd also taken to the road, hoping to get back home to India, Matthew's letter to Susan lay unfinished.

His main concern in that letter now was to allay her fears for his safety as news was relayed to England about the fall of Hong Kong and the air attacks on Rangoon. That city would surely be next to fall. Any time Matthew had he scribbled words of reassurance. Above all else, Susan, pregnant, must not be alarmed. He assured her that the bombing had been minimal no matter what the wireless said, but whether some censor would allow that piece of information in his letter to get through was out of Matthew's hands, though he felt better having put it in.

By the middle of January the Japanese were reported to be already concentrated on the Siam-Burma border, the speed of their movements stunning everyone. Matthew's troop found themselves suddenly attached to an Indian brigade very much in need of a signals unit and ordered forward to establish a line of defence just east of the Sittang River which ran into the Gulf of Martaban some eighty miles away.

Gathering up their kit, boarding trucks, they had no time to send last letters home even if they had been allowed to. By the time Matthew was able to scribble a page to Susan, Moulmein to the south was in enemy hands, so fast had the Japanese moved through what had been thought impenetrable jungle.

Two weeks later the letter still lay in his shirt pocket,

darkened by sweat, as he crouched by the side of a dirt
road passing on crackling coded messages over his field
radio, his nerves jumping, his eyes alert to any movement
from the dim jungle on either side of the road.

As yet they had seen no action, the enemy being busy
around the Bilin River fifteen miles away. But everyone
knew by now just how swiftly that enemy could move
through this tangle of rainforest, how adept it was at
easing around a battalion, small lightly equipped figures
appearing out of the greenery in front of their prey like
spectres, cutting off whole battalions without warning. It
had happened more than once these last few weeks and
no one wanted to be caught napping. Orders had come to
withdraw to the railway bridge over the Sittang, to guard it
until all transport and equipment was safely across. Then
the rest were to cross prior to its demolition to prevent any
enemy advance upon Rangoon itself.

As Matthew moved back along the road with his
platoon, a staff car passed him, empty but for the Indian
corporal driving it. Remembering his letter, Matthew
frantically hailed the man and as the car slowed he pulled
out the letter and waved urgently at the driver.

A slow gleaming smile split the dark aquiline features.
There was no need for any exchange of words; the
beseeching look on the taut face of the English corporal
brandishing his stained envelope spoke volumes in any
language. Stretching out a hand, the driver took it, nodded
understanding, and tucking it into his uniform sped off
westward in a cloud of dust.

*

Three months she had been here. Three months and still a guest, not one bit a part of Matthew's family, and she wondered if in fact she wanted to be.

Yes, of course Mrs Ward looked after her, saw she wanted for nothing and was apparently very happy with the knowledge of her son's wife bearing his child. It was the way she went about it, the way she always conducted herself, that made Susan feel like an outsider.

She yearned for home, for the noise and laughter, for her father's uncouth manner and her mother's brassy warmth, the sharp quarrelling of her sisters and the tormenting of her younger brothers, neighbours coming in and out as free as they liked. Their own doors too were open to anyone who wanted to come in for a chinwag and a cuppa. Three months here and she knew none of the neighbours, except Jenny Ross. But she looked for her in vain to unburden her troubles on. It seemed Jenny Ross was too taken up with her work nursing, her own friends and no doubt some young man, to come home at all the right times. Susan had seen her only once since that time they had spoken together, but it had been cold with a threat of more snow when she had glimpsed her entering her house, head down, glad to be out of the bitter wind and Susan had felt it too much an imposition to go across and make herself free as she might have done at home, especially as it was obvious Jenny Ross was eager to get indoors and relax.

Life, with winter closing in, the sounds of the world deadened by the first snows, was turning into a gaol, her gaoler a well-meaning but dictatorial Mrs Ward whom she couldn't bring herself to call Mum. Susan merely cleared her throat should she need to gain her attention, which was as seldom as she could get away with. Mr Ward, whom she did feel she could happily have called Dad except that she couldn't address one in-law that familiarly without the other, was so different. He had the same way of looking at her as Matthew had, as though concealing some joke. He said little, but possessed a sort of warmth his wife did not have, and for Susan any tiny port in a storm was a haven. When the weather had been more clement she'd been able to take a walk down to his shop and spend her time there helping a bit, making tea or serving customers with small items or talking to him in the back room when things were quiet. Now that the weather had turned foul, she was stuck here with her mother-in-law, yearning desperately for her own mother. But her mother was far away and in no way could Susan find courage enough to make an excuse to leave and go off to live up there.

In her own way Mrs Ward was kind enough, but Susan could not master her awe of her. And when she'd found herself pregnant, she also found herself practically in close confinement, watched over night and day by a woman with the eyes of a hawk watching its prey, or so it seemed.

'You must stay in bed longer in the mornings. Don't go out of the house without first telling me where you are going. Don't try lifting that on your own, it could be too heavy and cause the baby an injury, I'll do it for you. Don't upset yourself so about Matthew – it's not good for you in your condition. Try to content youself more, my dear – there's plenty of books to read. If you need to go to the library, tell me and I will accompany you. Is it not time you started knitting for the baby? That would help you. We could get some wool and you can make a start.'

And this when she'd only been two months gone. No better, in fact worse, now she was four months. What would it be like by the time she was seven or eight months? Life threatened to become unbearable.

Early Sunday morning, the fifteenth of February, came, with little to do but sit indoors all day as with most Sundays, and probably get on with her enforced knitting. Mrs Ward inspected it every now and again, helping her with dropped stitches, advising her on how to keep the knitting even: 'You knit far too tightly, my dear. That's because you're too tense. Then when you relax, you knit looser. The result is an uneven garment. Try to remain relaxed all the time.'

But how could she? She hated Sundays. She wished Matthew was here. But he was thousands of miles away, in a sunny climate, enjoying himself. Jenny Ross had told her, when she'd got into a panic over the news of war opening up in the Far East, that Pearl Harbor and Singapore which had been bombed at the same time were far far away from him. Mr Ward had confirmed that, adding – she suspected to make her feel better – that Matthew was probably living it up in India. Not that she didn't want him to enjoy himself, wasn't glad he was in no danger from this distant war; she just wanted him back here, a buffer between his mother and herself.

This Sunday she was feeling particularly desperate. It was the baby, beginning to twitch ever so slightly, already seeming to be pushing out the walls of her stomach. She needed to get out of the house without Mrs Ward there to hold her firmly by the arm, like some sergeant major.

That woman, why did she behave as if she had to be responsible for everyone else's well-being? Was it because she herself lacked something, was nursing a sense of inferiority, deep inside, needing to combat it by bossing everyone about? Perhaps it was a way of proving something to herself. But could anyone visualise Lilian Ward as ever having lacked self-confidence? Susan could imagine her at four years old, bossing all the kids about, even then managing everything for them; could imagine her in her crib consciously manipulating her mother with a cry, a squeal, a smile. Lilian Ward had been born managing. But she wasn't going to manage her!

Susan made up her mind. The weather looking passable, Mrs Ward was upstairs clearing out a cupboard in one of the back rooms, which she loved doing on Sunday mornings, Mr Ward looked ready to settle back with his Sunday paper, which he was never allowed to read over breakfast. Susan hastily donned coat, scarf, boots, and gloves and quietly opened the front door to let herself out. Just a short walk. She'd be back before they knew she'd gone. Mrs Ward might even assume she'd gone to lie down in her room for an hour though there was a chance she might look in to see if she was all right. There was never any need. Susan felt her health was magnificent. Gone was all that dreadful morning sickness when Mrs Ward would hurry into the bathroom after her, embarrassing when she was being sick, to wipe her brow and advise on how to prevent morning sickness: drink cold water, eat an apple.

'Is that you, Susan?' Her mother-in-law's bat-hearing had detected the door opening. Now she must answer.

'I just thought I'd wander down the road a bit. I need some fresh air.'

'Oh, no.' Already Mrs Ward was coming downstairs. 'The pavement is still a little icy. You'll slip and fall. You must not harm that baby.'

It was all she cared about, Susan thought uncharitably, the baby, the mother just an incubator for her son's child, someone else for her to fuss over, think for, do for, the way Matthew had described on one occasion.

'I just want to go out,' Susan blurted. 'I need to go out.'

'I'll come with you. I think I need a little fresh air myself.'

There was only one thing Mrs Ward really needed, to keep an eye on her. Slumping a little, Susan waited as the spotless flowered apron was taken off and outdoor clothes put on, the lightly greying short hair given a brief tidying pat and a hat put on over it. Mrs Ward had a wonderful clear skin, virtually unlined, and Susan thought as she waited for her that when young she must have been a very handsome woman. She still was, but so forceful. Meekly, Susan allowed herself to be conducted a short way across the icy road, in through the park gates, as far as its nearest bench and then back – a distance of no more than five hundred yards, not really a walk at all, and all the time with the woman's arm stayed tucked through hers, practically holding her up as though she were crippled or something. Susan was glad to get back indoors if only to escape to her room on the pretence of a lie-down after the walk, Mrs Ward approving wholeheartedly.

She had hardly closed her door and gone to her bed than she heard voices slightly raised downstairs. While Mrs Ward's voice had a penetrating quality to it, her husband's was always soft and thoughtful. Now, however, his could be heard above hers. Susan got up and opened the door again, the better to eavesdrop on this mystifying rise of voices.

'I think we should let her sleep on, rest, before we say anything,' he was saying.

'I think she should be told immediately,' came the reply.

'I don't think so, Lilian. You know how quickly she gets herself into a state.'

They had to be talking about her. What had she done to cause an argument? They had a damned cheek discussing her when she wasn't there. Becoming angry, she crept out on to the landing.

'Even so, he is her husband. She has a right to be told and as soon as possible.'

Susan made for the stairs. What had Matthew done that she must be told immediately of it? He hadn't found someone else, all those thousands of miles away? She felt sick as she ran into the living room. The two people were standing, their backs to her.

'What mustn't I be told?'

They had turned, were looking at her with a sort of dumb fear in their eyes. It was Mrs Ward who moved towards her first. Susan noticed that Mr Ward was holding the Sunday paper, half folded, half crumpled.

'My dear . . .' Mrs Ward began.

Her voice broke. She reached out and took Susan's arm in a vice-like grip but which Susan felt had been meant to be comforting. 'My dear, you must be strong. You mustn't allow yourself to become panicky.'

'What is it?' Susan asked, her heart already pumping like a little frightened animal behind her ribs although she had no idea why except the two people before her looked frightened and anxious, lending their anxiety to her.

'It's Matthew . . .' Mr Ward began, then checked himself. 'Well, not exactly Matthew, but it concerns him.' With that, he unfolded the newspaper and held it out for Susan to read. She had read with dismay of the fighting that had broken out in Singapore, how the Japanese had come down from the north through hundreds of miles of tangled jungle hitherto thought impassable for any human being, taking that city by surprise, and she had been mildly worried, but Singapore was still a long way from India.

Taking the paper from him while Mrs Ward turned away to gaze out of the window at the bare trees of the park opposite, Susan stared at the large black headlines:

SINGAPORE FALLS. GENERAL PERCIVAL SURRENDERS ON
ORDERS OF MR CHURCHILL TO PREVENT LOSS OF LIFE.

and then a smaller heading:

CHURCHILL TO ADDRESS NATION TONIGHT ON RADIO.

Susan looked up, imploring the couple as though they might

be able to do something to make it all better. 'But they said Singapore could never fall. How could it happen?'

With the Japanese capturing Singapore, would Matthew be with those sent to recapture it? He would have to fight, and she had thought him safe. He could be wounded, killed. She'd never see him again. The thought filled her whole being as though glue was being poured into her body. Susan felt herself beginning to sway. The baby seemed to be jumping about inside her.

'I don't know,' Mr Ward was saying. 'All their defences point out to sea, they were so sure no enemy could ever come from the north. But they did. That's all I can say.'

But she hardly heard anything he said for the buzzing in her head. The room had begun to spin. The floor was coming up to meet her and she felt her body grow limp and lifeless. She vaguely felt someone catch her, felt herself being picked up and carried upwards in a jerky manner, guessed in her faint that this was the stairs. But her faint had become complete before Mr Ward ever laid her on her bed.

Chapter 15

It was a day of stifling heat. Vehicles lurching from one bomb crater to the next sent clouds of dust over the sweating shoulders of those trying to clear the road of stricken transport on this twenty-second day of February.

The railway bridge over the Sittang River, hastily converted to allow single-file traffic, was making progress slow and hazardous, on top of which a truck had run off the temporary decking, hopelessly blocking the bridge, the tailback now grinding to a standstill.

They were at the mercy not only of enemy aircraft, but of Allied planes who had been ordered to attack the advancing Japanese but not informed that any troops west of Kyaikto would be British, and thus were strafing the waiting columns out of hand. With more transport being knocked out and more men being killed and wounded, the state of the road became steadily worse.

Beneath a smoking carrier a dozen men lay huddled, heads down, as dive bombers screamed over the muddle of men and machinery. Bullets whining like angry hornets ricocheted off the metal sides of the vehicle, and in the ensuing din Bob Howlett's voice had as much power as the squeak of a mouse, begging that they make a run for it to the safety of the jungle.

Some had already sprinted for the trees looking for an easier way to the river, but orders were to hold the bridge for as long as was needed to get the transport across before they were all cut off.

Matthew held on to Bob's shirt to prevent him from making for the deceptive shelter of tangled greenery each side of the open road. 'Stay put! The Japs could already be there. A whole platoon of 'em would be on top of you before you could see them.'

Scarcely any of his mob was left. Taffy – poor libidinous Taffy – dead. Hadn't known what had hit him. Ronnie Clark with his hankering for the excitement of battle, dead. Eddie Nutt, Lieutenant Grice, dead. Sergeant Pegg, somewhere back there along the road, both legs gone, had grabbed Matthew by the shirt front and pulled him close, his bullet-head unbowed, his eyes still glaring through his pain. 'Yer in charge now, Ward. Yer wanted t'be an officer. Now see if yer c'n make somefing of yerself, prove yer can ... Now git to it!' Letting go Matthew's shirt he sank back to stare at the bloody earth where his legs should have been and waited for the stretcher bearers, if there were any and if he was still alive by the time any did come for him.

Others of his platoon had been separated; of the survivors lying here beneath the shielding carrier, none of them was worth a light: Jeff Downey with chubby cheeks flabby and pallid with terror and fatigue, one side of his shirt stiff with blackening blood, his or someone else's, Matthew hadn't felt inclined to find out; Farrell nursing a shattered hand wrapped in a piece of his shirt; Bob as yet unscathed but becoming rapidly shell-shocked; a few men he didn't know, and himself, feeling as little like a leader as any could, his eyes sore from dust and lack of sleep, his throat clogged and burning, his cheeks sporting several days' stubble, his shirt and trousers caked with sweat and blood, thankfully not his own apart from digs and scratches collected from the lengthy retreat. But most of all his mind had gone quite blank as to how and whom he should be leading as Sergeant Pegg had demanded.

The rising crescendo of dive bombers seemed to expand inside his brain, smothering all ability to think. A bomb blast threw earth and rock high into the air beside the carrier with an ear-splitting fulmination of blinding light, making the vehicle jerk alarmingly as blast and chunks of white-hot metal slammed into it. One piece hissed past Matthew's cheek. Behind him came a gurgling, high-pitched shriek, a brief threshing about; then warm liquid gushed on to his back and he saw the victim flop and lie still.

Beside him Bob was curled into a tight foetal position. Downey was scrambling forward on all fours in an effort to get out from under the carrier and was screaming at the top of his voice: 'Oh, Jesus! We're gonna die – we're gonna die!'

Matthew threw himself on the man, hung grimly on to the squirming body as another string of explosions rocked the vehicle. 'You'll die all right out there.'

Farrell's voice was high with panic. 'Let the bleeder go, can't yer?'

'Shut your bloody mouth, Farrell!' His own voice sounded demented. So much for wanting to be an officer. He could hardly control himself, much less half a dozen panicking men. He felt utterly helpless.

The aircraft were wheeling off, leaving a strange silence. Ears accustomed to the din felt as though cotton wool had suddenly been stuffed into them. The planes would be back. Or perhaps they had realised they were bombing their own side. Oh, God, he hoped so. The panic under the carrier had melted away into shuddering breaths, trembling grunts, but for the moment it was safe to creep out and take stock.

Slowly, buzzing, deafened eardrums began to pick up sounds; the crackle of burning vehicles, the moans of the wounded, the urgent tone of men calling to each other, the crunch of boots running, the spasmodic revving of a lorry.

Shakily, shoving Bob ahead of him, Matthew crawled out, stood up, his legs feeling like rubber. Shattered transport lay everywhere. A truck with a cargo of wounded under a shredded tarpaulin had slewed across the road, its rear wheels in a bomb crater, gripping nothing while its excited Indian driver was revving the thing like a madman. Beside him an officer was leaning from the cab yelling orders to some Indian soldiers already trying to heave against its rear end without falling into the crater themselves.

Seeing the few men who had scrambled from under the carrier, he screeched, 'You lot, there! Give a hand. Give a hand.'

Matthew stared blankly at him, as yet incapable of a response. 'We've hurt men here.'

'Then get 'em on board and get this damned thing moving.'

The order brought Matthew back to his senses. No longer needing to be a leader, he could take relief in letting someone else do the leading. He and Bob, Bob now coming back to himself with an apologetic grin for his previous show of weakness, helped get their own wounded aboard. Farrell was the first to climb in.

Men's weight was pitted against machine. 'One – two – three, heave!' the officer shrieked. The vehicle lifted, its back wheels back on firm ground; the driver touched the accelerator. The wheels spun, briefly spraying dust over the men, then slipped back.

'Hold it! HOLD IT!' The officer's voice was full of panic. 'Again. One – two – three, heave! For Chrissake, HEAVE!'

From the direction of the crossing came the sudden rapid hammering of Bren-gun fire followed by the staccato crack of rifle fire. Caught by the knowledge that those at the river were having to turn and fight an enemy that had crept up on them, the men struggling with the truck paused.

The unsuspecting driver braked frantically but ineffectually and the vehicle slipped violently backwards. Cries of pain came from the wounded unceremoniously thrown about. Eyes rolling, the Indian soldiers exchanged cries of alarm in their own tongue, but it was Farrell leaning out over the tailboard of the stricken truck who said it explicitly.

'Oh, my bleeding Gawd, we're cut orf. We've 'ad it.' Very agile for one who a moment ago had been counted among the helpless injured, he was over of the tailboard and off, bolting towards the jungle.

'Stop that man!' To the officer's yell, Matthew added the power of his own lungs.

'Farrell – stay where you are!'

Farrell paused, Army training prevailing for all his panic, but his face as he turned twisted in an animal snarl of fear. 'Yer can't stop me. I've got a right ter git back ter me own lines. I'm pissin' orf.'

In one quick movement, Matthew unslung the rifle he still had on his back, levelling it at the man's groin. 'You do and I'll cripple you.'

In that moment he knew himself capable of carrying out the threat. It was as though he were another person, not because of his dislike of Farrell, but cold, clinical, the indurate soldier, Army-crafted, a machine, hating what he had become. But he'd halted Farrell who for a moment stood uncertain, though whether he would have defied his corporal's threat or not was not to be discovered as twin dark shapes roared over the rim of the trees, their shadows passing between the sun and the men below. A clatter of machine-gun fire scattered men in all directions, as though a stone had dropped on a cluster of marbles.

Matthew did a nightmare scramble for the carrier again, it seemingly a mile away as he felt rather than saw a line of dust spurts heading his way. In his own panic, he never even heard the explosion of the direct hit on the truck he had been helping to shove.

The attacks continued into the afternoon. In the centre of the road the truck was ablaze, now interlocked with a ten-tonner that had come from nowhere it seemed. From the smoking cab the officer's body hung amid shreds of burned clothing gently wafting away in the upcurrent of heat from the vehicle. Of Farrell there was no sign. He had legged it to the trees and was gone.

The sun going down saw the waves of planes depart. The bridge was at least still being defended, with the heavy hammering of a Bren-gun which sounded almost dignified against the excited clatter of an enemy machine-gun. Occasionally there came the dull flat detonation of a mortar bomb. At one time he fancied he could hear the hollow cough of a bomb as it left the mortar's barrel, the enemy too close for comfort if he was right. After a while it ceased, the operators perhaps moving closer to their goal, ignoring the broken vehicles nearby, but his uneasiness lingered. Those passing him in the sudden darkness that descends in the tropics trod warily, bent double, weapon held tense as they tried to probe the shadows either side of the road.

It made the flesh creep, this sensation of being watched, imagination magnifying fear tenfold. But fear had no place here. There was work to do, a way to be made for vehicles laden with wounded and supplies to get through to the bridge. In the darkness lit by lurid flashes, Matthew heaved and sweated helping to clear blockages While all around came the incessant chirruping of insects impervious to the racket of men locked in battle. At least while the sound of fighting continued there was hope of getting through.

Should it cease, it would mean the enemy had taken control.

It was with relief that he saw a staff car approaching out of the darkness, followed by a lorry full of Indian troops. The staff car held two obvious junior officers, even though they had ripped off their lapels and thrown away their caps, and a burly senior officer also minus his insignia.

With the road narrowed by the shattered ten-tonner, the car stopped. The burly officer got out. 'Where's your officer, corporal?'

Matthew indicated the body hanging from the burned-out truck. The man sighed, surveying the tangled wreckage. 'Not having much luck here.'

As Matthew explained his lack of men and tools, the lips beneath the dusty moustache gave a small, tight, tired, smile. 'My men will take over, corporal. Corporal . . .?'

'Ward, sir,' Matthew supplied.

'I'm Captain Weatherill. You and your men get some rest. You may need it.' He nodded towards the flashes around the bridge up ahead. 'By the way, the Japs have cut the road at Mokpalin,' he added as calmly as if announcing a cricket score.

Mokpalin, only three miles back, meant they were virtually caught in a neat pincer movement. For a moment, a feeling of doom spread through Matthew together with an irrational impulse to run towards the bridge, to race across and keep going until he got home to Susan and safety. It came to him that he might very well never see her again.

'Dear God,' prayed the panic within him, 'please, get me out of this. Let it all be a dream.'

Beside him Bob's voice came hollow. 'You mean we're trapped?'

The sound of that voice returned Matthew's sanity to him in a rush.

'We're going to get out okay,' he said, more to still his own fears than to reassure Bob. His mouth sour, he lifted a hand to his eyes and with finger and thumb grubbed out the caked dust that had collected at the inner corners. To ease the ache between his shoulder-blades he straightened his back. It was a gesture Weatherill immediately took as determination.

'Good man,' he grunted and left them to find a hole by the road to creep into and rest for a while.

Beside him Bob was fast asleep. Other men also were sleeping, but his own rest was fitful. For something to keep his imagination at bay he took a sip of the warm metallic water from his canteen, rinsed it around his mouth and spat it out, thick and evil, then took another sip and swallowed it. In the canteen the water slapped hollowly. How grand to have been able to wash, if only his face. To think of millions of gallons of fresh water flowing by just half a mile away. He listened to the spasmodic firing and wondered how much longer the two sides would continue taking pot shots at each other. He thought of Susan, the child she bore. He thought drowsily that if he were to get up now before it got light and go towards the firing, the river, there might be a chance . . .

A hand on his shoulder brought him awake, grabbing for his rifle. The grip tightened.

'Easy, lad.' Weatherill stood over him. 'Be light in a few minutes. Get your men together.'

Firing could still be heard from the bridge, a little more energetic in the fast-brightening tropical morning. The driver of the staff car, a cheeky Cockney, was handing out cubes of corned beef, the tin opened with his bayonet. 'We're orf, mate,' he said to Matthew. ''Ad a dekko darn the road. It ain't so bad furver along. A few obstructions but we can all git fru. Once we're over that bleedin' bridge we'll all 'ave a nice cuppa tea at HQ.'

Matthew grinned at his Cockney optimism and was on the point of helping himself to a greasy cube of the corned beef when a terrific triple explosion rocked the already pink dawn.

For a second or two the firing from both sides stopped as though paralysed by the tremendous paroxysm, and in the lull its echoes rumbled away into the distance with slowly diminishing reverberations.

'Mother of Jesus! What the hell was that?' one of the junior officers called out, running over.

Weatherill's answer was one of incredulity. 'They've blown the bridge.' A pall of smoke was spiralling slowly above the tree-tops.

The other man's voice shook. 'Bloody HQ. Couldn't wait for us. Left us in the lurch, thousands of us. They panicked.'

Weatherill didn't dispute him. Headquarters had probably had no alternative if the Japanese had been threatening to swarm across. It had been the plan, to delay the enemy's advance on Rangoon enough to allow Allied reinforcements to arrive.

After the first shock of the explosion, hostilities resumed with even greater ferocity, each man now desperately fighting for his own life, gone all thoughts of saving transport and artillery.

Weatherill lost no time. 'We'll try the river further upstream. Thank God this isn't the monsoon. The river should be low.'

'What about the wounded?' Matthew asked. The enemy, it was rumoured, had its own methods with casualties. Weatherill didn't even look at him.

'If they can walk and if they can be quiet, they come too.'

His words were met by silence, the men around him knowing there was no other suggestion to be made. He waited a moment or two for any there might be, then turned and without a word moved towards the trees. The others followed mutely, the green world closing in barely thirty feet into the trees, hiding the abandoned wounded quickly from guilt-ridden sight.

Here even any continuing rifle fire was muffled, the canopy a hundred feet or more above them cutting out all sunlight in a tangle of vines and parasitic growth, echoing only to the whirring of insects and the bell-like early-morning calls of forest birds. Grey wreathing mists of morning lay in motionless flat layers, but as the sun rose they turned delicate pink and lifted steadily through the ceiling of miniature jungle above to disappear. Within minutes that ceiling was pressing the heat down on the men, saturating them with sweat, the soft and spongy earth under their feet smelling dank.

Progress remained snail-like. In some areas the great mottled tree-trunks stood like dead-straight pillars of some vast cathedral, lianas draped from one to the other with curtains of green moss hanging from them. Sometimes the forest thinned enough to allow shafts of sunlight through and vegetation to become rampant, scrambling for light with vivid colouring, thick clumps of bamboo around which the men must time after time make diversions. In half an hour they had covered just half a mile, bearing northeast as much as those diversions allowed.

Breathing heavily from the now steamy heat which by midday would reach ninety degrees or more, arms aching from pushing aside the tough, woody creepers, legs aching from negotiating a surprisingly undulating terrain, from somewhere to their left came the gurgle of water.

'Should see some open space soon,' Weatherill predicted in a whisper. 'Paddy fields probably. We could be easily spotted. Keep your heads down.'

After ten more minutes pushing through undergrowth, they came upon a proper path, the forest beginning to thin.

In the sudden brilliant sunlight, Weatherill crouched just off the path, beckoning to his men to follow suit. 'I think there's a village ahead. Could be sitting ducks if we blunder in there. We'd best skirt it, find the river and somewhere to swim across. Come on, but quietly.'

He stood up, the rest taking their cue from him. A sudden movement of foliage, the metallic sound of hands on rifles, froze the group. In a strange language, a guttural voice grated out a command.

From nowhere there appeared small men in drab tunics with double belts, short legs bound in puttees to the knee, and split canvas boots that divided the big toes from the rest. Black shoe-button eyes trained on the group from behind levelled rifles with incredibly long bayonets; for all their size each man looked strong, immensely capable and very much a fighting man, utterly at home in this hostile environment.

One by one the surprised men let their rifles fall and lifted their arms in the time-honoured abject signal of surrender as their captors moved closer. There were some twenty-five of them plus their officer – that many moving so silently no one had heard them at all.

With a sickness pounding in his chest, Matthew lifted his arms with the rest, submitted himself to be searched by a soldier reaching only to his shoulder in height. His pockets and ration pack were emptied of all he possessed: silver cigarette case, lighter, a little Burmese money, a photo of Susan. It was the photo that hurt most, seeing it scrutinised then torn into four pieces and flung away. The silver cigarette case and lighter were handed to the Japanese officer who immediately pocketed them with a satisfied smile.

Chapter 16

'We'll get another letter from him very soon. You really must stop fretting, Susan. It isn't good for the baby.'

Susan eyed her mother-in-law, just managing to hold back the tears that threatened and which always annoyed the woman. But every time she thought of Matthew's last letter she couldn't help them rising to the surface.

The one prior to that had said he had been over the moon about her news of the baby, and she'd been so happy that he was happy. It had said they were leaving Bombay though where for, as usual, hush-hush.

His last letter had come two days ago, a single page written in pencil in such an obvious hurry she could hardly read it, the soiled notepaper in an even more soiled envelope telling her not to worry, he was all right, that in itself worrying her more although she wasn't sure why. It bore a military Rangoon postmark. Rangoon was in Burma, Mr Ward had told her, and she had heard fear echoing in his tone.

Her geography never good, she'd quickly consulted an atlas, alarmed how near the fighting Matthew had been sent. News from that part of the world had all been of disaster: the sinking of two large Royal Navy ships, the

Prince of Wales, and the *Repulse*, the fall of Hong Kong on Christmas Day, then Singapore on the fifteenth of February four weeks ago. Now it was March. There was fighting in Burma and Matthew's last letter, grubby and stained, made her shiver with imaginings she daren't voice; none of them dared, though the look on their faces said they were thinking the same as she was.

Why was it, Jenny thought, that when she was with Ronald she could talk without a pause about all sorts of things, completely at ease in his company, yet the very anticipation of going to meet him never failed to fill her with strange reluctance, wishing she didn't have to?

'Have a quick drink in the pub tonight?' he'd whisper as they passed in a corridor, if their off-duty hours coincided. 'Wait for you outside.'

She would nod, smile, aware of a sinking feeling, a wish to be doing anything other than meeting him, even preferring to go home to spend a dull evening with Mumsy. There was none of that excited palpitation a girl in love was supposed to experience – the way she used to feel all those years ago when Matthew Ward came into sight or inadvertently touched her. The touch of Ronald's hand on hers did nothing, though if he kissed her, her body would stir, responding of its own accord. Then her head would start to send messages that this wasn't love, but a natural response to the touch of any man halfway handsome. Yet it made no sense to shy away from the knowledge that marriage to Ronald could be the best thing to happen to her; she would become the wife of a general practitioner.

'It's still early days,' she'd hedged. 'Too many people are rushing into marriage because it seems the right thing to do.'

'Don't you want to marry me?' he had asked only last week, towards the end of February. What could she say?

'Of course I do.'

But was she lying, to him and herself? They had had their very first row, as far as it was possible to row with Ronald, who was always even-tempered.

'Then for God's sake why delay it? It's not as if I've nothing to offer you. My family's pretty well off. My father's a GP. Soon I'll be one as well.'

She knew that. He was taking his finals in a couple of weeks and was more than certain that he'd pass. He had talked often of the day when he too would be a GP expected to go in with his father as a junior partner. Perhaps it was that which made her so reluctant about marriage and the assumption that she would accompany him to Bristol. It meant leaving her mother, who still deemed herself lonely after all this time with Jenny not getting home regularly each night. Her mother was destined to become even more isolated if Jenny went off to live on the other side of the country – the other side of the world as far as she was concerned.

'If you go into your father's practice I shall end up in Bristol,' she argued obstinately and saw his lips tighten a fraction. 'There's my mother to think of. I can't leave her all on her own.'

She could have suggested he find some other practice around here, but some quiet little voice said it would be tempting fate – he might agree and she would then have no option but to say yes to his expectations of their marrying.

He had fallen quiet, had sat away from her, his brow furrowed. She too had sat silent over her mild ale and the evening during which they would normally have chattered away like a couple of monkeys had become long and tense until it was she who said she ought to be going to catch the last bus home. He had nodded, got up, got her coat for her and helped her on with it and had said, 'See you tomorrow then. I'll see you to the bus stop.'

This week, during another quick drink in the pub opposite the hospital, the row that had been simmering, exploded. Quietly, but it exploded just the same.

'I've had enough of this, Jenny.' Ronald's voice was harsher than she had ever heard it. 'What the hell do I have to do to show you how much I love you?'

She had to say it now. 'I don't want to go to live in Bristol all that way away.'

'I can't go without you.'

And now she must add: 'Then can't you try for a practice somewhere local, around here?' There, she had said it, had burned her last bridge.

Ronald looked at her, his brows meeting in anger at her selfishness. 'You want me to scratch around here looking for some half-baked practice that'll take me years to get anywhere with when I've an already made place with my father? You must be mad, Jenny. Don't you want to see me get on?'

'Of course I do.' She felt lame.

'Don't you love me?'

'Yes, Ronald.' She wished he wouldn't keep pushing that question.

'Well, it doesn't sound like it to me.'

A group of American servicemen with smooth smart uniforms and girls on their arms, bustling past, filling the pub with their loud easy twang and high spirits, put paid to the couple's quiet argument. Ronald threw them a frown, and repeated his statement a little more audibly. 'It doesn't sound like it to me.'

'Because I don't want to go traipsing all the way to Bristol, leaving my mother? What is this, Ronald – a demand for self-sacrifice?'

'In a way, yes.'

'But you're not prepared to sacrifice yourself when it comes to you.'

'Look, I shall be the breadwinner. I've got to consider what's best for our future. Can't you see that? If you really loved me, Jenny, it wouldn't seem to you like self-sacrifice – as you call it.'

There came screams of laughter from the GIs' girls. Jenny felt tears come into her eyes. 'If that's what you think of me, Ronald, the little lamb ready to follow its shepherd up hill and down dale, I've got a career too. I've studied hard, and I've still got a lot of studying to do, and I want to get somewhere, not just be a GP's wife, sitting at home, joining nice little ladies' clubs and doing your book work. Eventually I'd have liked to go into the QAs.'

This was the Queen Alexandra's Imperial Military Nursing Service Reserve. She hadn't really thought about going into the QAs before, but she thought of it now, more out of anger than ambition.

Ronald was staring at her. The ruckus from the GIs and their girls was getting worse, but they had good money to spend and the landlord would suffer them. The look on Ronald's face tore at Jenny's whole being.

'I had no idea that was all you cared for me, Jenny. You'd sooner join up than marry me.'

'No, darling, that's not what I meant. I want to marry you.' Now, suddenly, she did, seeing herself throwing away the chance of a lifetime. Did she really think she wanted to go on nursing for the rest of her life, to go off and be a Queen Alexandra's nurse, to take orders when she could live in comfort with a man who loved her? 'Ronald, I really do love you.'

He sat looking at her for a long while, as she watched him, visualising what was going on in his mind, her protestations fallen short. Then he stood up, and got her coat, as always helping her on with it, for he was a caring man even when hurt and angry. Wordlessly, she let him guide her from the now noisy pub. Outside, he took her in his arms and kissed her.

'Perhaps I have been rushing things,' he said in the quiet night, the sounds from inside muffled by the closure of the pub door. 'What I wanted to tell you, darling, is that I got my results today. I've passed.'

She leaned back from his embrace. 'Why didn't you tell me?'

'I don't know. I was going to, but somehow we ended up discussing something else instead.' He wouldn't say row. Easier to call it discussing. But he wasn't finished yet.

'Jenny, darling, I know now that you're not yet ready to commit yourself – not to me or to anyone. But I love you. And I think, deep down, you love me, but there's something in the way. Maybe it's your mother. But you must break away from the hole you're stuck in. So I think it best I let you consider things before you make up your mind what you want to do. In a week or two I'll be leaving to go home to start up in my father's practice. I'll write to you and if you do change your mind about coming to Bristol, I'll be waiting. I'll keep on loving you, Jenny. I won't give up hope. I just want you to think about everything and what we are throwing away.'

Tears were streaming down Jenny's cheeks. Now was the time to burst out that she did love him, that she wanted to go with him. But she didn't. For the most futile of reasons. And the moment vanished.

A bleak spring had followed a bleak new year, that first elation at the United States coming into the war dissipating; everywhere Jenny saw set faces that spoke of grim determination to believe things must only get better.

In the Middle East, Rommel, seemingly invincible, had struck back and recaptured Benghazi. At sea the German battleships *Scharnhorst* and *Gneisenau* slipped their hideout at Brest under the very noses of the British Navy and in attempting to sink them the RAF lost forty planes. Ceylon was raided by the Japanese, the British Eastern Fleet withdrew to Kenya; Britain had abandoned the Far East.

The London Hospital's outpatient department seemed to

be full of women showing the strain of trying not to dwell on loved ones away. Women with drawn faces, complaining of backache, neuralgia, stomach pains, stiff necks, strange agitation, trembling hands, 'I c'n 'ardly keep meself still in the mornin', doctor'; 'I'm fair sick of this bloody back of mine'; 'I've got these legs, doctor, wot keeps on swellin''; and usually as he examined whatever complaint presented itself, came the inevitable self-diagnosis: 'Wiv'art me ole man at 'ome I feel lorst.'

Jenny, helping in outpatients, knew how they felt thinking of those absent faces. Too often she thought of one absent face in particular. Since the fall of Rangoon in Burma, Susan Ward said she'd not had any letters from her husband and the Wards were growing anxious. Lots of wives and mothers were going through that strain, added to which was the constant worry of eking out the rations for those still at home. Shoppers needed to be ever more watchful for opportunities to present themselves in the food line.

It wasn't unusual to see whole streets come to life with hurrying women. Coats, aprons, scarves billowing like schooners in full sail as they converged on some butcher's shop from which whispers had emanated: ''E's got offal!' Jenny's mother and even the proud Mrs Ward joined in the hasty advance. Jenny would pass a growing queue of women now waiting patiently and not leaving until every last scap of off-ration meat had gone. Nothing stopped the unending search for something nutritious to fill a plate: horse meat, goat, stringy fishy-tasting whale meat being tried out.

'I got a little bit of goat meat,' Jenny's mum told her on one occasion – succulent, tender meat it was too, except, unused to such rich fare, they were both sick. Jenny stayed off duty all next day much to the displeasure of the ward sister. Otherwise, things went on as normal, the tip-and-run daylight raids on country towns like York and Bath and Exeter (Jenny thought of Jean Summerfield whose family had left London to escape all that) virtually ignored by Londoners, who had suffered the Blitz.

The evening she came home from the hospital, still a little queasy from the enjoyable meal of goat meat, she met Susan wandering along by herself, her coat tight about her stomach. The early March evening was still light, summer time's extra hour still prevailing. Susan looked wan, and hardly smiled as she saw Jenny coming towards her from the bus stop.

'Have you heard from Matthew yet?' was the first question out of her mouth. Susan shook her head.

'Nothing yet. I hope he's all right.'

'He's bound to be. Otherwise they'd have said. You'd have heard.'

'It's been nearly three weeks. I've not been out of the house in ages. I'm so fed up. I'd like to go to the pictures or something, but his parents don't go. I can't go on my own, so I'm stuck.'

Jenny found herself amazed at how easily the girl had slipped from concern at not hearing anything from Matthew to talking at far greater length of her own boredom. She would have thought the former worry would oust everything else from her mind.

'If you like,' she offered, giving Susan the benefit of any doubts, 'we could go to the pictures together. I'm off next weekend. *Casablanca* is on at the Regent in Mare Street. There are bound to be long queues, but we could go early on Saturday afternoon, if you can stand lining up.'

Susan's face was a picture of eagerness. 'Oh, that's ever so nice of you. I'd love to do that, I really would.'

'Then that's what we'll do.'

In her bedroom Susan stared into the mirror at the hardly noticeable lump. It would get larger and larger and she'd never be able to escape. Going to the Regent with Jenny Ross looked like being her last trip out, with Mrs Ward getting ever more attentive.

Just over four months pregnant, and being slightly built, even that tiniest bulge made her look dreadful. There was no one to reassure her that she still looked beautiful, no one to lay a loving hand on her stomach or to gaze on her with pride in her and himself at what they had achieved, no one to tell her she was a clever girl and that he adored her. When this baby was born there'd be no one there to hold it and gaze down on it in wonder. Only God could say when Matthew would return home. As yet she'd not heard a thing from him since that last letter at the end of February. It was March now. Early March, it was true, but waiting made it seem longer. She trembled for him, dared not think of his never coming back. Whatever would she do without him? The thought made her feel sick.

Hastily, she turned from the mirror, trying to push such dreadful thoughts from her, and feverishly got dressed.

They'd get his letter soon. Military mail from that part of the world was a bugger, the time it took.

A ring on the front doorbell swept away all her dismal anxiety. Maybe it was the postman. Hurrying from her room she leaned over the banister in time to see her father-in-law closing the door. Aware of her standing there, he looked up, his eyes wide as though with guilt, but she knew it was fear for she had seen the telegram he held. Even from here the blurred bold black letters OHMS leapt out at her, searing through her brain, sending her rushing headlong down the stairs. 'Matthew! It's about Matthew.'

Leonard caught her as she reached him, took her arm and guided her into the lounge through which the early March sunlight was slanting.

'Lilian,' he called as he sat Susan down in one of the armchairs; she felt struck dumb with growing terror. 'Lilian, come here, dear. It's important.'

As Mrs Ward came hurrying in, Susan found her voice. 'It's Matthew! Oh, God, it's Matthew!'

Neither took any notice of her or seemed to hear her as Leonard tore open the envelope, extracting the buff paper to read. He looked up bleakly.

'It says Matthew's missing.'

'No!' Susan's voice rose to a scream. She leapt up, tore the telegram from his hands, but the words blurred, her brain seemed to be exploding and the scream that came from her lips seemed not to be her own, a hollow screaming that went on and on: 'He's dead . . . Matthew's dead . . .'

The telegram fell from her fingers and she felt herself taken on a blind, headlong rush from the room, though where she was going she had no idea; she found herself clinging on to the newel post of the stairs, unable to let go of it. And still the hollow, terrible screaming continued, consuming her.

What happened next was a vague blur of being picked up, of being carried, of being laid down, then shaken until her head felt it would fall off her shoulders. That irrational fear was what brought her to her senses and she found herself looking into the stern face of her mother-in-law.

'Get a hold of yourself, Susan. You must remember the baby – his baby.'

Damn the baby! Tears squeezed between her eyelids as she screwed them tight. 'Matthew's dead . . .'

The hands holding hers were like stiff, dry claws giving no comfort at all. 'He's not dead, Susan. It says he's missing. They will trace him soon. We must cling to that hope. You must cling to it. For his sake. For the sake of his baby.'

'That's all you care about,' she burst out in her grief. '*His* baby – a baby to take *his* place. You don't care about me at all, how I feel.'

'We do, Susan.' They didn't, but she had no strength left to argue.

'The pain's still there in my stomach,' she complained from her bed. She'd been in bed for two days, ever since the dull ache had started. Now she saw Mrs Ward's expression of sympathetic concern change to one of apprehension.

'The doctor said it isn't what we thought it might be, but that you are upset and probably strained yourself when you lost control of yourself, and that we must just keep an eye on you. But doctors can be wrong and I really think we ought to get you to a hospital if this doesn't improve.'

'No!' Susan's voice rose in terror. She had a naked fear of hospitals; it dated from when she had been a child and had had her tonsils out. It had been an awful experience. The smell of the place, a mixture of antiseptic and ether, its green and cream tiled walls and age-yellowed ceilings, all pressed in on her, and the hush of the ward as night had come down emphasised the feeling of being alone away from her parents, shut away from the cosy world outside as though it was a different place – as hell might be, or death. She'd cried for her mother and a stern-faced nurse had told her to be quiet. Taken on a hard, rumbling trolley along corridors and into a stark white room with horrid glittering steel instruments hanging from the ceilings, an evil-smelling rubber mask had been put over her face until her mind seemed to swirl away into a roaring blackness. The next day her throat had hurt terribly and she wasn't allowed to eat and when she cried another nurse had told her off. And all the time that peculiar rustling hush and muted voices and that horrible disinfectant smell. She'd never been near a hospital since, unable even to bring herself to visit anyone in there. The mere thought of going into one brought back the memories of its smell. It must have done something to her because to this day her whole body would cringe from anything savouring of it, from those with a hacking cough to someone with a cut finger. Even an unsightly scar could make her body tingle with revulsion. How Jenny Ross or anyone could bring herself to be a nurse was beyond her.

Mrs Ward was looking down at her. How could she be expected to understand? 'If the pain gets any worse, you will *have* to go to hospital.'

This left Susan gritting her teeth against the dull ache for fear of the threat being carried out. Bidden by the doctor to lie as still as possible in bed for the next week, she did all that was asked of her, determined no one would get her anywhere near the gates of any hospital.

Mrs Ward wrote to Susan's parents. They came hurrying down from Birmingham; the content of Mrs Ward's letter had frightened them. They found Susan looking much better than they had thought, with the pain almost gone, but she was still confined to bed – just in case, said the doctor.

As soon as Susan saw them, she burst into tears and, when Mrs Ward prudently retired from the room, she threw her arms around her mother to be cuddled and crooned over in privacy. She hadn't realised until then how much she had missed her mother.

'Mum, oh, Mum – take me home. I hate it here.'

Her mother let go of her slightly to gaze around the pretty pink bedroom. 'Whatever for, love? This is really lovely. Matthew's parents look after you so well, better'n like I ever could in our crowded house.'

'Don't talk of Matthew,' Susan pleaded tearfully. 'The telegram said he's missing, but it's only another way of telling us he's bin killed.'

'Don't say things like that, Sue.' Her mother leaned

back to look up at her husband, seeking help from him, to which he responded in his usual way, merely repeating what had already been said as though that cemented it all perfectly.

'No, don't say things like that, Sue.'

'You've got to 'ave faith, love. He'll come back, right as rain, you'll see. When this war's all over, love, you and him, you'll both pick up like where you left off, and you'll 'ave a little baby then to look after, like. So you got to be strong and look after yourself, for Matthew and for his baby's sake.'

'I could do, at home,' Susan whimpered as her mother gently broke free of her arms, almost as though she were glad to be released of them. 'If I was home, Mum, with you to look after me, everything'd be all right. I hate it here. With Matthew gone, I don't feel I've got any business here.'

'Sue, love, he ain't gone. He's alive somewhere, waiting to be found by the Army. You make it sound as if you think he'll never come back. And look, love, we couldn't have you home with us. You know there's no room. There was hardly no room when you was single, much less when you've got a baby with you. And honestly, our Sue, look what you've got here. No, love, I do think you're better off staying here with Mr and Mrs Ward. They really are nice people and you're being so well looked after.'

So that was that. Abandoned by her own family. Over the next couple of weeks, she rested, slowly recovering, the baby still firmly entrenched inside her. There had been moments when she would have put her hands together

if she had lost the baby. Growing more convinced that
Matthew must have been killed, lying unfound somewhere
in the jungle with creepers and undergrowth hiding his
body and (the mere thought made her weep until her
eyes appeared permanently red and swollen) the horrid
creeping things slowly devouring it, a baby would only be
a painful reminder of the love and happiness they'd once
shared. She couldn't give her love to a baby when her love
for Matthew was of no use to anyone any more. Then, as
she recovered, she wasn't so much glad as relieved that she
hadn't lost the baby after all. It hadn't grown so much that
she was yet attached to it in her mind, but if Matthew had
really been killed and was at this moment actually looking
down on her, he'd never forgive her for such thoughts
about it as she'd had.

If only she'd been asked to go home, it might all be so
different. But now she was being pampered all the more
by Mrs Ward, who was nothing to her, this in-law business
thrust on her, yet was assuming the role of loving mother.
She could see no escape. At home she might for the time
being go out and enjoy herself, still go off to dances,
perhaps dance with some of the young servicemen, Yanks,
Canadian, the Free French, the Polish and the British boys,
and still be admired for a while. Here, she was trapped,
expected to play the wife when there was no one to play
wife to.

To escape the sensation of being smothered and continually watched over, she would spend hours in her
room reading the limp, buff-coloured magazines that
wartime austerity forbade shiny covers. Sometimes she

read increasingly tatty books from the library, love books mostly – easy-to-follow love stories with handsome heroes and violet-eyed heroines. They'd bring back a flood of memories, desolate now, of when she and Matthew had made love, had been in love. She'd pretend he was still making love to her, but it brought such wishing that she tried not to imagine it too much. Then she'd throw the book down and weep with loneliness, stifling her sobs in her pillow in case Mrs Ward came hurrying in to see what was the matter. As if the woman couldn't see why she was crying.

Chapter 17

Halfway through April, when her stomach was really beginning to show and not much chance of going out anywhere presented itself, there was no one to talk to. With Matthew's sister serving as a Wren in Southampton even Louise's company was denied her. She'd have felt even more trapped if it hadn't been for Jenny Ross popping in now and again. She'd become a good friend and confidante.

For Jenny, an hour or two with Susan on those evenings when she wasn't with her friends from the London could be a change from sitting with her mother who seemed to want to lean on her more and more. She often wondered how Mumsy would have coped had she married Ronald.

It had been strange not seeing his face about the hospital. She had found herself looking for him, missing him, but as anyone would miss a face no longer there, she told herself. One didn't have to love the person in order to feel keenly that empty place his going had left. She busied herself and put him from her mind.

As promised, he had written to her, a friendly letter, a little formal perhaps, wondering if she had thought any more about the things he'd last spoken of. He phrased the question itself slightly obliquely – no mention at all about the ring, which she still had tucked away in a box. She had replied, sounding just as friendly, just as formal, skirting the question. She had not meant it to be such a short letter, but there wasn't much to say. Time had gone on too long for that. She had wanted so much to say she'd changed her mind but when it came down to it, couldn't.

As time went on the wish had diminished, the dilemma's sharp edges had blunted somewhat. His departure had left a hole, but had she truly loved him, surely it would have left a much larger hole that would have taken a lot more to fill. And that impulsive statement she had made at the time about joining the QAs, then just a silly idea to get out of a spot, began to take more shape. The more she thought about it, the more attractive it was becoming. She'd be given a chance to travel overseas, to see the world, to meet new people, to expand her life. Mumsy wouldn't be too pleased but she had to get out of the rut that Ronald had accused her of being in. The QAs had such smart uniforms too, grey and scarlet with ties and snappy-brimmed hats, unlike the drab dress of ordinary nurses. She'd be tending fighting men instead of, now the Blitz was over, ordinary civilian ills and ailments. But first she had to pass her remaining exams. Prepared to work hard, she'd thrown herself into her work and looked very like passing her exams with flying colours come summer. All that would remain then would be to sit her finals that would turn her into an SRN. Then it would be off into the QAs in earnest.

She sat now talking to Susan in the living room. Mrs

Ward was out at one of her many women's meetings, Mr
Ward in the lounge listening to the evening news on the
wireless and reading his evening paper.

'The Red Cross hasn't come up with anything at
all,' Susan was saying, sitting back in a fireside chair
nursing the growing bulge over her stomach. She looked
particularly down this evening. 'His parents have made
lots of enquiries, but he's never been traced. They can only
guess he might be a prisoner of war but the Japanese aren't
giving out any lists.'

'But they should,' Jenny said, aghast. She had felt the
news of Matthew, or lack of it, as keenly as anyone, and
in private had shed tears. 'The Geneva Convention says all
sides must declare lists of prisoners.'

'The Japanese apparently think they're exempt because
they never signed anything, or whatever. So no one knows
if Matthew's been captured or gone missing or been . . .
you know.' Tears flooded the deep blue eyes.

'You mustn't give up hope,' Jenny said in an effort to
console.

'What's the point?' Susan got up and began pacing the
room, going to fiddle with the heavy curtains that concealed
the blackout material, drawn now with the gathering dusk
outside. Jenny watched her.

'If he's been taken prisoner, that has to be better news
than it might have been.' Meant to give comfort, it only
came out clumsy and tactless. She tried to amend it.
'You've just got to hang on to hope.'

Susan swung round, almost viciously. 'Hope! It's all
right for you to talk. You didn't love him like I did, so how

do you know what it's like not knowing what's happened to him?'

To combat the pain that retort invoked, Jenny got up and came to stand beside her. When she spoke her voice sounded flat even to her. 'Can you be that sure no one knows how you feel?'

Susan gave a sullen shrug. 'All I know is that if he's a prisoner of war, it'll be years before he ever comes home again, not till the war's over, and that could be God knows how long. And in the meantime, there's me stuck here. If I go on living in this mausoleum much longer, I'll go mad. I've got to get away from here before I get any bigger and can't at all.'

Again came the feeling that Susan wasn't thinking so much of Matthew, possibly in danger if indeed he hadn't been killed, as of herself and the loneliness *she* felt. Everyone was lonely who had a loved one away fighting, not knowing if they'd be killed or captured, but they usually kept it to themselves. Susan was too outspoken for her own good. It made her look bad.

'Where would you go if you left here?' she asked.

'Home. And as soon as I can. Trouble is, there's no room at me mum and dad's with our Robert and Les and our John there, and June and our Beryl. I'd rent a room somewhere nearby, but at least I'd be near my family. I'd have me mum near me. If only I wasn't having this baby . . .'

She broke off, not in shame at what she'd said, but swamped by the injustice of it all; Jenny could hear it in her tone. The girl's next words confirmed it.

'Why did all this have to happen to me? It's not fair! Landed with a baby, and Matthew God knows where.'

She began to pace around the room again while Jenny followed her with her eyes, the sympathy she had initially felt for the girl draining away.

'Haven't you stopped to think how dreadfully unfair it must be to Matthew?' She couldn't control the anger in her voice. 'Wherever he is, he can't be having much of a time either.'

She refused to think him dead. It was unthinkable. One day he would come home and take up his life again. That was all she ever wanted, to see him come home and be happy. The wish for that caught her like a pain. But not as great a pain as being compelled to keep her feelings for Matthew to herself when all she wanted was to sing them from the rooftops.

A day didn't go by that she didn't pray for his safe return. The notion of never seeing him again tore her to pieces. It was bad enough to know that if and when he did come home he and Susan could go off into the blue, that she would never see them again. But at least he would be in this world, somewhere. Far worse to know that he was gone from this world entirely. How dare this girl, his wife who professed to love him so dearly, take the news of his being missing as though she alone suffered – *her* loneliness, *her* grief, *her* plight, not his plight, not the worry and grief of his family, but hers.

Beneath the anger that welled up in Jenny was a dull ache for Matthew which she was sure would stay with her the rest of her life if he never came home again.

And here was Susan thinking of him only in terms of herself.

'Wherever he is?' Susan's voice had risen in near hysteria. 'Wherever he is? Don't you understand? He's dead. Matthew's dead! And here I am trying to be a wife, living with people that mean nothing to me.'

'You're carrying Matthew's child. His parents' grandchild. That's what they should mean to you, Susan.'

'Well, they don't. Everyone keeps saying he's been taken prisoner, but I *know* he's dead, lying out there somewhere in that terrible jungle where no one can find him, his body being . . .'

'Don't talk like that!' Susan had conjured up visions in her mind too awful to bear. 'There had to be others with him. They'd have reported . . .'

'I don't care! All I know is he's not here and I am, and I can't take much more of this living with his parents. They're not *my* family.'

'They're your baby's family.'

'I don't care,' she said again. 'I don't want this baby anyway, not now Matthew's gone. All I want is to get away from here. I have to get away.'

She broke off in a flood of tears and threw herself back into the fireside chair, head twisted into one of its wings, her small body convulsed with weeping.

The door opened. Mrs Ward in hat and coat came hurrying into the room. 'Susan! What is the matter? I could hear you shouting as I came in.'

Mr Ward had followed her in, also alerted by the cries. 'What in God's name is going on?'

'Susan is upset,' Jenny offered but neither of them looked at her.

Mrs Ward came forward and lifted the still-weeping girl from her huddled position in the chair. 'This happens each time someone tries to offer sympathy,' she said sharply, and Jenny might have taken umbrage had she not seen the girl's reaction for herself and heard the things she had said.

'Come on now, Susan,' Mrs Ward was ordering as Jenny stood aside, unsure whether to stay or go, both of which seemed ill-mannered. 'Pull yourself together now. We're all worried and anxious, but it does no good to give way like this. We all have to be strong. We all have to believe he'll be returned to us. You're doing yourself and the baby no good. Matthew wouldn't want that. I'm taking you up to your room and you can rest there.'

Helping the girl to her feet, she looked at Jenny for the first time.

'Having visitors seems to upset her even more,' she said with a small, cold smile which Jenny could only take personally, this time smarting from the rebuff. But the things Susan had said made Jenny herself prefer not to pop in and see her again. Let the girl do what she wanted. It was none of her business. And yet came the thought that in the depths of her, Matthew *was* her business, would always be her business wherever he might be.

She had intended to wait until at least after the baby was born. But after one miserable evening in early May, still with no news at all of Matthew, and with Mrs Ward telling her for the umpteenth time that they were all worried and anxious for him, Susan made up her mind. Early next morning, she got up before Mr and Mrs Ward were awake and feverishly packed her suitcase with a few essentials. It mustn't be too heavy. She was nearly seven months and she didn't want to harm herself in any way carrying it.

She had enough money, thank God, something under twenty shillings a week serviceman's wife allowance, and her National Savings book. Mrs Ward had never taken anything from her for her keep and she had been able to save quite a bit.

She left a scribbled note to Mrs Ward on the kitchen table, lacking the courage to face her. Retrieving her ration book from the shelf where they were kept, she silently let herself out.

The sun hadn't yet risen. The horizon of Victoria Park with its trees clad in young green glimpsed between the houses opposite was a mere blush, and seemed to emphasise the quietness. It was Tuesday, just gone four thirty, too early even for workers to be up off to work. She couldn't remember the road feeling so quiet or looking so wide. Lined by trees in new leaf, it was filled with the fresh, clean fragrance of the park and the new day, in May not even tainted by chimney smoke. She mightn't have been in London at all. It was a morning that should have been savoured, but it only made her shiver.

Alone in this empty road, all the large bay windows of the bedrooms looking down at her like empty eye sockets witnessing her flight, for a few seconds Susan stood uncertain, fighting the impulse to run back indoors away from those accusing, silent windows that seemed to be asking what she thought she was doing. At least her mother-in-law's home offered protection and comfort. With no idea exactly where she would go, a strong temptation to run back was growing stronger. Then she thought of the woman becoming even more dictatorial once the baby was born. With a final shiver, not at the silence of the morning, but at the well-intentioned if unwanted help of her mother-in-law, Susan turned her face towards Mare Street and Cambridge Heath Road, the bus stop and freedom. Once she got back to Birmingham and her own family she would be all right. It was her only comforting thought on this lonely morning.

Euston was a mad-house of hurrying people by the time Susan got there. Panting engines, the sudden shriek of released steam, the rumble of trolleys full of mail and parcels, deafened her. The last time she was here had been on Matthew's arm, with him to defend her against all this. Now she was on her own, her figure pulled out of all shape by the baby it carried inside it. She felt lost, conspicuous, but no one took a blind bit of notice of her, being more locked up in themselves: people getting to work; couples saying farewell to each other; the men going back off leave. Uniforms of other countries jostled past her, the ever-attentive Americans alone giving her pretty face a quick appreciative glance until seeing her condition and looking away.

By now her mother-in-law would have been bringing her up a cup of tea, telling her she could get up when she felt like it or could have breakfast in bed if she didn't, coddling her, concerned and managing. Suddenly that managing seemed preferable to standing here not knowing where to find the platform she was supposed to be on. Panic came and went in waves as she tried to gather her thoughts together, attempting desperately to hold back the tears her plight was prompting.

Once she found the right platform, the man at the ticket barrier told her the train would be leaving in five minutes. Hauling her suitcase, five minutes seemed hardly long enough to find a carriage and she worried that the train would pull out to leave her standing helplessly on the platform. So few trains ran these days, she could be stranded for hours. She struggled on, the suitcase banging against her legs, almost ready to turn round and head back to Hackney.

The first four carriages were full of people standing in the corridors. The fifth carriage seemed less full and with a struggle she got herself in. There'd be no seats, not here with the corridor partially occupied by servicemen. How could she face standing all the way to Birmingham? If an empty seat couldn't be found, she would go back home. Home. It seemed odd that she should think of it as that now she was away from it. Her heart seemed to sink down at the realisation. She had no home. Common sense told her there was no room for her with her family, and she had shunned the one she'd left behind. Mr and Mrs Ward would be up by now, would have read her note, devastated, not knowing how to find her and bring her back. And she so desperately wanted to be brought back at this moment.

Just as she was on the verge of turning round and forcing her way off again, a voice with a faint northern accent spoke in her ear.

'Pardon me, my luv.'

She turned to see an elderly man in a cap rising from a seat in the near corner of the apartment beside which she was standing.

'Have my seat, luv,' he said, and taking hold of the suitcase, added, 'Allow me,' and hoisted it up on to the string rack above.

'When you want, I'll get it down for you, like.'

Indecision had been taken neatly out of her hands, and she accepted gratefully. The sailor next to her looked a little crestfallen that he'd not offered his seat as the train gave a jerk, then with several more slowly began to move.

'Ooh, love, what you doing here?'

Her mother, her blonde hair in curlers, stared at her from the back door on which Susan had prudently tapped rather than surprise her mother by walking in on her after all this time away. 'How'd you get here? Is anyone with you? You're not on your own?'

'I've come home, Mum,' was all Susan could gulp.

'Good Lord. You'd best come in, love. How'd you get here?'

'I came on the train.'

It had been a long, drawn-out journey, the train stopping and starting as all trains seemed to do in wartime, sometimes to let a troop train through or one carrying munitions, sometimes for no known reason at all. She'd eaten a Spam sandwich she'd bought at Euston, somewhat stale, its grey corners turned up, but there'd been nothing to drink; that train had not carried refreshments. People going on journeys usually brought their own, just in case.

At New Street station she'd had some baked beans on toast and a much-needed cup of tea, then had come straight here on a bus. She felt tired and a little sick from the rather strong-tasting baked beans that were already repeating on her.

She was glad to follow her mother into the single living room. Nothing had changed, the room still looked worn, shabby, comfortable.

Susan had expected to find no one at home other than her mother, with everyone this afternoon still at work or school. So she was surprised to see her grandparents sitting there, having looked up expectantly at her entrance. Now her grandad was rising on his rickets-curved legs to greet her.

'Now then, there's a surprise, gel. Didn't expect to see you, like. What you doing 'ere?'

'That's what I asked her,' her mother put in as Susan leaned forward to give his lips beneath their bristling grey moustache a kiss.

She went over and kissed her grandmother too, feeling the bristles on her chin dig sharply into her like tiny needles. Her grandmother cut them with scissors.

'Nice to see you, luv. Y'look a bit peaky, love. 'Spect it's the baby. Y'r mam told us, but you ain't never come a-visiting. Is y'r husband with you, love?'

'He's away,' her mother explained quickly as Susan's

eyes began to mist. 'An' she will look a bit peaky, like, not getting any news about him. I told you, Mum, they reported him missing, like, and nothing more's been heard. Come on, now, our Sue. Sit down and tell us why you're here and I'll get you a nice cup of tea. And I expect you're hungry an' all. So why're you here then, luv?'

'I couldn't stay with Matthew's people any longer – not now he's not here.'

'They ain't turned you out, have they? I wouldn't think . . .'

'No, Mum, I left there.'

'Whatever for? A nice cosy place there to live, every-thing you want there.'

'I can't stand it there, Mum. I can't stand being told what to do and when to do it and what I should eat and when I should rest, and when I should go to bed, and I mustn't do this and I must do that. I can't stand it.' The words flowed out of her, all the pent-up things she'd been unable to say to anyone.

'But . . .' Her mother was looking at her, bewildered, a little concerned and, with the truth of her visit dawning on her, a little wary. 'But where d'you think you can go? Look, love, I don't want to appear hard and unkind or not caring or anything. I do care. But there's no room here at all, if you're thinking of coming here. I'd love to look after you, you and the baby, when it comes. I'd love to. My first-ever grandchild. Y'r grandma here'll be a great-grandma. Y'r looking forward to that, ain't you, Mum? But staying here, that's another thing, love. Y'see, last week they was bombed out in one of those daylight tip-and-run raids. House was condemned. Cracked walls and the roof's had it. Until it's repaired they've had to come here to live. That's why they're sleeping down here, don't y'see?'

For the first time Susan noticed the sagging double bed in the corner where the old scratched oak sideboard used to be. The sideboard was probably down in the cellar with all the other junk. Too damp for anyone to sleep down there even though during the night-time raids before she'd met Matthew, all the family had endured its damp conditions for safety's sake.

'I didn't know,' she mumbled. 'What am I going to do now?'

'Well, I think you ought to go back to Mr and Mrs Ward. They won't be cross with you, I'm sure. Just say you wanted so much to come and see us all up here.'

'Like this?' Susan looked down at her small bulging stomach.

'Well, you've got to say something. They'll understand. But you do see you can't stay here.'

But she could find somewhere to live nearby, some cheap room for the time being, until her grandparents could return to their repaired home. Her mother must have read her thoughts.

'The council people said your gran and grandad's place might not be repaired until the war's over. There's so many homes needing repair. Some people've had to be evacuated all over the place for the duration. At least your gran and grandad won't have to do that at their age when we can at least give them a roof over their heads, awkward as it'll be for them. You do see, love, don't you? I don't know what you can do except go back to London and I don't think you'd want to bunk in with any of your aunts and uncles, would you?'

No, she wouldn't. Go begging cap in hand to any of them, asking to foist herself on them, saying her own mother couldn't put her up, and them all knowing she already had a posh roof over her head down south.

Her mother appeared to think the problem solved. 'You can't go back tonight. You look all in. We can make a bit of room for you in with June and Beryl. It'll be a bit awkward for them but it'll only be for one night. But you can see, it couldn't be permanent, not with a baby to look after when it comes – nowhere to put a cot or anything. You do see, our Sue, don't you? Well . . .' She brightened as though everything was solved. 'I better get you this cup of tea and a quick sandwich of something. And when the boys come home and your dad and the girls, we'll all have a nice tea. I've got a nice big stew for us all.' Susan had smelled it as she came in and her mouth had watered and her stomach rumbled at the lovely aroma.

'I can get a better bit of meat with your gran and grandad's ration books added to ours,' her mother went on.

Susan fished into her handbag. 'I've got mine.'

Her mother looked horrified. 'Good Lord, love. I don't want yours, not for one meal. We've got plenty of stew. We won't even know it's been stretched. But, Sue love, you must go back home in the morning. Dad'll see you to the station all right. It won't matter if he's a bit late going into work.'

'I shall be all right, Mum.' It sounded pathetic, her
mother using the word 'home'.

'No,' her mother argued as though bequeathing some
bountiful gift. 'I won't have you going back to New Street
on your own with the workmen. Y'r dad'll take you. He'll
see you all right.'

Chapter 18

She hadn't felt so tired in all her life. The suitcase seemed to weigh a ton. Outside Euston station Susan checked the money she had left. There wasn't a lot, not enough to waste on a taxi back to Victoria Park Road and she just couldn't face the bus ride, nor see herself creeping back mollified to face Mrs Ward's wrath or relief, whichever it turned out to be. But where else was there to go? No one here to help her, no one to care for her, she felt as lonely as it was possible to be. She just wanted to sit here on her suitcase and burst into tears.

Nearby a news vendor's raucous voice was calling out: *'Standard, Ev'n Standard*! Get *y'r Standard.'*

It was getting late though daylight was still being drawn out. It had taken more than half the day travelling from New Street to Euston. And now she had either to go home to Mrs Ward before it got dark or find somewhere to stay at least for the night, she was so weary. But her remaining money for this week wouldn't stretch to any hotel. Misery rose again in her throat, which she fought to hold back with large gulps. She had been such a fool, it had been such a daft escapade. And now even her brain couldn't think properly. She saw herself sleeping here where she sagged, a policeman moving her on in the night like he might a tramp. She wasn't a tramp. She was a fool and she was seven months pregnant. If only she could stand here and cry her eyes out.

'Get y'r *Standard*! Fifty farsand at Second Front demonstrashern.'

Of course, buy a paper, look in the rooms-to-let columns, the logical thing to do. Feeling uplifted, Susan bought a paper. She wasn't going back to Mrs Ward, she would stand on her own two feet. At least for a while.

Half an hour later found her on the doorstep of one of the somewhat shabby-looking houses off Mile End Road whose address was the one she'd selected from the to-let column: 'Two furnished rooms, large family home, shared bath/wc, seven and six pw.' She had to knock twice before anyone answered.

She felt and looked sick, and the woman who finally came to the door took one look at her condition, her suitcase, and said: 'Gawd 'elp us – you orlright, dear?' the Cockney accent closing around Susan like a warm blanket.

'I . . . I saw your ad,' she began, unable to say any more for the sick giddiness that was overwhelming her.

'Better come inside, dear,' the woman was saying. 'You don't look too good, and that's a fact. I'll take yer case for yer. Come on in.'

Taken into a cavern of a room, Susan gratefully allowed herself to be eased down on to a sagging brown leatherette sofa that puffed explosively under her small weight. The suitcase was plonked at her feet. 'You stay there, dear. I'm gonna make yer a cuppa tea. Look as if yer could do wiv one. I won't be a tick.'

Left alone to recover, Susan stared about her. The room had a high ceiling and a huge, stained marble Victorian fireplace but was bare of all ornaments and embellishments, almost as though the family were on the point of moving out and had packed away everything easily movable. All it held was two large armchairs that matched the sofa, half a dozen straight-backed chairs and a scratched oak sideboard with a radio on it. There was only lino on the floor and set in the centre was a circle of linked-up toy railway lines with a couple of Hornby trains, their carriages lying on their sides, and nearby some very battered toy cars.

As she sat looking at it, a boy of about thirteen came in. Staring at her from under a thatch of unkempt tawny hair, he said, ''Ello.' Susan smiled through her tiredness.

'Mum's gorn ter make yer some tea,' he announced gravely. When Susan nodded, he went on, 'I'm Malcolm. I've got two bruvvers. They're Percy an' 'Enry. They're younger'n me.'

Again she nodded, too weary to make conversation with small boys. A silence fell and finally Malcolm wandered off leaving her to continue gazing at the square-patterned lino and the indifferent beige wallpaper. The once-heavy green brocade curtains at the long Victorian bay window were faded at the edges by sunlight. Against the wall were propped makeshift blackout shutters of thick black paper in flimsy wood batten frames. The woman returned with a steaming basin-like cup on a wide saucer which she put into Susan's hands.

'Yer'll feel a lot better after this,' she said and sat on one of the chairs while Susan sipped what was the best cup of tea she'd had in what seemed like ages.

'About the advert,' she said at last.

'Oh, yes,' said the woman as though only just recalling that was why Susan was here. Now Susan felt better enough to take note of her, she saw a smallish woman of about thirty-five with uncurling fair hair roughly cut straight about her ears and forehead. Her hands were rough and she wore a washed-out flowered wrapover pinafore over a green dress.

'Well,' she said now. 'I'm Emma Crawley. Me 'usband's often away fer days on end – works fer the Gas Board, reserved occupation, but 'is job takes 'im all over the place and I get a bit lonely. I need a bit of company. That's why I'm lettin' out the rooms.' She eyed Susan. 'An' your 'usband?'

'In the Army,' Susan obliged quickly. 'Abroad. At least he . . .' She faltered to a stop, then added hastily, 'I've got my marriage certificate.'

Mrs Crawley burst out laughing. 'Lord luv us, I don't disberlieve yer, dear. Where is 'e, or is that 'ush-'ush?'

'He's . . . he's been posted missing.'

'Oh, yer poor duck!' Her earlier hilarity swept away, the woman's face creased with pity. 'An' you wiv a baby on the way. But ain't you got no 'ome or anythink? 'Ave yer bin bombed out, then? Not in London though, dear?' She had taken note of Susan's accent. 'D'yer come from Manchester way?'

'No, Birmingham.' Susan was surprised that tears

hadn't flooded her eyes at the mention of Matthew, but guessed she was too tired for that.

'Birmingham. They've 'ad it nasty up there too. 'Ad some of them daylight raids. They've left London alone this time, thank Gawd. We 'ad enough of our share in the Blitz. Shockin' it was rarnd 'ere, flames . . .'

She pulled herself up sharply. 'Look, come upstairs and take a look at the rooms, see if yer like 'em. Yer can cook up there. I've put in a gas ring but there ain't no place fer an oven. But yer can eat wiv us if yer like. Might save yer a few bob in the meter. Don't s'pose yer get much allowance from the Army. Come on, dear, I'll show yer. Leave yer suitcase there fer the time bein'. What's yer name?'

'Susan. Susan Ward.' She got up, put the cup and saucer on the floor because there was nowhere else to put it and followed Mrs Crawley out and back along the passage, its thin runner rucking up under her tired feet, and up the narrow lino'd stairs.

Opening the door to the large bedroom which had been divided into two at some time to form a sitting room as well, Mrs Crawley stood back for Susan to enter.

'Everythink's nice an' clean,' she said. To someone who had been travelling for much of the day, it looked like heaven, despite the well-worn furnishings and, if one had been finicky, really only being one divided room. 'I 'ope it's suitable for yer.'

Suitable! Susan could have cried at the sight of the large brass bed on which she could have flopped this very second, it looked so inviting and comfortable. She turned to the woman. 'I'd like to take it. But do you mind me being . . . like this?' She nodded towards her midriff.

'Bless yer, no. I like kids. Got free of me own – all boys. Wot I'd like is a gel. Well, yer never know. Ain't too old yet. An' Geoff, that's me 'usband, it's Geoffrey really, but 'e's called Geoff by everyone – when 'e comes 'ome, yer never know, it could 'appen and I could spark again. But it'd be nice 'aving a bit of female comp'ny in this family of boys. Me 'usband too – as much boy as any of the kids, I can tell yer.'

'Well, if it suits you to have me here, Mrs Crawley . . .'

'Call me Emma. An' I'll call yer Sue.'

Susan smiled. The woman was motherly, and she needed someone motherly right now, someone like her own mother. Her mother spoke real Brummy, Emma Crawley spoke Cockney; it was all the same when someone saw no point to putting on airs and graces.

'Emma,' she repeated, already feeling at home.

The first thing she intended to do once she was settled in was to write to her mother telling her of her good luck. As to writing to Mr and Mrs Ward, she would think about that one, but she supposed, as their son's wife, she really should let them know where she was. This she did and bravely prepared herself for their onslaught. It wasn't long in coming.

'What did you think you were doing, Susan? You had us worried out of our wits. You seem to have no conception of what you have put us through. No consideration. Didn't you ever stop to think how worried we'd be?'

In her room, which she had already made even more cosy, Susan withstood the tirade by keeping her head bowed and saying nothing.

'After all we tried to do for you. I don't think we've been unkind or made you do anything you didn't want to do. We've treated you as though you were our own daughter and done all we can to make you feel at home. Not only for Matthew's sake but your own, a girl away from her parents, her husband . . .' Mrs Ward gulped back a wave of emotion, thankful the landlady Mrs Crawley wasn't present to see it, having decently left this family to its argument. 'Her husband, our son, not with her,' she finished.

Collecting herself, she paused again, this time for some sort of reply. When none came, she pushed on. 'How could you have been so thankless, so unkind, so thoughtless as to cause us all this worry?'

'Don't you think you were being just a bit unfair?' Mr Ward added with a little more calm, saving Susan the awkwardness of answering his wife's angry question. 'God knows, we've done you no harm to have been treated in such a way. What *have* we done to you, Susan, to deserve it?'

This was said in such a heartfelt manner, tears began to surge up in Susan's eyes. She hadn't meant to cry, had even steeled herself against crying. So finding herself on the verge of doing so made anger rise up instead.

'You've never let me lead my own life,' she blurted. 'Watching every move I made, you made me feel like I was a prisoner. I want to lead my own life. I'm not a kid. I can look after myself.'

'It looks like it,' Mrs Ward remarked, gazing about her, exactly as she had done on entering the house. 'This place is disgusting.'

'But it feels more like home to me than your fine house ever did.' It didn't matter that she sounded rude. She felt angry. 'Mrs Crawley's like a mother to me, which you never was.'

'Well, that is the absolute limit . . .'

'Now look here, Susan,' Leonard Ward cut in again. 'There's no call to talk to us like that. We have, truly, tried to do our best for you. If the way we did it wasn't what suited you, I'm sorry, it's the only way we know. You must admit, you wanted for nothing. Did you?' he ended firmly.

'No,' she said in a small voice.

'Then where have we failed?'

She was crying now. 'You haven't failed. I didn't mean to upset anyone. I suppose I should have told you how I felt. But it's done now.'

'It isn't. You can come back with us.'

'It is. I want to live on my own. I'm sorry, but I feel smothered. I just want to live on my own.'

There was a long silence, both of them looking at her, she not daring to look at them.

'But the baby . . .'

'I'm all right,' Susan cut across her mother-in-law's lame words. 'Mrs Crawley's got children. She's made me feel wanted and comfortable here.'

'Meaning we haven't?'

'It's like I said. I don't feel comfortable in your home.

I want to be on my own. I need to be on my own. I don't want to be smothered.'

'Well, all credit to you, Susan,' Leonard Ward muttered then turned to his wife. 'I can't see anything we can say altering her mind. I think we'd best go, Lilian.'

'I'm not . . .' she began, but again he interrupted her, firmly raising his hand towards her.

'There's no point us trying to argue any more. I give you credit for wanting to stand on your own two feet, Susan. I didn't think you had it in you, but obviously you have. Well, we're not far away if you need us. If we hear anything from Matthew, we'll let you know immediately. Obviously we have no way of writing to him except through the Red Cross, which we will do, and I expect you will too. You're as anxious as us to hear something, no matter what. I expect it's the strain of all this that's made you do what you did. We're going now. But, Susan, keep in touch. Don't alienate yourself against us, whatever it was we did to displease you. Of course, we want to know when the baby is born and if you're all right. You will do that, won't you?'

Dismally she nodded. He came forward, laid a kiss on her downcast cheek and took hold of her shoulders to give them a small encouraging shake. It was like having Matthew touch her and it was all she could do not to fall into his father's arms to receive his hug. Instead, she stepped back, lifting her tear-streaked face, shaking her dark hair from her eyes, a small defiant gesture, and he too stepped away, defeated. It showed in his eyes, again so like Matthew's though a few shades lighter.

Mrs Ward just stood there, not quite looking at her, her face set like granite.

'Take care, child,' Leonard Ward said and his wife, still without looking at her, gave a stiff nod of concurrence and turned, leading the way out of the room.

Susan stood listening to their footsteps echoing down the uncarpeted stairs. She heard Mrs Crawley saying to them before they left, 'I'll see she keeps in touch. She's in good 'ands 'ere.' Then the door closed and Emma Crawley's footsteps came quickly back up the stairs.

'I'm gonna do yer a nice cup of tea, Sue. Make yer feel better.' It was Emma's way of solving all crises. More often than not it worked a treat, just as it did now as Susan smiled at her through her tears.

A fierce stab somewhere in her stomach awoke Susan with a start and for a moment she lay rigid, frightened by a pain that could bring her out of what had been a deep sleep. There was only a dull ache now that wasn't really an ache at all – she wasn't sure what it was – just a feeling. The clinic had told her she had only a week or two to go now, though no one could say quite when. So was this her time? No, it couldn't be. Probably just wind. The fear began to subside but it had left her wide awake.

Turning over she closed her eyes again and tried to sleep. But sleep had gone and all that were left were thoughts, the sort of reflections that come at night, persistent, refusing to be ignored.

All this time, there had been no news whatsoever of Matthew. But she wouldn't think about that. Once on that track it would persist, plaguing her with memories of those wonderful days with him, thoughts of the days that now stretched ahead of her without him, forever and ever. She would end up crying into her pillow. She mustn't think of him. She would try to think of something else. Something positive. Something happy.

It had been the best move she had ever made getting away from his parents. Emma was such a wonderful, motherly person, she couldn't have wished for a better landlady, more a friend than anything, so free and easy. It was a rough-and-ready-come-and-go-as-you-please sort of home. Meals were never the ritual they'd been at the Wards' home. The only time anyone sat around a table – the big bare table in the back room – was when Geoffrey Crawley was home, and even then everyone came one after the other as each plate was filled, leaving the same way, as soon as the plate was empty – no waiting for anyone else.

Helping around the house, going shopping with Emma who held her arm as she got bigger around the middle, was enjoyable. So were these long July evenings. As the sun went down on kids playing in the street, the drawn-out twilight of double British Summertime fading, the Crawleys' flimsy blackout shutters would go up amid a dozen bits of advice how to make them fit so no light finally showed. With the sounds in the street finally muted by the closing of the thin curtains, they'd all settle down to an evening around the wireless, laughing at ITMA, Arthur Askey and Stinker Merdock, Vic Oliver, Ben Lyon and Bebe Daniels; listening intently to the news read by Alvar Lidell or Bruce Belfrage, hoping to glean a little joyful tidings from the war front. Sometimes she and Emma would have a go at one of the dozens of old jigsaw puzzles that lay around the house, the wireless still blaring to itself, while young Malc sat at the other end painting from a tin paint box on bits of old paper, his brothers playing noisily with some toy or other, Geoffrey in his creaking old fireside chair reading the evening paper or studying his work sheets for the following week. All nice and cosy.

With all this going on around her there was little time for fretting any more, although now and again she did, picturing herself and Matthew together in a little home of their own. But this was the nearest to it, and Emma and Geoffrey were so nice, she should think herself lucky. Geoff was an easygoing man. It wasn't at all difficult to talk to him. Mr Ward had been nice too, but it had not been so easy to talk about things that she liked – films, popular songs, singers, the big bands, her life in Birmingham. Geoff would talk about his life too, telling outrageous tales of the people he met in his work, making them all laugh. He told her how he had met Emma, how she'd caught him on the rebound from a girl who'd given him up for a prizefighter. The girl had been a real wow and Emma hadn't measured up to her, he said, but Emma fell for a baby and they'd hastily married. 'Had to,' he said, 'for her sake.' Susan felt a little sad for him that he'd had to take, as it seemed, second best, though Emma had, he admitted, been a bloody good wife to him, more than the other girl might have been.

If Matthew were to come home now, Susan mused as

she lay wide awake, she would make sure no one else could match her . . .

A second stab of pain broke into her thoughts, making her gasp. It was not as bad as that first stab had been, but she was consumed by a sense of urgency, an ancient instinct that lies dormant within each woman so that she knows instantly what it is without being told.

Swinging her feet out of bed, she hoisted herself up and, holding her stomach in which there was now only a dull grinding feeling, she got to the door and out on to the landing.

'Emma.' Her raised voice sounded small and terrified even to herself. 'Emma, quick. Something's happening.'

Geoff was away. Emma came running out from her room and guided her downstairs to sit her in one of the old armchairs in the cavernous front room, the most comfortable place she could find. 'Stay 'ere,' she ordered. 'I'll go up an' get yer clothes an' fings for yer.'

She was back within seconds with a shopping bag holding a towel, flannel and soap, hairbrush, a change of nightie, and over her arm, Susan's coat and a scarf, and a pair of shoes dangling from her fingers.

'Can yer put yer coat and shoes on yerself?' she queried anxiously. 'I've got ter get meself dressed. D'yer think yer can walk? We've got ter get yer to the 'orspital. It's only half a mile darn the Mile End. Yer've only just started. Yer'll be able to make it if we walk slow.' To which Susan let out another gasp at a fresh small onslaught of pain.

Lights were on all over the house; the boys wandered out of their bedroom asking, 'What the 'eck's up?' before being told by Emma to go back to bed – it wasn't none of their business.

There came a loud hammering and knocking on the street door, a harsh voice shouted: 'What th'ell are you lot up ter? Yer showin' a bloody great light – like a bloody searchlight art 'ere.'

'Oh, Gawd, the blackout!' Emma rushed in panic to the window to find one corner of the blackout frame leaning inward towards the room, not having been put up properly. Only then did she run to the door, flicking off lights as she went, leaving Susan in pitch-darkness.

Her voice was breathless at the street door. 'Gawd, I'm sorry. We've got an emergency 'ere. Me lodger, she's only young, 'er 'usband's overseas, an' she's just started 'er labour pains. I've got ter get 'er to the 'orspital.'

'Can't yer get an ambulance?'

'It's only 'alf a mile ter the London.'

'Yer can't ask 'er ter walk 'alf a mile, not in labour.'

In pitch-dark, Susan felt the pain returning. In panic she cried out. From the door, the voices grew more animated. 'Can't she 'ave it 'ere, in the 'ouse, save walking all that way in 'er condition at one in the mornin'?'

'It's 'er first. She ought ter be in 'orspital. I told 'er 'usband's people I'd look after 'er. I can't be responsible for anyfink goin' wrong.'

'Well, she can't walk. Tell yer what. I've got a bike. We could put 'er on that and wheel 'er. Save 'er walkin'. It's got a wide saddle. And paddin' as well. I got piles an' I 'ave ter 'ave a wide saddle wiv a lot of paddin' on it.'

Sitting in the dark listening, Susan wasn't sure whether

to laugh or cry as the present bout of pain began to fade a little.

The baby, a girl, arrived the next day around three in the afternoon. 'Quick for the first,' a nurse told her, but it had seemed like eternity to her as she writhed in terror and pain, a young mother not knowing what was expected of her, what to expect. Throughout she had been alternately encouraged and scolded, assured that it wouldn't be long now, that she was doing wonderfully, then in the next breath upbraided for making a fuss, getting into a needless panic, yelling when there was no need, not co-operating. And when during easier moments she wept for Matthew, she was told she must be brave for him, that he, a stalwart fighting for his country, wouldn't want to see her less brave, breaking down like this.

She couldn't bring herself to tell them he'd been reported missing. Though his family hung on to the hope of his having been captured, she knew deep inside her that he was dead, that she'd never see him again and would have to bring up his child alone.

Chapter 19

Jenny stood by Susan's bedside. Susan's in-laws had just left and her parents, who had further to come, had yet to see her.

Jenny herself had heard of the birth of Susan's baby by chance, being told at teatime by one of the nurses, creased up with laughter, of a woman in labour having arrived at maternity around one thirty in the morning on a bike. 'What people don't do in wartime,' the nurse had giggled over her bread and jam sandwich.

'You mean she rode herself here on a bike?' Jenny had joined in the general laughter. Odd things happened in hospitals, but that one had taken the biscuit.

'Well, not exactly rode herself. An air-raid warden was pushing her. And her landlady apparently kept helping her off every time she got one of her pains. They had the saddle all padded.' This last brought a fresh gale of laughter.

'I'm not surprised,' Jenny had said over the laughter. 'Where were her parents then?'

'She said they lived in Birmingham. She'd walked out on her in-laws or something and lives about half a mile from here. Seems it was easier to get here on a bike than having to walk. I ask you! Can you just see it – some old

air-raid warden wheeling a pregnant woman on a bike all
the way to the hospital, her hopping on and off every so
often? It must've looked a sight. Lucky for her it wasn't
midday. Honestly, some people!'

But Jenny had no longer been laughing. Now she stood
looking down at the girl's face, pale from the hard work of
bringing a baby into the world, looking wan and down in
the mouth when she should have been glowing with pride
at her achievement.

'Have you seen the baby, Susan?' she asked for something to say after having enquired how she was, a question
which had been met by a tear being squeezed from between
the closed eyelids.

'What did you think of her?' she pressed as Susan
merely nodded without speaking.

'I'm too worn out to think anything. Except that
Matthew's not here and I'm all on my own. I'll never see
him again, and no one cares.'

'Of course they care. His parents care. And your family
– they care.'

And Matthew, he'd be over the moon with joy and pride
if he was here to know about his baby daughter. But there
was no way he could know, no way he could be told, could
be contacted. Her mother had relayed what little news she
happened to glean from his parents, which was hardly
anything. And having for a while lost the run of Susan, all
she knew of Matthew was of the ongoing but vain efforts
of the Red Cross still to trace him, one way or the other.
Wonderful people, but as far as she knew they'd hit a
complete blank.

Gazing down at the despairing Susan, Jenny bit her lip, refusing to believe Matthew could be dead. Somewhere he had to be alive. She clung to that hope with all her heart, and inside that heart those feelings she had always had for him beat as strongly as ever.

She had tried to put it away from her, had assumed she had at last conquered it when she had written to Ronald Whittaker, finally confronting the stupidity in letting such a chance go of getting Matthew out of her system once and for all by marrying Ronald as he'd once asked. His parents had replied for him, saying they were sending her letter on to him, that against their wishes he hadn't gone into practice with his father but instead had joined the Army Medical Corps. Slightly dismayed, she had got in touch with him at the address they'd given. Ronald's reply had been kind and friendly but said that he had met a girl to whom he'd be getting engaged on his next leave; that he was sorry Jenny hadn't written earlier because they'd got on well together but it wouldn't be right for him to drop the girl he now loved for the one he had thought at the time he loved. He'd always remember her with affection and hoped that it wouldn't be too long before she too found herself someone to settle down with. She had felt hurt, angry with herself and very aware that her only avenue of escape from the love inside her for Matthew had been cut off.

It made her furious that Susan could lie here lamenting her lot and assuming her husband dead when she should at least be fighting to fill herself with optimism that he would eventually come back to her. She didn't even seem interested in her baby as a mother would normally be.

'What are you going to call her?' Jenny asked and received an apathetic shrug.

'I don't really know. I've not really thought about it.'

'Then don't you think you should? What do Matthew's parents say?'

'They suggested a few names.'

'And?'

Another shrug. 'I can't seem to like any of them. I got confused and said I'd think about it. Mrs Ward said don't take too long about it.'

'You'll have to come up with something.' Jenny herself thought about it for a moment, then said, 'How about Mattie?'

'Mattie?'

Yes, it was a lame sort of name and sounded even more so on Susan's amazed lips. 'It's short for Matilda.' Matthew had always loved shortening names. '. . . Hi there, Jenny . . .'

Jenny swallowed back the sentimental restriction of her throat. 'Matilda is the feminine of Matthew. It would remind you of him, and . . . when he comes home.' He would come home. 'When he comes home he'll know you were thinking of him. Make it Mattie, Susan. It sounds better.'

She spoke positively. Susan was by nature a malleable person and she was at her most malleable now. 'Well, I hadn't got any name ready for her. I suppose it's as good as any.'

She couldn't care less, Jenny thought angrily, but she smiled. 'I had better go or I'll get into trouble,' she said brightly. 'I'm supposed to be on duty. Another nurse is covering for me, so I could only have a few minutes. I'm glad you're okay and I'm glad the baby, Mattie, is okay. She'll be something for you to cling to until Matthew comes home.'

Giving Susan no opportunity to argue with that, she turned smartly on her heel and with a quick wave went back to work.

Sitting by the lounge window for a better light by which to see her knitting pattern, Lilian Ward glanced out at the dull November weather, her fingers still busy with the clicking needles. She had no real need to look at them; the pattern itself had become partially imprinted on her brain so often had she used it to knit the exquisite little dresses for Matilda. The weather was getting colder. Wool was hard to come by, so second-hand woollen garments were usually found in jumble sales, unravelled and re-knitted, but the child needed some warm clothing. Left to Susan, she'd have nothing warm to wear. It seemed to Lilian the mother had no interest whatsoever in Matilda. She insisted the child's name be spoken in full. None of this silly Mattie business. But in truth the shortened name reminded her too much of Matthew. Where was he?

Nothing, absolutely nothing. The Red Cross were even mentioning the dread word. But she wouldn't have it that Matthew was dead. He was *somewhere*. He had to be. Why *couldn't* they find him? Not trying, too many other missing servicemen to trace. But her son was as important as they. Meanwhile this war was dragging on. So what if on the fourth of this month came the long-awaited tidings that German forces were at last in full retreat in Egypt, the wireless announcer hardly hiding his excitement? So what if the Allies had landed in Algeria? So what if the church bells had rung across the whole country to mark Montgomery's victory? One or two swallows didn't make a summer. Meanwhile Matthew continued to be missing. His daughter was going to grow up not knowing him. Susan, his wife, was gadding about as though she hadn't a care in the world, leaving Matilda in the dubious if willing care of her landlady, just as if her husband, missing or dead, meant nothing to her. No sighing after him or, Lilian was certain, tears, except, when she and Leonard went to see her – then she'd weep buckets. Lilian's needles clicked angrily in the dull November daylight.

Crumpling the brief letter into a ball, Susan threw it across the kitchen.

'She never gives up, does she? Says she's got another cardigan for Mattie. I don't want her making clothes for my child. Anyone'd think I can't dress her myself. She looks all right, don't she, in what I put her in?'

Carving hunks of bread for when the boys trooped in from school for their midday break in half an hour, Emma looked up from the kitchen table. 'She means well, Sue. She knitted you both lovely Christmas presents.'

'Means well? She always means well. It's the way she goes about meaning well that gets my goat. Treating me as though I've not got a clue on how to bring up a baby. I know she doesn't approve of me going out every once in a while. That's all it is, once in a while. I'm not gadding about with soldiers. I just need a break now and then.'

'Of course you do.' Emma continued spreading the doorsteps with the thinnest scrape of margarine, her family's rations dwindling towards the end of this week's allowance. She put a small smear of plum jam on them and pressed the slices together, the resulting sandwiches almost too wide for any child's mouth.

'The way she talks,' Susan went on, 'you'd think I was on the streets. I like going dancing with Edie. And we know how to behave ourselves.'

In September, for a bit of extra money, she'd started a part-time job in the Whitechapel High Street near Aldgate East station in the stockroom of a wholesalers of men's underwear and hosiery, Fishman & Sob. The owner's son had been called up. Edie Barrows, who worked with her, also had a husband in the forces, and like herself needed to get out now and again and see a bit of life rather than be stuck at home – it was easier for her, having no children. There was no harm in it, the way Mrs Ward intimated.

'Neither of us are going to go off the rails, both married. We just need a break now and again, that's all,' Susan repeated.

''Course yer do,' Emma murmured. 'Do yer want jam or a bit of yer cheese ration in this sandwich?'

'Jam'll do.'

She began mixing Mattie's bottle with dried baby milk and a tiny drop of cod-liver oil. Her own milk had dried up earlier. Susan wasn't sorry. Though making bottles was a chore, she wasn't confined to the house or to rushing back home having to breastfeed at inconvenient hours.

She set the bottle in a saucepan of cold water to cool for when Mattie woke up. 'I think I do all right with Mattie's clothes. That exchange shop's a real godsend.'

In the Mile End Road near the old Empire Music Hall, a small derelict shop had been set up with a system whereby mothers could barter clothing their toddlers had outgrown for larger clothes. It saved on clothing coupons and it was cheap. Mattie looked a treat in some of the baby clothes Susan had managed to find.

'Trouble is, she inspects everything I buy for Mattie, as if I'm putting her into something lice-infested. The way she purses her lips if Mattie looks the least bit messy! You can't keep babies clean all the time. She's bound to sick up a bit of food on her clothes, and she always manages to come in when Mattie's messy, never when she's clean. I'm sure she times it.'

Emma laughed and glanced at the battered alarm clock on one of the kitchen shelves. Twelve thirty. The boys'd be home any minute, all three of them bursting into the house as ravenous as if they hadn't eaten for a week.

'Wait till she starts feeding 'erself, then yer'll know what messy is.'

When the post fell lightly through the letter box, Lilian was neatly folding the finished baby dress, ready to take with her tomorrow morning. It looked pretty; the pink and white wool she'd picked up from the WI skeined and washed, almost new. Susan should be pleased, though

Lilian could bet she wouldn't show it if she could help, merely look askance at it as though she, Lilian, were interfering. How could she be interfering, the child's own grandmother? More than them up in Birmingham ever bothered themselves – she allowed herself that little grammatical lapse in referring to Susan's people who as far as she knew hardly ever came down to see their daughter, much less sent her presents of clothing. Out of sight out of mind. They probably wrote now and again and thought that good enough.

At the sound of the post, she left the dress on the round occasional table in the bay window and hurried into the hall to see what had arrived. Always in the back of her mind was that one day the post would contain a letter from the Red Cross or some other authority to say her son had been traced. At the same time there lingered that fear of being informed of his confirmed death, so that she never approached the envelopes lying in the wire cage attached below the letter box without pausing, to carry on more slowly in trepidation at what might be there.

This procedure she followed now. Pray God there was no bad news, bills excluded of course. But what was bad news and what was good if it concerned Matthew? Was missing good news? But surely better than that dread which invariably throbbed in her mind. Whatever it was, it had to be faced.

There were several letters, most of them bills and invoices concerning Leonard's business, two private letters, both face down. What would they contain? One had an official look to it. It was that one which she swept up almost in a single movement, knowing even before she turned it over that it bore the small red cross on it.

Feverishly she ripped open the envelope. Her heart thumping heavily, she pulled out the single sheet of limp recycled note-paper and unfolded it swiftly, hardly daring to breathe, hardly daring to let her eyes scan what it had to say. It took only the first two lines to send a sensation of debility spreading through her limbs so that she had to clutch at the newel post to keep her from falling. The waiting was at an end. At last they knew.

Tears she had kept unshed all this time started to flow and she didn't try to prevent them as she sank down on the stairs and, all alone in the house, gave herself up to weeping, the letter crumpled in her hand. Slowly, though, she gathered her thoughts. She must let Leonard know. Her hand automatically reached for the telephone on the hall stand, she dialled the operator, gave her the number of Leonard's shop and waited. It seemed to take forever before his receiver was lifted, but she felt too drained to think in the interval. Her brain seemed quite dead. She actually gave a small start as Leonard's voice sounded close to her ear.

'Hello? Ward's Electrical Shop.'

'Leonard! We've heard. We've heard from the International Red Cross – a letter – this morning. Leonard – they've found him. He's a prisoner of war. That's all they know. But, Leonard, he's alive. Our Matthew's alive.'

There was a second or two's silence, then his voice came, trembling, just as hers had. 'I'm coming home. I'm closing up and coming home.'

'But your customers. You can't . . .' It sounded quite inane. News of Matthew traced and she was worrying about customers?

'Sod the customers!' He never swore in her hearing. She wouldn't have it. But today she forgave him.

Chapter 20

The rain had ceased. The flood within the railway cutting
had subsided and with it part of the earth wall which must
now be shored up. The guards, tempers uncertain at the
best of times and now made more vile by the appalling
conditions which they and prisoners alike were compelled
to share, were calling for more speed. Anxious to return to
their dry quarters and some warm food, they backed their
demands with stick and stone aimed at any prisoner who
flagged at his task.

The cutting rang to their demented yells, to the screech
of steel being dragged from antiquated lorries, the clang
of hammers on the metal spikes securing the rails in place
while the sickly glow of carbide lamps gleamed on the
glistening shoulders of those who toiled into the night.

To Matthew's fevered mind the whole thing resembled
scenes from Dante's *Inferno* as on hands and knees he
groped in the yellow mud for the bolts of the fishplate that
would join together the two rails placed there.

His last meal of cold boiled rice diluted by monsoon
rain had been eaten at mid-morning, eight hours ago. He
would not eat again until their overseer, the shoko, called
a halt to measure the day's quota of work sometime just

before midnight. His brain felt it was bursting from the most recent attack of malaria; he dared not dwell on how he would get through the remaining hours, but get through them he must.

Evading the prospect, he found himself turning his thoughts inward – a sort of mental escapism he'd long ago learned – a way of withdrawing into the depths of his own brain as into a dark little world secluded from all this misery outside. Slowly a wonderful phenomenon would occur, though it was only imagination. Inside his head there would appear a bright disc and within the disc he'd visualise Susan's face, smiling, gentle as she reached out to him. The clamour around him would recede and he would seem to float on a tiny island of peace, remote from the violence and hunger that made up the world he now existed in. A figment of a feverish mind, perhaps. What did it matter? It sustained him, and with a fanaticism born of sheer desperation he clung to that wavering disc with an insane – because one could become insane in this place – but obdurate conviction that while he could conjure up that disc of light inside his head, he would survive.

He had never dreamed he would, that day of his being taken prisoner. Hands raised, his pockets being rifled, he'd protested at Susan's photo being torn into pieces, had taken a step forward. One of his captors had sprung at him, bayonet whipping round. It was then he'd thought his life over, but the bayonet just scored his outstretched forearm.

The captives, bound together by their own belts in twos, had been pushed and prodded along jungle tracks with the noise of the river, which had meant safety, receding; they had finally been incarcerated in a small bamboo enclosure, full of Indian and British soldiers, which became filthier as the days passed with no latrines and a constant scramble for water. His arm had swollen to twice its normal size from the shallow bayonet wound bound by a piece of his own shirt.

Rangoon fell a week later. He had joined a lengthening column of POWs, taken back across the Sittang River, by then spanned by a hasty bridge flung up by the Japanese, past shattered metal and unburied bodies and into the city.

The poison from his festering wound had spread and he remembered little of the trek across the Irrawaddy Plain beneath a burning sun, but it was then that the strange disc-like brilliance with Susan's image inside it began to fill his head. Bob, who had been with him, and still was, had said that he was holding whole conversations with her. But he'd been convinced then as now of the telepathic origins of that bright light. Susan's thoughts were encouraging him, spanning the thousands of miles between them.

It had been Bob Howlett who'd practically carried him into the Rangoon jail from that seventy-mile trek, who had badgered him into putting one foot before the other, holding him up, telling him not to give up, that he had Susan and a baby to get home to; Bob who had fed him with tiny morsels of watery rice and bits of fruit as he lay desperately ill.

Now it was Bob who lay desperately ill with dysentery, so pernicious that Matthew feared he would lose him. So many friends had been parted, they had been fortunate staying together this long. If Bob died, there'd be no panacea of shared comradeship, nights spent in their rotting tent talking quietly of their hopes of what they were going to do when they got back home, their wives, their memories of happier days. If Bob died, he'd be totally alone.

With the wall shored up and this particular group of railway workers at last clear of the cutting, a whistle blasted; work ceased abruptly while the shoko went forward to inspect the quota completed. Silence fell, broken only by the dripping of rainwater from sodden vegetation, the drowned earth sucking and bubbling, the laborious breathing of the men, a cough or two, the idle clink of a metal tool and the sigh of the sick, their mates waiting to help them back to the huddle of tents they called home.

With the shoko signalling permission, each man lined up for his mess-tin of cold rice doled out from an old oil drum positioned under a strip of leaking tarpaulin, afterwards to slither their way along a morass of a path to their tents and sleep. But first there was water from the river to be boiled, to cook the edible lizard he'd caught and killed that morning. Anything caught was supposed to go into the common pot, but he meant to cook it himself and feed the broth to Bob, who would have done the same for him.

Armed with a bent and battered petrol can, he made his way from the tent designed to hold three Japanese schoolboys comfortably but now used by eight men, and headed a quarter of a mile down the slippery path to the stagnant backwater of the river. It had to be the backwater. The torrent of the main river could wash away a man, especially one in a weakened condition. Men were already there scooping up the cloudy liquid, a perfect breeding ground for disease. The last to arrive, Matthew sank down on a decaying log to wait for the pool to clear, his head buzzing from his malaria. He watched each man depart with a full container, slipping, sliding, shambling back up the greasy track, all the spring of youth gone out of their step. Sitting here, he too felt like an old man, trying to summon the will just to raise himself up and fill up his can with the cloudy water.

Holding the petrol can below the surface to fill, he stared across the river into the darkness of the jungle. The roar of the river was deafening. A slow, lethargic thought came. What was the point of it all, squatting here, a half-naked, emaciated travesty of a man, shaken by fever, tongue raw from pellagra that made every mouthful of what food he got an agony? Would he drag on for a few more months in this hopeless corner of the world, or somewhere like it further along this growing railway, lost, forgotten, to succumb and be buried under a bamboo cross, one among all the countless other bamboo crosses that lined the route?

'God! Why in Christ's name did you do this to me? Why in Christ's name won't you help us?'

The roar of the river bore away the insane cry. The buzzing night-jungle swallowed it whole. There was no one to hear, just some unseen monkeys disturbed by the strange man-cry, replying with a distant demented howling while the incessant chirruping of myriads of insects in this primeval tangle of sodden vegetation continued uninterrupted.

There was a reply – voiceless in his own head, the memory of a smile, Susan hovering in his head across thousands of miles of sea and desert and mountain and jungle, waiting for him. He couldn't let her down. He couldn't let Bob down, sitting here nursing his own misery while Bob hovered at the edge of death. Rationality returned. The can was full and he had jobs to do.

It was heaven to close the door, to curl up in one of the old armchairs in the partitioned-off part of her room upstairs, to be alone.

Emma was a wonderful and supportive friend, but her chatter could get a bit much sometimes. With Mattie being looked after downstairs by a willing Emma, who adored girls, she could relax with the latest paperback romance, identifying with the beautiful heroine in the embrace of the dark handsome hero, who in her imagination was Matthew, until it was Mattie's bedtime.

But all the imagination in the world could never compensate for the real thing. She and Edie spent most Saturday nights being whirled around a dance floor by Uniformed worthies, one of them invariably whispering a certain invitation in her ear. It was a source of pride to her that she resisted, loyal still to her married state. But sometimes she envied Edie leaving with a partner's arm around her waist. 'You be orlright goin' 'ome without me?'

She'd nod and watch her leave then go and sit at the side of the hall knowing that the next partner – there always was one – asking her to go for a walk with him, the question heavy with innuendo, would get a short answer. But oh, how she envied Edie.

Once, hurrying to catch her bus home, she'd passed a couple hidden in a dark doorway. In the blackout she would have missed them but for a girlish giggle she recognised as Edie's. She heard the deep drawl of a GI and knew that tomorrow Edie would be displaying a fancy bar of toilet soap, or a bar of chocolate or a pair of nylons, perhaps even, with a brash flourish, bring out a packet of US government-issue contraceptives to shock her friend.

'It's safe as 'ouses, Sue, an' what 'arm are yer doing, keepin' the poor things 'appy, far away from 'ome, making yerself feel better in the bargain?'

But she couldn't do that. What if she did fall by accident? How would she ever face Matthew's parents? Yet it had been so long since a man's hand had touched her, really touched her. Her whole body ached at the thought of it. It was now August. August 1943, seven months since she'd heard Matthew had been made a prisoner of war; almost two years since she had last seen him; at times she couldn't remember his face unless she looked at a photo of him first; Mattie's first birthday had come and gone two weeks ago and he had never seen her. She often thought nowadays of herself and Mattie, never herself, Matthew and Mattie.

'I wish I had your courage,' she said to Edie on the Monday morning, knowing Edie had throughly enjoyed her Saturday night by evidence of yet another handful of Hershey bars and a pair of nylons.

Edie ran the gauzy stockings through her fingers. 'Can't get these in this country,' she tempted.

It wasn't the gifts American boys could dish out that made Susan squirm at Edie's efforts to tempt but the thought of someone's arms around her. It was a terrible thought and made her want to cry. Her first joy at the news of Matthew having been traced had long since dwindled. She had been allowed to send him a message if that was what it could be called. Fifteen words on a form, all the Japanese permitted. Whether Matthew received it who was to say? There had been no reply. It felt for all the world as though her message had been written to a ghost. She had never dared voice those sentiments to his mother, who had sent off her own forlorn fifteen words of encouragement and love that day. She would have been appalled. How much more appalled would she be were she to know how his wife yearned for the feel of a man's hand fondling her even though it wasn't her husband's. No, she couldn't.

All very well for Edie in the arms of some frustrated warrior far from home. Edie had changed a lot this year, voiced a different slant on her husband these days.

'Two years away – and God knows 'ow many more years. I mean, the man's stuck out in the Falklands. When're they goin' ter give 'im leave from there? Meanwhile I could go barmy waiting fer 'im ter come 'ome and make love.'

'But don't you feel some loyalty to him?' Susan asked and received a sceptical chuckle as Edie sorted out men's small from men's large, ready for despatching.

''Ow do I know 'e's not 'aving it off with some Falklands floozie? I do know 'e 'ad a rovin' eye, even when I first married 'im. It didn't matter then, I was there to keep my eye on 'im. But now, miles away. Why shouldn't I 'ave a bit of pleasure too? You must feel the need too, Sue? Keepin' yerself like a nun – it ain't natural. What the ole man don't know won't 'urt 'im. You ain't gonna confess all when 'e comes marchin' 'home, are yer? Fer God's sake, Sue, you'll be a physical wreck by the time 'e does if yer don't let off a bit of steam now and again.'

Frustration had its own way of dealing with things. Alone in her room, her senses keened from reading cheap romances about larger-than-life heroines and handsome forceful heroes, she would furtively turn the key of her door, quietly so no one would hear it. Secure behind the lock, she would slip out of her clothes and survey herself before the mirror, run her hands slowly, slowly, over her body, gently following the curve of her small breasts, still firm; over her flat stomach that child-bearing had not marred at all. Closing her eyes she would imagine her fingers to be those of Matthew, tenderly exploring, growing urgent until her disquietened senses shrieked for relief. Then, throbbing from the lack of fulfilment she would fling herself on to her bed to squirm and weep in self-torment. How tempting it would be at these moments to follow Edie's example, to find herself someone to fondle her, fulfil this emptiness inside her – surely more honest than this pathetic self-pleasure that was no pleasure at all and left only misery in its wake.

'I wish I knew if Matthew was all right,' she confided in Emma. 'It could be years before I ever know. I'm so lonely.'

'At least yer've got Mattie,' Emma said, busily darning one of her Geoffrey's socks. He'd gone away for a day or two as usual.

'You have her most of the time these days,' Susan said.

Emma looked up sharply. 'It's you wot asked me ter look after 'er. You goin' ter work an' all. I'm not keepin' 'er away from yer.'

'I know. I didn't mean anything.' She was glad of Emma's help. She wasn't cut out to be a mother, she didn't think, driven to distraction when Mattie got herself into a temper, shrieking at the top of her voice. A child's shriek could be like a hot iron searing right through a person's eardrum. Smacking only made things worse. Many times Susan had been forced out of sheer frustration to resort to a smack on her legs, finally having to rush her down to Emma to pacify her. Emma was a natural mother. At times Susan felt quite envious of her.

'I'm just a bit down, I suppose,' she excused herself now. 'I hope she don't play you up too much.'

'Good Lord, no. She's a real dear. 'Cos, the only fing is we 'ave ter put everyfink up out of 'er reach now she's 'oisting 'erself up on 'er feet. Got 'er little 'ands inter everyfink. Real explorin' character she is. Quick. An' if she don't get wot she wants, gets a real tantrum on 'er. Strong-minded. It's good. She probably takes after 'er dad. You're more of a pliable person, you are. She don't look as if she's gonna be. She ain't gonna be moved from wot she wants in life.'

'Sounds like she takes after Matthew's mother. Nothing can move her either.' She didn't say it in bitterness, just stated what was the truth. Mrs Ward had never deviated from the certainty that Matthew would come home, even though her poor little message hadn't been answered; had not deviated from continually telling Susan that she must be strong and pray for him to come home and not to give way to 'any temptation that may come along'. Such instructions made Susan shudder. What did the woman know of the feelings she harboured? Probably nothing. She was merely wise to such things, being older and having seen and learned more, for all her primness.

'I miss Matthew so much,' she said in an effort to evade thoughts of those temptations Mrs Ward hinted at with more emphasis than Susan cared to acknowledge. 'I know Geoffrey's not in the forces but he's away a lot too. Don't you miss *him*?'

'Miss 'im!' Emma put away the sock she had darned and picked up another, studying the dangerously thin place on the heel that next week would become a hole. 'I'm glad to see the back of him sometimes.'

Shocked, Susan stared at her. 'You don't mean that.'

'Yes, I do.' Emma gave a good-tempered chuckle. 'So will you when he's bin home fer a few years. Most wives do. Not nasty-like. But it's nice ter 'ave 'em out of the way occasionally and get on wiv yer own fings. Before 'e 'ad this job of 'is, it was, "Wot yer goin' out fer? 'Ow long'll yer be? I don't feel like goin' ter the pictures ternight." So I couldn't go either, could I? Not on me own an' leave 'im 'ere on 'is own. Married people don't do that. An' when yer spend all day mendin' 'is socks an 'ironing 'is

shirts, an' bringin' up 'is kids, an' gettin' 'is breakfasts
and dinners, an' makin' 'is sandwiches, an' bein' woken
up out of a deep sleep because 'e wants a bit of the other
... well, yer've had enough, ain't yer, an' yer want a bit of
time to yerself. Miss 'im? I think this job 'e's got 'as bin a
godsend. I know 'e's safe, not overseas somewhere in the
fick of it all. But Geoff's the limit sometimes – expecting
me ter be runnin' after 'im. The least sneeze and I'm 'is
nursemaid. Men!'

Her darning needle flew fast but without ill will.
'Babies, most of 'em. I expect they're brave enough
amongst themselves, but get near their wives an' they're
little babies, straight they are. I'm a bloomin' muvver to
Geoff.'

She stopped to tap the hand of her youngest trying to
fish into her workbasket for the glass marbles that always
got in there. 'Yer'll prick yer fingers, yer silly little bugger!
I'll get 'em out for yer after I've done this. Jus' wait!' She
directed another laugh towards Susan watching. 'Even
at that age. You 'ave ter fink for 'em. Mind, I don't mind
Geoff wantin' his rights. I'd love ter 'ave a little daughter,
just like your'n, it's just 'im waking me up out of a sleep
fer it ... .' Another tolerant laugh. 'My mum use ter say,
"Before yer married yer could feel yer could eat it. After
yer married, yer wish you 'ad!" '

'I hope I never feel like that,' Susan said fervently.

'You will, luv. You will. Anyway I've got my little
remedy – just tell 'im I'm out of bounds fer a week. I've
told 'im, if 'e wants more'n I can give 'im, 'e can find it
wiv a bit of skirt on 'is travels.'

She glanced up at the domed clock on the mantelshelf and sighed, ignoring Susan's look of horror as she put the rest of her husband's socks back into the workbasket to finish off later. 'Come on, you kids, time fer bed. Yer've got school in the mornin'.' Mattie, just a baby, had been put to bed ages ago. Emma's edict was met with a howl from the younger two, because Malcolm was still out playing.

'It's still light, Mum.'

'This time of year, it's always light. It's still eight o'clock and time fer bed.'

'Malc's not bin called in yet.'

''E will be. Soon as you two are up them stairs. Come on now.' She threw Susan an amused backward glance as she ushered them from the room in front of her. 'I was only jokin', Sue. My Geoff'd never go off wiv anuvver woman. 'E knows only too well where 'is bread is buttered, don' you worry.'

In the flimsy bamboo and attap construction they called the hospital, Matthew eased his way between the low platforms of sick men, some still as death, some tossing and turning in delirium, some bloated by beri-beri or calling for a pan as they strained to the flux of dysentery, or waited to have tropical leg ulcers attended to.

Bob lay at the far end, a cadaverous figure whose hair had mostly fallen out to leave just a few dry tufts. His dull eyes glowed in the depths of their sockets and his lips parted in a grin at Matthew's approach.

'Hi.' He was unable to say more.

'Hi,' Matthew returned. 'How goes it?'

The thin shoulders hitched a fraction. 'Fine,' croaked the voice.

Kneeling beside him, Matthew recounted the day's news as he gave him a drink and then the soup he'd concocted from rice and a tiny bit of dried fish, but Bob turned away after the first mouthful, appetite destroyed.

'Cream of asparagus,' Matthew made the pathetic joke, 'straight from Harrods.'

But Bob's body had doubled up in pain, and Matthew held the panshaped piece of tin beneath his pal as the bowels evacuated the black blood-stained fluid. He felt helpless. How Bob had stayed alive for so long was beyond him. Sheer will-power sustained him and nothing else, for he no longer ate.

There were no drugs and food was his only chance. But rice alone was not food enough. For his friend, Matthew stole, but not well. Bob had always been better at it than he, his cheerful slant on life serving him well in the face of the anger of their conquerors if caught. Even for them food was not all that forthcoming and understandably they were apt to become overwrought by light-fingered prisoners purloining the tiniest portion of what small comforts they did receive. But stealing was a necessary part of survival. Bartering what inedibles he stole called for patience, and again Bob's stolid approach to life had allowed him to stand the strain of it and the disappointment that often followed. Wily villagers knew they had the edge on British POWs with half a mind on prowling guards. The Nippon cigarettes or stolen truck spares they'd risked their lives for would reap a couple of tiny eggs or a pomelo or two or a scrap of dried fish. But beggars couldn't be choosers.

The watery dawn coming up, Matthew turned his face towards camp with a lighter heart than usual. Under his loincloth hung half a tiny chicken, a bit high but edible. It made him walk oddly but the gait of anyone with a raw scrotum was easily ignored. Once the chicken was made into a soup, Bob must surely find the appetite to take a few mouthfuls.

The night shift had been unusually short. Yamagata, their shoko, had miscalculated the quota and his pleasure at their apparently superhuman efforts to reach the target he'd set showed on his round face, his tone almost pleasant as he'd called out *'Yoroshii,'* which meant things were good. Or men finish.

With the railway growing apace it was a long march back to camp. By the time they reached it, Yamagata would have eaten and been in the arms of Morpheus. It was a surprise then to see him coming back to meet them, his short arms flailing like stubby windmill sails, his face animated. He had obviously discovered his error in judging his quota and intended putting it to rights; no doubt he'd been hauled over the coals himself for the mistake. But instead of marching the men back to the railway, he took them down another narrow path into the jungle to arrive at another camp.

It was empty. It didn't take long to discover why. Every one of the native labourers there was dead. Ordered to burn every corpse, a strong suspicion grew that they were disposing of cholera victims and Matthew thought that no Japanese could ever have seen men work faster. Two hours later they were marching back to their own camp, a very sober, thoughtful bunch. But worse was to come. In their absence three British POWs had died of something also strongly resembling cholera.

Matthew felt his flesh creep, seeing the Japanese running about making ready to flee before it struck them also. He noticed too that the guards with his column had disappeared. Nothing would prevent a man escaping except the jungle itself; thousands of square miles of rainforest; a mapless terrain where he would climb and slither endlessly; inedible plant life, poisonous insects, evil water; he would go round in circles until he died. No iron bars could have made a better prison.

In a steady rain that had again begun, the camp was a nucleus of panic, the sick being transported from the hospital on makeshift stretchers to be unceremoniously dumped on the bare, wet ground. Catching the panic, Matthew grabbed the arm of one of the helpers.

'I'm looking for Bob Howlett.'

The man looked put out. With over a hundred sick to get out of this place at the double, who the hell remembered one man's name? 'Go and ask the bloody MO.'

'Where's the MO?'

The orderly shrugged free of his grip. 'Listen chum. We've got just five minutes to get these poor buggers out before them bastards set fire to the hospital. They're bleedin' terrified. If you can't help us, sod off!'

He had jerked a thumb towards three guards, no doubt ordered by their CO to stand their ground, which they would, more frightened of his wrath than cholera. Two had set up a machine gun, obviously meant for any protesters as the third stood by with several cans of kerosene. Their faces, full of terror, were the colour of putty.

'There's blokes gonna die being moved like this. But they ain't gonna burn. Now leave us alone if you ain't gonna help.'

Matthew found the MO inside the hospital frantically supervising the exodus. 'Bob Howlett,' he enquired urgently. 'Lantern-jawed chap. Has dysentery.'

The distinguishing feature had made an impression. The MO paused in his work, his expression one of commiseration. 'Were you the mate who used to feed and wash him?'

There was no need for the man to say more. Matthew felt numbed.

'When?' he whispered.

'Buried him last night.' The statement was almost callous. The MO had expended his compassion in this direction. Now he must return his attention to the living.

'Where was he buried?' Matthew persisted.

'Cemetery.' The soldier with the kerosene can was coming forward, approaching cautiously as though the dread killer might pounce out on him.

'Where in the cemetery?'

'I don't know where!' The MO pushed past, pointing to his helpers. 'You, over there with that one. Quick now!' His shout was one of exasperation. Two British officers, identifiable by the tattered shirts they still retained, were arguing with the soldier.

'Wait – please – wait.'

But he pushed them aside, shaking his head. *'Iie! Dame desu! Kirai! Hayaku!'* He was demanding they move out of his way. Those with the machine gun had grown tense. Defeated, the officers fell back. The can at arm's length splashed against the hut. Numbed by his own grief, Matthew watched a lighted match thrown into the place, heard the fuel ignite with a soft roar. Flames met rain-soaked material, hissed, spluttered, hesitated. A pall of yellow smoke rolled the length of the hut. Men running in and out, bearing their occupied stretchers, coughed in the smoke, shouting, getting in each other's way. More fuel was splashed on, another match struck. A growl rose up from the rescuers, but the Japanese had the machine gun and were trigger-happy.

Conquering the wet bamboo and palm-leaf roof, the flames leapt, and still the rescuers ran in and out, the sick draped over their shoulders, men, hardly able to stand, clambering over the open sides of the hospital.

His own personal loss dulling his senses, Matthew ran with the others, blindly helping the last of the sick to safety until the heat finally forced him to retreat. With the flames crackling behind him he went towards the cemetery at the far end of the camp where a tangle of jungle prevented any further intrusion. There he stood gazing at the rows of bamboo crosses, each tilted in the sodden mud, each bearing a pathetic attempt to inscribe the name of whoever lay beneath.

It was very still here. Just the sound of pattering rain on the soft earth and the distant cries of those still helping with the rescue and the red glow from the burning hospital flickering on the drunken crosses in the monsoon-dulled morning like something in a weird dream.

Which cross belonged to Bob? Was he yet to have a cross? So many crosses. So many. From some of them a fine rivulet of mud was trickling. By the end of the monsoon many of the markers would be horizontal. As the camp moved on, following the railway, the jungle would return, cover them with vines and roots and fungus, all signs of them obliterated as though they had never been. By that time he and others would be far away, perhaps themselves beneath the mud under a rough bamboo cross out there in this senseless tangle. All were living on borrowed time. All a man could hope for was a mate to hold his hand so he would not die alone.

But Bob had died alone. The man who'd been his friend from almost the beginning of their Army service, who had carried him for two days on the march to Rangoon, who had bathed him so many times when he had been sick and helpless, had been denied the privilege of a companion to ease his last moments. Amid other dying men he had gone unnoticed, alone.

The thought of that loneliness constricted Matthew's throat muscles. He should have been with him, should have been there to put an inscription on his pitiful bamboo cross, to honour Bob's burial with his presence.

Without strength Matthew let his knees buckle, sank down in the mud which, disturbed by his light weight on it, offered up a fulsome stink. And as he had failed to comfort his dying friend, so there was no comfort for him – only the rain mingled with salt dribbling down his cheeks; only the empty silence of the lonely graves, the intermittent calling of the wild things of the rainforest, and, faintly, the shouts of men trying vainly to help each other.

Chapter 21

'I really enjoy these moments of peace and quiet.'

Geoffrey Crawley lounged in one of the sagging arm-chairs in the living half of Susan's partitioned room. 'Between you, me and the gatepost,' he continued, 'Emma's jolliness can go right through one sometimes.'

'She's a very nice person,' Susan defended, handing him the cup of tea she'd made on the small gas ring she seldom used except when he came up here to escape the constant din of wife and kids downstairs.

'Oh, don't get me wrong.' He took an appreciative sip of the tea. 'I'd be the first to challenge anyone who says anything against her. Salt of the earth – Emma. But sometimes . . .'

Susan smiled. He seemed to like her as an audience, to get off his chest the little things that bothered him or to regale her with little anecdotes of his travels which Emma, managing three growing boys and a house, had no time to listen to and had probably heard before. At first it had been a little embarrassing, him coming up here. What if Emma got the wrong idea?

She'd said as much to Emma who had promptly viewed the whole thing with amusement. 'Keeps 'im out of my way while I'm gettin' dinner. S'long as yer don't mind 'im. If yer don't want 'im up there, just send 'im packin' back down 'ere. Yer don't 'ave ter put up wiv 'im. Need yer own privacy sometimes, I expect. Just turn 'im out when yer've 'ad enough.'

But she didn't want to turn him out. It was nice having a man's company all to herself. He made good conversation but his was quiet where Emma's could be so noisy. He brought her little things, sweets he'd got from under the counter, most of them for his children and for Emma and even Mattie, but a few for her. Lately he'd been giving her more and more little presents: a pair of nylons; a length of parachute silk from which she made herself a couple of slips; a lipstick on her birthday – Max Factor – not easy to come by. The ends of previous ones were melted down and poured in to one container to make them go further. Emma didn't wear lipstick since having the boys. 'He knows what I look like,' she'd said when Susan had offered her a touch of hers. ''E'd 'ave a fit, me dolled up. Think I'd got meself some other bloke.'

Susan accepted them all gratefully. At least she didn't have to go with some GI like Edie to get them. On her first Christmas with the Crawleys – she'd refused to spend it with her in-laws – he had brought home a tiny wooden doll for Mattie. At Easter a real chocolate egg, not a cardboard one. On her first birthday a pink dress, and on Susan's birthday, lace hankies. Where he got these things from she never asked; she was just flattered by the attention. And ever since her birthday he'd come up to sit in her armchair and chat for an hour or so, whatever

Sunday afternoon he was home. It had become almost a habit.

Christmas came round again, and again she refused to spend any of it with Mr and Mrs Ward, nor, to be fair, with her own family. They were too much of a journey away and the house remained crowded with her grandparents still there, their home still uninhabitable. She sent them a card though, one of those postcard things that now took the place of the fancy pre-war ones.

But Mrs Ward was as put out as she'd been the previous year. 'We never see Matilda unless we come to you. Surely one Christmas with us.'

Susan had remained silent, sullen, but she had her way. Here was fun, she could be herself with an easygoing family. The thought of spending it with the Wards, the long silences, the brooding atmosphere she always sensed there, though it was probably of her own making, made her cringe. She turned from the knowledge that there would be just three people at the Wards' house this Christmas, Mr and Mrs Ward and Louise, home on leave, and they would sit and mourn the absence of their son through the whole festive season. She wanted none of it.

On Christmas Eve came an uproar from below, exactly as last year, when Geoffrey arrived home with presents. As before she remained in her room, not wishing to intrude. But soon footsteps echoed up the stairs and she heard a light tapping on her door.

Opening it she saw Geoff standing there, face flushed from the many whiskies and gins offered by various customers and reps who could still get hold of it. Swaying slightly he held out a large square brown paper parcel with a smaller one on top.

'Happy Christmas!' he burst out, thrusting the packages at her, and, too excited to wait for her to open them when the time came, announced in a slurred voice: 'Dolls house f'r Mattie. Cardboard I'm 'fraid. The small one's f'r you, pair o' gloves.'

Susan felt her face flush with pleasure. 'Geoff, you shouldn't have.'

'Part o'th' family, hey?'

Even tipsy, he spoke much better than Emma. A Cockney twang could still be discerned there but Susan supposed that his work called for better speech. He was the exact opposite of Emma in every way; she bonny, sloppy, talkative, animated, her hair fair and frizzy; he slim, neat and quiet, brown hair slicked back by brilliantine. He was something like eighteen years older than Susan – Emma said he was nearing forty though she hadn't said how near – but he looked younger than that. Although shorter, he resembled Matthew in some way, but was more sleek and not so dark-haired and his eyes looked an indeterminate shade of blue where Matthew's had been brown. (She had used the past tense when that thought had come to her, though it had gone unnoticed.) But Geoff was here, and she had begun to notice him a lot. Not only was he nice to look at but he smelled nice, from lotions she supposed he picked up on his travels.

'I've got everyone something,' he was saying, still swaying in the doorway. As she stood back to let him in, he plonked the packages on a chair.

'I've got something for everyone too,' she said. They were already wrapped and waiting, in brown paper. Christmas wrapping had become a thing of the past. 'Wooden toys for the boys,' she announced. 'Someone I know makes them out of old furniture.' It was a man who worked next door to where she worked. 'I've got a brooch for Emma.' That too was made from wood with a picture painted on it by the same man, making quite a trade out of it, it seemed.

'And this is for you.' She handed him the tiny package. 'What is it?'

'I'm not saying. Wait 'til you open it.'

He giggled. 'I've told you what I got you. Tell me what you've got me.'

'It isn't much.' They were cuff-links, not expensive.

'Ah, th' best things always come in li'l packages?' He was regarding her closely and she felt he was referring to her personally. She felt herself blush.

'Don't be silly.'

'No.' He swayed towards her. 'I mean it.' His breath smelled sweetly of whisky, not at all unpleasant. Leaning forward, he laid a kiss on her cheek. Suddenly all the loneliness she'd been pretending wasn't there whenever Edie regaled her with what she'd been up to the evening before welled up inside her. She lifted both arms and put them around his neck and at the obvious invitation, his lips settled on hers.

Susan felt herself trembling with all the longing that had lain inside her, and she realised that he too harboured a certain loneliness, though why he should, with Emma there for him, she couldn't understand. But at the moment she didn't want to understand. Her whole being was crying out for comfort. For a second, her thoughts flew wildly to the bed behind the partition. Her heart seemed to be pounding through her entire body, her blood throbbing to its thumping. Then suddenly he released her.

'God, I must be more stoned than I thought. God, Sue, I'm sorry.'

How could she cry out, 'Don't go'? How could she make herself look cheaper than she must already look? She stood watching him back away towards the door. It was all she could do. What her expression was like she didn't know, but she hoped it wasn't imploring. He was still apologising, clutching the present she had given him. This would be the end of their moments together up here in this room. She'd driven him away by her own stupid actions and now she'd have no one. There was a dull ache where the throbbing had been while he stood teetering in the doorway, apologies still on his lips.

'If you knew, Sue, what I was thinking just now, you'd throw me out,' he said, and it was then that she found her voice.

'Geoffrey, don't go.'

She waited. Then very slowly he closed the door and came back into the room.

She had got through her finals, she was a State Registered Nurse at last. Jenny telephoned her mother, then armed with a four-hour pass went out to celebrate in a local pub with the others of her group who had passed.

'What d'you plan to do now?' asked mousy-haired Molly Fergusson who'd become her best friend. Everyone was asking the same question of each other.

Sipping her third Sanderman's sherry, Jenny thought about that one. The idea of applying for the QAIMNS/R made itself felt again. This time she would apply. Mumsy would be distressed, but she needed some of that freedom she had always dreamed about, which even becoming a nurse had not as yet fulfilled. It meant she could be sent abroad; she couldn't help it but somehow the idea identified her with Matthew, silly fool that she was. When would she ever grow up?

She knew of course that he was a prisoner of war. Susan walking out on his parents as she had, knowing how things stood, had to her mind been a terrible thing to do. Now she lived with some rough family off Mile End Road rather than the nice home into which she had been so generously accepted. Susan must have been off her head. But it was none of her business. She had to get on with her own life. And how often had she told herself that as soon as Matthew came into mind? As he came to mind now, so she pushed the thought away and told Molly of her plans.

'Watch it,' Molly said ominously. 'They could send you anywhere.'

But she was adamant now. It was what she wanted, to be sent anywhere. It was what had happened to Matthew. And she was thinking of him again. All these years and she still thought of him.

Quickly she stopped thinking of him. Even so, she applied, and soon found herself saying goodbye to all the friends she'd made at the London Whitechapel, except for Molly who having readily told her to watch it, had decided to go with her. It felt good to have someone, not exactly to hold her hand, but to be a support in a corner, to be in the same boat with. Paddling one's own canoe could be all very well, but a lonely business, and Molly had become a good friend. It would have been hard to say goodbye to her.

'I feel a bit guilty leaving here at a time like this,' Jenny confided. Air raids had begun again, this time more concentrated, the bombs heavier and more destructive. Dispirited Londoners who'd thought they'd seen the end of the Blitz called it the little Blitz; almost as many victims were being brought into the London as before. The second front was still being talked about, but this time everyone knew it would come soon. Guilty feelings or not, she was determined nothing should stop her now, visions of being sent overseas filling her mind.

'Adventure at last,' she said, shrugging off feelings of guilt.

'Aye, adventure at last,' Molly Fergusson agreed.

Conditions overseas could be uncomfortable, Jenny was told at her interview. She didn't mind. She could be sent anywhere. She didn't mind. A medical was followed by a lengthy shopping list, with her expected to pay for the items it contained.

'We'll be out of pocket a whole month at least,' she grumbled. 'I never considered us needing these things.'

They were items that very few of the nursing recruits had considered: folding camp bed and bedroll; a collapsible canvas bath, wash bowl and bucket; gumboots; portable paraffin stove. Even the uniform, grey suit and greatcoat with scarlet facings, a change of grey shirts and ties, hat, a change of grey cotton dresses, cape trimmed with scarlet, a lawn veil, had to be bought. Her mother generously sent her a bit of money to help out along with her laments at her daughter no longer coming home most evenings – not coming home at all. She was in the forces, it hadn't properly registered until now. She'd be called sister. Nursing Officer J. Ross number T/348509. And she and Molly were to be sent off to a military hospital somewhere in England. So much for going abroad.

In fact they ended up in Essex, at a large manor called Hamdon Hall, now a military hospital in a village of the same name – far from being hundreds of miles from home, she could have cycled there!

New Year's Eve, like Christmas, had been wonderful, the house filled to overflowing with all the Crawley family: friends, relatives, mostly women and children or men too old to have been called up, a sprinkling of uniforms of those who had been lucky enough to be home on short leave. The New Year seen in, the party had lasted until around one in the morning, until slowly growing stale and dwindling as one after another relatives yawned, remembered their own homes, minds on a cup of cocoa and bed. Now they had all gone. All were living close by and did not need to stay the night.

In the now-quiet kitchen surrounded by the debris of the party while Emma said goodnight to the last of them at the door, loath to see them go, when she would have to come back and face the clearing up, yapping away with them in the silence of the freezing early hours of 1944, Geoffrey gave Susan a long, searching look.

'Fancy a nightcap? There's some whisky left, or a drop of port.'

She shook her head. 'I think I've had enough.'

She started to leave but he took hold of her hand. 'Look, Sue, I'm sorry about the other day.'

She wanted to say, '*I'm* not,' but she wasn't even sure about that. It had been so wonderful, then afterwards so wretched knowing what she'd done, and then she had wanted it to happen all over again. She ended up saying, rather stupidly, 'Emma must have wondered why you was so long delivering the Christmas presents.'

'Probably reckoned I was just chatting,' he mused. He moved nearer to her. 'Are you sorry about what happened?'

It was a direct question, one she couldn't answer except to give a small shrug, her eyes lowered. Taking her silence for collusion, he drew her gently to him. 'I love you, Sue.'

His breath smelled of alcohol. She held herself stiff in his embrace. Any moment Emma would be back in, her goodnights said. Fear made her body grow even more tense. 'You don't,' she whispered. 'You had too much to drink that day. You've had too much to drink tonight. We mustn't . . .'

He put a hand gently over her mouth. 'I love you. I can't remember when it started. All those times I sat in your room I could hardly keep from taking hold of you and kissing you and telling you how I felt. But you gave me no encouragement – no sign. I knew how you felt about your husband so I didn't dare . . . I wouldn't muck you about, Sue. You're too nice for that. But that day, when you asked me not to go, knowing by then how I felt . . .'

He let his words drift off, his hand falling away from her mouth. In his arms she felt limp. 'But I don't love you,' she managed to say. She had to be honest with him. But what was honesty? What was truth? 'I was lonely.'

The strength went out of his clasp on her, his tone took on a touch of harsh disappointment, bitterness. 'And I came in handy.'

'No.' She heard Emma call out a last goodnight, the night air making her call sound flat and far away. She would stand watching her guests until they disappeared into Mile End Road, a woman so full of demonstrative affection that she couldn't bear to let those she was fond of fade from sight until forced to by the intervention of something like a street corner. There were a few more minutes left before she came back indoors. Meanwhile Susan gabbled what she needed to say to Geoffrey.

'That's the trouble, all I could think about was you, you near me and the wonderful feeling it gave me. I should've thought about my husband, but I didn't. He's like a dream – something that never really happened.'

'Then why hold me off?' He too was talking fast, knowing his wife would be back any moment.

'Because,' she said, 'I don't know how I feel – if I was trying to put you in his place . . . Geoffrey, I could let you love me, easy as anything. But I must have time to think.' Any minute now Emma would be back indoors. Susan pulled free of the hand still holding her wrist. 'You must leave me alone, Geoffrey. And don't come upstairs to see me any more, please.'

The street door scraped to and closed with a tortured grating thud. The wood had swollen in the damp winter weather. Susan fled to the kitchen door and stumbled past Emma coming along the unlit passage.

'You all right, Sue?' came the startled voice.

'Just want the lav,' she mumbled, making for the stairs. 'Think I'll go straight to bed.'

'It's all that beer – makes yer run. Wanna nightcap? Tea? Cocoa?'

'No thanks.'

Reaching her door she stumbled into her room. Closing the door she leaned against it. Her body felt like an empty sack as she let herself slide to the floor to give herself over to weeping, ceasing only when Mattie stirred in her cot, dreaming, giving a small whimper.

For three months they hadn't moved from where they had been quartered. In huts erected in the grounds of Hamdon Hall, in the depths of January and February and March, they looked forward earnestly to the warmer spring weather. With the second front still being talked about, they treated cuts and bruises on men returning from training manoeuvres, saw to fingers squashed in lorry bonnets, dosed sore throats, winter colds, caught colds themselves and dosed each other.

'Fun, don't ye think?' Molly said, her nose red and sore from the constant application of unforgiving hankies.

Jenny chuckled and wiped her own tender nose. Molly was a tonic. Always jolly, always looking on the bright side, a girl to turn every soldier's eye. She was tall, like Jenny herself, but whip-thin, and looked as though the smallest breeze would knock her sideways. Like all women with such figures she looked wonderful in her smart grey and scarlet uniform, whereas Jenny saw herself as doing her uniform no justice whatsoever despite the appreciative remarks of the soldiers about the colour of her hair and the lovely grey-green of her eyes. She took it with a pinch of salt. They'd pay compliments to any nurse in uniform attending their trivial medical complaints.

So their lives continued, spring sunshine lifting the spirits as they went on occasion to the local pictures in nearby Chelmsford, attended the village fête at Easter, went to the community hall dance that had once only catered for a sprinkling of villagers but now was crammed with a variety of uniforms, hospital staff, and patients. Molly hardly ever danced with the same man twice; she went into town on the arm of every Tom, Dick and Harry. Jenny did the same but somehow could never allow herself to get close to any one man, so she supposed she too lingered on every Tom, Dick and Harry's arm and it was an ever-changing foursome that marched off into Chelmsford for an evening at the pictures or a better-class dance at the town hall.

The next two months passed like a dream, surrounded by the gentle warmth of the Essex countryside, by contentment, comradeship, and all the while learning ever more of the skills and requirements of her chosen career. At last she was forgetting to think about Matthew. This was a different life, her old life and all its sense of confinement and commitment left far behind. As for the yearning to go overseas, although the QAs were an overseas division of nursing, it seemed this was where they would remain for the duration of the war.

Things, however, were to change. Towards the end of May the whole unit of QAs upped stakes and moved to outside Deal in Kent to meet a mounting stockpile of ammunition, military vehicles and chaos. They got fitted out with sloppy dungaree-like garments, heavy boots, webbing, respirator and haversack, raincape-cum-groundsheet and all the other paraphernalia that was designed to hang around the frame of military personnel.

Miles from anywhere, for the last weeks of May life assumed a state of utter immobility beyond the vast camp site with its growing mass of men and military machinery. The first week of June began wet and windy, the wind at times whipping to gale force, making life under canvas more than miserable.

Emerging from the prefabricated canteen that first Tuesday in June to a newly washed morning after the gales of the previous few days, Jenny became aware of a low and steady distant roar that made every girl look up, wonderingly. Within seconds the distant roar was filling the air.

'Christ! Look at that!' Molly's voice had to screech over the growing racket.

As though being raised on a vast curtain, a cloud of dark shapes had begun to loom over the tree-tops from the west. Bearing down on the awed, open-mouthed watchers below – the whole hospital had turned out to see what the thunderous noise was all about, the building itself being shaken by the weight of it – wave after wave of planes began to pass overhead. Each bomber towed a glider, Halifaxes, Lancasters, Blenheims, the huge Flying Fortresses, moving almost wingtip to wingtip in steady purposeful majesty, deceptively slow, forming a virtual ceiling above the upturned faces.

'It's the second front,' shrieked Molly, the deafening roar practically carrying her voice away. 'It's started. At last!'

But with the last waves of planes receding into the distance, silence descending strangely upon ears still ringing from the earlier noise, Jenny and Molly looked at each other, as did all the women of their unit.

'We'll probably be following them soon,' Molly said, serious for once.

Chapter 22

Obeying her wishes, Geoffrey hadn't visited her room again. Downstairs he was polite to her as though nothing had ever occurred between them. Weeks stretched to months; for Susan it was a most miserable time. The colder he seemed towards her, the warmer he appeared to become towards his family, playing with his boys far more than she was sure he once did whenever he was home. He was good with Mattie too, bouncing her on his knee until she chuckled fit to burst, but not one warm glance did he cast towards herself. She ached for him to give her just one look that said he too remembered Christmas Eve in her room and yearned to repeat it.

Even Emma noticed. 'You done somefink ter upset Geoff?' she asked. When Susan raised her shoulders sullenly without offering any explanation one way or the other, he laughed, assuring Emma he was being a perfect gentleman to their tenant, the innuendo not escaping Susan who wanted to burst into tears and tell him that if anything he was behaving perfectly rotten to her.

She even contemplated giving up her rooms and moving on, but how could she explain why to a bewildered and hurt Emma? Not only that, the courage she had possessed on that one single escapade when she'd left the Wards now evaded her; she couldn't repeat that, not with a twenty-month-old child in tow with all its attendant toiletries, nappies, clothing. And she'd never find herself another place like this with such wonderful people. She gritted her teeth and forced herself to stick out Geoffrey's horrid attitude, knowing it had really been of her own making.

He had even managed to avoid her during the little Blitz when they'd all huddled in the Morrison shelter in the tiny cluttered basement, the air raids less regular but as devastating as the real Blitz three years before – incredible to think the war had gone on so long.

In April they also had ceased as abruptly as the first Blitz, leaving the big cities in a period of quiet, Hitler foiled again. For Susan, terrified as she had been of a direct hit, the debatable closeness of Geoffrey, who continued virtually to ignore her, was taken away. A month had gone by since then and this weekend was only the second time Geoffrey had come home, she and he, as usual, avoiding each other like the plague.

After putting Mattie to bed, she had stayed up in her room, sick of looking at his averted face as he played with his sons. She'd been up here some time and when a gentle knock came on her door she guessed it was Emma wondering why she hadn't come downstairs again. Emma worried that way. She opened the door ready with an excuse, to find Geoffrey standing there. He looked apologetic.

'I'm sorry, I had to come up. Emma's been asking why

I never come up here now. I thought I'd better make it look good – just for half an hour. Do you mind?'

'No,' she answered woodenly and stood back for him to enter.

'I could go if you want.' But he was already sitting in the armchair. She stood near hers, not sure whether to sit down or not and make this seem like the cosy little times that once had been.

'Do you want me to make you a cup of tea?'

'No, I shan't stay long. Fact is, after the boys went to bed, Emma went next door to Mrs Fulham for a chat. She'll be in there about an hour, if I know her.'

'Oh,' her voice sounded flat, neutral. Suddenly he was out of his chair.

'Sue, I can't go on like this. I'm in a state. I can't work, I can't think, I can't think of anything but you. Sue, I'm so bloody unhappy.'

She wanted to say that he looked happy enough to her, but she said nothing. Her heart was racing. This was what she had wanted to hear all those months, and now her heart was going like a steam hammer and her mind was in confusion and she could find nothing to say. The fact was, she had no need to say anything. He was saying it all for her, still in the same place where he had stood up from the chair, as though his feet were nailed to the floor, his pale blue eyes trained on her.

'I really do love you, Sue. I'm not a man of any special talent. I don't know what to say on these occasions. All I know is what I feel for you. I've tried to conquer it, as you'd asked me to.'

'I never . . .' But he was rushing on.

'I *know* it's wrong. I'm a married man, but I've never felt for anyone the way I feel about you. I *know* you said you love your husband, that you were just lonely when I . . . when we . . . I'm married. You're married. But we can't help these things happening.'

'Geoffrey.' She tried to stop the flow of pitiful clichés, but he did not hear her.

'I know you love me – the way you look at me. Sue, darling, if you feel anything for me you can't possibly feel the same for – well, anyone else. Do you still feel anything for . . . anyone else?' She knew who he meant, loath to say the name.

'I – don't know,' she stammered.

'You do feel something for me?'

'I – Geoffrey, I don't know.'

'You must know. If I didn't matter to you, you wouldn't go around looking so downcast. I know you love me. You do, don't you?'

She allowed a glum nod, a half-nod really, but enough for him. He came forward and his arms were about her, the sweetness of his breath flowing across her face, she in turn clinging to him, needing this reality.

She couldn't remember reaching her bed, but she would never not remember the delicious, the overwhelming joy of being made love to, all the more wonderful for the mad snatched affair it was, filled with need and with tension and with fear of time overtaking them. She had never felt so fulfilled as when he came inside her, she rising up to meet him.

Afterwards she didn't feel at all ashamed as she had that first time. Lying in Geoffrey's arms, luxuriating in the contentment that flowed over her, she found herself drawing a veil over the man she had once adored, found herself forming a mental note to put his photo away from its place on the bedside table. What could be gained by staring at the flat, lifeless image of a smiling man that a scrap of paper proclaimed was her husband? How did she know where he was and if he still existed? Nothing was ever heard of those whom the Japanese had captured. They stubbornly recognised no conventional rules of war, were said to be fanatical about dying for their emperor and to see captives of war as unworthy of respect. Fearful tales had come out of the Far East of massacres and terrible deeds done by them. How was she to know what might have happened to Matthew?

In Geoffrey's arms, seeing her vigilance as a waste of effort, she blocked out everything else but the hope that this would be the beginning of a long summer of ecstasy, perhaps a lifetime. Only later when he left, dressed and dapper as always as his wife came in through the front door to get his evening cup of cocoa, did she give some thought to what they'd done and what they intended to go on doing. With Emma suspecting nothing. But one day she would, or would have to be told. And then . . .

A shudder passed over Susan at the misery that awaited Emma, and she felt suddenly sick.

The doorbell, of course, didn't work. It had never worked. Lilian would have liked it to work so that she could have kept her thumb on it indefinitely, displaying her anger until the door was eventually opened. Instead she must use the door knocker which wasn't the same thing for she'd be disturbed by the noise as would the neighbours, whereas a bell upset only those on the other side of the door.

It was Mrs Crawley who answered, but that didn't matter. Lilian's wrath was directed as much to her as to Susan. She'd promised she'd make herself responsible for the girl and she had let the side down.

Susan's letter had completely taken her breath away, shocked her to the very core. Unabashed it was, no matter how shamefacedly worded, the grammar and spelling, bad as ever, adding to the ill grace of it.

. . . I've got to tell you sometime. I feel I've got to be honest, because Emma Crawley's walked out on Mr Crawley as him and me are living together you might say. It all just hapened. We couldn't help ourselfs, and now I've found out I'm pregnant. So I thought it was best to tell you the truth. I know it sounds bad, but it wasn't intended to be like that. It just what happened. I don't expect you'll forgive me and I know you'll say I should wait for Matthew but I could just be waiting in vane? But now there's Mattie to think of. Mr Crawley don't like her around now Emma's not here to give eye to her. He askd me if I'd ask you if you'd like to have her for a wile, being her grandparents . . .

She'd crumpled the letter up and thrown it from her half-read, only to retrieve and re-read it, still with disbelief. How anyone could be so shameless, so brazen? And to choose now of all times to write such things, three years almost to the day Matthew had gone away, had kissed his wife – his *loyal* wife – goodbye to march off into captivity. *Three years!* How could anyone be so faithless? She couldn't wait, could she?

Her mind again seething with the contents of that letter, Lilian had begun to wonder if there was anyone at home. Her knocking was taking so long to be answered. As if there wasn't enough to put up with, she continued to wait for news of Matthew that never came, clinging desperately to the belief that one day she'd hear, that one day, when the war drew to an end, he'd come home.

But this war was on their doorstep yet again in the shape of the doodlebug. Just as the news of Allied advances had everyone reading the papers as though following the football results, excited by it all, there had come the spluttering-engine roar of those V2s, like black crosses spouting blowlamp fire in their wake. From D Day and throughout June, July and August they had laboured across the sky. All warily watched their course as they cut out, soughing on ominously, the watchers unsure whether to duck or not. When they finally came plunging to earth they demolished homes in huge explosions that fanned out flying glass and debris, killing scores of people, for no one knew where they'd fall. Sometimes a hundred would come over in a day, several at once so no one knew where to look or run. The old air-raid shelters proved of no help;

cowering in them would have halted all normal life, they chewed up a body's nerves. Several had fallen near to her, too near for comfort, and people had again left London in droves.

Yet, as though none of this mattered, Susan had had the audacity to carry on an affair with her landlady's husband, heedless of his wife who'd befriended the girl, of her own husband who was a prisoner of war. She was thinking only of herself, her needs, her pleasures.

Lilian's first thought had been to seek out Leonard and show him the letter. On Saturday the shop stayed open until five thirty, but she had eventually decided against going there and demeaning herself by telling him such news in front of goggle-eyed customers. She had to deal with this herself. Making up her mind in a fit of anger, she had got herself ready and now, half an hour later, was waiting for someone to answer her knock.

But she had not been prepared for it to be Mrs Crawley herself. Even so, she collected herself, fluttering the letter in the woman's face. 'This arrived from my daughter-in-law an hour ago. She gave me to believe you'd left. I hardly expected to find you here, circumstances being what they are.'

Mrs Crawley's face was bleak. No longer the amiable woman, she regarded Lilian with a steady pride in her eyes. 'It's still my 'ome, Mrs Ward. I just come back fer a few fings wot's mine.'

'I see.' For a moment she was stumped. 'Is my daughter-in-law here?'

'Upstairs.'

'Is he . . .'

'Wiv 'er? Yes. 'E's wiv 'er.'

Again she was caught by the simple truth spoken so directly, without inflection. 'I need to see her,' was all she could find to say.

Without a word Mrs Crawley stepped aside, allowing her to enter. Her face lifted briefly towards the top of the stairs, indicating for Lilian to go up. She too said nothing, but nodded her head in Mrs Crawley's direction as she passed, noticing a battered suitcase in the hall with a hat balanced on top.

Mounting the stairs, there was no sound behind her but she had the feeling that the woman hadn't watched her go, and reaching the door to the room where Susan resided, she heard the front door close quietly and knew that Mrs Crawley had let herself out.

For the first time she felt fear. What would she find on the other side of that door? It took all her reserve of courage to rap on it with her knuckles. Then she remembered the letter, how she'd felt reading it, and her rap became firm.

'I couldn't tell you before. You were at work.' Leonard was visibly upset by her going off like that without a word to him.

'You should have allowed me to be there, Lilian. I'd have been able to lessen the impact rather than you having to deal with it alone.'

'I managed well enough.'

She had managed, facing up to the situation that had confronted her on stepping inside Susan's rooms, seeing the state the girl had allowed it to get into. And that poor little mite, Matilda; she could have cried for her.

Entering, she'd been met by the sight of Geoffrey Crawley. In white shirt, brown trousers, plain brown tie and sleeveless pullover, he presented quite an elegant figure until one noticed the pale stubble on his chin. The man hadn't shaved that morning. Lilian knew immediately that her entrance had been heard downstairs. There must have been an unholy rush to dress, making it seem as though they had been up for hours.

Eyes sharpened by the sight of that stubble saw more telltale things: through the open door in the partition wall, a glimpse of an unmade bed and this at eleven thirty in the morning; clothes left on the floor; breakfast cups unwashed. The two must have been idling around the place in a state of undress. The knowledge brought bile into her throat as she swallowed fastidiously. Worst of all, Matilda, who was standing up in her cot, the covers twisted into a heap, was still in nightclothes, her dark curling hair dishevelled, her little face unwashed and still sticky from a piece of bread and jam that now adhered to the cot rail. She'd been crying, no doubt for attention that wasn't forthcoming as these two indulged in each other – evidence of her distress was visible in the mucus drying around her nose. Lilian had never seen the child in such a mess. Usually Mattie looked quite presentable at other times when she had visited, but now she knew that had been Emma Crawley's doing, never the mother's. And there had stood Susan in a clean dress and hastily applied lipstick, though her long hair had not been

combed quickly enough, for Lilian had seen one or two
tangles that had been missed because of this couple's vile
goings-on earlier this morning.

It was then she had found her voice. With the letter held
at arm's length to the girl, she demanded what was the
meaning of it. 'Are you saying that this . . . animal has got
you pregnant?' she'd asked, quite illogically, for had it not
been written there in black and white?

Crawley had stepped forward, full of indignation. 'I
say, hold on.'

Lilian had recalled her words all the way home and
recalled them now with a mixture of pride in her own self-
control – her ability to find the right words about which she
was now justly satisfied – and of controlled anger which
now struck her as totally correct in the circumstances.
'Yes, animal. That can be the only word to describe the
sort of person who leads a young woman with a child
away from her true path, loyalty to a husband who is not
here to fight for her. I call it despicable. It is nothing less.
That you, who have so far kept yourself out of the forces
by your job while young men are fighting and dying for
you, can find it in yourself to break up my son's marriage,
is a despicable act. A different story, I can vouch, if he
were here. Then a coward like you would run with your
tail between your legs. You are a coward, a traitor, a
parasite. And you,' she had turned on the trembling girl,
her daughter-in-law, 'you are a harlot. I'd rather see my
son dead than take you back!'

That had been a mistake. She shouldn't have said that.
On reflection it seemed she was condemning her own son.

That was when she had nearly broken down. To combat her weakness, she had gone into the other room to stand over Matilda, the other two following at a distance.

Looking down on the child, averting her eyes from knickers, bras, stockings and men's pants that draped every chairback, she'd been revolted by the musty odour that rose up to meet her from the cot itself, an offensive effluvium of urine, long-unbathed skin and unwashed bedclothes. She'd half expected disorder but not this abomination. The cot, like the bed, must have been crawled in and out of for weeks without any change of linen, and looking at Crawley with his fresh-looking skin and his attention to dress, it was unbelievable he would put up with such squalor as met her eyes. There had been another smell too in that room. A faint reek that she could not at first place. Susan and her abominable lover had been crawling all over each other night after night, filling the room with the reek of their coition. One word had escaped her as she lifted the child, who must have witnessed this copulation time after time, out of her cot: 'Slut!' And again, enlarging on the word: 'You disgusting slut!'

In a smouldering fury she had commanded Matilda to be washed and dressed, a process that had involved a great deal of perseverance to control the miniature tempest at the unaccustomed washing. Susan had told her this was how Mattie always was and that it was easier not to bother and upset her, a likely excuse for laziness. Finally, Lilian had borne the child home with her, as Susan had asked.

It still escaped her how the child's mother had stood by and watched her being taken away without one word

of protest. The last she had seen of Susan, as she bore
Matilda down the stairs and out of the house, was her
standing there leaning slightly against Crawley, his arm
protectively about her, a declaration if ever there was one
of her intention never to go back to her husband when he
finally came home. Lilian was still certain of that.

She now cuddled her granddaughter to her. After a
proper bath, her hair now brushed to a dark sheen, the
little body still convulsed with the occasional sob from
screaming at such mishandling. One would think she'd
never seen water in her life, which must almost be true,
sad to say, and Lilian again felt hatred build up against the
mother.

'You should have seen those rooms,' she said to
Leonard. 'She was never like that when she lived here. I
took her always for a clean girl, clean-living. You could
have knocked me over with a feather. And her cries when
Matthew left, I'd never have believed she could turn so far
the other way.'

'Well, she's here now,' he soothed, his arms opening
for Matilda to come to him, which she did readily, to lie
against her grandfather, thumb in mouth, dark eyes slewed
round towards the grandma who had so handled her.
'She'll be with us until Susan wants her back.'

To which Lilian huffed, 'We'll see about that.' And
smiling at the child, added, 'One day, you'll thank
Grandma. When Daddy comes home.'

As the year drew to its close, that he would come home she
was more than certain. And soon. Of that too she had no

doubts, the news being what it was, all good. This year of
1944 marked a turning point if ever there was one; despite
buzz-bombs, despite frightening V2s that had come after
– in June alone Rome was captured and the landings in
Normandy took place, but much more heartening, for her
at least, was the defeat of the Japanese invasion of India.
For her it was a light at the end of the tunnel. A few more
months and they'd be defeated entirely and Matthew
would come marching home. In the face of that thought,
all other victories had paled, even when Paris was liberated
in August, then Brussels. And then on the twentieth of
October had come the most wonderful news of all, of the
Americans' re-landing in the Philippines. Not long now
before she saw her son again. Then another heartache
would begin when he learned that the wife he loved so
much had been and still was unfaithful. At least they had
his child here. A beautiful two-and-a-half-year-old to be
introduced to him, to call him Daddy, compensation for
the loss he did not yet know of. Lilian's heart almost broke
for him at what faced him on his return.

Meanwhile it was a new half-forgotten world she and
Leonard had entered, taking Matilda into their home.
They'd scarcely remembered what it was like to bring up
an energetic young child. Louise had been quiet, doing all
that was asked of her, never resorting to tantrums, when
hurt, running to her parents for it to be kissed better in the
stubborn knowledge that all would be well. She could be
quite self-willed when the fancy took her, but Lilian had
always managed her.

Even Matthew, who had been the harder of the two to

bring up, a rebel always wanting to kick over the traces, going into a corner to nurse his hurts, brazening out hurt pride with abrasive flamboyance – even with him she had managed. Until, that is, he'd gone against her advice to go for a commission, instead joining up as a mere private. She still felt he had done it just to spite her, though why, she had never been sure, she with only his well-being at heart. And look where his action had got him.

But all the good and bad in her two children had become a distant memory as they'd grown away from her. Louise was now an independent young woman, hardly ever coming home when on leave and, so her letters said, going out with a young Canadian by the name of Ken Turnbull from Winnipeg. They planned to go steady and, reading between the lines, she was hoping to go back with him to Canada after the war. With Matthew a prisoner far away, Lilian prayed daily, if God were willing, that he would come home, but she knew he would probably be a changed man.

Yes, her memories of bringing up a child had dimmed considerably. Matilda, however, altered all that. Invading her grandparents' stagnant lives, she hounded them, small as she was. Being a demanding child, rather like her mother, but charming with it, she made her grandmother's head spin and sometimes ache with her liveliness. With no idea how to stay neat and clean, her clothing coupons never went far enough, and to keep her prettily dressed, Lilian dragged out her old sewing machine, cutting down her own dresses, unravelling old cardigans and often sacrificing her and Leonard's own coupons. But there were rewards, seeing a child they'd brought home looking and smelling like some workhouse waif transformed into the pretty little thing she was. And so like Matthew that it hurt.

It had pained them at first hearing Matilda's plaintive cries of 'Mummy, Mummy'. She said little else, for she was terribly behind with her talking, not yet chattering as a child that age should. It passed, as she was too young to sustain a memory, but Lilian took care not to take her to see her mother and awaken the child's renewed distress. Susan seemed not to mind.

There was never a word from her unless Lilian made it her business to seek her out.

'Aren't you interested in how your daughter is getting along?'

Susan, displaying sullenness at her insistence in coming, had merely shrugged. 'I know where she is if I want her.'

Come Christmas, heavy with her bastard, off-handed and rude to her mother-in-law, Susan had apparently made up her mind that she had been right about Matthew. Now certain she was a widow, she treated Lilian as an interfering old busybody who no longer had any jurisdiction over her actions. Lilian, keeping to her rigid faith, fostered hatred of the weak-willed girl for it.

The International Red Cross, with so much on their plate, were still working hard tracing prisoners of war, and had said that they'd made contact in certain quarters and the name Matthew Ward had been on a list which the Japanese had reluctantly released just prior to Christmas. It could have been any Matthew Ward, the name was not an uncommon one, but Lilian saw it as too much of a coincidence for it not to be her son. His wife had no such weight of faith, continuing to prefer her life with the abominable Geoffrey Crawley. Her and Matthew's child was slowly becoming Lilian's whole life, a straw to cling to, someone to take the place of her son in the unlikely event of his never coming home. But that thought she put from her.

Chapter 23

Sister Ross moved briskly across a quadrangle of the Shaftesbury military hospital.

Hard to believe the war was over at last. Having only just returned to England, she'd missed the VE celebrations here, and could only hear about it from her mother and from the nurses here.

From her mother she had gleaned all sorts of news, amazingly detailed for one supposed to be reserved, unless of course Jenny's absence had brought her out at last. She heard how Matthew's wife was living with the husband of her erstwhile landlady. Jenny wasn't a bit surprised by that, only sad. Sad for Matthew who would learn of it when eventually he came home, soon, because the war in the Far East couldn't last much longer for all the tenacity of the Japanese in refusing to surrender to superior forces, their allies in Germany allies no longer. He would discover that while he had been sweating it out in Japanese hands, his wife had been enjoying the comfort of another man's arms.

Jenny learned too that his parents had charge of his child, were bringing her up admirably; that his wife had had a baby by her lover, a boy; that she had nothing now

to do with Matthew's parents, considering herself wholly
a widow. The war had passed her by.

As she walked on, Jenny thought back over her own
war, over all that had happened to her after landing in
Normandy. Having crossed the Channel in a full gale that
seemed at the time to have been waiting just for them,
making the whole unit, herself included, seasick, they'd
moved forward with the advancing Allies, tending the
wounded as they were brought in. Some were injured so
grievously it had taken all her resolve not to show revulsion
or pity before the sights that greeted her lest she undermine
the brave face the wounded had put on. She marvelled at
the resolve of most of them not to be done down by their
ghastly, disfiguring wounds before their comrades.

She had seen foreign towns and cities, Bayeux, Caen
completely in ruins from Allied bombardment, Rouen
which had been let off relatively lightly as the troops went
through. The gunfire always ahead of them, their trucks
had rumbled along in the wake of the advance, bucking
and pitching over the shell craters they'd left. And always
the grey-faced wounded, the air filled with their moans,
the hospital tents packed with hardly room enough for
stretcher-bearers, medics, and nurses to go about their
business, usually all under a continuous relentless barrage.

She had learned swear words she had never before
known existed. She'd also learned a smattering of German
as, success following success, German prisoners began
being brought in, wounded prisoners in as much need of
attention as Allied wounded. The QAs tended them all.

She'd seen Paris and had been entranced by its beauty,

and finally, with the guns falling silent, she had been posted to a town called Rotenburg, not far from Bremen, to a small hospital to help nurse the pitiful victims of Sandbostel, a concentration camp in the north of the country. After all she had seen of the wounded and dying, that place had provided the sights she most wanted to erase from a heart still apt to sink with sickening regularity at the slightest recollection.

Finally home, leave, and transfer here, caring for servicemen who had contracted tuberculosis, mostly ex-prisoners of war, victims of conditions they'd been compelled to live under. She had seen a little of the world. In time she'd return to civilian nursing. But she would never forget.

Shovelling sawdust into sacks wasn't pleasant at most times. Now, as with most things in Japanese hands, the extractors had long ago fallen apart and no longer sucked away the fine dust. Despite strips of sacking tied over nose and mouth, it got into the lungs to be hawked up later in thick yellow phlegm.

The officers complained regularly. The gaol commandant, Major Tanaka, listened sympathetically and did nothing, just as he did nothing about the diabolical bullying by his men, especially one known as Valentino from his handsome narrow face and the dramatic way he swivelled his eyes.

Having felt the weight of his bullying, Matthew trudged back through the gates of Rangoon gaol at sunset in a black mood. Loading sacks on to a barge, one had slipped, spilling sawdust everywhere. Valentino had pounced, wielding his bamboo stick like a samurai warrior, ending up by booting him headlong into the water, strutting off to leave his victim to be fished out by his workmates.

Showering briefly under the Heath Robinson contraption built by the POWs which the Japs allowed to be turned on for just half an hour each evening, subsequently causing long disappointed queues, Matthew worked to take his mind off his treatment, thinking instead of Susan. She no longer floated in his mind as during the days of the railway. He'd come through it, just, though he still suffered malaria from time to time. Almost callously, he had fought to put behind him thoughts of comrades who had died on the way. He had survived. He was determined to continue to survive, and to this end, he put behind him too today's thrashing, and thought only of Susan, of going home to take up their lives together, when all this would become a thing of the past.

In the midst of thinking that as he soaped himself with the tiniest sliver he'd been handed by an officer – told not to overdo it as others had to use it too – the name Jenny flashed into his mind and for a second he saw her quite clearly through the thin curtain of dripping water: her flaming hair, her wide smile, her well-formed features.

Strange though, he thought a lot of Jenny Ross; she came into his mind at the oddest of moments, like now. Mostly it was to recall that ardent kiss she'd given him in the street, right out in the open, all that time ago. Typical of her to do a thing like that. Never seemed to get it right.

Matthew lifted his face up to the drips falling from the makeshift shower head, a perforated canvas bag being spasmodically filled by a pipe from a tank someone in turn kept refilling as long as the water would last.

Her kiss had been a fleeting thing, leaving him to smile reflectively at the lingering sensation it had brought, one that had stirred him enough to make him want to write to her, perhaps further the relationship she had begun. But then his unit had been transferred to Birmingham and he'd met Susan. From then on *she* had taken up all his thoughts.

Strange he should think of Jenny Ross now, and with a small pang of sadness to go with it that he'd let her down. Where was she now? Was she still a nurse or had she married someone, was she raising a family? Without warning an empty place took up residence inside him, a sudden longing for things to be again as they had once been, carefree, safe, full of fun. He could see them all now. And Jenny, she had been a stunner, hadn't she? Just that she hadn't been his type. But a stunner just the same. He should have told her so. He regretted that now. Pity she hadn't had as much confidence in her looks as some men had in them – that Dennis Cox – he'd been smitten by her but hadn't the nerve to tell her. Someone had said Cox had been killed. Well, lots of blokes had been killed. Women too. Serving abroad, nurses being sent overseas, their ships sunk. Perhaps Jenny had been one of them. He wouldn't know, would he? Not here. A stab of panic gripped him then sank away, leaving a sort of empty grief that had no substance because it was unfounded, all in his mind. He had begun to fall in love with Jenny at one time, he was sure, but then he'd met Susan . . .

'F'Chrissake, y' doughy Pom – get a bloody move on,

bloody mooning about. Y'r thirty seconds was up bloody ages ago.'

Shot back to the present, Matthew slipped hastily out from the dribbling shower to receive a basinful of ripe epithets from the Aussie waiting to take his place.

'Keep your hair on,' Matthew growled irritably as the man named Phil shouldered roughly past him. Phil glared at him but Matthew's mind was now taken up with more immediate interests, even above thoughts of Susan and Jenny, as he walked away still dripping wet. So were his ragged shorts, with his time under the shower too brief for them to be taken off. They would dry as he dried. His thoughts now were on what news there might be, if any, over the grapevine.

Hidden beneath the dirt floor of a low wooden lean-to, once a tool shed belonging to the saw mill, then a makeshift latrine but now just a haven for flies and maggots, was a radio, constructed by some boffin or other. With a look-out squatting idly against the sagging rotting walls, certain chosen men – not himself, thank God, for it was an execution if the Japs ever discovered it – would take it in turns, a couple at a time, to squeeze under the floor of the lean-to, lying flat, and follow the crackling news of Allied invasion in Europe, American successes in the Pacific or how many tons of bombs B-29s had dropped on Japanese-held territory, very little of it accurate, being mainly from Japanese sources rather than Allied.

But the news they most sought was lacking – the Fourteenth Army's penetration into Assam and northern Burma five months ago had gone silent, and along with it any speculation of an early release from captivity.

He turned as an angry snort was heard directly behind him, Phil having caught him up after his own thirty seconds had been apparently cut short by two seconds owing to Matthew's delay in getting out as promptly as was required. Phil, a dismal-faced individual who shared the next cell to his with a dozen other Australians, was in a bad mood and obviously wanted to make it plain to the miscreant. Giving him little time to finish his complaint, Matthew turned on him. His own temper was none too good, his shoulders smarting still from Valentino's cane.

'Why don't you put a fucking sock in it?'

The Australian looked hurt. He wasn't a brave man, at least not rash in the face of the other's baleful glare that threatened a punch on the nose.

'Don't bloody take it out on me because yu've had a bloody blue with some lousy bloody Nip.'

Crisis over, Matthew continued walking in the direction of the three steaming oil drums from which wafted a bland aroma of saltless boiled rice.

'I'm not taking it out on you.' A fit of sawdust-laden coughing prevented him saying any more and gave Phil possession of the argument.

'We've all got bludgers t'put up with. Ain't no sense antagonising 'em, is there?'

Harry Hope, who shared Matthew's cell, once a short, naturally chubby man, but now from whose skeletal back, ribs and hips protruded, unhealthy skin hung fleshless like thin grey rows of pelmets, caught the two up, his brief shower over as well. The last of it dripped off his ridged skin like raindrops off a gutter. His voice was soft, with a West Country accent. 'Stay off our Matt's back, old son. He's been a mite touchy all day.'

'Too right, he's touchy.' But Harry ignored the man as he surveyed Matthew's shoulders.

'It do look bloody zore.'

'It is bloody sore.'

'You need to keep that covered. Got a shirt?'

'Flogged it last week for a bag of bran.'

Rice bran, discarded during milling as fit only for animal feed, was a precious commodity, rich in vitamin B, and coveted because it helped avert beri-beri and other deficiency diseases. It was consequently hard to come by. Matthew's haul had amounted to under a quarter of a pound, for which he considered himself fortunate all the same.

'I've got a shirt you can borrow until you've healed a bit.'

Giving Matthew no time to thank him, shirts too being precious commodities, Harry made off towards the queue forming behind drums of steaming rice, their supper, leaving Matthew to stare after him until the small dry cough caught him again and he followed after Harry.

Leaning down from his rickety bunk Harry surveyed him lying directly below. He'd been disturbed by his cough. All those in the cell were disturbed by it. ''Bout time you saw the quack on that, Matt, old son. Don't like the zound of that. Zounds loik a touch o' TB ter me. Don't loik your colour either.'

Matthew raised his eyes to the head hanging upside-down. 'You really know how to cheer up a bloke, don't you?'

'Only an opinion, Matt, only an opinion. But if it be TB I don' wanna catch it.'

From the next cell, divided only by open bars, came Phil's monotone drawl. 'Not as it makes any difference. All gotta go sometime, so what's it matter, hundred years from now, if yuh died at nineteen or ninety? Tryin' to live a long life – you're just a bloody gnat on an elephant's arse. Fifty years after they shove yuh under, forgotten, what's it matter if you lived at all?'

Angered, fighting another cough, Matthew turned away from the would-be philosopher. 'You're just a miserable bugger. You might not have anyone to go home to, but I've a wife and a baby waiting for me.'

On that score, senses heightened to the possibility of tuberculosis, next evening after work found him outside the TB outbuilding transfixed by the sight of those within its open door, chests sunken, eyes unnaturally bright, cheeks with that peculiar transparent flush, as his were.

An orderly, just finishing ministering to a frail stick of what three years ago had been a strong young man, now having to be fed sips of watery rice gruel from a tin cup, looked up at Matthew.

'Looking for someone, chum?'

Feeling suddenly fraudulent, Matthew shook his head; he watched the man gently ease his patient down on the platform that served for a bed and with a piece of khaki rag wipe the residue of gruel from the man's lips. The tenderness of the action touched Matthew more than anything had done in a long time. This man with his gentle hands, these men quietly heroic in their suffering, they humbled him. This endless stream of sufferers, crippled by tropical ulcers, blinded by vitamin deficiency, swollen with beri-beri and withered by dysentery, so many struck down by all the diseases the tropics could throw at them; many died without fuss lest they undermine the will of others to struggle on. None had distinguished themselves in battle but they were heroes just the same in their silent acceptance of death. And here he was shivering in fear of his own miserable life as though he were someone special, as if he were the only man who yearned to make it home to wife and child.

The orderly had stood up and was coming towards him. 'Can ah help ye, laddie?' The soft Scots accent emphasised the hush of this place. He gnawed at his lip. He had no right to waste this man's time.

'It's nothing,' he blurted.

The man was looking at him with the eye of the experienced. 'Ye think ye're tubercular then. Hold on a minute.' Drawing Matthew into the outbuilding with him, he began fishing into a box nearby, drawing out a stethoscope, home-made from rubber tubing and the handles of a metal filing cabinet he'd probably come across at some time. 'Let's have a listen.'

Submitting himself to the examination Matthew breathed, coughed, uttered thirty-three when told to. The stethoscope was put slowly away. When the man looked back at him, his smile was fixed, too reassuring by far.

'Ye was reet to come here. But it's no' too bad. In a cool dry climate, why, it cud be cured in three months, Ah'd say.'

But the look on the man's face told its story. In a cool dry climate with good food and rest, of course recovery would be certain. Here, in this humid heat, watery rice for fare, working without respite, it was a death sentence as surely as if he stood before a firing squad.

These three years he had stared at death. Now it had arrived. He nodded casually at the advice to take it easy. 'At least I know where I stand,' he murmured and received a short nod. As he left, an insane notion went through his head. Why wait for death? Why not go out in a blaze of glory, a heroic act of sabotage, take a few of those sons of Nippon with him? But he knew he would do no such thing. Like those who had gone before him, like Bob Howlett, he would await his time, quietly, patiently, reluctant to make a fuss, and carrying Susan's image in his head, would silently say goodbye to her and hope to find courage and a small semblance of dignity when his time came.

'Ain't no good, the bloody thing's had it.'

He and another man named Derek gazed down at the now silent wireless that had crackled itself to its death. From now on they could receive no news of the outside world, no heartening snippets about Germany herself being overrun by the Allies.

'No chance getting hold of another valve?' It was a valve that had gone. It might as well have been the whole set for all that could be done.

Derek shook his head viciously. 'Just when something good came over. Something about the Fourteenth Army fighting around Mandalay. Mandalay's only just up country. Didn't you hear it?'

The sound had been so faint, Matthew hadn't heard. Within days, however, rumours were going around. And the Japs were looking decidedly jumpy. Perhaps Derek had heard right. But everyone had grown concerned by their captors' attitude. If rumours were correct and their liberators not far away, what would the Japs do?

'Don't look too good,' Harry said. 'They're sayin' if the Fourteenth Army do make it to Rangoon, the Japs'll start usin' us for sandbags.'

'If that's the case,' Matthew said grimly, 'I'd sooner be shot running than being a shield for some . . .'

The rest of his words were drowned in a fit of coughing from which Harry moved hastily away. But it didn't matter. He now had hope to cling to and his spirits lifted of their own accord.

May, the monsoon yet to begin, the weather still as sweet as any tropical climate allowed, Matthew came awake from a sleep already disturbed by the bouts of sweating peculiar to his condition and a wonderful dream about Susan to a hand shaking his shoulders. Phil was standing over him, all his worldly goods draped about his waist like tarnished charms on an old bracelet. Above it all the normally doleful hatchet face looked grim.

'Sorry t' disturb your sleep, Matt. But us lot 're movin' on.'

The Japs had been growing more and more jittery of late, even their interest in forcing their prisoners to work all hours dropping off. The air was still full of rumours, all of which the prisoners believed purely because they needed to feel that soon they must be released by the fabled oncoming Fourteenth Army. Now all the rumours suddenly took substance as Phil went on.

'They say your blokes're just up the road. Nips're movin' out. Taking all us *healthy* buggers with 'em. To Moulmein ready for shipment to Japan. You cripples are stayin' behind.'

It was meant to be witty but the grin was one of sick disappointment. From the courtyard, came the bellow of the retreating Japanese assembling their 'fit' prisoners.

'S'long then, sport. Take care of y'self. Yuh gonna make it y'know. Bet y'shirt on it.' The grin widened determinedly, the first time Matthew ever remembered Phil smiling without it being a sneer. 'Send yuh a postcard from Sydney one day.'

Going to the now wide-open door of his wing of cells Matthew watched the long gangling figure, deprived of freedom that was nearly his, shoulders hunched in despondency, go off to join the men assembled. He'd never liked Phil all that much but now it felt he was saying farewell to a comrade in a chain of comrades to whom he'd said farewell, one way or another. He should have been feeling elated by the news he'd been given. Instead he felt he wanted to cry. In fact, he was looking at this gangling bundle of misery through a mist and one of his cheeks was being dampened by a thin rivulet.

He forgave himself the tears; TB made a man over-
emotional. But in his way, Phil had been close to him,
perhaps by his very dolefulness. Watching him go,
Matthew thought of all those he'd known, some closer
than others: little Taffy Thomas, the endearingly libidinous
Welshman blown apart in the retreat to the Sittang River;
Bob Howlett, the gentle man who had succoured him on
that long march to Rangoon, himself dying alone; another,
Colin Pardoe, a religious man of simple faith who had
dragged him back to sanity after Bob's ignominious death
– where he was now God only knew, might even be sitting
at His feet right now for all Matthew could tell what had
happened to him. There had been others, and Harry Hope
was still here, but one by one they had all gone. Now he
felt only utter loneliness as Phil, the man of misery, turned
and waved for the last time.

Dawn broke grey and heavy, announcing the coming
monsoon season. The sick awoke to find the prison
gates standing open, the guardhouse deserted – a faintly
bewildering experience after so long close-confined.

Matthew and a few others wandered through them just
to savour the sensation of this new freedom. They found
a note in English nailed to one of the gateposts: YOU ARE
FREE TO MOVE AS YOU WISH. FOOD AND MEDICAL SUPPLIES
HAVE BEEN LEFT FOR YOU. THE BRITISH WILL SOON BE
HERE, YOU MAY WAIT FOR THEM OR GO TO MEET THEM AS
YOU CHOOSE.

Thus, as the British had fled Rangoon three years earlier,
so the Japanese, who'd scorned them for their cowardice,
had likewise fled before the conquerors. The wheel had

turned full circle. Slowly. But it had turned. He was going home, home to Susan. How she must have wept over him, worried herself silly over his well-being, how lonely she must have been.

And himself? The years spent struggling to survive yet seeing death at every turn waiting to pick him up, were over. Death had been waiting for him to thumb a lift from all the misery and degradation that had almost sucked him down into its depths. Thank God he had resisted that dark presence, even through the worst of times. It was over. It hardly seemed true that soon he'd be going home, picking up the threads of his life.

He felt all in, very near to tears at the enormity of this moment as he stood in the emerging sunlight with all the others waiting for their liberators to appear down that road. When they did he would show them that his head had not been bowed, that his spirit had remained strong, had endured. He would throw them a cheeky wave, perhaps even chuck up a smart salute, and not show the true emotions that were ruling inside him. His throat ached from the effort.

All the good intentions. When the first well-clad, sturdy, full-cheeked soldier came marching up to the gaol gates, he could only stand there staring at the health of the man, who smiled at him with such pity in his expression that Matthew found himself stumbling towards him. And as the soldier held out a hand to him, he laid his emaciated arms about the man's neck and sobbed.

Chapter 24

Matilda was not an easy child. Lilian, with recollections of her own, had been taken by surprise. Her little hands were in everything. She was so quick, and it was all her grandmother could do to run after her, those sturdy little legs going like pistons as she found her feet.

It had taken a while to find them, left as she had been in her cot for days on end where she could come to no harm, Susan had said, from the stairs which she could have fallen down, the gas ring from which she could have pulled a kettle of water over herself, the sharp corners in the room. Excuses. Children came to know these dangers by having an alert parent watching them. No, the real reason was that vile man Crawley who didn't want a child that wasn't his hanging around.

Emma Crawley had taken their boys with her to stay with her sister in Valance Road a couple of streets away so that the boys hadn't had to change schools or anything. And of course, in the quieter house, the cries of Susan's baby to be given more freedom had disrupted his enjoyment with his mistress when he was home.

Let free in her grandmother's large airy house, the child found her feet. Five months later and still she was wearing out her indulgent grandparents.

'She's as energetic and high-spirited as Matthew was,' she said to Leonard one night, once the child finally fell asleep after lying wide-awake and bored in the drawn-out daylight of long May evenings, taking up time they would have preferred to have to themselves.

Leonard looked up from his *Evening Star.* 'We should have known what we were taking on. Do you regret it, Lilian?'

'No, I don't,' she answered emphatically, picking up the embroidery she was doing on a dress for Matilda – when she had the time. 'All I dream is for her father to come home and see the pretty little daughter he has. That's worth all the trials and tribulations we've undergone in taking Matilda on.'

She fell silent, bending her head to the rosebud she was fashioning on the front of the cotton garment. It had been a cream skirt of hers. Now it was a dress, needing just this sprinkling of rosebuds to lift its plain colour. Leonard went back to reading his paper.

A quietness descended on them both; it brought thoughts drifting through Lilian's mind as she worked. The war in Europe was over, Hitler dead by suicide. He had deserved a far worse death. Mussolini too was dead, his body afterwards hung by its feet from a lamppost by a mob, those he'd once ruled as dictator, his face kicked in. Lilian shuddered. That should have happened to Hitler too. The ghastly pictures in the papers revealed the horror of those terrible concentration camps. And poor President Roosevelt, a natural death, but a sad, sad loss.

Now there was peace, but not everywhere. The news-papers, when they weren't reporting about the Nuremberg Trials, now concentrated on the Far East and what the Japanese regime was really like. A statement made in January by Anthony Eden in the House of Commons had described the fearful treatment of prisoners by the Japanese, and later, a Japanese prison ship transporting prisoners of war to Japan, had been sunk. The state of the surviving captives showed them to be in the most appalling state.

What then of Matthew? He could easily have been on that ship, one of those who had not survived. No news, never any news. The war in Europe was over, but they might still find that their son had died perhaps a year ago or more.

Holding her baby in her arms, Susan went to answer the knock on the door. She was not really concerned who stood there, except that whoever it was had interrupted her quiet afternoon nap. Trevor, a good baby, unlike Mattie, slept in the afternoon, allowing her to do likewise until Geoff came home. Since the war had finished he'd applied for a transfer nearer home to be with her more, and now worked at a Gas Board office in London. Wonderful. She saw him every night. Well, almost, because some evenings he went round to see his sons. She hated those evenings.

Casually she opened the door, then gasped. Mr and Mrs Ward stood there with Mattie between them, Mrs Ward holding the child's hand in her usual iron grip. Mattie, now nearly three years old, looked happy, her small face animated at seeing the mother she seldom saw these days, but the look on the faces of her grandparents suggested they had received bad news. Susan's mind flew to Mattie with a stab of dismay. Had they brought her back? What the hell was she going to do with her? She had Trevor now. How could she deal with two children?

'What's the matter?' she blurted, hitching Trevor to a less weighty position in her arms. 'What's she done?' She had to have done something awful for them to look like this. Not angry; strange, strained.

'It isn't Matilda,' Mrs Ward began, but Mr Ward cut in. 'We've had news of Matthew,' he said.

Another stab of dismay. If they'd had news that he was dead, she'd be sorry, thinking back to that glorious time they had spent together making love on Beacon Hill, then their wedding day and the little love nest he had found. She saw again the cramped little room with the sunshine coming through the window lighting everything golden. The cosy silence they had shared, the way he had so masterfully commanded her to make love to him, laughing; the love they had made. They had been such wonderful days, but so brief. So long ago. A blur, a photograph, a faded photograph.

And what if the news was that he was alive . . . She tightened her lips, all the complications it would entail filling her head. Did she love him after all this time? She tried in those few seconds to feel what she once had for him. But it wasn't there, only fond memories that could have been those of someone other than her, someone not her any more, totally different.

And what of Geoffrey? She recalled those twinges of excitement when Matthew had talked of the trust made for him, enough to buy a house, live comfortably. His father of course had a shop, so there was money there too. But Geoff had a house, here. She felt comfortable in it. She could imagine the home Matthew would make for them. His mother would constantly be popping in, criticising this wasn't right and that wasn't right, looking askance at her for not keeping the place spick and span and sparkling. She almost shuddered at the thought, knew immediately, staring from one to the other of his parents, that if he was alive she'd still have to choose Geoffrey, comfortable, dependable Geoffrey, who treated her like a goddess, and no one to interfere in what they said or did.

She became aware that Mr Ward was saying something to her which she hadn't caught and had to beg his pardon to ask what it was he'd said.

He looked irritated. 'I said . . . Look, Susan, may we come in. I can't stand here on the doorstep explaining news as important as this.'

Automatically she stepped back, allowing them inside. She'd had fish and chips for dinner (she'd get Geoff's tonight when he came home) and the smell of it hung in the house – she knew it did by the offended twitch of Mrs Ward's nose, though she said nothing.

They followed her into the still-cavernous front room, no longer with the old blackout frames stuck in the corner. Letting the two sit on the huge sofa, she positioned herself on one of the upright chairs, laying Trevor in one of the armchairs where he wouldn't roll off while Mattie went exploring the room.

'I'm sorry I wasn't quite listening when you were

speaking,' she said looking at Mr Ward, but it was his wife who reacted with a disapproving sniff.

'I would have thought you'd at least be attentive seeing that it concerns your husband.'

Mr Ward raised a mollifying hand. 'I said, Susan, that we'd had good news of our son, your husband. He's still your husband, Susan.'

'Yes, I know.' It sounded fatuous, but he'd said it with such distaste for what she supposed he saw as her carrying-on behind Matthew's back. What did he know of how she felt? No one could turn love on and off like a blessed tap.

'Our news,' he continued, 'if it's worth anything to you now, is that Matthew has been released.'

Susan stared. 'But the war out there's not over yet.'

'You *may* have read,' put in Mrs Ward, her tone intimating that Susan's reading power was limited to say the least, 'that the Fourteenth Army recaptured Burma some weeks ago.' Even so excitement rang in her voice. 'They found Matthew there.'

Responding more to her own churning of feelings than the news itself, Susan wasn't sure how to react. To give herself time to analyse how she felt about all this, she merely said, 'Oh.'

Mrs Ward's eyebrows shot up into her forehead, her controlled joy smothered instantly by exasperation. 'Aren't you going to enquire how he is? Aren't you interested?'

'I'm glad he's safe,' Susan offered automatically, taking it that was what she was expected to say. Uppermost in her mind, however, now she'd had time to sort out her reactions, were the complications this news brought. She saw a line of legal wrangles, divorce courts, three years at least being fettered to a man she'd all but forgotten, never again to feel at ease with her Geoffrey without her husband's mother breathing down her neck. She would be marked as the guilty party. She was the guilty party, true, but how can anyone turn aside natural feelings, the way she felt about Geoffrey? A tiny place in her mind cried, why couldn't he have died, a voice she brushed aside the instant it spoke, shuddering that she could even harbour such an evil thought. She wouldn't wish that on Matthew, on anyone, for a million pounds.

In the nurses' home Jenny opened her mother's letter. The hospital overlooking the Blackmoor Vale had a time-less charm; with its smooth grey stone over which this hot, sunny June day seemed to slide like treacle left the interior cool, placid and airy. The windows stood wide open to the fresh breezes essential for those with half a chance of recovery; tuberculosis was a known killer, fresh air, rest, good food were all they could hope for. There was talk of some drug called streptomycin; the press had called it a miracle cure, promising to make TB a thing of the past, but it was still in its experimental stage. The papers hadn't referred to it again, the headlines bowing out to more important political news. The first peacetime general election was set for the fifth of July. Small things like reporting work on a wonder drug took second place. What a glory if it could be used on the patients she cared for. It was heartbreaking to see those glowing-faced young men, the deceptive transparent bloom a cruel symptom of the disease, slip away. Heartbreaking when they died so young, having come through all the perils of war. It was only when Jenny opened her mother's letter, the usual two closely written pages relaying all the home gossip, that the disease suddenly became a personal thing. Halfway down the letter, her eyes paused over the next words:

> . . . You remember Matthew Ward, don't you? He was a prisoner of war and they lost trace of him. Well, they've heard from him at last.

Jenny's heart leapt inside her chest, continuing with a thumping of joy and anticipation as she skipped the observations on how it couldn't have been jolly for them, everyone celebrating VE Day, the other war still going on.

> Matthew's parents had no idea he was in Rangoon. He could have been anywhere. It must have been absolutely marvellous, our boys recapturing Burma like that. Mrs Ward's been telling the whole street about it. He's in hospital in Ceylon. They think he's got TB. Isn't that dreadful, after coming through all he's been through . . .

There was more about the bits she'd found out about Matthew's wife. And a part that made Jenny go suddenly cold with anger. Hearing of his release, the girl had written to him telling him about the man she was living with.

What an awful thing to do. Some people can be so
cruel. How he must feel I just don't know. How could
anyone do such a thing? She should at least have
waited until he came home, I would have thought.
But I gather she doesn't have much sense, or so Mrs
Ward once said, a long time ago now. But . . .

Jenny lifted her eyes from the page of neat, tight little
writing, her head a hotchpotch of thoughts, silent prayers
touching her lips in a gush of thanks for his safety, of
pleading for his health, of joy, of hope for him to be sent
back to England very soon and for her to see him again,
and the opportunity for her to be at his side should he need
someone, anyone.

Quickly she scanned the rest of her mother's letter but
there was nothing more about Matthew. He just constituted
a passing bit of information among all the other snippets
her mother had written, the letter closing with a hope that
Jenny could be allowed a holiday soon so she could get
home.

I don't know why you want to work so far away. The
war is over and there are adequate hospitals around
here. But if you must work with TB patients, and I
hope to God you don't catch it, tuberculosis is so
infectious but I expect you're immune by now, we've
one just the other side of the park where you first
went to get a job, do you remember? You could find
a place there . . .

Yes, she could. But not yet. First she'd set about making enquiries about Matthew, find out where they would send him once in England. A lot of the boys from that area came here after landing, because it was convenient from Southampton. If she could ask the right people.

Whether her efforts had anything to do with it, there was no way of finding out; a few replies came from different quarters saying it would be looked into in due course but no one could give any promises. Her case, she suspected, was put aside, for the months had gone by and she'd heard no more.

Two weeks earlier the dropping of the atomic bombs on Hiroshima and Nagasaki had brought about Japan's capitulation. Great Britain celebrated VJ Day but, less energetically than VE Day, having done it all once. Her mother's letters no longer mentioned Matthew or his family. Jenny made her way across to the TB wing, under a clearing September dawn which promised to become a fine day after twelve hours of rain, to relieve Staff Nurse Merriman from night duty.

Merriman leaned back on her chair, flexing her stiff shoulder muscles, and yawned widely.

'Ooh-ahh . . . What's it like outside?'

'Beautiful. It's going to be a fine day. What sort of night has it been?'

'Pretty quiet,' came the answer. Merriman was already gathering up her bits and pieces. 'Corporal Douglas haemorrhaged and got a bit panicky. Otherwise all quiet.'

The wards were coming alive. Strident voices of nurses

were urging patients not to fall back to sleep after having been aroused at five thirty with tea and wash basins. The clang of bedpans resounded from the sluice, and the corridors echoed to the rattle of crockery-laden trolleys bringing the breakfasts. A nurse going off duty hurried in to deposit an admission file on the desk, gave the incoming sister a brief smile, grabbed her cape off the peg behind the door and departed.

'Oh yes,' said Merriman, pushing the notes across to Jenny. 'I meant to tell you, Admission phoned a few moments ago. He's probably on his way up now. Everything's ready for him, so there's nothing to do.'

Jenny laughed. 'Thanks.'

She took the cup of tea handed to her by a skinny first-year nurse who surveyed Merriman with tired, hopeful eyes.

'Is it all right for me to go off now, please, Staff?'

Merriman was in an authoritative mood, still in charge for the while. 'If you've left the sluices clean, yes.'

'Thank you, Miss Merriman.'

'And charted the temperatures?'

'Yes, Miss Merriman.'

'Is the kitchen tidy?'

The girl nodded vigorously. 'Can Harvey go as well, Miss Merriman?'

'If she has finished everything.'

'Oh, she has. Thank you, Miss Merriman.'

As the girl's flat heels clicked urgently away along the corridor to be joined by Harvey's, Merriman sighed and stood up. 'Time I was off too. I need my bed. And I want to wash my hair.' She made a stack of her notes on the desk, laying the admission file on top. 'There, over to you.'

The day staff were coming in, chattering. Jenny heard Staff Nurse Reid's sharp tones reminding them who and where they were. The chattering ceased abruptly. Jenny reached for the admission folder as Reid burst in, her voice querulous.

'You'd think this was a four-ale bar, not a hospital. To hear those girls, you'd never guess there were sick people here.'

Jenny's gaze was fixed on the now-open folder. She hadn't heard what Reid was saying. Reid leaned over her shoulder to see. 'Oh, no, not an admission this early in the morning. I'll take it.'

The file was snatched up from under Jenny's eyes. 'Why can't they come at a convenient time? And we've a probationer coming on the ward today. All our time will be taken up telling her what to do.'

A porter popped his head around the door, his attitude full of self-importance. 'Where d'yuh want this one?'

'I'll deal with it,' Reid said briskly and clutching the folder waved the porter on, leaving Jenny staring into space. After all those letters she had written, all those enquiries, entreaties. They had paid off. Unbelievable. Quite unbelievable. If she hadn't been on duty she'd have burst into tears.

At first she thought she must have been mistaken, misread the file in that short time before Reid had snatched it so imperiously from under her hand. For a moment it was impossible to associate this patient with the man she had once known, the young man full of laughter and abrasive wit, the khaki-clad soldier she last remembered, so certain of where he was going, carrying himself with all the zest of life.

This man, propped up with pillows, bore no resemblance to that one. Her practised eye already noted that he did not yet have the high colour that went with his disease, which hadn't yet secured such a hard grip on him as it had done on others. It was possible that with care and attention he'd overcome it. But of the man himself? The eyes, deep in their sockets, looked out not on a sunny ward but back in time to an existence that had all but destroyed him as it had so many thousands whose lives he had shared. Everyone now knew of the Burma Railway, the prison ships, the conditions of men incarcerated in jails throughout the Far East, the ghastly massacre of men and women in hospitals as they lay sick and wounded. Some, if not all of that, men like this one must have seen, struggling single-minded to survive. Here was such a man. It glowed from his eyes and Jenny shuddered.

It was only after a moment or so that a slight movement of his head touched her as singularly familiar, at first vague but growing stronger so that all at once she wondered why she hadn't been able to recognise him instantly. Gaunt, cheeks still sunken from years of starvation, eyes that dwelled on the past, it was nevertheless Matthew.

As she spoke his name he looked at her, in those few short seconds his regard blank as hers had been: puzzled, uncertain, trying to pinpoint a memory. A spark of recognition lit up his dark eyes, coupled with disbelief.

'Jenny?'

She tried to laugh. 'Jenny Ross. Sister J. Ross, Q.A.I.M.S.'

It was a poor joke and she felt immediately ashamed, seeing the smile trying to reach his eyes, ridden as they were by dark ghosts. Her own eyes filled with sudden tears she tried hard to keep from showing. The last thing a man wanted was what would appear as a superficial show of sympathy, the giver with no idea what it had been like for him.

Instead, she said simply, 'I'm glad to see you, Matthew.'

'Oh, Jenny.' With a cry from the heart, that bond they'd once known formed itself anew, the way it had done when the promise stretching before them had been bright upon a horizon they hadn't then known concealed the shadows of what was to come. It hadn't been a bond of love then, and now it was more a renewing of a friendship that had flourished briefly only to be interrupted by circumstance. But now he was here, she'd nurse him back to health and for her, for the time being, it was enough.

Thank God the disease was proving less advanced than she'd first feared. Despite the conditions under which he'd lived these last three years he'd retained a strong enough constitution to fight it in its early stages.

For that at least, Jenny offered up prayers of thanks. If only his state of mind showed as much promise. He'd sit in the hospital grounds, wrapped up with a coat against the stiff, health-giving breezes from the Blackmoor Vale which patients were expected to endure daily, staring ahead, seldom glancing around him as people normally do. If she approached him, he'd tense, his gaze averted. Asked how he was – a nurse's question after all – his reply would come back in a monotone. He offered no conversation, no observation of his own, leaving her to maybe lift the wrist, feel the pulse, play the nurse's role. Should she try to further her concern for him she'd inevitably be fobbed off with a terse reply that nothing was the matter and why should there be?

At these times Jenny would feel a blaze of anger against Susan Ward, for it could only be she who was the cause of such anguish. Of course some of his attitude stemmed from what he'd endured as a prisoner of war. But with a loyal woman at his side he'd have surmounted it in time. His wilful, selfish wife had let him down – if her mother had been right, and no reason why she shouldn't be. Susan's letter to him had revealed her adultery while he'd been away and helpless to do anything about it. After all he'd been through, to come home and hear something like that! Worse, he never spoke about it and Jenny felt powerless to alter the situation. Even as she came up to him now, she knew there would be no help she could give him.

To think she'd offered the girl friendship. Had she known what she was like, she'd have had nothing to do with her. Reaching Matthew's side, she found herself hating Susan as she'd never hated anyone in her life before.

As Jenny had anticipated, he did not look up at her as she too let her gaze wander to the trees on the horizon, their billowing of full-leafed heads darkened by distance against the sky with its small lamb-clouds marching in procession across the azure expanse. Matthew had said nothing and she tried not to see herself as an intrusion as he continued to ignore her, his hands curled into tight fists against the arm supports of the hospital Bath chair in which he sat. Yet she couldn't walk away, not with the torment she could see in the tightness around his mouth, the fine brows drawn together, the eyes seeing nothing but what must be seething inside his head.

Unbidden, she sank down on the small bench beside him. This time she didn't go through the motions of taking his wrist ineffectually to feel the pulse. He would know it as only a ruse. Nor did she speak. Making smalltalk would only reap a sarcastic response and send her away hating herself for having stupidly intruded. The time spun itself out, slowly, the silence between them heightening the faint hum of traffic on the road, the musical trill of a nearby thrush, the soft twitter of a myriad other birds in the grounds, the distant intermittent conversation of people further off, enlarging the silence between them as though they sat within a vacuum. When he did speak, low as his voice was, Jenny's nerves jangled sharply although her body itself did not move.

'I'm trapped here,' was all he said. She remained silent, encouraged for a hopeful moment or two, but he didn't appear to want to say anything more, and her hopefulness died.

She reached out and laid a hand on his clenched one, letting it lie there. He didn't draw away as she had half expected. The fist remained there, unmoving beneath hers, the warmth of the skin penetrating hers, her nurse's enquiring mind immediately registering that he might be feverish. A little maybe, nothing to be concerned by; temperature could go up and down. It was expected, so long as it did not flare. She did note something else, that the fist began slightly to relax. He moved his head a fraction and let his gaze fall on to her consoling hand. Did it seem to be a consoling hand to him?

A nurse's voice nearby startled them both. Then the nurse and her charge moved on, the voice fading. Jenny followed their departure with her eyes, so it was a second or two before she became aware of Matthew speaking, of what he was saying, his voice halting and so low as to be hardly audible except for the sibilant sounds.

'Places like that – you need someone. Something. To cling to. In my head. She was in my head. Fever. Does weird things to you. But she *was* real. Thinking of me. Far away. Thinking of me.'

He was talking about Susan. 'But for her I'd have gone under. She kept me going. Once – a mouth full of ulcers – vitamin deficiency – couldn't eat . . .' There came a low mirthless chuckle. 'Starving, and I couldn't eat . . . She kept me going. In my head. And all the time I didn't know. Had no idea she was . . .'

He broke off this time with an intake of breath that sounded more like a sob caught in his throat.

Jenny had said nothing, letting him talk. She hadn't expected this. His need to talk had come out of nowhere, unprompted, unless it had been the way she had lain her hand on his. But she'd done that before only to have him snatch his hand away. There was no reason for her to congratulate herself, nor did she try to probe what had prompted him. She merely sat saying nothing, letting him get it all out of himself, or praying that he would.

He hadn't looked at her once. He seemed to be trying to fight the emptiness that was consuming him, but she was glad he hadn't given way to tears which she knew instinctively would have destroyed his dignity in his own mind. All she could do as he lapsed into silence was to wait and listen if he chose to say more, and if he didn't then she must let it go at that and keep her platitudes to herself. But the emptiness he nursed proved too strong for him. Startling her, he suddenly pulled his hand from under hers and she thought he was about to reject her. Instead, he took her hand and lifted it to his forehead as though in dire need of her comfort. No sound came from him, though she could feel his silent grief as a faint vibration on her arm. When again he spoke, the words were muffled by the cuff of her uniform. 'I love her, Jenny. I should hate her. But I can't.'

Jenny nodded, stifling emotions of her own. The comfort she'd thought he sought from her was merely what he would have sought from anyone. He still loved Susan.

Chapter 25

People were putting the war years behind them; forgetting was perhaps another matter. Rationing still gripped hard, so Christmas had still been frugal, but it had felt more relaxed than for six years. New Year 1946, this first full year of peace, held out fresh promise for the future.

Spring, welcomed in with open arms, saw hoardings going up around bombed areas, cranes being ferried in to shift the rubble in preparation for rebuilding. Soon, the damage covered over with new buildings, no one who hadn't been here would know there had been any. The old raw fear for one's life was giving way to all the petty concerns of peacetime – politics, nuisance neighbours, making ends meet, keeping children clean. Demobbed men, this time in orderly fashion unlike the mad release of the First World War, were going back to old jobs to demand the sort of wages enjoyed by those essential workers who'd been kept out of the forces. For some the way ahead looked rosy. For those still nursing grief, remembering loved ones never to return, it hardly glimmered.

Watching Matthew's slow progress, Jenny knew it wasn't glowing for him either. He had at last been told the whole truth about Susan by his well-meaning parents: how she'd walked out of the house while heavily pregnant, not a word of warning, not a word of thanks for all they'd done for her; how she had treated them when they'd found where she was living, was still living (they told him the address); the affair she'd had, still ongoing, with her landlady's husband, Geoffrey Crawley; Mrs Crawley finally leaving him; how distant and rude Susan had been to them when they had called on her to persuade her to go back home with them; how they had found her and this Crawley fellow living together, but how without a qualm she had let them take her daughter – Matthew's daughter – away from her, the child in a terrible neglected state, as though she had no care or love for Matilda at all; how not once from that day to this had Susan asked after her. (They brought photos of Matilda, now a bonny three-year-old, but they hadn't brought her in person, for fear of infection.)

He had listened to it all without comment, but afterwards Jenny had found him abstracted and unresponsive, his expression frozen, his lips a tight white line in his narrow, set face. Jenny had wondered if now had been the best time to tell him everything. Of course he would have had to know at some time, would have known soon enough once he went home. The drug Streptomycin was now helping to save sufferers from the old resort to surgery. Matthew had escaped the trauma of the knife, and was declared fit to go home and attend checkups at a local hospital. But how would he face going home, knowing what he did? Not only from his parents but from Susan herself. She had not once visited him or written to him, but she did that Christmas.

It was just after Christmas when Jenny came upon him asleep on his bed one cold afternoon. The windows as ever stayed open to admit draughts of vital fresh air against which patients must huddle under blankets and wool cardigans.

For a moment Jenny allowed herself the luxury, or perhaps the imposition, of watching him asleep, an intrusion upon his privacy she knew, but he looked so peaceful that she needed to take more than a brief glance at him. It was then she noted that his sleep wasn't as peaceful as it first appeared. Nothing specific, just something about the expression, even with his eyes closed, caught her attention and made her frown.

Her gaze travelled to the hand lying limp above the coverlet where she saw that his fingers, that had been curled about a sheet of notepaper, had loosened their hold. Without touching the letter she bent forward, conscious of the cruelty of her intrusion into an unsuspecting person's privacy, to read what she could see of it, a few words only. But they were enough. In fact one word had been enough: divorce. The childish handwriting was that of Susan.

Compressing her lips to stem the seething anger that rose up in her, she could only hurry away, knowing there was nothing she could do to help him. She could not know, not until he told her, and he would not do that. He would keep his pain to himself as he'd learned to do all through his three hard years of suffering while Susan, the treacherous little bitch, had been having a good time with some other man.

*

All this time, Jenny felt instinctively that her presence had been a bolster for him; she sensed that he clung to her as a friend who would hold his hand should he need it. Now he was leaving. Who would he have to hold his hand against the onslaught of Susan's infidelity? Not his mother, who meant well but who found it impossible to unbend. His father? Perhaps. What he needed was someone who loved him as she loved him. Yet what right had she to presume that her silent love, which would always be there for him although he wasn't aware of it, was what he needed?

On the day of his leaving, he took her hand, grinned up into her face and said, in the same way as he had once told her she would be one of the nicer of his memories, 'I'll miss you, Jenny. Keep in touch.'

He had needed her throughout his time here, sometimes desperately. But love? There were all kinds of love. Maybe he did feel something towards her, something deeper than just friendship, and perhaps such a relationship could grow into something more meaningful given time, but it would never be what people called being in love. And for all Susan had done to him, Jenny knew he still loved her with a desperation that pulled him apart.

So she smiled at him as he got into his parents' car, and said with cheery encouragement, 'Of course I'll keep in touch.'

Mrs Ward smiled her wintry smile at her and nodded her gratitude for all the nursing she had given Matthew, and Jenny, returning the acknowledgement, knew the woman was grateful, although her nature was unable to allow her to express how she really felt.

Mr Ward, coming round the car to take Jenny's hand, was more open and forthcoming. 'He wrote, you know, to tell us all about you. You mean more to him than I think even he realises. You've been a tower of strength to him and I don't think he'd have got this far, little as it is, but for you. I wish . . .' He paused and his eyes studied hers. 'I wish you and he . . .'

Jenny knew what he was trying to say but felt it right that he shouldn't be urged to further it. She broke in quickly. 'Matthew and I are very good friends, Mr Ward. Have always been that. He needs friends.'

'Yes, of course.' The relief that he hadn't had to say what was on his mind was apparent, that and a depth of understanding between them in the significant way he added before going back round to the driver's side of the car, 'Don't lose touch with us, Jenny.'

Watching them go, Matthew appearing wretched and somehow defeated, looking neither right nor left, not even waving to her, she thought about his father's parting words. 'Don't lose touch.' An ordinary saying, but expressed so earnestly that she knew it carried a totally different meaning to the normally light-hearted one. Yet her heart did not rise with hope. It was up to Matthew, not his father, how far their friendship progressed, and Matthew would never let go of Susan. His love for her would forever haunt him, fill his heart, and Jenny Ross would have no chance to squeeze into whatever minute portion of his heart might be left free.

Matthew's going was a signal for her to leave the QAs.

She had no more use for them, nor they for her. But it was impossible to see herself as leaving the profession. The mere idea of going back into office work after all she had experienced made her feel like a deflated balloon. She would stay a nurse to the end of her working life. She'd become a civilian nurse. Ignoring the vision of the years stretching on, while she, unmarried, dedicated herself to moving steadily up the ladder one day to become a matron, she applied for a post of nursing sister at the London Chest Hospital, and got it. That she was back near to Matthew's home and would still see him from time to time, she chose to ignore. She had come back for her mother's sake and nothing else. Except for her mother she might possibly have applied for a place elsewhere in any of the distant counties, pastures new, Matthew a closed book. This she told herself, almost convincing herself that he had nothing at all to do with her return home.

But it was good to be home again, with her mother cooking for her in the evenings, seeing the pleasure and contentment in her face. It was good to spend her days off with her, pick up where she'd left off. But that part of it wasn't quite true. The threads of that old life before the war had been well and truly cut. The friends she had known had gone their own ways: Matthew's sister Louise had married and gone to Canada; Jean Summerfield's people were still living wherever they'd gone to (she could no longer recall where it was) and Jean no doubt was married by now; Freddy and Eileen Perry, with their two children, lived in Romford, Essex – she had their address but probably wouldn't bother writing to them; Dennis Cox, poor Dennis, was dead . . . she felt sad for a young life lost, so many young lives lost. But for the war she might have ended up marrying Dennis, settled down to being the wife of a successful solicitor, perhaps with one or two children, attending social events. But there *had* been a war and it *had* altered all their lives, their once carefree, happy lives. Now this was her life and she must settle for that.

'It's nice knowing I don't have to be sent anywhere and everywhere,' she told her mother who, at last convinced that her daughter would be home almost as regularly as if she had gone back to office work, was happily setting the table for this, their first evening meal together for some considerable time. 'Though all the friends I used to know around here are all gone now.'

'There's still the church, dear. You might find someone there.'

'I think I've got a bit old for that, Mumsy.'

Her mother shrugged as they sat themselves down to the table. 'Well, I expect you'll soon make new ones, dear. Perhaps from the hospital. And there's still young Matthew Ward across the road. Now he's home again, I expect he'll be attending there for check-ups. It's the nearest place, easy for him to get to. You'll probably see him now and again.'

Blithely she prattled on this new tack, how ill he was looking, as she began on the stew she'd prepared. 'To think how he once was, poor dear.'

Jenny too remembered.

She had an old photo somewhere around the house of them all, her old friends, all of them happy and unsuspecting of what lay ahead, snapped in the act of fits of laughter. She remembered it being taken by Louise, then a girl of sixteen. Matthew had made a quip in his usual mocking manner: 'Look at her, worst photographer this side of Lower Wallop and west of Katmandu!' Coming unexpectedly, it had them all falling about so that the snap was slightly blurred. It still lay in her dressing-table drawer. He'd been so debonair then, and now looked so thin and ill and haunted.

'His mother looks worried lately,' her mother was saying, chewing on a piece of the precious still-rationed scrag end of lamb. 'For him I suppose, him and his so-called wife. I think I said something about it in one of my letters to you, that they were more or less separated? She really let him down while he was away, poor boy, a prisoner of the Japanese, and nothing he could do about her so far away. His mother looks after their little girl now, you know. That's a comfort to him at least.'

Jenny nodded obligingly as she ate. She had never divulged her secret feelings to her mother, to anyone. She vowed to find an excuse to pop across the road at some time or other and see how he was.

It was with some surprise one bright Sunday afternoon to be welcomed in by his mother on her first tentative visit. Much of what she had always considered the woman's frigid mien melted at the sight of her.

'Of course, my dear, come in,' she said readily. And then, her voice dropping to a whisper, 'He certainly needs someone else's company than just ours. It's hard for him, going nowhere, doing so little. He sits in the garden doing nothing. It was suggested he go to Southend sanatorium for a while. Sea air. Good for his chest. But he won't go. It's a good job we have the park nearby, the air's fresher here than most places in London. Mr Ward thought we should move to the country for his health, but Matthew got himself into such a state about it, we've dropped the idea. He's in the garden.'

All this she relayed as she conducted Jenny along the bright, neat hallway and through the spotless kitchen to where Matthew was sitting in a deckchair on a narrow paved patio which the sun at its summer height could just about touch for a couple of hours.

His head was bent over a photograph but as he looked up at her emerging from the house with his mother he quickly slipped it out of sight between himself and the deckchair fabric, but not before Jenny glimpsed the glossy black and white image of a young woman. That and his reaction to her coming upon him could only mean it was of his wife.

Jenny pretended she hadn't noticed. 'Hope you don't mind me popping in. I just wanted to see how you were.'

He was trying to smile. Watching the effort it was obvious he'd been tormented by the now-hidden photo. Now he must look at this visitor as though nothing had happened, and Jenny felt the weight of guilt at her intrusion, wishing she hadn't so blithely taken it into her head to come over here. His mother having gone back into the house, leaving them to it, she could hardly depart the second she had arrived. Best to brazen it out and make an exit as soon as decently possible.

'See you're taking advantage of the sunshine,' she said brightly. He nodded and she gazed about the long, narrow garden for some inspiration. 'This garden's bigger than ours, but then, your house is larger too. These are nice houses. I see your dad's already taken out the old air-raid shelter. I think ours will stay there permanently if we're not careful, though I suppose in time we'll get a man to take it out for us and grass it over.'

She was talking rubbish, anything to fill the threatening silence.

He was saying nothing. She wondered if he was even listening. What was he thinking? It was hard to tell and she was beginning to feel a virtual idiot standing here talking nonsense about gardens and air-raid shelters.

She stopped, regarding him. What had she come here for? To cheer him up? To give him a pep talk? To pry? All she wanted to do now was say, 'Nice to see you again, Matthew – goodbye,' but she merely stood looking at him, desperately probing her mind for something to say. What else? Glad you are looking better? But he wasn't looking better. He was looking . . . not ill; he had filled out a little from that first time she'd seen him brought into the hospital. No, not exactly ill, but drawn, pulled down, despondency oozing from him because he saw no hope of any future for himself. And didn't she know why? Of course she did, and prayed to be able to put it right for him, without becoming an interfering nuisance. He wouldn't welcome her interference. His pain was private and it was obvious he intended to keep it that way.

So it took her by storm when he said, as though to himself, 'It's her photo. I was looking at her photo.'

She could have said, 'Were you?' and nearly did, but that would have been crass, false innocence. She had seen him, and he knew she had. She could have said, 'Whose photo?' but she knew whose it was, and he knew that of her as well. So she stood silent.

'There's nothing I can do,' he said in the same flat tone.

Now was the time to say something. 'What can I do?' she said simply.

He turned his eyes to her, dark with the grief that was eating him. 'I don't know.' He wasn't telling her to mind her own business, that there was nothing she could do, just that he didn't know.

'If there is anything I can do, Matthew. If you need me. I'll be here.'

She spoke few words now, not that earlier inane chatter. Words that had some meaning, she hoped. She saw relief flow into his eyes, saw him incline his head in a small gesture of acceptance and she knew they would talk again and little by little he would release into her keeping all the suppressed grief and rage and hopelessness that was within him and perhaps in this way she would lighten the burden that at this moment seemed unbearable.

Even now he was on the verge of saying something. She waited while he contemplated what he needed to say. He, who had once been unstoppable with ready quips and digs and careless laughter, must force himself to look at every word, each drowned in a mire of unspeakable memories, having to be wrung from him, and now with an added reluctance after what had been done to him by one who he had thought had stood by him.

'Jenny . . .' he said at last. 'Jenny . . . I have to see her. I've got to talk to her. Somehow. If I could see her . . . There's no one, no one who'll help. They say I . . . I mustn't . . .'

Now he halted altogether, but she knew what he was trying to say. His parents' well-meaning efforts to defend him against the wife who'd caused him such hurt had resulted only in antagonising him more. They were too close in their shared grief to be of any good to him. But could she do any better?

Now wasn't the time to broach it. The least said at this moment . . .

There was movement in the house, the sound of voices, one of them high, childish. Matthew brightened immediately as a small figure came out in a rush. Jenny turned to see a small girl of around three-and-a-half pull up sharp at the sight of her, a stranger, while Jenny, relief surging over her at this timely interruption, smiled down at her. 'Hello.'

Mrs Ward stood behind her granddaughter. 'Matilda, say hello to daddy and Miss Ross.' Jenny caught the coupling of her and Matthew's names, as though she'd have liked to see them as such.

Shyly, Matilda stood her ground, her head dropping as she surveyed Jenny from under a generous dark fringe of hair. She was a beautiful child, softly rounded, sweet-faced, her eyes cornflower-blue, the rest of her hair cascading down behind her small shoulders.

Jenny glanced at Matthew. He was regarding his daughter, his eyes suddenly tender, a faraway look in them. Was he thinking of Susan? Did his daughter look like her?

She turned back to the child. 'And where have you been?' she asked.

No reply was forthcoming and the little rose-red lips began to pout in childish self-consciousness. But her grandfather, who appeared in the doorway, went to her rescue.

'We've been out, haven't we?' he said in an indulgent voice. 'We've been to Epping Forest. I came by some extra petrol so I took her out for the day. Matthew's mother stayed here for Matthew's sake. He didn't want to come along.'

'Not much point, was there?' Matthew's remark was sharp, but his father chose to ignore it, turning his attention to the child, bending towards her encouragingly.

'And what did we see in the woods? We saw squirrels, didn't we?'

'Squiddles,' repeated Matilda, picking up the spirit of it.

'And what else? What else did we see?'

'Squiddles.'

'And? Tell daddy what you saw. And . . . what flies in the air?'

At last she was in full command, embarrassment forgotten. 'We seed some birds and squiddles and . . .' She broke off to twist round to consult her grandfather who mouthed something at her, she in turn working at it. 'Pheasints!' she cried in triumph. 'And lots of sheeps.'

'That's really nice,' Jenny offered, bending down to be rewarded by the girl coming forward to put a small soft hand in hers. 'She's lovely.' Jenny turned to Matthew but his eyes had grown hard, not looking at any of them, so she turned hastily back to his parents, who nodded their wholehearted concurrence.

'She is,' Mrs Ward said, a little sadly. 'And very well behaved.'

'Yes.' More a sound from Matthew than a word, it was weighted with bitter incrimination leaving Jenny wondering if it had been directed at his mother, who would have insisted on good behaviour even from a three-year-old, or at his wife, whom this child obviously took after. Not a bit of Matthew could be seen in her.

'At least in that,' his mother turned on him, 'she takes after you, thank the Lord. And she has your colour hair, and . . .'

'So Susan's hair isn't dark?' he shot back at her, almost viciously. 'She takes after her in everything. *Her* eyes, *her* stature. And who does she take after for tantrums? There's only one. Well-behaved, yes, sometimes, but there are times when even you can't control her. If that's not Susan I don't know what is. Why don't you bloody well admit to it?'

'Oh, Matthew,' his mother's exasperated voice rang out. 'Why can't you put that woman out of your mind? Why must you always bring her up?'

'Because I still love her. You can't see that. All you can see is your own damned righteousness. She was alone. She had no one. I wasn't there. I should have been. Instead I was . . . I was . . . Christ, if you'd only see how it must've been for her. So she's done the dirty on me, found someone else. But you're not helping make it any bloody easier for me.'

Jenny got to her feet awkwardly, an outsider witnessing family dissension. This was a side to Matthew she had never seen. Even all that time ago when he had spoken against his mother's efforts to encourage him to go for a commission at the beginning of the war, it had not been this acrimonious, his hatred of people trying to help, the world itself. It wasn't what he was saying but the way the words were being spat out with such vehemence that was so frightening.

Matilda was looking from one to the other, her pretty face animated with anguish, nearing tears. On impulse, Jenny gathered her to her with one arm around her and the child came readily, huddling against her.

Matthew had got out of his deckchair to stand glaring at his mother, and without thinking Jenny found her voice, directing it at him.

'You're frightening your daughter, Matthew.' It amazed her how calm her voice sounded and he shot an enraged glance at her, instantly modifying it as their eyes met. He took a deep breath, a shuddering sigh, and his posture sagged a little.

'I'm sorry, Jenny, that you should hear all this.' His whole mien seemed to diminish and, appalled, Jenny let go her hold on Matilda and went towards him. He must not be diminished.

'Oh, my dear. Don't. It's not your fault. I started it.'

Of course she hadn't, but it felt like it. He was breathing hard. He began coughing, small, sharp little coughs. He looked all in, had worn down what energy he had; the disease still lurked in him. She put an arm about him, supporting him while she looked at his parents.

'I think he ought to rest,' she ordered, she the nurse in charge, and they, like admonished children, moved back before her as she went with their son into the house.

Once Matthew was installed in bed in his room, she apologised as a formality to his parents for her being here, for being a disruption to their private life. She waved away their insistence that she hadn't been, but she was still in her role of nurse, advising as she saw fit.

'I think he ought to be got to a sanatorium for a while, you know. His mind must rest as well as his body, and it's not being rested here. He's too near his wife. I think he needs a few months away, in spite of what he says.'

It was gratifying to see them nod agreement, but Mrs Ward surprised her on taking her to the door by putting a hand on her arm before opening it.

'You are of course, quite right, my dear.'

Chapter 26

There wasn't a lot he could do about it. Between them all, his parents, his doctors, Jenny Ross, whom he alternately turned to for support and backed away from, he knew that if he wanted to get better he must bow to their superior judgement, submit to being packed off to the sanatorium.

He did need to get better, to be well again to claim Susan back from that bastard who'd tempted her away. Susan was easily led. It wasn't her fault. She had this thing about sick people, but once he got himself back on his feet, all that would disappear.

The sanatorium was bright, two-storeyed, with more windows than walls, and verandas positioned to catch every vestige of sunlight. The grounds had the benefit of sea air to help with the cure, and with one of the mainstays of cure being to keep up the patients' spirits, make them feel at ease with the world, the nursing staff were attentive and cheery. He too was expected to feel at ease with the world, but he wasn't. He was an inconvenience, to be put away. He had no means of getting to Susan from here, for the sanatorium was effectively a prison too. At home he might in time have evaded his mother's eagle eye, boarded a bus for Mile End Road and burst in on Susan in the hope, vain perhaps, of getting her back. Here he could only wait to be declared fit before ever being allowed to escape and be his own man to do as he pleased.

Do as he pleased! That was a laugh. It seemed all his life he'd been in captivity. Home, the Army, prison camps, hospitals; his mother, even Jenny Ross joining the ranks of his keepers. Where had all that free spirit gone he'd dreamed of in his youth? At twenty-eight he felt every bit an old man. There had been such thoughts before the war of one day leaving home to soar free as a bird. He had left, but merely to swap one form of imprisonment for another, and there was no way he would ever be free. Only with Susan had he been free, tasting a tiny morsel, enough to reveal the golden glory of it, before it had all been snatched away.

Stuck here in this place, this morning watching his parents' cautious approach like that of people about to confront a time bomb, he wondered what was the point of all the efforts to make him well while inside memories both wonderful and evil entwined in a form of torture until he could no longer tell them apart. These memories could not be shared with anyone because no one understood what it was like to love and have it snatched away, to be strong and have that snatched away, to ache for beauty and see only misery and privation and degradation and betrayal, to contrast the wife he had loved and trusted with the truth he had come home to face. Only one sure way to be free remained. This he contemplated with strange detachment as he sat watching his parents' progress along the clean, bright ward towards him, and when they had each kissed him and asked how he was, he answered with a sort of perverse wish to witness their horrified reaction, a despondent need to gain their attention.

'Tell the truth, I've just about had enough of everything. What's the point of it all? I'd be better off finishing it and being no more worry to anyone.'

His remark was ignored.

'It's time you started thinking what you're going to do about Susan.' He turned his face away from his mother's probing eyes. 'All this hoping for miracles, it's just ludicrous, Matthew. She wants a divorce and she's not particular how she gets it.'

His eyes remained averted. No point responding when she got on this track, leaping on it the moment she arrived, and Dad putting his oar in as well.

'If you think she'll ever come back now, Matthew, you're just banging your head against a brick wall, son.'

'If she did come back,' his mother's tone sounded righteously adamant, 'I for one wouldn't give her the smell of my dish rag, much less house room . . .'

But she wasn't in love with Susan. At times his chest felt as if it was being torn out. Even his father no longer took his side. Matthew felt totally alienated seeing his father nodding at every word his mother said.

'We've spoken to a solicitor, Matthew. He has written to her on our behalf advising her to get one of her own in this matter, and she's done that now.' All this had been done without once consulting him. 'They both agree that the marriage is unsalvageable. Susan is quite happy to be cited as the guilty party.' She was as eager as that? Something inside Matthew plummeted. 'Apparently this Crawley fellow has no objections to being cited as her lover. His wife is apparently thinking in terms of divorcing him anyway. Pity it all has to take so long, and meantime the solicitor is running up a nice fat fee.'

Was that all they cared about, costs? He kept his face turned away.

'It's up to you, Matthew. How much longer are you going to let things drag on? There's nothing you can do. She's made up her mind, the slut.'

Now he turned. 'Don't say that!'

'I will say that, Matthew. Because that's what she is. How can you feel anything for her after what she's done to you, you a prisoner of war, all you went through, while she enjoyed herself playing fast and loose.'

How could he, even if he wished, tell them what he'd gone through and how it had been Susan alone who had kept him going? He still believed that, fervently, still believed she *had* thought of him, willed him to live. This adultery had come later. It didn't matter what they said, there had been a time, at first, when she had willed him to live, prayed for his safe return, cried for him. If everyone would only stop interfering, he and she could come together again. He would forgive her everything. The war had done this to them, had taken all good things out of their hands. And he could, would forgive her. If only she would come back to him.

'There's nothing you can do about it, Matthew.' This from his father, his tone pleading. 'It's gone too far. Gone on too long. You've got to file for a divorce, son. There's nothing more you can do.'

What did they bloody know? He looked at each of them, his eyes ice-hard, but there were no words he could say and he turned away again. Let them get on with it. They would, no matter what he said. But once he was out of here, then they would see a different Matthew. No longer did he contemplate suicide. He'd fight for what was his – once he was strong again.

'I just feel I'm being buried here, Jenny, bit by bit.'

The words seemed to come from deep inside his soul and Jenny fancied she felt every iota of his pain as if it were her own. She counted the days to each visit, coming to see him whenever she could get time off from her work.

There had been a wild idea when he'd gone off to the sanatorium to give up her present post and follow him, but in time he would leave there and come home for good. It was always a fool's game following others around the country. They always moved on, leaving behind a void much as before. Not only that, here she was a visitor, a friend, a confidante. As a nurse she would have become an overseer, an official figure, not to be trusted. Things were better as they stood.

She sat now beside him on the veranda that caught the slanting, fast-diminishing warmth of an October sun. He was in a wickerwork easy chair, a cardigan about his shoulders, she on a hard chair that made her back seem unacceptably rigid. She would rather have been allowed to recline a little, to look more at ease. This way he had to look up at her which didn't help an easy relationship. Though mostly he stared at the tiled floor as he emptied out his heart to her.

'If I could only go to see her.' He seldom mentioned Susan by name. By this time they all knew who *her* referred to. 'I know I could sort things out. But no one agrees, they keep telling me it'll put my health in jeopardy, but that's an excuse. They don't want me to try getting her back. They hate her so I must hate her too.' He let his voice trail off and they sat on in silence for a while, then suddenly he looked up at Jenny, his eyes brightened by new hope.

'But you could go.'

'Me?' She was startled, lost for words. How could she go to his wife, trying to convey to her what was in someone else's heart? It was impossible.

He was looking at her from under his brow, his eyes slewing sideways towards her. She hurried on. 'It wouldn't be right for me to pay her a visit on your behalf. What could I say to her?'

'No one has ever bothered to talk to her,' he said bitterly. 'Except to condemn her.'

She waited. He had dropped his gaze and she could see his face working very slightly, could almost see the thoughts going through his head, the pain, the longing, the hope and the hopelessness that seethed there. And memories too, memories that would never die. All he'd suffered these past years would be with him always. But none of it, looking at him now with grief and emptiness showing on every part of his face, had scarred him as Susan had.

Jenny could foster only contempt for the girl which instinctively she knew she must smother for his sake. If she did consent to being his errand boy, she would have to be sweet and understanding to gain Susan's confidence. It smacked of an unsavoury business because subterfuge did not come easily to her. But wasn't she resorting to subterfuge at this very moment, visiting him in the guise of a friend, when her whole being cried out to touch his hand in love, to kiss his lips and be kissed in return, the way he had kissed her before he'd gone away and it had all gone cold for her when he had met Susan?

'Please, Matthew, don't ask me to do that,' she pleaded. But for his sake, for the sake of the love she had for him, if he pressed the point . . .

As well she had been looking at him or she'd have missed the hand half-raised in a small poignant gesture of defeat, of humiliated pride, an effort not to recognise that he must rely on her to do his work for him. He needed help yet felt belittled by that need. Innocently she *was* belittling him. He would not ask her again, that she knew. She knew too that their friendship was being placed in jeopardy, that he would never trust her again. She needed his trust as much as he needed hers. It was a kind of love in its way.

'I'll have to see,' she added lamely; not a promise nor a denial, neither one thing or the other, a way of avoiding the total commitment she knew she was in danger of being held to. To escape it, she got up to gather up her coat and handbag, preparing to murmur some sort of farewell, when, only halfway out of her seat, she was taken by surprise as his hand closed about her wrist.

'You will see her, Jenny? You promise.'

'I haven't . . .' The commitment was already being made for her. Blackmail, trading on the affection she had for him, the thought shot through her head. He knew, he must know, how she felt about him, and was using it. That was unkind, cruel. For a second Jenny was aghast at the anger that swept through her. But the eyes staring up into hers were filled with pleading, not craftiness, were sunken with desolation, dark with pain, and though that in itself was a form of blackmail, how could she refuse him?

Yet still she hesitated. He was asking too much of her love. And she had expected him *not* to ask again, so was now taken off guard. 'What on earth could I say to her, Matthew?'

'Just that I . . . I want her to come back to me.'

'I can't tell her things like that. If you wrote a letter, I could take it to her.'

'I've written letters.'

'This time I'd be there to hand it to her, while she reads it, tell her how you are, how you feel.'

Oh God! She had walked right into it. Hope had begun to glow in his eyes. Hope was filling him as a deep hole is filled with lifegiving soil to nurture the tree with which it is about to be planted. And it was glorious to see him come suddenly alive. How could she destroy that?

'All right, Matthew. Write to her. I'll wait.'

She sat down again, put her hat and handbag aside and watched him fish a small writing case from his locker, feverishly open it and pull out the fountain pen resting inside to write his private letter to his wife.

All the while Jenny's heart was pounding against her chest wall, partly at the prospect looming before her, partly at feeling herself being used as a sacrificial lamb, partly with the same emotion he himself suffered – love that tore at the very being but which the sufferer knew to be quite futile no matter what they did.

The feeling of being made a sacrificial lamb still lingering, she reluctantly prepared herself to visit Susan.

She made three calls that week, during break times from the London Chest Hospital, none of them successful. She received no reply to her knock and had no way to tell whether they were out or merely pretending to be. Each time it had rained, not heavily but with miserable persistence that carried all the odours of the East End with it, and after her three separate attempts, standing on the doorstep wet and fed up and growing more and more annoyed, she gave up. There was only so much one could do. Besides, it was all pointless anyway. Susan would never go back to the man she had rejected. Obviously happy with her lover, what did she want with a sick man? Which Matthew still was.

In a way it was a relief not seeing Susan, loathing the girl as she did for the way she'd behaved. But more than that, a tiny spark kept leaping into her mind that the longer Susan stayed away from Matthew, the more chance there was of his coming to terms with it. Would he one day see the futility of chasing after her and turn to someone else – herself perhaps? His friend all these years, always there for him, he was fast becoming dependent on her. Could that one day lead to love?

The thought made her laugh. Little hope of that. But a week from now she'd have to confront him with her admission of failure, see his face. She found herself putting it off and on that Saturday decided to postpone seeing him until another of her days off. Instead she'd try to see Susan one last time, have something she could tell him. But that morning it rained again . . .

It was his mother who forced her hand that very morning. It came as a shock to open the door and find his mother standing there, an umbrella above her head. Mrs Ward demeaning herself to come across in the rain to a lesser neighbour's door revealed the extent to which some of her high-necked values had taken a nose-dive since the war.

She looked almost supplicant, the weight of her son's plight making her a wholly different woman from the one who'd once lorded it over others. Her principles, however, had not slipped to the extent of agreeing to Mrs Ross's invitation to come inside.

'It's Jenny I wish to speak to,' she said, her voice as sharp as it ever was, and turning to Jenny she asked directly, 'When do you next hope to be visiting Matthew?'

'I was thinking of perhaps going this afternoon,' Jenny lied, trying hard not to sound reluctant.

'That's what I thought.' Mrs Ward compressed her lips in a manner natural to her. 'We'll be seeing him too today, as soon as Mr Ward gets the car out. You can come with us. Save your train fare. Could you be ready in, say, half an hour?'

Still some of the old Mrs Ward there. Assuming everyone would fall in with her plans came as naturally to her
as breathing. Jenny chewed on her lip. She and Mumsy
had planned on a quiet afternoon together, but it could
probably be put aside. They'd have all evening. And part
of her did want to see Matthew very much, despite her
trepidation at what she had to tell him.

'Yes, I could be.' His parents being there might soften
his reaction.

Mrs Ward inclined her head in a small gesture of
acknowledgement. 'He often asks after you, Jenny,' she
said, but broke off abruptly as though that information had
embarrassed her in some way.

This woman would never let her high standards slip
entirely no matter what the circumstances, but Jenny
had detected more than once, as she did now, a ring of
suppressed hope in Mrs Ward's voice that she might
one day see her as part of the family. A daughter-in-law
perhaps? Vain hope, that, but she smiled as Mrs Ward
added a little too briskly, 'Well, we'll pick you up in half
an hour then,' before turning and going down the steps and
back along the road to her own house.

Matthew was in the day room, it being too wet to go
outside. October, nearly at its end, already heralded a bad
winter, and the room buzzed with families and patients.
Jenny prayed he wouldn't ask her what she had achieved.

She sat by while his parents put their offerings of fruit
and a bar of Fry's chocolate from their sweet ration before
him, asked him how he was and began on all the trivialities
of their lives since last seeing him. He murmured his

thanks for the gifts, after a while turning aside from what they were telling him, his attention wandering while he muttered occasional comments in whatever seemed the appropriate place.

Several times Jenny saw his eyes come to rest on her, saw the query in their depths. She smiled weakly, knowing he would wait for a moment when they were alone. As if he had planned it, his father went out on to the veranda to smoke his pipe; his mother joined her husband, leaving Jenny to hold the fort. It was a moment she had been dreading.

The second they were out of hearing, his question came direct. 'What did she say?'

'Your wife?' She stalled, trying to remember how she'd rehearsed this moment. He said nothing, but the look in his dark eyes said, 'Who else?'

Jenny steeled herself, 'I went there several times, Matthew, but there was never any answer to my knock.'

He sat silent for a moment, then said, 'You didn't speak to her.'

'I tried. Oh, Matthew, I did try so hard.'

'I expect you did.' His tone was soft but full of condemnation. 'It was unfair of me to ask that of you.'

'No, it was right.'

He shook his head, throwing off the failure. 'I've let myself down. The only one to go and see her is me. Can't ask things like that of you. My fault, expecting too much.'

'No, Matthew. I understand how you feel.'

He looked directly at her. 'Do you?' The look made her

squirm, a look one would give one's executioner, defiant
yet resigned.

'I want to.' That she'd let him down she felt keenly. 'I
want to help.'

'You're putting yourself in a high place, aren't you,
Jenny, thinking you can do anything for me? I could tell
you all of what's inside me. I could tell you for a hundred
years, you still wouldn't know.'

'I feel so useless.'

'Then how the bloody hell do you think I feel?' His
voice had risen, bringing all heads turning in his direction.
'You all think you know how people like me feel. Trotting
out your damned platitudes. "It's all behind you now
– forget it – we'll make it better – tell you some jokes –
snap you out of it. It doesn't matter that you wake up in a
cold sweat, crying out for the friends who died while you
stayed alive, feeling bloody guilty for surviving, feeling
that you'd trodden on them to stay alive while they died.
Why d'you keep crying for the girl whose picture you kept
inside your head through all those years, who you thought
was waiting for you to come back home, to find it was
only a dream? You must get over it." Well I can't get over
it. And all your bloody understanding, Jenny, isn't going
to help me get over it.'

He stopped as suddenly as he'd begun. Now he stood
up, staring around him at the faces turned to him in
stunned silence. His parents had come back in to gaze at
him in alarm. For a moment he regarded them, then with
all those in the day room watching him open-mouthed
in the manner of people who feel unable to pinpoint any

reason for odd behaviour, he strode from the room.

No one, not even his parents, moved, but Jenny was already on her way, hurrying after him. Thus when she caught him up they were alone. Just one other person could be seen in the corridor, a porter at the far end going about his business.

Taking Matthew by the arm she swung him round to face her and pulled him to her, gathered him in her arms. He came without protest, his head turned so that his cheek rested on her shoulder, allowing his face to bury itself in the hollow of her neck.

Cradling him, she could feel his body being shaken by quiet sobs. She heard herself crooning soft, half-formed words as a mother might do to a hurt child. 'No, no, dear, no. It's all right. It's all right.' Silly words to a grown man but they afforded the comfort of understanding and shared feelings.

But he was right. How could she share what went on in his mind? Who had any idea what it had really been like for men like him, only from what papers and newsreels showed? She had seen a Nazi concentration camp after its liberation and had been horrified. But by the time accounts of the experiences of the freed emaciated British lads had reached the papers, too much coverage had been devoted to those newsreels of Nazi atrocities for much more to be given to the horrors of Japanese prison camps. The inmates had been too far away. Also they'd been British and American and Australian, men who surely hadn't succumbed to such barbaric treatment as had those Jews of the concentration camps, their skeletal corpses piled high in ditches for the public to see on cinema screens and the front pages of newspapers. No one saw the thousands of crosses lying deep in the jungle, too deep for photographers to penetrate with their cameras. Why bother? They had the groups of smiling if skeletal freed prisoners to snap. Brits, Yanks, Aussies, Kiwis, with bottles of beer in their hands given them by their rescuers, all doing thumbs-up for the cameraman as they held each other up on matchstick legs, bony arms around each other's necks. They were all right. They weren't lying in obvious piles of dead. They were coming back, all of them looking cheerful and victorious as though they'd won a war, and no one saw the horror that lay behind those smiles, the dead comrades who'd forever haunt their dreams. Jenny's arms tightened about Matthew, imagining the pain for some like him whose wife or sweetheart hadn't waited for them.

'It's all right,' she murmured again, her face buried in his dark hair that smelled of him, spicy, and of shampoo. 'Just let me be here for you.'

Suddenly she too was crying. 'I love you, Matthew. You're all the world to me. You've always been all the world to me. That's why I've never got married. I hoped . . . I never gave up hope of you coming home. I kept it alive because I . . .'

She realised all at once what she had been saying. His body had grown calm and he lifted his head, his dark eyes still shining with moisture, looking into hers. Flustered, Jenny dropped her eyes from the gaze that seemed to bore into her. Then she heard his voice, hoarse from grieving for the woman that was his no longer, 'Jenny, I didn't know.'

Still looking down, she shrugged dismissively, no longer in command of herself, embarrassed by having her adoration revealed.

'It's a private thing,' she managed to say. 'It doesn't matter.'

'It does.'

He was looking down upon the crown of her still-bent head, she could feel it. 'I don't deserve you, Jenny. If only . . .'

She looked up as he broke off, but he was moving back from her, putting her from him. She took a deep, fortifying breath and gathered herself up. 'I'm sorry I let you down, Matthew. I did try hard.'

'I know.'

Footsteps hurrying along the corridor invaded the private moment. Voices broke in, at once irate and concerned. 'Matthew! What on earth's going on? What upset you? You'll do yourself no good getting so upset. Jenny, what upset him?' As though he couldn't talk for himself.

Jenny looked at him and a mutual spark passed silently between them. He was aware now of her feelings, but he had to bow to the stronger obsession that drew him, and she accepted that he felt tenderness towards her, a caring love which couldn't match that which was destroying him.

'I have to do this myself,' he said, mouthing the words so that only she heard them as his parents reached him. Wondering at the words he'd mouthed at her, she had a vision of a man walking knowingly to his doom. He would let Susan destroy him because he wanted her to and there was nothing anyone could do about it.

Chapter 27

'When do you think you'll be bringing Mattie to see me again?'

The last time he'd seen her had been August. It was now November. His daughter would be left with the woman who cleaned for his mother a couple of days a week with a few shillings extra to keep an eye on Mattie when they visited.

He'd liked to have said, 'ordain to bring her', his mother having the final say in things concerning him, even whether he saw his own daughter or not. Matthew felt bitterness run through him like a trickle of acid as his parents sat looking awkward and concerned. His mother frowned.

'It's too cold these days.'

'It's warm enough in here.' Weak as the autumn sun filtering through the conservatory roof was, it was enough to warm up the place considerably apart from a constant draught from the obligatory ever-open top set of windows. Used to so-called healthy draughts, it felt warm enough to him, but his mother had another ready excuse up her sleeve.

'During the summer, Matthew, she could play in the open, but with winter coming on, it's boring for her cooped up inside. It would be for any child her age. She'd get on the other patients' nerves. It's not fair on them or her.'

And besides, he finished in silent sarcasm, a sanatorium's no place for a child. True, it wasn't, but he missed her; missed Susan; felt rebellious.

'She's my child.' His and Susan's, so like Susan, even at four. He'd feast his eyes on her, still filled with wonder at this his daughter, a surge of love for her twisting inside him so that he wanted to hug her to him. Of course as yet he dared not. TB was catching, not so much from him now, as because all patients came here to this out-of-quarantine visiting area. Visitors were safe at arm's length, but Mattie had to be discouraged from approaching too near, for her own sake.

Not that she ever came that near to him. To her he was a stranger still, a man she had been told to call Daddy. As a child who had never known one and was still only four years old, she hadn't any real idea what a daddy was meant to be. His father she called Grandad, his mother Grandma, and she had experienced the feel of that, but him, he was Daddy in name only. How he longed to clasp her to him and show her what it meant. But if he did, she might ease away from him, his hug unfamiliar, maybe even a little alarming. And that was another reason why he did not try to embrace her.

The weak sun had disappeared without anyone seeing it go. A pale fog moving in from the estuary had begun licking cold white tongues against the glass, promising to rime the lawns outside with frost before morning. His father noticed it and looked at his watch.

'Nearly four o'clock. We best be getting along, son. You'll be coming home soon. By the New Year. They're pleased with your progress. You'll be with Mattie then, for all the hours you want.'

'Do call her Matilda, dear,' interjected his mother, but Matthew hardly heard her.

Five weeks and he'd be home, to do what he liked. And he knew exactly what he would do. But that he would save for later. Five more weeks cut off from outside contact, seeing only the other patients, their visitors, the staff, and occasionally Jenny when she could get time off from her work. He had no letters to read, except from Louise, who was married and in Canada now. There seemed little point in anyone else sending letters when they came each Sunday.

Nor did Jenny write. What would she write about? Work, her life, his health, hers? She knew better than to resort to all that rubbish. His heart lifted at the thought of her. Since that unexpected episode a few Saturdays ago he hadn't been able to get her out of his mind, the way she had folded her arms around him, drawn him to her, the way she'd whispered her love for him; seemingly it had burst out of her.

And him? Something had stirred in him, but the image of Susan had immediately made him push Jenny away. To feel anything like that for her would destroy the love he nurtured for Susan and he couldn't bear that. It felt like being caught up in the strangling tendrils of a vine but not wanting them ever to fall away. Yet other than the unlikely hope of any visit from Susan, he found himself waiting for Jenny's visits more than anyone else's. But she wasn't visiting so often as before. She had embarrassed herself too much that day. He wanted to see her to tell her she had no need to feel bad, that he understood. But when she did finally arrive, alone, the first Sunday in December, he said nothing, seeing his planned comment as a platitude, an insult to her feelings.

He was reading Louise's letter when she came in. Louise sounded full of her life in Canada, making it seem romantic and exciting. She and her husband were so much in love with each other. He was miserably comparing his wrecked marriage to her successful one, wishing she didn't have to be so full of it. She was promising to come over to see him when they could get the money together for the flight. She'd gone out there by sea, but swore she would never set sail on the sea again; she would use one of the new airlines opened up since the war. However they had started a family, 'at last', and she didn't think it the right thing to do in her condition. She would make it next year once the baby was born, if they could still afford it. 'You know how much money a baby takes.'

No, he didn't know. He hadn't been there when Mattie was a baby. He had just screwed up that letter in a fit of suppressed hate, against whom he wasn't sure, perhaps circumstances, perhaps himself, when Jenny came in. Thus he was not exactly in any receptive mood to see her.

Sensing it, Jenny sat awkward and self-conscious. 'I hear you'll be coming home soon,' she said for want of something better to say.

She had been to see him only once since her outrageous

performance in the corridor, when his parents had caught her in the act of cuddling him. Not that they mattered. Mrs Ward had appeared highly approving. But *she* had felt a fool, them seeing her holding their son, a married man, to her bosom.

'When I come home,' Jenny became aware of a mordant edge to his tone, 'I might finally be allowed to think for myself.'

'Don't you do that now?' Immediately she saw the inanity of the remark. Here, everyone thought for him, he was powerless to do what he wanted. She knew what was in his mind. Once home he would go and find Susan with no one to stop him, probably taking her daughter with him, confronting Susan with her duties as wife and mother. It would be a disaster. Jenny could see it a mile off, the selfish, spoiled, wilful bitch throwing his pleading back in his face. And where would that leave him? Didn't he realise the harm he'd be doing himself? She wanted to tell him, warn him, but it would sound presumptuous, could even wreck their friendship, certainly any hope she fostered of anything more than that. Again she squirmed at the way she had held him to her, murmured her stupid words of love. How he had looked at her then, his eyes dark and deep. Recalling it now, had his look been one of understanding and mutual affection, or merely fear and rejection?

It was the best Christmas Susan felt she had ever spent. Just her, Geoffrey and little Trevor. She wondered how Emma Crawley was. She hadn't come nigh or by since leaving. She and Geoffrey's boys were living with her sister not far away, but she might as well have been in Timbuctoo. Geoffrey never spoke about her, though now and again he would go and pay a visit for the boys' sake. It annoyed Susan a bit, but she shrank from complaining, a little superstitious that if she did, she might lose him.

From Matthew's parents there had been no sound, other than letters from their solicitor to hers. Nothing as yet was moving regarding the divorce, with Matthew playing at delaying tactics all the time. She would have gone to tell him how useless these were, that nothing would induce her to go back to him now, but her solicitor had discouraged it, urging her to leave it all in his hands. But he was taking such a bloody long time about it. Still, he was right, no point rocking the boat. Matthew was well out of the way in that sanatorium near Southend.

She didn't wish him ill, didn't hate him or loathe him. Just the illness made her shudder to think how he must be, handsome looks all gone, in their place a gaunt individual who coughed and spat blood and lay pale and vapid – she'd seen it portrayed in films, the victim wasting away, dying in the arms of a lover. She'd always hated hospitals. Even setting foot in one as a visitor made her feel sick and shaky. Having Mattie in one had been bad enough. Thank God she'd had little Trevor at home.

None of these thoughts did she impart to Geoffrey. Why spoil things? Christmas passed like a dream; they'd had a wonderful time indulging in all the goodies he'd brought home. Nineteen forty-seven waited two days off and rationing was becoming less harsh even though the winter was already proving one of the severest they'd known since the one at the beginning of the war. But settled before a bright fire whose rising heat stirred the now-dusty Christmas trimmings, Susan's whole world was lit up and life couldn't be sweeter. Matthew was just a memory, at least until the divorce came through. After the New Year the solicitors might get their silly fingers out and get things moving.

But she wouldn't think about that. She'd just think about her and Geoffrey. Little Trevor was safe asleep in bed, she and Geoffrey had the evening all to themselves. Already in a slinky black nightdress, her dressing gown open to reveal her at her best behind the lace and satin, she was beginning to feel worked up by the way he was looking at her over his glass of whisky. Both their minds were focusing on the same thing. Her insides crawled deliriously as she thought how she intended to make him really happy tonight. In fact they might not even wait to get to bed. She came over, put an enticing arm about his neck, easing herself into his lap.

He grinned at her, and, the whisky glass still in one hand, fondled her breasts with the other, easing them from their flimsy lacy covering. That he kept the glass in his hand while doing so added a certain masterful casualness, heightening her senses even more to see how far this would go before he was compelled to put down the glass. Her dressing gown fell from her shoulders, the straps of the satin nightdress also slipped from her shoulders, letting the garment slither to her waist. Geoffrey's free hand was beneath the material, fingers manipulating firmly, teasing her desire with uncontrollable force. She moaned. When

would he put down that damned glass? What was she –
his bondmaid to do what he liked with, arousing her until
she screamed? Already urgency was rising faster than
she could ever remember. She cried out to him, sobbed
for him to put down the glass, for God's sake, she could
take no more of this. And yet how wonderful it was – this
awakening without him even entering her. What a man she
had.

She was hardly aware of the glass finally being put on
the sideboard, of him easing her down on the hard lino, but
only of his weight on her.

From somewhere came a pounding, like iron being
bashed against wood. A voice raised outside in the street
came dimly to her. She heard Geoffrey swear, felt his
weight ease, became suddenly aware that the street door
seemed in danger of being broken down.

'What is it?' Angry, she lifted her head that a moment
ago had seemed to be spinning, now completely still
and filled only with disappointed anger at this untimely
disruption.

The voice in the street was demanding entry, the street
door rattling on its lock and hinges with a resumption of the
pounding it was taking. All sorts of thoughts raced through
Susan's mind. Fire? Trevor fallen out of the window? A
drunk? The police – what would they want, bashing on
the street door? She thought of Matthew – perhaps he
was dead, her husband, and they were here, to inform her.
Geoffrey was on his feet, frantically buttoning his fly. Still
sitting on the floor, she was equally frantically dragging
on her nightdress, gathering her dressing gown about her.

Even so, she hissed to him, full of fear of the unknown: 'Don't answer it.'

'I've got to. Someone might be in trouble.'

'It's not our business, Geoff.' But she was thinking again of little Trevor upstairs. Was he all right? And then she too was on her feet, trying to find her slippers as Geoffrey, now respectable, made for the hallway.

She heard him open the door, waited to hear a policeman's voice. What had he to tell them? What she heard made her clutch at her throat. All these many years since she had heard that voice, its deep timbre, yet she recognised it instantly. 'Where is she?' it demanded.

Though his parents didn't know it, he spent Christmas at the sanatorium at his own request. He felt in no hurry to celebrate it at home with them carping at him to do something about his marriage. But yesterday he'd been obliged to concede. He was due to leave anyway, now or in a week's time. Two days before New Year's Eve, with the sanatorium nursing staff stretched because of leave through the festive season, his parents thought it only right that he make it now and welcome in 1947 with them as a family.

'Start the New Year afresh. Let's hope that will be the last time you have to go into hospital. They said you're clear, at last, and so long as you look after yourself and don't fret, you can only look forward.'

His first night home had to have been the worst he had ever spent under this roof, lying awake in his room while his parents slept, their sleep sound and contented in the assumption that with their anxieties for him a little easier for the present, he must be at ease too. How could he be?

Letters were lying on the doormat as they'd come in from collecting him. His father had picked them up, sorted them out, selecting one above the rest to hand to him.

'Looks like it's from your wife's solicitors.'

Taking it, he'd put it in his jacket pocket, and saw his father's face draw together with concern.

'Aren't you going to open it? It could be important.'

'It can wait,' he'd told him and, parrying his mother's arguments that followed, refused to open it for them to see what Susan was asking. He already knew what she asked, the same request kept being trotted out – for him to divorce her, she would give him grounds enough, she was in love with . . . He couldn't even read the name without a burning rage compelling his fingers to screw each letter into a ball. He would give no answer to any of these letters until he saw her face to face. This statement he'd written repeatedly, but she (or her solicitor on her behalf) had not once acknowledged them. He might as well be crying into the wind.

But whatever it contained wasn't for others to cluck over, full of their damned advice. 'Divorce her, Matthew, and get it over with. She's no good to you. You wouldn't take her back after all she's done.' No, he wouldn't give them the satisfaction of raising his voice against their demands.

The letter had stayed firmly in his pocket. Finally he opened it in the privacy of his room, hating the task and what would be written there. As he had suspected it had been the usual cry. But this time a small sealed envelope had been enclosed, the flap signed across with her small uneven signature – no, not signature, just the Christian name, Susan. She didn't even deign to include her married name, which in itself provoked anger and remorse from him.

What she'd written had taken his breath away. 'I'm tired of asking. If you can't grant me a divorce, it's no skin of my nose. I'll carry on living with Geoffrey until I die wether you like it or not. What I really want to tell you once and for all is I don't ever want to set eyes on you. It would make me sick. I wasnt never cut out to be a nurse for anyone and I'm not ready to start with you. I'm sorry if I hurt you but I don't no how plane I can make it.'

Hurt him? With a seething mind he'd risen, dressed himself, fumbling in his fury and pain at her words that seemed to so encase his brain in iron that no thought could get through but the one intent of getting to her, half killing Crawley and taking whatever came from that. He'd had sense enough to creep from his room without making any noise and waking his parents up, downstairs to where his father's car keys lay on the kitchen sideboard. The car had once been given to him as a twenty-first birthday present in the happy certainty that he would have years of pleasure from it, not knowing what had awaited him. They'd kept the car, during the war years of petrol rationing, on the gravel driveway under a tarpaulin, his father cleaning and servicing it with loving regularity. This ritual silently declared the certainty that Matthew would indeed return. 'It's yours again, Matthew,' Dad had said, but until he came home and felt well enough to drive, Dad continued to use it to keep it in running order. A way of encouraging him to get fit, Matthew supposed. Well, tonight he'd be fit, if necessary.

Muffled in an overcoat, he'd driven off almost blindly in the rage that still consumed him. It was ten thirty and people were still about. Only turning into the Mile End Road from Cambridge Heath Road was his brain cooled by force as a man coming out of one of the pubs made straight across his path. The car's tyres screeched to a skidding halt, in front of the man swaying and glaring at him. 'Gerrout, y'silly sod! Watch where yer goin'. Nearly knocked me darn.'

The man had staggered on across the road, as Matthew leaned his head on the steering wheel for a moment to clear his thoughts.

Geoffrey Crawley had no notion what was in store for him. Opening the door to the frantic yelling and thumping, uttering, 'What the hell . . .' he was taken totally by surprise when a hand thrust itself against his chest with such force he was thrown back against the wall, his head connecting with solid brick with a whack that for a second sent him dizzy. He had the presence of mind at least to lunge back, enough to deny the intruder entry for a brief moment during which his attacker shouted again, 'Where is she?'

Crawley, indignant now at his home being invaded, held the man with both hands on the shoulders, countering inanely, 'Who are you? What d'you want? You can't come barging in here like this!' All of it ran together like a single sentence. The man was leaning against his efforts to hold him off.

'I said where is she?' he repeated.

'Get out of here!' Frightened, Crawley felt thin fingers begin to force him from the hold he was vainly trying to retain on the man. 'Go away! Who the bloody hell are you?'

For an answer, Matthew let go of the hands trying to prevent his entrance, reached back with his right and took a swing at his wife's lover. It grazed past the man's cheekbone, making his head connect again with the passage wall though less violently than the first time. The man let go of him to clap a palm to his abused cheek.

'Godawlmighty!' he screeched. 'I'm calling the police. Sue! Sue! Get out at the back, quick, get Mr Adams next door.'

Matthew heard her voice come plaintively, quavering with fear and perturbation, from a room down the passage. 'I can't. I'm not dressed.'

Not dressed? Visions of her and this bastard naked together a moment ago assailed him. He lunged, grabbing the coward by the throat, bearing him down the passageway with the force of the rush, taking him to the floor as Susan tried to run out from the room, screaming, finding her way blocked by two grappling men at her feet.

'Matthew! Oh, God, leave him alone. You'll kill him. Leave him alone!'

Crawley was making strange choking, rasping sounds as his hands flapped about, in turn trying to break the hold on his throat or scratch his assailant's face. The choking and rasping were becoming more pronounced, the defending hands weaker, now flopping to the floor between attempts to release the grip. The face had turned puce, the eyes were beginning to stare, bulge. At first deaf and blind to all else but wreaking revenge, Matthew became aware of that dreadful colour. Sights and sounds came leaping back into his brain, as Susan screamed and beat on his shoulders, plucking at them in an effort to tear him away. Yet he couldn't let go. His fingers seemed to have locked about that neck. Meantime, the face below him was darkening rapidly. Geoffrey's eyes were closing; his mouth was falling open but no sound came from it now except for a faint and fading hiss. The hands, which had ceased to flap, lay quite still against the floor, flung out as in a posture of crucifixion. It didn't need Susan's cry, 'You've killed him!' for his own brain to cry out, 'God, I have. I've killed him.'

Standing there, knowing he must go, yet feeling utterly incapable of moving himself, Matthew heard a small sound like a tiny rasping intake of breath. He saw one of the dead man's hands stir ever so slightly, turning over until the palm lay downward instead of limply on its back. Susan heard and saw it too.

'Geoffrey!' Her scream rang through the house. At the same time a small fretful cry came from upstairs. A child had awakened. Susan's child. Hers and this man's: the man who lay in her arms, miraculously stirring.

'Geoffrey, Geoffrey,' Susan continued to shriek. She was trying to shake him awake. He had begun breathing again in pain-racked, difficult gasps. It would take a stronger grip than that of a man still weak from his years of captivity and illness to kill a man in his prime, well fed, well paid, and at ease with his world.

Matthew moved forward instinctively. 'Susan?'

She turned on him like a tiger, blue eyes blazing. 'Get out! *Get out*! I never want to see you again. I hate you! I hate everything to do with you.'

'Susan.'

But she was crying, her head bent over the stirring, gasping Geoffrey. Her muffled words sounded full of unhappiness now. 'I did love you, Matthew. I did love you. But you weren't here.'

'That wasn't my fault.' It was a silly thing to say but all he could find.

Crawley was trying to sit up, his hands carefully feeling his throat. Susan held him to her, her glare moderating.

'It don't matter now, Matthew. It just happened. A long time ago.'

She was trying to help Crawley to his feet. Matthew watched the manoeuvres dispassionately as though this was all happening on a screen and he, the watcher, stood apart from it all, unable now to feel any emotion as to whether the man lived, died, took his wife from him, or even sprang up to murder him on the spot. Nothing inside him seemed to care any more. Nothing mattered. What was it someone once said in the prison camp – a long-faced, miserable Aussie – does it matter if yuh die now or when yuh ninety; hundred years from now, no one'll remember yuh or care and yuh certainly won't care when it was yuh died? Nothing mattered.

So why not make it now rather than lingering on with memories of a love that had vanished? Quick. Easy. No time to think. A tall building, a few tablets sending one into endless sleep, a gas-filled room, a passing train. So many ways. And yet he knew he'd do none of those things. Like the coward he was, the coward he'd been in the prison camps, dreaming of going out in a blaze of glory taking half a dozen Japs with him but too weak-willed to do anything about it, he was weak-willed now; would live out his natural lifespan and take his memories with him to the grave. He wanted to weep. But he wouldn't let her see him weep.

He left the house, left Susan still cuddling her Geoffrey to her. In a daze he got back into the car and headed east towards his home, his parents and – an odd thought filtered into his head – Jenny Ross.

Chapter 28

'Look, you're going to have to make a decision very soon, Matthew.'

He heard her well enough but chose not to heed her. It would mean committing himself and he wasn't ready, couldn't see a time when he ever would be. Far preferable to keep his eyes closed, think instead of the sun bathing him with its heat, of sitting here enjoying his surroundings; anything but the making of decisions about signing those divorce papers.

High summer. The winter had been fierce and hard. The Big Freeze they'd called it, with everything, transport, power, everyday life, paralysed by deep snow drifts right into March, then devastating floods. Now summer was making up for it.

Jenny had become his constant companion since his return from the sanatorium; the night he'd thought he had killed that bastard Crawley seemed years ago instead of just a few months as he lolled now on a bench in Victoria Park. During that dragging eternity of waiting he met each day with hope of a letter from Susan that might contain a change of mind. Such a bloody forlorn hope. All that ever arrived was legal, concerning the divorce. He had finally

capitulated, the decree nisi having been granted with what
had struck him as indelicate haste. Now screeds of legal
correspondence followed, designed to drag as big a fee
from both parties as possible. Everyone was looking to
the main chance. What did they care how he spent days,
weeks, months, sick with desolation while it was all going
on? Now the decree absolute loomed.

Jenny was waiting for him to answer her, but he didn't
want to. She too was looking to the main chance. Why else
devote her time to him? He felt no swollen pride in the fact.
What the hell did she see in him? He had become a man
ravaged by circumstances, churlish, his thoughts invariably
centred on the past, on memories best forgotten but which
still persisted, emotions that tore him still with guilt and
remorse. Bob Howlett dying alone still haunted him; and
the sweet face that had lived in his head all through the
terrible years haunted him too. The once-loving face that
had hovered had grown twisted with loathing.

'Matthew, did you hear me?'

Yes, he had heard. He kept his eyes closed, pushed
away a moment of irritation at her persistence. He
needed her support more than he cared to admit; at times
he wasn't sure what he'd do without her. With her he
felt safe. When she wasn't with him, he felt lost. She
remained patient and understanding when he used her as
his sounding board to beat out his bad moments on, even
when he sometimes went too far. He would apologise and
she would accept his apologies, kiss his cheek lightly and
say it didn't matter.

But it did matter. He wasn't worthy of her love. She

had told him she loved him though had never said so again after that one time. He wished he could return her love, for her sake, but that would mean rejecting the feelings he had for Susan, and lying to Jenny, who didn't deserve to be lied to. Susan had become an obsession, a part of him he could not ignore.

'Matthew.'

He opened his eyes. 'I heard you.'

'Then you can't keep putting it off. You've got to start getting on with your life. I know all about getting on with one's life, Matthew. I've done it.'

The statement sounded vehement. Was it a hint that he might one day take up his life with her? He wished she wouldn't make those sort of comments. He loved Susan. But what was love? A bonding of two like souls, each helping the other without thought of self? Or was it this overwhelming, mindless desire for someone who selfishly destroyed? One endured of course, yet the other was all-consuming. What if he were to take Jenny on and Susan came crying back? Would he have strength enough to reject the one who'd torn him apart and cling to the one who'd been steadfast all these years without hope of gain? The thought frightened him, but he wasn't contemplating proposing marriage to Jenny, was he?

'Let's leave it,' he told her almost savagely. 'Just enjoy the afternoon, shall we?'

She was equally sharp. 'Yes. Shall we? If that's what you want.'

'That's what I want,' he snapped back, faintly surprised

at her tone. It wasn't like her. She was usually so mild-mannered.

He lifted his face to the sun and tried to forget it as she went quiet. Not moody, Jenny was never moody, but he could sense anger simmering inside her. This was a side of her he'd not seen before. An odd tingle of new respect for her went through him, warm as the sun on his face. He let the warmth soak in and tried not to think of Jenny or Susan or anything.

It was a sweltering summer. Temperatures had been soaring into the eighties; newspapers announced it as sizzling, with photos of eggs frying on pavements, toddlers naked by the sea, tarmac bubbling. Only the holiday-makers revelled in the heat. For himself, having known the humid sweat-bath of a Burmese jungle, this English summer could be comfortably endured lounging on a bench beside a shingle path. Victoria Park again looked beautiful, its railings restored, its lawns, where he'd been told ack-ack guns had once run up and down ploughing up the grass, once more verdant and immaculate. What had been allotments were now replanted with shrubbery and bright flowers.

It was peaceful sitting here, far from the problems the country faced. Food rationing was still going on, the government was still trying to repay America's Marshall Aid loan. Attlee talked of the country as being engaged in another Battle of Britain and the cost of cigarettes had risen to three shillings and fourpence. India, Ceylon, Pakistan and Burma all wanted to break away from British rule with resultant massacres; at home the rising cost of living plagued everyone.

It all came a poor second to his own problems, with this damned divorce business. For all his efforts trying not to think about it, he was. He felt so powerless even though he could stop it at any point. But soon it would be too late. It was as if he was being driven towards a cliff edge, unable to cry out, but he could watch the precipice drawing nearer, his life ceasing to exist. Why didn't he call a halt? He could still grab the wheel of his own fate and turn it from what they were all telling him was inevitable. Why didn't he? Because breaking this marriage *was* inevitable, if not now, then at some time. He couldn't *make* Susan love him, could never reawaken those feelings she had once had for him. But, dear God . . .

'I still love her, Jenny,' he said, and his voice broke.

Sitting beside him, Jenny knew he hadn't heeded a word she'd said. He remained lost in his own world, hoping all would come out the way *he* wanted it to come out. But it couldn't. Others were making sure this broken marriage did not mend, his parents, his solicitors, his wife.

Then there was herself – she too exerted an influence on him. She knew it from the way his face brightened when he saw her, though since that day in October he seemed to be holding her at bay. Before then their friendship had been easy. Now, when she came to his home, he would get up and go out into the garden or somewhere upstairs, anything to avoid being with her in the presence of his family. Yet he readily accepted the opportunity to be with her alone, as he was now.

'I expect you'll always feel that way about her,' she returned, studying a squirrel that had scurried down from a tree to investigate a bit of dry bread dropped by children going to feed the ducks. As it nibbled it kept one eye on the couple on the bench for a more likely morsel.

She was conscious of her voice sounding strained. 'But it'll serve you to no avail, you know. You do know, Matthew?'

She felt her heart shrink as he turned on her. 'What do you know about it?' Immediately he caught himself. 'I'm sorry, Jenny, I didn't mean that to sound like it did,' he said, then justified it by repeating himself in a different way. 'But you can't know how I feel about her.'

'Perhaps I do,' she countered softly, only to reap more bitter reaction.

'You sound like my mother.' This was accompanied by a cynical curl of his lips.

She had no reply to that. Something inside her was growing angrier by the second. Usually she curbed it, waited until he calmed down and tried to vindicate his hurtfulness, but this time her patience had no power and the anger exploded before she could catch it to hold it back. She turned on him, her grey-green eyes blazing.

'That's it, Matthew. Go on feeling sorry for yourself.' At her raised voice, the squirrel dropped its piece of stale bread and scurried back up the tree, but she did not see it go. 'I've just about had it up to here, Matthew. I do try to see your point of view. I do feel sorry for what's happened to you and I know I'm being unfair, that no one who's not suffered what you have can know what it was like, for all the stories and pictures we've seen. And now this on top of everything. But I'm only flesh and blood. Now do I sound like your mother? I want to help and I feel so useless, and I love you so much, Matthew. Yes I do know *exactly* what it's like to love someone who doesn't love you, when nothing can be done about it. I know it like mad.'

Tears were springing from her eyes. They rolled down her cheeks. 'I wish I was small and dainty and had someone to be crazy over me, as you are with *her*. But I'm not the sort of girl you fancy, am I? I've never been the sort of girl you fancy. Well, if she's the sort you fancy then you're welcome to her. That's what I say. But is that supposed to alter what I feel inside? You'd rather run after someone like her and let your heart be torn out of you while you grovel at her feet, pleading for her to come back and hurt you all over again. Well, honestly, Matthew, if that's what you want, I might as well just give up. No point me being your friend forever and ever. Damn what I feel.'

He was staring at her, the expression on his thin, handsome face one of confusion. Surely he couldn't be so naive as not to have some inkling of how she felt about him? She had said too much, had revealed her heart to him when she hadn't intended to. She felt exposed, but she was too angry with him to care. And now she fought to recover her composure, savagely sweeping the tears away with the back of her hand.

'What does it matter anyway? I've got a good career in nursing and that's all right with me. I don't suppose I'll ever marry, not now. I'm not the wife type. I'd only start bossing him about, whoever he'd be. I'm the bossy kind, you said so yourself. Like your mother. I suppose if I was like your wife you'd be letting me wipe the floor with you. I don't think I could ever bear that – from you.'

He was looking at her in a strange way, studying her, his dark brows drawn together. 'Jenny, I'm sorry. I didn't intend to upset you.' He was always being sorry.

She shrugged and looked away from him as he went on inadequately. 'You're the last person I'd want to hurt, you know that.'

Jenny said nothing, very much in danger of refuting the statement. He didn't seem aware of it.

'I've only been thinking of myself all this time. I never once stopped to consider how you feel in all this. Even when you said you loved me, I could think of no one else but Su . . .' he hesitated over the name, but plunged on. 'Susan. All I've ever done is abuse your friendship. Your real friendship. Using it and giving nothing back, especially knowing how you felt about me. Jenny, I wouldn't hurt you for the world. You're the only decent thing that has ever happened to me, and . . .'

As he broke off, she turned to see him still gazing at her, realised he hadn't once ceased looking at her, even though she had turned away from him. Now he put his hand out and laid it on her upper arm. She could feel the warmth of the hand penetrating the thin material of her summer dress.

He was drawing her gently towards him, his voice husky. 'I couldn't have gone on without you. I know the thought of her still consumes me, and I know I've got to fight it. But I know you're worth two of her, Jenny.'

His other hand took hold of her, he was pulling her

closer to him. When his face was inches away from hers, she felt his lips touch her cheek.

No, it was too much. He had no right. He was taking it upon himself to offer comfort with a kiss on the cheek. She made to turn her face aside from the insult of that friendly peck, the sudden move causing her lips unintentionally to brush his.

All at once she found herself unable to break away as the pressure of his lips on hers became instantly firm. In that second all her love for him poured out to encompass him. With a small choking sob, Jenny let her arms wrap themselves about his neck as if they had a will of their own, and to her astonishment his arms encircled her in response. The squirrel in the tree ceased scratching at the bark to look down at a young couple in a close embrace, the girl crying, the man holding her, kissing her gently now, and murmuring soft words of comfort.

'It's all right, Jenny. It's all right.'

'I'm sorry, Matthew. I shouldn't have . . .'

'No, you should. I've been damned stupid, selfish.'

'But you don't love me. You can't. You love . . .'

'I don't really know any more what love is. What I do know is I can't imagine being without you, Jenny. You've become part of my life.'

The squirrel, looking down, heard only a meaningless chatter of human sounds and went on exploring his own world, seeking food and, instinctively searching for a mate with whom to procreate his own species.

Below, if Jenny was expecting the words, 'I love you, marry me?' she was doomed to disappointment. The kiss had been emotional but an accident. She knew that later he would be embarrassed at having been carried away on a wave of brief, profound affection. She knew that too. She'd ruined everything in a weak, thoughtless moment. In the meantime they would walk home together as though nothing had happened.

What she didn't know about were the new feelings she had awakened in him.

Jenny took the envelope her mother held out to her: 'It's addressed to you, dear,' and stared at the unfamiliar handwriting. She rarely received mail other than *The Nursing Journal*. Her friends were local nurses with no need to write, seeing them every day. Her first thought was that it was from one of the old group in the QAs but the postmark was local. It was the small uneven handwriting that gave her the first clue as with the edge of a thumbnail she slit open the flap to withdraw a single sheet of cheap, blue-lined notepaper. She cast her eyes to the foot of the letter, noting the name.

'Who's it from, dear?' queried her mother with interest.

'Matthew's wife. Why should she be writing to me?'

'Odd.' Mrs Ross moved to lean over her shoulder. 'She won't be his wife for much longer. The divorce comes up in two weeks' time, so I hear.'

Jenny nodded, already reading, ignoring the misspellings:

Dear Jenny, I thought I'd write to you becaus I need some advise from you if its possible. Im ever so worried and I don't know what to do. As you know the devorce comes threw in a couple of weeks time and Geoffrey. Thats the man I am living with. Geoffrey is acting very strange. I think he's worried about the devorce but he is not as nice to me as he used to be. Im getting ever so worried. I wanted to talk to Matthew but I cant very well ask him direct after all this time and I was wandring if you could have a word with him on my behalf so as to pave the way so to speek. I know youve always been a good friend of his and perhaps you can act as a go between like. I will be waiting for your reply and hope you can help me. Thank you. Susan Ward.

'Well I never,' breathed Mrs Ross in Jenny's ear. 'That's a cheek if ever there was. You're more than friends with him nowadays from what you've told me.'

Jenny had told her about the incident in the park several weeks earlier, full of hope that in voicing it she could make love come true. What she hadn't mentioned was Matthew's reticence since then, just as she'd predicted but hadn't wanted to believe. His true feelings remained a mystery, leaving her alternately filled with hope and despair: perhaps he was battling within himself as to whom he needed most, perhaps needing to come to terms with it; or again perhaps his inane pursuit of that worthless cat dominated him still and he hadn't the heart to tell her she must forget what had happened. Maybe he'd been too taken up with the finalities of the approaching divorce to think of anything else as yet, but would once it was all over. Then again, maybe he still had hopes of the divorce never taking place and hadn't the courage to tell her that either. Time and time again a flood of anger would pour through her at the unfairness of being strung along. He was not man enough to tell her the truth and still her churning soul one way or the other.

This time she held it in, so as not to give him even more reason to fend her off. Outwardly they behaved as they had always done, still talked about all sorts of things – everything but the one thing that mattered to her. Her pent-up emotions were doing odd things to her. One minute she saw him as weak, the next she swept the thought aside in a fit of remorse, for whatever he was, she loved him. And he wasn't weak. He wasn't. He was merely terribly confused. Once this divorce was over he'd have to forget Susan.

But now she must hand him Susan's letter, stand by and watch his reaction; felt she knew already what it would be.

These closing hot days of summer they had continued to frequent the park together. He seldom wanted to go any-where else, but now as they sat on a bench or on the lawn watching other late-summer sun-worshippers, picnicking families, children, people walking dogs, they didn't touch. They spoke of trivial things. Matthew never spoke of his wife now or the imminent divorce. It was as though neither existed and she hadn't dared bring up the subject lest she drive him further from her.

There seemed to be a dull, flat ache in her soul as she folded Susan's letter and put it back into its envelope.

'I'd better hand it to him straight away,' she said

defeatedly. It went without saying what his reaction would be. A ray of hope. Jenny would be forgotten in an instant as he embraced the marvellous knowledge that Susan at the eleventh hour wanted him to take her back. He would forgive her all she had done to him and Jenny Ross would be put aside, told of his wonderful good news, thanked for all she'd done for him, and forgotten.

'He'll be pleased,' she said simply as she slid the envelope into the pocket of her nurse's dress to hand to him on her way to work. Then she would hurry off before seeing his reaction and get on with her day, get on with her own life, as she had vowed so many times before. But this time it held all the characteristics of finality.

Chapter 29

It was Saturday night, nearly ten o'clock. Little Trevor, in his cot since eight, had waited for his father well past his bedtime, and Geoffrey's key was only now just turning in the street door lock.

She stood waiting for him, the whole of her slight, small body quivering with fury.

'What bloody time do you call this?' she attacked him as he came into the cluttered living room, still innocently pocketing his keys in the jacket he'd already taken off to drop over a nearby chair.

He looked at her astonished, his jovial, 'Hello, love,' frozen on his lips. 'You know I always see the boys on a Saturday.'

'Not until this bloody hour of the evening. And you already see them twice during the week too. You never used to. So what's so special about them now? You used to come home before eight so you could see your own son before he goes to bed.'

He glared at her now, his jacket hanging by its collar from one finger. 'They're my sons too, don't forget. I owe them some of my time.'

'Not every bloody day of the week.'

'It's not every bloody day of the week.' Angered now, he flung the coat at the chair, which it missed. It slid to the floor to lie in a crumpled heap. 'It's twice a week and once on a Saturday.'

'That makes three times,' Susan stormed, standing her ground on the rug before the empty firegrate. She had no intention of moving from the spot to welcome him or go off to get him cups of tea as once she always did whenever he came in the door. This time she was going to have it out with him, one way or the other.

'I'm not putting up with this, Geoffrey. Not for much longer. Why do you have to keep going to see them three times a week? It was four times last week.'

'Four?' he blazed at her.

'Yes, *four*. What about Monday? You went there on Monday as well.'

'For an hour, that was all. You're begrudging me one hour with my own boys, now?'

'It's one hour too many, Geoffrey. What about me waiting all hours God sends for you to come home and give me a bit of your time? I mean, I'm important to you too, aren't I? You used to think so. You used to be a lot different to what you are now. I need to have you here.'

'You've got me, haven't you? Nearly all the time.' He went and threw himself down in one of the pair of sagging fireside chairs. It creaked under the sudden violent weight. 'Don't start an argument, Sue,' he sighed. 'I'm tired.'

'And *I'm* tired,' she railed on at him. 'Tired of being a doormat for you. For you to come home any old time you please. And I suppose you expect to make love to me, as always, as if nothing's happened.'

'You like it.'

'That's got nothing to do with it. You come home from *her* and your blessed sons, and clamber on top of me and make love as if you've not had it for weeks. How do I know you haven't been making love to *her* as well?'

He sat bolt-upright. 'That's not fair, darling. You know I don't have nothing to do with Emma and she don't have nothing to do with me. It's just for me to see the boys, that's all.'

'What proof have I got of that?' she continued to blaze. 'And don't darling me straight after you've seen *her*. What's going on between you two?'

Geoffrey shot out of the chair and stalked about the room, flinging irritated, disbelieving glances at her. 'This is getting bloody silly. I thought our row in the week was bad enough, and over the same bloody thing. But you're going right over the top again. Nothing's going on between Emma and me. Can't you get that straight? She's just the mother of my sons and they live with her. Of course I have to see her when I go there, but she don't have nothing to do with me.'

'But you wish she did.'

'Of course not, darling. I love you. I left her for you and that's not changed.' His voice had grown softer, more persuasive. 'It's you I love, Sue, and no one else.'

'Huh!' She moved at last to the window to straighten the already moderately straight gold-patterned curtains. 'Love me? You don't care anything about me, only to get your oats, that's all you care about me. It's all I'm good for.'

'Don't be silly. And don't be selfish.'

'Selfish!' The curtains received a tug, almost dislodging the pelmet they hung from. 'Me? Selfish? I should think you're the one who's selfish, leaving me alone half the week.'

'You *are* bloody selfish, Sue, sometimes.'

'I'm not. I'm not selfish.'

This was how it was lately, arguments going round and round, silly and pointless, ending up unsolved unless she gave in, threw herself at him and burst into tears. Before, he would kiss her better, take her to bed to assuage his need with her. She adored being made love to in that way, the rougher the better, with her the object of his lust, the helpless recipient. But these last couple of weeks, he hadn't made love to her after any row; he had merely extricated himself from her pleas for him to forgive her and had gone sullenly to bed; he would be asleep or apparently so by the time she came to him. Any attempts to wake him up had been met with a deep snore and a mumble of protest. Many a night she had lain awake beside him, her eyes wet with what she hated to admit were self-induced tears. Her sniffling and snuffling sounded loud enough to have disturbed the devil, but not Geoffrey, even though to her mind he must have heard but ignored the noise. The next morning he would leave for work after breakfast, through which he said little but read the morning paper that fell through the letter box at six thirty. His departing peck on the cheek seemed a condemnation of her attitude of late and left her to weep silently the rest of the morning as she got his son from his cot to feed him.

Slowly she was coming to feel that their relationship was beginning to fall apart, that he was tiring of her. But why now? In less than a couple of weeks her marriage would come to an end. She couldn't let Geoffrey lose interest in her now, not after all that had happened. She was being silly of course. He hadn't lost interest in her. His lovemaking said as much, or had done until lately. It was her fault. She *was* being selfish. He did need to see his sons by his wife. Soon she would be his new wife when his own divorce came through. This wouldn't be for several months yet; Emma had only filed for it a little while ago.

Tomorrow she would have him all to herself, all day. She would make up for her foolish, groundless tantrum by being all sweetness and light, and on Monday would run to get him his evening tea, for that evening he'd be home at the proper time. Last Monday had been the exception, because of his middle son Percy's birthday.

Sunday passed blissfully. They made love in the afternoon, with Trevor safely asleep in his cot. She bit back the cries of ecstasy Geoffrey forced from her in case she awoke the child and put an end to the unbelievable climax to which her lover was capable of bringing her. And they made love again that night with her happy cries ringing out abandoned enough to wake the neighbours.

All Monday she went about the house, content that all was well again and waited for Geoffrey to come home from work. Five thirty came and went. Six o'clock. Seven.

Susan, watching the clock, the egg and bacon she'd cooked dried up in her efforts to keep it warm for him, began to seethe afresh. There was no reason for him to have been kept at work. It was obvious he had gone round again to where Emma and the boys still lived with her sister. But there was no birthday to celebrate this Monday. And hadn't she heard from Geoffrey last week that the youngest would be at a friend's birthday party this evening and that Percy and Malcolm were going off on a school coach trip to Southend and wouldn't be home until after seven thirty? And didn't Emma's sister do evening work in some nearby pub? If Geoffrey had gone round to Emma's tonight, he'd really blotted his copybook this time.

Sick at heart, Susan waited, put Trevor to bed and waited some more. It was nearly nine before Geoffrey came in. In the ensuing row, he ducked and dived like mad. He didn't admit it for one second but Susan knew he had been with Emma, really been with Emma; there was something in the look of him that showed he had. When she accused him outright, his protests were too violent to be true, so she *knew* he had.

It was then she began to be really frightened, knowing just what she had done and how her life could go. Were he to go back to his wife, what would she have left? Geoffrey's son – that was all. Suddenly she didn't want to be left just with Geoffrey's son. She didn't want to be the spurned mistress saddled with a baby. She could see it all looming before her like a great yawning canyon. She thought voluntarily of Matthew, for the first time in months. It was then that she wrote a scribbled, frantic letter to Jenny Ross in the hope that she would speak for her to him. Jenny had always been a saviour of lame dogs and desperate souls. She would not fail this desperate soul – for once in her life, Susan waxed poetic as she wrote her letter, then sat back to await the results, which she knew could only be to her advantage. Matthew would have her back in the blink of an eye, still madly in love with her as he was.

Susan rather liked that word, desperate. She said it over and over again to herself as she sealed her letter and went to post it. Her heart, though, still ached for Geoffrey and she prayed he'd have a change of heart and carry on their relationship as though nothing had happened. Then of course there would be no need for Matthew and no harm done because from past knowledge of Jenny, the girl would be very careful how she worded her errand and might even delay it in rehearsing the words she would use to him. There would still be time enough to rescind her plea. After all, Matthew had recovered, hadn't he? He was no longer the sick and ravaged person she imagined he had been after coming home. Look how he'd belted into poor Geoffrey. Geoffrey, the apparently healthier man, had been unable to defend himself. At the time she had hated Matthew, seeing a savage, embittered, degraded man. But thinking about it, his face, at the time twisted and suffused by fury, had still retained much of that which had attracted her to him that first time. Half crouched in rage as he'd been, he still looked tall and slim, a far cry from the sick wretch she had imagined. Memories of what he had been now flooded back. In time he would become that again and perhaps they would pick up the threads of those beautiful if brief months they'd had together before he'd gone away. She hoped so. That was if her and Geoffrey's affair was over, which in her heart she hoped was untrue. All she wanted in life was a stable, loving relationship with someone, to be looked after, to be loved, to be given security.

Matthew took little notice of the ringing of the doorbell. He and Dad had not long got up; both were washed and dressed and waiting for their breakfast, the nutty fragrance of toast creeping from the kitchen. He listened idly to his mother going to answer the door. Probably the postman. A parcel perhaps?

'Matthew. It's Jenny, here to see you.'

He stood up, curious, as she came in with his mother. She seldom came here on a Wednesday, and never in the morning, never so early, her nurse's coat, spattered by light, early-morning rain, showing she was in fact on her way to the hospital. She was looking a little strained.

'Anything wrong?' His first words showed his concern.

'I can't stay. I'm on my way to work.' She sounded breathless as if she'd been running, but the breathlessness seemed to have something to do as well with the strained look on her face. She was holding an envelope, holding it out in a way that did not exactly ask for it to be taken from her. 'This arrived for me in the post, but it has to do with you rather than me. I was going to pop it through your letter box but it needs some explanation why it was sent to me and not to you.'

'Shall I take your coat?' His mother eyed the rain-spotted garment with concern for her furniture lest Matthew's visitor sit herself down. Jenny shook her head quickly.

'I can't stop.' She was looking at him, her expression apologetic in a way, her high brow furrowed with concern the way it used to furrow when she had tended him in that first hospital in England.

'What is it, Jenny?' He ignored his father, who had also stood up sociably at Jenny's entrance, and came round the table towards her. Perhaps being nearer she might hand him the letter she said so concerned him.

'This isn't possible to break to you gently, Matthew. It's from your wife. I was supposed to explain, tell you what she wants. I suppose what she is hoping me to do is to . . .' She broke off with an impatient tut. 'Well, read it yourself. I can't be . . . I don't want to be her go-between. It's nothing to do with me, anyway.'

Thrusting the letter into his hands, she turned and with a little nod and a thank-you to his mother, allowed herself to be conducted out.

Left holding the envelope, he instantly recognised Susan's laboured handwriting. By the time his mother came back, eager to see what it was all about, he had the letter open, his eyebrows drawn together in a frown.

'What is it, dear?'

'As Jenny said,' his father's deep voice was deadened by the well-furnished little breakfast room, 'it's from Matthew's wife.'

'Well, what does she say? What does she want?'

'She wants to come and see me. I shall have to see her.'

'Matthew.'

'I want to hear her say this to my face.'

'You can't. You can't see her. The divorce case . . .'

'I have to.' Screwing the letter up, he thrust it into his trouser pocket and made out of the room.

'Your breakfast,' she called after him, but received no reply.

The night he'd attacked Crawley, his first glimpse of her in years had been a fleeting, distorted one, seen through a mist of rage. Now as he opened the door to her knock, she stood before him, as he remembered she had done years before that, still with the same petite build, the same blue eyes wide and timid. Perhaps she looked a fraction more mature but still vulnerable and unsure of herself, prompting a natural reaction in others to take her under their wing.

'I got your letter telling me to come here,' she began tremulously. 'I'm glad you wanted to see me.'

He didn't smile. He dared not. He stepped back to let her in and she followed him into the sitting room like a small, subdued dog at his heels. He closed the door and they stood facing each other in the filtered light of a drab September afternoon. The room was very quiet. They were alone, his mother reluctantly and full of disapproval of his request leaving them to themselves. It occurred to him that he hadn't yet asked Susan to sit down, but to do so would be an acceptance of her and he was wary of betraying how he felt looking at her. Seeing her again had resurrected that surge of adoration the sight of her had always brought and it alarmed him.

To cover the discomposure her nearness aroused, he said stiffly: 'You said in your letter you weren't happy.'

She nodded, catching the fuller part of her lower lip briefly between her small teeth, an endearing little habit that had always stirred his emotions to see. Matthew clenched his hands against them.

'So what did you want from me?'

She came forward a fraction, a small movement of appeal to that love he'd once had for her, an attempt to awaken it if it now slept. She couldn't know how easily the single movement could awaken it, for its sleep had never been total. Her eyes were glistening.

'I'm so sorry, Matthew, for everything I've done. I know I was wrong, but you were so far away and I didn't know if you was . . . oh, Matthew.'

Tears had begun trickling gently down her cheeks. He was in danger of being disarmed by them. He didn't want to look at them, so lowered his eyes, remembered all the crying he too had done; the pain remembered was becoming insufferable.

'Matthew, don't turn away. Look at me. I'm sorry. I really am.'

Now he looked up, surprised at his own reaction. What did she expect of him? That he'd take her in his arms, soothe away all the sorrow she was displaying, tell her it was all right, that he forgave her and wanted only to take her back as though nothing had happened? His whole being cried out that that was what he wanted to do. He felt his lip curl contemptuously with the knowledge of how easily he might, contempt for himself that he knew how close he was. But he had grown embittered. Her tears, they weren't for him. She wasn't hurting for him, only for herself, had always only ever thought of herself.

Rationality seemed to spear through his body, but its searing pain was his only salvation. He kept hearing Jenny saying, 'It's nothing to do with me.' But it was everything to do with her, rationality, security, trust. He could trust Jenny. He could never trust Susan – ever again.

When he did speak his voice seemed to be conveying every vestige of that agony spearing him. It was an effort to talk at all.

'I'm sorry too, Susan. I can't . . . I can't have you back. I know I can't. You see . . .' He stopped as her eyes opened wide with terror. His immediate instinct was to grab her to him to stop that awful look of desolation. Fighting it, he shut his own eyes so as not to see how she was looking at him.

'I need to trust someone,' he heard himself saying. With an effort he pulled himself together, willed himself to look at her while trying to keep the mirror of his soul closed to her. It made his stare harder than he intended. He saw her shrink back a little, the gesture almost destroying his resolve until he remembered again the agony she had caused him over the years of wanting her.

'You see,' he began again. 'It wouldn't be any good – not now.'

'Matthew, no!'

He pushed on, ignoring the cry. 'The first sign of

anything not going your way, any inconvenience, any outside temptation, and you'd be off again. It's not your fault. It's how you are. When we married, I'd no idea. All I knew was I loved you, adored you, thought you could do no wrong, that you were perfect. But it wasn't enough, was it? I couldn't hold you. I'll never be able to hold you.'

She had been gazing up at him, the dawning of what he was saying growing apparent in her gaze, but her protest came in a wail of disbelief. 'I don't know what you're saying, Matthew. I know I was wrong. I *am* sorry. I'll make it up to you. I will. I still love you. I'll make everything up to you.'

He wanted to counter, 'What about Crawley?' But that would be dragging it down to the level of a slanging match. Suddenly he wanted to be rid of her. He was beginning to feel unsteady, shaky, a dull nausea in the pit of his stomach. He wanted to sit down but he dared not.

'I want you to go.' His voice sounded hoarse, strangled.

'Matthew . . .' Her eyes suddenly hardened, narrowed with suspicion. 'Is it someone else?' He almost laughed. 'It's that Jenny Ross. You've fallen in love with her, haven't you? You don't want me now.'

He didn't reply. Every word she said seemed to be driving her further from him. He couldn't believe that he could ever *not* be in love with her. It would hover inside him, a small devil, to the end of his days ready to resurrect itself the second his guard was lowered. But at this moment he was merely beginning to feel sickened. That she could say Jenny's name with such contempt! Jenny could make six of her, ever willing to take on his burden of fears, his indecisions, and not complain. Yet his fear was that he'd burden her too much, more than she could stand. Not for himself, but for her. Was that true love? If it was, then Susan paled into insignificance beside it.

'I might've known.' Her words pierced through his thoughts, her tone contemptuous, covering the fear that consumed her.

He blinked. 'I think you'd better go, Susan. Back to Crawley – try to make the best of it. You can use your charm on him, Susan. You know how to do that, don't you? You're good at it. He won't be able to resist. As I once couldn't. You'll be all right. You'll always be all right.'

Bitterness rose up inside him without bidding, like some other self. He was astounded by his own words, their harshness. All at once the past had become another country. He held her look of disbelief, aware that his was arid.

She took a step or two towards him, her expression still one of abject pleading, but his arid stare remained a wall of glass. Realisation began to dawn on her and she gave a small defeated sob, turning from him like a rabbit released from a car's headlights. She had no idea how near she had come to shattering that fragile barrier.

Making blindly for the door, her sob breaking into full-blown weeping, she pulled it open, fleeing past his mother whom he saw standing just beyond. A bitter grin twisted his lips that she had been there listening to it all.

'She's gone then?' The stiff statement reached his

hearing, but he found himself incapable of answering her. What in hell's name had he done? Susan had been in his grasp and he'd thrust her away. For a moment there came an urge to run after her, but he let the moment pass.

Chapter 30

It was the dim light of October making her feel low. The days had begun rapidly to shorten, the promise of a long winter already dulling the sky. It had to be; people were usually affected by the weather. Even so, she should have felt brighter than this. After all, Matthew was now a free man.

Jenny looked across the dinner table at her mother. 'Matthew Ward's divorce came through last week, did you know?'

Mrs Ross smiled as she chewed, her fork engaged in selecting a piece of potato. 'He should feel easier now. I suppose you do too.'

Jenny's knife and fork lay idle each side of her plate, although she gripped them as though gripping a pair of lifelines. 'I suppose I do in a way.'

'You and he might spend more time with each other.'

'We already do.'

'You know what I mean.' Her mother hadn't once lifted her eyes from her plate. Jenny knew exactly what she meant. It was a pity Matthew didn't.

For days he had been moping indoors. Off duty this weekend, she'd gone over to his house yesterday, been heartily welcomed in by his parents, invited to stay for a bit of tea with them. But seeing Matthew's obdurate expression of moodiness, his apparent lack of joy at seeing her, wrapped up as he was in his own sullen grief of his lost marriage, she had felt a flush of anger at him and excused herself, saying she didn't want to leave her mother on her own on a Saturday night.

She hadn't gone across today at all. He could stew in his own morass of misery if that was what he wanted. Of course she ached to see him but she was no longer prepared to be his whipping boy whenever he felt like it. She had made up her mind about that. He was free now. Divorced. Nothing he could do about it. It was up to him to get on with his life. But she wished she was included in that life, and still had no idea whether she was or not.

'I'm sure I don't know what he's going to do,' she said to her mother, a little sharply.

'Are you going to see him after dinner?'

A ring of the doorbell interrupted an awkward denial. Jenny leapt up from the table. 'I'll go.'

She left her mother murmuring that she couldn't think who that could be on such an overcast Sunday afternoon and hurried to the door.

For a split-second her mind wouldn't work, having a problem placing the face. But already the name had burst from her lips in disbelief.

'Ronald!'

He looked awkward, a man faintly aged since she had last seen him. 'I remembered your address,' he began. 'I was going to write, but I was in the vicinity, attending a medical seminar, and I thought before going home I'd look you up. Hope you didn't mind.'

She could only stare at him. 'Er . . . no.'

He gave her a somewhat silly grin, slightly apologetic. 'I was at a bit of a loose end.'

'Oh.'

'I'm a free agent, you see. Nothing to rush back home for. Of course there's surgery in the morning, but it only takes a few hours in the car to get back to Bath, so I thought why not look up an old friend?'

'Oh.'

'My marriage broke up,' he continued by way of explanation for his unexpected appearance.

Jenny heard her mother's voice filter faintly from the dining room. 'Who is it, dear?'

Hastily she called back over her shoulder. 'An old friend, Mumsy.'

'Well, ask her to come in, dear. Don't let her stand on the doorstep.'

Jenny ignored the invitation but any moment her mother would come to see why.

'Look,' she said quickly, lowering her voice so that Mumsy wouldn't hear. 'Can you wait outside while I get my coat?' Somehow she didn't want to go through lots of introductions and explanations to Mumsy. 'We can take a walk and you can tell me about yourself and why you're here.'

He was looking embarrassed. 'Perhaps I'd better go, Jenny. I didn't mean to . . .'

'No,' she cut in. 'I'll only be a tick. I'd like to know

how you are.' After all, it was only polite. She couldn't turn him away.

She closed the door, gently so as not to seem rude, and hurried back along the hall. She felt flustered, not from renewed affection but by the fact that Matthew might have seen him at the door. Silly really – it could have been anyone. But he might see her walking with Ronald. What would he think? She felt suddenly unaccountably rebellious. What the hell did it matter what he thought?

'Didn't you ask her in, dear?' Her mother, coming from the dining room, regarded her a little bemusedly as Jenny quickly gathered her coat from the skeletal stand that held their everyday coats.

'I'm just going for a walk, Mumsy. Shan't be a tick.'

'It looks rather like rain. Silly going for a walk when you could have asked her in. I wouldn't have minded. You'd best take a brolly with you.'

To appease her, Jenny grabbed one of the two umbrellas sticking out at an angle from the guard rail around the foot of the coat stand.

'Don't be out too long, dear,' her mother's plaintive departing call followed her as she made towards the door. 'You don't want to get wet. And bring her in when you get back.'

'She has to get straight back home,' Jenny returned on the point of closing the door on her. And Ronald could go straight back too. Said he was divorced. If he had come here hoping to pick up where they had left off years ago, the cheek of it!

He was leaning on the gatepost looking somewhat

woebegone. As she reached him he straightened up, taking her arm and threading it through his as though it were his right, whether she objected or not. But it would have seemed rude to have shrugged away from him. He was only trying to be amicable and he did seem a little uncomfortable.

'It's so nice to see you again,' he was saying as he conducted her, guiding her before she realised it away from the main road from where he had obviously come. Still confused by him turning up like this out of the blue, it did not dawn on her until they had gone some way that this would not have been the route she would have consciously chosen. She took a quick glance up at Matthew's house as they passed it, but there was no sign of life. Jenny breathed a small sigh of relief.

'It's nice to see you again too,' she said.

'Well, as I was nearby.' He looked abruptly at her. 'You know, I was pretty broken up when you gave me up, Jenny. I really thought we had something going for us. I kept hoping. But I know you weren't the sort to play a chap along, so I had to decide to put it all out of my mind. I joined the Medical Corps, you know. That's where I met Penelope. We got married. We didn't see each other all that much. Then I came home unexpectedly one day and found her in bed with someone.'

'I'm sorry,' Jenny said as he paused.

'I don't know why I'm telling you all this,' he went on. 'After the divorce I began thinking about you again, wondering if you'd got married. I found out the hospital you're working in and that you were still single, and I thought there might still be a chance for you and me to, well, perhaps pick up where we'd left off. The war's over. Things are different now. Settled. I just hoped you might feel, well, perhaps a bit more ready to . . . well, us to, you know, start going out together again.'

So there had been a method in his coming here.

They had gone some distance when the first tiny droplet of rain made itself felt on the back of her hand. Jenny welcomed it with a stab of utter relief.

'It's started to rain. I'd best be getting back,' she said just a little too enthusiastically. She turned to him. 'Ronald, there is someone, you see. I'm going out with someone.'

It wasn't exactly an untruth, was it? She and Matthew. Friends. Not lovers. No proposal. But there was always hope. 'We're more or less going steady,' she said.

Working the rest of the week, there had been no chance to see Matthew. Most of the time, Jenny's mind was centred on Ronald Whittaker and the heartbreaking disappointment that had showed on his face when she had lied to him. Yes, it had been a lie – Matthew no more wanted her than he'd wanted his divorce. She found herself dreading her next evening off duty when she would have to pop over to see him, imagining his off-handed greeting. But she couldn't avoid going. They were friends.

She'd been so sorry for Ronald as he walked her back to her gate that she had leaned towards him and given his cheek a brief consoling peck, purely on impulse. He had read its message clear enough. He had taken her by surprise in catching her to him in a gentle hug. Not knowing how to break away and further hurt his feelings, she had stood thus in an embrace, half her mind thinking unkindly that the rain was getting heavier. He must have felt her tense. When he let her go, he smiled at her, such a sad smile.

'For old times' sake,' he'd murmured, then, 'Be happy, Jenny.'

With that he had walked away, leaving her standing there with tears misting her eyes, beginning to trickle down her cheeks, the spots of rain splashing them away.

She'd felt, still felt, oddly empty after his going. It created a strange sensation knowing he had walked into her life again, briefly, and as quickly walked out of it, leaving behind reawakened memories of that part of her life which felt as though it had never happened. She wondered what his world would be like, what he would do, who he would meet eventually to continue his life with? She would never know.

'Oh, Jenny, come in. I'm so glad to see you.'

Mrs Ward's expression was at once relieved and concerned. She had become a different woman lately. Jenny could almost read her mind, an ability few were privileged to possess. It invariably registered optimism whenever Mrs Ward's eyes fell upon her. It said: My future daughter-in-law, please God, as surely as if spoken aloud. This evening however, concern overrode the pleasure of seeing her as she bade Jenny to come in.

The evening was proving a busy one. For the first time since the war ended, Guy Fawkes Night was being wholeheartedly celebrated, the puny explosion of fireworks no longer conjuring recollections of wartime bombing raids.

Further down the road on a cleared-up bombsite, children had a large bonfire going. The stink of burning wood, rubber and old furniture and the acrid tang of saltpetre hung in the air. But Jenny no longer noted it, the look on Mrs Ward's face alarming her.

'Is anything wrong?' she asked as she was let in.

Mrs Ward lowered her voice, hovering with her in the spacious hallway. 'It's Matthew. Perhaps you can do something with him. He's hardly spoken two words to us and then only to snap at us. Even his father's becoming angry with him, and his father is normally a mild-mannered, understanding man. Neither of us know what to do with him.'

'What's wrong with him?' Jenny whispered back in the same conspiratorial undertone.

'We just don't know. He won't tell us. If we ask, he just snaps at us, tells us to mind our own B. business.' Mrs Ward never swore, not even in quoting. She loathed the mildest epithet in her hearing, much less her home. Jenny smiled to herself. She'd heard some ripe ones from Matthew before now; had heard some even riper ones from soldiers wounded and in pain. Mrs Ward should have been a nurse. That would have broadened her mind.

Jenny's smile, a tiny one that Mrs Ward hadn't even noticed though the hallway was brightly lit, vanished as fast as it had come and she turned her thoughts to what she was telling her.

'He's in his room. He must have seen you coming up

the path. But he hasn't even come down. I just don't know what's wrong with him.'

Jenny followed her into the lounge, returning Mr Ward's nod of welcome. He sat in an armchair by a low fire lit against the growing autumn damp, though it was not cold enough yet to warrant a larger blaze. He had been reading an evening paper, now folded on his knees. At Jenny's entrance he half rose then sat back down again. With a regular visitor, there was no call to stand on ceremony. His whole mien held a defeated look about it.

'Park yourself, Jenny,' he muttered, his terminology so like his son's, a breath of fresh air compared with his wife's self-conscious articulation.

'Is Matthew coming down?' Jenny asked as she sat herself on the sofa. It was him she had come to see, not his parents. The room had an odd atmosphere to it without him, almost as though he no longer lived here. She felt uncomfortable, an interloper.

'Hope so,' his father returned. 'Call him, Lilian, say Jenny's here.'

'He knows she's here,' she snapped.

'Then tell him again,' he snapped back.

It was unlike him. Jenny could sense the tension, the anger, the bewilderment that resided here, a tendency to bicker at the slightest provocation, something they'd never have done under normal circumstances. Yes, Matthew since returning home had been hard to deal with, the careless and debonair youth gone for good, in his place an embittered man tormented by evil memories. He was bound to be edgy and perverse. But not like this.

Jenny heard his mother call up but there was no reply. 'Should I try?' she said awkwardly as Mrs Ward came back into the room, her face tight with annoyance and embarrassment.

'You can if you like. Try knocking on his door.' It was a privilege Mrs Ward allowed no caller; to explore her upper floors was not their business. There was a significance in this acceptance. 'I think he might talk to you, tell you what the matter is with him.'

The newspaper rustled on Mr Ward's knees. 'You being a nurse, Jenny. If you can't pull him round, who can?'

What could she say? She nodded and got up from the sofa, wishing she was indeed wearing her uniform. It would make this confrontation with him official. Again perhaps not – it might drive him further away with whatever was worrying him. It had to be something dire. She couldn't think what.

Leaving them in the lounge she mounted the stairs and tapped lightly on the door his mother had indicated. His voice came muffled.

'It's open. We don't have keys to bedrooms in this house.'

Tentatively she pushed the door and came in, taking care to close it behind her, a signal that no one else would be an audience to whatever he said to her.

He was standing at the window gazing out, his back to her. With the light on and the curtains open, neither the lamplit road nor its lurid bonfire further down nor the flash of fireworks penetrated. Yet he seemed mesmerised by what was going on outside. Above that faint infiltration of wood smoke peculiar to Guy Fawkes celebrations, the room smelled slightly of cigarette smoke and she noted a nearly empty packet of cigarettes on the bedside cabinet next to a saucer acting as an ashtray with several butts in it. Jenny doubted whether there were any actual ashtrays in the whole house.

He shouldn't have been smoking; hadn't done so at least since his illness; it was detrimental to anyone recently recovered from such a condition. It spoke of rebellion, but what rebellion? She ignored the packet and sat on the foot of his bed looking at him across this rather spacious bedroom. Only the main bedroom in her house was nearly as large as this one. Hers was much smaller and the box room was exactly what it sounded like, a box room.

'Your mother said I could come up,' she began.

He didn't respond. He hadn't turned round to look at her at all. No use sitting here looking at someone's back. She might as well get up and go. His back had a very straight look to it. He did look very tall standing there, but not so painfully thin as he had been. He had put on a little weight at last and his shoulders seemed to have broadened again. Seeing them, she felt a thrill of love pass through her. She got up and went across to him.

'Matthew,' she whispered. She touched his shoulder, surprised and alarmed to have him shrug the shoulder away from her as though stung.

'Good God, Matthew, what is the matter?' The profile of his face in the light from the street lamps seemed chiselled in granite, exactly as his mother's sometimes appeared when in a dilemma.

There was nothing for it but to force him to turn away from the window where he seemed to be staring out, not at the celebrating children and the lingering parents, but at something entirely disconnected from them. The look he gave her on being turned to face her was no different, as though it were not she but someone else who stood there. Then he blinked, seemed to come back to himself, recognise who it was standing beside him.

'Jenny . . . Jenny . . . I don't want it to happen to me again. I don't want to be in love with someone and find they don't want me.'

So he was frightened of ever falling in love again. A sense of deadness began to grow inside her. He had made up his mind and was letting her down gently. There was a strange expression in his dark eyes, so dark they seemed to have buried themselves in the depths of his skull. There was a look on his face she couldn't understand. A silent request for her to leave, she guessed. He seemed in pain, his brows drawn together, his lips twisted.

'So if he's the one you really want.'

What was he talking about? 'Who?' she interrupted weakly.

'The chap you were out with last week.'

Oh, God, Ronald Whittaker. Matthew had seen them together, must have watched them come back, watched their embrace. It was imperative to explain. She started to but he wasn't listening, was still talking.

'I don't blame you, Jenny. What've I got to offer someone like you?'

'It's not like that, Matthew,' she blurted, but he still wasn't listening.

'I don't love you, Jenny, I just felt – watching you . . . I don't love you. You don't have to feel bound to me if there's someone else. I don't love you, you know. I really don't . . .'

Her heart plummeted in shock and misery. He stopped suddenly, his expression like one of desperation. It confused her. It also dawned on her that he was denying just too vehemently this love he was supposed not to have for her. What was it Shakespeare wrote? 'The lady doth protest too much, methinks.' Matthew too was protesting too much. He did love her.

From its downward flight, her heart was lifting up, a soaring bird within her breast.

'Oh, darling, it was someone I knew years ago. He came looking for me. I told him I felt nothing for him. And I don't. It was over long ago. He's married.' The lie tripped easily off her tongue. All she wanted was to hear Matthew translate into words that which was contorting his features. But she must be the one to say it, she knew. She didn't hesitate a single second.

'The only person I love is you, Matthew. It's always been you.'

She saw his brow clear, his eyes become brighter, his lips lose their tightness to quiver and part in a disbelieving, hesitant smile. Seconds later she was in his arms, hearing him whispering fiercely to her.

'You don't know how I felt seeing you, down there with someone else. You'll never know. That feeling of jealousy, like a huge black insect inside me, I wanted to tear it out. That was when . . .' A small ragged laugh, hardly a laugh at all but a sound, escaped him. 'That's when I knew. For the first time, I really knew.'

He didn't have to say it. She knew as well. All these years. All these wasted years. They were over. From now on she and Matthew would be able to look forward. There'd be times, of course, when sullenness overwhelmed him, old memories, old regrets maybe, the empty years of want raising their ugly heads in a dream, an unguarded moment. But she would be silent or encouraging, whichever his mood called for. There would also be the happy times, the loving moments, the quiet times.

'I love you,' she murmured, for the pair of them.

She felt him nod against her cheek before he kissed her, and knew he felt the same way about her. And it didn't matter that he did not put it into words.

Beyond the window a firework exploded in a protracted series of crackling – a jumping cracker. Perhaps in a little while she would suggest they take Mattie outside to see the fun. It would be Mattie's first time. She might be a little scared, but with a packet of hand-held sparklers Mattie could be gently coaxed into holding one to watch their fairy-like corona of sparks darting out like stars. This would soon inure her to the noise and the gleeful shouts as sky rockets whooshed up into the dark heavens.

It was in triumph that she and Matthew came downstairs and into the room where his parents waited in tense vigilance. It felt wonderful to witness their utter delight in seeing the smile on his face, his arm about her.

'We're taking Mattie out to see the fireworks,' he said simply, and for once his mother did not upbraid him for not calling his daughter Matilda.

Matilda sat half asleep in one of the armchairs, a little unnerved by the bangs and cracks outside. Jenny hadn't noticed her in the fraught moments earlier on, but now she was roused, still sleepy, and had her coat and hat put on her while Jenny made off down to a shop in Mare Street to buy the packet of sparklers. On the way she stopped off to tell her mother her news that Matthew had declared he loved her. Well, declared as much as he dared.

Matthew stood by the school railings, muffled in overcoat and scarf against the December cold, watching the children spilling out of the dim building into a sleet-spattered playground as the muffled echoes of the hand bell ringing home-time died away inside.

He thought of the night nearly four weeks ago, when he and Jenny had stood together with Mattie watching the fireworks and the bonfire, Jenny holding tightly on to her as she screamed in initial fright at the sudden noises, coaxing her to hold a sparkler by its thin stick between her small fingers until alarmed cries turned to squeals of delight.

At five years old, Mattie had suffered no fear of war. Her only trauma seemed to be the school where she had been started in September. She hadn't adjusted to it as well as she'd been expected to, and would throw herself into her grandmother's arms on coming out, saying she hated everyone there. The children were noisy and rough, the teachers frightened her; every morning she burst into tears, fighting every inch of the way as she was taken there, sometimes saying she felt sick, until on several occasions her grandmother relented and brought her home again.

Jenny had expressed concern. 'There's something worrying her.'

'Other kids cope,' Matthew had said.

'Mattie's not other kids, Matthew. She was taken from her mother, though she was too young to understand, and it must have been unsettling. She's only been with grandparents all this time. Then suddenly she had to adjust to a total stranger she is told is her father. And now she's whipped off to a school full of strangers and expected to cope. No, Matthew, she's not like other kids.'

For a moment the old ache had welled up inside him, thinking how like her mother Mattie was, wilful, at times almost uncontrollable, quick to burst into tears. Yet she could be so charming, endearing herself to everyone at first glance. She was so much like Susan, in ways and looks, that it tore him apart to watch her. Jenny was right, he often found himself actually avoiding her so as to lessen the pain it gave him.

'She'll just have to learn to adapt. We all have to learn that,' he had said, remembering that he too had had to adapt over the years after knowing only a youth full of being molly-coddled. It had come as a shock.

But Jenny had been firm. 'A child's view of things is different to ours. We know we have to put up with what comes, or go under. We learn to fight adversity. A child doesn't even know what adversity is, only that they're unhappy and can't understand why. It makes them behave oddly, and when we get confused by them, they get even worse in sheer frustration. There's something underlying all this. Something even she doesn't remember, but it's there lurking in the back of her mind. She needs a real parent, which is what you are.'

Now he was being a real parent, waiting for Mattie to come out of school.

He was remembering how Jenny had clutched Mattie to her as a banger went off nearby. The houses around them had danced and shivered in the shadows of the lurid flames leaping high into the air from the bonfire. Jenny had given a visible shudder. 'She's had enough of this. I think I have as well.'

They had walked back down the road towards his house, Mattie walking between them, each holding her hand. She had seemed happier away from the violent fun, enjoying the fireworks from a distance. Small rockets had streaked thinly up into the sky over the rooftops, dimmed by bright street lights before which the once practically touchable moon and the pure discs of stars receded, never again to be seen in their full glory by city dwellers in the way they had been during the years of blackout.

Walking back slowly, he had thought what a wonderful mother Jenny would make. And at his gate he had proposed to her and Jenny had said yes.

Recalling it all with a light feeling inside him, he waited for his daughter to emerge from the school exit.

First came the very young, protectively shepherded by a tweed-skirted, motherly teacher into the chill afternoon already gathering into dusk. They were followed closely by exuberant older children: girls in neat hats, precisely buttoned overcoats and shiny strap shoes; boys with caps askew, blazers and coats open and flying, socks concertinaed and shoes with the mud of clogged playing fields clinging to them, laces already coming unravelled.

Taking leave of their teacher, the younger children ducked in and out of the bigger ones, seeking mothers who stood in groups with craning necks to collect their offspring.

Matthew stood a little apart from them, the only man, looking for his child. He saw her moving sedately among the others – small neat figure in her blue overcoat, her short dark curly hair peeping from under the small brim of her blue school hat. Blue suited her, as it had suited her mother.

Swallowing the lump that came into his throat, Matthew called out to her. Catching sight of him, her face lit up, but she walked across the playground and out of the gate to him with all the nonchalance of one having survived a traumatic experience and come off triumphant. The first time ever, he calculated with pride in his daughter's achievement.

She looked up at him with those great soulful blue eyes, so like her mother's. 'Are *you* taking me home today, Daddy?'

'Yes, Mattie,' he replied, love swelling within him as he gazed down at her, that love filling every dark place her mother's going had left inside him. She would fill it every day from now on. She and Jenny between them. By them he would survive. 'I'm taking you home.'

'Is Jenny going to be there?'

'Yes, she'll be there.'

Jenny had come over early. They had talked while his mother had taken Mattie to school, for once without tears with Jenny – he guessed he would always call her Jenny – promising to bring her sweeties if she didn't cry. 'And next week I'll go to school and wait for you to bring you home. Is that all right?' And Mattie had squealed that it was and had taken her grandmother's hand almost with enthusiasm. Jenny was good for her, would always be good for her.

'And you should call her Jenny, not Jenny,' he said solemnly. 'Or if you like, you could call her Mummy.'

Mattie thought for a moment, regarding him steadily. 'I like Mummy, it's easier.'

Matthew felt a small pang for her. She had never truly known her real mother, had she?

She was looking up at him, her mind gone entirely off names. 'Can we go home now, Daddy? I'm cold.'

Home. He held her hand as he led her to the car, which was warmer than having to walk in this weather. Home. By Christmas it would be a new home, his and Jenny's home, paid for from the trust money he'd been given on his twenty-first birthday, put away to accrue interest through the years, once intended for him and Susan. That was in the past now. The rest of the money would go to resuscitating the partnership – his father's wedding present to him, saying he himself was too old to manage alone any more. From now on the past would be put aside, only the future of importance.

He held out a hand and felt the soft fragility of Mattie's

small fingers twine around his, trusting, possessive, confident of both present and future.

What of the future, he mused as they went towards the waiting car. Two weeks from now he would be married. In two weeks' time he would begin his life anew, perhaps regain a small part of what he had lost, after all those promises so carelessly made so long ago, so lightly taken for granted. He knew better now. He would make new promises to himself now; would never again take them all for granted, but he knew it would never again be quite the same.

Guiding his daughter to the car, he opened the rear door for her to scramble gratefully in. Then he went around the front, slid into the driver's seat, started the engine and pressed down on the accelerator with a force that made the thing roar wildly into life, driving off sharply enough to toss Mattie back into her seat with a delighted giggle.

Also by Maggie Ford:

The Servant Girl

She is the downstairs maid; he is the Master's son...

Forced to become a kitchen maid at Fortune Hall, Hetty Pearson
strikes up an unlikely friendship with the younger son of the
house, Richard.

But Hetty is just a poor servant girl: what hope does she have
of either winning Richard's heart or escaping his older brother's
more base attentions?

EBURY
PRESS

Also by Maggie Ford:

A Mother's Love

Can she escape the hardships of her past?

Growing up in London's tough East End, young Sara Porter has had to learn to take care of herself. Her mother resents her maternal responsibilities and has never shown her daughter the slightest bit of love.

Starved of affection, Sara vows not to let anyone get close and focuses instead on getting out of the East End. But still she hopes that one day she'll find a real family to call her own...

EBURY
PRESS

Also available from Ebury Press:

A Wartime Wife

By Lizzie Lane

Trapped in a marriage to the wrong man...

Struggling to make ends meet, Mary Anne Randall is offered no
help by her drunk and abusive husband. A pawnbroking business
run from the wash house at the back of her home is the only way
she can hope to keep her three kids fed and clothed.

But, as storm clouds gather over Europe, can Mary Anne break
free from her loveless marriage for what might be a last chance
at love...?

EBURY
PRESS

Also available from Ebury Press:

A Wartime Family

By Lizzie Lane

A scandalous woman?

Having left her abusive husband for very good reasons, Mary Anne
Randall finds herself judged harshly by her neighbours, especially
after she has the courage to risk a second chance at happiness.

But with the only man she has ever loved away fighting, Mary
Anne is less concerned by her tarnished reputation than with
keeping her children safe, as the bombs fall on Bristol – all too
close to home.

EBURY
PRESS

Also available from Ebury Press:

The Downstairs Maid

By Rosie Clarke

She is a servant girl...

When her father becomes ill, Emily Carter finds herself sent into service at Priorsfield Manor in order to provide the family with an income.

He will be the Lord of the Manor...

Emily strikes up an unlikely friendship with the daughters of the house, as well as Nicolas, son of the Earl. But as the threat of war comes ever closer, she becomes even more aware of the vast differences between upstairs and downstairs, servant and master...

If you like Downton Abbey you'll love this!

EBURY
PRESS

Also available from Ebury Press:

Like Mother, Like Daughter

By Maggie Hope

Sadie Raine has a bad reputation...

When she runs off with a Canadian airman, her two young
daughters are left behind to pick up the pieces.

But Cath Raine is determined to rise above the local gossips.
Only, when she meets the upper-class Jack on the grounds of
his father's estate, she is tempted by the thought of an affair.
Is she destined to follow in her mother's scandalous footsteps
after all...?

EBURY
PRESS

Dear Reader:

What a privilege to partner with my publisher, WaterBrook Press, and our friends at LifeWay Christian Stores to bring you this special edition of *Directed Verdict.* I've tried to pen a story that would capture the twin wonders of God's justice and grace.

You'll meet some lawyers you might actually like and a missionary you're sure to admire. You'll learn about the high cost of following Jesus in other parts of the world. More Christians have been martyred for the faith in this century than in all the previous centuries combined.

Readers frequently ask if religious persecution is really this brutal in places like Saudi Arabia. I have seen firsthand the courage of missionaries in this corner of the world. And I've had one church planter (who I first met after the book was complete) tell me—"This is my story! This is the kind of thing that happened to me!"

Why is LifeWay helping to make this specially-priced edition available? Because as an organization, LifeWay has a heart for missions and stories that inspire missions. As individuals, hundreds of LifeWay employees participated this year in mission trips to places like Bangladesh, Brazil, and Tanzania—with incredible results.

Which leaves one final question that some people ask: Would an ambulance-chasing lawyer like the one in *Directed Verdict* really risk everything just to help one missionary obtain justice? Hey, folks, it's fiction! Anything is possible.

Enjoy,
Randy Singer

DIRECTED
VERDICT

DIRECTED
VERDICT

A Novel

RANDY SINGER

WATERBROOK
PRESS

DIRECTED VERDICT
PUBLISHED BY WATERBROOK PRESS
12265 Oracle Blvd., Suite 200
Colorado Springs, Colorado 80921
A division of Random House, Inc.

ISBN 1-4000-7249-2

Library of Congress Cataloging-in-Publication Data

Singer, Randy (Randy D.)
    Directed verdict / Randy Singer.— 1st ed.
      p. cm.
    ISBN 1-57856-633-9
    1. Americans—Saudi Arabia—Fiction. 2. Religious tolerance—Fiction.
  3. Missionaries—Fiction. 4. Saudi Arabia—Fiction. 5. Deportation—Fiction.
  I. Title.
    PS3619.I5725 D47 2002
    813'.6—dc21

                                                              2002007027

Printed in the United States of America
2005

For Rhonda, Roz, and Josh.
You're the best. Ever.

■ ■ ■

ACKNOWLEDGMENTS

I owe much to many for the words on these pages. The following are among my largest creditors:

Palmer Rutherford, Conrad Shumadine, Bruce Bishop, John Pearson, and Gary Bryant, my mentors and partners in the practice of law. You showed me how to practice with honor and passion. The best traits of the lawyers in this story come from you; the worst traits I discovered on my own.

Bob Reccord, my mentor in the ministry, who taught me the value of friendship. Thanks for daring me to dream and write.

Erin Healy and Carolyn Curtis, two great editors and mentors in writing. You taught me the value of words, and you didn't mince them in your unfailing efforts to make this story better. Thanks for your patient persistence.

The class team at WaterBrook Press, who gave this story a chance to live and provided expert help at every step of the process. Thanks for believing.

Those who inspired this book: the missionaries of the North American Mission Board, who take the gospel to the hard places on this Continent, and the lawyers of the American Center for Law and Justice, who defend their right to do so. Thanks for making the kinds of sacrifices that others only write about.

And finally, my awesome family and incredible friends, who provided encouragement, insights, and kind-hearted critiques all along the way—this story exists because of you. For that, I will always be grateful.

Part I

PERSECUTION

1

_____

"S arah, the Muttawa found us! They're coming. Maybe tonight." The caller paused, his voice trembling. "Arrests. Interrogations. Executions. They'll stop at nothing." He whispered rapidly in Arabic.

Sarah tried to answer, but the words stuck in her throat. She clenched the receiver so tight her knuckles turned white. She was suddenly out of breath, yet she knew she could not allow the man on the other end of the line to sense her fear.

"Sarah, are you there?"

"Is this Rasheed?" she asked in her own low murmur. She, too, spoke in Arabic.

"You must cancel the services tonight. And Sarah?"

"Yes?"

"Get the kids out of the apartment."

The kids. Twelve-year-old Meredith. Ten-year-old Steven. Of course she would find a place for the kids. But what about her…and Charles? They couldn't just run and hide at the first hint of an investigation. But if this were not a false alarm…

"Sarah? Remember, we are not given a spirit of fear but of power and love and a sound mind."

"Um, okay…we'll be all right. As she spoke her voice grew steadier, but she still whispered. "Pray for us."

"I will," he promised, and the line went dead.

Sarah kept the phone against her ear, not yet ready to hang up and face Charles and the kids. A million questions screamed for answers. It was Rasheed's voice, but how could he possibly know about the Muttawa? And if they were coming tonight, what did they know? Who told them? And why? She tried to gather her thoughts, calm her fears, stop the spinning sensation in her head. She lowered the phone and stared down at it.

"Is everything all right, hon?" asked Charles. He crossed the kitchen and began massaging her shoulders. She closed her eyes and felt his fingers penetrate the knotted muscles. They did not relax. "Hey," he asked gently. "What's got you so tight?"

Sarah turned and let Charles embrace her. She trembled in his arms then stood on her toes and whispered in his ear. "The Muttawa have found us. They may be coming tonight."

Tilting her head to look at him, she searched his eyes for the comfort and strength she had found on so many occasions during their twenty-three years of marriage.

Instead, she saw nothing but terror.

■ ■ ■

There were few empty seats in the cavernous courtroom, and the marshals were on full alert. The middle aisle divided the spectators into two camps. They had nothing in common.

The left side, behind the prosecutor's table, was jammed with the local defenders of a woman's right to choose. Employees of the Norfolk Medical Clinic were there, as were leading pro-choice advocates from across Virginia. Joining them, so as not to be associated with the fanatics on the other side, were court personnel who had taken time off to see the defendant get what he deserved.

The other side of the courtroom—the right side—was populated with members of Chesapeake Community Church. Many kept their heads bowed in silent prayer as their pastor, the Reverend Jacob Bailey, came to a critical point in his testimony. The church members were joined by some hard-core veterans of the pro-life movement, men and women who had served time for chaining themselves to each other or to abortion clinics. They had seen some irate judges and pit-bull prosecutors in their day. But, as they eagerly told any reporter who would listen, they had never seen a judge as biased as this one—the Honorable Cynthia Baker-Kline. And in this case, with no jury, she had the sole power to convict or acquit.

Two sketch artists, drawing fast and furiously, sat with the reporters on the left side of the courtroom. The woman wearing the robe was easy, a sketch artist's dream. Behind her back, the lawyers called her Ichabod Crane. She had angular features—a long pointed nose, wire-rimmed glasses, accusatory bony fingers, a perpetual scowl, and a jutting jaw— the quintessential schoolmistress. She had not smiled the entire case.

The Reverend Jacob Bailey would prove more difficult for the artists. Try as they might, neither had succeeded in making the defendant look like a criminal. His face was thin and pale. Twenty days of a fluids-only fast had rendered him gaunt. Static electricity charged his wispy and unmindful blond hair, and he slumped forward as he testified, his bony frame engulfed by the witness chair. He talked so softly that Ichabod had to keep reminding him to speak into the mike.

The man presently questioning Bailey was defense attorney Brad Carson. He fared better with the artists. He was thin, possessing a runner's build, a chiseled jaw, deep-set and expressive steel-blue eyes, and jet-black hair. He had the comfortable bearing of a man without pretense and a quick and easy smile that charmed both witnesses and spectators.

The artists put down their pencils as Carson got to the crux of the matter.

"What were you doing outside the abortion clinic on September 13, Reverend?" Brad addressed the witness from behind the podium. Yesterday his efforts to pace the courtroom had generated a stern lecture from Ichabod on proper decorum.

"Praying," said the reverend, softly and simply.

"Were you talking to God or talking to men?"

"I pray to God," answered the reverend, "in the name of His Son, Jesus Christ." Brad had not put that last part in the script, and he shot Bailey a reproving look.

"Did you have your eyes closed as you knelt to pray?" Brad emphasized that the reverend was on his knees; it would make his conduct seem less threatening.

"Yes, of course."

"Did you even know whether anybody else was around?"

"Not really," said the reverend. "When I pray I try to focus on God and block out everything else." Another bonus answer. Brad got the impression that the pastor was juicing it up a little for the congregation.

"Were you within one hundred feet of the clinic?" asked Ichabod sharply, leaning forward so she hovered over the witness.

Her question, though an easy one, seemed to startle the witness. He looked up meekly at the judge. "Yes ma'am," he said.

Brad watched Ichabod make a check on the legal pad in front of her. The criminal statute applied to any speech or activities within one hundred feet of a medical facility.

He moved quickly to regain the initiative. "May I approach the witness, Your Honor?" Brad started walking toward the witness box.

Ichabod glared at Brad and waited a few painful seconds. He stopped. "Yes," she said, when she had his full attention. Brad sighed and moved forward. Out of the corner of his eye he watched Ichabod return to doodling on her legal pad, doing her best to look bored.

"I'm handing you a copy of the criminal statute in question," Brad said as he extended a single sheet of paper to the reverend. The paper trembled as Bailey held it. Brad knew this would happen. It was part of his plan to generate sympathy.

"Look down at the second paragraph," Brad continued, moving back to his own counsel table and pulling a pair of reading glasses from his suit coat pocket, "and follow with me as I briefly read the things this statute prohibits. Did you try to obstruct, detain, or hinder anyone from entering the facility?"

"No."

"Did you knowingly come within eight feet of any patients for the purpose of passing out a leaflet or handbill?"

"No."

"Did you knowingly come within eight feet of any patients for the purpose of engaging in oral protests or persuading the patients not to proceed with an abortion?"

"No," said the Reverend Bailey, his voice picking up some confidence even as his hand continued to tremble. Brad was pleased with the witness; it had not been easy to convince the pastor to answer so succinctly.

But Ichabod was not through.

"When you pray," she asked, looking thoughtfully out toward the audience, "does your religion require that you pray at a certain spot?"

"No, Your Honor," admitted Bailey, looking befuddled.

"So you can pray anywhere in the country, and God will still hear?"

"Yes, of course. He's omnipresent."

"And can your God hear you whether you pray out loud or to yourself?" the judge asked, still staring off into the distance.

"Sure," said Bailey. He had leaned too close to the mike, and it squealed. He jumped back as if it had bitten him.

"On the date in question, were you praying out loud or to yourself?" Ichabod queried.

"Out loud."

"Loud enough for others to hear?"

"Yes."

Ichabod made a few more check marks on her pad. Then she turned and gave the witness an icy stare. He shifted uncomfortably.

Brad felt like he was watching a train wreck develop in slow motion and was powerless to stop it. He took off his glasses and began gnawing on them.

"Then do you expect this court to believe that you just *happened* to pick this spot to pray and just *happened* to pray out loud, but really had no intention of persuading the women who might just *happen* to walk by?" Ichabod raised her inflection and eyebrows in a show of disbelief.

"Your Honor," said Brad quickly, drawing attention away from the witness box. "I find myself in the unusual position of objecting to the court's own questions." He flashed a disarming grin that the judge did not return.

"While I've got a suspicion that my objection will be overruled," he continued, "it does seem improper for you to be asking argumentative questions of this witness. Particularly when the question implies that this statute prevents someone from praying out loud on a public sidewalk. My reading of the statute does not suggest that interpretation."

"Is that your objection?" Ichabod turned her icy stare to Brad.

"For now," he added quickly.

"Overruled. The court is entitled to develop a full record. Now, Mr. Bailey, answer the question."

Reverend Bailey hesitated and exhaled deeply. "Honestly, Your Honor," he said in a soft-spoken plea, "I felt burdened to pray about this." He paused and looked down at his folded hands, his voice softening even further. "This sin that is plaguing our nation…this killing of unborn children. And I felt led by God to do so in front of the clinic, regardless of the consequences."

Attaboy, thought Brad. *Show a little spine.* Brad jumped on the chance to regain control.

"Why did you feel so burdened?" he asked, leaning forward, feigning interest.

The question elicited a quick response from the prosecuting attorney, a severe-looking woman in her midforties named Angela Bennett, who rose immediately to object. She could have saved her energy, because Ichabod, the self-appointed guardian of the Norfolk Clinic, was all over this one.

"Mr. Carson," Ichabod hissed, staring at him over the glasses perched on the end of her nose. "That question's improper, and you know it. I've told you before, we are not going to get into the reverend's personal views on abortion—"

"But Judge, motivation is key. The statute requires that Reverend Bailey intentionally come within eight feet of abortion patients for the *purpose* of persuading them not to—" The judge held up her hand and Brad stopped in midsentence.

"Mr. Carson!" she snapped. "I am not finished!"

"Sorry, Your Honor," Brad said, without the least hint of remorse.

"You *will not* inject the issue of motivation into this case. This is basically a trespass case. He either violated the law, or he didn't. His purpose for being there—and whether it was to persuade women not to have an abortion—can be determined from his actions. His motivation for being there does not concern me. Is that clear?" She gave Brad her most intense federal judge stare.

He wanted to tell her she was splitting legal hairs, that she was a disgrace to the bench. He wanted to tell her off the way he had in his dreams, the way he had while driving to work, the way he had a thousand times this morning in his own mind. He felt the heat rising in his neck, and he knew how good it would feel to unload. But he also knew it would be pointless.

His plan called for a far different approach. And his client's future hinged on Brad's ability to keep his cool and execute the plan.

So he just glared back, his eyes flashing with equal intensity.

"Mr. Carson, I'm speaking to you," Ichabod said, her voice nearly cracking.

"Sorry, Judge," he replied at last, "I just wanted to make sure you were finished this time."

His impertinence caught her speechless. Her eyes were mere slits, with the nostrils on her enormous nose puffing in and out. When she finally did speak, it came in short, staccato bursts.

"Don't you ever…treat this court with such disrespect again! Next time…I'll hold you in contempt. And Mr. Carson?"

He raised an eyebrow, determined not to speak.

"Get back behind that podium and resume your examination from there." She watched warily as Brad retreated to the podium. "Your juvenile shenanigans do not impress me."

Brad shuffled his notes on the podium, then leaned down to whisper in the ear of the heavyset woman seated at counsel table, his longtime assistant, Bella Harper.

"Watch that vein on her neck," whispered Brad, "I'm going to make it explode." Even as he spoke, the prominent vein on the right side of Ichabod's neck was pulsing visibly, in and out with every heartbeat.

"Don't be a hero," whispered Bella.

But Brad realized he no longer had a choice. He could not win this case in front of Ichabod. She had already made up her mind and would not be confused by the facts. His best chance now was to demonstrate her bias and set her up for reversal on appeal.

To do so, he would have to provoke the full fury of the judge and put his own reputation at risk—a reputation that had taken twelve years to build. It would make matters unbearable at trial but give him a shot on appeal. As an unpleasant by-product, it would make him the poster boy for the Christian Right, a martyr for a cause he did not embrace.

He would do it anyway.

He would do it because he had taken an oath to represent his clients zealously. He would do it because it was the right thing to do.

Brad paused for air and braced himself. Ichabod had not heard the last about motivation.

It was time for Plan B.

■　■　■

On the other side of the world, a warrior stalked his prey.

Ahmed Aberijan was a holy warrior, and he was in a holy war. His official title was director of the Muttawa, the Saudi Arabian religious police. His colleagues called him the Right Hand of Mohammed.

His agency was the last bastion of religious purity in a society ravaged by the cancer of Western culture. For Ahmed, Islamic law was all that separated his country from the degradation of the West. Without it, Saudi Arabia would become America's puppet, its Arab slave. America sickened him—the haughty women, the crass materialism, the arrogance of the weak Western politicians. He had secretly gloated when the Twin Towers of the World Trade Center collapsed, watching with pleasure as radical Muslims danced in the streets. Like the infidels in the trade towers, all Christians would one day face the fierce wrath of Allah and answer for their transgressions.

In the meantime, they would have to deal with him.

He lived for nights like this one; he could feel the blood racing through his veins, each nerve-ending fully alert. His target was the underground house church of an American missionary named Charles Reed. But his ultimate goal, as always, was purity for the people of the Kingdom.

Prophet Mohammed himself—peace be upon him—had declared that there should be no religion but Islam on the Arabian peninsula. It was holy ground. Sacred. Not to be desecrated by Western infidels.

For that reason, non-Islamic sects were prohibited from holding public meetings or worshiping. And converting from Islam to another religion was still punishable by death.

A young Ahmed had cringed when the Muttawa enforced religious purity with unfeeling brutality, torture, even beheadings. But as he grew in strength and fervor, Ahmed began to understand that advancing the cause of the Great Prophet sometimes required the shedding of blood. He still remembered the first time he had personally exacted revenge for Allah. He was overwhelmed with a euphoric sense of passion and peace. He experienced, like never before, Allah's pleasure. And that day, he dedicated his life to advancing the cause and punishing the infidels.

Tonight, that mission required Ahmed's presence on the other side of town at a run-down apartment complex. Though he could easily have done so, he never dreamed of delegating this task, of sending someone else to do the hard work for Mohammed. And as his caravan sped through the dark side streets of Riyadh, he sat alone in the back seat of the first unmarked car, interior lights on, reviewing the file and savoring his plan.

The Reed file was thin, the information sparse. Page one contained the summary. Dr. Reed's official occupation in Saudi Arabia, as listed on his visa application, was that of a private school teacher. His wife, Sarah, posed as a school administrator. But Ahmed knew the Reeds were, in fact, American missionaries, sent to deceive and proselytize the Muslim people.

According to his source, a loyal Muslim who had feigned conversion and joined the Reeds' church, the combination of Dr. Reed's passionate teaching and his wife's administrative skills had proven effective in leading more than a few Muslims astray. Tonight he would put an end to their crimes.

Page two of the Reed file contained the affidavit from the source. The Reeds and their followers crammed themselves into the stuffy family room of the Reeds' apartment every Friday night at seven o'clock, the source said, forming one of Riyadh's fastest-growing underground churches. The Reeds were passionate about converting those who attended and equally passionate about the secrecy of the service, which lasted about two hours.

But it wasn't the Friday night service that bothered Ahmed. The names and addresses of those worshipers could be—in fact had been—acquired from his informant. One small church gathering did not merit a minute of Ahmed's valuable time. But the affidavit alleged that the Reeds were also the catalysts for a network of underground churches. They would pray for these other churches on Friday night. Some were led by the Reeds and worshiped at other places. Some were led by other pastors who were in turn mentored by Reed. They never used names, and the informant did not know the leaders or locations of these churches.

But Reed knew. And if he cared about his wife and children, tonight Reed would tell.

Ahmed stared at the passport photos of the couple. The years of pastoring had not been kind to Charles Reed. Ahmed smirked at the pale and pockmarked skin of the pudgy American, the thick glasses, the receding hair, the deep wrinkles that spread like vines from the American's eyes. He would be easy prey. Soft. Pliable.

Sarah Reed had aged more gracefully. Her short, wavy blond hair framed a face of gentle lines and smooth skin. High cheekbones complemented deep blue eyes that glistened with life even in the photograph. Ahmed was surprised that Sarah Reed made no effort to accentuate those features with the detestable makeup or jewelry of the West. Her looks communicated a natural and comfortable warmth, a woman who would become an immediate friend and confidant to the unsuspecting Muslims she was leading into heresy.

He was sure, just from looking at the photographs, that Charles Reed would love his wife deeply and do anything to protect her. He was also sure that the men he had brought for this raid, with their lust for subjugating Western women, would give Charles Reed sufficient cause for concern.

■ ■ ■

Hours after the phone call, Sarah was beginning to think it was a false alarm.

Shaken by the call, she had first suggested leaving.

"Where would we go?" asked Charles. "Who would we stay with and place in danger?"

Sarah looked down and did not respond.

"Sooner or later, if we're going to stay in this country and reach these people, we'll have to face them," Charles said softly.

Without another word, Sarah picked up the phone and started making calls. She called some trusted friends to take care of the kids. She called every family in the church, explaining the situation, telling them the service was cancelled, and asking them for their prayers. Only three members of the church were not home, and though it was against every rule of the fledgling underground movement, she left a vague warning on their answering machines.

When Meredith and Steven were safely out of the house, Sarah and

Charles went about the job of sanitizing the apartment of all things religious. Charles started on the computer. He deleted Bible software programs, e-mails, files, and backup files. He transferred lists of church members to CDs.

Sarah collected all the CDs, Bibles, song sheets, address lists, and papers from the mission board and put them in two large green garbage bags. She even took down the refrigerator magnets with the Bible verses on them. She wrapped the bags in a second bag for safekeeping, then carried them outside.

The Reed's apartment building was in a forgotten part of the bustling city of Riyadh. It housed hundreds of residents, mostly foreign nationals, in look-alike apartment boxes distinguished only by the apartment number. The place smelled like stale urine. The apartments had not seen a fresh coat of paint in many years, and the Dumpsters in the parking lot were overflowing. Ignoring the full bins, Sarah walked past them and carried her heavy trash bags to a Dumpster in a complex three blocks away.

By the time they were done with their "spring cleaning," the apartment could just as well have belonged to a couple of atheists.

It was time to pray. And for the next few hours, Charles and Sarah sat next to each other and talked—to each other and to God. "Lord," Charles said quietly as he held Sarah's hand at the kitchen table, "if it be Your will, deliver us from the Muttawa and keep us safe. But if it is Your will that we suffer, give us the same power and courage through the Holy Spirit that you gave to the apostle Paul. And give us the grace that allowed Paul to say he counted it a joy to suffer for Your name's sake. Above all else, put a hedge of protection around Meredith and Steven and keep them safe."

Charles squeezed Sarah's hand. She squeezed back.

"In the name of Jesus, amen."

Sarah stood to survey the apartment one more time. It was getting late. Maybe they wouldn't come. It was nearly eight o'clock. Maybe the Lord had already answered their prayers.

She looked at Charles and forced a small smile. He was trying to act calm, but Sarah had felt the sweat on his palms as they prayed, and the look of terror had never left the depths of his eyes.

As she stood, she jammed her hands into the pockets of her jeans. Then she felt it. Her prayer card. The daily list that reminded her to pray every time her fingers reached into her pocket. She smiled at the way the Lord had just reminded her to get rid of it. She had gone over the house with a fine-tooth comb and totally forgot about the list in her own pocket.

She pulled it out to read the names one last time as she headed for the door. It would go in the trash bin with the other stuff. But first, she would try to remember. "Pray for salvation," the list said, "for Hanif, and for Khartoum, who has attended, but never—"

She stopped reading in midsentence and froze in midstep. A noise—maybe a shuffling—from the landing outside her door. Her eyes darted over to Charles, who put his index finger to his lips. She reached inside her blouse and stuffed the list in her bra. Another noise, muffled words…

■　■　■

By 8:02, Ahmed and his thugs had crept up the stairs and assembled outside Apartment 3C. He gave his orders in a low and hoarse Arabic.

In the next instant, he and his men crashed through the wooden door of the apartment and unleashed the fury of Mohammed on Sarah and Charles Reed.

2
_____

For Sarah, events became a blur, jumbled images on a screen that changed so quickly the eye could not focus.

Without knocking, two large Muttawa agents blasted through the wooden door, destroying the deadbolt and shattering the door itself. Two others quickly followed, guns drawn, orders flying in Arabic.

An older man entered next, walking quickly through the splintered door, clearly in charge, his eyes blazing as he assessed the apartment. He was not a tall man, but he had a linebacker's build with a dark complexion and a darker scowl. Deep wrinkles creased his leathery face, and a thin and wiry beard covered his chin. His penetrating eyes stared straight through Sarah until she diverted her gaze.

The man unleashed a vicious stream of Arabic curses. Sarah couldn't catch it all, but she got the gist. He expected a worship service. He had been double-crossed. They would pay. The traitors would die. The other men began moving toward her and Charles.

Sarah instinctively backed away toward the family room adjoining the kitchen, her empty hands raised over her head. She glanced at Charles, who still stood at the kitchen table, frozen in time. He had placed his own hands behind his head, like they did in the movies. His countenance quickly changed from consternation to calm, and he shot Sarah an almost imperceptible nod. For some reason the terror was gone. His reassuring look calmed Sarah.

A slender agent with small, dark slits for eyes and a scar that ran down his left cheek began shouting orders in English at the Reeds. "Hands on your head! Spread your legs and face the wall!"

Sarah immediately turned to face a wall in the family room, craning her neck slightly sideways toward the kitchen table and Charles. He was slower to move, and she saw another of Ahmed's men jam a forearm into Charles' back and slam him into the wall. His nose hit hard, and blood started trickling to the floor. Charles kept his hands on his head, with the agent standing right behind him, fists clenching and unclenching.

Sarah took a quick look over her shoulder at the apparent leader. His hooded eyes were red and wild with emotion, like a badly developed photograph. Though she immediately diverted her gaze back to the wall, she knew those eyes had been etched into her memory forever, tattooed as a grim reminder of this horrible night.

She wished she had never looked.

She could sense the man moving slowly and purposefully behind her. Within seconds, she smelled the stale breath coming from over her shoulder and felt the callused hand squeeze the base of her skull. He exerted pressure, and the pain shot through her head. She wanted to scream but could only whimper.

"Do not defy me," he whispered hoarsely. "Do not look me in the eye." The other men in the apartment stopped moving. Sarah heard nothing but the man's heavy breathing in her ear.

He closed the vice again between his finger and thumb. Her knees buckled from the pain, and she groaned pitifully in submission. He released his grip and took one step back.

Sarah took an uneven breath and let out a slow groan. She tried to focus on standing, leaning heavily against the wall. The room spun, and the throbbing at the base of her neck would not let up.

She would not look at them again.

Someone began to pronounce the charges. Perhaps the man with the scar; the broken English sounded like his.

"We have reason to understand you are leaders in a criminal…how do you say…plan or conspiracy," he announced. "We have reason to know you sell cocaine through a group of people who, ah, pretense to act like church. We have papers of arrest and search."

"Let me see your credentials." Sarah heard fear in Charles' words.

His voice, an octave higher than normal, sounded more like a whimper than a command. But he bravely stammered on. "These charges are ridiculous."

A sickening thud caused Sarah to glance at the kitchen. Charles' face and bloodied nose had been crushed against the wall, his glasses knocked to the floor. Charles moaned in pain as a thick agent ground the glasses with his heel and pressed Charles' face harder into the wall. The blow had opened a gash above Charles' left eye, and more blood trickled down his face and splattered on the floor.

Sarah shrieked at the sight of the blood, then she stopped abruptly when the barrel of a gun touched the back of her own neck. She began to shake and quietly sob. She closed her eyes to erase the images. But all she saw in the darkness was the face of Charles covered in blood. And the vicious eyes of the Muttawa leader.

In the next few moments, the men began ransacking the apartment. Sarah tried to fight off the pain and fear, her slender body convulsing silently as she sobbed. She kept her eyes closed as she listened to the agents move from room to room, dismantling, destroying, searching.

She prayed for courage.

A commotion in the bedroom indicated they had found something. The men huddled briefly in the hallway and then began turning the rest of the apartment upside down with renewed vigor. The man behind Sarah jammed the gun harder against her skull, a warning not lost on her, and then pulled it away as he joined the others in the search. Sarah finally mustered the courage to look discreetly over her shoulder as the men attacked the family room. Her heart skipped a beat as the agents cut open the cushions of the couch and withdrew packages filled with a powdery white substance.

We've been set up, she realized. *What now?*

The search complete, the small apartment looked like a war zone. The agents marked and stacked the plastic bags neatly on the family room coffee table.

"Ahmed!" The agent with the scar called to the leader and pointed to the stack. "Ten kilos," he said with a cruel smile.

Sarah questioned Charles with her eyes, the silent language that flows from years of marriage.

What do we do?

Peace continued to fill his steady gaze, a coming to terms with the reality of being persecuted for his faith. His composure was her strength, and for a moment she believed they would actually be all right.

The man called Ahmed dished out more orders, and the agents jumped into action again. They turned a kitchen chair to face the family room, threw Charles into it, then wrenched his arms behind it. Ahmed leaned over in front of Charles, his face inches away.

"We find ten kilos of coke," Ahmed bragged. "You will soon be famous drug king. But you are also an American missionary—yes?"

Charles Reed did not speak. He locked his eyes on the floor.

"Do not ignore me!" Ahmed demanded. He grabbed Charles' hair and jerked his face upward. "Look...at...me," he growled.

Charles narrowed his bloodied eyes and glared back. Defiance filled his look in a way that Sarah had never seen.

"I want names and addresses of other church leaders," Ahmed spoke in a low and gruff voice. Without thinking, Sarah slowly started shaking her head from side to side. Her husband could no longer see her, his view blocked by the bulky body of his interrogator. But Sarah willed her husband to defy this evil man. *Just hang tough,* she pleaded silently, *don't give even one name!*

"I see," snarled Ahmed as he let go of the hair and watched Charles resume his stare at the floor. "You make this difficult."

He turned to the agents in the family room. "Continue the search," he commanded in Arabic, but this time he gave the orders slowly, enunciating the words carefully so the Reeds could comprehend. "Remove the woman's clothes and search her for drugs, every hiding place on her body. Enjoy yourselves."

Sarah went numb.

As if fueled by his wife's fear, Charles reacted with the desperate impulse of a man who had nothing to lose. He jumped from the chair and shook off one agent just as Ahmed turned again to face him. Charles lowered his head and drove himself forward. He landed a perfect head butt, driving his forehead as a battering ram into Ahmed's chin.

Ahmed reeled backward, spitting blood, but quickly regained his footing. With the fluid motion of a martial arts expert, he spun and landed his foot squarely against the side of Charles' face, the sound of cracking bone a testament to the blow's force. Charles' head snapped to the side, and his body hurtled against the kitchen wall, collapsing helplessly on the floor.

Sarah dropped her face into her hands and screamed.

A large agent instantly jerked her around and clamped his hand over her mouth. She bit. Hard. And she brought up her knee with all her might. He yanked his hand back, doubled over, and cursed.

But now two more agents were up against her, pinning her to the wall, stuffing her mouth with some type of cloth. Her small frame was no match for these men. They were in her face, pinning her arms and legs. Then they went after her clothes with a vengeance, ripping open her cotton blouse, gawking and grinning stupidly.

The prayer list, she remembered, *they'll see the prayer list!*

This thought energized Sarah, and with an adrenaline-fueled explosion she slipped away from one assailant and lunged at the other. He barely averted her wild swings, wrapped her in a bear hug, and threw her backward to the floor, landing squarely on top of her. Her neck snapped back, and her head bounced hard on the thin carpet.

Everything went black.

■ ■ ■

Brad checked his notes and his nerve one more time. Ichabod would never let the witness answer these questions, but still he had to ask.

When you try a case with one eye on the appeals court, you have to preserve the record. Make the judge rule. Demonstrate her bias.

"Do you believe that human life begins at conception?" Brad bluntly asked Reverend Bailey.

"Objection."

"Sustained," ruled Ichabod, "that question ought to be taken out and shot."

"Do you have a basis in the Bible for your belief that human life begins at conception?" Brad persisted.

"Objection, Judge," prosecutor Angela Bennett whined. "That question assumes that the witness answered the prior question, which he didn't."

"Sustained," snapped Ichabod. "Mr. Carson, move on to something relevant."

"Do you believe abortion is murder?"

Bennett stood but had no time to object. "Mr. Carson," Ichabod's voice had a hard edge, "do you understand English? The reverend's personal beliefs about abortion are not relevant. *Not relevant*. Now move on to something that is or sit down so the witness may be cross-examined."

"May I at least explain the basis for asking the questions?" Brad asked, a trace of sarcasm in his words.

"No."

Bennett smirked and sat down.

Brad's eyes locked on Ichabod as he planned his next line of attack. His next question dripped slowly from his mouth, but he kept his stare fixed on the judge, daring her to rule the question out of order. "The statute requires that you purposefully try to persuade a woman not to enter the clinic and have an abortion," Brad explained. "What was your *purpose* in praying on the sidewalk in front of the clinic?"

Ichabod frowned but did not speak.

"To petition God for mercy," the reverend said. Brad returned his attention to the witness. The man looked paler and more fragile than ever.

"And why did you choose to have this prayer meeting in front of the abortion clinic?"

"Because that's where the evil was happening," the reverend said softly.

"Speak up," demanded Ichabod, "and move closer to the microphone."

"Because that's where the evil was happening," the Reverend Bailey repeated. "That's where the babies were dying."

"Is the front of the abortion clinic the only place you have conducted this type of prayer meeting?" asked Brad.

The prosecutor was on her feet, but her objection was forestalled by a quick look from Ichabod.

"Don't bother," the judge said testily. "Don't bother objecting, because I'm going to let it in. I'm going to give Mr. Carson all the rope he needs to hang himself."

Bennett shrugged and sat down.

"No it's not," said the reverend, leaning into the mike.

"It's not what?" asked Brad.

"It's not the only place we have petitioned God for mercy and to halt evil. My congregation and I have prayed over the last few years in front of our local pharmacy when they started dispensing the RU-486 pill, and in front of some of the bars down on Military Highway, and, you know, places like that…" His voice trailed off, and he leaned back from the mike.

Brad gave him a sideways look of reproach. "Any other places you can think of…where you have petitioned God to end some perceived evil?"

"How can this be relevant?" asked a frustrated Angela Bennett.

"Because it shows the Reverend Bailey didn't go to the abortion clinic with the purpose of persuading pregnant women as prohibited by the statute," answered Brad. "His purpose was to petition God, and that's not prohibited. And it shows he has prayed with his congregation at other places where he perceives evil influences exist, also for the purpose of petitioning God. In short, it demonstrates a pattern."

Brad looked at the judge and waited for her ruling. He knew she didn't like this line of questioning, but neither did she like getting reversed on appeal for making bad evidentiary rulings.

"Go on," Ichabod said, without hiding her impatience. "Is there anyplace else you have done this prayer meeting thing?"

"Just one other place," said the Reverend Bailey meekly. He paused. The entire courtroom waited.

"The steps of this courthouse."

"That's ridiculous," said the prosecutor sharply.

"I agree," barked Ichabod. "The remark will be struck from the record."

Her face flushed and the vein pulsed.

She had taken the bait.

3

Charles Reed tried to focus. His mind swirled in a rage of anger, pain, and helplessness. Two muscular agents forced him back into the kitchen chair and pinned his arms behind his back. Ahmed was in his face. Sarah lay motionless on the family room couch.

She was alive, he knew. And by the grace of God, she had not been molested. After she blacked out, Ahmed started barking orders again. Check the pulse. Lay her on the couch. Grab that list from her bra. Leave her alone.

Charles did not know the reason for the last order. Maybe they were waiting for her to regain consciousness. Maybe they could get whatever they needed from him. Maybe even these men had limits on what they would do to American citizens. Maybe it was just a miraculous answer to his prayer. Whatever the reason, it gave Charles hope.

"Who is Hanif?" Ahmed demanded, reading from the list.

Charles stared at the floor. His face throbbed. The taste of blood trickled through his mouth.

"Who is Khartoum?" Ahmed continued.

More silence.

One of Ahmed's men removed a sleek black stun gun from its holster. He held it inches from the base of Charles' neck and looked at Ahmed, apparently waiting for his cue. Ahmed grinned at Charles and boasted about the weapon. It would immobilize any man, Ahmed told him, with two hundred thousand volts of electricity. And the best thing, Ahmed claimed, was that the instrument left no marks on the victim except two small burn spots where the probes of the gun contacted the skin and unleashed the electricity. Only the central nervous system would suffer permanent damage, and the cause would be difficult to prove.

Charles wondered for a fleeting instant how bad it could be.

He soon learned. And for the next twenty minutes—for what seemed like an eternity—his hope for survival faded with every passing question, with every mind-searing jolt.

"I need names of the leaders of the other church groups you have started," Ahmed spoke deliberately and calmly, as if he knew Charles was beginning to have trouble understanding the words. "Don't play games with me."

The waiting was the hardest part. Knowing what was coming—the surging current of the stun gun—and being powerless to stop it. How many times had they been through this? How much more could he take? How long ago had Sarah gone down? And what would happen to her now? His mind raced, chasing questions with no answers.

Charles sensed movement behind him and convulsed at the thought of another jolt from the hated gun. "Please...I'm begging you," he trembled, struggling for breath. "You've got to believe me... I don't know what churches you're talking about... These names on the card are just friends—"

"Shut up," snapped Ahmed. He grabbed Charles' hair and jerked his head backward again, demanding eye contact.

Charles prayed for strength.

Ahmed slowly raised the corner of his mouth, a small and sick smile, then spit in Charles' face, letting go of his hair. Charles' head dropped hard against his chest. The saliva dripped from his cheek.

"You think you are strong," Ahmed whispered through clenched teeth. "But you are stupid. You will talk, my friend," Ahmed paused, letting the words hang in the air. "You will talk."

Ahmed held out his palm to stop the agent with the stun gun. This time Ahmed himself would do the honors. He took the gun and jammed it furiously against the base of Charles' neck.

Burning flesh, surging electricity, searing pain. Charles shook and yelped as his body twitched involuntarily, the pain affecting every nerve ending, the electricity jolting his brain. His body was on fire from the inside out. His screams did not seem to belong to him, and he jerked uncontrollably in the chair, unable to escape the gun or to bear this new round of torture.

Finally, mercifully, Ahmed disengaged the gun. Charles' seizure continued, blood and saliva flowing from his contorted mouth into his lap. The smell of burning flesh filled the kitchen.

Charles was losing his will to endure. He prayed for strength for the next minute, nothing more. He tried to focus on Sarah and the kids. He would make it one more minute for them, for the church members, for his Lord.

Images flashed through his mind in rapid succession. Images of his wife and children, of baptisms of church members, of the face of Christ as it had been portrayed in his childhood picture Bible. Ahmed's voice brought the parade to a stop.

"We are just beginning," Ahmed said gruffly, without emotion. "Do not be a fool. My men are anxious to finish what they started. On both you and your wife. Your wife needs help, and I need names. Let us make a deal."

The threat to Sarah brought Charles back to reality. He raised his head, looked out toward the living room, then locked eyes with Ahmed. *What does he mean?* Charles wondered. The eyes told him nothing. *Can you deal with the devil? God, give me wisdom!*

Sudden clarity came over Charles in the midst of the pain, an immediate answer to a desperate prayer. *This man is just keeping Sarah safe so he can use her as leverage against me. If I give up the names, he will have no reason to let either of us live, no reason to protect Sarah from his men. The informant must have told him the names of the Friday night worshipers. But the other names he does not know. My silence keeps Sarah alive.*

Ahmed narrowed his eyes. Charles was sure the man could read his thoughts. As Ahmed reached again for the stun gun, Charles mumbled a sentence and dropped his chin to his chest.

"Again," demanded Ahmed. "Say it again."

As if possessed by a force greater than himself, Charles repeated the words, slowly, and in a barely audible whisper.

"He was led like a sheep to the slaughter," he paused, taking a labored breath, "and as a lamb before the shearer is silent, so He did not open His mouth."

Ahmed's silence caused Charles to raise his head. When he did so, Ahmed turned and looked at Sarah, sprawled on the couch, the only sign of life in the heaving of her chest. "Some men need a little extra persuasion," the Muttawa leader growled. He turned back to Charles and, with great force, pulled Charles' right arm from behind his back and grabbed Charles' wrist. He pushed hard against the back of Charles' hand, nearly bending the wrist in half as he forced the hand toward the forearm. Charles flinched and ground his teeth, swallowing the scream that welled up in the back of his throat. Surely his wrist would snap in two.

The pain was back. Searing, debilitating pain. And then Ahmed backed off slightly on the pressure but continued to hold the wrist. "Speak to me," Ahmed said simply. "Or you will beg me to stop, and there will be no end."

Once again Charles summoned courage he did not know he had for another symbolic act of resistance. He gritted his teeth and made a futile effort to yank his wrist away from Ahmed's iron grip. Charles knew immediately that he had made an awful mistake.

Ahmed reasserted the pressure with a vengeance. This time he did not let up as Charles begged for mercy. Ahmed pushed harder; the pain intensified. It shot up Charles' arm and engulfed his brain. And then it happened—the sickening snap of the wrist bone as his hand went limp.

His bloodcurdling scream echoed throughout the apartment.

■ ■ ■

"When did you hold a prayer meeting on the steps of this courthouse?" Brad asked innocently.

Angela Bennett bolted from her seat, hands spread in protest.

"Mr. Carson, that's not relevant," Ichabod said gruffly, leaning back and folding her arms.

"Judge, it *is* relevant. If you give me a few minutes, I'll link it up," Brad promised.

The judge hesitated, then scowled. "Go ahead, Mr. Carson. But it better be good."

Oh, it will be, thought Brad.

"Reverend Bailey, when and why were you praying on the court-house steps?"

"It was in the summer of 2000," he said, "after the *Stenberg v. Carhart* Supreme Court case in which the Court sanctioned partial birth abortion. I just couldn't believe that in this country our courts would defend a procedure like that—a procedure where a viable fetus is delivered into the birth canal, and then…" The reverend paused, pursing his lips and sadly shaking his head. "And then the skull is torn open with scissors, and the brain material is extracted to reduce the head size and ensure the child dies before delivery."

He did not look at Brad as he finished his answer. Brad chose to let the silence linger.

"God help us," the reverend mumbled into the silence. "I knew then it was time to pray."

Ichabod appeared unmoved except for the telltale vein, now a bit larger and pulsing a bit faster than before. She had been duped; Brad saw the realization in her eyes. The volatile issues she had worked so hard to keep out of the case were now cascading around her, and she was powerless to stop them.

"Did you read the opinion in *Stenberg* before you went to the court-house to pray?" asked Brad, pushing the point.

"Yes, I pulled it off the Internet."

"Was there anything in the opinion that surprised you?"

"Yes. I had heard so many news reports about the gruesome proce-dure referred to as partial birth abortion. But until I read the *Stenberg* decision, I had never focused on what really happens during a normal D and E procedure, not a partial birth abortion but the kind of abortion performed every day right here at the Norfolk Clinic."

"And is that what motivated you—" Brad began.

"Stop! Right there!" demanded Ichabod, her harsh words echoing off the courtroom walls. "You are flaunting this court's rulings, Mr. Carson." She clenched her teeth and hunched her shoulders. "Move off this line of questioning."

"Doesn't the prosecution have to make her own objections anymore, or are you just—"

"Don't push it, Mr. Carson," Ichabod snapped. "Don't push it."

Brad pulled a copy of the case from his counsel table and turned to the dissenting opinion of Justice Anthony Kennedy. "Do you recall these words from the opinion?" he asked the reverend. He began reading as if Ichabod had never spoken. "Are these the words that caused you so much anguish that you went first to the courthouse and later to the clinic for the purpose of begging God to stop these procedures?"

Ichabod looked stunned, but Brad could sense the wheels turning. Would she dare rule out of order, as being too emotionally charged, the very words from an opinion of the U.S. Supreme Court?

"In a D and E procedure," read Brad, "the fetus, in many cases, dies just as a human adult or child would: It bleeds to death as it is torn from limb to limb…"

The prosecutor jumped to her feet again. "I strongly object to this inflammatory tactic," Bennett shouted in an effort to be heard over Brad's reading.

"…the fetus can be alive at the beginning of the dismemberment process and can survive for a time while its limbs are being torn off…"

Ichabod started banging her gavel. "Mr. Carson! Mr. Carson!" The prosecutor continued objecting, and a loud murmur rose from the left side of the courtroom. The Reverend Bailey's eyes widened.

Brad increased his volume and continued over the rising din, "…mere dismemberment does not always cause death. Dr. Carhart knew of a physician who removed the arm of a fetus only to have the fetus go on to be born as a living child with one arm." The gavel was still banging, Bennett objecting, and Ichabod was repeating the word "sustained" over and over. "At the conclusion of a D and E procedure, no intact fetus remains. In Dr. Carhart's words, the abortionist is left…"

"That's enough!" Ichabod screamed. The intensity of it stilled the courtroom. Nobody moved.

"…with a tray full of pieces," Brad said into the silence.

All eyes turned to the seething form of Ichabod, still hunched forward, wild-eyed, her face crimson.

"That comment, Mr. Carson, will earn you contempt of court and a ten-thousand-dollar fine," she said coldly, straining every muscle to keep control. "I have never, in twenty-six years on the bench, seen such obnoxious behavior." As she spoke, her voice shook, the anger etched deeply on her face. "In addition," she continued, "your contempt citation will carry a five-day prison term…" An audible gasp went up from the right side of the courtroom. Brad averted her gaze.

After an exaggerated pause Ichabod continued, "…to be suspended on the condition of an apology to this court and good behavior befitting a member of the bar throughout the remainder of this case."

She glared at Brad. "Does counsel wish to make a statement or comment?"

Brad knew the drill. She was waiting for a humble and contrite Brad Carson to grovel and apologize, and then she would probably consider some leniency. Even Ichabod was not in the habit of sending lawyers to jail. The ball was in his court.

For this moment, Brad was ready. He had done his homework. He had mulled this scenario over in his head during the prior sleepless night. He knew that only one word could have the desired effect and consummate his plan. He weighed his response carefully.

Then he shrugged.

"Whatever," is all he said as he turned to take his seat.

"Get him out of here!" Ichabod barked to the marshals, her voice thick with emotion. "Cuff him and get him out of my sight! You have five days minimum, Mr. Carson. And you will stay behind bars longer than that unless and until you apologize to this court and promise to show this court proper respect in the future. This case is hereby suspended until Mr. Carson can finish serving his time."

She slammed her gavel.

Two hefty marshals grabbed Brad and placed handcuffs on his wrists. The Reverend Bailey looked aghast at the sight of his lawyer being treated like a criminal.

The church members prayed.

Brad turned and caught the eye of Bella as he was being escorted from the courtroom. He stared at her for a second, and then he winked. These were not the actions of an unbiased judge. Perhaps now the appellate judges in Richmond would understand.

Plan B had worked to perfection.

■ ■ ■

Charles Reed had no plan. He simply wanted to die.

He curled on the floor in a fetal position, left arm wrapped tightly around his legs, his broken right wrist dangling at his side. Nausea had overcome him. The thought of more torture, the shooting pain from his wrist, the throbbing of his temple and face—it all seemed to lodge momentarily in his stomach. The vomit was the least of his worries. He made no effort to clean himself.

He had given names. He couldn't bear the thought of another jolt from the gun. But the names were just the Friday night worshipers, names that Ahmed already knew, and so the ordeal continued. Other names had not yet crossed his lips, but he knew they had broken his will; he was ready to talk.

Instead, he prayed.

Lord, take me home. Let me take these names with me. Take me home before I talk.

It was all so confusing now, so dark. The images morphed into one another with increasing speed. He tried to focus on the kids, on Sarah, on the suffering of his Lord. He remembered the cross, the nails driven into those hands of mercy. And then the nails became a needle. A needle Ahmed drove deep into Charles' left arm. There was talk of cocaine. Then his arm became Sarah's, and he saw the needle again. They made him watch. She didn't even move as they emptied the contents of the needle into her arm.

The images blurred, the pain became distant. And then he felt it. The cold touch of the two metal prongs on the base of his neck. The voice of Ahmed in the background, demanding more names. The involuntary tightening of every muscle as the current began its deadly course. He squeezed his left arm tighter around his legs. He tried to scream.

This time the pain stuck in his chest, as if he had been stabbed. He struggled for air, but the tightness overwhelmed him.

Jesus loves you, he said to his tormentors. But the words clung to his vocal cords and reduced themselves to a gasp.

His last thoughts were of Sarah and the kids. He subconsciously committed them into the hands of his Lord, and then prepared his soul to die. In the distance, he could hear Ahmed barking orders to his men.

■ ■ ■

Ahmed looked down at Charles Reed in disgust. The American was ghostly white, his chubby face distorted by pain. He gasped again and went still.

As his victim succumbed, Ahmed felt himself begin to relax. The adrenaline that had been fueling his body slowed, the savage vitality of the torture gone.

"Scrape his knuckles against the wall," ordered Ahmed. "Make it look like a fight."

He glanced at Sarah, still motionless on the couch. He saw the lust in his men's eyes.

"Don't touch the woman," he ordered, "except to put another shirt on her. These are American citizens, and every injury will be endlessly investigated."

Ahmed motioned to one of the officers who had been holding Charles Reed. The officer approached Ahmed and stood in front of him.

"Did the American not try to resist us in his drug-induced state?" asked Ahmed.

The officer nodded in nervous agreement.

"And did he not break his wrist as he lashed out at us?"

"Yes."

"Then we must have more evidence of a fight," said Ahmed. And with lightning quickness he drove his powerful fist into the cheekbone of the agent. A gash opened and blood flowed.

The man reeled backward, clutching his face, fear in his eyes. He did not raise his hands in defense.

"You," said Ahmed, "are Exhibit A." Ahmed rubbed his fist and smiled. "Now call an ambulance."

He turned to one of his officers and asked for the two lists of names they had compiled. He compared the first list, provided by the informant, with the list that they had coerced from Charles Reed. Reed had coughed up twenty-one names. All but two had been previously divulged by the informant. Their efforts had fallen woefully short of Ahmed's expectations.

"Deal with the infidels on these lists," he said as he handed them back to the officer. Such common church members did not merit a personal visit from Ahmed Aberijan.

Even without giving an explicit order, Ahmed knew exactly what would happen. The Muttawa would combine with local authorities to handle the more prominent members of the church. Drugs would mysteriously appear at residences. The church members would be arrested, threatened, then released after they signed detailed confessions. They were the lucky ones.

Islamic radicals from the Wahhabi sect would be dispatched to handle the lesser-known members of Reed's group. No arrests would be made. If the church members recanted, they would be severely beaten and released. If they did not recant, they would not survive the night. Their gruesome deaths would serve as a graphic warning for anyone inclined to doubt the Great Mohammed.

4

A few minutes after midnight, the U.S. Embassy in Riyadh began making calls. The embassy had been alerted by a friend of the Reeds, the pastor of another church the Reeds had helped start. The pastor and his wife were taking care of Meredith and Steven. Just before midnight, the couple went to the U.S. Embassy and breathlessly told their story.

Sarah Reed had called earlier in the day and asked them to care for the children. She was worried about a surprise raid from the Muttawa. The pastor began phoning the Reeds' apartment a few minutes after nine o'clock, but nobody answered. After almost an hour of phone calls, he assumed the worst and headed to the Reeds' place. The apartment looked like it had been hit by a hurricane. There was blood on the kitchen floor. He had photographs to prove it.

He had already called the Muttawa, but the Muttawa said they were not in the business of giving out confidential information about arrests and pending investigations.

The embassy officials did not fare much better. They confirmed, through the Muttawa, that the Reeds had been arrested. In fact, the Muttawa claimed the Reeds had resisted arrest and were being treated for injuries. Dr. Reed and his wife were not school workers, as they claimed on their visa applications. Instead, they were drug kingpins, and tonight their tawdry enterprise had been quashed. It was a major drug bust for a nation like Saudi Arabia, netting an estimated two million dollars worth of cocaine. The Reeds themselves were high at the time of the arrest, and tests would soon confirm the levels of cocaine in their blood.

The Muttawa wanted to be helpful but could give no further information. No, the embassy officials could not speak to the Reeds until the investigation was complete. No, the Reeds did not have legal counsel and had not requested counsel. No, the Muttawa were not willing to make an "educated guess" about the possibility of bond or how the process would unfold. And so it went, one governmental bureaucracy stalling another, the Muttawa getting the better of the exchange.

The situation escalated throughout the morning. Higher-ups in the embassy contacted higher-ups in the Saudi government. First one department then another. Officials who were needed to make decisions could not be reached. Those who could be reached had no authority to decide.

Late Saturday morning, the embassy officials finally learned that the Reeds were in the King Faisal Specialist Hospital in Riyadh. Charles Reed was in critical condition. Drug charges had been filed.

The potentially explosive situation had international implications. Both sides were motivated to deal. The Saudis wanted the drug lords deported. The Americans wanted the missionaries safe. And so they agreed, early in the afternoon, that the two Americans would be transferred to a military base hospital thirty miles from Riyadh. American specialists would assume their care. The Reeds would surrender their visas, and the charges would be dropped.

Charles Reed was transferred against the medical advice of his surgeon. He was post-op, and his prognosis was not good. His heart surgery had been complicated by the cocaine racing through his bloodstream, the delay in treatment, and his preexisting heart condition.

Surgery had taken more than three hours. Ventilators, tubes, monitors, and other gadgets kept him breathing and his heart beating. But it would be a stretch to say he was alive. His surgeon's prognosis was dismal. A transfer would only hasten the inevitable.

The embassy, however, desperately wanted to get Charles under the care of American physicians. They ignored the Saudi surgeon's advice and authorized the transfer.

■ ■ ■

Brad awoke Saturday morning to the smell of coffee. He was groggy and disoriented—that brief moment between being fully asleep and fully awake—and he couldn't quite make sense of his surroundings. He rubbed and squinted his eyes as the bright sun streamed through the barred windows toward his cot. The warm rays cleared his head. *That's right*, he remembered. *A federal holding cell. A prisoner of my own government.*

Brad beamed at the logic of his plan. Sure, he would have preferred to plot his appeal in a place where he could use the bathroom unchaperoned, but for the pure brilliance of the legal strategy, Brad was sure he had outdone himself. Yesterday his case was going nowhere fast; today he had a serious issue for appeal. It was a long shot, but it was a shot.

It had dawned on him late Thursday night: Quit trying this case against the government in front of the judge; try the case against the judge in front of the government. Put the judge on trial. Aggravate her in such a way that the record would unmistakably reflect her bias. Appeal based on judicial misconduct. Ask the appellate court for a new trial in front of an unbiased judge. Trade what little chance you might have for a trial-court verdict for a much better chance at a successful appeal. Roll your dice with the boys on the Fourth Circuit.

To Brad's surprise, he was now something of a folk hero among the federal marshals who ran the Norfolk detention center. They confided in him last night that they couldn't stand the brooding arrogance of Baker-Kline either. She was impossible to please, they said. And the marshals, who were occasionally assigned to her courtroom for the judge's own protection, were some of her favorite whipping boys. Brad got the distinct impression that his captors dreamed of spouting off to the courtroom despot just as he had.

The night before, Brad had been allowed a private shower. He had his own holding cell—small, dank, and musty, with only one cot and an open toilet sitting against the far wall—but at least it was private. No drug lords as roommates. And now, at 7 A.M. Saturday morning, his day started with hot coffee.

"Mornin', Brad." It was Clarence, one of the marshals who had swapped stories with Brad the prior night. Clarence stood outside the cell holding two Styrofoam cups.

"This ain't the Hilton, but we make some mean coffee."

"Thanks, man."

Clarence grunted something, carefully placed the two steaming cups of black coffee on the floor, and went about the business of unlocking Brad's cell. "You got a visitor, Brad. She's pushy. If she were visitin' somebody else, I woulda told her where to go. But I figured you might need to hear from her this mornin'."

Brad couldn't resist a grin. He knew who it was.

"But hey, tell her to chill out or next time she's not gettin' through. And, if she works for you, put her on a diet." This said by a man who had obviously devoured more than his share of doughnuts.

"You try telling her that," Brad said, stretching his back. He was not surprised that Bella had come so early. "Is there some kind of private conference room where we can meet? It won't take long."

"Well, technically it ain't visitin' hours." Clarence handed Brad the hot cup. "But I'll see what I can do." He turned his back, left the door unlocked, and lumbered slowly down the hall.

Brad took a sip of the scalding coffee. Terrible. Twice as strong as the stuff at his law office, and no cream. As soon as Clarence disappeared, Brad flushed the powerful black liquid down the grungy toilet. He sat down gingerly on his stained cot, resisting the urge to simply walk out the door.

■ ■ ■

For a lady who stood only five feet two inches, Bella Harper was imposing. The source of her stature was her personality, definitely not her looks. She was a bulldog in every sense of the word.

She packed some serious weight on her short frame. Nobody dared ask how much. Nor did anyone have the guts to ask her age. Bella didn't celebrate birthdays.

Bella featured a butch cut for her salt-and-pepper hair, precious little makeup, a pack-a-day cigarette habit, and a constant scowl that let people know she was not a woman to be trifled with.

She was also the world's best legal secretary.

Bella had been with Brad since he hung out his shingle after graduating from William and Mary Law School. Her outward personality aside, she had been a tough-loving mother to Brad, particularly when Brad's wife divorced him, claiming she could no longer compete with the law for his attention. Bella, however, was fiercely loyal, both to Brad and to her own ailing mother, whom Bella cared for with the attentiveness of a master gardener.

And today Bella was a sight for Brad's sore eyes. She was booting up her laptop when he entered the room and slouched into the bolted-down chair on the other side of the bolted-down metal table.

"You look like death on a bad day," Bella said in her New York accent without looking up.

"Thanks." He rose from his seat and started pacing on his side of the conference table. "You don't look so hot yourself."

Brad was not lying. Bella's eyes were more bloodshot than normal. Because it was not an official workday, she was not dressed in "professional" attire. Her black stretch pants seemed two sizes too small.

"I've called the three largest law firms who have the most federal court experience." Bella wasted no time. As if Brad had important places to go that day. "None of them will handle this emergency writ of mandamus. They've all got the same lame excuses—too busy, schedule conflicts, you know the routine. Everybody's scared to take on Ichabod."

This part of the plan had always worried Brad. He knew he couldn't contact lawyers to represent him before he pulled his little stunt. It would look too calculated. Now he was at the mercy of the local bar as the wagons circled. None of the usual federal court firms would take on a sitting federal court judge. Brad had lots of friends who would do it in a heartbeat, but he wasn't about to ask. He would not poison those friendships just to get out of the can a few days early.

His pacing intensified. He ran his hand through uncombed hair.

Bella rambled on, "Harris, Clark & Yarbrough; Day & Adams; Kilgore & Strobel. They're all runnin' scared. I offered to pay full hourly rate. You could almost hear 'em laugh through the phone. Brad, you've already sued half their clients. Representing you would be suicide."

"Somebody needs to tell them not to take those suits so personally," Brad muttered.

"Right."

Bella absentmindedly reached into her purse and pulled out a pack of Camels. As she lit up, the rancid smoke filled the poorly ventilated room. Brad continued pacing in silence, altering his path and cutting Bella a wider berth.

"By the way," Bella said between puffs, "I had to fire Tina."

Brad stopped midstride and let out a groan. "C'mon Bella. We're already short-handed. Tina was doing a good job. How many times have we discussed this?"

"Tina was a parasite," snapped Bella. "She'd come in late, take two-hour lunches, and be gone by five. Should have fired her a year ago. I'd rather do her work myself."

"She wasn't even with us a year ago," protested Brad. "And now you *will* be doing her work yourself."

He waited for Bella to respond, but she just puffed in silence.

"Put in the usual classified ads. Make sure you hit the legal periodicals," Brad said. He really needed some caffeine to clear his head. "And this time, Bella, I want the paralegal reporting directly to me. I hire them, and only I fire them."

He looked at Bella again and waited for confirmation. She ignored him and pulled some more files out of her briefcase. It was no use getting mad at her now. He would deal with her attitude later. At least she was here, first thing on a Saturday morning. And they had more important things to talk about than office management.

He switched gears. "We've got to get a brief and petition for a writ of mandamus hand-delivered to Judge Baker-Kline and a Fourth Circuit judge by the end of the day to have any chance for a hearing on

Monday. We'll have to write it ourselves. I'll need you to help with the research. I'll sign it and argue it in front of the Fourth Circuit."

In response, Bella took another long draw on her Camel, then tossed a manila folder and an extra pair of reading glasses onto the table in front of Brad. He put on the glasses, opened the folder, and was not entirely surprised to find a twenty-two-page brief and accompanying petition. Bella couldn't suppress a grin. Her bloodshot eyes twinkled.

"I stayed up all night drafting this baby," she said proudly. "I had a little help."

Brad sat down and started reading, ignoring the smoke that came in waves across the table. Ichabod sounded like the Ayatollah. The brief was fat with applicable case law—precedents where more egregious conduct by other lawyers was found insufficient to justify contempt. By page eleven, Brad was ready to sign.

"That won't be necessary," said Bella. "You know what they say. A lawyer who represents himself has a fool for a client."

"Somebody's got to sign it."

"Why don't you check the last page before you go startin' another argument you can't win."

Brad looked and his jaw dropped.

The signature belonged to Jay Sekulow, renowned constitutional law expert and lead counsel for the American Center for Law and Justice. Sekulow had the personal reputation and legal firepower to get the attention of the Fourth Circuit judges. The smell of victory began to replace the stale fumes of Bella's cigarettes.

"I didn't even have to beg," said Bella curtly. "Turns out he's been following the case closely. His group is big on religious liberty cases. All I had to do in return," her voice lowered as she mumbled the rest, "was to promise you'd appear on *Jay Sekulow Live* when you get out."

"You *what?*" Brad cocked his head sideways, as if eyeing Bella at a new and skeptical angle would change this news. "Just what I needed. A nationally syndicated radio show. Brad Carson, the new lap dog for the Christian Right." He took off his glasses and placed them on the table.

Then he hunched forward, narrowed his eyes, and locked in on Bella to make his point.

"Whatever," she said with a wry smile.

■ ■ ■

By midafternoon Brad was sitting in the regal chambers of the Honorable Cynthia Baker-Kline. It was a surreal scene and a humiliating one. The judge sat behind her large oak desk, dressed in a black pinstriped suit. Assistant district attorney Angela Bennett sat next to Brad and also sported a power suit, even though it was Saturday afternoon. Brad wore his orange jail jumpsuit, his feet adorned by the standard-issue jail flip-flops.

Brad knew the fix he was in when he got to Ichabod's office on time and discovered that the judge and the ADA were already meeting. Such ex parte meetings were technically improper—a judge should never discuss a case with only one lawyer present—but when Brad entered the office, the two women started chatting aimlessly about everything but the law. The message was clear: We were not discussing the case, so don't even bother complaining.

Ichabod pretended not to notice his jumpsuit. But Brad sensed a perpetual smirk on the lips of Bennett, who seemed to be enjoying herself way too much.

"How's it going?" she asked snidely.

"Better if I'd remembered to bring my toothbrush with me to court on Friday."

Ichabod did not smile. She began laying out a proposal that Brad was sure she had already discussed with ADA Bennett. It was damage control and face-saving time for Ichabod. She clearly did not want this case appealed. Now that she had calmed down, read Brad's brief, and seen the name of Jay Sekulow, she was apparently willing to do everything within her power to keep the appeals court in Richmond from considering the case and evaluating her conduct.

"This is a no-win situation," Ichabod was saying, her elbows on her desk, fingertips tented together. She was looking back and forth at Brad and Angela Bennett. "I've been giving this a lot of thought. Mr. Carson's ill-advised actions have escalated the emotional nature of this highly charged case and created a difficult situation for everyone."

Brad suddenly noticed there was no court reporter present to record their conversation. "I have every right, and half a mind, to keep you in jail for as long as you stubbornly refuse to apologize for your childish conduct," she continued, giving Brad her holier-than-thou look.

Brad spread his palms—bring it on.

"But I won't," announced Ichabod, "because I refuse to let counsel drag me down to his level."

Bennett's smirk widened.

"Instead, I want to propose an agreement that could turn this into a win-win situation." Ichabod shuffled her papers and began reading from some notes.

"I strongly suggest that counsel consider a plea bargain in this case, and I have given some thought to the types of terms I would accept. Let me be frank with you, Mr. Carson. Your client has no chance of being found innocent."

She said it and paused, as if it were some shocking pronouncement. In truth, Brad knew this from the moment he drew Ichabod to hear the case. Years earlier, when she first ascended to the bench, some pro-life senators had delayed her confirmation hearings for more than eighteen months, digging for dirt they never found. It was common knowledge around the courthouse that Ichabod had a long memory and painted those responsible with a broad brush.

Brad had spent a long time kicking himself for suggesting to his client that they waive their right to a jury trial and take their chances with a judge.

"I assume the Reverend Bailey's conscience would not allow him to plead guilty to this charge, so I would be willing to accept a plea of 'no contest.' It would have the same effect, of course, except he wouldn't have to admit guilt. You will withdraw any defense and any rights to appeal, and I will find the reverend guilty. I will sentence him to serve only four days in jail, to be done on four consecutive Saturdays. No overnight stays. I will also sentence him to a total of six months in jail but will suspend that part of his sentence conditioned on good behavior for the next year, including no more protests or prayer meetings within one hundred feet of any abortion clinic."

Ichabod quit reading and looked at Brad. He sat absolutely stonefaced, determined not to give her the satisfaction of a reaction. It *was* a good deal. And he knew it was motivated by Ichabod's desire to avoid looking bad in front of the appellate judges in Richmond. But he didn't want to look too anxious to jump on it. Better to make the judge sweat a little.

"I'll have to discuss it with my client," Brad said, thoughtfully rubbing his unshaven face.

"Judge, I don't know if I can agree to this," Bennett blurted out. "It's very lenient. But this case is getting out of hand, and I would love to put this matter behind us." She paused for effect.

All part of a carefully choreographed show—with me as the audience, thought Brad. He was flattered.

"I'll agree to it," Bennett finally said, trying to sound reluctant, "but only if we can wrap it up by 5 P.M. I'm not willing to spend all weekend wondering about what we're going to do. I've got a closing argument to prepare for this trial…assuming, that is, that Mr. Carson will find the good sense to apologize."

"Oh, that's another thing," said Ichabod, looking back at her notes like she just remembered something. "If we can all agree to this plea bargain, I will release Mr. Carson from custody on Monday morning."

What a surprise.

"So, Mr. Carson, what's it going to be?"

He was tempted to say "whatever" again. He was tempted to tell Ichabod how much he liked jail, and how much the marshals liked him because he had stood up to her. Instead, he just stared down at his flip-flops. It really was a good deal for his client, and he didn't want to say anything to jeopardize it.

"My client is a man of strong convictions," Brad said solemnly.

"And I'm not sure he'll go for it. But I'll talk to him, and I'll recommend it. And I'll let you know by five o'clock."

"Thank you, Mr. Carson," said Ichabod, sounding both sincere and smug at the same time. Then she looked at Bennett. "I'd like a moment alone with Mr. Carson, please."

The government lawyer quickly excused herself. Brad studied his flip-flops some more, knowing what was coming. No court reporter, no witnesses. Ichabod was going to lower the boom.

"Mr. Carson," she began, her voice low and even as she measured each syllable, "you may think that you are clever. And, I will admit, you have done well for your client by your little stunt in this case. But the most important thing any lawyer brings into my courtroom is his or her own credibility. And once you lose it, you can never, ever, reclaim it. You have lost every ounce of your credibility with this judge, Mr. Carson. In my courtroom, you are a marked man. And I have a very long memory."

Brad felt a deep breath leave his body, and with it went some of the pride of his cunning achievement. He had indeed done well for his client, but at what cost to his own career? Did he really want to be known as a lawyer who couldn't be trusted, even by someone as petty as Ichabod?

He began to carefully choose the words for his response, but Ichabod didn't give him a chance. She simply pushed a button under her desk, and a marshal appeared at the back door.

"Clarence," she said, "give Mr. Carson a half-hour leave from his contempt sentence so that he can go buy a toothbrush."

Brad stood and flashed Ichabod a puzzled smile. He waited for her to look up so he could offer to shake hands. *No hard feelings?*

But Ichabod began reading some more papers, not bothering to stand or extend her hand or even look at him.

"Good day, Mr. Carson," she said without taking her eyes from the page in front of her.

∎ ∎ ∎

"What did he say?" asked Bella.

She was sitting in the muggy, dank jailhouse conference room with Brad. He had recounted the plea bargain offered by Ichabod, then called the Reverend Bailey on a cell phone that Clarence allowed Bella to bring into the conference room.

"He said if I recommend it, he'll take it."

"The man is clearly a poor judge of character," offered Bella.

Brad ignored her sarcasm and pensively stared at the floor. He was pretty sure he had won this case. He just didn't think winning would feel this bad.

■ ■ ■

Sarah Reed tried to open her eyes, encountered blinding lights, and closed them again. Her head was throbbing, and she could not seem to get out of the haze. She heard voices in the distance but couldn't make out the words. She tried to speak, tried to scream and tell someone about the pain, but the noises just tumbled out of her throat, making no sense.

She tried to sleep, but sleep would not come. Her mind swung in and out of consciousness, while nightmares blurred the lines between reality and dreams. She tried to reach out and grab something real, to get her bearings, but her arms would not respond. *Where am I? Where is Charles?* Then the haze became darker, and she floated away, voices mocking her in the distance.

"Sarah?"

A disembodied voice cut through the thick fog engulfing her. A touch on the arm, an insistent shaking, then the same kind voice.

"Sarah, do you hear me?"

It was a man's voice. *Maybe Charles?*

She reached out for him, finding comfort in the soft and understanding eyes. He moved closer, bringing a peace and order to her thoughts. Without even knowing why, she took comfort in his presence. She couldn't remember what had happened, but she had a feeling of great danger and great loss. And then…he changed. The face hardened before her eyes, transforming into the leathery image of the Muttawa leader, the eyes turning rabid. Sarah heard his heinous laugh…she recoiled, fear wracking her.

"Sarah."

Another gentle touch. This time she opened her eyes, then squinted to protect them from the lights' harsh glare. She could make out the silhouette of a figure standing over her.

"Sarah, my name is Dr. Rydell," the soft voice said. "Do you know where you are?"

Sarah nodded her head ever so subtly. At least she tried to. She didn't know if she actually succeeded. She tried to focus. She could feel the sleep coming back and somehow knew she didn't have long to get an answer about Charles.

"You're in a naval base hospital outside of Riyadh. You took a pretty nasty blow to the head, but you're going to be all right. You're going to need some rest."

Even as the haze started closing in, Sarah felt the images cascading around her. The Muttawa. Charles. Blood dripping from his face. The men coming at her. She closed her eyes and felt a stream of tears running down her face and toward her pillow.

She had to know.

She struggled to form the words, to fight off the fog for one last critical moment, but her tongue was thick and uncooperative. Still she managed to mouth a single word, inquiring with her eyes and lips.

"Charles?"

The doctor reached out and touched her arm again, bending forward and nearly whispering. "I'm afraid we weren't able to save him," the man said. "We tried everything we could, but he passed away a few hours ago from massive heart failure." He paused for a beat as the awful news penetrated the fog and pierced her heart. "I'm sorry, Sarah."

No! she wanted to scream. Bring him back! It can't end like this! Not for those who love God and are called according to His purpose…

More images flashed into her mind—unheeded—of their last struggling moments together. She remembered now. Vividly. The way Charles courageously refused to give up the names of other pastors. The brutal reaction of the Muttawa. The pain and the blood.

She needed to hold her husband one more time…say her good-byes…tell him how much she loved him…how hard it would be without him…how much he had taught her about the love of Christ.

But Charles was not there, and even in her drug-induced state she understood with awful certainty that he would never return. She found herself clutching the arm of this doctor, her lips forming one final haunting question as she slipped back into the darkness.

"Why, God? Why?"

Part II

THE LAW

5

Six months later

Leslie Connors looked down at her watch and could hardly believe it was already 11:30. The law library would close in thirty minutes. As usual, she had run out of time before she ran out of work.

She leaned back in her chair and stole a quick look around. Not surprisingly, she was the only one left on the basement floor. Most students avoided the loneliness and despair that seemed to linger in these parts of the catacombs. No windows, no noise, no socializers, no distractions. Just the way Leslie liked it.

She put in her time at this same carrel night after night, grinding away and chasing her dream. She owned this carrel, not in a legal sense, but through the personal effects she had scattered around the small cubicle and her chastisement of any intruders. After all, she was a second-year law student and already a bit of a legend. She was on track to graduate second in her class. That feat alone would take her one step closer to her goal of becoming one of the top international law practitioners in the country. The world was shrinking, and the global village was becoming a reality. Leslie loved the thought of the travel, the prestige, the intellectual challenge, and yes, the money. For a girl who grew up in a doublewide trailer, a career representing multinational corporations seemed like the perfect ticket to a better life.

There was no sacrifice she was not willing to make.

Her carrel was lined with law books across the back. Pictures, yellow Post-it notes, and to-do lists filled the sides. One of the faded color photos reflected the happier times in her life. It was a picture of Leslie and

Bill, her late husband, with their arms around each other, standing on the steps of the U.S. Supreme Court.

At the age of thirty-three, Bill had been diagnosed with an aggressive form of prostate cancer that had already metastasized. In the bittersweet nine months that followed, a nostalgic Bill made Leslie promise to pursue the legal career that she had sacrificed in the real-life compromises made by a young couple trying to make ends meet. And so, at the age of twenty-eight, and without Bill for the first time in eight years, Leslie enrolled at William and Mary Law School. She had been tearing the place up ever since.

"Ready for Friday?"

Leslie jumped and turned quickly around. Her friend Carli was smiling. "Little edgy tonight, aren't we?"

Leslie shook her head and returned the smile. "Didn't know you were sneaking up on me."

"Just stopping by to see if maybe you had died down here or needed a sleeping bag or something."

"Very funny."

Carli surveyed the casebooks and legal briefs scattered around the carrel. "So…you ready?"

"Not yet, but I will be."

"Right," teased Carli. "No pressure, but the law school bookies have you as a five-to-one underdog. They're sayin' you'll wilt under Strobel's withering questions."

"And what do you say?"

"That Strobel will be so amazed, he'll offer you a plum job in his international law practice on the spot."

"Just in case," said Leslie, "you might want to put down a few bills against me."

Carli laughed and gave Leslie a playful push as she walked away. "You kidding?" she said over her shoulder. "I already did."

Leslie's thoughts lingered for a moment on Maximillian Strobel, the managing partner of the largest law firm in southeast Virginia. Strobel was one of three moot court judges who would hear and decide the finals in two days. More important, he also headed the only thriving international law practice outside of Washington, D.C., New York, and Los Angeles. Because Leslie had promised herself that she would never live in those mammoth cities, Strobel was her only chance at a serious career in international law with a quality of life she could tolerate.

She glanced again at her watch. It was now fifteen minutes until midnight. Six in the morning would come quickly. She reached into her backpack and popped a couple of sleeping pills. They would kick in about the time she got back to her little studio apartment. In the meantime, she would use fifteen minutes wisely. She picked up a brief and began reading through it for the third time.

■ ■ ■

The next morning, Sarah Reed walked into the law offices of Carson & Associates, not at all confident she was doing the right thing. She had a nagging conviction that Christians should avoid lawyers in general and lawsuits in particular. Still, the insulting letter she now carried in her purse had overridden her feelings, and the Reverend Jacob Bailey, her pastor in Chesapeake, suggested she come here. She knew of no other attorney she might be able to trust.

But as she got off the elevator at the fifth floor of the Tidewater Community Bank building on the outskirts of a Virginia Beach shopping mall, she started to have second thoughts. She had never been in a law office before. She would rath er be going to the dentist.

She followed the signs for Carson & Associates to the end of the hallway. She hesitated in front of the oak door with the name of the firm emblazoned in gold letters. Then she took a deep breath, said a quick prayer, and entered the waiting area.

The receptionist did nothing to put her at ease.

"Yeah," said the squat woman. She didn't bother to pause her typing. The nameplate on the desk identified her as Bella Harper. Smoke wafted upward from the ashtray next to her, where a half-gone cigarette smoldered.

"I'm here to see Mr. Carson," said Sarah timidly.

"Do you have an appointment?" asked Bella.

Sarah immediately felt stupid. She knew she should have called and scheduled in advance. But that would have locked her in. She needed the freedom to bolt if she got cold feet. Like right now.

"No. Reverend Jacob Bailey referred me. I was hoping I could get just a minute of Mr. Carson's time. I'll come back later."

"Honey," Bella said, finally deigning to look up. "We don't take drop-ins. I can get you an appointment, but it'll probably be about three weeks before Mr. Carson can see you. He's in court this morning on a trial that will last a week. Then he's got back-to-back appointments for two weeks after that."

Three weeks!

Legal matters were something Charles would have handled. The thought of it made Sarah's eyes fill with tears, which made her feel even more self-conscious. It didn't help that Bella was eyeing her up and down. Sarah had become so emotional since Charles died, and waves of grief would wash over her at the most inopportune times.

"I'll just make an appointment some other time if I can't get this resolved on my own," she said to Bella, swallowing hard and forcing a plastic smile.

"Suit yourself." Bella resumed her typing.

Sarah stared at Bella for a moment, dumbfounded. *No wonder lawyers have such a bad reputation.*

This was obviously God's way of telling her to drop the matter. She shouldn't have come in the first place.

As she turned to leave, a slender, well-dressed man burst through the thick oak door and nearly ran over her.

■ ■ ■

"Sorry," Brad said, stopping just short of a collision. He gave the woman a quizzical look. "Do I know you?"

She shrugged her shoulders. "I don't think so."

"I'm Brad Carson," he said, sticking out his hand. *She looks so familiar.*

"Sarah Reed," she said softly. *Even her name sounds familiar.*

Brad noticed a trail of smoke from the ashtray where Bella had just stabbed out her cigarette.

"What happened?" Bella called out. "I thought you were in trial."

"We settled."

Then it hit him. He had seen this lady on the news. The missionary whose husband had died in Saudi Arabia. CNN had run live coverage of her testimony before the Senate Foreign Affairs Committee. The government of Saudi Arabia had denied Sarah's allegations of murder. They claimed her husband died from a heart attack unrelated to the injuries he received from resisting arrest on drug charges.

In the end, the importance of the vast Saudi oil reserves won out over the testimony of a missionary. The committee authored a scathing report but avoided any real sanctions against the government of Saudi Arabia, and the Saudis agreed to conduct an internal investigation and punish any renegade police officers. The Senate placed the Saudis on probation for a while, and the Saudis agreed to diligently protect human rights.

The oil kept flowing.

"I remember now. I'm sorry about your husband," said Brad earnestly. "And I'm sorry about the way your case was handled by the government."

Sarah shrugged and seemed to relax just a little. "Thanks. I'm just trying to move on. One day at a time."

"Can we help you with anything?" Brad asked. Bella shot him a look.

"She was referred by Reverend Bailey," said Bella, as if that explained everything. Reverend Bailey's church members had not given up on their abortion protests, and many had tried to solicit Brad's representation.

Once had been enough.

But Brad could sense that Sarah had not come for that reason. He saw something else etched in the soft lines of her face. She looked tired, older now than she had seemed just a few months before when he saw her on television.

"Well," Brad said, "as fate would have it, my day just cleared up. Come on back to the conference room, and we'll talk." He turned to Bella with a playful smile. "Bella, could you get a couple cups of coffee?"

Bella grunted and stalked down the hallway to the kitchen. Brad ushered Sarah into the conference room.

■ ■ ■

"This is ridiculous," Brad said, slapping the letter down on the large oak table. "Unbelievable."

The letter came from Charles' life insurance company and denied Sarah's claim for one hundred thousand dollars in death benefits. Brad glanced down to the operative paragraph:

> The investigation of Trust Indemnity has revealed that, according
> to tests performed at the hospital and during the autopsy, the
> Insured had a lethally high dosage of cocaine in his bloodstream
> on the night of his demise, and the Insured's heart attack was pre-
> cipitated in part by this self-induced overdose of cocaine. Accord-
> ingly, Trust Indemnity cannot honor your claim for insurance
> proceeds in light of Exclusion 4 Section A(2).

Brad stood up and began to pace, still holding the letter. To line their own pockets, the insurance company had chosen to disregard Sarah's version of the facts and to conclude that Dr. Reed had died from a self-inflicted drug overdose. And, Brad knew, this was par for the course with Trust Indemnity. He had sued them twice in the last year alone for bad faith.

He looked at Sarah's expectant expression. She was just sitting there, engulfed by the deep leather swivel chair, her hands folded on the table, concern etched deeply into her brow.

"We'll sue," Brad promised. He said it with that air of authority that clients loved. "This is outrageous. We'll sue for every penny of the hundred thousand, then we'll sue for bad faith and punitive damages. I've had lots of run-ins with these folks, but this is the worst." He paused for emphasis. "It's time to teach these guys a lesson."

Brad was surprised that the look on Sarah's face did not change. He didn't get the same sparkle in the eyes, the you-tell-'em look he was used to receiving from other clients when he uttered the magic words "punitive damages." If anything, the creases of concern on Sarah's forehead burrowed deeper.

"Couldn't you just send a letter and see if we could handle it that way?"

"A letter won't do any good, Sarah. The boys at Trust Indemnity understand two things: lawsuits and punitive damages. Nothing else gets their attention."

Sarah shifted uncomfortably and looked down at her hands. "I don't want to file for punitive damages, Mr. Carson."

Brad tried not to look at her as if she were some kind of freak. *Doesn't want to file for punitive damages? Does God still make people like this?*

Still looking down, Sarah continued softly. "I really don't want to even file a suit. But I've got two kids to think about, and the money…" Her voice quivered then broke off.

Brad leaned forward on the table, looked directly at Sarah, and lowered his voice to its most comforting tone, perfected by years in front of the jury box. "Okay, Sarah, listen to me." She looked up, and Brad continued. "There's nothing wrong with filing a lawsuit," he said it with real conviction, his voice comforting and steady, "sometimes it's the only way in our society to obtain justice. These guys owe you a hundred thousand. To let them get away with that is to admit that Charles committed suicide and died from a self-inflicted overdose of cocaine. And I know you don't want that."

Sarah forced her lips into a thin smile and shook her head.

"Then here's what I'm going to do. I'll draft a lawsuit and have it served on Trust Indemnity. My guess is that they'll pay immediately once they know you've got a lawyer involved. If not, we'll talk about a fee agreement at that stage. I won't charge anything for drafting and sending the lawsuit."

It was not good business, but every once in a while Brad believed he owed it to the profession to take on a case pro bono. If ever there was such a case, this one was it. At least that's the way he saw it; Bella probably wouldn't speak to him for a week.

"Reverend Bailey said it would be just like you to take this case for free," Sarah said. "I don't want that. I want you to take your normal fee. In fact, I insist on it, and I'll go to another lawyer if you refuse."

Brad gave Sarah another sideways look. Where did she come from? It was hard not to be charmed by this lady. "I seldom see clients so insistent on giving me their money. But if you insist, I'll sic Bella on you, and we'll have you sign our retainer agreement."

Sarah paused before answering. "If I've got to deal with her again, maybe I'll reconsider." She smiled, and her moist blue eyes lit up for the first time. Brad laughed politely, struck by the warmth of her smile.

He stood up and shook hands with his new client, walked around the table, put an arm around her shoulder, and gave her a squeeze. They chatted for a few moments, then he ushered her out of the conference room and into the clutches of Bella.

Brad watched Bella attack the fee arrangement with gusto, placing one form after another in front of Sarah for her signature. Carson & Associates would receive one-third of any money recovered "against Trust Indemnity or otherwise" as a result of the death of Charles Reed. Brad knew Bella had another form that actually placed the fee at 40 percent, but apparently even she could not spring that form on a grieving widow like Sarah in such a simple case.

■ ■ ■

Rasheed turned over and reached out to stroke his wife's hair. As he touched her cheek, he felt the warm tears. He leaned up on one elbow and tried to focus in the dark.

"What's wrong, Mobara?"

He sensed a slight movement, perhaps a shudder, perhaps a shrug of the shoulders. "Nothing," she said.

Rasheed knew better than to accept that answer.

"You just decide to start crying in the middle of the night for no reason? Come on, you can talk to me."

Mobara wiped the tears away with the palms of her hands. "I feel so guilty," she sobbed. "I've felt this every day and every night since the Muttawa came…" Her voice faltered. Rasheed reached over and drew her to himself. He held her softly as she cried.

When she regained control, she spoke again in a desperate whisper. "We denied our Lord, Rasheed. I can't live like this."

He squeezed her tighter in the silence. "Nor I," he said at last.

"What…are we going to do?" Her sobbing intensified.

Rasheed gently released his wife, then drew her out of bed to kneel together. "We must pray…ask forgiveness…trust God to give us another chance."

Mobara joined him and put her hand on his.

"What if they come back, Rasheed? I'm so afraid."

"I know. Let's pray. Remember, God has not given us the spirit of fear."

Mobara looked intently at her husband. "I love you, Rasheed. And I'll be okay if you're with me."

Rasheed put his arm around her again and drew her close, still kneeling, preparing to pray.

"Are you afraid?" she asked.

Rasheed thought for a moment and looked down. He couldn't lie to Mobara. She would know. "Yes," he admitted.

Together, they began to pray.

Leslie took another sip from the glass of water on her counsel table. It was half-gone, her mouth was still dry, and she hadn't even started her argument yet. She tapped the sides of the typed pages in front of her, perfectly lining up the edges of her notes, then surveyed again the panel of accomplished lawyers who would act as judges for the moot court final.

Seated on her left was Professor Lynda Parsons. She was rumored to be tough, fair, sarcastic, and witty. Leslie had skillfully avoided taking her classes, but now she had to face her as a judge in the moot court final.

In the middle, and acting as chief justice because of his experience and reputation in international law, sat Mack Strobel. He was already staring down the litigants.

Leslie stared back.

She had read the book on Strobel. *Don't let him intimidate you. He's from the old school—blunt and full of bluster. Respect him but don't trust him.*

It was hard not to look away. Strobel's eyes became piercing. His clean-shaven head, close-cropped goatee, and fierce scowl gave him a draconian look—like some type of WWF wrestler dressed up in a business suit. His leathery skin and bald pate were well-tanned, though summer was months away. He had broad shoulders, above average height, and he seemed to dominate the courtroom without trying.

After making her point with Strobel, Leslie diverted her gaze to Brad Carson, who sat to Leslie's right. Carson shuffled some papers and looked absent-mindedly around the courtroom. He caught Leslie's gaze and smiled. Compared to Strobel, Carson was not an imposing figure, but he seemed so sure of himself and so natural in a courtroom setting that he, too, commanded respect. He also seemed bored and ready for some action.

"Be seated," barked Strobel, obviously ready to get down to the business of beating up the litigants.

■ ■ ■

The sizing up went both ways. Brad had already decided that Leslie would win if points were awarded for style.

"Is counsel for appellant ready?" asked Mack.

"Ready, Your Honor." Leslie stood and flashed a nervous smile.

"Is counsel for appellee ready?"

"Yes, Your Honor."

Brad studied the young man opposing Leslie. Stiff posture, short cropped hair, and precise movements. Probably active duty military, attending school on a JAG scholarship. Long on discipline, short on creativity, Brad figured.

Leslie was more of a mystery. She was attractive but trying hard to look more like a lawyer than a beauty queen. She wore her shoulder-length auburn hair in a tight braid, and her traditional dark-blue suit camouflaged a tall, thin frame. Intense sky-blue eyes seemed to sparkle with anticipation. She had the high cheekbones and long neck of a model, but none of the makeup that would accentuate or draw attention to those features. Her pale skin had probably been weeks without seeing a ray of sun, and red blotches marked her neck where she had probably scratched nervously. Brad pegged her as a hardworking over-achiever who was taking this event way too seriously.

She stood and addressed the panel.

"May it please the court, my name is Leslie Connors, and I represent the appellants—the former Taliban regime and the nation of Afghanistan. The issue in this case is whether a U.S. federal court has the jurisdiction to hear the case and award damages to certain female Afghanistan refugees against the Taliban and the nation of Afghanistan for the alleged torture of these refugees. Let me make myself perfectly clear. The issue is not whether the Taliban abused these women and should be punished for their heinous conduct; it is whether a U.S. court should usurp the role of the international community and set itself up as the final tribunal to judge that conduct."

"Counsel," Strobel interrupted. "Would you agree that your clients committed some of the most despicable and far-reaching human rights violations since the atrocities of Hitler?"

"Your Honor, that is for the international community to decide, not this court."

"But, counsel," drawled Strobel, "do you deny that the Taliban regime deprived women like yourself of the most basic human rights?"

"No, we do not deny it." Leslie appeared uncomfortable making even this obvious concession. Brad watched as she shifted her weight from one foot to the other, then nervously tucked an imaginary strand of stray hair behind her ear.

"Do you deny that the Taliban beat and tortured women if they attempted to run away from an abusive husband? Do you deny that the Taliban treated women as something less than human, as property of their husbands?"

"No. But the international community addressed that in removing the Taliban from power—"

"Counsel," interrupted Strobel, immediately silencing Leslie. "This court has now been petitioned by a group of refugees to grant redress for these terrible acts of torture. Are you suggesting that this court just sit idly by, refuse to take jurisdiction over this case, and let the Taliban get away with rape, murder, and torture?"

"We are a nation of laws," responded Leslie, slowly and evenly. "And on this point the law is very specific and very clear. All nations have the privilege of sovereign immunity, a basic and fundamental privilege that prevents them from being hauled into the courts of another nation as a defendant. We must respect the sovereignty of other nations and not drag them into our courts as if they were just ordinary American citizens, especially since a new government in Afghanistan has replaced the Taliban—"

"I'm well aware of the law, counsel." Strobel used a tone a parent might reserve for scolding a young child. "So let's talk about the law for a minute. Under the Foreign Sovereign Immunities Act, there are certain exceptions. For example, a foreign nation can be hauled into our courts if that nation causes harm associated with a commercial activity, such as breach of a contract. Is that right?"

"Under some circumstances."

"And a foreign nation can be hauled into our courts if an agent of that nation causes injury on the high seas, right?"

"That's correct."

"And if an agent of a foreign nation injures someone on American territory, then that nation gets hauled into American courts?

"Yes, in most cases."

"So let me get this straight," Strobel stroked his goatee as if he were deep in thought. "A foreign nation can get hauled into American courts if they hurt us in the pocketbook, or if they injure someone on the high seas, or if they breach a contract, but there is some overwhelming reason that says we can't drag them into American courts if they systematically torture, rape, or kill innocent civilian women. Is that the way you read the law?"

Leslie shifted her weight. The red blotches grew. She pushed at more imaginary hair.

For his part, Brad was growing weary of the bullying. He was always one to cheer for the underdog. Especially an underdog as pretty as Leslie.

"That's not exactly the way I would phrase it," said Leslie. "There are important foreign policy reasons—"

"Counsel," said Brad, coming to the rescue. "Did you write this law? Justice Strobel seems to think you did." He shot a sideways glance at Strobel. No love lost there. "Last I checked, Congress wrote the law, and it was the job of courts like this one to apply it."

Leslie looked relieved to get a pitch she could actually hit. "Congress had to balance numerous important factors in drafting the Foreign Sovereign Immunities Act. There are delicate foreign policy issues at stake—there is a new regime in Afghanistan, put there by our own country, and that regime should not be undermined and held accountable for the actions of the Taliban. Plus the governments of other countries must be respected by the courts of the United States, or those other countries will reciprocate by hauling the United States into their courts as a defendant. The role of this court today is not to question the wisdom of the Sovereign Immunities Act passed by Congress, but to apply the law even if we don't necessarily like the result."

Brad looked at Strobel and nodded.

"The court should not open this can of worms," concluded Leslie. "Otherwise, plaintiffs' lawyers will clog our courts with all manner of bogus claims against foreign governments, just trying to get lucky and hit it big."

Brad winced. Now Strobel smirked.

Brad was fully engaged. The game was clear: It was Brad against Strobel, head-to-head. The litigants were just allies—pawns to move around the chessboard. Brad thought it worked out nicely to have the attractive one on his side. Strobel could have the drill sergeant.

"You are aware, counsel," Strobel's voice boomed again, "that all civilized nations acknowledge certain generally accepted principles of international law?"

"Yes. These fundamental principles and values common to all mankind are called *jus cogens* laws and are considered binding."

"These are the highest forms of international law, is that correct?"

"Yes, they are."

Brad leafed through his materials for a copy of the Foreign Sovereign Immunities Act. He could not put his finger on it, but this moot court argument was giving him a strange sense of déjà vu.

"And one of those norms widely recognized as a *jus cogens* norm is the right of people everywhere to be free from torture at the hands of their own government, right?" asked Strobel.

The trap was set. Brad could see it about to snap.

"Basic human rights, such as the right to be free from torture, would be considered *jus cogens* laws," admitted Leslie.

A mirthless smile formed on Strobel's lips. "Well then, if a nation violates a basic human right, like the right to be free from torture, they have violated one of the most basic tenets of international law. Shouldn't a nation that breaks one of these most basic tenets of international law, a *jus cogens* law"—Strobel let his deep southern drawl lengthen the phrase like some religious incantation—"by torturing and killing its own citizens be seen as waiving the protection of sovereign immunity?"

Strobel leaned forward, elbows on the bench, waiting for an answer. The phrase *jus cogens,* majestically Latin in its origin, seemed to echo around the courtroom.

Leslie cleared her throat. "If we start weighing violations of international law, and decide that some violations are worthy of the protection of sovereign immunity while others are not, then we will find ourselves in an ambiguous area. If nothing else, international law requires certainty and predictability—"

"But aren't we already making exceptions?" Strobel insisted. "It's just that now we make exceptions for commercial cases, and I'm suggesting that the far more important cases for exceptions are violations of basic human rights—violations of *jus cogens* laws."

Leslie let the question hang in the air. She looked at Brad—an appeal for help.

Brad and Mack each started a question at the same time. Brad raised his voice and continued.

"Ms. Connors, you are an American lawyer representing the Taliban and Afghanistan, is that right?" he asked.

"Yes," said Leslie tentatively.

"Do you remember when the American jets were relentlessly bombing cities in Afghanistan and there were numerous reports of civilians being killed during the bombing raids?"

"I believe so," Leslie answered, apparently hedging her bet.

"Would you say that killing innocent civilians violates one of those, how do you say it?" Brad wrinkled his forehead, a picture of naiveté and perplexity.

"*Jus cogens* laws," replied Leslie.

"Yeah," said Brad, "would you say killing innocent civilians with a military jet would qualify?" He took off his reading glasses and began chewing on them.

"You bet."

"Do some of the people in your client's country, including some of the judges, still dislike the American troops who bombed their cities and killed their civilians?"

"I think it's accurate to say that some detest Americans," Leslie volunteered.

"If an Afghan court, which as I understand it is still governed by Islamic law, were allowed to put the United States on trial for the bombing of those civilians—in other words, if the shoe were on the other foot—do you have any prediction as to the amount of the judgment that an Afghan court might render against the United States in such a case?"

Brad expected the answer was obvious to everyone in the courtroom.

"I'm sure the judgment would be in the billions," Leslie answered enthusiastically. "The U.S. courts would then retaliate with a judgment against Afghanistan for billions more. Pretty soon we're heading down a slippery slope of retaliation—nations slapping each other with billion-dollar judgments and throwing international law into total chaos."

Leslie looked thankfully at Brad and, for the first time during the argument, flashed a relaxed smile.

■ ■ ■

Driving home it hit him—the reason for his déjà vu. The case of the Afghan refugees reminded him of the abuse that Sarah Reed endured at the hands of government officials. Slippery slopes aside, why should foreign governments be allowed to torture innocent civilians, then hide behind the doctrine of sovereign immunity? Why should the Saudi Arabian police be allowed to torture and kill an American citizen and not be held accountable in an American court?

Brad was not familiar with the vagaries of international law, but he had a keen sense for justice and fairness. And in the case of Sarah Reed, justice demanded that the Saudi police pay for what they did.

He picked up his cell phone and dialed directory assistance. He needed an international law expert who could exhaustively research this potential cause of action. He knew just the person.

■　■　■

Leslie could not stop fuming. She had lost the final round of the moot court tournament and spent her drive home ruthlessly critiquing her own performance. She second-guessed every word and every gesture, replayed the entire argument in her mind, thought of things she should have said, and hated herself for not having said them.

She lived twelve miles from the law school in a quaint studio apartment above a detached garage in the country. A law school professor owned a majestic estate about two miles off the main road on the banks of the scenic Chickahominy River. Because the professor had taken a two-year assignment at another law school, she'd hired a contractor to build an apartment in the attic space of her three-car garage. She'd offered the apartment to Leslie rent-free so long as Leslie kept an eye on the estate.

Leslie's friends thought she was insane for living alone in such an isolated setting. But Leslie loved the seclusion, the scenery, the wildlife on the riverbanks, and the price of the apartment. Besides, Leslie practically lived in the law school library. Her apartment was just a way station for sleeping, showering, and licking her wounds.

By the time Leslie turned off the main road, she had pretty much concluded that she would always be second best. She had also decided that she had no desire to practice international law at the firm of Kilgore & Strobel. She dreamed of a day when she, a big-city lawyer, would try cases against Strobel and his small-town law firm. She would crush him with superior resources and clever lawyering. She had a sudden hankering for the Big Apple, where she could plot her revenge.

Leslie parked her car in the garage and slowly climbed the steps to her apartment. The sun was just beginning to set over the Chickahominy, and the light show was spectacular. She planned to microwave dinner, grab a law book and a bottle of wine, and sit on the dock until the sun completely disappeared.

She had struggled with dependency in the days following Bill's death, and she had therefore not allowed herself even one drink since the start of the semester. But after a day like today, she had earned it. She would indulge just this once. As she popped a Lean Cuisine into the microwave and poured her first drink, she also checked her phone messages.

The first caller had not left a message. The second one was a consolation call from Carli. You did great. You should have won. Sweet lies to make Leslie feel better. The third call made her quickly forget the other two.

"Hello, Leslie, this is Brad Carson. Listen, great job in moot court today. I know this sounds a little strange, but I'm actually investigating a real case that is similar to the hypothetical case we were discussing. I need someone familiar with international law to do some research and help me determine if we've got a cause of action. Uh...I'm willing to pay enough to make it worth your time, and you can work around your school schedule. Anyway, if you're interested, give me a call, and my secretary will set up a meeting."

Leslie replayed the message twice, wrote down the number he left, and weighed her options. She didn't have time for this. She needed to stay focused on school to maintain her class ranking. Good offers from top firms would follow. Besides, it was March, and Leslie planned on spending the summer abroad as part of the William and Mary study program in Exeter, England.

But as Leslie walked down to the dock, the lawyer in her couldn't help but argue the other side. She owed Brad a favor since he had saved her from complete humiliation. Maybe this would be her big break in international law. She was tired of studying concepts and arguing hypotheticals. The thought of a real-live case with a real-live client was intoxicating. Besides, she needed the money.

She debated with herself vigorously until the sun finished its descent and she had polished off the tiny helping of Lean Cuisine lasagna and two glasses of wine. By then she had rendered her verdict. She would call Brad first thing Monday morning.

After another glass of wine, she finished critiquing her performance and decided maybe she hadn't done such a miserable job after all. She was ready to practice some real law and work with a real lawyer. Forget Monday. She would go to the library first thing tomorrow morning. She would call Brad tomorrow afternoon and sink her teeth into a real case by the beginning of the week.

It was a beautiful night, and her head was starting to spin. She lay on her back on the dock and watched the stars as they circled the sky. A chorus of bullfrogs serenaded her, accompanied by the steady rhythm of small wind-blown waves lapping against the bank. She felt her nerves relax as exhaustion overwhelmed her weary body. Before long, she closed her eyes and drifted away.

She dreamed of humiliating Strobel.

7

M iles of tree-lined sidewalks snaked their way among the tall and stately brick colonial buildings, each adorned with beautiful white columns, that made up the City of Virginia Beach municipal complex. The sprawling office park boasted plenty of green space and immaculate landscaping, adding to its bucolic appeal.

The courthouse building was always a beehive of activity. And on this Friday morning, as on most Fridays, large crowds crammed themselves into the courtrooms for "motions day," the weekly cattle call where lawyers hashed through all their motions on their cases so they could reserve the other days for trial work.

Two weeks after her moot court argument, Leslie walked into the weekly melee of Virginia Beach Circuit Courtroom Number 7 and took a seat in the back. Brad had told Leslie he didn't know what time he would be done with his motions, but afterward they would have lunch and discuss her research.

She decided to come a few hours early to see how motions and other important legal issues were decided in the real world. Her valuable time bought a study in mediocrity that made Leslie thankful for her class ranking and more determined than ever to avoid the slosh pit of mundane law where most lawyers wallowed.

The cases of Billy "the Rock" Davenport dominated the morning's hearings. Leslie immediately recognized the name. The widely known senior partner of Davenport & Associates was the genius behind his firm's irreverent and ubiquitous television ads: "When trouble rolls, call the Rock." It was the kind of advertising Leslie detested, the kind of exposure that gave all lawyers a bad name. Turn the television to Jerry

Springer, and the breaks would be accented by a tough-sounding and mean-looking lawyer with boxing gloves ready to deck the insurance companies. Watch ESPN, and another lawyer, this time fit and in jogging shorts, told you how to avoid the insurance company runaround. Tune in to your favorite soap, and a young and handsome lawyer assured you that Davenport & Associates literally feels your pain. Of course, none of the lawyers on television looked even remotely like the short, bald, pudgy man who meekly took his place behind the counsel table in Courtroom Number 7.

For forty-five minutes, defense lawyers of all stripes took their turns pummeling the Rock. The cases were different, but the themes were the same—the Rock had not answered interrogatories in a timely fashion, the Rock had failed to provide required medical reports, the Rock had failed to show for a scheduled deposition, the Rock had failed to name expert witnesses in a timely manner, and so on and so on. The lawyers asked for sanctions against the Rock, or that the cases be thrown out, or that the Rock be forced to concede major points in penance for his failure to comply with discovery rules.

The Rock was clearly on the defensive, shuffling papers, mumbling lame apologies, trying to survive the morning with some of his cases still intact, and above all, avoiding eye contact with the judge. By the end of his time on the hot seat, Leslie couldn't help but feel a little sorry for the hapless Rock and desperately sorry for his clients. She sighed with relief when Brad finally got his turn at the counsel table.

By 1:15 the judge had ruled on the last case, and Leslie was ready for lunch. Brad insisted that they eat at one of his favorite restaurants on the Lynnhaven River. He offered to let Leslie ride with him. They could talk business on the way.

She was not looking forward to this. Leslie's initial enthusiasm for this assignment, which waxed so strong in the beginning, had been decimated by her sobering research into the black-letter law. Sarah Reed had no case. And now it was Leslie's job to ruin Brad's lunch and explain to him the harsh realities of sovereign immunity law.

■ ■ ■

The three adults waiting anxiously in the dimly lit apartment had little in common except a dangerous faith. They had all been members of the church in Riyadh formerly led by Charles and Sarah Reed. They had been severely beaten by the Islamic radicals unleashed by Ahmed Aberijan. To their great shame, they had recanted with their lips, if not with their hearts.

But now Rasheed and Mobara Berjein had boldly reinstated the weekly prayer meetings. These two young schoolteachers were joined by Kareem Bariq, another former member of the Reeds' church, who drifted from one construction job to another and was presently unemployed. The Berjeins were doing what they could to help Kareem both financially and spiritually, with mixed results on both fronts.

The Berjeins had been overjoyed to reunite with Kareem and to learn that he had struggled with the same feelings of guilt and conviction. The tiny church of three rededicated themselves to the cause of Christ and the study of His Word. Over time, forgiveness replaced guilt, and courage began to take the place of fear.

The Berjeins became so emboldened that on this night they had invited another couple from school, close personal friends and spiritual seekers. When Rasheed heard the special knock at a few minutes past ten and welcomed his friends to the meeting, he was expecting nothing short of a miracle.

But now that the guests were there, Rasheed didn't really know where to start. He looked at Mobara with rising panic in his eyes, and asked her to share a little about her own spiritual journey. Mobara smiled warmly and launched right in, as if it were the most natural thing in the world. Before long, she was fully engaged, passionately telling of her own feelings and faith. She talked about her life as a devoted Muslim, as an ardent follower of Mohammed and the teachings of the Koran. She talked about how much she had learned from her time as a Muslim and what great respect she had for other devout Muslims. But she also shared about an emptiness, a longing for something more than the discipline and sacrifice of the Islamic faith. She longed for peace, she longed for joy, she longed for assurance of eternal life. In a word, said Mobara, she longed for a Savior.

Without realizing it had happened, Rasheed found himself entranced, on the edge of his seat, as if he were hearing his wife's story for the first time. He loved to watch Mobara's ever-changing expressions as she took her listeners through a gauntlet of emotions, every feature on her face going all-out to accentuate her words. And then Mobara seemed to notice this as well—that she had become the center of attention—and she suddenly seemed self-conscious about it. Perhaps only Rasheed, who knew his wife so well, noticed the slight change in her countenance. And he was not at all surprised when she turned to him and flawlessly asked him to tell how they had found the answers to all their spiritual searching, to all of their many questions, in the Bible.

Rasheed swallowed hard, cleared his throat, and suddenly realized how thick his tongue had become. He said a quick prayer, licked his parched lips, and opened his Bible. He began sharing some stories that were not found in the Koran. He started with some of the great teachings of Christ, common ground for Muslims and Christians. As he talked, with his guests listening politely and Mobara nodding her agreement, he grew bolder. He felt a power not his own, an eloquence he did not know he possessed.

Oh, he still stammered around some, and he couldn't remember half the Bible passages he wanted to explain, but he was now ready to hit the issues head-on. He explained how Christ had suffered and died on a cross. How Christ had paid the price for sins. He knew this was a major sticking point for Muslims; it had been his own greatest obstacle.

"I couldn't believe that a God of love would actually let His own Son die on a cross," Rasheed admitted, looking at his guests. He saw the same question register in their eyes. "If God is all powerful, why did He allow this to happen?" A long pause. "But then I realized that the very love of God required this—that He loved us so much He was willing to pay any price, including the death of His own Son, to provide us with a way to be brought back into relationship with Him."

He couldn't tell if he was getting through, but there was no stopping Rasheed now. He talked about Christ's resurrection and the historical evidence for this miracle. He said that new life in Christ was available to everyone—Jew and Muslim, male and female—that God was the Father of all.

"In the Christian faith," Rasheed explained earnestly, "salvation does not come from sacrificial living, faithfulness in prayer, or following a certain set of rules. Christ obeyed all the rules, kept the entire Law, something we could never do. And He did it for us.

"Salvation comes through faith in Jesus Christ."

It was time to put the choice squarely to his friends, Rasheed could feel it. And he knew that these words were not his own, that somehow the Holy Spirit prompted them. "Christ cannot be regarded as just another good man, or even another great prophet in a long line of prophets culminating with Mohammed. Christ claimed to be God and wants to be Lord of your life. We must either accept Him on those terms, or reject Him as a liar or a lunatic."

Rasheed put down the Bible he had been holding in both hands and looked squarely at his guests. "Does that make sense to you?" he asked.

There was a long and uncomfortable silence as his question hung in the air. His guests looked down, quietly studying the floor, and Rasheed had no idea what to do. He had blown it. He had gotten so excited that he had overwhelmed them. He had not communicated clearly. He had turned them off. Here he was, a trained teacher, and for some reason he couldn't explain the most basic thing in the world—the simple gospel of Jesus Christ.

And then the woman looked up. Rasheed saw the tears welling in her eyes. Her husband reached over, gently taking her hand. He nodded his head ever so slightly, almost imperceptibly. He was saying it all made sense!

"It does?" Rasheed asked, more surprised than anybody else in the room.

The man just nodded his head again. "What do we do now?" he asked softly.

Startled, enthused, bewildered, and excited, Rasheed looked at Mobara. She smiled and turned to the guests. "Rasheed will lead you in a prayer," she suggested. "A prayer that can change everything."

Hesitantly at first, then with great enthusiasm, Rasheed led the couple in a prayer that ended their separation from God and started their relationship with Christ. They talked for an hour afterward.

That night the small church grew by two. That night Rasheed became a pastor.

They ended, as always, in another prayer. And their prayer ended, as always, with the petition that God would help them to remain faithful to Christ, "no matter the cost." They did not have the option of the cheap and easy Christianity of the West. Their faith, with its great reward, would also demand great sacrifice.

■ ■ ■

Brad didn't spend one minute talking about the *Reed* case on the way to the Lynnhaven Mariner. A master storyteller, Brad entertained Leslie with improbable tales of quirky lawyers, convoluted cases, and irascible clients. After they arrived, he made the long wait longer by insisting they hold out for a table on the dock overlooking the bay, and Leslie surprised herself by not minding any of it. At one point she laughed and realized her anxiety about this bad-news meeting had faded.

Brad didn't get down to business until their lunches sat before them.

"So, counsel, do we have a case for Sarah Reed? Don't pull any punches."

Leslie hesitated for just a second. "It doesn't look good, Brad. I wouldn't say impossible, but the next thing to it." Her eyes met his. He stared at her intently, and she felt her throat constrict. "I've got a complete memo in my car, but I can give you the nutshell." Was that her voice? Was she going hoarse?

"Go for it." He continued staring.

She took a quick drink of water and collected herself. "Sarah would have a potential cause of action against both the individuals who tortured her as well as the government of Saudi Arabia for the actions of government officials. There are different laws and procedures for each. With regard to the individual police officers, there is a cause of action under the Torture Victim Protection Act.

"That part of the case is pretty straightforward," Leslie continued. "We would have to prove that Sarah and her husband were tortured by official representatives of the Saudi government. We could recover against those persons who performed the torture and against any higher-ups who authorized, tolerated, or willingly ignored these acts."

"Sounds good to me," quipped Brad. "Where do I sign up?"

Leslie risked looking Brad in the eye again. "As you know better than anyone, the issue is not whether you can get a verdict, but whether you can collect against the defendants. Even if you can pinpoint the police officers who were involved, they probably don't have a dime to their names. And you can't even try to collect against them unless they have property in the United States or enter the country personally."

"What about Prince Asad?" Brad asked. "There's no one I would rather sue…with the possible exception of Bill Gates."

"There is no indication that the prince either authorized or sanctioned this conduct," said Leslie in her best professional mode, trying hard to burst Brad's bubble. "The real issue is whether you could win a judgment against the government of Saudi Arabia for the actions of their agents."

"I'm pretty sure the Saudis have the bucks to satisfy any billion-dollar verdict we might get." Brad shooed away the waiter who was coming to refill their drinks. "So what's the answer?"

"I think it's a loser, Brad." Leslie knew it was not good news, and she liked him too well to sugarcoat it. "Foreign countries and their agencies have enjoyed immunity from suit in American courts since 1812 with only a few minor exceptions. And none of them apply here." She stopped abruptly. Brad was leaning forward, chin propped on both hands, looking directly at her. She found it hard to read his eyes. "Is this boring you?"

"Not at all," he said, then smiled. "I was just thinking how much I could use someone like you to help research some of the issues I'm constantly running up against. You sound like an encyclopedia."

"Thanks. I think." She couldn't help but blush. She felt like a schoolgirl with a wicked crush. *I don't even know this guy!*

She cleared her head of these distracting emotions—purposefully, clinically, she willed herself to disregard them—and continued with her rehearsed synopsis of sovereign immunity law. "In 1976 Congress codified the issue of sovereign immunity with the Foreign Sovereign Immunity Act. That law basically provides that foreign governments cannot be sued in U.S. courts unless one of five exceptions applies."

Brad's eyes lit up. "Loopholes are my specialty." He smiled playfully.

Leslie maintained her game face. "Maybe so, but I doubt any of these exceptions would apply. The Reeds are not the first U.S. citizens to be tortured by another country. Let me put it this way: If the Nazi holocaust victims could not successfully sue under this act in New York City, it's hard to think we could do it here in the conservative federal courts of Norfolk, Virginia."

Brad fell silent and stared pensively at the ships motoring slowly by on the Lynnhaven. Leslie thought she perceived a slight sag in his shoulders.

Brad turned from the horizon and picked at his food. "If you had to file suit on the *Reed* case, if you had no choice but to file suit, what approach would you take?"

Leslie furrowed her brow and took her turn staring at the river. "I would argue the implicit waiver clause…that when other nations torture U.S. citizens in violation of *jus cogens* norms, they waive their immunity from suit. This theory has never been squarely addressed by the U.S. Supreme Court. I would stress the fact that Charles and Sarah Reed were U.S. citizens tortured for religious reasons, and that our courts have a special role to play when the fundamental rights of U.S. citizens are involved."

Brad thought about this for a moment. "Oh, you mean the Strobel argument."

Leslie winced. "Yeah, I guess so. But I'd prefer not to call it that."

"Call it anything you want, as long as it works."

"I didn't say it would work. Only that it was our best argument."

"What are our chances?" asked Brad. He sat up straighter, taking a big bite of a crab-cake sandwich. "I'm ready."

"What?"

He chewed for a minute, then swallowed hard. He chased the sandwich with a gulp of tea. "I said…I'm ready. I just want to know what our chances are."

Leslie put down her fork. This was not going as she had planned. "Nearly impossible. Didn't you hear me? Brad, every effort by every lawyer to haul a foreign government into court based on human rights violations for the past hundred years has been unsuccessful. And there are lots of cases with facts every bit as horrible as yours."

She said it with an edge. And either the tone or the bluntness of the assessment caused a long silence between the two. Leslie became uncomfortable and resumed working on her meal. Brad gazed down the river some more.

After what seemed like an eternity, he spoke. "There's got to be a first time," he mumbled.

Leslie put down her fork. "What do you mean by that?"

"Leslie, with every new breakthrough for justice, there's got to be a first time. How do you think we got our civil rights laws? Some lawyers were sitting around, just like we are today, knowing they had justice on their side, but not the law. That didn't stop them, because they knew the law was meant to serve justice, not the other way around. I know this may sound corny, but it's true. Ninety-nine percent of the lawyers in the world see the law as it is, but the few really great ones see the law as it ought to be."

Brad spoke as if the law were a sacred thing. He leaned forward, his voice reverent, barely above a whisper, and suddenly Leslie saw Bill leaning toward her, his voice coming out of the past full of captivating idealism. She gasped before she could stop herself.

"What is it?" he asked.

Leslie felt her cheeks grow hot. "Nothing," she murmured. "You were saying?"

Brad now focused on the horizon and continued in the same passionate tone. "Most lawyers think the laws are written in law books, but a few lawyers understand that the fundamental laws of justice are carved deep in the human spirit, that the law books just try to capture those transcendent laws that are already there. And when the laws on the books don't match what justice requires, you change the laws on the books, not the definition of justice.

"You wait your whole career for a case like this. There's got to be a first time, Leslie. And I think this case just might be it."

Brad finished his impromptu speech, and more silence followed. He fixed his gaze on Leslie, beseeching her with his steel-blue eyes. It was, without a doubt, one of the most intense looks she had ever experienced—one of the most intense feelings she had ever felt.

She couldn't look away.

Get a grip, Connors, she told herself. *It's just a case. It's not a crusade, and it won't bring world peace. He's just another guy.*

Yeah, right.

"If I decide to go tilting after these windmills," Brad was asking, "will you join me? I could really use your help on the research. And I'll pay twenty bucks an hour."

Leslie had predicted this scenario. She had practiced saying no the entire trip from Williamsburg to Virginia Beach. She had finals coming up and the trip to England. It was not a good time.

"Thanks for the offer, Brad. But I just can't…I don't have time." She looked down at her food; it had not moved. "I promised myself I would study abroad this summer, then slow down some my third year and enjoy law school. I just…I don't know…"

Her voice trailed off, and she knew she had left the door open, cracked ever so slightly. It was not part of the plan.

Brad apparently sensed it too. "Law school will always be there, Leslie. England can wait. But this case," he paused, "a case like this comes around once, maybe twice, in a lifetime. Don't you see it, Leslie? The moot court argument. Sarah Reed just walking into my office on another matter. It's destiny, Leslie. You can't say no to destiny."

Brad was playing hardball, but Leslie had steeled herself. Sure, she would like nothing more than to work on a potentially groundbreaking case. But she had already decided. She had other plans. Plans that had been two years in the making. Plans that would cause less pain than working on a case for another widow—a case that would remind her every step of the way of the devastating loss of her own husband. And she couldn't throw out her plans just because some irresistible man across a lunch table asked her to.

Could she?

"Okay," she said, stunned by her own words. "But I'm worth at least fifty an hour."

Brad smiled broadly, white teeth flashing, and lifted his tea glass for a toast.

"Deal," he said. "You can start Monday."

Leslie touched his glass gingerly with her own, convinced she had just made a huge mistake.

■ ■ ■

The driver of the large rig had been at it for twenty-two straight hours. His logs would say differently, of course, so that his company would not be cited for violating FTC regulations. The money was good, but he was getting too old for this. He would dump his load at the depot on Military Highway, then push on through to a rest area outside Richmond.

It was warm for an April night, so he kept his windows down. The fresh air would help keep him awake, keep the heavy eyelids open, and might even help him shake off those brews he had thrown down at the truck stop in Suffolk. He was pretty sure he had stopped after two or three, nothing he couldn't handle, nothing he hadn't handled before.

Blasts from a car horn stunned him awake. He jerked his head up just in time to see the driver of the car, wide-eyed, looking out the driver's side window in horror at the truck careening toward him...a jolt, the surreal sound of shattering glass and smashing metal, and the sickening thud of a car under the truck chassis.

■　■　■

Nikki Moreno heard it on her police scanner. A bad accident, possible fatality, at the intersection of Military Highway and Battlefield Boulevard—less than four blocks away. With any luck, she could beat the police to the scene.

She wasn't dressed for this. It was Friday night, and she had gone straight from the beach to the parties. She was wearing shorts, a bikini top, and sandals. It would have to do.

She reached under the seat and pulled out a half-empty bottle of Jack Daniels. She made a mental note to replenish her stock. You never know when opportunity might knock.

"Hang in there, pal, you've got to pull through," she mumbled to herself as she gunned the engine. "You're never worth as much dead."

E ven Bella had to admit the case sounded good. The caller was Ralph Johnson, who had first come to Brad five years ago after losing two fingers in a saber-saw accident. Bella remembered how Brad had parlayed those two fingers into a nifty structured settlement with a total payout of more than $150,000. After Brad took his third, Johnson would have had enough for a down payment on a new home. In his euphoria, and without even consulting his wife, Ralph decided to get a new pickup, stay in the rundown shack they lived in, and have a little money on the side to party.

Five years later, the party money was gone, and the house was feeling cramped, but the pickup was still going strong. Like a rock. Ralph never regretted the way he spent his windfall.

Now Ralph called from the bedside of his brother Frank at Norfolk General Hospital. Misfortune had again visited the Johnson family, and Ralph was hoping Brad could find another pile of cash to ease the pain. Frank had had the bad luck of navigating an intersection at the same time a sleeping drunk driver in an eighteen-wheeler blew through a red light and demolished Frank's vehicle. Ralph was sure this was a case for Brad Carson.

Upon learning the facts, Bella transformed herself into a sugary-sweet grief counselor. But she had a hard time disguising the glee in her voice as she offered Ralph and his brother her deepest condolences. She assured them that Brad would be on the way immediately. Justice would be done. The jerk who caused this terrible tragedy would pay. Dearly.

She talked of justice, but she thought about cash. The case was a gold mine. By the time she hung up the phone, she was practically drooling.

■ ■ ■

Brad took the call from Bella on his cell phone and was at the hospital in a flash. He waited briefly for the elevator, lost patience, then bounded up the stairs to the third floor, where Frank Johnson was being treated. He took the stairs two at a time, his feet barely touching the floor, the adrenaline pumping. He always felt this way when he landed a promising new case.

This feeling, this sense of excitement at someone else's misfortune, always prompted a bout of guilt followed by the same Brad Carson pep talk. The practice of law was so competitive, he reminded himself, there was nothing wrong with feeling good about landing a new case. After all, the damage had already been done, and *someone* needed to help the man get the money he deserved to get on with his life. Brad was convinced that nobody could do that better than he could. Apparently Frank's brother agreed. Brad worked hard and got an honest referral. No need to feel bad about that.

Brad put on his best look of professional compassion and stepped inside the door to Frank Johnson's room. He surveyed the small crowd of people and immediately sensed that something was wrong. Frank was lying uncomfortably in traction, hooked up by tubes to a computer contraption that monitored his vitals and fed him intravenous fluids. Frank's wife sat by his bedside, holding his hand. Ralph stood next to her with downcast eyes. All of this was typical of the hospital room of an injured client. But the woman with her back to the door was the source of Brad's discomfort. She was clearly not medical personnel, and Brad sensed trouble.

Ralph sheepishly introduced the stranger as Nikki Moreno, a paralegal for Billy "the Rock" Davenport.

Brad extended his hand to Nikki. In her other hand, and clearly visible to Brad, was a typed contract for legal services. At the bottom of a full page of small print was a signature that Brad assumed belonged to Frank Johnson.

Brad gave her hand a menacing squeeze. Nikki lifted an eyebrow.

She did not look the part of a professional. She was thin—too thin for Brad's taste—and all legs, which she showed off with a tight miniskirt and three-inch heels. Nikki apparently believed that the gods of style required her to lavishly decorate and puncture her smooth olive skin with a small tattoo on her ankle, a more prominent one on her left shoulder, a pierced navel clearly visible under her cropped blouse, and numerous holes in her ears. Despite her over-the-top presentation, Nikki's face had an exotic Latino allure that came from sharp, angular bones, deeply tanned skin, long black hair, and dark-brown eyes— accentuated with generous amounts of dark eye shadow.

Brad immediately determined he would not be outhustled by a legal assistant for a second-rate ambulance chaser like the Rock. "What are you doing here?" he asked bluntly.

"Our firm represents Frank Johnson. What are *you* doing here?" Nikki fired back.

Brad shot a glance at Ralph Johnson. Ralph pinned his eyes to a spot on the floor.

"Mr. Johnson"—Brad pointed to Ralph—"called *me* to see if I could help his brother the same way that I helped him. I didn't know that you were tailgating the ambulance to the hospital."

"It's not my fault you're a day late and a dollar short," retorted Nikki. She turned to Mrs. Johnson. "Brad's a pretty good lawyer who could do a pretty good job if this were a garden-variety personal injury case. But he works alone. In a complicated case involving serious injuries, you'll be better off with the resources of a firm like Davenport & Associates."

Brad snorted. "Your boss doesn't know the first thing about trying cases." He turned from Nikki to Ralph. "Tell your brother about our case, Ralph. Tell him how a real lawyer operates."

All eyes turned to Ralph, who was still mesmerized by the spot on the floor. He stood silent and unmoving, like a statue.

"A real lawyer," interjected Nikki, "does not act up so bad in court that he gets thrown in jail in the middle of his client's case. It's hard to be effective for your client when you're sitting in jail."

"I wasn't talking to you," snapped Brad.

The statue cleared his throat. "It's like this," said Ralph haltingly, "Ms. Moreno, here, brings some things to the case that no other firm brings. She can help us prove the other driver was drunk. She's an eyewitness to his drinking—"

"I can always subpoena her," Brad interrupted. "I'm telling you, Ralph, you don't want Davenport trying your brother's case. The other side will laugh all the way to a defense verdict."

"You can't subpoena me if I'm representing the truck driver," Nikki said, raising her voice. She waved the paperwork under Brad's nose. "And believe me, if Mr. Johnson reneges on this contract, the truck driver will hire me in a heartbeat."

Brad rolled his eyes. "If you're a witness, I'll subpoena you. And why would the truck driver hire *you?*"

Brad knew this argument between him and a second-class paralegal was totally undignified. *But what are my options? Let her steal the case so the Rock can sell out Frank for a quick and easy settlement?*

Not in a million years.

A nurse wearing the most severe scowl imaginable stepped between Brad and Nikki—*where did she come from?*—and unceremoniously asked them to leave the room. "My patient has enough trauma in his life right now," she said scornfully. "Why don't you take your little disagreement into the hallway?"

Chastised and feeling like a total idiot, Brad murmured an apology to the family, flashed another angry glare at Nikki, and walked quickly from the room.

Nikki followed.

"What a coincidence," Brad lectured, "that you just *happened* upon this accident and *happened* to witness the other driver slamming down a few drinks. What do you do, spend all night listening to a police scanner, waiting for some poor soul to get killed or injured? I ought to report you to the bar."

Nikki just stood there, staring at Brad.

"Are you finished?" she said at last.

"For now."

"Good, because then maybe you'll listen. We were doing just fine here until you showed up, hotshot. If you don't mind, I'm going to go back in there to confer with my client. You, by the way, are not invited." She turned on her heel.

Brad saw his window of opportunity closing quickly. He could not stand the thought of a hapless lawyer like the Rock representing Frank Johnson. He had to do something. Fast.

"Wait," Brad said. "We've both been called on this case." He paused. He was having difficulty forcing out this next sentence. "Let's work as co-counsel and split the fee."

Nikki stopped at the door and turned. She brushed her long dark hair back over her shoulder. If it was designed to impress, it didn't. Brad was already starting to hate himself for suggesting this pact with the devil.

Nikki glanced around the hallway and took a step toward Brad. "Okay, here's the scoop," she said in a hushed voice. "If you want a piece of this case, you hire me. It's a package deal. The case and I come together."

Brad was stunned. Slack-jawed. If he told her off, he would lose the case for sure.

"I did hear about this accident on the scanner," Nikki whispered. "I got to the scene before any help arrived. The other driver smelled like a brewery. I asked if he was okay. Somebody else was already helping Mr. Johnson. I looked into the truck and saw an open bottle of Jack Daniels. I told him I worked for a lawyer and suggested he have a drink to calm his nerves."

She paused, allowing the audacity of what she had done to sink in.

"I've been hanging with the Rock long enough to know the protocol. You tell a drunk driver at the scene to drink some more and then not talk to anyone. The blood-alcohol test will not be able to distinguish what percentage is due to alcohol consumed before the accident and how much is due to alcohol consumed after the accident and before the police arrived. The only person who knows how much the truck driver drank after the accident, as opposed to before the accident"—Nikki again paused and checked the hallway, looking this way and that—"is me. That's why both you and Mr. Johnson need me on this case."

Brad just stood there, shaking his head, condemning her with his eyes. He had never seen such outrageous conduct.

"Of course," continued Nikki. "I didn't want to see the guy get away with drunk driving, so I came over here as soon as Mr. Johnson could have visitors. I told Mr. and Mrs. Johnson that if they retained our firm, I would be happy to testify on their behalf."

"That was big of you," Brad huffed.

"If the Johnsons decide to use some other firm—including yours," continued Nikki in her conspiratorial whisper, "I'll just give the truck driver a call, and he'll retain us. That way any information I have will either be protected by the attorney-client privilege or I'll just conveniently forget it."

"You've got no morals," Brad said, stating the obvious.

"Says the man who purposefully baits a judge and gets himself thrown in jail."

"That's different."

Nikki shrugged. "Whatever." She smiled. "My morals are beside the point. I'm not stupid. I've got a case you want, and you need a good paralegal." She looked down the hallway one more time. The coast was still clear. "And if you repeat this, I'll deny I ever said it—but I also know you're ten times the lawyer Davenport ever dreamed of being. Take the deal, Carson."

Brad did some quick math in his head. Even if he gave Nikki a huge salary out of his one-third contingency fee, he would still turn a handsome profit. If he didn't like her work, he could fire her. If she was good, he did need a paralegal, and he could sure use a hustler like Nikki. But he would lay down some strict ethical guidelines on acceptable behavior in soliciting cases.

"Here's the deal," said Brad. "I can't give you a percentage of the case because it's unethical to give a nonlawyer a percentage for bringing a case to the firm. And despite the way you operate, some of us still believe the ethical rules that govern lawyers ought to be followed every once in a while. But if you bring this case to our firm, and you agree to abide by our code of conduct, I'll give you a one-year contract for fifty thousand dollars." He frowned to emphasize his displeasure at making such a distasteful offer.

Nikki scoffed. "This case alone is worth half a million to your firm. And I can bring in a bunch of other cases like it. But I'm willing to prove myself in the first year." Nikki furrowed her brow and glanced at the contract in her hand, as if she were trying to calculate the combined worth of the contract and her own brilliance. "I'll come for a mere seventy-five thousand, plus a bonus if we do well on the Johnson case. We can talk about the amount of the bonus when we negotiate year two."

Brad pushed a sharp breath out through his nose, like she had just asked him for the Grand Canyon. He shook his head. "Sixty thousand."

Nikki didn't hesitate or blink. She just turned on her heel again and headed straight for the hospital room.

"Okay," Brad fumed, "Seventy-five."

She turned. "Plus medical benefits, parking, and a 401(k) plan."

"You're hired," said Brad quickly.

The two new partners walked down the hall to the waiting area and drew up a short contract on the back of the paper that Johnson had signed. The knot in the pit of Brad's stomach reminded him he would have to break this news to Bella. He prepared himself to offer her a raise.

"One more question," Brad said to Nikki as he signed the makeshift agreement. "Where did that truck driver really get the Jack Daniels."

"If you want the answer to that one," said Nikki smiling, "you'll have to give me a raise."

Just as Brad expected. He made a mental note to keep an eye on Nikki Moreno.

9

I can't do it," said Sarah. "I won't do it. It might endanger the members of our church still worshiping in Riyadh. It may hinder the efforts of the World Mission Society to send other missionaries. But, most important, it would probably mean I could never go back to the Saudis again—never return to the people I love."

Brad shot a sideways glance at Leslie. He had not anticipated this reaction to his proposal that Sarah file suit against the Saudis as well as the insurance company. Brad had predicted Sarah would balk at the prospect of risking any money on the case, so he offered to take the case on contingency and fund the expenses strictly out of firm reserves. Sarah would pay absolutely no fee unless they recovered. But Brad never dreamed that Sarah would still object for philosophical reasons. Clients never objected to the potential for a huge recovery when lawyers took all the risks.

"Well," Brad said after a long silence. He stared at his legal pad on the conference room table. "Nobody is going to force you to file this case. But it seems to me that there are times to turn the other cheek and times to fight back." Brad made a desperate mental search for some biblical arguments, but his repertoire was limited to what little he could remember from his Sunday school days.

He vaguely remembered that Christ Himself got angry a time or two and beat up on some guys in the temple—he could recall the picture from his Bible. "I mean, even Christ turned over the tables on those men selling pigeons in the temple." He looked up and noticed Sarah trying to suppress a grin. Maybe he should stick to logic. "I think it all comes down to the greater good. You could go back into Saudi Arabia and reach dozens of people, maybe even hundreds, as a missionary. But what if this lawsuit resulted in real religious freedom in Saudi Arabia? How many Sarah Reeds could minister in the country then? And not under cover of darkness, but in the light of day. And what if this case results in similar cases against China and other repressive countries? Could it be that God is calling you to take this stand, at this time, to pave the way for thousands of others to go where they could never go before?"

Brad finished talking and waited patiently for Sarah's response. She was deep in thought, not smiling at all now. Leslie fixed her eyes on Sarah as well.

"Brad, I just don't know." Sarah replied tentatively. "I've got to have some time to think about it, pray about it. What you say makes sense, but only if we win. If we lose, it's not just a case, and it's not just money, it's my calling at risk. I could never go back. You can shake off the dust and move on to your next case. But I couldn't live with myself if I made it any harder on the converts in Saudi Arabia."

"What would Charles want?" Leslie asked softly.

Sarah studied her folded hands. "What would Jesus do? If I knew the answer to that question, then I'd know what Charles would want."

More silence followed. The threesome eventually agreed that Sarah would take a few days to think and pray. Leslie would start drafting the lawsuit just in case. Brad made a note to get his hands on a Bible and muster some support for the proposition that Jesus would have filed suit. But he had to admit, it seemed odd to imagine the Man who went without objection to His death on a cross filing suit over a human rights violation.

Brad didn't have the foggiest idea what Jesus would do. But he did know what he wanted to do. He had to get Sarah's permission to file this case. And he had to find a way to win.

■ ■ ■

Nikki enjoyed the first five minutes of her new job. She spent the time unpacking her personal belongings in her new office, waiting for Brad to arrive with instructions.

But at 8:35 Nikki's solitude was shattered when a thick woman in a foul mood parked herself at Nikki's office door. She stood there with one hand on her hip, the other handling a cigarette, while she huffed and puffed about the traffic, the miserable weather, and the other evils of living in Tidewater. "You must be Nikki Moreno," she finally said, her voice filled with scorn.

"Yep," replied Nikki. "Do you mind putting out that cigarette while you're standing in my office?"

Bella pointed out that she was not technically in Nikki's office, and even if she were, she'd put the cigarette out when she darn well pleased. Nikki pointed out that Bella was the only person she knew who was big enough to be technically in Nikki's office at the same time that she was technically in the hallway and technically in the reception area. The conversation went downhill from there.

They argued about the evils of smoking and the danger of second-hand smoke. They argued about whether Bella would do Nikki's typing and answer her phone. They argued about whether miniskirts were appropriate office attire. Bella told Nikki she was so thin she looked sick. Nikki said at least nobody had mistaken her for a beached whale lately. In honor of Nikki's tattoos, Bella called her "the Dragon Lady." In turn, Nikki dubbed Bella "Willy," in honor of the famous orca.

■ ■ ■

By the time Brad arrived, the two women were almost at blows. "I see you two lovebirds have met," said Brad. "Bella. My office—now!"

Brad spent the rest of the morning talking both women out of quitting. By noon he was nursing a splitting headache. As expected, Bella demanded and received a raise, even though she was already probably the highest-paid legal secretary in all of Tidewater.

Even after the raise, Bella told Brad she just couldn't understand why she should be making less than the arrogant and inexperienced Nikki Moreno. Especially, claimed Bella, since her mom was in a nursing home and Bella had to single-handedly pay all the bills. Bella had used the same sympathy ploy for the last two years.

Later that afternoon, Brad heard Bella calling the office-supply company and ordering a brass nameplate for Nikki's office with "the Dragon Lady" etched in black. When he poked his head into Nikki's office, he saw her hanging up framed pictures of dolphins and whales that she had picked up on her lunch break at the mall, as if she had always been an ardent fish lover.

The psychological warfare was well under way.

■ ■ ■

Sarah plopped down on the worn recliner in the small family room. It was nearly 10:30, and there was still so much to do before she could crawl into bed. Two more loads of laundry, dirty dishes all over the kitchen, lunches to get ready for school tomorrow, bills to pay that should have been sent yesterday—well, actually last week.

This was not the way she wanted to end her day. Meredith had just copped an attitude and been sent to her room. The walls were thin in this single-story ranch house, and now Sarah could hear the music from Meredith's CD player infiltrating every nook of living space. Before long, Steven would probably come out of his room and complain he couldn't sleep. Then there would be another battle with Meredith, who had grown increasingly distant and rebellious since Charles' death.

Sarah didn't know if she could take one more battle. Not tonight.

She sighed heavily and reached for the worn Bible—Charles' old Bible, sitting on a small coffee table, right where she had left it two days ago. When Charles was alive, they had devotions together nearly every morning, when they were fresh. Now she struggled to get out of bed in the morning, already running behind, and she would not get to her devotions until the evening. She often couldn't stay awake for the duration.

Before she began, she prayed the same little prayer she always did. "Lord, show me something from this Book tonight that is just for me...as I live for You."

She picked up her reading in the book of Acts. Chapter by chapter. The difficulties that Paul faced and his obedience to his mission in the face of extreme trouble inspired Sarah and made her long for the mission field again. She would go back some day. She loved the Saudi people so much.

She started relaxing as she read God's Word, and her eyelids became heavy. Paul had been arrested, for about the third or fourth time, for preaching the gospel, and he was being tried in front of some Roman governor named Felix. As usual, Paul was giving the governor fits, as he defended himself and witnessed about Christ and the Resurrection. Sarah's mind started to wander, imagining the bandy-legged little Paul, dwarfed by the grandeur of this Roman tribunal, wagging his finger at the great Felix and telling him about the resurrection of the dead. She could see the astonished looks on the faces of the Roman dignitaries as this ornery little Jewish man made his case. Sarah's eyes were blinking more slowly now, the music from Meredith's room drifting into the background, and the words on the page in front of her blurring into a sea of black ink.

And then a tiny phrase jumped off the page. "I appeal to Caesar," Paul said. The words pierced through the fog of impending sleep and slapped Sarah awake. "I appeal to Caesar," Paul insisted. And then Festus answered, "You have appealed to Caesar? To Caesar you shall go!" She sat up straight in the chair, her eyes wide.

The words spoke to Sarah, shouted to her from two thousand years ago and half a world away, as if Paul himself were in her family room at that very moment. "I appeal to Caesar."

Suddenly, Sarah was energized. She couldn't read fast enough. Why did Paul appeal to Caesar? Didn't he just want to get back to the mission field? Didn't he know that appealing to Caesar could take years away from his work? Why was this man, who rejoiced when he was abused for the sake of Christ, suddenly so insistent about his legal rights?

She stood up from the chair, gathered a pen and tablet, and cleared herself a place at the kitchen table. She made some quick notes and outlined the history of Paul's legal troubles and options. She read earlier chapters to put it in context. More notes. More excitement. She was onto something. The answer was here, somewhere.

Some time and several pages of notes later, she found the answer in the ninth chapter of Acts, right after Paul had been converted from a persecutor of the church to a missionary. She had read it so many times before, but she had never seen it. At least not like this.

The Lord called Paul a "chosen vessel" and said that Paul would "bear My name before Gentiles, kings, and the children of Israel. For I will show him how many things he must suffer for My name's sake."

There it was! Her answer. God had given Paul a threefold mission. To share with the children of Israel, which Paul did when he preached at Jerusalem. To share with the Gentiles, which Paul did when he planted churches all over Asia Minor. But Paul also had a mission to share with kings. And how did Paul do this? Through the court system! The Sanhedrin, Governor Festus, King Agrippa, and ultimately to the leading ruler himself—Caesar!

Paul's plea wasn't about winning or losing. He wasn't plotting some kind of legal strategy. In fact, Acts ended with Paul imprisoned in Rome, ready to testify before Caesar. How that trial ended, who knows?

But Paul fulfilled his mission.

To the children of Israel, thought Sarah, Paul's own people. In her case, these would be the Americans. To the Gentiles, foreigners despised by Paul's people. These would be the Saudis. And the kings, the court officials. They would be the federal court judges, the world's media, and the leaders of nations as they followed this international case through the eyes of the world's press.

A threefold mission.

"I appeal to Caesar," said Sarah solemnly.

Without bothering to check the clock, she picked up the phone and dialed Brad.

Leslie filed the suit papers when Norfolk Federal Court opened for business on Good Friday. The timing was Brad's idea. The press would be looking for some good religious news on Easter weekend. Brad was more than happy to oblige. The poisoning of the jury pool had begun.

The suit was a whopper. It spanned an impressive fifty-six pages, encompassing seven separate causes of action and containing enough whereas, heretofore, and hereinabove clauses to choke a horse. Leslie's masterpiece contained impressive citations of various international human rights laws as well as graphic references to specific acts of torture inflicted on the Reeds that would be good grist for the papers.

The suit named the nation of Saudi Arabia as a defendant and at least nine separate "John Does," references to the unknown individuals who had assaulted Sarah and killed Charles.

After detailing the heinous conduct of the Saudi officials for more than fifty-five pages, Leslie demanded, in capital letters, the handsome sum of ONE HUNDRED FIFTY MILLION DOLLARS as compensatory and punitive damages.

The suit requested trial by jury on the counts against the individuals and trial by judge on the count against Saudi Arabia. Brad insisted they file in Norfolk, home of the famed "rocket docket," where cases were always tried within six months of filing. Brad also wanted to file in Norfolk because the court had a legacy of gutsy judges who made tough calls on racial-integration cases. Although those judges had since retired, Brad hoped to tap into this legacy of pioneering civil rights decisions.

While Leslie filed the suit, Nikki hand-delivered courtesy copies to the local newspapers and television stations. Both women returned to the office to help answer the phones. Leslie smiled as she listened to Nikki act surprised at all the media attention.

By noon, the phones were ringing off the hook. Local network affiliates wanted interviews; the newspaper wanted a comment. Even the Associated Press called with a few clarifying questions. It was heady stuff for Nikki and Bella, but poor Brad was mired in a medical malpractice deposition with a cantankerous defense lawyer paid by the hour who had no intention of finishing early.

At 12:30 the defense lawyer came up for air, and Brad sprinted out of the room to claim his rightful place in the spotlight. He called the newspaper first and spent the next thirty minutes explaining the case and waxing eloquent about the importance of international religious freedom. His opening statement in this case would start long before the jury ever assembled.

Brad ran out of time in his lunch hour before he ran out of interview opportunities. He told Leslie he was going to make her a star. He had Bella schedule a press conference for the local television stations for 4 P.M. Leslie would experience media baptism by fire.

Brad was right. Good Friday was a slow news day. National networks picked up Leslie's earnest face and lawyerly remarks from the local affiliates. Soon the cable networks picked up the story, and Leslie's face could be seen both at her apartment in Williamsburg and around the world on CNN.

Leslie watched her debut with Brad that evening on the local network affiliates. A few friends called to say they thought she came off cool and sophisticated. A professor left a message suggesting next time she should clarify she was only a law student. Brad heaped praise on her and toasted her brilliance.

Later that night, Leslie took a tape of the newscasts back to her apartment and replayed it several times. She was brutal in her analysis of her own premier. She promised herself to do better next time.

■ ■ ■

Frederick Barnes, a short bowling ball of a man who ran a Washington-based "consulting firm," made a small fortune from his Saudi account alone. Barnes took great pride in representing a stable of unsympathetic clients with deep pockets and a willingness to pay almost any price for services and information that fell just short—in Barnes' opinion—of espionage or treason. He knew how to navigate the seedy underbelly of Beltway politics in a way that generally pleased his clients and lined his pockets.

Not all his clients were satisfied customers. Ahmed Aberijan had not been on the phone long before Barnes concluded he would have to find satisfaction in taking Ahmed's money even as he endured the Saudi's verbal abuse. One of Ahmed's men had seen reports on CNN of a lawsuit filed against the nation of Saudi Arabia. The suit alleged that the Muttawa tortured and killed an American missionary. All lies, according to Aberijan.

Incensed and derisive, Aberijan spent most of the call railing at Barnes as if Barnes himself had filed the lawsuit. When he finished venting, Ahmed outlined several schemes designed to quash the lawsuit in its infancy. Even with Ahmed's invectives ringing in his ears, Barnes tried to focus on the merits of the plans Ahmed outlined. Barnes had to admit he was impressed with both the complexity and temerity of the plans hatched by this Saudi Arabian hothead on such short notice.

■ ■ ■

Ahmed hung up and placed a call directly to the office of the crown prince. Prince Asad agreed that the case must be contained. The prince had no desire to dirty his hands in the details of the case. Ahmed would take the point. The official statement from the crown prince would reiterate his confidence in and support of the Muttawa. The crown prince would again express his sorrow that an American citizen had died after an unfortunate but unavoidable arrest. Prince Asad would make no other statement about the case and had no intention of answering questions from anyone.

Ahmed was instructed to keep the crown prince informed as the case progressed, and Ahmed knew how to read between the lines of that order. His job was to win the case at any cost, and it would be better if the crown prince did not know the details of what that might entail.

The first phone call between Ahmed and the crown prince on this subject would also be their last.

■   ■   ■

Within twenty-four hours, Barnes called Ahmed back with his first task accomplished.

"I found just the lawyer," Barnes reported. "He knows international law, he's ruthless, and he's rumored to play dirty when necessary."

"Perfect," replied Ahmed.

T he Monday of her second week at Carson & Associates, Nikki
  burned up the phone lines talking to friends. As usual, she closed
her office door, both to keep Bella from prying into her personal business and as a buttress against the cigarette smoke that wafted in whenever Bella came within spitting distance.

The phone calls were, of course, done on company time. Nikki
believed it critical, for a variety of business reasons, to stay plugged into
the paralegal rumor network.

"No way!" exclaimed Nikki. She wore a headset and spoke into a
small mike hanging on an attached wire, freeing both hands to type an
e-mail to another friend. "Who told you that?"

"I heard it from Jessica, that new paralegal at the Jones firm. She's
good friends with Marisa, who, as you know, has a thing going with a
certain unnamed partner at Kilgore & Strobel."

"You mean a certain unnamed partner with wavy dark hair, broad
shoulders, two BMWs, and a cute little tush?"

"You didn't hear that from me."

"Hear what?" Nikki laughed.

Her friend cackled, then started off on another story of romance
and intrigue. But this time Nikki wasn't listening.

She was already formulating a plan.

■   ■   ■

By the time he finally touched down in Norfolk, Ahmed was irritable
and exhausted. The flight from Riyadh to Norfolk took a full nine hours.
Even on board the Saudi government's luxury jet, he felt cornered and

caged. At least he wasn't flying with the unwashed masses on a cramped commercial airline.

The unimpressive size of the Norfolk airport surprised Ahmed. He found it hard to believe that the mighty government of Saudi Arabia was being forced to answer groundless legal allegations in a city like this.

The palpable decadence of the American people threatened to smother him. He could see it in the magazine and bookracks, in the billboards lining the concourse, in the spring dress of the women. In his country, women saved themselves for the pleasure of their husbands. Here the women seemed to strut, to advertise themselves, to dominate the men. Surely it was only a matter of time before Allah judged this pagan culture.

Ahmed would spend as little time here as possible. And he would hate every minute of it.

Tidewater was hot, but he could handle hot. The humidity, however, threatened to undo him. Though it was nearly ten in the evening in the first week in May, Ahmed's short walk caused him to break a sweat. He enjoyed nothing about America. Except, perhaps, the ease with which he might successfully execute his plan.

■ ■ ■

At five minutes after ten, Nikki's cell phone rang. The caller identified himself as Johnny, the desk clerk at the Marriott.

"He's here," Johnny whispered. "His name is Ahmed Aberijan, and he has checked in for just one night. As we discussed, I cannot give you his room number."

"You're a sweetheart," said Nikki, also in hushed tones. "Did he sign the paperwork?"

"How 'bout that!" Johnny exclaimed. "It seems I forgot to have him sign the rate sheet."

"I'll be there in twenty minutes."

Nikki hung up the phone and grinned at her luck.

Eighteen minutes later she entered the spacious lobby of the Marriott and glanced in Johnny's direction. After she caught his eye, she crossed the lobby to the winding, open staircase on the other end that ascended to the second-floor restaurant and bar. She climbed the stairs and crouched behind the railing where she could inconspicuously observe the first floor and the check-in desk. She winked at her new friend behind the desk, and he picked up the phone.

When Johnny finished his call, he gave her a thumbs-up. She crouched down, eyeballed the elevator, and waited.

A few minutes later, the elevator door opened, and Ahmed stepped out, heading straight for the front desk. Nikki watched an animated discussion between Ahmed and the clerk, voices raised, hands expressing frustration. Finally, Ahmed leaned over and signed the cards with a flourish, threw his pen down on the counter, and turned around. In one quick motion, he glanced around the enormous lobby and then up, looking straight in Nikki's direction. She ducked, hugging her knees behind the railing.

Even as she held her breath, not daring to look, she realized how much she loved this element of risk and danger.

Ahmed would be out of range in a matter of seconds. If he saw her, she was history. If he didn't, she must work quickly.

She exhaled quietly and raised her head just over the railing. He had leveled his gaze and was crossing the lobby. She raised herself up a few more inches. He kept walking, unaware of her. *There. Keep going. Don't look up now, buddy.* A few more steps and he would be in the cross hairs.

She focused, aimed, squeezed her finger, and took three shots head-on.

■ ■ ■

Rasheed Berjein responded quickly to the secret knock. The special sequence and rhythm always made his heart beat faster. His mind raced with expectancy, and with dread. It could be another visitor, any one of a number of people he had mustered the courage to tell about this worship service. Or it could be the Muttawa. They had infiltrated the church once. There was no guarantee they would not do so again.

Rasheed looked through the peephole.

To his great surprise, the eyes that greeted him belonged to his brother, Hanif. Rasheed had shared his faith with his family and mentioned these meetings, but so far they had responded with only scorn and ridicule. Still, he prayed for his family morning and night. And now this! With tears welling in his eyes, he flung open the door, threw his arms around Hanif's neck, kissing each cheek, and invited him in.

As Rasheed introduced his brother, he thought about the phone call many months ago that had already meant so much to the struggling Christian churches of Riyadh. Hanif, a police officer for the city, had learned about the planned raid by the religious police. Though Hanif detested the church his brother attended, he was still family. Hanif reluctantly tipped off Rasheed, who in turn called Sarah. It was the only thing that kept the Muttawa from discovering records in the Reeds' apartment exposing a whole network of churches. It was no stretch to say that Hanif had saved them.

And so, tonight, Rasheed wanted to return the favor. He wanted nothing more in life than to show his little brother a very different type of salvation.

■ ■ ■

The Berjeins' living room boasted only sparse furniture—one old couch, a recliner, a rickety coffee table, and a wooden chair. Most guests sat on the floor. None noticed, or could even see, the small electronic listening device that Ahmed's men had placed on the underside of the couch. Nor did they notice a similar device stuck to the bottom of the kitchen table. Nor the device embedded in the receiver of the phone. As soon as Ahmed received word of the lawsuit, he'd instructed his men to plant similar devices in all the homes of the former members of the Reeds' small church.

Tonight's service would be special not only because Rasheed's brother was present, but also because the listening devices would transmit every word by shortwave radio to a nearby van where two of Ahmed's men would join the worship. The church in Riyadh now had an un-planned media ministry, but there was no chance that the sinners in the van would think of repenting. Instead, they recorded the service on state-of-the-art digital equipment and smiled. Ahmed would be pleased.

■ ■ ■

On this night, with a family member present, Rasheed was more ner-vous than ever as he started preaching. His voice was hoarse and high, hardly recognizable in its nerve-induced tone. *It's so hard to share these things with my own brother. He knows me too well—knows every character flaw and shortcoming I have. How can I have any credibility with him?*

But as Rasheed talked, with the faithful church members spurring him on and muttering their amens, he gained confidence and began focusing less on himself as the messenger and more on the message. He kept it simple and delivered it with a genuine sense of humility—one sinner to another, one blind beggar telling another blind beggar where to find bread.

Hanif responded immediately, with tears flooding his cheeks. Rasheed embraced him again with a huge bear hug of acceptance, mak-ing no effort to stem the tide of his own tears. Others formed a close circle around Hanif, reaching out to touch him as Hanif prayed a prayer of repentance and committed his life to Jesus Christ. By the time the last amen was uttered, there was not a dry eye in the place.

Rasheed felt like he was floating, and he couldn't stop himself from slapping Hanif on the back and exclaiming, "Unbelievable," over and over. *My brother! My own brother!* thought Rasheed, shaking his head. The entire group seemed caught up in the enthusiasm and soon broke into spontaneous praise songs. Nobody sang louder than Hanif, though he obviously didn't know the tunes. The service lasted thirty minutes longer than normal, and even then, Rasheed had to practically force the people out the door.

Hanif was the last to go. As he stood in the doorway, Rasheed grabbed him by both shoulders, squeezed tight as if making sure that this whole scene was real, then looked him square in the eye. "I love you, brother," Rasheed said for the first time in his life.

The new convert glanced down at the floor. "Thanks," he said softly, fighting back more tears. Then he kissed Rasheed on both cheeks, smiled broadly, and disappeared into the night.

The door had hardly closed before Rasheed dropped to his knees in grateful prayer.

■ ■ ■

The phone's harsh ring woke Sarah. She sat straight up in bed and tried to focus on the clock. It was nearly 11 P.M. She picked up the receiver before the phone could ring again and wake the kids.

"Hello."

"Sarah, this is Nikki Moreno, Brad's new paralegal. We spoke on the phone last week. Brad's out of town doing some depositions, and I've got something real important I need to discuss with you about your case. I can't talk about it over the phone. Can you wait up for another half-hour or so?"

Sarah was bewildered. She could tell Nikki was calling from a cell phone. She didn't like the idea of this lady she had never met coming to her house in the middle of the night.

"Can't this wait till tomorrow morning?"

"It really can't, Sarah. When I explain it, you'll understand. It's like, you've got to trust me on this one. I promise I'll be there before midnight, okay?"

After a long pause, Sarah agreed. She hung up the phone and headed to the kitchen to fix a pot of coffee. She wondered what she had gotten herself into.

■ ■ ■

Just before midnight, Nikki arrived at Sarah's home in a quintessential Chesapeake suburb, located on a small postage-stamp lot on one of the hundred cul-de-sacs in this residential neighborhood. Standard-issue beige vinyl siding and blue and red trim lined the "Great Bridge Special," so named because it had the same floor plan as a thousand other single-story ranch houses in the Great Bridge community. As she pulled into the driveway, Nikki reminded herself that she never wanted to live like this.

Sure, the houses here were a step up from the shacks in South Norfolk where Nikki spent her childhood. But inside the four walls, inside the *home*, the struggles would be the same—single parents, dysfunctional families, constant friction. As she walked from the driveway to the front stoop, Nikki found herself wondering how Sarah was really doing. Nikki knew how deceptive appearances could be.

Forbidden thoughts of her own childhood flooded forward, unleashed by subconscious forces beyond Nikki's control. But as she knocked quietly, she banished those thoughts completely. That was behind her. Ancient history. She had overcome.

"Hi," said Sarah, sticking out her hand and forcing a smile. She answered the door in some worn-looking pajamas, with a housecoat thrown over top. "Come on in."

The two women settled in at the kitchen table and got right down to business. Nikki declined coffee. What she really needed was hard liquor, but Sarah said she didn't even have beer.

"As you know, when we filed this case, we sued Saudi Arabia and nine John Does," Nikki explained. "The John Does were named to represent those men who actually abused you and killed your husband. We didn't name specific individuals because the U.S. courts would not have what lawyers call 'personal jurisdiction' over someone who had never actually been inside the United States. Under our Constitution, individuals can generally be served with a lawsuit only if they actually appear on U.S. soil. Does that make sense?"

"Not really," admitted Sarah. She looked bewildered and only half-awake.

"Anyway, here's the bottom line. I took some pictures tonight at the Marriott hotel in downtown Norfolk of a guy from Saudi Arabia who is here to meet with some lawyers. If you can identify him as one of your torturers, we can legally serve him with an amended complaint tomorrow while he's still in this country. That way, even if the judge throws out the case against the nation of Saudi Arabia, we can still proceed against this guy and the other John Does."

Nikki slapped the photos down on the table, proud of her handiwork. The zoom had worked nicely; you could see every wrinkle on the man's leathery face. You could see the hatred in the bloodshot eyes, the wiry black beard, the broad nose, and the dark eyebrows.

"The clerk said his name is Ahmed Aberijan," Nikki said. "Isn't he the head of the Muttawa?"

Sarah picked up the photos, and her hands began to tremble. Tears started rolling down her cheeks. She made no effort to stop them.

"Are you all right?" Nikki asked.

The question seemed to jar Sarah back to reality. She nodded a yes and took a few deep, jagged breaths.

"He was the leader," Sarah offered. "He's the one who told his men to strip me and search me." Her voice was hoarse with emotion, her gaze far away. "I'm sure he's the one who ordered Charles killed. I can't believe he has the audacity to come to this country as if it never happened."

"Then he would be John Doe Number 1 in the lawsuit." Nikki said softly. She shifted in her seat, never taking her eyes off Sarah. "Here's what I'm going to do," said Nikki, as reassuringly as possible. "I'm going back to the office right now to rework this lawsuit. We will substitute Ahmed Aberijan for John Doe Number 1 and file the amended complaint first thing in the morning. By noon, we will personally serve the amended complaint on Mr. Aberijan, and there will be no question as to whether he is subject to the jurisdiction of this court."

Sarah looked at Nikki with hollow eyes. Nikki dropped the professional demeanor and lowered her voice again. "Are you sure you're okay?"

Sarah pursed her lips, nodded her head slowly, and promised she would be fine.

■ ■ ■

After Nikki left, Sarah slouched over the kitchen table and stared at her coffee. She was suddenly so very tired, so very lonely. The man in the photos had reached out and delivered a gut punch that knocked the wind out of her, destroying all of her heroic efforts to put this behind her.

She needed, at this moment perhaps more than any other, to be held by Charles. She missed him so very much. She could not go to bed, because closing her eyes would simply bring back the face of Ahmed Aberijan. The flashbacks would overcome her: the shattering front door…the men hitting Charles…the blood pooling on the kitchen floor…the stench of the man's sweat and breath as he manhandled her…the heinous laughs as they ripped off her clothes…the struggle…the blackness. The nightmares were always the same. The faces of the Muttawa, the bloodied face of Charles, his hand reaching for her but never quite connecting, then visions of the casket.

She gently whispered Charles' name, while the tears dripped off her chin and onto the table.

■ ■ ■

Nikki called Bella on her cell phone as soon as she pulled out of the driveway. It was now after midnight.

"What?" answered Bella, always the charmer.

"I need you to come into the office right away. I'll meet you there in about fifteen minutes."

"Fat chance." Bella slammed down the phone. Nikki hit redial.

"What?"

"Bella, don't hang up, this is serious. It's about the *Reed* case. A guy named Ahmed Aberijan is in town…" Suddenly Nikki was listening to a dial tone. She hit redial again. She would have slapped Bella if they were in the same room.

Bella didn't answer, but after five rings her answering machine kicked in. Nikki punched "one" to leave a message.

"Listen, you lazy slug. We have less than nine hours to prepare an amended complaint in the *Reed* case, file it, and have it served tomorrow on one of the jerks that tortured Sarah and killed her husband. I can't get access to the documents I need because they're on your hard drive. If I have to, I'll go in alone and retype everything, even if it takes me all night. But Bella, I could really use your help. I wouldn't call you this late at night if I wasn't desperate."

When Nikki arrived at the office fifteen minutes later, Bella was already at her desk. One cigarette smoldered in the ashtray, a second hung from Bella's lips. She looked worse than usual, and for a fraction of a second, Nikki felt sorry for her.

"What took you so long?" Bella asked.

At seven the next morning, Nikki and Bella camped out in the Marriott lobby's overstuffed chairs with strong coffee and the local paper. Every twenty minutes or so, Bella slipped outside for another cigarette. Nikki was grateful to see another desk clerk in Johnny's place. She didn't want to start the day by breaking his heart.

At ten minutes before nine, Ahmed came out of the elevators carrying his briefcase. Nikki and Bella watched Ahmed go straight out the front door of the hotel, then followed him across the street, where he disappeared into the rotating door of the twenty-story office building immodestly labeled One Commercial Place. They entered the lobby just as Ahmed elbowed his way onto an elevator that serviced floors eleven through twenty. As the elevator doors closed, Ahmed and the other grim-faced office workers stared straight ahead.

Once the Saudi disappeared, Bella headed straight to federal court to file the amended complaint and obtain a service-ready copy to be handed to Ahmed. In the meantime, Nikki hunkered down for a stakeout in the lobby. She determined from the directory that Mack Strobel's office was on the twentieth floor. Though she couldn't be positive, the bigger-than-life Strobel was an obvious choice from the many lawyers at Kilgore & Strobel to handle such a high-profile case. She called the commercial airlines, posing as Ahmed's secretary, and determined that he was not flying commercial. With nothing left to do but wait, she bought a magazine from a small deli and studied the latest fashions, leaning against the wall but always keeping at least one eye on the elevator doors.

Less than an hour later, Bella returned with the necessary papers.

The two women would wait patiently for the chance to slap a $150 million lawsuit into the bloodstained hands of Ahmed Aberijan.

■ ■ ■

Twenty stories up, Mack Strobel suddenly felt cramped in his large corner office. Despite its spacious decor and expensive Persian rugs, it did not come close to being big enough or plush enough to comfortably handle the egos that now filled the room. Mack had suggested just talking over the phone, but Frederick Barnes wouldn't hear of it. "The client wants to meet his lawyer face-to-face," Barnes had insisted.

Mack strategically suggested they work at the small round conference table in one corner of his office, immediately under the expansive picture of Strobel's alma mater, the Virginia Military Institute. He made the suggestion to Barnes, who translated the request to Ahmed, who nodded his assent.

As Mack warily took his seat, Barnes reached into his suit-coat pocket and pulled out a small plastic cylinder containing an expensive Cuban cigar. Barnes removed the cigar from its case, gently licked one end, and placed it in his mouth as he patted down his other pockets in an apparent search for a lighter.

Mack looked on in disgust. He would have let it slide if Barnes intended only to chew on the nasty thing. But Mack was a reformed smoker himself and considered it his mission in life to keep others from lighting up.

"The air breathers would appreciate it if you would refrain from smoking in here. That stuff'll kill ya, you know."

"I don't inhale," replied Barnes as he finally found his lighter and flicked it to life. "Besides, I didn't think I'd get any flack from the firm that represents Phillip Morris."

"If you don't inhale it, we'll have to," Strobel growled.

Barnes ignored him and watched with detached satisfaction as the cigar's sweet, putrid smell quickly engulfed the room.

Client or not, Barnes knew how to push all the wrong buttons. Mack pushed politeness aside. "Either put that thing out, or go find yourself another lawyer. If you represented Phillip Morris, you'd stop smoking too."

Slowly and deliberately, cigar hanging out of one corner of his mouth, Barnes stood and walked nonchalantly to the office door, opened the door, still puffing on his stogie, and smiled at Strobel's young assistant sitting at her desk.

"Got an ashtray?" Barnes asked.

"No sir, but I can get one for you," Mack heard his assistant say.

Barnes just nodded and leaned against the doorframe, his eyes following the woman as she raced off down the hallway. She returned with a clear glass ashtray and offered it gingerly. He took it, turned to face Mack again, and begrudgingly ground his stogie into the glass. Barnes closed the office door, then slowly returned to his seat at the table, chewing on the cigar, and smiling broadly at Strobel.

In that moment, Mack resolved to cut Barnes out of the loop at the first opportunity. He would earn Aberijan's exclusive loyalty as the case progressed. Mack had seen it happen a thousand times; he could always earn the grudging respect of even the most hard-to-please clients. When he did, Barnes would become expendable, and Mack would set him up.

"You ought to try one," Barnes said, eyeing the unlit stogie as he twirled it around in his fingers.

"Let's get started," replied Mack gruffly. "Mr. Aberijan didn't call this meeting so we could discuss cigars."

For the next two hours, the men talked legal fees and strategy. Despite the rocky start, Mack soon negotiated a premium hourly fee for himself and the host of other lawyers who would work the case. Four hundred dollars an hour for Mack. A new record. A new cash cow. There would be excited whispering over the phone lines and in the hallways as Mack's legend grew. There would be joy at Kilgore & Strobel.

■ ■ ■

In the lobby, Nikki fretted. Ahmed had disappeared into the elevator more than two hours ago. She knew his luggage was still at the hotel, and she was pretty sure he would have to come back through this lobby on his way out, but still the possibilities kept bubbling up in her brain.

What if someone from Kilgore & Strobel had seen her and Bella hanging out in the lobby? What if Ahmed took the stairs and slipped out one of the stairwell doors? What if he took the elevator down to the loading dock in the basement, where a car was waiting for him? What if, somehow, he just avoided Nikki altogether and made it back to Saudi Arabia without getting served?

How could she ever explain it to Sarah if Ahmed got away?

For reasons Nikki could not yet put her finger on, she knew the case had now become personal. Something had snapped in her when she saw Sarah's distressed reaction to Ahmed's photo. She had to serve this man. He had to be brought to justice. He must pay for what he had done to Sarah and undoubtedly to hundreds of others like Sarah.

He would not get away with it again; not on her watch.

Two hours was too long. She explained her plan to Bella, who immediately shook her head in protest.

■ ■ ■

Twenty stories up the phone rang. Barnes watched Mack answer it in a huff. He enjoyed seeing lawyers flustered.

"I told you to hold my calls. You know I can't be interrupted in this meeting." Mack listened and frowned. "Okay, put her through." Another long pause while he listened some more. His voice dropped, but not out of Barnes' hearing. "Bring me a copy immediately. Thanks for the heads up."

He put down the phone and looked at Barnes.

"We've got some trouble here," said Mack. "One of our paralegals just returned from federal court. It seems an amended complaint naming Mr. Aberijan as an individual defendant has been filed. The plaintiffs also requested process papers so that Mr. Aberijan can be served personally with the suit while he is on American soil. This is the very thing I was talking about earlier when I explained that Mr. Aberijan should stay out of the country from now on. We've got to get him back to his plane before the plaintiffs serve him."

Barnes spoke to Ahmed in Arabic. Ahmed nodded his head and responded vigorously.

"He left some items at the hotel," explained Barnes. "I can go pick those up if you can get him to the airport."

"I'll call a limo to meet us in the basement. We'll be at the airport in twenty-five minutes."

■ ■ ■

Nikki got off the elevator at the twentieth floor and stepped onto the thick Persian rug of the reception area. Lavish testaments to the prowess and wealth of the boys at Kilgore & Strobel surrounded her. Polished oak floors, mahogany trim, stylish antique furniture. Even the receptionist, barricaded behind a beautiful oak workstation sporting the firm's gold logo, looked like she had just stepped off the cover of a fashion magazine.

She flashed Nikki a blinding white smile and asked with sickening sweetness, "May I help you?"

Nikki returned a smile with her own lips closed—no sense trying to compete with those teeth. "I've got an appointment with Mr....um..." Nikki shook her head in frustration at her own stupidity, "I can't believe I forgot his name... I was just in his office a few weeks ago."

The receptionist gave her a wary look.

"Oh, you know," Nikki continued, "I've got his name in here somewhere." She started opening up the manila envelope she was carrying. She read a few lines of one document. "Here it is...that's right. The guy I originally came to see was a Mr. Strobel," she pointed down a hallway toward her left, "but then he hooked me up with the guy whose office was right next to his, and I can't remember his name..."

The receptionist checked some papers in front of her. "Actually, the office right next to Mr. Strobel is one of our female associates, Andrea Gates." *Of all the luck—the Kilgore firm couldn't have more than a couple female lawyers total, and one of them had to be next to Strobel.* "Are you sure—" began the receptionist.

"Which side of his office?" interrupted Nikki. "His office is in a corner, right?" *That was a safe bet.* She motioned to an area behind her, on the northwest corner of the building. *Where was Bella? What was taking her so long? Couldn't she even do a simple thing like—*

"Right, but it's this corner over here," said the receptionist helpfully, motioning to the southeast corner. Nikki gave her a puzzled expression and an innocent shrug.

"Okay…right," Nikki said, turning a half-circle as if getting her bearings.

"And the guy next to him on the other hallway is Brett Aikens," said the receptionist. "I'll give him a call."

Don't bother, Nikki wanted to say. Instead, she forced out a thanks. Still no Bella. She'd kill her later.

"Your name?"

"Oh." The request caught Nikki off guard. She'd forgotten to plan an alias. In the pressure of the moment, she said the first thing that came to her mind. "Bella Harper."

"Thanks."

The receptionist called the lawyer and, to Nikki's great relief, he was not in. But Nikki insisted on waiting for him to return. It was a very important meeting, Nikki said. So she took a seat in the reception area, checked her watch, and began silently cursing Bella.

Five minutes later, precisely seven minutes behind schedule, Bella stepped off the elevators. Nikki picked up the manila envelope lying next to her on the floor.

The receptionist was on the phone and lifted a finger, indicating to Bella that she would be right with her. Bella glanced over at Nikki, who glared back, jaw clenched, showing her displeasure with the timing. Bella responded with a quick roll of her own eyes and a little headshake that just made Nikki steam even more.

"May I help you?" asked the receptionist.

"Yes, I'm Bella Harper, and I'm here—"

Nikki nearly jumped out of the chair. *What kind of idiot gives her own name when she's part of a scam and hasn't even been asked her name?* The receptionist's puzzled look lasted only a moment, for in the very next instant a bigger problem demanded her immediate attention.

Bella clutched her chest and groaned loudly. The eyes of the receptionist widened. Bella's face turned red, and she began staggering, fighting for air. With a fitful gasp Bella collapsed in a heap on the floor, falling thunderously and gloriously on the Persian rug, then flopping on her side, still clutching at her chest.

The receptionist put a hand to her mouth, stifling a scream. She looked down at Bella and frantically dialed a number. "Are you all right? Are you all right?" she kept saying.

Nikki wanted to watch this drama play itself out, but that was not the plan. "I'll go get help," she called out, and bolted for Strobel's office.

She had taken no more than five or six steps down the long hall—a virtual gauntlet of secretaries at computer terminals and open work stations—when three men emerged from the corner office at the end. She recognized one of the men as Mack Strobel and one as Ahmed Aberijan. The third man she couldn't place. They huddled outside the doorway momentarily, talking to each other, no more than eighty feet away.

Nikki fixed her gaze straight ahead and quickened her pace.

She was halfway down the corridor when Mack Strobel noticed her coming and took a step in her direction. The shorter man grabbed Ahmed's arm and steered him down the perpendicular hallway, away from Nikki.

"Who are you?" demanded Strobel, walking toward her. Some secretaries stopped typing, others put a momentary freeze on their phone gossip, almost all of them glanced up. "What are you doing here?"

When she was just a few steps away, Nikki started speaking rapidly, motioning wildly with her hands to emphasize the urgency of her message.

"Dónde está la oficina de Señor Aiken?" she blabbered. A puzzled look crossed Strobel's face, they were now standing no more than two feet apart. *"No entiendes ni una palabra que he dicho verdad, tonto?"*

Strobel gave her a blank stare, and the muscles in his face relaxed ever so slightly. "Anybody know Spanish?" he asked, glancing around.

Sensing her chance, Nikki exploded past him, shoving him slightly with her free hand, deftly sidestepping the startled lawyer. She broke into a sprint, quickly turning the corner.

"Stop her!" Strobel yelled.

The shout got the attention of Ahmed and his sidekick, who were still half a hallway ahead of Nikki, ready to turn a corner down another adjacent hallway. They both pivoted on their heels, a brief look of astonishment on their faces. Nikki locked eyes with Ahmed and ran straight toward him.

Before she reached Ahmed, his burly sidekick barreled into Nikki with a force that sent her crashing against a wall. Nikki gasped as the air left her lungs, and she collapsed to the plush floor. Pain shot through her left shoulder, which had hit the wall first, bearing the main brunt of the brute who assaulted her. He stood over her now. Her world spun, and she blinked to fight back the converging blackness and stars.

Dazed but still conscious, Nikki realized she still held the envelope containing the suit papers. She threw the envelope across the floor so that it slid within inches of Ahmed's feet.

"Congratulations," she gasped. "You've been served."

Ahmed sneered, his lips curled ever so slightly into an arrogant little smile, and the eyes sent an unmistakable message of their own. She had seen the same eyes before, the same pent-up fury, the same smoldering violence. It was the look of her own father, remembered across a decade of time, as if it were yesterday. It was the look she remembered from that split second in time before he would strike out at her mom…

"Get up," barked the stocky man as he yanked Nikki to her feat. Mack Strobel was telling shell-shocked secretaries to call security.

"Get your hands off me," Nikki shouted back. "You're hurting me. Someone call the cops!"

But the man just twisted her arm tighter, and with pain shooting through her shoulder, Nikki stopped resisting. One gawking secretary found the presence of mind to get security on the phone and hand the receiver to Mack Strobel. With the envelope still lying unopened on the floor, and Mack Strobel preoccupied on the phone, Ahmed came over to Nikki and leaned so close to her that the hot stink of his breath brushed across her face.

"You will pay." Ahmed said slowly and emphatically.

The words shot through Nikki's rattled nervous system, putting her flight instincts on full alert. Yet her sense of bravado never betrayed her.

"Promises, promises," she snapped back.

She stared hard at Ahmed, unblinking, until his friend yanked her back down the hallway and toward the lobby, ignoring her threats to sue the pants off him. He marched Nikki right past Bella, who was now sitting in a chair, wet paper towels plastered on her forehead, breathing fitfully. Nikki glanced sideways at her compatriot, who in turn acknowledged Nikki with an almost imperceptible nod of the head, then resumed her tortured performance as a heart attack victim and her loud complaining about how long it was taking the ambulance to arrive.

Ahmed Aberijan had been served.

A special sense of relief washes over the body of a law student as she puts down her pen at the end of semester exams. Sagging shoulders straighten, a smile replaces a furrowed brow, and a bounce in the step replaces the exam-week shuffle.

For Leslie Connors, this invigorating relief was underscored by the anticipation of spending the evening with Brad. He had asked her to dinner, ostensibly to discuss her work on the *Reed* case. But Leslie believed—and hoped—that the real reason had more to do with personal motives. Leslie had not seen Brad since she started exams two weeks ago, and she did not look forward to spending the summer away from him in England, separated by the Atlantic Ocean rather than the Chesapeake Bay.

Leslie was nearly thirty years old and experiencing emotions from her schoolgirl days. She felt a bit guilty for craving his attention so much. Though her tidy life plan left no room for a relationship with Brad, her emotions suggested such a relationship was exactly what she needed.

Tonight she vowed to throw caution to the wind and enjoy herself. Brad had insisted she choose the restaurant. It was an easy choice. The most romantic restaurant around was The Trellis, a quaint and elegant throwback to another era in the heart of Colonial Williamsburg. The Trellis sat on prime real estate, fronting on Duke of Gloucester Street, strategically located in the middle of Williamsburg's historic district.

Duke of Gloucester Street, or "Dog Street" in the parlance of the locals, was a passageway to a simpler time. The colonial architecture, the gravel road, the manicured lawns, the authentic historical costumes of the workers, and the exact replicas of the colonial buildings, all combined to make visitors a part of history. Any tension remaining from exams left Leslie's body entirely as she strolled down Dog Street, killing time. It was the perfect setting for a promising night.

■ ■ ■

Like all drivers in Tidewater, Brad despised the bridges and tunnels that surrounded Norfolk and Virginia Beach. He hated them most when, like tonight, he was running late and heading north, because traveling in that direction meant crossing the Chesapeake Bay through the mother of all traffic jam generators: the Hampton Roads tunnel. The tunnel *never* backed up on those rare occasions when he was on time. But somehow, the desperation of his personal situation seemed to trigger the most gnarly jams. Tonight, with Brad running late, a stalled car performed the honors of backing up traffic for nearly a mile.

Inching his way along, Brad whipped out his cell phone and dialed.

"Strobel here." The words blasted. Strobel was on his speakerphone, and the echo made him hard to understand and louder than life.

"Take me off the box," said Brad.

"Who's this?" Strobel bellowed. He had the tone of a man who was not used to taking orders from a stranger.

"It's Brad Carson, returning your call, and I'm not going to talk to you if you don't take me off that blasted speakerphone."

"Bradley, thanks for calling back." Strobel was still on the speakerphone. Brad simmered. Nobody called him Bradley. "Look old boy, as you obviously know based on that cute little stunt your paralegal pulled, we've been hired to defend the *Reed* case, and I thought I owed you a courtesy call before we file the kinds of motions we're preparing. You still there?"

"Yeah, I'm still here," Brad responded. He had now put his cell phone on speaker mode and laid it in the seat next to him. Two could play this game.

"What types of motions are you talking about?"

"Say what?" shouted Strobel.

"I said, what kinds of motions are you going to file?" Brad said it slower and louder, emphasizing each word.

"Well, Bradley, I've been practicin' law a long time, and you're a good lawyer, but I've never seen a case more desperate than this one, except maybe some of those *pro se* cases filed by prisoners complaining about jail food. Unless I'm missing something, you don't have squat. Am I out in left field here? Are you aware of some case law or authority I haven't stumbled across?"

Strobel was obviously on a fishing expedition, trying to flush out Brad's best arguments so he could address them in his opening brief. Brad was not about to bite that hook.

"You're the expert on international law. You tell me."

An audible sigh. Strained patience. "All right, Bradley, I will tell you. Your claims against Saudi Arabia are barred by the doctrine of sovereign immunity. In addition, Bradley, the only witness you have to support your claim of torture is your own client. And her credibility is—how shall I say this?—shaky at best." Strobel paused, apparently wanting the thinly veiled threat to sink in.

"Our only choice, under these circumstances, is to file a motion to dismiss and to also ask the court for Rule 11 sanctions against you and your firm for filing a frivolous claim. I don't like filing such motions against my colleagues, Bradley. That's why I'm calling. If you voluntarily dismiss the case by week's end, we'll forget the motion for sanctions. We all go home, on to the next case. Your choice, Bradley, what's it gonna be?"

■ ■ ■

Mack stopped pacing and yacking long enough to listen. Only then did he realize that the sound on the other end of the phone line was a dial tone.

Mack had his answer. This case was about to get personal.

■ ■ ■

Leslie arrived ten minutes before seven o'clock and verified the reserva-
tion. By 7:15 there was still no sign of Brad. Leslie knew Brad typically
began meetings and appointments by apologizing for being late.
Tonight would be no exception.

As the minutes clicked by, she felt the magic of Dog Street waning.
Leslie and Bill had eaten at The Trellis just once, a few months after the
diagnosis. The evening was quite possibly the first since the disease
became part of their lives that they spent the entire evening without
mentioning it. Bill had resolved not to spoil a perfect date, and Leslie
had followed his lead.

Now, as she sat here waiting for Brad, the memories of that night—
the smells of fresh bread from the ovens, the sounds of laughing tourists,
the sight of William and Mary undergrad just a few blocks away, the
very feel of this area of Colonial Williamsburg—simply overpowered
her. She felt a sudden need to be alone, to savor one more time the
special relationship she had had with Bill, the one man who knew her
completely—warts and all—and accepted her totally. She stood up to
go home, pour herself a nice glass of wine, and unwind on the dock
overlooking the Chickahominy.

She sighed and sat back down. All at once, tonight felt like such
hard work, like it would be her job to impress Brad with an outgoing
and fun-loving personality. She would have to guard against lapses in
the conversation, against saying anything that might betray this building sense of depression eating at her. Why was it so hard to enjoy a night
with someone she liked so much? Why did she suddenly feel so much
pressure to make this work? And why, on tonight of all nights, was it so
hard to get Bill out of her mind?

By 7:30, when Brad finally came jogging over from a nearby parking lot, Leslie's anxiety was in full bloom. As he approached, she felt her
pulse quicken, but she put on her poker face and did not smile, a little
psychological punishment for being late.

"Hey, Leslie. Sorry I'm late," Brad said, catching his breath. "Hope
you haven't been waiting long."

They faced each other awkwardly as Brad seemed to vacillate between a quick hug and shaking hands. Leslie stuck out her hand as further punishment, and Brad took the cue. She immediately felt silly. She decided to put him at ease. Her poker face disappeared, replaced by a bright smile. She followed the handshake with a quick hug. She congratulated herself on her studied act of spontaneity.

"Don't worry about it. For the first time in weeks, I've got no deadlines." She was keenly aware of her unenthusiastic tone and wondered if Brad noticed. "But I am starving. Let's see if they've still got a table for us."

"I really am sorry," he repeated as they walked into the restaurant. Brad opened the door and placed a gentle hand on Leslie's shoulder as she passed through. The spontaneous touch sent chills through Leslie's entire body. The ghosts of Bill again. The gentle hand on the shoulder as she entered a restaurant, the soft spontaneous touch—these mannerisms belonged to Bill. Leslie had never realized how much she missed them, these little habits, until this moment.

"We should have something in about twenty minutes," promised the maître d'.

Brad leaned close to the man and whispered intently, as if the two were lifelong friends. Two minutes and twenty bucks later, the host seated Leslie and Brad at a remote window for two that overlooked Dog Street.

The conversation started slowly, weighed down by Leslie's melancholy. But before long, her queasiness began to melt away in the face of Brad's relentless determination to have a good time. He put his personality on overdrive. He had quips and stories galore, and he even managed to strike up a nice conversation with the waitress, whom Leslie suspected of trying to hit on her date. But that was one of the things she liked most about Brad—his ability and desire to put people at ease. To make them feel good about themselves.

Despite her formidable defenses, Leslie found the Carson charm working. The conversation flowed more easily through dinner, time disappeared, and suddenly the server asked if they wanted dessert. Brad allowed the flirting waitress to talk him into Death by Chocolate. Leslie passed.

Brad didn't mention the *Reed* case until after his first bite of the life-threatening dessert.

"I talked to Mack Strobel today," he said out of the blue.

"You know how to ruin a perfectly good meal."

"He's going to file Rule 11 sanctions against us." Brad said it matter-of-factly, then took another bite of the rich, dark chocolate cake with chocolate icing and smothered in chocolate sauce. "Wants to give me another taste of jail food."

"Speaking of which, how's Nikki?"

"Bella didn't call you?" Brad pushed the dessert toward her. Leslie started to push the plate back, then caught herself. She shook her head in answer to his question and sliced off a small piece with her fork. No telling what this one small bite would cost her—probably three pounds, directly to the hips. But it tasted great…actually, beyond great, though the guilt of the calories hit before she swallowed.

She pushed the plate back.

"Four hours in jail, and we pled her out on misdemeanor trespass. I did the whole thing over the phone. Six months' probation—no time. I think the prosecutor actually thought it was funny."

Leslie eyed the chocolate. It was disappearing fast.

"But then this assistant U.S. attorney gets involved," Brad continued. "Angela Bennett—colder than ice—and threatens to file charges for assaulting a foreign dignitary."

"What'd you do?"

"You mean after I peeled Nikki off the ceiling?"

Leslie grinned at the thought of Nikki's reaction.

"Bennett was in our conference room, making these accusations face-to-face," a smirk curled across Brad's lips as he recalled the scene, then he chased the smirk away with another bite of chocolate. "So Nikki flashes her bruises, then stomps over to the phone and starts dialing a friend at a local television station. 'Let's just give the media a call,' she says, 'and let them know that this *foreign dignitary* beat me up, threatened me, and now you're going to pile on by filing charges.'"

Brad smiled broadly. He held his fork up with another bite of dessert, as if toasting Nikki's brilliance.

"Case dismissed," he said, then devoured the forkful.

"Was she hurt?" asked Leslie.

"She's pretty bruised, still threatening a lawsuit, but she'll be fine. She said that jerk from Saudi Arabia threatened her, but Nikki doesn't scare easy."

"She's got to be more careful."

Brad suspended his fork in midair and seemed to ponder this off-hand comment.

"No," he said, looking serious. "The practice of law is the art of taking risks. You prepare and calculate the best you can, but at the end of the day, you just roll the dice, and your client's entire life is changed by what comes up. You can't be effective if you're not comfortable with risk."

Leslie thought about this as she watched Brad devour the remaining dessert. Risk was not her thing. Perhaps it was just Brad's style, or perhaps he was right. She would force herself to take a few more risks. She would start now.

She picked up her fork, thought about the calories again, and set it back down. She wondered what risk-taking Nikki would do with this dessert.

And the thought of Nikki behind bars suddenly struck her as funny.

"Did you ever think about doing lawyer ads featuring you and Nikki in jail?" Leslie reached out her hands and grabbed the imaginary bars. "Carson & Associates, it takes one to spring one."

"Very funny," said Brad. But he couldn't help smiling.

■ ■ ■

An hour later they walked in silence down Dog Street, enjoying the brisk night and basking in the tradition of Colonial Williamsburg. Brad had stopped his running commentary, sensing a comfort between them that did not need to be broken with makeshift conversation.

While they strolled, Brad quietly fought his own inner war. He had mixed business and pleasure before with disastrous results—including devastated feelings and a lost case. The pressures of litigation had ways of forging romances that never lasted under normal circumstances. He had long ago established a hard-and-fast rule that he would never again date a lawyer involved in one of his cases.

Besides, his lifestyle left little time for meaningful relationships. At times he regretted that fact. More often, he realized he was still not ready to trade the thrill of pursuing the big case for the mundane life of a sub-urban husband and dad. But tonight his heart told him he should allow himself a loophole for a romance with this beautiful law student, a loophole that seemed particularly compelling as he glanced at Leslie's auburn hair shimmering in the soft moonlight. What made her even more beautiful, Brad decided, was that Leslie had no idea how pretty she was.

■ ■ ■

Her earlier anxieties entirely gone, Leslie desperately wished the night had just begun. She stood in the shadows of Dog Street, facing Brad, inches apart. Brad reached down and took her hands in his.

"I had a great time," he said. "I really wish you weren't going to England. It could be a long two months."

"I know," said Leslie, surprised by the intensity of her inward response to the warmth and strength of his hands. She could not move or think; she could only shudder.

"Can we do this again when you get back?" Brad asked. He released one hand and gently brushed her hair back over her shoulder. She hadn't felt this way in so long.

"I'd like that."

Brad gently drew her close, and she did not resist. The warmth of being held by him, the security of his arms—she had forgotten how special the nearness could feel. She breathed deeply, filling her lungs with the presence of Brad Carson. And then, suspended in time, she closed her eyes and gracefully tilted back her head. Their lips gently touched. Dog Street spun; the passion flowed. It was, in Leslie's considered opinion, an awesome kiss. One that lasted longer than she intended. One that surprised her with the intensity of her own passion, the tingling of her skin, the release of pent-up emotions. It was at once tender and exhilarating. It was only a few seconds, but it completely carried her away.

Dog Street was indeed magical.

But for Leslie, it was also confusing. She pulled slightly away from Brad, thoughts racing through her mind too fast to process, a jumble of emotions and feelings from past and present colliding.

"I can't do this Brad. I'm not ready; it's still too fresh." Even to Leslie, it sounded crazy. How could she not be ready to move on after three years? When would she be?

But it was also true. She needed more time. The emotions she had just felt, that she hadn't felt since she lost Bill, she had believed she would never feel them again. It was just too raw. Too overpowering. And Leslie cared too much for Brad to tell him anything but the truth.

"I lost a husband to cancer three years ago," she whispered. "I'm sorry." She took a half-step back, looked down, and shuffled her feet. Her guilt was magnified by the knowledge of what she was doing to Brad.

"Leslie, I didn't know… I would have never…" He paused and gently took her hands. "You've got nothing to apologize for."

His kindness only made her feel worse. She could think of nothing to say, completely embarrassed by the unfolding events she was powerless to change.

"Do you want to talk about it?" he asked gently.

Leslie shook her head.

"If you ever do, just let me know."

She nodded.

"C'mon," said Brad. "I'll walk you to your car."

14

————

His threatening overtures to Brad Carson aside, Mack Strobel was a sensible lawyer and would not file a Rule 11 motion lightly. He wanted nothing more than to see Carson taken out to the proverbial legal woodshed with a whipping stick, humiliated by the sanctions. But since the courts used the Rule 11 woodshed sparingly, Mack would have to exercise caution to prevent his request from blowing up in his own face. As he always did when he needed advice, Mack summoned the other members of the firm's informal brain trust.

Though Kilgore & Strobel had an official executive committee, everyone knew it was the four men assembled this day at the Norfolk Golf and Country Club who called the shots. They gathered informally to plot strategy on every major case or business deal the firm ever handled. It was their way of rewarding each other with easy billable hours at the expense of clients who would never notice the difference. Today, after a grueling eighteen holes in the heat of a May afternoon, they were paying off bets and throwing down a few cold ones to lubricate their brain cells.

Mack polished off his second glass, surveyed the group, and found himself silently shaking his head. *If this is the A team,* he thought, *it's a wonder that our firm can function at all.*

Seated directly across from Mack was a wrinkled man with sad, droopy eyes, stooped but still vigorous, with a pointed face and tufts of gray hair on the sides of his head. Nothing grew on top and had not for as long as Mack could remember. His name was Theodore "Teddy" Kilgore, the grandfatherly patriarch of the firm and the only lawyer who outranked Mack. He no longer actively practiced law, but he was still the firm's premier "rainmaker," snagging well-heeled clients so the young bucks could work on their cases.

To Mack's right at the small table was Melvin Phillips, a brilliant Harvard graduate and a first-rate tax attorney with no social graces. The boys at Kilgore & Strobel valued his big brain and frequently came to him with their thorniest problems, but they also kept him well hidden from the clients. He never combed his thick gray hair, and he wore ill-fitting suits that looked like hand-me-downs from a traffic court lawyer. Melvin housed his huge cranium inside a round head, precariously perched on a round body with not one discernible muscle. He had an enormous chin and small beady eyes, shrunk further by the magnification of thick glasses, so that he always sported an out-of-touch look.

On Mack's other side was the member of the brain trust with the best pedigree, a man whom Mack personally despised because of his genteel arrogance and condescending ways. Winsted Aaron Mackenzie IV came from good stock. His father was a prominent Virginia politician, his grandfather an appellate court judge, and his great-grandfather, the original Winsted Aaron Mackenzie, fought for the Confederacy. "Win" was the pretty boy of the firm—tailored suits and monogrammed shirts, silk ties and wavy brown television-evangelist hair that never moved, even in the stiffest breeze. Win was fifteen years younger than Mack, but already he had a reputation for hard-nosed trial tactics that rivaled Mack's folklore. There was no small amount of professional jealousy between the two.

"The issue I need this group's help on," Mack finally announced, "is whether we should file for Rule 11 sanctions against Carson."

"I would," said Win predictably. "This is one of the most outrageous claims I've ever seen. We aren't aggressively serving our clients if we don't go after Carson. It's a no-brainer."

Melvin Phillips nodded his approval, then raised his hand to flag down a waitress. "What's the deal? All the waitresses on strike? I'm dying of thirst here!" Everyone in the room, including the waitresses, ignored him.

"I don't know," said Teddy. "This whole Rule 11 business is bad for lawyers. We file against Carson on this case, some other lawyer will file against our firm on the next one. Pretty soon cases just become personal wars between attorneys. We oughta be able to disagree on a case without getting personal."

Mack knew the old man would be cautious and reluctant to file. In many ways, Teddy still lived in a bygone era inhabited by gentlemen lawyers. He was not in touch with the age of Rambo litigation.

"Teddy, things have changed," Mack said dispassionately. "Carson would slit our throats in a heartbeat if we gave him the chance, and so would half the other lawyers in Tidewater. Litigation is not a gentleman's game anymore; it's war. And in war, you take no prisoners."

"I agree, Teddy," said Win. "If we don't file Rule 11, we're just enabling guys like Carson to file more junk lawsuits."

Melvin finally flagged down a waitress. "Anybody need another?" he asked. He replenished his drink, and the skull session continued. This time Melvin was engaged.

"What are the chances?" asked Melvin.

"What do you mean?" countered Mack.

"Exactly what I said. What are the chances that you'll win on Rule 11? To my thinking, it's purely a tactical call. If you have a fair chance of winning, file the motion. It will send a signal to the judge that you really believe this case is nonsense. It makes it more likely that the judge will throw the case out. It also gives the judge a compromise. He can deny your Rule 11 motion, thus throwing a bone to Carson, but then grant your motion to dismiss and get rid of the case. Judges like to play Solomon and split the baby like that, and you like it because you get what you are really after—a dismissed case." Melvin stopped for a long gulp of beer.

"But if your chances are bad," he continued, "the judge will just hammer you, because judges hate Rule 11 motions. What's more, you'll encourage Carson to make all kinds of other frivolous motions. Like Win just said, you become the enabler of his conduct."

The others thought about Melvin's comments. For a long time nobody spoke.

"I think Carson's claim against Saudi Arabia is totally bogus and Rule 11 has a good shot," said Mack, sensing that the others were waiting on his analysis. "But his claims against Aberijan and the individuals are based on a different set of laws and may have some merit. At the very least, he could avoid Rule 11 on those claims."

Melvin finished another long gulp and set his glass down hard on the table, as if banging a gavel. "That's your answer then. You file Rule 11 but limit it to Carson's frivolous claim against Saudi Arabia."

"Makes sense," conceded Mack, though he was actually hoping for a broader and more aggressive filing.

"Let's not make this a common practice of the firm," said Teddy. "I don't want a reputation as the firm that always files Rule 11."

The other partners nodded their approval. Mack would humor the old man for a few more years. Even Mack was not willing to take on Teddy just yet.

"Let's talk about Sarah Reed for a minute," said Melvin, rolling his huge head around to survey his audience. "Have you looked at the case from her perspective? If her allegations are true, what are her weaknesses and how can they be exploited?"

"Of course I've considered that," said Mack. Of course he had not, but he could not concede as much to this bunch. "We've looked at this from every possible angle."

"Since our last session, I've been putting myself in Sarah Reed's shoes," continued Melvin, as if Mack had never spoken. "There's one thing she fears worse than losing this case." He paused, apparently trying to create a little mystery. He took another long swallow of his beer. This was one of Melvin's annoying habits that Mack particularly despised. Start a sentence, then take a bite or a drink while others sit in suspense. "And that is revealing the names of the church leaders in Saudi Arabia. According to her own allegations, her husband died rather than reveal those names. She would undoubtedly dismiss this suit, rather than expose these people, for fear they would be persecuted. That's her weakness; figure out a way to exploit it."

I waited for that?

"That's a great theory," scoffed Mack, "but impossible to implement. I intend to push for those names in discovery, but Carson will object. The judge will probably not think they are relevant to our defense of the case."

Melvin smiled, squinting his beady eyes. "Figure out a way to make them relevant, Mack. You're the litigator. Make them a central issue in the case. Force her to chose between revealing the names and dropping the case. Now, if you'll excuse me, I've got to take a little trip."

With that, Melvin staggered off toward the rest room, leaving the others shaking their heads.

"Old Melvin, frequently wrong but never in doubt," said Win.

But Mack just sat there, staring after his quirky partner, his mind a thousand miles away. Abruptly, Mack turned to the two remaining members of the group. "Maybe so, but he may be onto something this time. I've got an idea."

For the next half-hour, they discussed and refined the details of Mack's plan. The entire meeting lasted two hours and cost the nation of Saudi Arabia $3,225. It would prove to be worth every penny.

■ ■ ■

Brad pretty much neglected the *Reed* case during the two months that Leslie spent in England. To be sure, the case proceeded, but Brad himself was too busy with other matters to devote his time to the file. His primary concern during the summer months was a tricky product liability case that went to trial during the last week of July. The case settled while the jury was deliberating, but preparing the case decimated Brad's summer.

While Brad deposed engineers and scrutinized product-testing reports on this other case, the trickle of paper from Kilgore & Strobel became a flood. Every day, the mail would be littered with pleadings, motions, or discovery requests from Strobel's minions. Brad didn't pay much attention to the growing mountain of paperwork. He knew nothing major would occur until after the court conducted a hearing on the motion to dismiss in late August. Fortunately, Leslie would be back in the country a few weeks early to help him prepare.

■ ■ ■

All summer long, Leslie and Bella wore out the FedEx planes between Virginia Beach and Exeter. Leslie attended class in the morning, worked on legal pleadings all afternoon, then reviewed her FedEx packages for more presents from Kilgore & Strobel. She was thankful her coursework was light but resentful that she had no time to tour the country. She could not take time off while there was work to be done on the *Reed* file, and there was always work to be done on the *Reed* file.

■ ■ ■

For Bella, it was just another lonely day in the office. Brad was in court, and Nikki and Sarah were huddled in the conference room working on answers to interrogatories. As usual, Bella held down the fort, answering the phone and doing the firm's filing. The clock on her desk barely moved, the morning stretched on forever, and she found herself counting the minutes until lunch.

At a few minutes before twelve, Bella put her phone on forward, rushed down to the firm's small kitchen, closed the door behind her, and lit up her fifth or sixth cigarette of the morning—she had lost count. She turned on the small fan strategically placed in the corner of the countertop and pulled a plastic chair up to the small table. She grabbed her bag lunch out of the refrigerator and picked up her sappy romance novel. The plot was all too predictable, but she had bought it for the picture of the strapping young gladiator on the cover with the long dark hair and the come-hither look. She settled in for another solitary lunch hour. It was, she supposed, the price you paid when you exercised your freedom to smoke.

There were no windows in the kitchen, just white walls stained yellow, a tile floor, a counter area, sink, refrigerator, microwave, and coffeepot. To Bella, it was as cramped as a jail cell. But thanks to some tense negotiations with Brad a few years ago, it was also the one place inside the office where she could still officially smoke. Until Nikki came, she could also sneak a smoke in the women's rest room, or light up when Brad was out of the office, but now even those minor luxuries had disappeared.

Bella indulged herself in a little self-pity. Discrimination against smokers seemed to be not just legal, but downright fashionable. It was not like she could control it. Someone ought to do something about this. Smokers have rights too.

As she worked her way through a salad and another unimaginative chapter of the book, the door burst open, and Nikki darted through. As usual, Nikki held her breath and went straight for the refrigerator to retrieve her lunch. She waved snidely at Bella and gave her a tight-lipped smile. Then she waved the smoke away from her face, neither talking nor breathing the entire time she was in the room.

"Hope you choke," Bella said as the door closed behind Nikki.

A few minutes later, three pages and two long, passionate kisses later, to be exact, the door opened again, but this time more slowly. Sarah Reed stuck her head in the kitchen and walked in with her own bag lunch.

"Hi," she said. "Mind if I join you?"

"Um…no." Bella put the book down and gathered her Tupperware a little closer to her own place, making room for Sarah. "That'd be great."

She watched Sarah spread out a sandwich, some carrot sticks, and an apple. Bella suddenly felt self-conscious about the cigarette smoking away on the ashtray in front of her. She liked Sarah—after all, no one else had dared join her for lunch in this smoking dungeon. But Bella decided not to put out her cigarette yet, as a matter of principle.

"What're you reading?" asked Sarah.

Would a missionary approve of a romance novel? "Just something I found lying around," Bella said. She gave the book a suspicious and unfamiliar look, as if somebody had just switched her book of choice when she wasn't looking. She turned the book over so it was lying with its cover facing down.

"It's probably a nice break after all those legal pleadings," Sarah said. "I don't know how you do it, day after day."

"Yeah, it is." Bella took a short puff on her cigarette and blew the smoke over her shoulder. "The other stuff does get pretty dry."

Sarah nodded. "Can I get your advice on something?"

"Sure."

"How do you keep everything around here straight? I mean, I'm finding as a single mom that I just can't keep up with everything. Seems like I'm always showing up late or missing something or not getting something done. Yet here you are, single yourself, and basically keeping this whole firm running on schedule." Sarah leaned forward and tilted her head a little. "How do you do it?"

It was, thought Bella, a good question. She pushed the novel aside. She was just thinking this morning about how she could see the strain showing on Sarah's face. Maybe this would help.

After a few minutes of time-management coaching, the conversation turned to other matters. Bella finished her salad, but still she kept talking. She seemed to mesmerize Sarah, who kept her eyes glued on Bella, asked the most insightful questions, and seemed enthralled with the answers. Before long, Bella found herself snuffing out her half-finished cigarette and laughing with Sarah, in spite of herself. She couldn't remember when talking to someone about nonlegal matters had seemed so natural.

"Tell me about your family," said Sarah.

Bella hesitated. The first noticeable pause in the conversation. What was there to tell? *I'm not married. Never been married. An only child whose parents are divorced. The only person who ever loved me—my mom—can hardly recognize me. Tell me about your family.*

What family?

"There's not much to tell," Bella said, looking down at her Tupperware. She began packing up. "Dad and mom divorced when I was in college. No sisters or brothers. And Mom, well…" She could feel the tears forming in her eyes, the words catching in her throat. "Mom's not well." She sniffled. "Sorry."

Bella stood to leave and threw her trash away. She felt stupid, tearing up about her mom, but she couldn't help it. She knew it would be better to change the subject and get back to work.

But there was something about Sarah. "She's in a nursing home," Bella heard herself say, "with Parkinson's."

Sarah stood now as well and reached out gently to touch Bella's arm. "Do you see her much?"

Bella nodded.

"Maybe I could go with you sometime," said Sarah softly.

"You'd do that?"

"Sure. And there's something else I'd like to do."

"Okay."

"Would it be all right if I prayed for her?"

"Right now?" Bella couldn't imagine praying right here, right now, in the middle of the smoking room. Was it legal? It seemed so…well, so unclean. So…unnatural.

"Sure. What's her name?"

"Gertrude."

And before Bella knew what was happening, Sarah was praying for her and Gertrude right there in the middle of the smoking room, her hand gently rubbing Bella's arm. Sarah was so sincere about the whole thing, this sweet missionary who had lost her own husband, passionately praying for Bella and her mom, that Bella felt guilty when she realized she had not once directed the conversation Sarah's way.

Bella never closed her eyes, for fear that Nikki would blow through the door. Still, she somehow felt God couldn't help but hear Sarah's prayer on her behalf.

"Thanks," said Bella when Sarah was done. "That's one of the nicest things anybody's ever done for me."

Then she hustled out of the small kitchen area before the tears could start in earnest.

■ ■ ■

Nikki spent most of her summer on the road, touring the continental United States, talking to potential expert witnesses, hunting down doctors who had treated the Reeds at the military hospital in Riyadh, and spending money on clothes. She hit real pay dirt with a young intern stationed at Fort Bragg, an Army doctor named Jeffrey Rydell, who had been one of Charles Reed's treating physicians in Riyadh. Nikki sat in a chair right next to Rydell, rather than across the small conference room table. She was wearing one of her stock-in-trade tight black miniskirts, and she crossed her legs provocatively, hoping the handsome young doctor would notice.

"How's Mrs. Reed doing?" he asked Nikki with genuine concern.

"If you mean physically, she's doin' great. On the other stuff, give her time. She'll be okay."

"She seemed like a fighter. I really hope she can get through this. I'll help any way I can."

"You can start by telling me your opinion of the cause of Dr. Reed's death."

Nikki placed her minicassette recorder on the table. She leaned forward and struck a pose, placing her elbow on her knee and her chin in her hand, letting the doctor know she was interested. She tried hard to ignore the wedding band on his left hand.

"Cause of death was cocaine injection by the Muttawa that in turn led to an acute myocardial infarction. Even before this happened, Dr. Reed had advanced coronary artery disease, and as a result, the flow of blood to his heart was severely restricted. The cocaine, in my opinion, probably stimulated the formation of a blood clot in a man who was already in extreme distress from being tortured. The blood clot might not have been fatal in the arteries of a normal man, but in Dr. Reed's case, it led to total restriction of the flow of blood to the heart, causing massive damage and ultimately death."

"You seem so sure that the cocaine was *injected* into his blood-stream, Doctor."

"I am."

"Based on?"

"Well, first, the word of Sarah Reed that she and her husband never even experimented with the stuff. Second, neither Dr. Reed nor his wife had any of the telltale signs of drug abusers, and I've been involved in the management of hundreds of critical-care patients with abuse problems. Third, the toxicological testing confirms that the concentration of cocaine in Dr. Reed's blood actually showed higher levels at the second hospital he was in, the base hospital, than it did from the first hospital, the King Faisal Specialist Hospital."

There was a pause, and a mesmerized Nikki realized it was her turn to speak. "What's the significance of that, Doctor?"

"Well, it actually means that the cocaine must have been injected fairly close in time to when Dr. Reed was admitted to the King Faisal Hospital, and that the cocaine was still being absorbed into his blood-stream while he was hospitalized. I was also shocked by the levels of cocaine found in the toxicological reports. They are not levels typically associated with snorting cocaine. When cocaine is snorted, it narrows the blood vessels in the nose, which in turn reduces the flow of blood, which results in a slower absorption rate. The types of elevated readings we saw in Dr. Reed's case typically come from either injecting cocaine directly into a vein or from smoking crack."

"Fascinating."

"And finally, and perhaps most important, a very peculiar aspect of the toxicological report that I didn't notice at first makes me certain the drug was injected." Rydell paused for a second. "But if I tell you, then you have to reveal it in discovery or make sure that I mention it in my deposition, is that right?"

The question hung in the air for a while, as Nikki realized she didn't have the foggiest idea what he had just asked. She had been too busy looking deep into his eyes, fishing for a sign of mutual interest.

"Huh? Oh, well, sure you would… What's your question again?"

"If I tell you this hunch I have about the lab report, do you have to tell the other side about my opinion prior to trial?"

"Yeah, we have to tell them about any of the opinions you intend to testify about at trial, and then they will ask you questions about those opinions in a deposition prior to trial."

"And then they will go out and hire sixteen other doctors to come and testify as to why I'm wrong. Isn't that the way it works?"

"Something like that. I can tell you've done this before."

Rydell looked pensive for a moment, perhaps conflicted on whether he should share his hunch with Nikki. "One more question," he said after a pause.

Nikki raised her eyebrows.

"If it really isn't my opinion yet, if it's just a hunch and I don't research this 'hunch' until just before trial, and if I can't really form an opinion until I've had a chance to research the 'hunch' further, then would you have to reveal it?"

"There's no rule that says we have to reveal a hunch," answered Nikki confidently.

"Good. Then let's just say I've got a strong hunch…" Nikki heard a vibration, and then Rydell looked down and checked his beeper. He looked worried. "I'm sorry, Ms. Moreno, but I've got to go. Like I said, I'll help however I can…" He was already up and out of his chair, heading for the door.

"Maybe I could come back for a follow-up interview… There's lots of stuff to cover," Nikki offered.

"I'd be happy to talk further anytime you need me, but don't feel like you've got to come out here. Just give me a call, set up a time we can get together by phone." And with that, Dr. Rydell was out the door, off to save another life.

Nikki looked wistfully at the conference room door. She turned off her recorder and stuffed it in her briefcase. She worried that she was losing her touch. As she stood to leave, she caught sight of her own reflection in the conference room window. She straightened her posture, sucked in her stomach, and smiled.

That boy must be blind, she said to herself.

15

By the first week of July, Nikki was preparing to take her investigation international. It had not been an easy trip to arrange.

For starters, a visa to Saudi Arabia was impossible to obtain without a sponsor from within the country. And obtaining a sponsor was not easy when the purpose for entering the country was to investigate a high-profile case against its government.

Nikki started with the large multinational law firms that advertised a stable of English-speaking lawyers. Her goal was to hire a lawyer who would later help with depositions in the country and on this initial visit could serve as a translator and consultant. No respectable firm, however, was anxious to bite the hand that fed them.

After three days of phone calls and three days of rejections, Nikki gave up her insistence on a respectable law firm with specialists in international law. She would settle for any semiliterate Saudi lawyer who could speak passable English. And she finally found her man in Sa'id el Khamin, a sole practitioner obviously hurting for clients and ready to make a quick buck. She agreed to pay him the exorbitant sum of twelve hundred Saudi riyals per hour, the equivalent of more than three hundred U.S. dollars. Somehow the amount felt like a bribe rather than a legal fee.

With el Khamin's sponsorship, Nikki finally obtained her visa and prepared to prove her worth in Saudi Arabia. With el Khamin at her side, Nikki would interview former neighbors of the Reeds and the members of the Friday-night church group.

Nikki arrived at the King Khalid International Airport in Riyadh late in the evening on July 8. She was bone weary after the brutal flight from Reagan National Airport, during which she sat sandwiched between two large Europeans who both slept soundly while encroaching mightily upon her shrinking space. When she arrived in the Kingdom, customs took forever, the process slowed by a shortage of agents and the fact that she was a single unaccompanied female.

She was finally rescued by her sponsor, a rumpled and bearded Sa'id el Khamin, who convinced the authorities that she was harmless and would behave. They allowed her to pass into his custody.

"Here, I bring gift for you… Wear this abayya please." Sa'id presented Nikki with the ugliest garment she had ever laid eyes on, an enormous all-covering black cloak. To Nikki, who had seen similar garments in news coverage of Afghanistan, it was the very symbol of chauvinistic oppression. She held the thing at arm's length, as if it contained the germs for some incurable disease.

"Change…here." Sa'id suggested, pointing to a ladies' bathroom. "No need to cover…" and he made a sweeping motion over his face. "But, please, Mees Neekie, put on over other garments."

Nikki smiled and graciously headed into the bathroom, wondering why she was doing this. Mumbling to herself, she wrapped the cloak around her until she felt like a mummy, then looked at herself disapprovingly in the mirror. She immediately began to sweat. This would be a long week in the Kingdom.

When she came out of the rest room, her peculiar little host bowed deeply and thanked her enthusiastically. Sa'id himself was dressed in a white floor-length shirt that looked like a dress. He called it a "thobe." As they walked through the airport, he pointed out items to Nikki and named them in Arabic, as if she were going to learn the language in the week or so she would spend in this place. Nikki had only two immediate goals: get to a nice American hotel room and get out of the oppressive abayya as soon as possible.

On the forty-five-kilometer drive from the airport to the Hyatt

Regency in Riyadh, Nikki sat in the backseat and gawked at the sites while Sa'id chauffeured. Nikki was told emphatically that women did not drive in the Kingdom.

Sa'id made some lame attempts at conversation, but Nikki was more interested in admiring the sights in this strange and foreign land. She expected a backward and dirty city. Instead, Riyadh was a high-tech oasis of glass, steel, and concrete rising up from nowhere in the desert. It boasted freeways, high-rise office towers, big hospitals and hotels, and modern-looking houses that stretched beyond the horizon. She was struck by the cleanliness of the city and its modern, glistening architecture. She was equally amazed by the glut of vehicle traffic and the absence of pedestrians. The roads looked like rush hour in L.A., but the sidewalks looked like a ghost town.

Nikki also noticed, much to her relief, that not all foreign women wore the stifling black abayyas. She decided that tomorrow she would not be wearing hers. Sa'id would just have to get over it.

■ ■ ■

By her third day in Riyadh, the city had lost its charm. There was absolutely no nightlife, and alcohol of any type was strictly prohibited. All restaurants and stores closed during prayer time, and most closed for the day at 1 P.M. Nikki's favorite pastime, shopping for clothes, might as well have been illegal. Many of the shops actually prohibited female shoppers, and she wouldn't dare wear any of the styles offered by those that didn't.

To her consternation, the culture rigorously enforced a strict separation between men and women. Families ate together in special sections of the restaurants, some of which refused to serve women at all. Women rode in the backs of busses, and a taxi driver refused to give Nikki a ride one night when she was unaccompanied by Sa'id. According to Sa'id, custom restricted women from looking men in the eye, a custom that Nikki enthusiastically violated by glaring at all sorts of Saudi males. Her behavior invariably resulted in loud arguments between Sa'id and the victims of Nikki's rude behavior, reprimands from Sa'id, and threats to get Nikki a veil.

Contrary to her earlier intentions, Nikki reverted to wearing her hated abayya. It was the only way she and Sa'id could avoid unwanted attention as they traveled together, pretending to be husband and wife. Sa'id seemed to enjoy this fantasy, his body language and mannerisms belying the huge crush he had on Nikki. She did not know if Sa'id was married. She was afraid to ask.

The first three days of the trip had been a total bust. Nikki and Sa'id could not locate several of the former church members, confirming the rumors about a general crackdown on the church the night the Reeds were arrested. Those members they did find steadfastly refused to talk to either Nikki or Sa'id, with many refusing to even answer the door. Nikki was hot, discouraged, and tired of being insulted by men whose language she did not understand.

On the evening of the third day, Sa'id and Nikki found their way to the small apartment of Rasheed and Mobara Berjein and knocked gently on the door. A hesitant woman cracked the door and looked suspiciously at the couple in the hallway. Sa'id began a rapid explanation in Arabic about the purpose for their visit, but the woman did not move, and the crack did not widen. Nikki did, however, detect a slight widening of the eyes when the name Sarah Reed was mentioned, and for the first time since landing at the King Khalid International Airport, Nikki allowed herself a glimmer of hope.

Impatient with Sa'id's slow progress, Nikki butted into Sa'id's polite inquiry and produced a photo of Sarah and her kids. To Nikki's surprise, the woman reached through the crack, took the picture, and studied it carefully. She murmured something to Sa'id in Arabic.

"She asks how she can know we speak the truth," Sa'id translated.

"Tell her Sarah sends her love and a message," said Nikki. Her words were translated by Sa'id.

Nikki could hear the woman speaking to someone behind her, then she peeked back through the crack and asked Sa'id another question.

"She wants to know what the message is."

"This is the message from Sarah Reed: God has not given us the spirit of fear, but of love, and of power, and of a sound mind."

Sa'id translated the message. To Nikki's astonishment, the woman slowly and cautiously opened the door. She smiled timidly, introduced herself as Mobara Berjein and the man standing next to her as Rasheed Berjein, and bid the visitors come into her home.

After Nikki and Sa'id took their seats in the living room, Rasheed and Mobara offered them some Turkish coffee. Nikki had already learned from Sa'id that it was extremely impolite to refuse such an offer. Etiquette, Sa'id had said, must be carefully followed. Patience would receive its reward in due time; impatience would arouse suspicion. Nikki wondered how much of this was true, and how much was motivated by the fact that Sa'id's patience was being rewarded to the tune of three hundred bucks an hour.

Mobara served the coffee in a tiny, handleless cup that held only a half-dozen sips. Following Sa'id's lead, Nikki asked for her coffee to be served *mazboot,* which apparently had something to do with the amount of sugar. Nikki had to muster every ounce of her self-control not to make a face as she drank the thick, gooey liquid in her cup and listened to the others chat in Arabic. She dutifully drank every ounce, right down to the pile of grounds left sitting in the bottom.

After ten minutes of pleasantries, the Berjeins were apparently ready to talk church. They began asking some questions about Sarah, and as Sa'id started translating, Nikki's paranoia took over. She thought it strange that no other members of the church would even talk to her and Sa'id. She worried about the ever-present eyes and ears of the infamous Muttawa. Her instincts told her the place might be bugged. She therefore suggested, through Sa'id, that Rasheed and Mobara join them in the car and talk about these sensitive matters where they could not be overheard.

They parked on an out-of-the-way side street in the city, then turned the radio up to an annoying level. The four of them huddled together in the middle of the car, Rasheed and Sa'id leaning back from the front seat while Nikki and Mobara leaned up from the back. After two hours of intense questioning, Nikki got what she was after. The Berjeins agreed to testify on behalf of Sarah Reed, no matter the consequences. To confirm their testimony, Nikki hand-printed an affidavit for Sa'id to translate and the Berjeins to sign. As Nikki drafted the affidavit, Mobara quickly wrote a letter to Sarah, telling her about the phenomenal growth of the surviving church, the conversion of Rasheed's brother, and Rasheed's valiant attempts to fill Dr. Reed's shoes. She folded it carefully and handed it to Nikki.

As they returned to the apartment, Nikki notarized the affidavit bearing the Berjeins' signatures and placed it in her briefcase. She laid out a plan that would secure the Berjeins' testimony in an American court of law while minimizing the risks to them personally.

Before getting out of the car, Mobara extracted yet another promise from Nikki to make sure that Sarah got the letter. The women parted with hugs and Nikki's promise to tell Sarah of Mobara's continuing love.

■ ■ ■

Rasheed held Mobara's hand as they walked back into their apartment, head held high. He was grateful for this opportunity to redeem himself and stand tall with Sarah Reed for the cause of their Savior. He locked the door behind him and immediately embraced his wife. No words were necessary, and no words could stop the trembling of Mobara in his arms.

They had done the right thing, but they would undoubtedly face consequences. After holding Mobara for the longest time and quietly stroking her hair as they embraced together just inside the door, he began to softly pray. It was only then that he felt Mobara finally stop shaking. And as soon as she did, almost as if events had been carefully choreographed and synchronized, a loud knock sounded at the door.

Rasheed turned calmly to the peephole, looking through as the impatient visitor knocked again, even louder than before. Four men stood outside his door, but Rasheed's attention went immediately to one. He had seen the face on television, seen the hatred in the eyes. And now, only inches away, the eyes were even more intense, causing Rasheed to shudder involuntarily.

"It's the Muttawa," he whispered over his shoulder as he reached to unlock the door. "And Ahmed Aberijan is with them."

L eslie had anticipated this day for two months.

Time crawled during the flight across the Atlantic. Leslie could think of nothing but Brad. There were so many things she would tell him when she saw him at the airport. Two months of thinking had cleared her head and calmed her mind. She was nervous but ready to pick up where they left off. She had dreamed for weeks of spending time with Brad, an afternoon at the beach followed by dinner and a long stroll on the boardwalk. She was determined not to compare Brad to Bill, since she was not at all sure who would win if she did.

There would be no handshakes this time. They would start with a hug. She was almost running as she approached the end of the concourse where he promised he would meet her. Two months of waiting. It would be worth it.

"Welcome back, Rhodes scholar," said Bella.

"Thanks, Bella. Where's Brad?"

"Great to see you, too," said Bella.

"I'm sorry, Bella. I just wondered if something was wrong."

"I'm parked in a metered spot out front, so why don't you grab your baggage and meet me at the curb. We've got trouble in the *Reed* case. I'll explain on the way to the office."

Leslie had not planned to go to the office, but she didn't complain. It sounded serious.

■ ■ ■

Leslie found Brad, Sarah, and Nikki waiting for her in the main conference room. The conference room table and floor were cluttered with law books, notebooks, legal pads, briefs, miscellaneous papers, and half-filled coffee cups. The phones were ringing unmercifully, but Brad and the others seemed oblivious.

After warm greetings for Leslie, and a hug fest that included everyone but Bella, Leslie pulled out a document she couldn't wait to share with the team and placed it on the table. It was labeled "Preliminary Game Plan for *Reed v. Saudi Arabia*" and contained Leslie's best thinking for the case—witnesses to call, experts to use, evidence that would hurt and evidence that would help. It demonstrated her trademark attention to detail. The others did not know that it was in the works—she wanted to surprise them with it and use it as the framework for preparing the case.

Brad didn't notice Leslie's document, and tossed another on top of it. It was an affidavit in support of Rule 11 sanctions, signed by Mack Strobel. It had been filed earlier that day. Leslie picked it up and began reading.

On May 11, I had a telephone conference with plaintiff's attorney, Mr. Bradley Carson, for the purpose of explaining our firm's intent to file a Rule 11 Motion against Mr. Carson based on the frivolous nature of this case. I called Mr. Carson, as a courtesy, in order to give him an opportunity to explain whether he had any cases or authorities that would support the unprecedented claims that he makes in this case.

In response to my question of whether he was aware of any cases or other authority that would support the filing of this case, Mr. Carson indicated that he was aware of no such authority. He also acknowledged our firm's greater expertise in international law and questioned whether we were aware of any authority that would justify the filing of this case. In this regard, his precise words, to the best of my recollection, were: "You're the expert in international law, you tell me whether you think there is any law or case authority to justify our filing." I responded by telling Mr.

Carson there was no legal basis for this case. I waited several weeks, fully expecting Mr. Carson to either drop his suit or provide me with legal authority that would justify the filing of this case. I have not heard back from Mr. Carson and accordingly file this Motion for Rule 11 Sanctions based on the enormous waste of judicial time and resources occasioned by the filing of this suit.

My client, the nation of Saudi Arabia, has incurred legal fees and expenses to date to defend this suit in excess of one hundred forty-five thousand dollars ($145,000) and, accordingly, requests sanctions in that amount against Mr. Carson.

Leslie's face turned one shade darker than her auburn hair. She cursed Strobel, then noticed the disappointed look on Sarah's face.

"Sorry, Sarah. I just don't understand how any officer of the court can just flat-out lie like this in an affidavit. It's outrageous."

"Welcome to the real world," said Nikki.

"This one's my fault," said Brad. "I thought he was fishing for information about our case, so I didn't give him any. From now on, if anyone talks to Strobel or another member of the defense team on the phone, follow it up with a letter confirming the substance of the conversation. We can't afford to have them misrepresenting us to the court."

"It's ridiculous that you can't trust the other lawyer any more than that," said Leslie.

Brad flipped his glasses on the table and picked up another document. He stood up to pace as he explained its legal import.

"This is another motion filed today by Kilgore & Strobel. It's a motion to compel answers to interrogatories. They have noticed it for a hearing on the same day as the motion to dismiss. Before I get into the details of this motion, let me make one thing clear," he paused and looked around. "This motion to compel is nobody's fault, and it won't do any good to beat ourselves up over this. There will be no finger-pointing on this team."

He then turned to Sarah. "As leader of this team, and the lawyer who you personally retained, I take full responsibility for any issues raised by this pleading."

Leslie's stomach began to churn. What was Brad talking about? Interrogatories were part of the typical discovery process in any lawsuit. One side would send a group of questions, or "interrogatories," to the other side asking about witnesses or exhibits or any other relevant facts or circumstances. The interrogatories would then be answered under oath, or objections would be lodged and a judge would determine whether the interrogatories had to be answered.

Leslie and Nikki had answered the defendant's interrogatories nearly a month ago. Leslie provided the legal objections, and Nikki provided the factual information. The objections and answers were full and fair. Leslie couldn't imagine what the defendants were complaining about now, but her instincts told her she had missed something. Something big. She tucked her cold and clammy hands under her legs.

"The motion to compel requests that the court overrule all of our objections as untimely, then require us to answer every interrogatory. Some of these interrogatories request information that is clearly protected by the attorney-client privilege. They are claiming that we missed the deadlines for filing objections—"

What?!

"That's ridiculous," Leslie interjected. She'd heard enough. "We filed all of our answers and objections within the thirty days allowed by the rules." She grabbed a code book and thumbed through it.

"I hand-delivered the objections myself," added Nikki.

"Here it is," Leslie announced. "Rule 33(b)(3): 'The party upon whom the interrogatories are served shall serve a copy of the answers, and objections, if any, within 30 days.'" She closed the book and placed it back on the table.

"If you two are done, let me finish." Brad was still pacing. "Under federal procedure, each district court can pass some of its own local rules to supplement the federal rules. Leslie, they don't teach you this in law school, and you had no reason to know it, but the Norfolk courts, in their infinite wisdom, have passed a local rule requiring that all objections to interrogatories be filed within fifteen days, not thirty." He paused for just a second, but to Leslie, it stretched out endlessly. The awful consequences of this blunder immediately numbed her brain and set her stomach on fire. She could barely hear Brad's next words for the ringing in her ears. "That's why I'm saying this motion is my fault. I should have warned you to read the local rules."

Leslie felt the blood drain from her face.

"Won't the court cut us some slack?" asked Nikki. "This must happen all the time."

"It does happen all the time. But the court has a history of not being very forgiving on these matters."

Leslie forced herself to move and to think. Fighting off rising panic, she pawed through the local rules in the book that Brad had dropped on the table. She read the rule three times and still couldn't believe it.

"There are lots of problematic interrogatories," continued Brad. "But none as bad as number 3. It requests the name of 'every alleged church member who ever worshiped with Charles and Sarah Reed during their tenure in Saudi Arabia.' Of course, we objected to this interrogatory, but now our objection may not hold up because it wasn't timely filed."

"What does that mean?" asked Sarah. It was the first time she had shown any interest in the legal issues.

"It means if we lose on the motion to compel, we must provide the names of every church member who ever worshiped with you and your husband and pray that they are not persecuted by the Muttawa, or..." Brad's voice trailed off.

"Or what?" insisted Leslie.

"Or drop the case in order to protect these innocent church members," concluded Brad.

"We can't give them the names," Sarah said firmly. "Dozens met with us on nights other than Fridays that the Muttawa do not know about. Charles died rather than divulge those names. I would do the same."

Sarah's uncharacteristic bluntness generated a long silence. A sickened Leslie was unable to speak.

"Then we'll have to win the motion to compel," said Brad at length, "and talk the court into granting some mercy on this one."

The scene unfolding before Leslie's eyes was surreal, a lawyer's worst nightmare. The case would be lost, not on the merits, but on a technicality. Just like that. Justice perverted.

"So it all comes down to one judge and whether that judge will allow us to file objections late?" Leslie exhaled sharply. "No matter what the law says, it all just comes down to the discretion of one judge, thumbs-up or thumbs-down, and the case is over just like that?" Her voice was full of disdain, her pristine view of the law crumbling by the second.

"That pretty much nails it," said Brad.

Silence took over, the weight of this precarious position sinking in. Tears of frustration and guilt welled up in Leslie's eyes.

"This is all my fault," she said, her voice wavering. "I was the one responsible for filing the objections. I sweat out every detail of this case. I dot every *I* and cross every *T,* and somehow I missed this. I spent the last four months of my life working like a dog on this case and the last two weeks working around the clock on a detailed game plan for the case, and now it's all just wasted work because of some idiotic local rule that nobody knows about.

"The law isn't about this stuff," she said, and with her left hand she made a clean sweep of the table in front of her, knocking law books and documents, including her beloved game plan, onto the floor. "It's about clever lawyers like Strobel taking advantage of fools like me."

Then, in front of her speechless colleagues, Leslie stood up and bolted from the room, leaving the others staring in disbelief.

■ ■ ■

Brad had a strong urge to run after Leslie, talk to her, somehow calm her down, and make everything right. But something else told him to stay put. Leslie would have to learn to respond like a professional. Running to her would not help.

Sarah stood and looked at Brad. "Let me talk to her."

"Good luck."

As soon as the door shut behind Sarah, Nikki started in.

"Leslie's got to get a grip. But I don't see why we've got to drop this case if we get a bad ruling. I mean, let's just ask the judge to allow us to produce the names to Strobel under a court order that says he can't share them with his client. That way, we can buy some time and settle this baby."

"Right," scoffed Bella. "Let's put our trust in Mack Strobel, boy scout that he is. Even if he doesn't tell the Muttawa, he'll want to take depositions, and how do you hide the names then?"

Brad sat back in his chair and turned toward Nikki, interested in this budding debate. Maybe it would help him sort things out. Right now, Bella had a point. Advantage, Bella.

"All right then, we just run a bluff," responded Nikki. "You give them phony names, which still buys you enough time to settle, then you get something out of this deal. You don't just cave."

Shaky, thought Brad. Bella will smash this one.

"Brilliant. The only difference between that and highway robbery is that we wouldn't be using a gun." Bella snorted. "Let me get this straight. We run a scam on the court, lie under oath, and try to obtain money under false pretenses in the meantime."

Match point.

"Well, what's your bright idea?" Nikki shot back, her voice rising in frustration. "Just let the creep go? Let him laugh at us all over Saudi Arabia?"

"Drop the case!" scowled Bella. "Cut your losses! Don't be stupid!"

Nikki didn't respond this time, she just glared straight ahead at Bella. She looked ready to pounce.

In an act of studied defiance, Bella whipped out a pack of cigarettes, shaking one loose, and lit it up in the middle of the no-smoking conference room.

"Nice," said Nikki, chasing the smoke away with a wave of the hand. "Black-lung cases, Brad, what do they go for these days—for an overweight single secretary with limited earning capacity?"

Bella stood.

"Sit down," Brad said sharply. He turned to Nikki. "That's not necessary." Then back to Bella. "C'mon, put it out." She sighed, dropped her cigarette into a half-full coffee cup, and plopped into her seat. Brad felt like he was lecturing a couple of kids. "Nikki, we don't handle cases that way here. If the client says drop it, we drop it."

Nikki snorted out a derisive little laugh. "Oh yeah. I forgot. Let's see... *Lewis* case, two weeks ago. Client wanted 150K, insurance company offers 100, you said 'take it.' *Pardee* case, last week. Defense attorney says 75K, client says 90, you take 85. *Migliori* case—"

"They're different," Brad argued. "Every one of those cases is about a greedy client, unrealistic demands. You agreed with every one of the settlements. It's our job to make the client see reality. Sarah...well, she's different."

"So it's our job to just sell her out, drop the case—"

"You don't get it, do you?" interrupted Bella. "Nobody's selling out. If we take this case all the way, it could bankrupt us. It's a dog, Nikki. And if we go bankrupt chasing this dog, then all of your well-intentioned crusading won't do anybody any good."

"Nobody's selling out," repeated Nikki, mocking Bella's tone. "Then what do you call it?"

"I guess if anybody would recognize selling out, you would," responded Bella. "It's how you got here in the first place—"

"Enough!" barked Brad. He wondered if the two women would ever get along.

"If we have to give up the names," he said softly. "We drop the case. I'm sorry, Nikki. But that's the way it's got to be."

Nikki began to calm down. "Shouldn't we at least get Leslie back in here and let her vote?"

"No votes," replied Brad.

"Oh, I see. And no respect either, huh?"

"C'mon, Nikki. You know that's not the way it is here."

Nikki pursed her lips and stared straight ahead, apparently not convinced. Bella, her victory secure, got up and headed for the door, a thin trail of smoke still slithering in her wake.

"Satisfied?" asked Nikki.

"Get over it," said Bella, and slammed the door behind her.

■ ■ ■

Leslie felt a gentle hand on her shoulder as she stood on the sidewalk in front of the office building and looked out over the parking lot.

"This isn't really about the case, is it?" Sarah asked.

"It is about the case," said Leslie, desperation in her voice. "It's about not letting Aberijan and the others get away with murder. It's about making your husband's death mean something."

The two women stood quietly for a moment.

"Listen, Leslie, I don't harbor any hatred toward these men. I miss Charles so much, but I know that if I don't forgive, it only eats me up and causes more pain. I trust God to take care of justice. That's His job, not mine."

Leslie could not fathom this forgiveness that Sarah so easily embraced. She loathed Ahmed for what he did to Sarah. She loathed Mack Strobel for being his hired gun. And right now was not a good time for the platitudes of a missionary.

You're sweet, Sarah, but you're not me. I'm not put together that way. I never will be.

Leslie turned and faced Sarah, but did not look her in the eye. "I don't know how you can forgive these men—God either for that matter. I've been in a feud with God ever since He took away Bill."

"Maybe that's the difference," said Sarah softly. "I don't blame God for taking Charles away. I just thank Him for giving me Charles all those years."

The words struck Leslie like another blow. Though they could not have been more kindly delivered, they brought to the surface a lingering bitterness Leslie had worked hard to deny.

The words stayed with her throughout the day and continued to echo long into the evening. She turned them over and over in her mind, and vainly searched her own heart for the type of peace that Sarah expressed. Instead, she found humiliation. Embarrassment. Defeat. And when she finally arrived back at her tiny garage apartment and crawled into bed, it was the missed deadline, and not the insightful words of a missionary, that caused Leslie to lie awake the entire night, staring at the same spot on the ceiling.

■ ■ ■

It came two days before the motion to dismiss hearing. It arrived in a plain 8½-by-11 manila envelope bearing a Norfolk, Virginia, postmark. Ahmed read the contents of the package for the third time, still incredulous at his good fortune.

The envelope contained two documents. The first document was one page long, and the second was nearly twenty pages. The long document was titled "Preliminary Game Plan for *Reed v. Saudi Arabia.*" It contained lists of potential witnesses, experts, exhibits, and relevant documents. It appeared to be some sort of analysis of the case by the plaintiff's lawyers.

The other document was a note composed of letters and numbers cut from magazines and pasted on a plain white sheet of computer paper. Ahmed would ask Barnes to analyze both documents for fingerprints and other trace evidence, although he really didn't expect to find anything. The note was simple and direct: "This first installment will cost you $50,000 U.S.D. More will follow if you obey my instructions and do not investigate. Make payment before the conclusion of the motion to dismiss hearing."

The second paragraph contained wiring instructions for a Cayman Islands bank account that undoubtedly belonged to a shell corporation whose officers and shareholders would be untraceable. The note was, of course, unsigned.

Ahmed called Barnes and speculated about the note for the better part of an hour. It could come from any number of sources, they agreed. The most likely scenario, offered Ahmed, would be an employee of Carson & Associates. A truly disgruntled insider who was fed up and saw this case as a surefire way to make big money fast.

But Ahmed also recognized that there were many other less desirable possibilities. In fact, the meager amount of money demanded concerned Ahmed. Perhaps the source was not a member of the plaintiff's team. Such a person would have placed a higher value on the case. It could be a roommate or friend. It could be their clumsy Saudi lawyer, el Khamin. It could even be a friend of Sarah Reed. For that matter, it could be the janitor in Carson's building or just a good old-fashioned thief. The possibilities were endless, but the promise in the note of future installments certainly had Ahmed's attention. He had to know the source so he could verify the credibility of this information.

"Frederick, why do you think I pay you all this money? I must know who sent this, and I must know soon. Is that understood?"

"You will know, Ahmed. Just give me some time."

T he alarm seemed louder than normal, partly because it was set an hour earlier and partly because Brad had never achieved deep sleep during the night. 5:30 A.M. He forced himself out of bed and stumbled downstairs to start the coffee. He would add two miles to his morning run today, an extra fifteen minutes, because he needed the additional time to clear his mind and prepare for the day's events.

His first mile was always a grind, and starting an hour early didn't help. The endorphins kicked in at mile two, freeing his mind for deep thinking. He hit his stride by 5:45 and started to sweat in the early morning heat and humidity of Tidewater.

By the end of mile three he was in the zone. He determined that the best way to combat a Rule 11 motion was to act the part of a reasonable and careful lawyer. He would save the dramatics for trial. Today he would argue the law in scholarly tones and be the very picture of an attorney who would never consider filing a lawsuit unsupported by the current state of the law. He would leave the name-calling and insult-hurling to Strobel. Brad promised himself he would behave.

He would have Leslie handle the motion to compel. She would fall on her sword, admit her mistake, and plead for mercy. She would undoubtedly generate sympathy. A judge would be more likely to feel sorry for a law student than a seasoned litigator.

On his fourth mile, he thought about how he would handle the motion to dismiss and adjust his style based on the judge assigned to the hearing. That was the one great wild card remaining to be dealt. Norfolk Federal Court was famous for concealing the judge's identity until the morning of the hearing. To keep the litigants guessing, the court would even change judges on a case from one hearing to the next, up until the morning of trial. The trial judge would remain a mystery until the morning of jury selection.

Brad dreaded the possibility that he might draw Ichabod. If she showed up today wearing the black robe, he might as well get out his checkbook to pay the sanctions and kiss the case good-bye. No adjustment to his style could overcome the ire of Ichabod.

If he could pick his judge, he would ask for Judge Samuel Johnson, the only African American on the Norfolk bench, and the only judge whose career did not include a stint with a big firm defending cases for corporate clients. More than any other member of the bench, Brad suspected Judge Johnson would be open to his argument that outrageous violations of human rights, like those at issue here, must have a remedy in international law. Johnson would understand the basic parallels to civil rights laws in this country and would not be intimidated by being the first judge to do what was right.

Brad used the last three miles of his run to rehearse his arguments. By the time he finished at 6:15, he was relaxed and ready for the day's maelstrom.

■ ■ ■

By 9 A.M., Norfolk Federal Court was a media madhouse. Though court rules prohibited cameras in the courtroom, the First Amendment kept the judges from extending their ban to the steps and sidewalks in front of the large brick building. Accordingly, the local media hordes transformed that area into a gauntlet of cameras and microphones poised to engulf the lawyers and their clients as they entered the sanctuary of the court.

Strobel and his entourage showed up first. They arrived simultaneously in several luxury cars, transporting no fewer than eight lawyers and paralegals. All were dressed in expensive dark-blue or gray suits. While the rest of the team busied itself by unloading boxes of documents and notebooks, Strobel held forth for the reporters.

"What are your chances of having this case thrown out today?"

"We think they are excellent, or we would not have filed the motion."

"Do you expect to get sanctions against Mr. Carson?"

"Will you be calling any witnesses today?"

"Will you appeal if you lose?"

"One question at a time please. No testimony is heard when the court rules on a motion to dismiss. We do not believe we will lose this hearing, but if we do, we cannot appeal a motion to dismiss ruling until the entire case is over. As for the sanctions against Mr. Carson, that will be for the court to decide."

"Are you pleased with the selection of Judge Johnson to hear this motion?"

Strobel hesitated. His eyes flashed, then his game face returned.

"I'm sure Judge Johnson will do a fine job. The judge assigned makes no difference to us. All of the jurists in this court are fair and impartial. Now, if you'll excuse me, we need to get ready."

■ ■ ■

Brad caught himself smiling as Judge Johnson took the bench, fashionably late to his own hearing. Brad wiped the grin from his face as the spectators stood and fell into hushed silence.

"You may be seated," said the judge in a rich, slow southern baritone. "Counselors, I've reserved two hours for your arguments, no more. The court has read every word of your briefs, so do not waste the court's time by simply repeating arguments you've already made. Is that understood?"

"Yes, Your Honor," Brad said simultaneously with Mack Strobel.

"Mr. Strobel, we are here on your motions, you may proceed."

Strobel strode confidently to the podium to address the court. He took a massive notebook with him and left another just out of reach at his counsel table.

"If it pleases the court, we are here today on a number of defense motions." His confident voice bellowed throughout the courtroom.

"I will address three motions: the motion to dismiss plaintiff's case because this court lacks jurisdiction, the corresponding Rule 11 motion we have made requesting sanctions against plaintiff's counsel for the filing of a frivolous lawsuit, and our motion to compel answers to the interrogatories that we filed based on the fact that counsel for plaintiff did not file any timely objections."

"Let's deal with the motion to compel first," suggested Johnson. "It seems like that issue is pretty straightforward, and we ought to be able to resolve it quickly before we get into the more complicated motion to dismiss."

A thin smile creased Strobel's face, and for the next several minutes he set forth his reasons for wanting every interrogatory answered, but particularly the one requesting names of every church member who ever worshiped with the Reeds. The names were relevant, he argued, so that he could take the depositions of these former church members and find out if the Reeds were really missionaries or just clever drug lords. Besides, he asserted, the plaintiff waived any objection when her attorneys missed the deadline for filing objections.

"Is that true, you missed the deadline?" Judge Johnson asked Brad.

So much for reading the briefs, thought Brad. *We only spent about ten pages on this issue.*

Though Johnson was looking at Brad, Leslie stood. "I'm afraid it is, Your Honor." She looked appropriately nervous, eyes darting around, voice slightly quivering. Brad was proud of her.

"And it's entirely my fault. I'm a rising third-year law student helping Mr. Carson on this case, and I missed the deadline for filing objections. I didn't know about the local fifteen-day rule, although I also recognize it is entirely my responsibility to be familiar with that rule. I bring the court no excuses, just a simple request that the court not hold my client responsible for my failure by making us produce the names. We are prepared to answer every other interrogatory, but if we have to produce these names, we sincerely believe that it is just a matter of time before they are tortured too."

Johnson thought about this for a second, indecision etched in the wrinkles on his forehead. Leslie gingerly sat down, never taking her eyes off the judge. He stared at the back wall, saying nothing.

Finally, he spoke.

"I read in the briefs that your client will drop the case rather than produce any names. Is that true?"

Whoa! He has read the briefs. The earlier question was just a setup, a credibility check to see if we would fudge the issue. We passed.

Leslie was on her feet again. "That's correct," she said tentatively.

"And if I give you a simple order to produce to Mr. Strobel all the names of alleged church members who worshiped with Sarah Reed, you would rather drop the case than obey my order?"

Leslie shifted her weight from foot to foot, the pain of this answer registering in her eyes.

"I wouldn't phrase it that way, Judge. But, with all due respect, my client has decided not to produce the names under any circumstances."

Johnson shifted his stare to Sarah.

"Is that true?" he inquired.

Sarah stood. "Absolutely, Your Honor."

"That's what I thought," said Johnson. "And it's the only thing that makes my decision easier." He flashed a quick grin at Sarah. "You may sit back down, Mrs. Reed."

"Thanks," she said, embarrassed.

"This case reminds me of the biblical story of Solomon and the two women fighting over the baby. Solomon said he would split the baby and give half to each woman claiming to be the mother. He knew the real mother would never allow that to happen. And so he awarded the baby to the woman who begged the king not to kill the child."

Brad felt a small smile creep across his lips.

"In the same manner, I am impressed by the sincerity of Mrs. Reed. She is prepared to drop this case rather than reveal the names of alleged church members. She must sincerely believe they would be persecuted for their faith. I realize that her lawyers missed a deadline, but this court is not willing to make Mrs. Reed pay so dear a price for the mistake of her lawyers.

"Accordingly," he concluded, "we will take a page out of Solomon's book and see if we can split this baby. Mrs. Reed must answer each and every interrogatory except she will not be required to reveal the names of the alleged church members unknown to the defendants. In exchange, Mrs. Reed will not be permitted to mention or testify at trial about any alleged church members other than the Friday night group that the defendants already know about. I know it's not a perfect remedy, and whatever judge tries this case may decide to do something different, but it's the best I can do for now. After all, I'm no Solomon."

A collective sigh of relief registered at the plaintiff's counsel table. They had dodged at least one bullet today. This judge was Solomon incarnate, as far as Brad was concerned. Brad leaned over and whispered to Leslie.

"Nice job," he said. "You looked pathetic."

"Thanks," she whispered back. "It's my specialty."

Strobel appeared unfazed. He had undoubtedly seen his share of surprises through the years, and you could never tell from his demeanor if he had been dealt a serious blow. He remained stoic, thanked the judge for the ruling, and launched into his argument on the motion to dismiss with undiminished vigor.

"The courts of the United States have honored the immunity of other nations from lawsuits for more than 180 years," he asserted. "From the time Chief Justice John Marshall decided the case of *Schooner Exchange v. M'Faddon,* in 1812, through this very day, courts have honored the bedrock principle of international law that each country has exclusive and absolute territorial jurisdiction over actions that occur within its territory. Therefore, countries grant each other immunity over lawsuits—"

"Skip the history lesson," cut in Johnson. "Let's bring it up to at least 1976, shall we? Would you agree that in 1976 Congress passed the Foreign Sovereign Immunities Act and that is the statute we need to interpret today?"

"Yes, Your Honor. And that statute makes it clear that the defendants are entitled to immunity from this lawsuit." Strobel looked the part of the big-firm defense lawyer. He stood erect, and his full and deep voice originated from deep down in his diaphragm, reverberating throughout the courtroom.

"Plaintiff claims there should be an exception to this statute for torture arising out of religious persecution," he continued. "She says that torture violates a fundamental norm of international law, also known as a *jus cogens* law, and therefore nations cannot claim the immunity of international law when they act in ways that violate the very essence of international law. But this claim has been considered and rejected by other courts. For example, the Ninth Circuit Court of Appeals, in the case of *Siderman v. Argentina,* rejected the claim of a Jewish citizen from Argentina who had been arrested and tortured because of his faith—"

"Speaking of the *Siderman* case," said Judge Johnson, waving the lawbook in his hand, "let me ask if you agree with some quotes from that case that I find very persuasive. Do you agree, sir, with the following quote: 'The right to be free from official torture is fundamental and universal, a right deserving of the highest status under international law, a norm of *jus cogens.* The crack of the whip, the clamp of the thumb screw, the crush of the iron maiden, and, in these more efficient modern times, the shock of the electric cattle prod are forms of torture that the international order will not tolerate. To subject a person to such horrors is to commit one of the most egregious violations of the personal security and dignity of a human being.' Do you agree with that, Mr. Strobel?"

Johnson glared down at Strobel, still holding the *Siderman* case in one hand as if it were an original copy of the Ten Commandments. For the first time all day, Brad slid back in his chair, crossed his legs, and relaxed.

"I agree that torture violates the personal security and dignity of human beings but—"

"Then don't you also agree, Mr. Strobel, that when a nation violates this fundamental rule of international behavior, the cloak of sovereign immunity that is provided by international law falls away, leaving the nation vulnerable to suit?"

"No, Your Honor," said Strobel with great confidence. Even when he spoke to a judge, he had a certain air of authority. "You quoted some select language from the *Siderman* case, but the ultimate decision in that case rejected the very argument you just raised—the court ultimately said that the act of torture did not strip away the right to sovereign immunity."

"Let me put it to you this way, Mr. Strobel: Suppose I agree with the language of the *Siderman* case but not the ultimate reasoning. I don't have to follow that court's reasoning. Are you aware of any U.S. Supreme Court case that says a foreign nation that tortures U.S. citizens cannot be sued in U.S. courts?"

"No, Your Honor, the Supreme Court has not squarely addressed this issue." Strobel's confidence took on a tone of frustration. "Based on other decisions regarding similar subjects, however—"

"If neither the Supreme Court nor the appeals court for this circuit have squarely addressed this issue, then it seems to me I've got to do what I believe is right. And it just doesn't seem right that foreign countries can torture American citizens and then scream sovereign immunity when they get sued in American courts. If all courts in the past had read the law as narrowly as you do, Mr. Strobel, we would still be in the Dark Ages when it comes to civil rights in this country. Justice and common sense require something more. Now that's just my initial inclination in this case. I'm willing to give you every opportunity to talk me out of it."

For the next hour, Strobel tried heroically to do just that. But Johnson's "initial inclination" proved to be a stubborn one indeed. The more Strobel talked, the bigger the hole he dug. And after exhausting every argument and citing nearly every case in his handy black notebook, Strobel reluctantly sat down, needing a miracle.

Brad practically floated to the podium. But before he could speak, Johnson put his upcoming argument into the proper perspective.

"Now, Mr. Carson, there's one thing I'd like you to keep in mind as you begin your argument." Brad listened intently to the soothing baritone drawl. He wanted to address every concern and allay every lingering doubt that Judge Johnson might express. "I've read all the briefs, and I've now heard Mr. Strobel's eloquent arguments. Despite those arguments, I'm leaning toward allowing the case to go forward. Of course, if I did that, I would also dismiss the Rule 11 motion, since you can hardly be fined for filing a frivolous case if I decide the case has enough merit to proceed. Now having said all that, Mr. Carson, I am certainly willing to give you all the time you need to help me rethink this matter and change my mind."

Brad glanced quickly down at his yellow legal pad and all the arguments he had worked so hard to refine. He thought about the press corps behind him waiting to be impressed with passionate oratory about the virtues of religious freedom and the vices of religious bigotry. He thought about his own reputation, about how few chances a lawyer had to mesmerize this type of gathering. But then he also thought about Sarah and the torture and her children being raised without a father.

Silence was, after all, a virtue.

"In that case, Your Honor, I believe I can be very quick. We would simply like to rest on the arguments previously submitted in our briefs."

"A wise choice," said Johnson, and Brad returned to his seat.

"The court will take a ten-minute recess," said Johnson, "and then I will announce my decision."

■　■　■

Thirty minutes later, Brad was in the process of reassuring Leslie when Johnson reentered the courtroom. The chattering immediately stopped. "Remain seated," Johnson said to the crowd.

"Don't worry," Brad whispered. He could tell his words just bounced off Leslie's furrowed brow.

"Then why did he take so long?"

"What did I say?"

"Do I look worried?"

Brad scrunched his face and nodded. "Yep."

"I will be filing a lengthy written opinion in the weeks ahead," Johnson said, "but I thought it only fair to the parties that I state for the record my intentions with regard to the ruling so they can plan accordingly."

The judge surveyed the crowd, put on his reading glasses, and commenced with the opinion he had written just minutes earlier in his office.

"The United States, Saudi Arabia, and most other civilized countries are members of the United Nations and therefore signatories of the United Nations Universal Declaration of Human Rights," he began. "Article 18 of that document states that 'Everyone has the right to freedom of thought, conscience and religion; this right includes freedom to change his religion or belief, and freedom, either alone or in community with others and in public or private, to manifest his religion or belief in teaching, practice, worship and observance.'" He stopped reading for just a moment and glanced up at Sarah. He looked back down and continued.

"Moreover, both Saudi Arabia and the United States have signed the International Covenant on Civil and Political Rights. That document repeats this commitment to religious freedom and also states that 'Each state party to the present Covenant undertakes to ensure that any person whose rights or freedoms as recognized herein are violated shall have an effective remedy.' Furthermore, as the court noted earlier, it is a fundamental norm of international law that citizens of all countries should be free from torture at the hands of governmental officials.

"In order to give substance to the international rights contained in treaties and charters signed by our own government, this court must open its doors for serious and substantial human rights claims against foreign governments. It makes a mockery of these treaties, and of the human rights that undergird them, to suggest that nations can violate these rights at will and then hide behind the doctrine of sovereign immunity. Accordingly, I am denying defendant's motion to dismiss and dismissing defendant's Rule 11 motion."

A murmur drifted up from the spectators. Hushed and excited whispering could be heard. Strobel stared ahead, his face betraying no emotion.

"I am also mindful that justice delayed is justice denied. This case has already been pending for more than three months. Plaintiff is entitled to her day in court. Accordingly, I am setting a trial date for the third Monday in October, less than three months from today's date."

After reading this last sentence, Judge Johnson banged his gavel, rose from the bench, and walked regally out the back door of the courtroom. Brad thought that the crusty old judge looked remarkably like an angel.

■ ■ ■

Later that night, after an impromptu celebration dinner died down, Brad walked Leslie to her car. He gently put his arm around her shoulder. She snuggled against him, and they walked slowly, completely in sync.

The adrenaline that had coursed so freely through her body earlier in the day was now completely gone. She was so totally relaxed, she felt like a limp dishrag. She wanted nothing more at this moment than the very thing now happening. The case was moving forward. And Brad Carson, the man she had thought about nonstop for two months in England, was walking with his arm around her and holding her close, like they would never be apart again.

"Leslie, I'm sorry about that night in Williamsburg…"

"You don't need to apologize."

"I do," he urged softly. "I'm sorry that I tried to push our relationship too far, too fast. I didn't know about Bill. I've been doing a lot of thinking since that time, and I've come to realize that you were right. It's not good to start a relationship in the middle of a pressure cooker like this case. Especially when you're still trying to recover from Bill's death. Let's wait till this case is over. That'll give us both more time to sort things out. If there's anything real between us, it'll survive. If there's not, then it wasn't meant to be."

They stopped walking, and Brad took her gingerly by both hands, the same way he had in Williamsburg. "Anyway," he said, "that's what I've been thinking."

It wasn't at all what Leslie had been thinking. And looking deep into Brad's penetrating gaze, those intense steel-blue eyes, was not helping to clear things up. At this moment, she was more confused than ever.

Should she tell him how she felt? *Forget that night in Colonial Williamsburg, Brad Carson. Forget my hesitation and second-guessing, my "I need more time" protestations. I'm ready now. I've thought this through. Banished my demons of doubt. And I've decided that I need you more than you'll ever know. Not when the case is over, but now. Right now. Tonight.*

But when she opened her mouth, none of those words came out, none of those feelings found expression. "Thanks, Brad," was all she could bring herself to say.

He kissed her gently on the cheek, then turned and walked away. He didn't even notice the mist gathering in her eyes.

Part III

DISCOVERY

It's one thing to allege torture at the hands of a foreign government; it's another thing to prove it. This harsh reality dawned on Brad and his legal team the morning after the hearing, as the euphoria of surviving the motion to dismiss gave way to the reality of the task before them.

To get this next phase started on the right foot, Brad called an all-hands meeting for 8:30 A.M. Nikki arrived at 9:15, and Bella pried herself free from the phone and a cigarette a few minutes later. Leslie had already been in the conference room for two hours, refining her preliminary game plan and developing a list of potential witnesses for trial.

Brad was pacing, thinking out loud, and twirling his glasses.

"These cases are won or lost with expert witnesses. Experts can give opinions about anything. If we get the right ones on the stand, experts that the jurors like and understand, we can blow this case wide open. We've got to have guys who don't condescend to the jury—juries hate that, you know—and guys who will stand up to Strobel on cross-examination without being obnoxious.

"Our deadline for naming experts is a week from Friday. How're we coming, Nikki?"

Nikki's head jolted up. "Yep, I agree."

Bella rolled her eyes. After twelve years working together, Brad knew what she was thinking: *We're paying Nikki how much for this?*

"You agree with what?" asked Brad. "I'm asking you, how're we coming on our experts?"

"Okay, I guess," said Nikki. She looked a little sheepish. "You said you knew an economist who could testify about the economic impact of Dr. Reed's death—lost wages, loss of services, that type of thing. So I haven't done anything yet on the economist."

"There's a surprise," muttered Bella.

Brad ignored her, as did Nikki. Leslie ignored everybody as she continued to write.

"Bella, get Nikki the contact information for Dr. Calvin Drake," said Brad. "Have him sit down with Nikki and Leslie and draft an opinion before the deadline. The total economic loss needs to be about two million. Who else have we got?"

Nikki casually checked some notes. "We've got the toxicologist, Dr. Nancy Shelhorse. She'll testify about the blood tests and urine tests given at the two hospitals and the toxicological tests that were part of the autopsy. It's her opinion that Sarah and Charles Reed were injected with cocaine by the police at the time of the arrest."

Nikki glanced up from her notes, this time looking extraordinarily pleased with herself. She smiled at Bella.

"Sounds pretty strong," said Brad. "What else do you have?"

"Our star will be Alfred Lloyd Worthington, a Washington lobbyist who works with multinational corporations and serves as an adjunct professor of international law at George Mason University. Worthington is a former congressman who got caught up in the demographic shift from Democrat to Republican in northern Virginia. During his time in Congress he served on the House Foreign Relations Committee. He's got a great résumé, and he sees this case as his ticket back into the spotlight. He's qualified to give opinions on international treaties and the miserable track record of the Saudis when it comes to religious liberty. He'll prove that the Saudi government knew all about the activities of the religious police and sanctioned this type of conduct."

Brad tried not to look as surprised as he felt. Nikki had been busy. "Sounds great. Leslie, can you spend some time prepping Worthington as well?"

Leslie nodded and made some more notes.

"How much are all these wonderful wise men and women costing us?" asked Bella. "I don't want to be the killjoy, but isn't three experts a bit much?"

"Not when the defendants have twelve," said Leslie.

"Three experts should be plenty," said Brad. "Having more than one expert on the same subject only gets confusing."

"Confusing and expensive," said Bella. "How much are these guys charging us?"

"The usual," said Nikki. "A couple hundred an hour each."

"A few million here, a few million there. Pretty soon you're talking some real money," Bella griped.

"Isn't it time for you to go get another cigarette?" asked Nikki.

Brad shot a warning look toward both Nikki and Bella.

"Brad, I just don't see how we can possibly get everything done," Leslie piped in, studying her notes. "Kilgore & Strobel sent deposition notices this morning for Sarah, her kids, all her doctors and counselors, and a number of former church members living in Saudi Arabia. Strobel's boys have been calling all morning demanding to know who our experts are so they can schedule their depositions. We will want to depose, at a minimum, all of their experts and Aberijan. The way I see it, we've got at least thirty days of depositions waiting for us, and you're the only one who can do them."

"Can't you take some of the depositions under third-year practice rules?"

"Not unless you or some other lawyer is sitting there with me, which defeats the purpose."

"Brad, you can't even start these depositions for thirty days," said Bella, ever anxious to be the bearer of bad news. "You're booked solid on other cases through the end of August."

"Look," said Brad, "we're into this case, and we've got to figure out a way to get it done. Y'all have been great at identifying problems, now how about a little help with some proposed solutions?"

The entire team silently mulled that one over. After a few seconds of avoiding eye contact with Brad, Leslie swallowed hard and spoke. "I'll take a semester off from school and work full-time on this case. An opportunity like this only comes along once."

Brad caught himself staring at her and thought about how great it would be to have her around more. Still, he forced himself to give an appropriately sensitive response. "I wouldn't ask you to do that," he heard himself say.

"You didn't ask, but I'm going to do it anyway. You wanted solutions, that's my contribution."

Careful, Big Guy. Don't give her too many opportunities to rethink this, to wiggle away. Having Leslie around full-time would be great for you and equally great for the case.

"Then let's at least get you an apartment here in Tidewater for the next several months," Brad offered.

Bella's face registered her disapproval. Brad was glad to be pacing, or he would have been kicked.

"No thanks," said Leslie, taking the tension out of the room. "I can do a lot of my work at the law library and stay in Williamsburg."

"I'll clear the decks of my other cases," offered Brad, inspired by this turn of events. "I can pass some off to my buddies and get continuances on others. It'll take me thirty days, but I'll clear the decks and focus entirely on this one."

He caught Nikki's frown out of the corner of his eye. "Every case except Johnson, of course."

"And I'll continue to perform my stellar legal work in the same manner as I have, even though I'm grossly underpaid," said Nikki. Nobody laughed, but Brad sensed Nikki said it less to draw a laugh than to aggravate Bella.

"All of this is wonderful," said Bella gruffly, "warm and fuzzy and all that. But it still doesn't solve the problem of covering the depositions. We need another licensed lawyer, a warm body to sit with Leslie."

Nikki sat straight up, her eyes suddenly sparkling. "Why didn't you say so?" she asked. "I know the perfect warm body, and he won't cost us a dime." She had Brad's attention. "We go to the Rock and ask him to sit in on a few depositions with Leslie. In exchange, we offer to make him co-counsel on the Johnson case, which Brad stole from him anyway, and we give him a small split on our fee. We also make him co-counsel on the *Reed* case and offer him no part of the fee. He's the one plaintiff's lawyer in Tidewater who will join us in the case and not charge us a dime just because it's megafree publicity. The Rock *lives* for free publicity."

Brad hated the idea. But no one offered a better plan.

By noon they had retained the Rock.

■ ■ ■

Mack Strobel was at his best when bullying younger members of his firm. On the morning after the motion to dismiss hearing, Mack was in rare form.

The unsuccessful hearing was, of course, the fault of the brief writers. Their prose failed to persuade Judge Johnson, and even the brilliant oral arguments of Mack himself could not salvage the situation. He ripped into the inept associates and sent them back to the library to work on a new set of briefs for other important pretrial hearings. One young female associate actually left the room in tears. Mack made a mental note to veto her from future high-profile cases.

The honeymoon was over, Mack announced. They had made the mistake of underestimating this case once. It would not happen again. No more country-club environment and twelve-hour workdays. It was time to buckle down.

Mack also called another meeting of his brain trust. There had to be a way—there must be—to ensure he did not get stuck with Johnson as a trial judge.

■ ■ ■

As Rasheed had requested, Hanif came a full hour early for the Friday night worship service. After affectionate greetings, Rasheed silently nodded his head toward the door, and Hanif followed him outside. The brothers walked several feet down the sidewalk before Rasheed started talking.

"The Muttawa know about us," Rasheed said. He waited a few seconds to allow the awful news to sink in.

Hanif did not break stride. "I am not surprised." He kept his eyes glued to the sidewalk.

"Our apartment is bugged."

No response.

"A few weeks ago, they came to visit."

The quiet padding of Hanif's shoes against the pavement stopped. "Why didn't you say something?"

"I wanted to so badly, but I needed time to sort it out, decide what to do." Rasheed's voice was cracking with emotion. He stared straight ahead and continued talking. "They made Mobara and me promise to disband the church. They made us promise to give videotaped testimony against Sarah Reed. They made us promise…" His bottom lip trembled, and his voice trailed off. Instead of continuing, he handed Hanif an envelope.

The letter inside was addressed to church members.

The letter said that the Berjeins' home had been bugged, and that the members should not say anything out loud but simply read the letter. The letter explained that, for the sake of the recording devices, Rasheed would declare the church disbanded. The members should act appropriately dismayed, but ultimately agree not to meet.

The letter also gave the location for the next week's meeting and told the members to never mention this location out loud. Each subsequent week, wrote Rasheed, he would provide a new letter specifying the meeting place for the following week. He instructed the members never to say a word about the chosen location and to destroy the letters after noting the next place of worship. They should not call or otherwise contact the Berjeins.

The second page of the letter had been the hardest for Rasheed to write. He watched as Hanif read it, disbelief slowly forming on his face.

"For reasons I cannot explain, I will only be able to meet with you for a few more weeks," Rasheed had written. "And it is obvious that I can no longer be the pastor of this fellowship. If you will allow me, I would like to pass that mantle of leadership to my brother, Hanif, whom the Holy Spirit will empower to lead this church through this most difficult hour. Please give him all the love and respect you gave me. Though I will only be with you a few more times, you will forever be in my prayers."

Hanif looked up from the letter and into the tear-filled eyes of Rasheed. "I can't…I just can't…" Hanif stammered. "I don't know how…"

"You must," Rasheed responded emphatically, grabbing his younger brother by both shoulders. "I will teach you. Quietly. Secretly. We will study God's Word together. The Muttawa promised to leave the others in the church alone, including you, if Mobara and I give testimony in the case against Sarah Reed. That testimony will take place in a couple of weeks. Nobody else in the church must ever know about this." Rasheed again fell silent, struggling against his rising emotions, taking a few fitful breaths.

"You can't do that," protested Hanif. "It doesn't matter what they promise."

"Leave that to me, Hanif. And trust me completely. I will do what I have to do. God has given me a plan." Rasheed squeezed his brother's shoulders. "Your job is to build this church. Nobody else can do that but you."

Hanif exhaled deeply, the weight of the responsibility already showing on his face. "Okay," he said, looking his brother squarely in the eye. "I will try."

Then the two men embraced, their strength flowing into each other. Rasheed had never been more proud of his little brother.

■　■　■

Worthington would be magnificent. Even during his prep session, Leslie could tell he would make a great witness. He had credentials, neatly groomed gray hair, and an extensive vocabulary befitting an international law guru. Leslie asked him the toughest questions she could fathom, and he handled them with ease.

"The Saudis have always given lip service to religious tolerance, but in point of fact their Islamic regime is one of the world's most oppressive governments," he explained. "They systematically violate the United Nations Universal Declaration of Human Rights. Their very own laws require that all Saudis be good Muslims, and the infamous Muttawa brutally enforce strict compliance with these laws. The crown prince of Saudi Arabia is fully apprised of the activities of the Muttawa, and the crown prince himself sanctions their use of the police power to keep the people in line."

"What is the basis for that opinion?" Leslie asked.

Worthington responded with a series of past examples, recalling precise dates, names, and places with an almost photographic memory. After three hours of probing for a chink in his armor, Leslie was satisfied none existed. He seemed too good to be true.

Unfortunately, he was.

Just before their time ended, Worthington hinted at the one skeleton in his closet.

"As I understand it, Leslie, the defense lawyers will be able to ask me only about past felonies and misdemeanors involving moral turpitude, but no others. And they can't ask about charges, only convictions. Is that right?"

"Sure," Leslie replied, her mental red flags suddenly flapping wildly. "Misdemeanors that go to the credibility of a witness, like lying, cheating, or stealing, are fair game. Other misdemeanors are not. Crimes charged are not relevant unless the charge results in a conviction. Why?"

Worthington's eyes darted around the room, as if there might be hidden cameras present. He lowered his voice. "Is our conversation covered by the attorney-client privilege?"

"Sure," said Leslie. *I think,* she said to herself. Technically, Worthington was an expert, not a client. But he had piqued her interest. She would tell him what he needed to hear in order to bare his soul.

"About two years ago, I was arrested and charged with disturbing the peace," he said in a whisper, staring down at folded hands. "My lawyer cut a deal, and we pled no contest. The judge took the case under advisement for six months, with the understanding that if I stayed clean, the charge would be dismissed. I didn't even jaywalk. At the end of that time, the judge entered a not-guilty finding. It's all in the court records."

"They shouldn't be able to ask about that incident," said Leslie, suddenly more curious than ever. "It's a misdemeanor, and you technically weren't convicted. We should have no trouble keeping it out. What was it for anyway?" She tried to sound casual, though her voice was noticeably higher.

"Is that really relevant?" His voice turned the question into a statement. He folded his arms.

"Just curious."

"If I told you, I'd have to kill you," said Worthington, forcing a chuckle.

Leslie smiled politely, determined to find out.

■ ■ ■

Nikki seemed to know every police officer in Tidewater. Those officers had friends in Alexandria, and friends of those friends included an officer who was part of the misdemeanor investigation of Alfred Lloyd Worthington.

"The guy is a wife beater," reported Nikki. "The Mrs. finally had enough and called the cops. But when the case went to court, she no longer wanted to press charges. They're back together now, the perfect suburban couple."

■ ■ ■

Never answer the phone after 5 P.M. This simple rule had spared Bella from a multitude of crises designed to destroy relaxing evenings. Answer the phone after 5 P.M., and you can kiss the evening good-bye.

Tonight, however, the logistical challenges of the *Reed* case and the financial challenges of the entire office had so completely distracted her that she did not notice the time until she held the receiver in her hand. 5:06.

"Carson & Associates, how can I help you?" Bella asked, not sounding the least bit helpful.

"By dropping the *Reed* case," said the muffled voice on the other end. "You tell your boss he's in over his head. If he doesn't, he'll wish he had never met Sarah Reed. And we'll come after you first." The caller paused. "You got that?"

The phone shook in Bella's hand. She had received plenty of prank calls in her time. This one was different.

"Are you threatening me?" she asked as bravely as she could.

"Drop the case and you'll have nothing to worry about. You've got one week."

What scared Bella most was the monotone delivery, the lack of emotion.

Bella was so flustered she couldn't think of a thing to say. Not that it mattered. The phone went dead.

She returned the receiver to its cradle with shaking hands. She stared straight ahead, alone in the office, suddenly feeling vulnerable. She would mention the call to Brad first thing in the morning—one more reason to drop this risky case—but she knew what his reaction would be. They had been threatened on other cases. "We can't let those nuts scare us off," Brad would say. But this one was different. She couldn't explain why. But she could *feel* it.

This guy meant business. And Bella would have to be prepared.

For the first time in weeks, she left work before six. Instead of heading to her small apartment in Chesapeake or to the nursing home to visit her mother, she took off in the direction of the strip malls on Military Highway. Shortly before seven, she walked sheepishly into the Military Highway Sports Shop. She headed directly to the sales counter, looked around at the few browsing customers to make sure she was unnoticed, then talked in hushed tones to the clerk.

"I need to buy a gun. Something small that I can carry in my purse."

In response, the clerk ushered Bella into a quagmire of hidden weapons permits and Second Amendment rights. He was more than happy to help her navigate these waters and collect both a consulting fee and a large commission on the fine piece he would eventually sell her.

Six days, one affidavit, two court hearings, one concealed weapons permit, and two store visits later, Bella was the proud owner of a Berretta 9-millimeter repeat-action handgun, and a new oversized purse that would be its home. She paid the clerk to take her to the shooting range and show her how to use her new equalizer. She was no expert markswoman, but she learned how to load, unload, and most important, unlock the safety.

If the coward on the phone ever came by the office to make good on his threat, he would first have to get by an armed and dangerous receptionist. For the rest of the *Reed* case, and maybe beyond, Bella Harper would be packing heat.

■ ■ ■

It came in the same type of 8½-by-11 manila envelope as before. It was again addressed to Ahmed Aberijan. Like the prior package, the only hint of origin was the Norfolk, Virginia, postmark.

But this time the envelope contained only one page. The sender had again meticulously cut out letters and numbers from magazines and pasted them on the page to form a message.

Plaintiff's expert Worthington has a crippling Achilles heel.
Check Alexandria General District Court records and talk to
Officer Beecher of the Alexandria police force. $100,000 keeps
more coming.

Wiring instructions to a different bank in the Caymans followed. Ahmed read the letter four times, thanked Allah, then got on the phone to Frederick Barnes.

"What have you learned about the first letter I received containing the preliminary game plan for Mr. Carson?"

"The *first* letter?"

"Answer my question."

"We have been unable to trace it so far. There were no prints or residue on the papers inside the envelope. The true owner of the bank account where we deposited the money is shrouded by a maze of off-shore corporations that are not required to do public filings. We hit a dead end."

"Frederick, I must know who is sending these letters. I just received another about Carson's expert witness. We will pay for the information, but I must know who I am paying."

"We will need a little time—"

"We don't have time!" screamed Ahmed.

"It's got to be an inside job," said Barnes calmly. "Nobody else could know the information or appreciate the significance of it. We can at least narrow it down to the members of Carson's team. I'll have them all followed."

"And you should tell Strobel of this information, but do not tell him of the source."

"Understood," said Barnes.

19

"If litigation is war, then depositions are hand-to-hand combat," Mack told one of his young associates as they drove to the offices of Carson & Associates for the second day of Worthington's deposition. "There is no judge and few rules, so the name of the game is intimidation and persistence. Get the witness talking long enough, and he's bound to make some mistakes. He'll either contradict something he's already said or forget some minor detail. Your job is to turn that minor detail into a federal offense."

The associate listened intently. He had watched the great man in action yesterday. He had now been given a rare invitation to ride with Strobel from their office in Norfolk to Carson's office in Virginia Beach. Strobel, the motion to dismiss now a part of the distant past, was in one of his mentoring moods.

"Take one of two approaches, depending on the witness. If it's a neutral witness, try to charm him. Get him relaxed and talking and keep him relaxed and talking. Find out everything you can about his testimony, and get some quotes you can use to trip him up at trial. That's easier to do if he's relaxed. If the witness is hostile, browbeat him into submission. Establish who's boss. Ask your questions with a sarcastic tone, stare him down, laugh at the lawyer if she makes objections. Drag out the deposition until you wear him down. Tired witnesses make mistakes."

"Will you finish with Worthington today, or are you going to stretch this out all week?" the young associate asked.

Mack just drove on in silence. A man of his stature did not have to acknowledge the question of a lowly associate. He would finish today. But he had a few fireworks planned first.

■ ■ ■

The chore of defending the Worthington deposition fell to Leslie and the Rock. She had prepared the expert carefully and was in the best position to guard against his weaknesses.

On this second day of Worthington's deposition, the Rock showed up an hour late, and by then Strobel was in a foul mood. Strobel started hammering on Worthington right from the start, and Leslie couldn't provide Worthington much cover from Strobel's bullying tactics. The Rock might as well have stayed home.

By midafternoon, the stale air in the conference room was thick with tension. The unflappable Worthington held his own in the face of Strobel's relentlessness, which only seemed to frustrate Strobel and make him more obnoxious and cantankerous than ever.

"Mr. Worthington, have you discussed this case with Ms. Connors or the other lawyers for the plaintiff?"

"I object," said Leslie, "those conversations are attorney work product."

"Don't mind her," Strobel said to Worthington, as if Leslie were an annoying child. "She doesn't know the rules for a deposition yet; she's just learning. Now answer the question please."

"Don't answer that question," said Leslie, seething at the arrogance of Strobel. "He's just being argumentative."

"That's a first," mocked Strobel. "Instructing your witness not to answer the question on the grounds that it is argumentative. Read the rules someday before you finish law school." Strobel's associate smirked at Leslie.

"Mr. Worthington, as I said, don't bother answering that question."

"Grow up," said Strobel. It came from deep in his throat—a guttural threat. Then he looked at the Rock and smiled. "Mr. Davenport, you've taken a few depositions in your day. Tell your little protégé that she can't just instruct the witness not to answer if she thinks the question is argumentative. Otherwise, we'll call the judge, and I'll ask for sanctions. This is ridiculous."

The Rock was sweating profusely. He had a nervous twitch in his left eye that was acting up noticeably. "Go ahead and answer the question," he said to Worthington.

Leslie stared at the Rock and frowned. The Rock pretended not to notice.

"I don't remember the question," said Worthington.

"That's because your counsel insists on littering the record with frivolous objections," said Strobel. "And I want the record to reflect that in my more than thirty years of trial practice, I have never heard more unfounded objections interposed in bad faith than I have today."

The court reporter, who worked frequently for Strobel, smiled as if she could type that line from memory. Leslie suspected Mack used it in every case.

"And I want to say for the record," Leslie responded, "that I have never seen a lawyer be more obnoxious and rude than I have today." Her hands were shaking, partly from nerves and partly from anger.

"Okay," said Strobel, turning his attention back to Worthington, "tell me everything you and your lawyers talked about."

For the next ten minutes, Worthington recounted in detail numerous conversations he had with Leslie, giving a full account of all discussions they had regarding why the Saudi Arabian government should be found liable in this case. When Worthington was finished, Strobel just smiled and asked, "Aren't you leaving something out?"

"Like what?" asked Worthington defensively.

"Like whether you've ever been convicted of a felony or misdemeanor involving moral turpitude."

Leslie knew this was coming. She had prepared Worthington for this type of question. All he had to do was follow the script.

"No, I have not been."

"Have you ever been accused of a felony or misdemeanor involving moral turpitude and pled guilty to a lesser offense?"

"Objection. That is not relevant or admissible and not likely to lead to admissible evidence," Leslie scooted to the edge of her seat.

"Are you instructing him not to answer the question, counsel?" Strobel asked with mock incredulity. "Does he have something to hide?"

"Of course not, but we both know the question is improper."

"Let me tell you what I know, Ms. Connors. And let's go off the record." Strobel turned to the court reporter he had hired for the deposition. She quit typing.

"I know that your wonderful expert witness is actually a wife beater with a real anger problem. I know that he likes to lecture juries about abuse of innocent victims overseas and then go home and inflict a little abuse himself on the missis. After this deposition, I'll add to my witness list the names of two police officers who will testify that Mrs. Worthington looked like a punching bag the night she finally summoned the courage to press charges. I know that our little choirboy here pled no contest to the charges and that a judge eventually let him off.

"I also happen to know that your Mr. Worthington has plans to run for political office again or at least get a plum political appointment. And finally, I know that if he takes the stand in this case, I will ask about these allegations, even if technically your objection will be sustained. The jury will hate this man, and his career will be over. Now, if you don't withdraw him as a witness, I'm willing to go back on the record today and ask these questions right now. If you are willing to withdraw him as a witness, we can let this deposition record be silent on the matter. And may I remind you that this deposition record must be made available to the press."

Leslie looked at the Rock, who stared at Worthington as if the man had some type of communicable disease. She looked at Worthington— the blood had drained from his face.

"I'll need a minute to confer with Mr. Worthington," she said.

"Request denied," responded Strobel, as if he were the judge. "This is an easy issue. Either you tell me today, right now, that you are withdrawing him as an expert, or I'll start interrogating him on the record about the fact that he beats his wife, and I'll release the transcript to the press."

"That's blackmail!" Leslie shot back, her voice rising. "And I will not be part of it. I'll move to seal the transcript and file an affidavit with the court explaining that you are trying to use inadmissible evidence to blackmail an expert witness. I'll also file a complaint with the state bar. You'll be lucky if they don't pull your ticket."

Leslie stood up and prepared to march out of the conference room with Worthington in tow. She would show Strobel she could not be intimidated. "C'mon," she said to Worthington as confidently as possible. "This deposition is over."

But Worthington remained seated. "No, it's not," he said, without looking at Leslie. "I'm withdrawing myself as an expert."

"What?!" Now Leslie turned on her own witness. "You can't do that. We've retained you."

"You're a free man," said Strobel. "They can only force fact witnesses to testify. They can't force you to testify as an expert if you have no firsthand knowledge of the facts."

Worthington looked sheepishly at Leslie then across the table at the expressionless Strobel.

"I've got to do what's right for me and my family," Worthington said. "Sorry, Leslie."

"Let's go back on the record," said Strobel.

"I don't want any part of this," said Leslie. "You two deserve each other." She threw her papers and legal pad into her briefcase and stalked out of the room. She slammed the door as she walked out, leaving behind her stunned co-counsel and her former star witness.

■ ■ ■

"He did what?!" screamed Nikki into the phone. "Why didn't you threaten to reveal his secret to the press if he didn't testify for us? That would at least give him a little incentive to do the right thing."

"Really, Nikki," said Leslie, "what kind of expert will he make if I have to object every time Strobel asks him if he ever beat his wife?"

"The guy is scum. What now?"

"Pray for a lenient judge who will not require that we provide direct testimony on how the government of Saudi Arabia sanctions the techniques of the Muttawa. We have plenty of circumstantial evidence against the government even without Worthington. It's just that he's the one guy who could have pulled it all together."

When Nikki hung up, she immediately dialed a friend at the local paper. Worthington would pay for his cowardice with a headline tucked away in the next day's local section. It would read: "Attorneys fire expert witness over abuse allegations." The story, citing unnamed sources, would detail the charges against Worthington and praise the law firm of Carson & Associates for boldly dismissing their own expert witness in light of his checkered past.

■　■　■

Rasheed knew his brother Hanif had a gift for teaching God's Word. He harbored no jealousy. The church would soon be led by Hanif, just as Rasheed had hoped. He sat back in the meetings and marveled at God's hand of anointing on his younger brother.

The crowd became so large on Friday night that Hanif told Rasheed he had decided to add another weekly service. With each new convert, though, the circle of danger broadened. Rasheed could not know whether each new member represented the blessing of another sinner saved by grace or the curse of a government informant. He always assumed the former.

Rasheed savored each night with the church, knowing his time was short. His deposition would take place in two weeks. He knew what he had to do, but he also knew it wouldn't be easy. No man should be put in a position of choosing between his God and his family.

■　■　■

Friday night, after a string of sixteen-hour days, Brad and Leslie hit the town with a vengeance. They gorged themselves at an Italian place, enjoying each other's company and temporarily forgetting the case that had brought them together.

They tried to burn off a few calories with a long stroll down the Boardwalk, taking time to admire the paintings of local artists and the trinkets of local artisans. Brad, ever observant, slyly took note of Leslie's admiration for a painting of the Cape Hatteras lighthouse. A little farther down the Boardwalk, as Leslie stood watching another artist dab at his canvas, Brad doubled back to pay for the painting under the guise of going to the men's room. He ran with the painting to a hotel across the street and left it, along with a substantial tip, with the concierge. He returned in a few minutes to Leslie, still mesmerized by the amateur painter and entirely unfazed by Brad's insistence that the nearest bathroom was half a mile away.

They completed their evening with a late movie. Brad wanted a thriller, but Leslie talked him into a chick flick. Brad slept through the last hour and was newly energized when the movie finally let out at 11:45. Leslie, however, fell sound asleep in the car within five minutes of leaving the theater.

Brad silently vetoed the original plan of taking Leslie back to her car at the office, and instead drove directly to his home in Virginia Beach. He pulled into the circular drive in front of his large house and turned off the motor. He reached over and gently touched Leslie on the shoulder. She started and jerked straight up in her seat.

"What the...where are we?" she demanded, as her eyes popped open.

"Calm down, girl. You're in good company. You were sleeping so soundly I decided to bring you to my place to crash."

Leslie relaxed and rubbed both eyes. "I'm sorry, Brad. I was just having these nightmares—"

"Hey. After a week like this week, you're entitled to a few nightmares."

Leslie's eyelids looked heavy. She shook her head to clear her senses and fought back a yawn. To Brad, this woman who couldn't get the sleep out of her eyes, whose hair was darting out in different directions from static electricity, had never looked more beautiful. "I'm fine, really. Just get me a little caffeine, and I'll hit the road." She gave him a sleepy smile.

"Yeah, right. Let's go." Brad got out of the car and went around to open Leslie's door. She got out and stretched.

"No, really, Brad, I'm fine."

"Look, I've got a guest room suite upstairs that never gets any use. I'd feel better if you wouldn't try to head up to Williamsburg without getting some sleep."

Brad was already on his way to the front door. Leslie protested as she followed.

"I'll just crash on the couch for a few hours."

"Leslie—"

She held up her palm, her eyes half closed. "It's the couch or nothing."

Brad shook his head. "All right, at least let me get some blankets, sheets, and a pillow."

After fixing a place for Leslie while she crashed in one of the chairs, Brad leaned down, gently brushed her thick auburn hair out of her beautiful face, and kissed her ever so softly. He was dizzy with emotion.

"I had a great time tonight," he whispered. His face was just inches from hers. He couldn't take his eyes from hers. He didn't dare blink.

"Thanks," she said and flashed a soft smile under heavy eyelids that lit up the room. "Me, too."

"I put one of my T-shirts on the couch, if you want something comfortable to sleep in. There are towels and washcloths in the bathroom. And a spare toothbrush."

"A toothbrush?" Leslie smiled. "I won't even ask."

He kissed her again on the forehead, brushed his hand softly against her cheek, then turned and headed for the stairs.

"We make a pretty good team," he said as he walked away.

He meant it in a lot of different ways.

■ ■ ■

Brad set the alarm for 6 A.M. and resisted the strong urge to go back downstairs before then. He slept fitfully, but he slept smiling. He woke up on his own a few minutes before the alarm and rose quickly to fix breakfast.

The couch was empty. Though the T-shirt was gone, Leslie left the sheets and blankets neatly folded on top of the pillow along with a note of thanks. Brad shook his head in disbelief. She must have called a cab. He would never understand that woman.

Later that morning, Brad drove a half-hour from his house to the beach to pick up the painting and then another hour to Williamsburg to deliver it. He left the artwork carefully leaning against the outside door of the garage that housed Leslie's apartment.

■ ■ ■

One of Barnes' men, increasingly bored with his uneventful surveillance of Brad, decided to have a little fun. As Brad drove away down the long dirt road that led from Leslie's home, the man slipped out of his car and placed the painting in the trunk. His wife would love it. One of the perks of an otherwise unrewarding job.

M ack Strobel personally counted no fewer than eighteen empties scattered around Teddy Kilgore's private yacht by the time he joined the brain trust. Teddy had docked across the street from the office, in a reserved slip at the Waterside Marina, to pick up Mack so the brain trust could plot Carson's defeat. The heat and stickiness of the mid-September day clung to Mack like a leech. He'd been working on the case all day while his cohorts hit the links and floated the waterways, drinking, eating crab, and billing their time to the *Reed* file. And what had they accomplished?

"Where's Phillips?" he asked without bothering to greet anyone.

"Gone below." Mackenzie gestured below deck with a low chortle.

Strobel leaned over the stairway and bellowed. "Mel! Let's get on with it."

Mackenzie slapped a hand on Strobel's shoulder. "No, I mean he's *gone* below," Mackenzie tipped his hand like a bottle to his lips, indicating that Phillips had downed more than his share of brew and would not be participating in this evening's meeting. Mack cussed. Mackenzie laughed, nearly giddy.

After delivering a scathing piece of his mind, a tirade that had no discernible impact on his partners, Mack kicked back in a lounge chair himself and opened his first brew. If he couldn't beat them, he would join them, and at least salvage what remained of this miserable autumn day.

Elbow deep in crab legs and failing miserably in his attempt to pry some meat out of the pesky bones, Teddy Kilgore played his usual role of conciliator.

"Mack, my man. The way I see it, you're just working too hard.

That's why we've got associates. Let them take all those depositions. Conserve your strength, that's what I say."

Kilgore took a break from his losing battle with the crabs, proud of his advice, and gloated in the manner of those who drink too much and say something simple that they find to be incredibly profound.

"Thanks," said Strobel sarcastically. He was tired of carrying this firm on his back.

Teddy smiled. "Don't mention it." He took another swallow of his Michelob and dove back into the crabs.

"The way I see it," said Mackenzie, "you've really only got one problem—Judge Johnson. You just pulled the wrong judge for that hearing. Otherwise you'd be home free."

"I never would have thought of that," said Strobel, even more sarcastically than before. "Unfortunately, the court doesn't consult with me when it assigns the cases."

"What judge do you want?" asked Win, tossing Mack another beer. "Here, Teddy, let me help you with that. I can't believe you've lived in Tidewater all these years and still don't know how to shell these things."

Teddy smiled as he let Win pick the good meat out of the crabs and put it on a plate for him. "I let the hired help take care of that," he said.

Strobel had witnessed this scene before. Teddy was probably the most skilled crab-picker of the bunch, but he was also the laziest. Teddy had learned a long time ago that the best way to get good crab meat without the hassle of picking the shell was to look helpless and wait for a volunteer. There was always a volunteer.

"Baker-Kline would be a home run for us," said Strobel. His mood was sweetened some as he saw Teddy sandbag Mackenzie. "She's usually pro-defense, and she hates Carson. Threw his sorry bones in jail for contempt last year."

"I know," replied Win. "That case was all over the tube."

As they talked, Melvin Phillips staggered up the steps, walked over to the cooler, and took out another beer. He belched loudly, then turned and looked at Mack.

"What do you think?" asked Mack sarcastically. "About the *Reed* case—the one you're billing your time to today."

"Mmm," said Phillips, as he carefully headed back toward the stairs, leaning on objects as he navigated his way. "Settle." Then he belched again and headed below.

"Any more beer in that cooler?" asked Teddy. He needed something to wash down the crab legs. "Who are the possibilities?"

"For what?"

"For the judge. What else are we talking about?"

"There are five slots for judges not on senior status," explained Strobel. "One of those slots is vacant, waiting for Congress to approve the president's chosen man. Judge Stonebreaker is about halfway through a major antitrust trial that has been dragging on for months, and the defense just started. Even if she finishes by mid-October, which I doubt, they would never send her right back into another long and complex case."

"Who does that leave?" asked Teddy. He threw an empty toward the cardboard box from the Waterside Wharf that they were using for trash. The can bounced harmlessly on the deck, several feet short.

"It leaves Johnson, Baker-Kline, and Lightfoot, who is too liberal for my liking."

"Then let's get rid of Lightfoot," said Win. "Let's do a little judge shopping."

"How?" asked Mack. "Call some of your Mafia buddies?"

"Don't need to with Lightfoot," said Win smugly. "Don't forget, before he was a judge, he was a career politician, and our family financed major portions of his reelection campaigns."

"That's probably why he lost," mumbled Mack.

Win ignored the comment. "Some of the money was dirty," he explained. "Dummy corporations set up to evade federal limits, that type of thing. I can tell Lightfoot our clients have been snooping around, that this guy Barnes got wind of those financing irregularities and is threatening to leak them to the press if Lightfoot comes near this case."

Mack was intrigued by the idea of knocking Lightfoot out of the running. "But even if we give Lightfoot an incentive not to hear the case, he can't take himself out because he doesn't make the assignments. That job falls to Baker-Kline, since she's the current chief judge of the Eastern District of Virginia."

"You're right, but a chief judge never messes with another judge's vacation. I'll explain the score to Lightfoot, then give him an out by inviting him to join our family at our vacation place in the Blue Ridge Mountains during the second week of October. It would be hard for him to try the case in Norfolk if he has plans to hunt with me in Charlottesville."

"The problem," replied Mack, " is that your plan leaves me with a tossup between Johnson and Baker-Kline. Heads I win, tails I lose. I think I would rather keep Lightfoot in the running and at least lessen the odds of getting Johnson."

Win Mackenzie caught Mack's eye and nodded toward Teddy, whose head was tilted back so far it looked like his neck might snap off at any minute. His eyes were closed, but his mouth was wide open, sucking in the humid Tidewater air. As usual, this strategy session had boiled down to the two hard-core litigators.

"How important is this case?" asked Win, lowering his voice. "I want a serious answer, not sarcasm."

"It's one of the biggest I've ever tried," Mack ruminated as he gazed out at the sailboats meandering down the river. "The publicity for the firm will be huge. Win or lose, we'll be a household name."

"Then let's pull out all the stops," said Mackenzie. "I've got a deal for you. Name me as the lead lawyer for the case on appeal, and the media spokesman during trial. I'll guarantee that you get Baker-Kline as your judge."

The prospect of getting Baker-Kline for the case struck Mack as too good to be true. But the price was high—letting Win have a piece of the glory. Mack leaned back in his chair, took a long pull on his beer, and chose his words carefully.

"How you gonna do that?" he asked. "And how could you be media spokesman if you're on vacation in the Blue Ridge Mountains?"

"I never guaranteed that an emergency would not arise and keep me from going."

"What about Johnson?"

Win's lips curled into a smug little smile. "Leave that to me. Some things you don't want to know." He paused and looked at Mack. "Deal?"

Strobel narrowed his eyes, pictured Ichabod seated on the bench— glaring down at Carson, slicing him down to size—then Strobel extended his light beer toward Mackenzie. They sealed the deal with a toast, set to the backdrop of a busy evening at the Waterside and the sound of Teddy's snoring.

■ ■ ■

Unlike the lawyers he had hired, Ahmed was more concerned with the jury than the judge. Accordingly, when he received the list of more than one hundred prospective jurors from his lawyers about a month prior to trial, he took immediate action. As usual, he started with a phone call to Barnes.

"Did you get the list of prospective jurors?"

"Yes, it came this morning. We're on it. Give us two weeks, and we'll have a complete report."

"I can get a report from the lawyers. I need more from you. We need some of these jurors in our pocket. Can you make that happen?"

There was silence on the phone line. Ahmed waited Barnes out. "I don't know," Barnes finally said. "That's serious stuff in the United States. You can pull time for messing with a jury."

"Humor me. How could you do it if you wanted to?"

Barnes waited a few more beats before answering. "Well, off the top of my head, I'd start with the first thirty or forty prospective jurors and ask Strobel who he'll strike with his preemptories. Then I would hire some local investigators to do some background work on the remaining jurors. Go through their garbage, check out their places of employment, talk to some of their friends, those types of things.

"We would pick the ten most vulnerable jurors and start laying the foundation for buying or blackmailin' 'em if they get selected. We prefer blackmail. It's cheaper and more effective. There's a good chance that 20 percent of these folks are cheatin' on their spouses, lookin' at pornography on the Internet, or stealin' from their bosses. We trade our silence for their vote.

"Any preliminary contacts with jurors would be done only by one of my top two men. We would be very discreet in our approach. You can usually find out if someone can be bought without ever asking the question. We only need one member to hang the jury in a civil case. But two can provide moral support for each other during deliberations."

"Make it happen," said Ahmed, "and you've increased your bonus by one million. Pay whatever it takes to buy the jurors."

There was a long silence. Ahmed sensed Barnes' reluctance and decided to wait him out again. Barnes was not used to refusing an order. And a million dollars was a lot of money, even to Barnes.

"No promises, Ahmed. I'm not willing to go to the big house over a civil case."

"Get it done."

Ahmed hung up the phone.

Justice in America was not cheap.

■ ■ ■

Brad had a less ambitious plan for the list of prospective jurors.

"Bella," he said into the speakerphone. "Have you got a minute?"

"No," she snorted. "But I'll come in anyway."

A few seconds later she lowered herself into one of the client chairs across the desk from Brad.

"Would you take the list of prospective jurors and send it to these folks?" Without looking up from his paperwork, Brad handed her a list of fellow lawyers he could trust. "Draft a cover letter asking them to take a minute and look at the list to see if they know anyone on it. Give them your number to call if they have any information. Let's get those letters out today, if possible."

Bella didn't move. As usual, Brad had been taking the lady for granted. When there was no discernible response to his request, he looked up from his work for the first time and noticed that her eyes were watering. He couldn't recall the last time he saw that happen.

"What's wrong?" he asked as he put his other work aside. She had his full attention.

"Brad, we've got a serious cash-flow problem. It hasn't been this tight since the first year we started." She placed a stack of papers on his desk. "These are the invoices just for the *Reed* case." She placed a smaller stack next to them. "These are the other invoices we've received in the last thirty days. If I paid everything in both of these piles, we'd have only fifty-five thousand in the bank. Between the experts, Nikki's trip to Saudi Arabia, the deposition transcripts, and the usual salaries and over-head costs, we're burning through almost seventy-five thousand a week. Even if we max out our line of credit with Virginia National and drag out our creditors as long as we can, I figure we could get through an eight-week trial, but no more. If we lose, we're sunk. Even if we win, we don't have the cash flow to get us through an appeal."

She sighed, as if a huge weight had just been lifted from her shoulders. The bills remained on the corner of Brad's desk. Bella was the master of anxiety transfer.

Brad was used to Bella being the purveyor of bad financial news. What struck him this time was the intensity of her emotions. They had been through tougher times when they first started, and Bella had never been so despondent.

"We've just got to settle some of these other cases we have kicking around the office," Brad suggested. "We'll get through this. We're survivors."

"What other cases? We've already settled or farmed out just about any case of value except the Johnson case. I think it's time to settle Johnson."

"Bella, we've had this conversation before. The insurance company always lowballs the settlement offers until the eve of trial. It'll be months before we can get a trial date and scare them into a reasonable offer. I won't sell out one client for the good of another."

"Brad, I'm telling you, we don't have any choice. We either settle Johnson, or we bankrupt the firm."

They were both raising their voices, each retort louder than the last.

"Bella, it's not an option. End of discussion. We would file for bankruptcy and drop the *Reed* case before we would start selling out our clients." Brad took a breath and lowered the volume, "Now, what are our other options?"

"You can take out an equity line on your house…"

"Good. Work up the paperwork. How much will that net?"

"About another 150 if we're lucky. You've already got a serious first mortgage on that monster."

"Okay, what else?"

Much to Brad's surprise, the tears welled up again. But this time Bella didn't hold back as the tears tumbled quietly down her cheeks and onto her lap. Brad had never seen her this way and didn't quite know what to do. He slowly rose, grabbed some tissues, and went over to put a hand on Bella's shoulder. He crouched down in front of her.

"This isn't about the money, is it?"

Bella shook her head. Brad waited patiently with his hand on her shoulder. She finally began forcing the words out.

"We could…should…stop paying salaries…for a little while. But I can barely afford…Mom's home. I'm in huge debt. She's all I've got. I don't want to lose her." The words came tumbling out in a fit of emotion.

"Bella," Brad said softly, "it's gonna be all right… You're not going to lose her… It's gonna be all right."

■   ■   ■

When Bella left, Brad closed his door and slumped into his chair. His head throbbed, and his chest felt tight. This was the price he paid for the freedom of being his own boss—the loneliness of leadership.

He leaned back in his chair, put his hands behind his head, and stared hard at the ceiling. He took inventory. In one month, he would be trying a case that many thought was unwinnable. His usually steady secretary was in a state of panic. He had fallen hard for a woman who he could not figure out. The steady barrage of sixteen-hour days had set his nerves on end. He had just lost his main expert witness in a bizarre deposition that made him think his office might be bugged. He had decimated his practice to handle this case and now risked bankruptcy even if he won. And, to add insult to injury, he would have to share the contingency fee on the only good case he had in the office—the Johnson case—with the most pitiful plaintiff's lawyer in Tidewater—the Rock.

There was only one solution. He would work harder. And he would streamline the case. He would cut expenses. He would take it one day at a time. If he won, other major cases would pour into the office. Even if he lost, it would be a glorious loss, and more cases would pour into his office.

Besides, his client was a missionary and presumably had a direct line to the Almighty. It was a good thing. He could use a little divine intervention, or at least a little luck.

■   ■   ■

Just down the hall, Leslie refined her preliminary game plan to reflect the recently completed depositions and other developments in the case. The fifty-page document outlined the witnesses and their expected testimony. It discussed various evidentiary issues and the law supporting the plaintiff's position on each issue. It outlined the exhibits and documents they intended to introduce at trial, together with any anticipated objections. Each page of the valued document was appropriately marked: Confidential: Attorney/Client Privilege and Trial Work Product.

As she prepared to leave the office, Leslie made four copies. She hand-delivered two copies in confidential envelopes to the desks of Nikki and Bella, and slid a copy under Brad's door. She tucked the fourth copy in her own briefcase and left the original on the corner of her desk.

✷ ✷ ✷

Nikki left the office a few minutes after Leslie at 6:30. Unlike Leslie, she had no intention of taking work home with her. Nikki did, however, return to the office just before midnight as she had for the last five nights in a row. The first night Leslie was still working at the office, so Nikki just threw a few things in her briefcase, said hello, and headed home. The other four nights, the office had been empty except for the occasional visit by the cleaning crew. Nikki worked each night for almost three hours, and tonight she would do so again. By her rough calculations, she figured that she should be able to mail the last letter out by 3 A.M. If not, she was determined to stay until she finished.

Nikki's advanced warning system consisted of a listening device of the type parents used to monitor their babies. She placed the receiver in the lobby in an out-of-the-way location. The monitor sat on her own desk as she worked. Each time that the cleaning crew came in the first few nights, the system had given Nikki the advanced warning that she needed to sweep the documents off her desk and into one of her empty desk drawers. Her office was at the end of the hall away from the reception area, a short walk that would take no more than fifteen seconds from the front door, just enough time to return her office to normal.

Nikki took the monitor with her as she headed to the kitchen to pour her first cup of coffee. As was her habit, she turned off the light to her own office and walked quickly down the hall. Just as she was about to walk through the reception area, she heard the distinct noise of a key being inserted, the doorknob turning, and the front door opening. She had no chance to get to the kitchen to turn off the coffee or to sneak back and clean up her own office in the dark. Instead, she slid into the nearest office, which happened to belong to Brad, and sat by the open door for a few seconds in the pitch dark.

She heard footsteps coming down the hallway toward the office. They were fast and determined, landing hard like a man's. She didn't hear the usual noise of the handcart or the clunking of cleaning supplies.

It must be Brad! It was Nikki's worst nightmare.

The hall light flipped on. Nikki froze in a moment of panic. How could she explain herself if he caught her in his office in the dark? She actually considered, just for a moment, hiding behind the door and slamming Brad in the back of the head to knock him unconscious. She would slip out, and the whole incident would be written off as a burglary gone awry.

Instead, she made a quick move for his massive oak desk and slid underneath it, in the hollow where Brad would put his legs if he sat in his desk chair. The man entered the room and flicked on the lights. She heard the deafening noise of her own heart pounding in her ears. She tried to control the sound of her breathing and found herself holding her breath to remain as quiet as possible. She covered her face with her hands, every muscle of her body tensed.

She fully expected Brad to sit at his desk and unavoidably kick her when he sat down. She would be discovered, fired, and perhaps arrested.

But the man in the room did not sit down or even move behind the desk. She heard him rummage around the papers on top of the desk, finally finding the object of his search. He seemed to hesitate, possibly reading the document, then turned and headed for the door. After what seemed like forever, the man turned off the lights and left the room.

Nikki sat shuddering under Brad's desk, doubled over in the fetal position, not able to move her limbs for several minutes. She eventually calmed her nerves, walked to the kitchen, and turned off the coffeepot. She went to her office and locked the door.

She left the offices of Carson & Associates and came back fifteen minutes later with a bottle of rum. She needed something stronger than caffeine to help get her through this night.

Three hours later, at precisely 3:30 A.M., she licked the last stamp and sealed the last envelope.

_____

The panic usually sets in about a month prior to a big trial, when the lawyers realize how much still needs to be done and how little time there is to do it. For Brad, the pretrial panic arrived right on schedule. He had four lousy weeks left to prepare witnesses, review depositions, prepare an opening statement, and complete a million other detailed tasks that would mean the difference between a good case and a mediocre one. The fact that he would have to spend one of those weeks in Saudi Arabia taking depositions exacerbated his jitters.

Complicating things even further were some lingering questions that Brad could not answer or ignore: How did the defendants find out about Worthington's arrest? And why did the defendants seem to anticipate every legal argument that Brad and his team made in their briefs? It was as if someone were reading their mail. Or worse. And it was this lingering paranoia that drove Brad, one day before leaving for Saudi Arabia, to the office of Patrick O'Malley, private investigator.

Patrick was a step above the average P.I. who worked out of his home and spied on unfaithful spouses. Patrick had an office in a run-down strip shopping center on Military Highway in Virginia Beach. He specialized in electronic surveillance and in finding missing persons.

Brad arrived at the office after a long day of depositions. He opened the door and looked around the reception area's yellow walls and stained carpet. The magazines were about two months old, which appeared to be the same general time frame of the last office cleaning. If O'Malley was making money, he had certainly not squandered any of it on first impressions.

O'Malley appeared from the back, a tall, slim figure with a bushy

Fu Manchu mustache from another era. He wore cowboy boots, faded jeans, and a denim shirt.

"Brad, my man," he said and gave Brad an enormous bear hug. "Why this sudden urge to slum it and meet in my office?"

"Just wanted to see what 'uptown' looks like."

"You are the personification of 'uptown,' Mr. Bradley Carson, attorney at law, proud owner of a Dodge Viper, and landlord of the estate on the river." O'Malley bowed deeply. "May I kiss the ring?"

"Give me a break."

"Just don't forget us little people."

"That's why I'm here. I want to hire one of the little people."

"This isn't about your ex, is it?"

"No," Brad laughed. "I wish it were that easy. Look, I don't have much time, and I don't have much information. But I'm working on this case, and the other side seems to know what I'm thinking even before I figure it out. I don't have any hard evidence, but I'm concerned the office might be bugged. Can you check it out?"

"Absolutely, man. Are you talking about the *Reed* case?" Brad nodded. "Saw your mug in the paper," O'Malley continued. "Want my advice?"

"No."

"Settle, baby. You're in the big leagues on that one. Take the money and run. You'll have a hard time winnin'. Just be happy with the publicity you've got and move on."

"Thanks for the encouragement," said Brad.

"You know how the song goes: 'Know when to hold 'em and know when to fold 'em.' Now, what do ya need?"

In five minutes the two men put together a plan to sweep the office for bugs every morning. Brad would have the locks changed on the doors and issue new keys to his team. He would hire a new cleaning crew for the next few months. He would have everybody change computer passwords, voicemail passwords, and phone numbers. Brad would have Bella send a list of the new passwords to O'Malley so he could check the computers and phones for outsiders tapping into the system.

Brad would tell each of his team members to be attentive for any suspicious signs.

Brad could not bring himself to believe that any member of his inner circle was involved. He may be paranoid, he told O'Malley, but he was still a good judge of character, and he knew he could trust Leslie, Nikki, and Bella. The Rock, on the other hand, would be totally cut out of the loop.

■ ■ ■

Chesapeake Estates looked pleasant enough on the outside. Manicured lawns surrounded the dark brick building with the huge white pillars, giving the place a southern colonial feel. It also featured a large front porch, on which the residents would sit and rock for hours while they discussed the weather and complained about the government. Unlike isolated nursing homes, the facility rested snugly on the outskirts of the exclusive Riverwalk development in the heart of Chesapeake. The nurses and staff seemed to genuinely care about the residents at Chesapeake Estates. The care didn't come cheap, but like so many other things in life, you got what you paid for. As far as Bella was concerned, there was no nursing home good enough for her mother—Gertrude Harper— but Chesapeake Estates came close.

The pristine appearance of the place stood in stark contrast to the turmoil going on in most of the residents' lives. Many struggled with Alzheimer's, dementia, Parkinson's, and other diseases that tormented an aging mind and body. Bella's mother suffered from advanced Parkinson's. She had her good days and her bad days. Lately, the good days were scarce.

It was a beautiful fall afternoon, and Bella intended to leave work early and take her mother for a walk. But nobody left Carson & Associates early these days. And so Bella did not arrive at Chesapeake Estates until nearly 7 P.M. She went straight to her mother's room.

Getting her mom out of that room had become more of a challenge as Gertrude's nervous system and muscle control deteriorated. Doctors told Bella the disease did not affect her mother's mind, only her physical ability to communicate her thoughts. Bella didn't believe it. Some days Gertrude didn't even recognize her and called out incessantly for Bella's father, who had divorced Gertrude more than twenty years earlier and been dead more than five.

Bella took Gertrude for a long walk and tried to convince her that her ex-husband was not coming back. Gertrude unloaded her many concerns about things that made no sense to Bella, undoubtedly driven by conversations she had overheard from the other residents. Bella found it nearly impossible to understand Gertrude, who shook uncontrollably as she talked. Her walking pace was incredibly slow, and she was stooped almost in half. Sometimes during these walks Bella would think about her mother in the vigor of her youth, how she would always have the answers for life's many challenges. Oh, how she wished she could turn back the clock and tap into some of that wisdom now.

At nearly 9 P.M., exhausted and hungry, Bella kissed her mom on the forehead—the same way that her mom used to kiss Bella when she was just a little girl—and told Gertrude she would be back soon. As Bella left Chesapeake Estates, she wondered if her mom would even remember the visit. Bella felt the tears welling up in her eyes as she turned to leave, desperately missing the only person in her life who had ever cared enough to wipe them away.

■ ■ ■

Win Mackenzie picked up the phone and dialed the clerk's office for Judge Samuel Johnson. He asked to speak with Alex Pearson, one of Johnson's two law clerks.

"Alex, this is Winsted Mackenzie, a litigation partner at Kilgore & Strobel. How's it going?"

"Great," said Alex. "Working with Judge Johnson is excellent. I've learned more in my first few months on the job than I did in my entire third year of law school."

Mackenzie, himself a University of Virginia man, did not doubt that. Alex had attended Washington and Lee.

"Alex, let me cut right to the point, because I know Judge Johnson keeps you hoppin'. Every year, Kilgore & Strobel gets literally hundreds of résumés for the few litigation spots that open up for first-year associates. I have personally reviewed your résumé and heard about your work ethic in federal court. We've checked out your references and law school class ranking."

Win Mackenzie paused for a second to let the suspension build.

"Alex, you are this firm's number one choice for next year. We'd like you to start full-time at Kilgore & Strobel next year as a litigation associate without the necessity of the interviews with firm partners we normally require. You'll be getting a letter confirming all this, but I wanted to personally call and tell you myself."

There was silence on the other end of the line. Win figured Alex was probably pinching himself to make sure it was true.

"That sounds great," Alex finally managed. "Will the letter give the details of the offer?"

"It will," said Win. "But let me also handle some of those myself."

For the next several minutes, Win Mackenzie, trained trial lawyer, put the hard sell on a flabbergasted Alex Pearson. The generosity of the firm and the flattery of Mackenzie just about rendered poor Alex speechless. When Win mentioned a special ten-thousand-dollar signing bonus, he could almost hear Alex panting on the other end of the line.

Oh, the innocence of the young, thought Mackenzie.

"Take your time making this decision, Alex. I know you'll ultimately make the right choice."

Win hung up the phone and dialed another number. This time it was not a law clerk but a federal appeals court judge who answered the phone. After exchanging pleasantries, Mackenzie got right down to business with his cousin.

"I hope this isn't improper, but I may need your help with something

that just came to my attention. Can I talk to you confidentially—
dead man's talk here—and get some advice about a potential conflict of
interest?"

"You know you can, Win. What's up?"

"Our firm has made an employment offer to one of Judge Johnson's
current law clerks, and I just found out we've got a small problem. I'm
trying to look out for Judge Johnson, who I know is a personal friend of
yours. He admires you greatly. Johnson is one of several judges who may
have an opportunity to handle the *Reed* case, in which our firm is representing the defendants. Word has it that the plaintiff's lawyer would
make a motion to disqualify Johnson based on a conflict of interest if he
were selected. They would say that he can't be objective when one of his
law clerks, who is helping him research the case, has an employment
offer to work for the firm representing the defendants. Their point has
some merit. Johnson doesn't need the bad publicity, and it puts him in a
no-win situation. You know him well. Can you say something to the
guy?"

"Sure, Win. Lots of other judges can hear that case. No sense in
Samuel putting himself in that situation. I'll call back if there's any difficulty. Thanks for the heads up. And Win…"

"Yeah."

"Good luck in the case. The nation will be watching."

■ ■ ■

After waiting forty minutes in Baker-Kline's reception area—the price
any lawyer pays for showing up unannounced—Win was eventually
ushered into the presence of the Haughty One. He filled the air with ten
minutes of small talk before Her Honor's impatience got the better
of her.

"I know you didn't just come here to talk about community politics, Win, and I've got to be back on the bench in ten minutes."

Perfect, thought Win. He leaned forward and lowered his voice a
notch. "What I'm about to say is just between us—stays right here?"

Ichabod nodded, her impatience replaced by curiosity. "Of course."

"It's about the spot on the Fourth Circuit Court of Appeals." He noticed Ichabod's eyes light up. That spot, one step below the Supremes, occupied every district judge's dreams. "As you know, my uncle sits on the Senate Judiciary Committee. The politics of these appointments is getting very interesting."

"I'm sure," said Ichabod, studying Win intently.

"Of course, the president makes the nominations, and you're not exactly—how do I say this discreetly?—his type of candidate." Win shifted in his seat, crossed his legs, and put on the most solemn, secretive face he could muster. "But we control the Senate Judiciary Committee. And right now, the president's candidates just can't seem to get out of committee."

This brought a knowing little smirk from Ichabod. Win was sure she had followed the proceedings carefully.

"As always in politics, talk of compromise has cropped up. My uncle and his buddies could let most of the president's nominees out of committee if he throws them a bone by nominating someone who cares about our agenda…like the rights of women."

Ichabod was nodding with her whole body now. She could obviously see where this was headed.

"Your name's been floated, and, well, my uncle is one of your strongest proponents. The problem is…" Win paused and pursed his lips, as if trying to figure out how best to say this without hurting the judge's feelings.

"Win," Ichabod said, "don't tiptoe around this. If there's a problem, I need to know."

Win still feigned hesitation. "Well, word is that the administration fears you might be anti–big business and adverse to the administration's foreign policy direction. I mean, they know they have to accept at least one pro-choice judge, just to get their own pro-life judges through, but they don't want it to be someone who's also going to create problems on other fronts."

Ichabod looked past Win, her brow furrowed, digesting this information. She had bought the whole thing. Now, for the delicate part.

"Judge, there's a high-profile case on the court's docket right now that could demonstrate just the opposite, that you are not inclined to counteract the administration on foreign policy. It's more or less a slam dunk, but our firm's involved, and I don't know if it'd be proper to discuss it with you..."

Ichabod looked at Win with narrow eyes. "Tell me about the case, Win." Then she tapped her finger on the desk. "But realize that I will not now, nor would I ever, commit to rule a certain way on the case until I've heard the evidence."

"I know that, Judge," Win responded quickly. "I just thought if you knew the facts of the case, you could decide if you even wanted to get involved. By a twist of fate, our firm has a conflict of interest with the one other judge who *could* hear it, so we could basically...well, we could increase the odds of you winding up with the case if that would be helpful."

"You understand," warned Ichabod, "that I'm making no promises."

"Yes, Your Honor."

"Then tell me about your case."

■ ■ ■

Though Brad's door was closed for privacy, Nikki barged in without knocking. She slammed the door behind her, loud enough for Bella to hear in the reception area.

Brad's head jerked up. "Sure, come on in," he said.

Nikki slapped a pink phone slip down on Brad's desk.

"This time she's really done it," Nikki fumed. "Either she goes or I do."

Brad put down his pen and raised an eyebrow. He glanced down quickly at the phone slip. "Can't be that bad."

"It is. And don't even bother sticking up for her—she's way out of line this time."

"Okay..."

Nikki paced furiously in front of Brad's desk. "The Trader's Insurance Company offers $550,000 to settle the Johnson case—$550,000!" Nikki yelled. "Chump change…ridiculous…insulting! I wouldn't even dignify it by taking it to my client—"

"Our client," interjected Brad.

Nikki scoffed and kept pacing. "The case is worth more than a mil…easy. Anything less is just a sellout so we can keep the doors open while we chase the *Reed* case. It's not right…"

"Settle down," Brad said wearily. "Nobody's telling you to take their offer—"

Nikki grabbed the phone slip and waved it under Brad's nose. "She already did! Bella found out about the offer and told my client," Nikki paused and looked directly at Brad, "*my* client—about the offer. He jumps all over it, desperate for cash, says he needs money right away, and tells her—tells Bella, who he has never met before—to take it!"

Just retelling the story made her blood bubble all over again. Johnson was her case, her bonus, her call as to whether it should settle. She looked at Brad expecting a confirmation that the firm's matriarch had seriously overstepped her bounds this time. Instead, Brad just gave her a sympathetic look combined with a "What do you want me to do about it?" shrug.

"What?" snarled Nikki. "You aren't going to try to defend her on this, are you?" She paused, waiting for some type of outburst, a threat against Bella, a reprimand…anything to indicate Bella would get what she had coming.

"Did you inform your client about the settlement offer?" Brad asked patiently.

Nikki threw herself into a chair, as if the question itself had knocked the wind out of her and sucked every ounce of energy from her body. "I knew it."

"Look. Don't get defensive. Bella crossed the line, and I'll talk to her about it."

Talk to her about it! Nikki nearly screamed aloud. *That's it?! I could have "talked to her about it" myself…*

"I'll make it clear she is not to speak with Mr. Johnson again," Brad continued, "except to take a phone message. But Nikki, if the client wants to settle, we've got to settle."

Nikki stared at Brad in disbelief, her jaw hanging open. She should have known better than to approach Brad with this mess. As usual, she would have been better off taking matters into her own hands.

Without another word, Nikki shook her head, stood up, and headed for the door. *Talk to her about it,* she repeated to herself.

"Her or me," Nikki said over her shoulder. "As soon as we get past the *Reed* trial, take your pick."

"Nikki," barked Brad.

She stopped and turned.

"I *will* talk to her about it. And it *won't* happen again. But if the client says settle, you settle," he said firmly.

She gave Brad a smart salute then marched out of the office, yanking the door closed behind her.

■ ■ ■

By now Ahmed had begun looking for the 8½-by-11 manila envelopes. He gloated at his good fortune in having this unsolicited, unnamed inside source, then seethed at the thought that the incompetent Barnes could not determine the identity.

As usual, the latest envelope contained a cut-and-paste message. It also contained a thick report entitled "Revised Preliminary Game Plan for *Reed v. Saudi Arabia.*" This second document set forth the plaintiff's revised strategy for the case: who to call as witnesses, what to introduce as exhibits, what objections and legal arguments to make. He would make sure Strobel received this updated information.

Like the first game plan he received, the revised game plan would prove invaluable, but the message intrigued Ahmed more:

Worthington worth every penny of $100K The enclosed will cost
you another. Same wiring. Shelhorse must come down too. More

details to follow. Real-time surveillance info is now critical. We need to meet. Norfolk General District Court, Traffic Division Room #2, Monday fortnight, 9:30a. Bring three phone bugs. Come alone or deal is off.

Ahmed read the letter over and over. His elusive and mysterious ally was going to march out in plain sight! The audacity!

Ahmed agreed about Shelhorse. She was a powerful expert; her toxicology evidence was the most damaging in the case. How could Carson possibly win without an expert in toxicology?

On the other hand, Ahmed was not convinced that bugging the office, which he presumed the informant planned to do, was the right strategy. It was risky and probably would not reveal much more than his source could provide.

Ahmed understood immediately the purpose of holding the meeting in Norfolk General District Court. The place would be crawling with police officers. The metal detectors at the door would screen out all weapons. The court would be incredibly hectic, with masses of people milling around. The best place for their meeting to go unnoticed was the middle of a large crowd.

Ahmed thanked Allah and started making plans for the rendezvous. Once he learned the identity of this source, he would again be in control.

A s Brad prepared to board the plane for Saudi Arabia to attend the depositions of former church members, he was unsure of how destructive to the case those depositions might turn out to be. Strobel had scheduled them. Sarah warned Brad that these particular church members, with the exception of Rasheed Berjein, had never really made all-out commitments to Christ or the church. They would probably say anything the Muttawa wanted. Unfortunately, because they lived outside the jurisdiction of the court, their videotaped depositions could be used in lieu of live testimony at trial.

Brad decided to take Nikki on the trip both because she knew her way around and because she knew Rasheed. Nikki's presence might give Rasheed some security and confidence. Besides, Brad would have fun seeing how Nikki handled the customs of this chauvinistic country. Bella had objected based on cost, but Brad overruled her and promised to pinch pennies while abroad.

Money would prove to be the least of their problems.

Weather delays caused Brad and Nikki to arrive late at Reagan National Airport and miss their connection to Riyadh. Hours later they boarded the next international flight, which promptly suffered a mechanical problem. After two hours of broken promises, the airline conceded defeat and announced that the next flight to Riyadh would not leave until the following morning.

While Nikki ranted, Brad contacted Sa'id el Khamin and told him they would be late for the depositions. They wouldn't arrive until late afternoon; get a one-day continuance, Brad instructed Sa'id.

The next morning Brad and Nikki slipped into their seats in coach, fulfilling their promise to Bella to avoid first class no matter what. Brad squeezed in between two heavyweights, one male and the other undecided. Nikki had the honor of sitting between a talkative and nervous older lady on one side and a six-year-old kid on the other. The flight seemed interminable.

■ ■ ■

As Brad and Nikki suffered over the Atlantic, Mack Strobel surveyed the small army of lawyers gathered in a plush office in the heart of Riyadh and prepared to commence the depositions.

The defense side of the conference table was full of dignitaries and heavy hitters. Ahmed himself was there, sitting next to Mack, along with another partner from Kilgore & Strobel and three local lawyers. The local lawyers had retained an interpreter, reputed to be one of the best in Riyadh. His language skills were good, said the lawyers, and whenever a controversial issue of interpretation arose, he always remembered who paid his bill.

The court reporter and videographer were poised and ready, and the first witnesses waited in a conference room down the hall. Nearly every witness had rehearsed their testimony ad nauseam, with Mack himself practicing the direct examination and his partner performing Brad's role on cross-examination. They had done this for all the witnesses except Rasheed Berjein, who steadfastly refused to practice what he would say.

The plaintiff's side of the conference table was inhabited only by the lonely looking Sa'id el Khamin, who would act as local lawyer and interpreter for Brad and Nikki. Sa'id had apologetically explained to Mack that Brad and Nikki were having flight problems and could not be there until the next day. Mack nevertheless insisted on proceeding with the depositions, and at 9 A.M. sharp, he marched the first witness into the conference room and had him sworn in.

"For the record," Sa'id said, his voice hoarse and shaky, "the plaintiff objects to beginning this deposition without Mr. Carson present. Mr. Carson called late last night and said that his flight had been canceled due to mechanical problems. We therefore respectfully request that the depositions be started one day later."

"For the record," replied Mack, his authoritative voice filling the conference room, "this deposition has been scheduled for more than three weeks. Mr. Carson is well aware of the vagaries of international travel and could certainly have scheduled himself a little lead time. Mr. el Khamin is a capable local lawyer retained by Mr. Carson and can handle the cross-examination of these witnesses. The depositions will go forward as scheduled. You can object if you want and take it up later with a judge, but the depositions will start on time."

Mack glared at el Khamin, practically daring the little man to provide any further argument. When none came, Mack turned to the court reporter, also hired by Mack, and told her, "Swear the witness in." El Khamin quietly mumbled, "We still object," and the depositions were on.

Tariq Abdul took the oath first. He testified that he and his wife, Semar, had been members of the Reeds' church. He described the enterprise, through the translator, as an attempt by the Reeds to proselytize Muslims and recruit them for a drug ring. Tariq and Semar attended several meetings of the group but, according to Tariq, were never converted to Christianity. Therefore, said Tariq, he was never fully trusted and never given an opportunity to use or sell the drugs that were in such plentiful supply for those who did convert. He quickly added, without being asked, that he would never have participated in such an insidious enterprise even if he had been given the opportunity.

Although he never personally used or sold any drugs, Tariq did witness others doing so firsthand. He provided specific names and instances. While he was not there the night of the arrest, it did not surprise him to learn that Dr. Reed had resisted arrest. He had seen the normally mild-mannered Reed lose his temper on more than one occasion, especially if anyone challenged his authority. All in all, Tariq was sorry that Dr. Reed had died while apparently resisting arrest, was sorry that he, Tariq, had been an unwitting part of this criminal enterprise, and was sorry that he had not reported these activities to the police earlier.

The necessity of translation made the testimony stale and laborious. Tariq stayed on script but testified without emotion. His direct examination lasted nearly two hours and didn't pack much punch. Worse, the man's eyes darted all over the conference room whenever he talked about drug use by the Reeds or other church members. Mack had coached him to look only at the camera, but apparently that advice was too difficult for this frightened witness to follow in the heat of the moment.

By the rules of court, the video shown to the jury would consist of a static headshot of Tariq. Mack made a mental note not to show this tape after a big lunch or in a warm courtroom. No juror could be expected to stay awake for two straight hours while watching a talking head testify with no emotion. On the other hand, with those shifty eyes darting this way and that, maybe sleeping jurors would be a good thing.

After a short break, Sa'id began his cross-examination, which consisted of only three questions, all translated by Mack's paid translator.

"You were not there when the Reeds were arrested, right?"

"Yes, that's true."

"So you have no firsthand knowledge as to whether they were tortured or beaten by the police?"

"As I said before, I was not there, and I do not know."

"So it could have happened just the way Mrs. Reed described it?"

"I don't know how to answer your question because I don't know how Mrs. Reed described it. But if she said the police planted drugs, I don't believe it. There were already drugs in that apartment."

"Thank you, Mr. Abdul, that's all I have for now."

Mack could hardly conceal his excitement. Three questions! And none of them even remotely tough! El Khamin was weaker than Mack had imagined.

So weak, in fact, that Mack shot a sideways glance at Ahmed, just to judge the man's reaction. Ahmed did not seem at all surprised by this turn of events; his intimidating glare never changed. Could el Khamin be in Ahmed's back pocket too? It seemed that every other person Mack met in Saudi Arabia, including each of the witnesses now testifying, was more than anxious to cooperate in this case. It made him wonder how far Ahmed's influence reached and what means had been used to gain such far-reaching complicity.

After el Khamin's anemic performance, Mack changed his strategy. He dispatched a local lawyer to find out when Brad's flight would land. He called and questioned the next witness quickly. With any luck at all, Mack figured he could blitz through five of the six witnesses before the end of the day, leaving only Rasheed Berjein for tomorrow.

By the mandatory midday prayer break, Mack had dispensed with the first four witnesses. In addition to Tariq and Semar Abdul, another couple also confirmed the Reeds were selling drugs and then pressuring Muslims, particularly young children and their mothers, to convert to Christianity. The second couple went a step further than the Abduls by admitting their own use of drugs, ultimately resulting in a guilty plea and a suspended jail sentence. Again the cross-examination was short and sweet, establishing nothing more than the uncontroverted fact that this couple had not personally witnessed the arrest of Dr. and Mrs. Reed.

After the prayer break, Mack swore in his fifth and final witness of the day—Omar Khartoum. Mack was anxious to get Omar finished before Brad Carson arrived, and therefore decided to skip most of the preliminary questions.

■ ■ ■

After wrestling his way through customs and surviving a frenzied taxi ride from the airport to the law firm, Brad Carson burst through the conference-room door. Chairs and startled faces swiveled in his direction as if he were a junior-high teacher who had just entered class in the middle of a spitball war. He sported jeans and a T-shirt, disheveled hair, and he smelled like a man who had spent all night on a plane. A flustered receptionist speaking rapid and forceful Arabic followed on his heels, complaining because Brad had ignored her protests.

Brad stopped in the doorway and pointed at the witness. "What's going on here?" he demanded of Strobel. The receptionist bumped into his back. Brad ignored her.

On the other side of the conference table, Strobel stood. "Counsel, we are in the middle of our fifth deposition of the day. We started this morning at the agreed-upon time, and you were not present. Unfortunately for you, the world does not suspend all of its activities while it waits for the great Bradley Carson to stroll in."

After a long day and little sleep, Brad was in no mood for Strobel's condescension. "You arrogant jerk..." Brad lunged around the conference table toward Strobel, but the granite figure of Ahmed Aberijan blocked him. Brad was lucky to be restrained, as the older but more powerful Strobel had two inches and fifty pounds on him. The two lawyers traded insults while Ahmed acted as a human barrier between Brad and Strobel and slowly nudged Brad back to his side of the conference table.

Brad got no backup from Sa'id, who sat frozen in his chair, his mouth wide open and his eyes even wider.

After the yelling subsided, and Brad had placed every objection fathomable into the record, Strobel concluded his direct examination. The parties took a ten-minute break while Sa'id briefed Brad on the testimony. Sa'id made his own cross-examination of earlier witnesses seem impressive enough, and Brad calmed down a little. From the sounds of things described by Sa'id, the little man had done a good and thorough job of discrediting the others. Brad was thankful that they had retained this quirky little lawyer, even if he was costing them nearly three hundred bucks an hour.

■ ■ ■

Forty-five minutes into the cross-examination, Nikki slipped into the conference room dressed no better than Brad and took a seat right next to him. She handed him two plastic bags under the table—one full of a substance that resembled marijuana, the other full of a white powder. She leaned over and whispered in Brad's ear.

"This better work, babe. It's not easy getting this stuff."

Brad squeezed her knee. "Thanks," he whispered.

He carefully placed both bags on the table in front of Omar Khartoum.

"I would like the court reporter to mark, for purposes of identification, plaintiff's Exhibits 1 and 2. And I would ask the witness to please identify these exhibits."

"I object," Strobel proclaimed loudly.

"There's a surprise," said Brad.

"This is obviously some kind of trick by Mr. Carson to bring in substances that look like marijuana and cocaine. Of course, if they were the real thing, Mr. Aberijan here is an officer of the law and would have to arrest Mr. Carson." Strobel said it calmly but forcefully, just the right tone for the video camera.

Khartoum heard the objection and seemed to take the hint. He looked at the materials in the bags. He reached in and touched the materials, then tasted a small portion from the tip of his finger.

"It is fake cocaine and fake marijuana," he announced proudly.

"How did you know it was fake from tasting it?" asked Brad. "How is this substance different from the real cocaine that you've tasted?"

After the translation, the witness pondered the question. "This substance is sweeter."

"Is that how you tell whether a substance is cocaine? You see how sweet it is?" Brad's toxicologist, Dr. Shelhorse, would testify that the telltale sign for cocaine was the numbness it caused on the tongue and mucus membranes.

"Yes," Khartoum replied; this time his tone of voice was a little less sure.

"But these exhibits at least look like the types of drugs you bought from Mr. and Mrs. Reed?"

"Yes."

"Did you buy these drugs by the gram?"

"Yes."

"How much did you pay for the marijuana, and how much did you pay for the cocaine?"

Khartoum was actually prepared on this point and answered quickly and confidently. "Two hundred riyals per gram for the marijuana. Fourteen hundred per gram for the cocaine."

"How many grams would you say are in this bag that we have marked as 'Exhibit 1'?" Brad asked, holding up a bag of oregano.

Khartoum stared at the bag for two full minutes. "I don't know," he said at last.

"Guess," insisted Brad.

"He doesn't have to guess," said Strobel. "If he doesn't know, he doesn't know."

"Humor me," said Brad. "He says he paid big money for these drugs. But he doesn't have the foggiest idea how much these substances weigh?"

"Thirty-five grams," Khartoum said. It sounded more like a question than an answer.

Nikki pulled out a small set of metric scales, and Brad put the bag on the scales.

"Would you read that please?" said Brad.

"Seventy-five grams," said Khartoum sheepishly. "But I could never tell. That's why we always weighed it."

"Did the Reeds always weigh these drugs?" asked Brad.

"Sure."

"Then why did the police not seize or inventory a scale when they searched the Reeds' apartment?"

"Objection," said Strobel. "He can't possibly know why the police did what they did."

"Nor can anyone else," said Brad. "Did you ever freebase the cocaine?"

"I do not understand," Khartoum replied.

"Let me ask it this way: What did you do with the marijuana and the cocaine?"

Khartoum looked puzzled, but he had apparently seen a few

movies. "We would smoke the marijuana and sniff the cocaine up our noses."

"Show me how you would 'sniff' the cocaine," said Brad as he handed the witness plaintiff's Exhibit 2.

Khartoum looked at the substance like it might bite.

"I object," said Strobel. "This is totally improper."

"You've made your objection," answered Brad. "Now let the witness answer the question."

Khartoum dumped the powdered sugar onto the table in a long thin line and put one nostril down next to the pile, closing the other nostril with his finger. "We would do like that and breathe in," he said.

"All of it?" asked Brad. This was too good to be true.

The witness shrugged when he heard the translation.

"No, just a small part of the pile," said Khartoum.

"Show me how much," demanded Brad.

Using a piece of paper, Khartoum gingerly separated out a portion of the substance. To Brad's delight, it was a large amount.

"Now weigh it," said Brad.

"I object," Strobel's tone was no longer controlled for the camera. "This is nonsense."

"Just weigh it," said Brad.

"About twelve grams," came back the translated reply.

Brad smiled. Dr. Shelhorse would testify that a fatal dose of cocaine is generally considered to be only one gram, although there were stories of experienced users surviving more than twenty grams. Certainly, the amount separated by Khartoum was not an ordinary dose.

"Did you ever *smoke* crack cocaine, or did you ever see the Reeds smoke crack cocaine?"

By now, Khartoum had apparently determined that vagueness was his friend, so he resorted to an appropriately vague answer.

"Sometimes," he said.

"Sometimes what?" pressed Brad. "Sometimes you smoked crack, or sometimes the Reeds did, or both?"

"Sometimes the Reeds did. They tried to get me to do it, but I wouldn't."

"Explain the process of how they would prepare the crack and then smoke it."

After hearing the translated question, Khartoum sat thinking for quite a time. His eyes were blank, wandering over to Strobel for help that was not forthcoming. Then he gave a slow, calculated answer.

"Because I wouldn't join them in smoking crack, I never actually saw them do it. I know they did smoke crack because I saw them heating the cocaine and preparing the crack."

"How did they heat it? How hot?"

Another pause. More vagueness. "It is a complicated process that I cannot describe. I believe temperatures would be very hot—more than 250 degrees."

Brad knew, again from information provided by Dr. Shelhorse, that the cocaine powder would vaporize at temperatures over 200 degrees Celsius, destroying most of the active ingredients. Crack was made by vaporization and extraction of the hydrochloric salt in the cocaine at a much lower temperature. Brad would not make these points now and give Khartoum a chance to correct his testimony. He would wait until Strobel showed the jury the videotaped deposition at trial, then Brad would call Dr. Shelhorse to the stand on rebuttal and prove Khartoum a liar.

■ ■ ■

As Khartoum fidgeted in his chair, dodging questions and glancing at Strobel for help, Nikki diverted her gaze to the stoic face of Ahmed Aberijan. She stared at him, though he refused to look back. She just wanted him to look over at her one time so she could despise him with her eyes.

But the man just sat there, across the table and two seats down from Nikki, glaring at the witness with a look that promised future pain. Nikki saw the fire smoldering in Ahmed's eyes, the all-too-familiar look of an abusive temper ready to explode. It was the same steeled look, the same glare, that Nikki had so feared in her own father's eyes. It was that point in time when the eyes go from fire to ice, from anger to a cold resolve to hurt somebody. It would be a signal to Nikki, even in grade school and then in junior high, to grab her sister and get out of the room. She would turn on her boom box and drown out the noise of another terrible argument, of her mother taking the abuse for all the girls in the family.

Nikki had always melted in terror at the same look that she saw now. And she had never forgiven herself for failing to stand up to the man.

But she was older now. And wiser. And stronger.

Look at me! she wanted to shout. *I will not turn away!*

But even as the thought flitted across her mind, she was not absolutely certain she could do it even now.

■ ■ ■

"One final question," announced Brad. "When you snorted cocaine, how long did it take before you felt the rush, and how long did the rush last?"

This question, like the others, had been suggested by Shelhorse. She had explained to Brad that smoking crack gives an immediate euphoria that lasts only ten minutes or so and is followed by an intense downswing of mood, leaving the smoker irritable and wired. On the other hand, explained Shelhorse, those who snort the drug will not obtain the rush for several minutes, as the absorption process takes place, but the euphoria would last longer, sometimes as much as an hour.

But apparently nobody had explained these facts to Khartoum. "I would get a huge rush right away," he explained, "and I wouldn't come down for hours."

"That's exactly what I thought," said Brad. "No further questions."

Rasheed Berjein did not match the mental picture Brad had constructed months earlier after talking to Nikki. Subconsciously, Brad had stereotyped Rasheed as a Middle Eastern version of Charles Reed— a soft-bellied and soft-spoken Christian about Sarah's age. But Rasheed looked ten years younger and far more rugged than Brad imagined.

Rasheed's thobe could not entirely cloak his athletic build. Thick, short-cropped hair framed his clean-shaven face, which featured a prominent, broad nose. Large, dark semicircles underneath his deep-set eyes mirrored the enormous eyebrows above them. His skin was leathery and tanned. He looked more like a young man you would want on your side in a street brawl than he did Brad's preconception of a shy and retiring Christian.

Brad was trained to recognize signs of distress, and in Rasheed he saw them all. The man entered the room with his eyes downcast, darting around as he took his seat. He made no effort to shake hands with or even look at the lawyers. Brad noticed his hands trembled, and he blinked his eyes frequently. Brad stared at Rasheed, hoping for some eye contact, but Rasheed pinned his gaze on his hands.

Brad had no doubt that Rasheed was about to fabricate testimony against Sarah Reed.

"Please state your name for the record," Strobel instructed.

Rasheed looked up from his hands and locked his mournful eyes on Nikki.

"Rasheed Berjein," he said.

He continued to stare at Nikki for a long second. Brad thought he noticed a slight twinkle of the eyes and an almost imperceptible lifting of the cheeks, but the signs of recognition disappeared as quickly as they came.

■   ■   ■

On the other side of town, Mobara Berjein sat quietly on a folding metal chair, her hands clasped in her lap, head bowed in prayer. The Muttawa stood by the door, staring impassively at Mobara, listening intently to the deposition being piped into the small room and silently daring her husband to deviate from the plan. Everyone in the room knew that Mobara's life depended on how well her husband followed the script.

■   ■   ■

Sarah Reed's closest friends started arriving at her small house at 12:30 A.M. Sarah had started the coffee at midnight and had not even attempted to sleep. But Sarah's preteen children could sleep through anything, and so she began the impossible task of waking them up only a few hours after they had dozed off.

She went to Steven's room first and was struck again by how much the boy resembled his father. Even when he slept, the similarities were unmistakable. They both slept on their backs with their mouths open, hands flung up somewhere over their heads, sheets and blankets strewn everywhere, the result of a hundred thrashing movements that were prerequisites to falling asleep. Steven had his dad's eyes, his dad's mouth, and his dad's mannerisms.

Steven also inherited his dad's undying optimism and unfailing loyalty. He had taken seriously his new responsibilities as "man of the house," and had proclaimed on more than one occasion that he would live at home even as he attended college and afterward when he began his hoped-for career as a major league baseball player. He shouldered heavy responsibilities for an eleven-year-old, and the thought of it made tears well up in Sarah's eyes. It was not the first time she had stood in the dark by Steven's bed and cried.

By 1 A.M., the cul-de-sac where Sarah lived had been transformed into a parking lot. Chesapeake Community Church members filled the family room, spilling into the kitchen and down the hallway. An excited buzz of conversation filled the tiny house as the church members anticipated this most unusual meeting.

Chesapeake Community Church did not have the most inspired preaching or the most moving music, but it was a praying church, and the people in Sarah's home had been called to prayer. And so, at the precise moment that Rasheed started answering questions in Riyadh, the Reverend Jacob Bailey quieted the conversation and pointed the group's prayers heavenward. They prayed for wisdom and courage for Rasheed, they prayed for safety for Rasheed and Mobara, they prayed for blinders on the eyes of Strobel and Ahmed, and for slowness of understanding. They prayed for Brad and Nikki and even Leslie, who had declined Sarah's invitation to attend. They prayed for God's work to go forward and God's will to be done through His church in Riyadh. For two hours, they prayed and they prayed and they prayed.

Reverend Bailey and his church in Chesapeake were not the only ones petitioning the God of the Universe for safety, courage, and wisdom. Rasheed's flamboyant brother, Hanif, led a similar prayer effort in Riyadh. The language was different, the style was different, and the intensity was very different. The raw emotion of the Riyadh meeting far exceeded that of the Chesapeake church. Many in Riyadh had been introduced to Christ by Rasheed, and all knew him personally. The meeting was characterized by a passion borne of persecution, the intensity heightened by the knowledge that this meeting could be their last. They shed tears unashamedly, and with loud voices they begged God to intervene.

■ ■ ■

Brad took copious notes as the object of everyone's prayers relentlessly blasted Sarah Reed's case. Rasheed confirmed that Charles and Sarah Reed had in fact sold drugs and admitted using the drugs himself. He was more articulate than Khartoum and came across as infinitely more believable. He preemptively handled all the issues Brad had used so effectively on cross-examination the previous day by describing in great detail the way the drugs were used.

After ninety minutes of damaging testimony, Strobel passed the witness for a cross-examination that Brad knew would not be easy.

No sense beating around the bush.

"Are you or your wife being threatened by the nation of Saudi Arabia and forced to give untrue testimony in this case?"

"Objection," interjected Strobel. "That's outrageous! You have no foundation for that accusation."

Brad leaned forward and pointed directly at Ahmed. "Why don't you ask Mr. Aberijan if there's a foundation for my question?" Then he pointed at Rasheed. "Why don't you march this man's wife into the conference room so I can ask her?" He turned to Strobel, who was by now also leaning forward on the table. "How can you sleep at night representing people who torture and kill and then intimidate witnesses into lying about it?"

Strobel responded with a withering gaze. When he finally spoke, he did so loudly and slowly, emphasizing every word.

"You listen to me, Mr. Carson. Don't you ever again make accusations you can't back up. I'm tired of your nonsense. If you have one more outburst like that, I'll leave, and I'll take Mr. Berjein with me to file a criminal complaint against you with the Riyadh police." Strobel turned to the translator, "Don't translate that last question. I objected to it, and it's not worthy of being translated."

Brad and Mack stared hard at each other for a few seconds. Brad leaned back first.

"Did you meet with Nikki Moreno and Sa'id el Khamin several weeks ago?" he asked.

The question was translated. Brad knew Rasheed wouldn't deny this meeting. Both Sa'id and Nikki could be called to testify. They could also produce the affidavit Rasheed had signed.

"Yes."

"Isn't it true, sir, that you told Mr. el Khamin and Ms. Moreno that either Charles nor Sarah Reed had ever used drugs?"

"Yes."

"Isn't it also true that you told Mr. el Khamin and Ms. Moreno that ou were tortured by the Muttawa the same night that the Reeds were ortured and Mr. Reed was killed?"

"Objection," said Strobel, this time in a more businesslike voice. The question assumes facts that have never been proven."

Rasheed's translated answer was really a question. "Should I answer it?"

"Yes," said Brad. "The judge will decide later whether to sustain the bjection."

The translator passed on the message. "That's what I told them," aid Rasheed.

"Were you lying when you talked to Mr. el Khamin and Ms. Moreno, or are you lying now?"

"Objection."

"Just answer the question," demanded Brad.

The question, objection, and comment were translated.

"I was lying to them," Rasheed admitted.

"Do you lie when it suits your purposes?" asked Brad.

"Objection."

"Sometimes," Rasheed said through the translator.

It was one of the more truthful answers Rasheed would give on oss-examination. He proved to be a slippery and skillful witness. And the end of two frustrating hours, Brad had still been unable to under- at his testimony. He decided to try one final, desperate question, one al stab at the truth.

"Look me in the eye and tell me that you are not being intimidated threatened by the Saudi Arabian authorities."

"Objection," said Strobel evenly, "but he may answer the question. take this objection up with the judge later."

As he had done all afternoon, Rasheed looked at the translator as he interpreted the question. But this time, rather than look at Brad when answering, Rasheed looked down at the table and muttered his reply.

"No such thing has occurred," said the translator.

"Then I have no further questions," said Brad.

The final image for the jury would be the top of Rasheed's head.

■ ■ ■

Bella cleared everything off her desk except the firm checkbook, the firm ledger, and the huge pile of bills causing her to lose sleep. Her new weekly ritual was to stare at the firm's checking-account balance and then prioritize the bills she could pay. The trial was still three weeks away, and the firm was burning through cash even quicker than Bella thought possible. The firm now operated off a three-hundred-thousand-dollar line of credit that had been drawn down to seventy-five thousand. All Brad's assets were pledged to secure the loan.

She wondered how long it would be until the Johnson settlement check came through. She certainly wasn't about to ask Nikki. Wrapping up these settlements could take weeks, even months, and Brad had admonished her to have no further contact with that file. Every other case with a potential for settlement had been put to bed.

Just in case, as a final contingency plan, Bella ordered twenty-five new credit cards for the firm, each from a different bank. The average credit limit for each card was a little over five thousand. If necessary, these cards could provide another $125,000 of operating income, but at a very steep price in terms of interest rate.

In the meantime, Bella would have to make do. Brad had stopped taking a salary several weeks ago, and that helped. Bella suggested that Nikki should also forego her salary, but Brad wouldn't hear of it.

As she always did, Bella put the bill from Worthington on the bottom of the pile. She couldn't believe he had the audacity to withdraw from the case and then send them a bill for expert services rendered. Bella wouldn't have paid Worthington if she had all the money in the world.

Bella unilaterally decided to cut several "discretionary" items from the firm's budget. Brad belonged to many legal associations but infrequently attended the meetings. Bella decided he wouldn't miss his memberships as long as she intercepted the letters asking him to reconsider his withdrawal. She also decided that legal periodicals Brad never read were a waste of money. No sense killing those trees for nothing. These were the easy calls.

Slightly more difficult was the weekly bill for the office cleaning crew. But even with the crew in full swing, the office looked like a hazardous-waste dump. Besides, Brad, Nikki, and Leslie were all grown-ups and could pick up after themselves. The cleaning crew would be suspended.

The three bills that almost made the final cut but didn't were the ones she would hear about. Carson & Associates not only paid Brad's salary and bonus; it also made his car and boat payments. Brad would be way too busy in the next few months to ever use his boat. As for the cars, she figured she could buy at least ninety days before the repo man paid a visit. With any luck, the trial would be over by then. Bella divided the bills into "pay" and "no pay" piles. She thought about all the money that had flown through the firm in the past twelve years. Until the *Reed* case became the sole focus of the firm, they always had enough cases in the pipeline so that the contingency fees would just keep rolling in, each seemingly bigger than the one before. But that was yesterday's money, and it had already been spent. Now Brad had decided to risk it all on one case, something they had never done before. A foolish gamble. And Bella was not feeling lucky.

As she had so often since Nikki claimed that whopping salary, Bella turned her attention from the firm's bills to her own financial obligations. Only one commitment really concerned her, but it was enormous. As much as she cared for Brad, she would not let his financial indiscretions rob her of her livelihood and her precious mother's care. If she kept at her plan diligently enough, with great care and caution not to misstep, that would never happen.

■ ■ ■

On the flight home from Saudi Arabia, Brad's mind raced with
thoughts of incomplete pretrial tasks, the impact of the depositions, and
his worries about confidential information leaking to the other side.

His thoughts also turned to Leslie often. He had grown accustomed
to seeing her every day and missed her greatly on this week-long trip. He
gave up trying to fool himself into thinking that their relationship was
just professional or that they were merely friends. You didn't think about
a "friend" every second you were away from her. You didn't find yourself
constantly wondering how a "friend" would react to the things you were
doing, or wondering what that "friend" was doing at that very instant.
You didn't spend your time in a strange and exotic land desperately
wishing that your "friend" could be there to share the memories.

Their kiss at The Trellis aside, he wasn't sure Leslie shared his feelings. Brad had dropped repeated hints about the lighthouse painting
but never received a word of thanks. This woman was indeed a mystery.
Was he the only one getting emotionally involved? Was it just the pressure and trauma of the case that sparked an occasional chemistry
between them—and his thoughts now? He didn't know much for sure
except that he missed her smile, her touch. He missed staring at her
when she wasn't looking. He missed the way she made him feel.

He was now three weeks from the biggest trial of his life, wholly
unprepared, and all he could think about was this strange and wonderful
woman who dominated his thoughts. This wasn't friendship; it was love.

There. He had said it, if only to himself. He loved her. It made no
sense, the timing was bad, and she might not love him. But none of that
mattered. This was an issue of the heart, not the head. He loved Leslie
Connors. And he would tell her that and let the chips fall where they
might. As soon as he had a chance. As soon as he got the courage. Brad
Carson, the intrepid trial lawyer, fearless in the courtroom, and a coward
in the game of love. He would tell her.

As soon as the case was over.

■ ■ ■

Back on American soil, as they waited for their connecting flight at Reagan National, Nikki slipped away and called her home answering machine. She had sixteen new messages, an average number for a socialite of her caliber. She skipped through the first twelve, then heard the voice she was hoping to hear. Rasheed Berjein. Sounds of vehicles punctuated the background. Rasheed was on a pay phone.

He softly but distinctly repeated a phrase in Arabic, then hung up. Nikki was not fluent in the language, but she had learned a few phrases during her trips to the Kingdom. She and Rasheed had agreed that they would use this one as the code.

"Everything is fine," he had said.

"Thanks be to Allah," Nikki mumbled sarcastically. She smiled and holstered the cell phone without finishing her messages.

24

————

Ahmed arrived at Norfolk General District Court, Traffic Division
ahead of schedule, at precisely 8:30 A.M. He passed through the
metal detectors without event, turned left down the hallway, and located
Courtroom Number 2, one of two traffic courtrooms in the building.
Ahmed sat in the second row and watched the parade of American
reprobates arriving for their day in court.

Ahmed's instincts told him to be leery of a setup, but reason told
him he had already gained too much advantageous information for this
to be a sting. Still, he would feel better once he met the informant and
gained some insight into motive.

Within a few minutes of one another, three of Barnes' best operatives took their spots in the courtroom. The first was a twenty-six-year-
old in oversized baggy jeans, a ratty T-shirt, lots of jewelry, and at least
two earrings. His keys and wallet were attached to his belt by a chain.
He took a seat directly behind Ahmed. The second posed in the front of
the courtroom as a washed-up attorney in a pair of frayed dress slacks,
stained red tie, matching suspenders, and an ill-fitting sports coat. A
third man, a middle-aged investigator with no distinguishable features
who could blend into any crowd, stood on the other side of the courtroom.

■ ■ ■

The informant entered the doors of the General District Court at 9:50,
fashionably late. She cleared the metal detectors and went straight into
the women's rest room. She leaned forward over the sink and looked
closely at her face in the mirror, giving herself a little pep talk, calming

her nerves. She washed her hands in hot water, vigorously rubbing them together and drying them roughly on the paper towels. Still ice-cold. She determined not to shake hands with Ahmed.

She walked slowly into the courtroom, eyes darting around the gallery, taking in every look, every movement, evaluating every person for whether they belonged. She had spent enough time here recently to know the lawyers, the court personnel, and the rhythm of the General District Court—who belonged and who didn't. She clung to a small leather briefcase with both hands. She walked deliberately to the second row and sat down next to Ahmed.

He stared impassively ahead. "You?" he hissed.

She ignored the comment. "I told you to come alone," she whispered, her voice hoarse with emotion.

"I did," Ahmed said calmly.

This whole meeting was high risk, but she had to raise the stakes. Ahmed seemed so at ease, so in control. She had to do something to rattle him. These first few minutes were critical.

"Just behind the counsel table on the left," she nodded toward a lawyer seated there. "Partially bald. Red tie. Red suspenders." She had never seen him in this courtroom before even though the same lawyers seemed to show up every day. Plus, he had only a few manila folders in his hand, each representing a separate case, and no traffic court lawyer could survive on such meager volume. In General District Courtroom Number 2, the lawyers handled cases by the truckload. The other lawyers had manila folders everywhere.

She stood to leave. "He's one of yours," she whispered. "The meeting's off."

Ahmed grabbed her forearm with thick fingers and jerked her back into her seat. The uninhibited force of it, right there in the middle of General District Court, made her tremble.

"Impressive," he hissed. Then he released her arm. "I'll send my men out."

Ahmed turned and nodded to the man sitting directly behind them.

"Leave. And take your friend with you." Ahmed nodded toward the man at the front table. The informant kept her gaze straight ahead, watching in silence as the men left.

She felt her heart pounding in her throat, each beat ringing in her ears. Goose bumps, clammy skin, her stomach in knots, the works. But still, she willed herself to relax—deep breaths, stone-cold face, deliberate movements. Who would take control? Who would blink first? Who would flinch from the task before them?

"If you ever try that again," she whispered, her voice steady now, "the whole deal's off. I deal with you. No intermediaries. No extras."

Out of the corner of her eye, she could see Ahmed swallow hard. He'd better get used to taking orders from a woman.

"Did you bring the transmitters?" she asked.

Ahmed held them out in his unwavering right hand. She took them, taking care not to touch his skin. She placed them in her briefcase.

"These are magnetic, just attach them to any metal surface," he explained, his voice barely audible. "They operate off shortwave radio technology and send a coded signal to a receiver."

He turned to look directly at her. She froze, then inhaled evenly. "I don't actually believe these are necessary," Ahmed said. "Do you really think that we couldn't have done this ourselves if we wanted to?"

Though Ahmed looked straight at her, straight through her, she kept her eyes pinned on the front of the courtroom. "I will attach them to the three main telephones," she said through clenched teeth. "Carson sweeps for bugs at the same time every day. I'll attach them after those sweeps and take them off at night."

She was ready to bolt. This man, inches away, penetrating her with his eyes and sickening her with his putrid breath, was almost more than she could take. She had accomplished her purpose for this meeting. Why wait?

"How do you plan to take out Shelhorse?" he asked.

"It is enough that you know it will be done. I'll contact you with our next meeting time and place. If you try to follow me or in any way contact me, we're through."

With that parting instruction she stood, glanced down at him— stared at him—as she hovered there for a moment, then walked quickly from the courtroom. She rushed past the metal detector and out the doors, anxious to fill her lungs with some fresh air. She glanced around, consumed by the suspicious looks of dozens of strangers, each a potential accomplice to Ahmed. She resisted the urge to run or scream or dart into some crowd and slip into some back alley.

What good would it do? They knew who she was now. The game was on. Her only hope was to stay one step ahead.

■ ■ ■

Later that day, Brad gathered his team in the main conference room, which Nikki had appropriately dubbed "the war room." It looked like Sherman had ransacked the place on his March to the Sea, leaving behind papers, deposition transcripts, folder files, empty cups, paper plates, and dirty napkins.

In the vortex of the mess, Nikki sat in one chair with her legs up on another, papers spread across her lap, the table, and the floor around her. Nikki's three Diet Coke cans, all partially full of flat soda, probably from yesterday, sat together on a paper sign that Bella had taped to the wall a week prior: "Your mother doesn't work here, so please clean up your own mess." Nikki had redeemed the stained sign from the floor, where it eventually fell, and now used it as a large coaster.

Leslie walked into the war room and cleaned off a portion of the table, stacking the clutter in a neat out-of-the-way pile. Next to her, Nikki spread out a stack of what looked like surveys. The corner of one drifted across an invisible boundary line. Leslie lifted an eyebrow, and without looking at Nikki, she pushed the page out of her way.

The clutter of the conference room was exacerbated on this evening, one week prior to trial, by large sheets of poster paper taped to the walls with the names of the first fifty jurors from the jury list scrawled across the top. As this was a civil case, the jury would ultimately consist of seven jurors, plus alternates. In Brad's experience, it could take up to fifty prospective jurors in a high-profile case like this one just to find the seven who would be qualified to serve. Brad stood next to a sheet titled "Model Juror Profile" and facilitated a discussion on desirable juror characteristics.

"Male or female?" he asked.

"Definitely female," said Leslie, making a neat notation on the legal pad in front of her. "Women will appreciate what it means to lose a husband and raise kids alone."

"I agree," said Nikki. "Plus they're smarter."

Bella grunted her approval, making it unanimous among the female team members. The Rock, of course, had not been invited to the meeting.

"White, African American, Hispanic, or Asian American?" asked Brad, rattling off the predominate ethnic groups he expected to see on the panel.

"Definitely black," decided Bella. She constantly had trouble remembering that Brad preferred she use the term "African American." "They'll have a natural distrust of the police and authority figures. They'll hate Ahmed. Besides, look at the good rulings we've already gotten from Judge Johnson."

"Hispanics have attitude too," claimed Nikki. "We just need jurors with attitude."

Leslie furrowed her brow and stopped writing. "Can we even ask this question? Isn't discrimination while choosing jurors prohibited by the *Batson* case?"

"Technically, yes," said Brad. "But we're not discriminating here against minority groups, we're actually expressing a preference for them as jurors. Kind of like our own little affirmative action program."

Leslie frowned. "That's weak, Brad Carson, and you know it."

"Ex-cuuuse us," said Nikki. "Where did that attitude come from?"

Leslie ignored the question, and Brad decided he'd better move on. The chemistry among the women was fragile at best.

"All right, let's move off that point," Brad suggested. "How old is our model juror?"

"Young." It was Nikki again. "The old geezers will trust the police and not want to rock the boat."

Nobody else spoke. Brad took that as consent. He wrote it down.

"Religion?"

"Thought you would never ask—" began Nikki.

"Wait. We can't ask that either, can we?" Leslie's furrowed brow was back, this time combined with a disapproving twist of the head.

"Under *Batson,* we probably can't use our preemptory strikes on the basis of religion," Brad conceded. "But in this case, because it's so uniquely religious in nature, maybe we can get the judge to strike some jurors for cause based on their religion."

"Whatever," said Nikki, dismissing the legal niceties with a flip of her hand. "We've got to have fired-up, hard-core Christians on this jury. No Muslims. No atheists. No lukewarm fence-sitters. We've got to have real Bible-thumpers. Hellfire-and-brimstone types."

They pooled opinions and justified their hunches for an hour. When they were done, Brad stood back and admired the profile of his dream juror: a young African American or Hispanic single mother with strong evangelical Christian beliefs, lower-income bracket preferred, and someone with at least one attempt at suing for personal injuries in the past. *Fat chance,* he thought.

Next they would rate the individual jurors on a scale of one to ten so the process would have at least the appearance of scientific exactitude. They all agreed that Brad would have the ability to change the ratings once they started questioning the jurors in court, but this would at least give him a starting point.

They came to a stalemate on the first juror, a single mother of two. Leslie gave her a five, Bella a two, Brad a seven, and Nikki a ten. Brad did the simple math, assigned juror number 1 a six, and then moved on to the second of the fifty jurors. It was getting late.

But Nikki was shaking her head. "Trust me on this one guys, she's a ten. If you get a chance, you've got to have her on your jury."

"C'mon Nikki," Brad groaned. "You had your vote. We'll be here all night if we all lobby for our favorite ones."

"Brad, I know what I'm talking about. Trust me."

"It's not a matter of trust," Leslie broke in. "It's a matter of fairness. We each get one vote, and then Brad can make whatever adjustments he wants at trial. We don't really have much to go on anyway. We don't even know what her race or religion is."

"What if I told you she faithfully attends an independent church named Grace Chapel and goes on at least one volunteer mission trip every year? What if I told you she seriously believes that everyone needs to hear about Jesus Christ? What if I could guarantee you she is a die-hard supporter of all mission causes?"

"I'd change my score," admitted Leslie. "But how could you possibly know all that stuff?"

The looks on the faces of the others confirmed that they were all thinking the same thing. Brad was chewing on his glasses and raised an eyebrow at Nikki.

"Well?" he asked.

"Let's just say I have inside information on thirty-six of these fifty jurors," said Nikki, almost in a whisper. Brad started to say something, but Nikki lifted her hand to silence him. "I know the rules, Brad. No direct contact with prospective jurors. Don't ask how I got this information, but it's all legit. For most of these jurors, I can tell you more about their religious beliefs than their own mothers know."

Brad stared at Nikki in silence, searching her face for clues. They stood on thin ethical ice. He wanted this information—no, he needed this information. Desperately. But at what price?

"Are you sure you didn't contact any jurors?"

"No way."

"You sure it's all legal?"

"You bet."

He studied her for another moment, and she still didn't flinch.

"All right, then I change my vote to a ten," Brad said.

"Me too," said Bella.

"I'm staying with a five," said Leslie. "I don't trust any source that is unknown and cannot be tested."

Nikki rolled her eyes.

"Juror 1 gets a nine," Brad announced, crossing through the old score on the poster sheet.

And so it went, juror by juror, Nikki providing her mysterious insights and the group arriving at a judgment. At a quarter till one, the exhausted crew considered juror number 50. They had abandoned extended discussion long before.

"You got any inside information on this one?" asked Brad.

"Yep," said Nikki. "I give him an eight."

"Me too, then," said Brad.

"Count me in," said Bella.

"Four," said Leslie.

"Juror 50 gets a seven," said Brad. "And I'm going home."

■ ■ ■

The tired crew all filed out to the parking lot and dragged their weary bodies into their cars to head home. Nikki hadn't been driving five minutes when the phone rang.

"It's me," Bella said gruffly from the other end. "What's the deal with these jurors?"

Nikki was amazed Bella would even call. But tonight Bella had voted with Nikki, not against her. Maybe it was Bella's way of reaching out for some middle ground. Nikki knew she could never expect a full apology, but she was willing to meet Bella halfway. After all, Bella had called her; Willy had made the first step.

"Promise not to tell Brad?"

"Yeah."

"Okay. Well, the first thing I did was to send out a religious survey to each juror and all their neighbors. I didn't send the letter in my name, so I was telling Brad the truth when I said I didn't contact any jurors. The letter said it was on behalf of a new church that was going to start a service in Tidewater. It asked about the juror's religious beliefs in general, where they attended church, and whether they would want to join a church that was 100 percent committed to mission work and taking the gospel to the whole world. Most jurors didn't send the survey back, though some did. For those we didn't hear from, I had the Rock call them and ask those questions. There were still a few we just never reached, or they refused to answer the questions."

Nikki's explanation was followed by silence. Nikki knew that Bella was impressed but would try hard not to show it. She second-guessed herself for telling Bella and figured that Bella would say something to Brad first thing in the morning.

"I figured it was something like that," Bella said.

"Haven't you guys ever done this type of thing on your cases?" Nikki asked.

"Oh sure, we just don't like to talk about it."

Right.

"Gotta go," Bella said with her usual diplomacy. Before Nikki could respond, Bella hung up.

Nikki found herself wondering how Brad's firm ever won a case when he obviously invested no time in the investigation of jurors.

"He must be good on his feet," she mumbled to herself as she gunned the engine of her Sebring. She was just a few short days from finding out.

Part IV

■

THE TRIAL

The sun smiled brightly on the brisk October morning that greeted the first day of the trial. A cool northern breeze gently buffeted Norfolk and chased a few puffy white clouds quickly across the sky. A perfect day for protesting.

The demonstrators started arriving at 7:30 and arranged themselves neatly on the sidewalk in front of the massive stone federal building on Granby Street. On one side of the courthouse steps, and stretching down the sidewalk, were about 150 Christians from every walk of life led by the Reverend Jacob Bailey and a loyal band of prayer warriors.

While Reverend Bailey and his team prayed, others turned the vigil into a picnic, enjoying coffee and doughnuts and all sorts of other fast-food breakfast treats. They did have a few signs, mostly quoting Bible verses like John 3:16 or urging the court to "Stop the Torture." And, at precisely 8 A.M., when the national morning news audiences peaked, they all stopped eating and joined Reverend Bailey in spontaneous prayer for persecuted Christians everywhere.

On the other side of the steps was a group of about eighty Muslims, there to support the freedom of the Saudi people to choose their own religion, free from Western interference. These protesters stayed entertained by a barrage of rhetoric from a small group of fiery leaders. Occasionally, they would break into chants, goading the more docile protesters on the other side of the steps. The press congregated with the Muslims, who tended to give more passionate interviews that lent themselves to better sound bites.

Not fitting into either group, but determined to exercise their First Amendment rights on such an important occasion, were a handful of miscellaneous protesters representing a half-dozen other causes. By far the most colorful of the bunch was the gentleman in a well-worn, bright-yellow chicken suit carrying a sign that read "Jesus was a vegetarian." Most assumed he was with the People for the Ethical Treatment of Animals, and everyone gave him plenty of space as he roamed the sidewalks, goose-stepping so that he would not trip over his own large webbed feet.

As usual, the media seemed to outnumber the folks they were covering, and the reporters had the best seats in the house. Cameramen, talking heads, and a bevy of print reporters dominated the sidewalk directly in front of the courthouse. Local and national news trucks, with satellite dishes on top, jammed the streets.

At precisely 8:30, a black stretch limo arrived in front of the courthouse steps carrying Ahmed Aberijan and Frederick Barnes. Barnes parted the way for his infamous cohort, and Ahmed looked perplexed at all the English-speaking journalists who shoved microphones under his nose and shouted questions.

Mack Strobel, Winsted Mackenzie, and several of their partners arrived next, each carrying only one small briefcase. The associates from Kilgore & Strobel had already hauled neatly numbered boxes of documents and exhibits into the courtroom. Mackenzie stopped at the top of the steps for an impromptu press conference. Mack and the others stood and watched for a moment, unsmiling, then slipped into the courthouse.

"Will the defense claim that Dr. and Mrs. Reed were drug dealers?"

"We won't just claim it, we'll prove it."

"Will anyone from the Saudi Arabian government testify, such as the crown prince?"

"Mr. Aberijan will testify. There will be no need for others."

And on it went, endless questions and answers. Mackenzie willingly obliged the media with regard to any question, regardless of how trivial, as long as the cameras were rolling.

■ ■ ■

At 8:45, Win lost his audience when Sarah Reed's team made its appearance. Unlike the chauffeured defense team, they parked two blocks from the courthouse and carted large briefcases and boxed documents up the street with them. Bella cleared the way and took no prisoners. Sarah walked between Leslie and Nikki.

As the only male in the group, Brad felt obligated to bring up the rear and pull the heavy dolly containing three large boxes of documents that would not fit into the briefcases. He struggled mightily as he yanked the dolly up the courthouse steps, feeling like a clumsy errand boy and not at all like a top-rate legal eagle prepared to handle a major case.

True to Murphy's Law, as he reached the second to last step, the top box wiggled out from under the bungee cord holding it in place and fell hard on the steps, regurgitating pleadings, exhibits, and deposition transcripts at the feet of the startled press corps.

What a way to make an impression on the morning news!

Brad smiled sheepishly and muttered the first thing that came into his mind: "Better not quit my day job." It sounded stupid, and he immediately wished he could take it back.

And then, to Brad's astonishment, he watched as reporters, cameramen, and protesters all leaned down to scoop up the documents and place them back into the miscreant box. Brad thanked them with a brief press conference, then carefully, ever so carefully, wheeled his documents into the courthouse and passed them through the metal detector.

He caught up with the rest of the team in the elevator and immediately noticed that the color was gone from Leslie's face.

"What's the matter?" he asked, out of breath from his work as the team's pack mule.

"We're in Courtroom Number 1," whispered Leslie, "the Honorable Cynthia Baker-Kline presiding."

■ ■ ■

A hush fell over the spacious courtroom on the second floor of the court building as everyone rose to their feet. Judge Cynthia Baker-Kline entered through a large oak door several feet behind her bench, her long black robe flowing behind her. Her fury was evident in the speed of her stride, the pursing of her lips, and the slits of her eyes. She arrived at the bench, glowered at Brad, then turned her stare to those standing across the back of the crowded courtroom. The nostrils on her long nose moved quickly in and out, like a bull preparing for the charge.

Ichabod was firmly in control.

"Oyez, oyez, oyez. Silence is now commanded while this honorable court is in session. All those with pleas to enter and matters to be argued step forward, and you shall be heard. May God save the United States of America and this honorable court."

"May God save us all," Brad muttered quietly to himself.

"May God grant us wisdom and allow us to glorify Him," Brad heard Sarah whisper.

"You may be seated," Ichabod snarled.

She leaned forward and glared down at counsel.

"Gentlemen," she barked, "I am about to bring in the jury panel so that we can begin the selection process. This is an important case, and the world is watching." She turned directly to Brad, narrowing her eyes. "I'll expect you both to comport yourselves like officers of the court."

A warning shot across the bow.

Brad nodded with all the solemnity he could muster.

■ ■ ■

"I do have a few questions for Mr. Robertson, Your Honor." Strobel rose confidently and approached the jury box to question juror number 3, the first Baptist to be interviewed. Strobel straightened to his full height, buttoned the top button on his blue pinstriped suit, and began by graciously introducing himself and his client. Even Brad had to admit that Strobel cut an imposing figure, authority oozing from every pore.

He stood directly in front of juror number 3, just a few feet from the jury box, thereby blocking Brad's view of the nervous juror. Brad assumed the block was intentional and slouched to his left in his chair so he could watch the juror's face.

"Are you a regular churchgoin' man?" asked Strobel in his best common man's vernacular. He undoubtedly knew the answer. So did Brad. According to Nikki, juror number 3 was a faithful member of Sandbridge Baptist Church. He had scored an eight on Brad's scale.

"Yes sir, I try to be," admitted Robertson, looking sheepish.

"Where do you attend?"

"Sandbridge Baptist Church on Shore Drive."

"That church is pretty committed to mission work, isn't it?" Strobel said it like he'd heard of the church before.

"Yes sir, it is."

"And, as a Baptist church, your congregation contributes to the Cooperative Program, which in turn helps support Baptist missionaries all over the world. Isn't that the way it works?"

Robertson appeared perplexed, his face flushed. He probably didn't have a clue how his church did its mission work. But how could he admit that to some pagan big-city lawyer?

"I...s-suppose that's pretty much the way it works," Robertson stammered.

"So, in a very real way, you and your church help to financially support every Baptist missionary who's sent out, correct?"

"I... I guess so."

"Well, do you give money to the church?"

"Oh, yes sir. Baptists are taught to tithe."

"And does some of that money go to the Cooperative Program?"

"That's my understanding."

"And missionary salaries are paid in part from the Cooperative Program?"

"I believe that's correct."

"And, by the way, you also pray for these Baptist missionaries almost every day, don't you?"

A pained expression jumped on Mr. Robertson's face before he could suppress it. Brad could tell the poor guy probably didn't know the name of a single Baptist missionary and certainly hadn't thought to pray for them in quite some time.

"Probably not as much as I should, but I try."

Brad decided it was time to make some friends on the jury panel.

"I object, Your Honor," Brad said loudly. "Mr. Robertson isn't on trial here."

Strobel turned on his heels and gave Brad one of his steel-melting stares.

"You can't object to a question about the juror's background," Ichabod said. "Overruled."

Brad looked past Strobel and into the eyes of Robertson, sensing he had made a friend.

Strobel turned back to the juror. "Thank you, Mr. Robertson, for your honesty in answering these questions." Strobel then turned to the judge. "May we approach the bench, Your Honor?"

Ichabod nodded.

Strobel and three lawyers from his firm huddled in front of Ichabod's bench, as did Brad and Leslie.

"I move to strike juror 3 for cause," whispered Strobel. "The man has a financial and emotional stake in missionaries all over the world. How could he possibly be unbiased?"

"I could see that coming from a mile away," Ichabod replied. "Any objections, Mr. Carson?"

"Of course I object, Judge. Striking this juror for a religious reason violates the principles set forth by the U.S. Supreme Court in *Batson*."

"I'm not asking the court to strike him because he's Baptist," whispered Strobel. "Sarah Reed's not Baptist. But through his church, this juror gives his hard-earned dollars to missionaries all over the world who are similar to Sarah Reed. Asking him to ignore that would be impossible."

"Can't I at least ask him some questions to prove he can be fair?" Brad raised his voice so the jury could hear. He wanted the panel to know he trusted their ability to be fair and that his opponent was secretly trying to get them dismissed.

"Keep your voice down," insisted Ichabod in a loud whisper. She gave Brad a chastising look, then lowered her own voice. "Now, we have several well-qualified jurors on this panel. Some are probably Christian, some are probably Muslim, and some probably put their faith in their morning coffee. That makes no difference to me. But I'm not going to allow someone to poison the panel when I see a potential bias, no matter how tenuous, in favor of one of the parties in this case."

Brad opened his mouth to argue the point, but he was stopped by the judge's outstretched hand. "I've ruled, Mr. Carson. If you don't like my ruling, you can take it up with the appeals court when this case is over. Now, counsel may return to their seats."

The other lawyers turned and walked away. Brad lingered and stared at the judge momentarily. Then he shook his head and slowly sulked back to his seat.

"Mr. Robertson, you are excused from service," announced Ichabod. "Thank you for your time and forthright answers. You are free to go."

■ ■ ■

At the end of the second day, Judge Baker-Kline swore in the jury charged with deciding the case of *Reed v. Ahmed Aberijan and Eight John Does*. Because of the procedural peculiarities of the Foreign Sovereign Immunities Act, Judge Baker-Kline herself would simultaneously render a verdict in the case of *Reed v. Saudi Arabia*.

Brad surveyed his jury—the jury that would decide the most important case of his career—with a growing sense of despondency. His model juror was nowhere to be found. One by one, Strobel had knocked out all the self-confessed mission supporters for cause. Then, with his preemptory challenges, Strobel eliminated three more jurors who had scored high on Brad's rating scale, including two churchgoing ethnics who had each earned a nine.

Of the seven jurors who would actually decide the case, there were only two minorities. One was an African American male who had not seen the inside of a church in years. The other was a female Hispanic who claimed to be Catholic but had trouble remembering the name of her church.

One Muslim left on the panel would serve as the first alternate. Despite Nikki's urgings to the contrary, Brad had refused to strike him. Any grounds for appeal based on Strobel's religiously discriminatory strikes would be worthless if Brad engaged in the same type of conduct.

As he prepared to leave the courtroom after the second day of jury selection, Brad studied the jury and alternates one last time, then glanced sideways at his client. Sarah the single mom, Sarah the missionary, Sarah the on-fire evangelical Christian was about to have her case judged by a jury of her "peers" that contained six men and three women, and only one person who looked even remotely like her. And that juror sat at the end of the last row, where she would view the trial as the second alternate.

■ ■ ■

Strobel regarded this jury as a coup. He had eliminated almost all of the Holy Rollers and outspoken minorities. He had a bad feeling about juror number 4, but Ahmed had been adamant that juror 4 be left on the jury. In the huddle around the counsel table, Ahmed, through a translator, said he had inside information about the juror that could not be shared with the legal team. Whatever else Strobel did, it was imperative that he leave juror number 4 securely in place.

■ ■ ■

The protesters were out with a passion at the end of day two. Despite the steady drizzle, the ranks of the Christians had swelled to several hundred. News that the defendants were striking evangelicals right and left had ignited the sidewalks. Now outspoken pastors matched the fiery speeches given by Muslim leaders. As the crowd noise and fervency grew, the Reverend Bailey and his band of prayer warriors moved a half-block away so that they could petition God in relative solitude.

Unlike the calm that greeted the participants as they exited the courthouse after the first day, the respective crowds erupted in cheers as their favorites emerged on day two. Even Bella had to smile as the Christian demonstrators assured Sarah she was in their prayers.

The escalating tensions delighted the man in the chicken suit, a veteran of many high-profile trials. He predicted that soon T-shirt vendors and other hawkers would start selling paraphernalia for both sides. A fight or two would likely break out, especially if the right-wing Christian militia groups could be enticed to enter the fray. It promised to be an exciting month on the sidewalks of Granby Street.

———

"Sarah, you're ready," Leslie pronounced. "The main thing now is t get some sleep."

They had been at it four straight hours, from 6:30 to 10:30, usin a clean end of the conference table as a makeshift witness stand. Lesli popped questions, Sarah responded, then Leslie critiqued Sarah's re sponses. Sarah's willingness to accept the criticism and carefully respon with another variation of the same basic answer amazed Leslie.

"Are you sure?" Sarah still sounded unconvinced. "Can't we g through the events on the night of Charles' death one more time?"

"Sarah, we've been through it three times already. If we do it agai it will sound like you've memorized it."

"If you say so."

"I do."

Leslie stifled a yawn and started packing her notes. The adrenalin from another day in court had long since seeped out of her body, takin every ounce of her energy with it.

"Leslie, I want you to level with me, okay?" Sarah looked up an waited for a promise.

"Sure."

"How bad are the judge and jury we ended up with?"

The frankness of Sarah's question caused Leslie to stop packing an look straight at her. Sarah's eyes, her most prominent and becoming fe ture, were bloodshot, the lids heavy, the wrinkles underneath more pr nounced than when Leslie first met her. In fact, Sarah's whole face w drawn and gaunt, her clothes now seemed to hang on her frail fram She looked so very fragile. Her husband's death, the posttraumatic stres the strain of being a single mom, and the pressure of the case had all taken a considerable toll.

Through it all, Sarah had remained stoic and determined. And Leslie had never sensed that she wavered in her optimistic faith. Until this moment.

"The jury's pretty bad," Leslie said. "The judge is worse." She wondered how much more Sarah could endure.

"I thought so," Sarah said softly.

They looked at each other in silence.

"Go home!" Brad shouted as he burst through the door.

Leslie jumped and grabbed at her heart. To her surprise, it was still beating.

Brad laughed. "This is a marathon, not a sprint. My star witness and my star co-counsel better get some sleep."

Brad's exuberance instantly lifted Leslie's spirits. But she couldn't let him know he had the power to alter her mood so easily.

"What are you so happy about, cowboy?" she deadpanned. "Did you go to the same trial we did today?"

"Yes, and we sandbagged 'em beautifully." Brad strutted around the room. "Strobel is probably out getting drunk and celebrating, and here we are working our tails off. They're overconfident. It's working."

"Yeah, and you've got the judge wrapped around your little finger," mocked Leslie.

"Mr. Strobel," she continued, taking on the tone and air of Ichabod, "do you have any other jurors you would like to get rid of so that I can watch your opposing counsel squirm and squeal like a boiled lobster?"

Brad twisted his face and contorted his body, doing a pitiful imitation of a boiling lobster. They all laughed.

He stopped suddenly. "Sarah, I thought I told you to keep her out of the sauce," he said. "Go home, that's an order. You're both getting a little punchy."

"Us?!" the women said in unison. But Brad was already halfway out the door, in full retreat. Leslie looked at Sarah and shook her head.

"What got into him?" Leslie wondered.

"Whatever it is, I want some of it," said Sarah. "I love that guy." She said it without the least bit of embarrassment, and apparently without even thinking about anything more than a fraternal attraction. "I'm so glad he's on my side."

"Mmm," muttered Leslie. She didn't understand the way Sarah spoke so casually of loving somebody. Leslie's own feelings for Brad went way beyond the "he's a great guy" attitude of Sarah, but she didn't dare call it love.

Then what was it, exactly? She had this longing to be with him. All the time. She came alive when he walked into the room, especially when he touched her. She studied his every move, loved the sound of his voice, every word. If this wasn't love…

Whatever it was, it scared her.

Her emotions had begun to decimate every detail of her life's plan that she had so carefully, so logically, constructed during the past two years. She needed advice.

"Sarah, do you think you'll ever remarry?" she asked before she realized she had verbalized the question.

Sarah's countenance fell. She sank back into her chair as if she couldn't will herself to remain standing. She had just answered dozens of questions about Charles and how much she missed him. But this unscripted query seemed to hit her so much harder.

"There will never be another Charles," Sarah said simply. "People tell me God has someone special for me—maybe not the same as Charles, but just as right for me. I smile and I nod, but I don't believe it. They didn't know Charles the way I did. Otherwise, they wouldn't say such things."

"Do you think it would be wrong to remarry? I mean, in the sense that it would somehow cheapen Charles' memory?"

"Heavens, no," Sarah exclaimed. "In fact, I believe Charles would want me to remarry. He's probably up in heaven right now saying, 'Sarah, have you thought about Richard?' or 'Sarah, Joe would make a great father for our kids; he's such a nice guy.'" Sarah smiled knowingly and sighed a beleaguered sigh. "It's just that I can't imagine ever loving someone as much as I loved Charles. But Leslie, it's only been a year. If I do meet the right man, I'll know. And if my heart says go for it, I'll go for it."

Leslie knew Sarah discerned the real reason for the question. "That sounded more like a pep talk than an answer."

Sarah reached over and put her hand on Leslie's. "I'd have to be blind not to see the chemistry between you and Brad," she said softly. "Trust your heart, Sarah. Bill would tell you the same thing if he could."

■ ■ ■

After chasing the women from the office, Brad polished up his opening statement and headed home. He arrived after midnight.

He had a good feeling about this opening. And a good feeling about Sarah as his first witness. Tomorrow, the momentum would shift. Tomorrow would be a good day for the good guys.

Brad kicked off his shoes and threw the morning paper and un-opened mail onto the kitchen counter, where it joined a pile of other unread papers and unopened mail. He slung his coat over a chair, loos-ened his tie, and went straight for the refrigerator. He chugged some 2 percent milk from a half-gallon jug. It had that tart taste of milk one day short of being sour, or maybe one day past. He made a face at the aftertaste, then twisted the top back on the jug and placed it back in the refrigerator. As he headed for the stairs, he noticed the red blinking light on his answering machine and punched in the code.

Four new messages.

"Brad, Jimmy Hartley here. Look, I know you're in the middle of a trial, but I've got to see at least some interest payments on the car loans and home equity line. I tried to call at work but—"

Brad hit star seven, and the message was gone. Bella would handle this. He made a mental note to remind her.

The next three messages were from Leslie. Strange that she would call the house instead of his cell phone. Leslie's first message came at 10:45 P.M. From the background noise, she was calling from her car.

"Brad, Sarah is ready. I mean…really ready. Direct exam will take about four hours. I'd like to talk about a couple of tricky areas at lunch tomorrow, or if it's not too late when you get this message, just give me a call. I didn't want to talk strategy in front of Sarah. She's nervous enough as it is."

The second message came five minutes later.

"By the way, Brad, I'm still concerned about the possibility of our office being bugged. I know we aren't using the office phones for anything confidential, but we are preparing witnesses in the war room. Is there any way we could get O'Malley to check for bugs at different times during the day? He always checks first thing in the morning, and if someone is taking the time and effort to bug our offices, they'd surely notice the pattern. Call me paranoid, but I'd feel better if he would check both in the morning and at some unpredictable time in the afternoon. Thanks."

There was a brief pause, and Leslie concluded, her voice uncertain. "And call me if it's not too late."

The third message, logged in nearly an hour after the first two, proved that Leslie was ignoring Brad's admonition to sleep.

"Brad, sorry to leave this on your answering machine, but it seems like we never get a chance to talk together…alone." Leslie's voice was tentative and so quiet that Brad pressed the phone harder against his ear. "And when we do…well, I've tried to say this a hundred times but never got it out. Brad, I know what you said about waiting until the case was over to, um, see where we stand. But that seems like such a long time from now and, well, I was just…um," after a noticeable pause the words rushed out in a torrent, "wondering if we could try to maybe start over again this weekend. Like maybe Friday night. Well, if that works for you, just let me know. If not, you don't need to say anything…and I'll understand. If you'd rather just wait until the case is over…um, that's okay too."

A short beep signaled that Leslie was almost out of time for her message. Her voice continued at an even more rapid clip.

"Anyway, I didn't mean to ramble on. Just thought you might want a distraction this weekend after staring at the lovely Ichabod all week."

Brad checked his watch. It was 12:45, probably too late to call. The first two days of trial had been tough and unproductive. But his instincts were right. The third day would be a charm. And it had just gotten off to a rip-roaring start.

M ay it please the court," Brad nodded toward Ichabod as he began his opening. He stood and moved with measured steps around the podium toward the jury box, buttoning his suit coat, and starting the timer on his wristwatch along the way. He half expected Ichabod to make him retreat to the podium. But he also knew she wouldn't want to jump on his case right away, for fear of alienating the jury.

He carried no notes or other distractions to occupy his hands. He wanted to have a little family chat, lawyer-to-jury, common allies in the search for truth. He moved as close to the jury box as possible without encroaching on the jurors' space. He stopped and made eye contact with each. He knew this first sentence was key. He had worked so hard to capture the essence of the whole case in the first few phrases that came out of his mouth.

"Ladies and gentlemen," he began in soft, confident tones. "This is the case of the lions and the saints. The persecution, torture, and abuse that is this very moment being inflicted on Christians around the world is both frightening and appalling. It is every bit as vicious and grotesque as when the first-century Romans marched the first-century saints into the Coliseum, cut them to watch them bleed, and cheered as the bodies of the Christians were shredded by starving lions. Many of the twenty-first-century victims, like Sarah Reed, have suffered similar fates. Many of the twenty-first-century victims, like Sarah Reed, have seen loved ones tortured and killed. And many of the twenty-first-century victims, like Sarah Reed, are U.S. citizens and deserve the protection of U.S. courts."

Brad delivered these words in a near whisper, and the entire court-room seemed to grow even quieter as he spoke. He knew those in the back of the courtroom probably couldn't hear, and he didn't care. It was the jury, and only the jury, that formed his audience. This was their case now, and they listened intently, nearly holding their collective breath. Brad paused, surveyed every face again, and started pacing to put them more at ease.

He raised his voice a notch and empowered them.

"You now have the collective power to end the madness. Like no jury before you, you can send a message that will be heard by every dictator and abusive ruler around the globe. You, and you alone, can strike a blow for religious freedom everywhere and for everyone. What you decide in this case can protect the Buddhist and the Baptist, the Muslim and the Methodist. It can protect those in Africa and America, in Sudan, and, yes, in Saudi Arabia. You, and you alone, can shut down this modern-day Coliseum."

Strobel was on his feet. "I *object!*" he bellowed. "Your Honor, I'm sorry. I hate to object during opening statements, but openings are supposed to be a preview of the evidence, not a sermon about human rights and worldwide—"

"Agreed," said Ichabod.

Brad checked his watch. A minute and thirty-five seconds. Strobel had disappointed him. Brad put five bucks on Strobel's objecting within thirty seconds. Nikki said less than a minute. Bella said ninety seconds based on tactical reasons, and Brad noticed Bella's "I told you so" grin out of the corner of his eye.

"Mr. Carson, please confine your opening to a preview of the evidence, not a stump speech. I will not have you turn this courtroom into a circus. And furthermore, please continue your opening statement from behind the podium."

"Yes, Your Honor."

Brad hid a smile and retreated to the podium. He not only anticipated the objection; he had instigated it. He wanted the jury to see him as a champion for justice, as the advocate for not just Sarah Reed but for persecuted persons everywhere. He wanted the jury to hear Strobel object, to see Strobel try to avoid the broader issues on everyone's mind, to sense that Strobel was trying to keep something from them.

Brad grabbed both sides of the podium and switched gears. The family chat through, he transformed into an evangelist for justice. The folks in the back row would have no trouble hearing this next bit.

"We will prove that this man," and here he pointed directly at Ahmed Aberijan, "is the ruthless and repressive leader of Saudi Arabia's religious police, a group called the Muttawa. We will prove that he learned about Charles and Sarah Reed and their young children, missionaries to Saudi Arabia, who were reaching out to the people of Saudi Arabia with the love of Jesus Christ.

"We will prove that this man, Ahmed Aberijan, masterminded a raid on the Reeds' small apartment for the sole purpose of torturing and humiliating the Reeds and learning the name of every church member, as well as leaders of other churches, so that he could terrorize and torture them as well. When Charles and Sarah Reed refused to give in to his demands, Aberijan and his men beat Charles Reed, breaking his wrist in the process, and repeatedly shocked him with a stun gun, sending electrical volts surging through his body."

Brad was in his rhythm now, his voice rising and falling with emotion. "You will hear testimony from Dr. Jeffrey Rydell, a physician who tried desperately to save Charles Reed's life. He will talk about the burn marks at the base of Charles Reed's skull inflicted by repeated use of a stun gun, even though Charles Reed could have posed no threat to the arresting officers.

"In fact, the evidence of that fateful night will support only one scenario. Based on the firsthand testimony of Sarah Reed, the marks on Charles Reed's neck, the broken wrist, and the autopsy finding that Charles Reed's stomach was essentially empty of all contents, it is clear that Aberijan first beat Dr. Reed and broke his wrist, then stood over Dr. Reed, screaming at him and torturing him repeatedly with the stun gun, while Dr. Reed lay helplessly on the floor in his own vomit, gasping for breath and begging for his life. With no mercy, Aberijan shocked Reed again and again, sending the electricity surging through Reed's body, frying nerve endings and singeing flesh, smiling in his arrogance while Reed writhed in pain. And all the while this man, Aberijan, was demanding names of other church members so that he could hunt them down like animals and torture them as well."

Brad shouted now as he glared and pointed at Aberijan. Aberijan glared back, smugly, as if he didn't understand the language. It was precisely the reaction Brad hoped he would elicit. Brad stopped to catch his breath. He had been carried away with his own passion and found himself exhausted by the intensity of his emotions. And he was just beginning.

The jurors were sitting forward, processing the accusations, waiting breathlessly for more. All except juror 4, who sat back with his arms crossed, trying mightily to send the signal that he was not impressed.

"Sarah Reed will testify about the events of that horrible night that changed her life forever. Judge for yourself her credibility. She will tell you how Aberijan gave the order for his men to 'have their way with her,' an order that his men understood as permission to rape her. She will tell you how these animals began ripping her clothes off, how she tried to resist them, how they threw her to the ground, bouncing her head off the floor and rendering her unconscious.

"And then this man, Mr. Aberijan," Brad sneered at the scum sitting at the defense table, "not satisfied with torturing Charles Reed and ordering the rape of his wife, thinking of nothing but his own reputation, committed another atrocity that night. With Charles Reed unconscious from the torture, and Sarah Reed unconscious from the blow to her head, Aberijan ordered that they both be injected with cocaine in order to set them up as common criminals deserving of such horrible mistreatment."

For one full hour Brad ticked off points of evidence and painted his client and her children as saints. He ran the gamut of emotions. Harsh and intense words for Aberijan and the government of Saudi Arabia. Words of compassion for the Reed family, for the children who lost a loving father, for the wife who lost her lover and best friend. He choked back tears, he shook his fist in anger. He mesmerized the jury. And he knew all the while that the reporters would eat it up; they loved this stuff.

At one hour, Ichabod began inquiring, in a studied monotone, as to whether Brad was almost done. Five minutes later she asked again. Ten minutes later she told him to wrap it up or she would cut him off. Brad decided it was story time. He knew it would be unorthodox…a calculated gamble, but he was banking on Strobel's reluctance to object during the opening statement and Ichabod's attempt to look like she wasn't paying attention.

"At the height of the degrading games and bloodshed of the Roman Coliseum, a monk named Telemachus lived in a monastery far outside the city of Rome. One day he heard God calling him to take a pilgrimage to the city of Rome, though he didn't know why. Small and stooped, he gathered all his belongings in a backpack and started on his long trip.

"When Telemachus arrived at Rome, he was swept up by the crowds and carried into the gore and violence of the Coliseum. There, to his horror, he saw the gladiators killing one another for sport. He could not stomach the shedding of innocent blood, and he knew he had to do something."

Brad noticed Ichabod shoot her eyes toward Strobel, trying to get Mack's attention, undoubtedly trying to prompt the man to object. *Speaking of doing something,* she seemed to be saying, *how about an objection here?* But Strobel seemed content to ride it out.

"So Telemachus jumped to the floor of the Coliseum, ran between two gladiators, held out his hands, and said, 'In the name of Christ, forbear.'" Brad stooped over and flung his arms wide—the very picture of Telemachus.

"At first, the crowd cheered, thinking Telemachus was a clown running around for their entertainment. But eventually, they began to boo and hiss as Telemachus continued to insert himself between combatants, trying to stem the flow of blood."

Brad sensed that this story had revived the jurors' interest. None fidgeted; none looked away.

"I object," Strobel finally announced. "This is supposed to be an opening statement, not story time."

Brad was sure story time was now over, but the mercurial Ichabod surprised him.

"I agree, Mr. Strobel," she said harshly. "But you should have made that objection a long time ago. By now, you've waived your objection. Mr. Carson, you may finish."

Brad figured Ichabod just wanted to know how the story ended. She could always gut its usefulness with a few well-placed words later.

"Thank you, Judge." Then Brad turned back to the jury, slipping out from behind the podium, wielding an imaginary sword. "Anyway, one of the gladiators got frustrated with this awkward little monk and ran him through with a sword. But even as Telemachus lay on the floor of the Coliseum in a pool of his own blood, he thought not of himself but only of those gladiators and of his mission that had now become so clear. And as life left his little body, with his dying breath, he lifted up his hands and begged one last time"—Brad lowered his voice, closed his eyes, and lifted weary arms ever so slightly—"'In the name of Christ, forbear.'

"A funny thing happened that day in the Coliseum. Disgusted by the bloody slaughter of an innocent monk, a spectator got up from his seat and left the Coliseum, never to return. He was followed by another and another and another. One by one, the spectators all rose silently in protest and left the bloody place. And history records, that from that day forward, the bloodletting in the Coliseum ceased forever."

Brad stopped speaking and stood perfectly still, letting the solemnity settle over the courtroom. The enormity of their task descended heavily on the jurors, as Brad stood before them with imploring eyes.

"In a real sense, you have been called, like Telemachus, as one man or one woman to make a difference. History will judge your verdict—"

"I must object," said Strobel forcefully, rising to his feet, "this is totally improper."

"Will you have the courage to end the bloodshed and violence?"

"Sustained!" said Ichabod. She slammed her gavel. "Mr. Carson, that is quite enough!"

"Are you willing to look at this animal, Mr. Aberijan—"

"I object," yelled Strobel. "The court has ruled. This is insane!"

"Mr. Carson, not one more word!"

"...and say, 'In the name of justice—forbear!'?"

"That does it," Ichabod screamed. "In my chambers. Now!" She bolted from the bench, her black robe flying behind her. She left a chaotic courtroom erupting in her wake, excited murmuring, reporters writing furiously, jurors sitting wide-eyed, and Strobel shooting daggers at Brad with his eyes.

In the swirling madness, Brad walked quickly but calmly to his counsel table. He stopped next to Leslie, placed an arm on the back of her chair, then bent over and whispered in her ear.

"I'd love to take you up on your offer for Friday night," he whispered, "as long as I'm not in jail."

I chabod took sixteen and a half minutes to restore the integrity of the court. She needed ten minutes to deliver a vicious tongue-lashing to Brad. Another minute and a half for Brad to write his check for ten thousand dollars, payable to the U.S. District Court, for his contempt citation. Then five minutes for Ichabod to lecture the jury and ensure that Brad's shenanigans had not improperly influenced them.

"What the lawyers say in opening statements is not evidence," she explained. "And that is especially true if they resort to extraneous matters like telling stories about unrelated events. On the other hand," she warned, "you should not punish lawyers with an adverse decision just because they ignore the orders of the court and wreak havoc in the courtroom."

Ichabod assured the jury that she would take care of such offenders, as she had in this case. It was their job to focus on the evidence in the case and nothing else. After setting the jury straight, Ichabod called for another short recess.

■　■　■

When court resumed, Strobel walked confidently to the podium, knowing precisely what he had to do. Years of experience had taught him that when you represent an unpopular defendant, you appeal to logic, not emotion. Take the heat out of the case. Become the master teacher. *Reason* with your friends on the jury.

"Ladies and gentlemen of the jury," Strobel's baritone voice filled the courtroom, "there are two sides to every case. That's why you took an oath to keep an open mind until you hear all the evidence." Strobel stood erect behind the podium, a model of decorum. "One of your greatest tools in your search for truth will be your own common sense. Don't allow Mr. Carson's emotional appeals to alter what your common sense tells you is true." He paused and searched the jurors' faces, looking for an implicit promise that they would indeed follow their common sense wherever it took them.

"Don't be afraid to ask the hard questions as you evaluate the evidence. Why would Ahmed Aberijan and his officers inject Charles and Sarah Reed with cocaine? The Reeds lied to get into Saudi Arabia and broke the law in their attempts to convert Muslims. What the Reeds did was blatantly illegal under Saudi Arabian law, and everyone knew it. Mr. Aberijan had every right to arrest them and deport them. He certainly didn't need to fabricate a drug charge to do that.

"And why would he allegedly torture them and then take them to a hospital for treatment? If he wanted to kill them, as Mrs. Reed claims, why would he take them to a hospital so they could get treated and survive?

"And why, if Mrs. Reed and her husband were just innocent victims, did the arresting officers have abrasions and contusions, including scratches inflicted by Mrs. Reed's fingernails and a large gash on the face of an officer from a punch thrown by Charles Reed?

"And where is the corroboration? Where are the witnesses? There are none to back up Mrs. Reed's fabrications. Yet numerous members of her alleged church have testified against her. They have confirmed that the so-called church was only a front for a powerful drug ring."

Strobel rolled highlights from the deposition videotapes. The jury soaked in the words of the first witnesses they would hear testify.

He took an hour and a half to methodically walk through the evidence he intended to introduce during the trial. It was show-and-tell time. He did his best to juice it up with multicolored charts and enlargements of documents, but as the minutes ticked by, several of the jurors checked their watches and began to fidget. Strobel noticed them stirring and decided to wind it down.

"I will close with a story too," Strobel said. "But mine is a true story.

It is the story of a twenty-first-century Muslim who has served his country well for many years. It is a story of how that man did his job, broke up a drug ring in his country, and had to endure vicious lies and accusations by a greedy plaintiff's lawyer in another country. It is the story of how that devoted Muslim and faithful civil servant put his faith in the American system of justice and in a jury that has promised to look at the evidence with an open mind and render an unbiased verdict.

"You will write the last chapter of that story, and you will determine whether our system can survive the test of being fair to those who think and believe differently than we do. You can write a chapter for religious freedom by honoring the freedom of the people of Saudi Arabia to chose their own religion and worship their own God, free from Western imperialism."

Strobel paused, looked the jurors directly in the eye, then strode confidently to his seat. Juror number 4 nodded his head in support as he rocked back and forth. The others cast thoughtful but suspicious looks toward Sarah Reed.

■ ■ ■

The rules of elevator etiquette had established themselves during the two days of jury selection. The lawyers and contending parties would let the jurors and spectators take the first few elevators down. Sarah Reed and her team took the next, reserving the last elevator for Ahmed Aberijan, Mack Strobel, and the rest of the defense team. As the participants headed to lunch after the opening statements, they followed the same unwritten protocol.

As a critical part of the plaintiff's team, Aberijan's informant joined Brad and the others on the elevator, all facing front, all carrying their briefcases, all waiting for the doors to close. Nobody said a word, but she could sense that the team would erupt in high-fives and back-slapping as soon as they got some privacy. Brad's opening fell nothing short of masterful.

But as the doors began to shut, a hand reached in and pushed against the rubber safety strip on the inside of the doors. The doors sprang back to reveal a beefy, middle-aged man who had been sitting in court behind the defense table. Ahmed Aberijan stood at his shoulder. Amid quizzical looks from Brad's team, the two men boarded the elevator.

Ahmed moved to the back wall, stood next to his informant, and silently watched the lit floor signs as they descended.

What's going on here? Is he trying to intimidate me?

She wanted to lash out at him, give him a piece of her mind. Such a bold move would enhance her cover, make her a hero to the others. But nobody said a word; they all just stared straight ahead. And as the doors opened at the ground floor, Ahmed and his ridiculous little sidekick stepped off first.

"What was that all about?" she said just loud enough for Ahmed and his partner to hear.

"Who knows?" said Brad.

She found out right after she had ordered lunch.

When she reached for her briefcase to retrieve some documents, she discovered a legal-size manila envelope wedged in the outside pocket.

Suddenly, the conversation around her faded in the background, like she was operating out of some deep well. She had to know what was in that envelope. Nothing else mattered. With a catch in her voice, she excused herself. She retreated to the rest room and opened the envelope carefully in a small stall. The note was short and to the point. Ahmed apparently thought he was back in control.

> The bugs are useless and create a grave risk. Remove them imme-
> diately and return them to us. We need details on the plan for
> Shelhorse. Meet at the same location, Friday at 8:30 A.M.

She read the letter twice. And she trembled. She was clearly in over her head, but she could not turn back now. She didn't like Ahmed's boldness in contacting her. She didn't like his giving the orders. This was not her plan. Things were happening too fast. She needed to think straight. She needed to act fast. She needed to get back in control.

■ ■ ■

Sarah told her story beautifully. She and Leslie started with the events of the night on which Charles died, and Sarah recounted those events with precise memory of what she had seen and heard. She told of the Muttawa raid, the beatings, the attempted rape, and the events at the hospital later that night. Her unconsciousness, of course, left a huge gap in the story surrounding Charles' actual torture.

Sarah hardly looked or acted like a drug pusher. She seemed on the verge of tears throughout the emotional part of her testimony but broke down only once, as she recounted learning about the death of her husband. Sarah was blessed with a slender build and looked absolutely diminutive as the large witness stand and the massive grandeur of the courtroom dwarfed her. Leslie thought she could sense an almost palpable empathy flowing from the jury box.

After the emotional testimony about the Muttawa raid, Leslie took Sarah through an hour of background information about her life with Charles and their mission work in Saudi Arabia. This part of the testimony gave Sarah emotional downtime and allowed the jury to gear up for the emotional dam that would burst when Sarah talked about her children.

"I loved the Saudi people," Sarah testified, "and I believed my calling was to share the greatest thing that had ever happened to me with them. Charles and I were called to take the gospel to the land of Saudi Arabia."

"Did you have much success at first?" Leslie asked.

"It depends on how you define success," explained Sarah. "If you mean did we have a huge church right away—no. But if you mean were we able to reach out and help some folks who were walking through some tough times—yes. Our first convert was an elderly lady who had no family and no way to take care of herself. Meredith—that's my daughter—and I would go sit with her for hours, listen to her stories, and while we were there we would clean her house and cook some meals. We tried to take care of her without hurting her pride. At her own time, and in her own way, she came to Christ."

Throughout most of the afternoon, Sarah described the life of a missionary. The heartaches and challenges, the love for the people, the fear of the government. Strobel made a concerted effort to look bored. At 4:30, Leslie decided to end with the impact on the family.

"How has Steven handled the death of his father?" she asked.

Sarah's top lip quivered. She dabbed at her eyes with a tattered Kleenex she had wadded up in her right hand and toyed with for the past few hours.

"Steven misses his dad so much, but he tries hard not to show it. He's had to grow up so fast. He sees himself as the man of the house. Every Saturday morning, when his buddies are off swimming or playing ball, he's mowing the lawn and helping around the house. I try to be both mom and dad, but it's not easy."

The tears rolled quietly down her cheeks.

"With my schedule, I've told him he can play one sport in city league. He loves soccer. Last Saturday, his team lost a game on penalty kicks, and Steven missed his. I tried my best to console him, but he didn't respond. As we drove off, I saw him looking out the passenger window at the field. He was watching one of the other kids who had missed his penalty kick too. The boy was out there practicing penalty kicks while his dad played goalie."

Sarah stopped for a second to wipe back some tears. Leslie found her own eyes burning.

"I knew he was crying and missing his dad," continued Sarah in a whisper, "because his shoulders were shaking. He kept his face to the window all the way home."

No one in the jury looked at Sarah now; her pain made them visibly uncomfortable. Leslie needed to move on, but she sensed Sarah was not yet done. She waited an extra beat.

"It's not easy raising a young man coming into adolescence without a father, even though I know God is the father to the fatherless."

"Do you need a moment?" Leslie asked. Sarah was crying harder now.

"No, I'd rather keep going," Sarah answered through the sobs.

"Tell us how Meredith is handling this," Leslie asked gently.

"Not as well as Steven," confessed Sarah. "Meredith blames God. She asks questions I can't answer. Like, 'Why would God allow Dad to die if he was doing God's work?' She's becoming rebellious and hard to control. She doesn't want anything to do with church." Sarah paused, searching for the right words. "Charles was always much better at handling her than I am. There's something special between a father and his daughter. I don't know what to do… I feel like a complete failure as a mom. I've tried so hard—"

Sarah couldn't finish. As the tears flowed freely down her cheeks, the Kleenex no longer of any use, she simply repeated the words "I'm sorry" over and over.

"May we take a short recess, Your Honor?" asked Leslie, fighting back tears of her own.

"Yes." Even the granite heart of Ichabod seemed to have been touched. "Court now stands in recess."

As the judge and jury filed quietly out, Leslie approached the witness stand and embraced Sarah. The two women hugged, mourning husbands they had loved and lost. For Leslie it was the first time in nearly a year she had allowed herself to cry over Bill. In an odd sort of way, she felt a release from her own guilt and a forgiveness that flowed as freely as the tears.

■　■　■

As he rose to cross-examine Sarah Reed, Mack Strobel knew the jury would despise him. But he also knew that Ichabod would call it a day in only thirty minutes, making it imperative for him to draw blood quickly.

"Good afternoon, Mrs. Reed," he stood comfortably behind the podium, smiling at Sarah.

"Good afternoon," she did not return the smile.

"I'd like to show you what has been marked for identification as Defense Exhibit 1. Do you recognize it?" Mack's smile was now gone.

"Yes."

"Well, what is it?"

"It's the application I filled out to get a visa to live in Saudi Arabia."

"Your Honor, I would like to move this into evidence as Defense Exhibit 1. I also have an enlargement I would like to show the jury."

"No objection," Leslie said nonchalantly.

"Is that your signature at the bottom of the document?" asked Mack.

"Yes."

"All right, then. Looking at the third-to-last answer on the first page. Tell me what this document says you will be doing while in Saudi Arabia?"

"It says 'school administrator.'"

"And isn't it a fact, Mrs. Reed, that your primary reason for going to Saudi Arabia was to be a missionary and as a missionary to try to convert Muslims to Christianity?" Mack's voice was loud and staccato, accusatory in its tone.

Sarah's answer was soft. "Yes, I went to be a missionary, but I did not intend to limit my work to Muslims; I wanted to share with anyone and everyone about how to be a Christian."

"You knew it was illegal in Saudi Arabia for someone to convert from the Muslim faith to Christianity, didn't you, Mrs. Reed?"

Sarah looked down at her folded hands. "Yes."

"And you also knew that if you put the word *missionary* on this visa application, you wouldn't be allowed into the country. Isn't that right?"

"I suppose so."

"Then is it fair to say you lied on a visa application to gain admittance into a country so that you could then teach others how to break the law and convert to Christianity?" Mack stared hard at Sarah, waving the visa application with his right hand.

Sarah bit her lip.

"I wouldn't phrase it that way," she said at last.

"Then how would you phrase it?" Mack loved it when witnesses fought with him. It only served to highlight his points.

"I don't know," Sarah admitted. "I guess I would say that we didn't reveal certain things on the visa application because we knew it would disqualify us from entering the country."

"I see," said Mack. "It's okay to withhold information from the authorities if you deem it to be appropriate…information like using marijuana and cocaine, Mrs. Reed?"

"No, we never used marijuana or cocaine," Sarah answered emphatically.

Mack would come back to that point later. But he only had a few more minutes on this day. He wanted to make them count.

"Do you remember testifying on direct examination about the night the Muttawa came to your apartment?"

"Yes sir."

"To your knowledge, had Mr. Aberijan or anyone else from the Muttawa ever been inside your apartment prior to that night?"

"No sir."

"And yet you watched them with your own eyes as they found small plastic bags of cocaine in places like the cushions of your couch. Correct?"

"Yes, it all happened very fast. But yes, that's true."

"And isn't it also true that they had to cut those cushions open to get at the bags of cocaine?" continued Mack.

"Yes."

"So it's not like they could have just dropped them in there the same night and pretended they found them a few seconds later."

"I guess that would have been hard."

"Mrs. Reed, are you telling the jury today that you have no idea how those plastic bags of cocaine came to be, among other places, sewn into the lining of the cushions of your own couch?" Mack sounded incredulous. Juror 4 raised his eyebrows.

"Objection, argumentative," Leslie called out.

"Overruled," snapped Ichabod.

"That's what I'm saying," answered Sarah.

She might be speaking the truth. Mack didn't know. He was more interested in the fire forming in Sarah's eyes. She was growing weary of being misinterpreted, misquoted, and misled. He could tell that she was ready to take the bait and do what Leslie and Brad had undoubtedly warned her against.

She was ready to pick a fight with Mack Strobel.

"Why would I leave plastic bags of cocaine just sitting around the house when I knew the Muttawa were coming?" she asked. "Why do you think we called off the worship service that night? We knew they were coming. How dumb do you think I am?" Her face was flushed, her voice rising in frustration.

He fought back a smile. "Mrs. Reed," Mack responded evenly, "You may very well have thought that hiding the cocaine in the couch cushions would keep the religious police from ever finding it. But it's not for me to testify. I ask the questions."

"I object and ask that Mr. Strobel's speculation be struck from the record," Leslie was on her feet again.

"Sit down," barked Ichabod.

"Does that mean my objection was sustained or overruled?" Leslie was still standing.

"It means you sit down and I'll tell you."

With a huff, Leslie sat.

"Overruled," Ichabod said.

"May I proceed, Your Honor?" Mack asked politely. He was amused by this turn of events and ready to turn the hostility of the witness to even greater advantage.

"Yes."

"Mrs. Reed, did you just testify that you knew the Muttawa were coming?"

"Yes."

"How did you know?"

"We had a source."

The answer was just what Mack wanted, just what he would have scripted. He turned and looked at Bard Carson and Leslie Connors, as if accusing them of hiding some critical piece of evidence.

Brad's head was in his hands. Leslie dropped her pen and stared at the witness like she didn't recognize the woman who had just spoken.

Mack turned back to the witness, twisting every muscle on his face to register surprise. "You had a source?" he asked.

The witness had opened the door. The name of the source was now relevant. There could be no more argument against it.

"Who was your source? Who told you the Muttawa were coming?" Mack pressed.

"I can't answer that question," Sarah said softly.

"Can't or won't?" bellowed Mack.

"Won't," confirmed Sarah.

"You will in my courtroom," said Ichabod, hunkering forward as she glared down at the witness. "You have testified that you knew the Muttawa were coming because you had a source. You testified that it would be ridiculous for you to knowingly have cocaine in your apartment since you knew the Muttawa were coming. The issue of a source is therefore relevant. For that reason, I am ordering you to answer the question."

"I won't," whispered Sarah, looking at the floor. "It might endanger his life."

"Mrs. Reed, this court is not asking you to think about whether you will tell me the name of the person, apparently a male, that you yourself made relevant. This court is *ordering* you to do it. You should have thought about these issues of confidentiality before you filed suit and certainly before you made his name relevant. You cannot use him to bolster your credibility and then hide him behind this cloak of anonymity."

Sarah simply sat on the stand, her lip trembling, slowly shaking her head from side to side.

"Bailiff, please dismiss the jury," ordered Ichabod.

The jury shuffled out in silence. Several jury members glanced over their shoulder at Sarah on the way out. Their sympathetic looks worried Mack.

"Mr. Carson," said Ichabod, "this has been a long and emotional day for everyone." Ichabod appeared to be working hard to maintain her composure. "I know your client is exhausted and not thinking clearly. We will reconvene tomorrow morning, and Mr. Strobel will again ask his question. You will have Mrs. Reed prepared to answer, or I will entertain a motion to dismiss her case."

Brad silently nodded his head.

Mack returned to his seat and found a note waiting from Ahmed's translator.

"Good work," it said. "Whatever it takes, get me that name."

She had to get to the office ahead of the others. Ahmed's note radically changed her plans. The first order of business was to retrieve the listening devices from the phones. The small magnetic radio transmitters, no larger than a quarter, were attached to the bottom of each office phone. It would take only a few minutes to retrieve all three, but to do so she had to arrive at the office first. Alone.

She left federal court slightly ahead of the others, hustled to her car, and drove like a wild woman down the interstate. She hit the inevitable backup a few miles outside Norfolk on Interstate 44 and was actually grateful. By weaving in and out of traffic, even using the HOV lane, she gained valuable time on the others.

She parked in the handicapped spot immediately in front of the building and took the elevator to the fifth floor. She took a hard right off the elevator and got out her key as she approached the suite. She slipped into the reception area. The lights were on, just as the team had left them that morning. She walked across the reception area and took a left toward Brad's office.

She turned the corner into the semidark hallway and gasped, stopping short. She was inches away and face-to-face with Patrick O'Malley.

"Sorry," he said. "Didn't mean to scare ya, but we got trouble here."

He held out his palm. In it were the three transmitters.

"I know," she said, still out of breath. "That's why Brad sent me ahead of the others. There's a few things he wanted me to talk to you about. Step in here for a second." She pointed to the war room, and the two of them stepped inside and closed the door.

■ ■ ■

Sarah stared out the window of Brad's car as though he were taking her for a date with the firing squad. She thought of Saudi Arabia and the struggling church she was trying to protect.

"We're dead in the water," she finally said.

"Ichabod won't dismiss the case," Brad said confidently. "We'd have her reversed in a heartbeat on appeal. And she knows it. She could possibly fine you. She could have the jury assume there is no snitch. She could even jail you. But she can't just dismiss the case."

"Oh, that's better!" Sarah groaned. "Jail."

"She's bluffing," promised Brad. "That's why she said she would *consider* dismissing the case. Don't let her distract us with a bluff. We need to prepare like the case is going forward tomorrow...because it is."

Sarah felt little consolation from Brad's assurances. The prospect of facing hours of cross-examination from Strobel tomorrow was nerve-racking enough. But now she also had to face an irate judge who had the power to throw her in jail for something Sarah couldn't control. She had a splitting headache. She closed her eyes and tilted her head back against the headrest, unwilling to go back to the office and into the war room to endure more hours of preparation. After all, it hadn't done much good today.

"What do I say when Strobel asks again?" She tried to rub the tension out of her neck. How did she get herself into this mess?

"The same thing you did today," responded Brad. "Just tell the court that you respectfully refuse to answer on the grounds that it will endanger the life of an innocent man. The jury will love you for it. Leslie and I'll take over from there."

"Yeah," said Sarah, eyes still closed. "And the judge will chew me up and spit me out."

■ ■ ■

"That's a no-brainer," said Win, slouched in a chair in front of Teddy's massive oak desk. "We start off tomorrow by asking Sarah Reed again for the name of her informant. She refuses. Ichabod dismisses the case. Carson appeals. If we're lucky, he wins the appeal and gets a new trial. We bill a couple more million and win it fair and square next time around. Everybody's happy—except Carson, and he doesn't deserve to be happy."

Teddy sat straighter in his high-back leather chair. "I hope you're not serious," he said sternly. "Our obligation is to do what's right for the client, not to figure out a way to bill this file until we all retire."

Mack knew Win was serious. But he also knew Win wouldn't argue. Poor naive Teddy. The times had passed him by.

But this time, Mack was thankful for Teddy's outdated ethical standards.

"That's part of my problem," explained Mack. "As ironic as it sounds, what's best for the client in this situation is probably not a dismissal this early in the case on a technicality. Carson would appeal, and our research guys tell me he would probably win. I think it serves the client better if we let Ichabod hear the whole case, then recall Reed and ask her this question at the end of the case. That way Ichabod can say she's dismissing the case both because the case has no merit and because the plaintiff refused to answer a relevant question.

"We'll have a much better chance of sustaining the ruling on appeal. And frankly, Win, I don't want to have to try this case again, even for all the billable hours in the world. Reed makes a good witness, and Carson's a tough advocate. At my age, you don't retry cases like this one."

"But you've already asked Reed the question," protested Win. "The cat's out of the bag. How do you get Ichabod to wait?"

"It's my question. I'll just withdraw it and ask the judge for permission to recall the witness at the end of trial."

"I like it," affirmed Teddy.

"I still say take the win and hope for the best on appeal," said Mackenzie stubbornly. He was probably counting on a controversial victory to land him an appearance on *Larry King Live*.

"There's another problem," Mack turned and looked hard into

Teddy's eyes. "I think Sarah Reed is right to withhold the name. I hate to even say it, but I think my client would order the informant killed in a second."

"Since when did you start having fits of conscience?" Win asked. "You can't start thinking that way, Mack. You owe your client zealous representation. You start believing the other side, and you might as well throw in the towel."

Mack walked over to where Winsted Aaron Mackenzie IV was sitting and towered over him.

"Listen, you little prima donna," Mack said slowly, each word crawling across his lips. "I don't need you telling me how to try this case. I'll chew Reed up tomorrow and spit her out without that ridiculous question. Aberijan and Saudi Arabia are getting zealous representation like they would get nowhere else. But that doesn't mean you put an innocent man's head on the guillotine."

Win's eyes widened as he looked up at his irate partner. He spread his palms and shrugged his shoulders.

"Gentlemen," said Teddy loudly. Strobel stepped away from Mackenzie. "I agree with Mack. Our firm will not be used as a stool pigeon so some autocrat from Saudi Arabia can get the name of an informant and wipe him out. On the other hand, I think Mack is worrying about nothing. Mrs. Reed has already shown her stubborn unwillingness to give up any names."

Teddy leaned forward with his elbows on the desk, lost in thought. He made a small humming noise from deep in his throat. Mack knew it was the noise Teddy made when he was racking his brain. He also knew that what followed this little humming display was usually pretty profound. After more than a minute, Teddy looked up.

"If Mack withdraws the question tomorrow and then calls Mrs. Reed back to the stand at the end of the case and asks her the same question, two things will happen. Both of them good. First, we'll have a better chance to defend this case on appeal. Second, if the informant ever was in danger, and his name is not revealed until the end of the trial, then he will have between now and the end of the trial to find a way to dodge the Muttawa. Mack, I am asking you, in my capacity as senior partner of this firm, to withdraw the question tomorrow."

"That's what I plan on doing," agreed Mack. "I just want you to be ready for an onslaught of bellyaching from our client."

"Let him complain," said Teddy. "Just make sure he pays the bills."

"What are your chances with the jury?" asked Win. The question signaled he would not challenge Teddy's decision.

"I'd say about fifty-fifty," Mack responded. He leaned back against the window. "It's still too early to tell. But one thing I do know. Sarah Reed makes quite a witness, and she wowed some jurors. It won't be easy."

"Then get a mistrial," advised Win. "Have your snoops follow the jurors for the next few days. They'll find enough for seven mistrials. I guarantee you that several of those jurors have been watching news of the trial or talking to each other about what the outcome should be."

Mack gazed across the room as if he were only half listening. But he was thinking that Win might have a point.

"If Ichabod dismisses the jury, then she'll declare a mistrial on the case against Ahmed only, since that's the only count on which the plaintiff gets a jury trial," Win explained in his annoyingly patronizing tone. "Ichabod will then decide the case involving Saudi Arabia, presumably in our favor, and grant a mistrial on the case against Ahmed because of jury misconduct."

He's right, thought Mack. *The prima donna is onto something.*

"Plaintiff will not even ask for another trial against Ahmed since there's no real money in suing Ahmed," Win continued. "Ahmed is just window dressing. Get a mistrial based on jury misconduct, and your problems will disappear."

Mack snorted, as if dismissing the plan without saying a word. Then he turned and strode purposefully out of the office and straight down the hall. He would make a call to Barnes. Win was right; the jury was undoubtedly cheating. They always did in big cases, and Barnes was just the man to catch them at it.

"You're welcome," Winsted Aaron Mackenzie III muttered to himself a few seconds after Mack left the room. The comment struck Teddy as funny, and he let out a rumble of laughter that Mackenzie had not heard in years.

■ ■ ■

"I can't believe you're doing this for me," gushed Bella, driving like a madwoman down 464 on her way to Chesapeake Estates.

Riding in the passenger seat, Sarah put her considerable faith to the test, as she watched Bella take up the better part of two lanes. Hailing from Brooklyn, Bella couldn't talk without using her hands, even while she drove. Nor could she really connect with someone while talking unless she looked them straight in the eyes. Hailing from the South, Sarah believed it would be rude to tell Bella to keep her eyes on the road.

"Thanks for stopping for pizza with me," Bella continued. "I couldn't take another night of Chinese at the firm. I know you weren't hungry, but girl, you've got to start eating something. Winning this case won't mean much if our client dies of starvation." She swerved into the exit lane at the last possible second.

"To be honest, Bella, I just want to get through tomorrow, you know what I mean?" Sarah referred as much to Bella's driving as she did to her second day of testimony.

"Yeah," grunted Bella. "That's the way I've been living since I put my mom into this home a year and a half ago—one day to the next. I just want to get through tomorrow too."

"Have you ever talked to your mom about spiritual things?" Sarah asked gently.

"Not really. At least not for a long time. When I was a little girl, she used to take me to church and stuff. But she always kept religious things to herself. After my dad left, she quit goin'. Divorce was pretty rare back then, and you know how church folks can make you feel uncomfortable. I don't really remember goin' to church after dad left, except for funerals and weddings."

Bella paused for a second, as if she regretted criticizing her mother. "She was a wonderful mother and a good person, she just didn't have time for organized religion."

Bella turned abruptly into the parking lot of Chesapeake Estates, and Sarah said a quick and silent prayer of thanks. She saw no reason to speak. Bella didn't seem to be looking for advice.

"Mom never did anything for herself," Bella explained. "She worked her fingers to the bone to provide for us. Dad's checks would show up some months; other months they wouldn't. He never did. Mom, on the other hand, never missed any of my school events. The older I got, the closer I got to my mom. She would drive me crazy sometimes because she was so protective and always worrying. But I realized a few years ago that she was not only my best friend; she was really my only friend. Now she's in this godforsaken home, and I can't do a thing to make things better."

Bella turned off the car and continued to unburden herself to Sarah.

"I don't think Mom has much time left. It's time for her to get things right with her Maker. I thought maybe you could help."

"What about you, Bella?" Sarah asked patiently as she climbed out of the car. The fresh air brought her relief from the stale cigarette smoke that saturated the car.

Bella opened the door and hoisted her considerable frame out of the driver's seat.

"Let's deal with Mom first," she quipped. "For some of us there's no hope."

"You might be surprised," said Sarah. But Bella was already hoofing across the parking lot, breathing heavily and burping up pizza.

■ ■ ■

They found Gertrude in her small sterile room, sitting in her favorite rocking chair. The television was blaring, but Gertrude was not looking at it. Bella turned down the television and plunked herself down at the foot of her mom's bed, next to the rocker. Sarah sat gingerly in the only chair in the room other than the rocker.

"Mom, this is Sarah Reed," Bella said loudly. Gertrude slowly turned toward Sarah and reached out her trembling hand. Sarah immediately got up, took the hand, and held it warmly in both of hers.

"She's a Baptist missionary," said Bella proudly. "Kinda like the Protestant version of Mother Theresa. Mom, does that make sense?"

Gertrude nodded her head, and Sarah felt the feeble woman softly squeeze her hand.

"I asked Sarah to come and talk to us about God and heaven, Mom. Is that all right?" Bella was shouting. Gertrude's door was open, and Sarah was sure that everyone in the building now knew who she was and why she was here.

Gertrude swallowed hard and struggled to talk. The words came out forced and breathy. "Okay... I always...liked missionaries." And then her eyes smiled. Bella looked at Sarah and nodded. This was evidently her cue.

"Bella has told me all about you," Sarah started. She talked softer than Bella. And as she talked, she moved her chair right next to the rocker so they could talk face-to-face. Gertrude reached out and took her hand again. "About how you took care of Bella. I can tell that Bella loves you very much. You must be very proud of her."

Gertrude squeezed Sarah's hand again.

"The way you love your daughter, Gertrude, that's the way our heavenly Father loves us. And the way you took care of Bella, that's the way our heavenly Father takes care of us. Have you ever heard of John 3:16?"

Gertrude furrowed her brow. She stopped rocking for a brief moment.

"For God so loved the world," Sarah quoted the verse, "that He gave His only begotten Son, that whoever believes in Him should not perish but have everlasting life."

A flicker of recognition crossed Gertrude's face.

"Have you heard that Bible verse before?" Sarah asked.

Gertrude got ready to respond, but Bella beat her to the punch.

"Sure you have, Mom," Bella blurted out. "You used to say it to me all the time when I was little."

"But it's not enough just to know the verse," Sarah continued. "You've got to do what the verse says. You've got to believe on God's Son, Jesus Christ, for your salvation."

Bella's mom closed her eyes and continued rocking. Sarah looked back at Bella, who motioned with her hand to keep going.

"There's another verse of Scripture I'd like to share with you," said Sarah. "It's Romans 3:23. And it says: 'For all have sinned and fall short of the glory of God.' That means no matter how good of a mother you were, no matter how much you loved Bella and took care of her, you still did some things wrong that the Bible calls 'sin.' And this sin separates us from God, because God is perfect and holy and cannot tolerate sin. And the Scripture says that the wages of sin is death. Does that make sense, Gertrude? Do you understand that you and I and every person who ever lived are sinners and deserve to be punished by God?"

Gertrude betrayed no visible reaction. She just continued to rock in her slow, smooth, rhythmic way. Her eyes remained closed, and her lips stayed in a tightly pursed line.

"Think of the worst thing you've ever done, your greatest failure as a mom or a wife or just a woman. Then think for a minute about the price of that sin. John 3:16 says that God gave His only begotten Son. For you to be reconciled to God and forgiven of your sins, God had to send His own Son to this earth. And Jesus Christ, the only begotten Son of God, lived a perfect life and died a horrible and violent death on the cross. Our sins were placed on Him so that by His death He took our place."

Though Gertrude gave no visible response, Sarah was talking faster and getting excited. It always happened this way when she shared the good news.

"But the grave couldn't hold Him, and on the third day He rose from the grave, conquering death once and for all. And because of everything He did—living a perfect life, dying in our place, and then conquering death—we can have forgiveness for our sins through the blood of Jesus Christ. And if we're just willing to repent of our sins and ask Jesus into our hearts to be our Lord and Savior, then Scripture promises that we'll be saved. We'll have a personal relationship with Jesus Christ and live eternally with Him."

As Sarah spoke, the significance of the day's events fell away. Strobel's tough examination. Judge Baker-Kline's unsympathetic rulings. Leslie's valiant but futile efforts. None of that mattered any more. Life wasn't about federal court and all its trappings. At least not eternal life.

Sarah believed that her real accuser was Satan, that God was her Judge, and that Jesus Christ Himself was her Advocate. In the only courtroom that really mattered, her Advocate had taken her place as the defendant and endured her punishment. As a result, the Judge of the universe had declared her not guilty. And now, more than anything in the world, Sarah wanted Gertrude to experience that same liberation.

"The Word says that if you confess with your mouth that Jesus is Lord and believe in your heart that God raised Him from the dead, you will be saved. Gertrude, Christ died for you. And for me. We are the ones who should have been on the cross, but He took our place so that we might have eternal life when we die and abundant life while we live."

Sarah stopped and took a deep breath. She was a little embarrassed that she had been talking so fast and with such animation. But she was not embarrassed about the message. Just talking about Christ, sensing that a soul was hanging in the balance, invigorated her.

"Does that make sense, Gertrude?"

The rocking stopped, but Gertrude didn't speak. She sat in the chair in complete silence and stillness. The sound of Bella's labored breathing filled the room.

Sarah noticed it then. A small tear fell silently out of the corner of Gertrude's closed eye. Then another. And another. She started rocking again, and after a moment she opened her eyes, exposing their redness and the ragged emotion of a woman coming to terms with her eternal destiny.

"Yes," she said.

Sarah got out of her seat and knelt beside Gertrude. The elderly woman bowed her head, reached out, and gently placed a shaking hand on Sarah's shoulder. With her other hand, she clutched Sarah's.

"I'm going to ask you to pray with me now," said Sarah. "If you want, I'll say the words, and you can squeeze my hand if this is your prayer. Is that okay?"

A squeeze told Sarah to continue.

"Dear God. I know I'm a sinner. And I know I don't deserve Your mercy and Your grace. But I also know You sent Your only Son to die for my sins and make forgiveness available to me. I repent of my sins and receive Jesus as my personal Lord and Savior and ask Him to come into my heart and be Lord of my life. Thank you, God, for giving me eternal life. In the name of Jesus, amen."

Gertrude clutched Sarah's hand during the prayer and forced out an amen as Sarah concluded. Sarah looked at Gertrude and recognized the countenance. She had seen it before. A look of relief. A look of freedom. A look of acceptance. Gertrude could not smile with her mouth, but her reddened eyes were dancing. She almost fell from the chair as she reached out convulsively and gave Sarah an awkward hug.

■ ■ ■

Sarah and Gertrude had not been the only ones praying.

Unnoticed, Bella had slipped off the bed and knelt beside it while Sarah prayed. To Bella, it seemed a fitting posture. It was how her mother had taught her to pray. But it also seemed appropriate to be on her knees, to actually humble herself, as she prepared to ask the God of the universe to forgive and forget a whole truckload of sin.

Bella mouthed the words silently as Sarah prayed. Like her mother, she followed Sarah's amen with one of her own.

When she stood, she felt a sudden need to sit again. She felt the unconditional love and acceptance that had eluded her throughout her life. The scenes of her past ran together in a swirling collage of misery—

a neglectful father, an overprotective mother, teasing classmates, failed attempts at relationships, the hardening of her heart, the cynicism and hopelessness that resulted. But in this moment, it all seemed to be washed away in a flood of forgiveness and acceptance. An uncaring earthly father replaced by a loving heavenly one. So while Sarah and Gertrude hugged, Bella simply sat on the bed and basked in a wave of love and forgiveness that was unlike anything she had ever experienced.

I withdraw the pending question, Your Honor," Mack Strobel announced as he stepped behind the podium Thursday morning.

"You what?" exclaimed Ichabod. She furrowed her brow in disapproval.

"I'd like to withdraw the pending question at this time," Strobel repeated confidently. "I would also like to reserve the right to recall Mrs. Reed at the conclusion of my case, if necessary."

Ichabod looked at Strobel like he had lost his mind. "It's your question," she said at last.

"Thank you, Your Honor."

Sarah couldn't fathom the reason for this surprising turn of events. From the witness stand she looked at Brad and registered her surprise. *What does this mean?* Brad could only shrug and smile. As Judge Baker-Kline permitted Strobel to proceed, Sarah realized she had been holding her breath and slowly exhaled. *Thank You, Lord.*

Her relief did not last, however, as Strobel spent the entire morning and most of the afternoon grilling her with misleading questions and innuendos. She hesitated and stumbled in several answers, fearful of misstepping again, and said a few things inconsistent with her deposition testimony. By the time Ichabod dismissed her from the stand, Sarah's credibility had been badly tarnished.

After Sarah stepped down, Brad called Dr. Patrick Rydell to the stand and questioned him for the rest of the afternoon. When court adjourned, Brad assured Sarah that she had done just fine and promised her that things would take a turn for the better on Friday.

■ ■ ■

At 8:15 A.M. on Friday morning, she pulled up behind Patrick O'Malley's van parked on a side street about a block from Norfolk General District Court. The timing would be tight. She was to meet Ahmed at 8:30. Brad expected her in Federal Court on the other side of town by the start of testimony at 9:00.

A nasty wind battered the streets of Norfolk, and it began to drizzle. She hopped inside Patrick's van. He handed her a manila envelope containing a note and the three transmitters from the office. The radio blared in the background as she unfolded the paper and read.

"I'll be listening on a frequency that picks up these transmitters. If anything goes wrong, I'll be there. These things don't have great range, so keep them close to Ahmed."

She nodded, glad to be operating with a partner now, and closed the envelope, leaving the note with Patrick.

"Good luck," he mouthed as she climbed out into the cold.

■ ■ ■

Ahmed stared ahead and did not acknowledge her presence.

"I thought I told you to come alone," she hissed.

"You're wired," Ahmed snarled back. He grabbed her left arm at the bicep and squeezed with powerful fingers, drawing her closer to him. She gasped. "And you're not in charge here anymore. The men stay."

"Of course I'm wired. I've got your bugs."

"Show them to me," he demanded.

"Then let go." She said it firmly. Could he sense her fear, smell her fright?

Ahmed waited for an instant, then released her arm.

She pulled the envelope out of her purse and handed it to him. He turned to face her, staring right through her with those cold, gray eyes. His lips curled into a vicious little half-smile. "You seem to be shaking, my friend." He had noticed; he knew he was in charge! He looked at the transmitters. "What's the plan for Shelhorse?"

Pull yourself together. Deep breaths. This guy is scum—treat him like it.

"As I told you before," she said evenly, "the plan is to prevent Shelhorse from testifying. When I do, you will deposit one hundred thousand dollars into the Cayman Island bank account referenced on this sheet." She handed him a slip of paper that contained the wire instructions. This time her hand was steadier.

She lowered her voice another notch and spoke slowly, deliberately.

"There is something else. I know a juror that we can buy. He's a leader. You buy him, you'll have your verdict."

Ahmed's eyes lit up. "Which one?" he demanded.

"None of your business." Her fear began to dissipate.

Ahmed turned to her and spread his hot breath across her face. "I'm making it my business right now. We already own one juror. I must know whether this is the same person."

He watched closely, unblinking. She could not hesitate on this, even for a fraction of a second. He was testing her. Her heart slammed against her chest.

"Juror number 6," she said calmly. "Which one do you own?"

"That truly is none of your business," said Ahmed. He paused, staring. "But it is not juror number 6."

The co-conspirators exchanged a look. She thought she could see a slight relaxation in his jaw muscles.

"What's the cost?"

"Two million," she said without flinching. "Here are the wiring instructions." She handed him a second sheet of paper, this time for a Swiss bank account. "If our juror doesn't deliver the rest of the panel, you owe us nothing."

"'Us'?" asked Ahmed.

"I'm no fool. And I don't trust you. What would stop you, once you get your defense verdict, from eliminating me?"

"You'll have my word," said Ahmed lamely.

"Worthless when I'm dead."

"What are you proposing?" asked Ahmed. His words had a sharp edge. His muscles were again tensed.

She waited just long enough to let him know she could not be intimidated. "The nation of Saudi Arabia deposits one hundred million dollars in trust in a Swiss bank account. I get a copy of this trust document"—she thrust it at him but held it tight—"signed by a Saudi official. *Not* you. That money serves as my life insurance. As long as I'm alive, the money stays in the bank. If I die, under the terms of the trust document, the person I appoint as the executor of my estate must perform an investigation of the circumstances of my death. If he, or she, concludes I was murdered or that there were suspicious circumstances surrounding my death, the hundred million goes to Sarah Reed and her children. If my executor determines that I died from natural causes, then the money goes back to Saudi Arabia."

She could sense Ahmed's rising frustration; the death stare was back. She kept her voice low and even. She leaned forward as she spoke, her mouth a mere foot away from the transmitters.

"By next Friday, I want the money on deposit, and I want this document signed by an authorized representative of the Saudi government and delivered to the Swiss bank. Questions?"

Ahmed took the trust document. He made a great show of studying it, turning the pages slowly and methodically.

He placed the document in his own briefcase, placed the transmitters next to it, then whispered in her ear, his words dripping with vitriol.

"You don't set deadlines; I do. I will have the document signed, but not until after you have delivered on your promise for Shelhorse. And I'll have the money in the account when I'm ready—sometime before the jury begins deliberations. Your arbitrary deadlines mean nothing to me. I'll call the next meeting, not you... And one more thing, which I'm sure you've figured out. If you don't get rid of Shelhorse, or for some strange and tragic reason, we don't get a defense verdict, then you will die. And no escrow account will stop us."

She hardened her features, narrowed her eyes, and stared back.

"By the way," Ahmed said brusquely, "two million is too much. I'll set that price later." He stood up, grabbed his coat, and headed out.

She watched him leave and clenched her jaw. She was at once frightened and angry. Her head throbbed as adrenaline coursed through her entire body. She had been threatened by a cold-blooded killer.

But she had looked him in the eye, backed him down, and demanded her two million. She willed herself to rise, thrust her jaw in the air, and walk fearlessly from the courtroom.

■ ■ ■

As the chauffeur maneuvered against the morning rush-hour traffic, Ahmed had time to call Barnes and fill him in.

"Find out if she's got a will, and if so, who her executor is," Ahmed demanded. "She must have let the executor in on this little blackmail scheme. Wait until we get our defense verdict. Then, within twenty-four hours, I want both her and the executor dead."

■ ■ ■

Patrick O'Malley picked up the conversation from a few blocks away on his digital recorder. He was now the executor, and he would have to be careful. But as far as he could tell, they would have at least until the jury returned its verdict to execute the plan.

He smiled as he thought about Ahmed arguing over the two-million-dollar price tag for the verdict. O'Malley had predicted that the Saudi would try to get by for half. And all the while, Aberijan had his eye on the wrong ball. Two million, one million, what difference did it make? A hundred million—that was real money. And that price was nonnegotiable.

O'Malley punched in the numbers on his cell phone and was not surprised to hear it answered after only one ring.

"It's me," an anxious voice said. "How'd it go?"

"Just like we planned," crowed O'Malley. "Hook, line, and sinker. He even tried to negotiate the cost of the verdict—"

His phone beeped with an incoming call. "Hang on a second," he said. He checked the caller ID.

O'Malley put the first call on hold and answered the second. "You were great," he said reassuringly. "The money's as good as in the bank. The Saudis will never miss it."

31

At 9:05 A.M., with all the players in their respective seats, Dr. Jeffrey Rydell took the stand for a second day. Brad noticed one female juror nudge the one next to her and wiggle her eyebrows. Rydell had boyish good looks, a full head of blond hair, and bright-blue eyes. He was the all-American boy next door, except that he also happened to be a board-certified internist and seemed to know everything about emergency room medicine.

Brad had spent the first day of Rydell's testimony rehashing his qualifications and his treatment of Charles and Sarah Reed. Today Brad planned to hone in on the critical medical issues of his case.

"Dr. Rydell, do you have an opinion, to a reasonable degree of medical certainty, as to whether cocaine was a contributing factor in the death of Charles Reed?"

"I do," replied Rydell. One of the things Brad loved about this witness was that he always answered only the question asked and did not prattle on just to show his intelligence.

"What is that opinion, sir?"

"Objection," said Strobel. Brad rolled his eyes. "Dr. Rydell is not a toxicologist and therefore should not be allowed to give opinion testimony on this subject."

"I tend to agree with Mr. Strobel," said Ichabod, to nobody's surprise.

"Your Honor," Brad pleaded, "he was the physician at the base hospital who personally treated Dr. Reed just prior to his death. Certainly he can give opinions as to the cause of that death based on what he observed."

"May we approach?" asked Strobel. Without waiting for an answer, he moved toward Ichabod's bench. Brad joined him.

"I don't object if he talks about his treatment of Dr. Reed and what he observed," whispered Mack. "But from his deposition testimony, it's obvious that he also intends to talk about the toxicological tests performed both at King Faisal Specialist Hospital and the base hospital and then discuss the differences in levels of cocaine detected. He was not there for the King Faisal tests and is not an expert on absorption rates and other factors that would affect the significance of those levels—"

"Judge, he relied on those tests from the King Faisal Specialist Hospital when he treated Dr. Reed at the base hospital," Brad's interruption drew a glare from Strobel, which Brad ignored. "The reason Mr. Strobel does not want those tests admitted is because the tests at the base hospital showed a higher, not lower, level of cocaine. This could only mean someone injected Dr. Reed with cocaine very close to the time of his admittance to the first hospital, so that as the injected cocaine became absorbed into the blood and processed in the urine, it registered progressively higher levels between the time of his first admittance to the King Faisal Specialist Hospital and the time of his later admission to the base hospital." Brad was speaking quickly, trying desperately to get Ichabod to appreciate the significance of this ruling.

She interrupted him with her outstretched palm.

"That's quite an elaborate theory, Mr. Carson, and based on no small amount of speculation. It does, as Mr. Strobel suggests, depend on such things as absorption rates for cocaine into the bloodstream. Mr. Carson, do you have a toxicologist you plan on calling as an expert?"

"Yes, Judge, Dr. Shelhorse, but—"

"Mr. Carson," Ichabod interrupted, "that was a yes or no question. Since you have a toxicologist, I'm ruling that the prior tests from the King Faisal Specialist Hospital are not admissible through this witness. We can deal with them when your toxicologist takes the stand."

Brad looked at the judge and registered a silent protest. "Thank you, gentlemen," she said.

Brad huffed and stalked back to the podium.

"Dr. Rydell, please state your opinion as to whether cocaine contributed to the death of Dr. Reed, but in doing so, please do not discuss the prior drug tests from the King Faisal Specialist Hospital. Does that make sense?"

"No," said the doctor, "but I'll try.

"In my eleven years of experience in the management of critical-care patients, I have treated many who presented with various complications associated with cocaine usage. Cocaine is a powerful central nervous system stimulant that heightens alertness, inhibits appetite and the need for sleep, and provides intense feelings of pleasure. It is either snorted as a hydrochloric salt or boiled with sodium bicarbonate to produce a substance referred to on the street as 'crack,' which is then smoked and absorbed through the lungs. In rare instances, cocaine can be diluted with water and injected straight into the bloodstream."

Rydell talked straight to the jurors, and Brad noticed that they all appeared to be listening—with the exception, of course, of juror number 4, who seemed to be much more interested in the tops of his own shoes.

"Regardless of how it is absorbed, cocaine causes a number of potentially fatal complications, including some that directly affect the heart. Even in relatively small doses, cocaine increases blood pressure and constricts blood vessels. It also stimulates the formation of blood clots, disrupts normal heart rhythm, and can bind directly to heart-muscle cells, thereby weakening the heart's ability to pump blood. A variety of cardiovascular conditions and diseases have been associated with cocaine use, including hypertension, arrhythmias, cardiomyopathy, strokes, aneurysms, myocarditis, and heart attacks. Many first-time users have experienced heart attacks that have proven to be fatal.

"In the case of Dr. Reed, the effect of an enormous dosage of cocaine, as revealed in toxicological tests taken at both hospitals—"

"Objection!" shouted Strobel.

"Sustained!" snorted Ichabod. "The jury will disregard that last statement. Dr. Rydell, you are in no way allowed to refer to the toxicological tests from the King Faisal Specialist Hospital. Is that clear?"

"It is now, Judge," Rydell said, unfazed. "I thought before that you were just saying I couldn't tell the jury about the precise levels."

As Ichabod shook her head in disapproval, Rydell turned back to the jury with a level gaze and continued his lecture.

"Charles Reed already had a bad heart. He had fairly advanced coronary artery disease, which means that the flow of oxygen-rich blood to his heart was severely restricted. In my opinion, a combination of the stress from being arrested, the effects of the cocaine injected into his bloodstream, and the preexisting coronary artery disease all led to the death of Dr. Reed. The cocaine stimulated the formation of a blood clot that may not have been fatal in the arteries of a normal man, but it led to a total restriction of the flow of blood to the heart of Dr. Reed. In medical terms, we call it an acute myocardial infarction, but it simply means that the heart fails to receive any oxygen and is severely damaged as a result. In Dr. Reed's case, it was fatal."

Rydell looked back at Brad, apparently satisfied with his answer. So was Brad.

"You said Dr. Reed died from complications associated with an injection of cocaine; is that your testimony?" Brad wanted to make sure that no juror missed this crucial point.

"Yes, it was definitely an injection of cocaine."

"Well, Doctor, how can you tell that the cocaine was injected into Dr. Reed as opposed to absorbed in some other way...like snorting or smoking?"

"My conclusion is based on the level of cocaine found in the urine of Dr. Reed at the base hospital," explained Dr. Rydell. He looked again at the jurors. "This is not a level typically associated with snorting cocaine. When the drug is snorted, it actually narrows the blood vessels in the nose, reducing the flow of blood in that area and creating a slower absorption rate through the blood vessels into the bloodstream.

"On the other hand, the types of elevated readings we see in this case generally come from either injecting cocaine directly into a vein or smoking crack cocaine. Smoking crack, as it is called, delivers a concentrated amount of the drug to the lungs, brain, and bloodstream in mere seconds. That is why injecting cocaine or smoking crack gives users an immediate rush, whereas snorting cocaine can take several minutes to deliver a high. It all has to do with absorption rate. In my view, it would be nearly impossible to obtain the level of cocaine found in Dr. Reed from snorting cocaine several hours before the lab tests were run."

"Dr. Rydell, that would seem to explain your conclusion that Dr. Reed did not snort the cocaine that led to his death. But how could you conclude that he did not smoke crack cocaine?" asked Brad. He was following the script that he and the doctor had carefully crafted the night before.

"Judge, I object," Strobel was out of his seat again, sounding annoyed that he would have to bother to make another objection. "Same basis as before. Dr. Rydell is not a toxicologist, and he is very far afield with this line of testimony."

This time Ichabod hesitated. "I'm going to overrule your objection, Mr. Strobel. If he strays outside his area of expertise while answering the question, I'll strike the answer and instruct the jury to disregard the testimony."

"May I answer?" Dr. Rydell asked politely, looking at the judge. Brad turned around and smiled at Leslie.

"Yes, just stay within your area of expertise," instructed Ichabod.

Rydell nodded his head. "In my line of work it is customary to consult with specialists while treating patients. That is essentially what I did in the case of Dr. Reed. In this instance, I continued to consult with other specialists even after Dr. Reed's death in order to piece together what happened.

"Do you have a copy of the lab reports from the hospital?" asked Dr. Rydell. This request looked spontaneous, but it was, of course, scripted.

Brad pulled out a thick black notebook and fumbled around until he found the right tab. "Let the record reflect that the lab reports from the base hospital have been previously admitted into evidence and marked as Plaintiff's 37."

Brad handed the report to Rydell.

"Here it is," explained Rydell, pointing to a certain page. "This really didn't mean anything to me the first time I looked at it because it wasn't essential to Dr. Reed's treatment, but this urine test has no positive finding for methylecgonidine."

"And what is the significance of that, Dr. Rydell?"

"Well, you don't really smoke cocaine, you smoke a form of freebase of the drug that we have been calling 'crack.'" Rydell resumed his role as professor. "That freebase is made by boiling powdered cocaine with sodium bicarbonate, a process that frees the cocaine base from the cocaine hydrochloride. The base separates in chunks of crack cocaine. Then, when this product is smoked and absorbed into the bloodstream, it is processed by the body and produces a metabolite that will show up in a user's urine. That metabolite is called 'methylecgonidine.' The presence or absence of certain quantities of this substance is how you tell a snorter from a smoker.

"In the case of Dr. Reed, after finding a positive screening for cocaine using an immunoassay test, the lab performed a more sophisticated analysis that tested for both cocaine and its metabolite. This more sophisticated test is called a gas chromatography with mass spectrum detection, which basically creates a drug fingerprint and quantifies the drug. The cocaine was confirmed, but its metabolite, this compound called methylecgonidine, was not present in quantities that exceeded a standardized cut-off level. Thus it was not reported as positive."

"So if the user smoked crack cocaine, you would expect to find this substance. But you did not find it here?" asked Brad innocently. He wanted to make sure that every juror heard this at least twice.

"I object," Strobel bellowed again. "That last question is a leading question and should be struck. But more important, Judge, this whole line of testimony is way outside this doctor's area of expertise. May I voir dire the witness to show the court what I mean?"

"You've got to be kidding," responded Brad. "He's not allowed to voir dire my witness in the middle of his testimony. He can deal with this issue on cross."

"I'll allow a short voir dire," ruled Ichabod, sitting back and crossing her arms.

Brad held up both palms in silent protest, then turned and took his seat. Strobel rose quickly to begin his examination, his look of disdain showing the jury he was not the least bit impressed with Rydell. Strobel started peppering the witness with questions even before he got to the podium.

"Dr. Rydell, you're not a board-certified toxicologist, are you?"

"No."

"In fact, if you had a patient who presented with an unusual toxicological symptom, you would get a consult from a specialist more skilled than you in this area. Correct?"

"That's correct," said Rydell, "but I wouldn't call a cocaine overdose an unusual toxicological problem."

"Your Honor," Strobel pleaded, "please instruct the witness to just answer the question."

"Dr. Rydell," chided the judge, "please do not volunteer extraneous information."

Before Rydell could answer, Strobel was on the attack again.

"These lab reports, including the urine test, were in Dr. Reed's medical chart all the time, is that correct?"

"Yes, to my knowledge, they were," responded Rydell.

"And as the treating physician, you would have presumably reviewed them. Correct?"

"That's also true."

"But the absence of methylecgonidine meant nothing to you at the time because you knew nothing about that substance. Correct?"

"The absence of the compound did not mean anything to me at the time. That doesn't mean I knew nothing about the substance."

"Well, Dr. Rydell, isn't it fair to say that even when your deposition was taken in this case, some three months ago, you still hadn't attached any significance to the absence of this substance?"

"Yes. At the time of my deposition, I had not realized the significance of this laboratory finding. Dr. Reed tested positive for a very high level of cocaine. The absence of significant amounts of its metabolite did not impress me at the time as being that important."

"Dr. Rydell, you stated that these drug tests were confirmed with something called a gas chromatography with mass spectrum detection method, what you called a 'fingerprint' of the drug. Is that right?"

"Yes, I think that's what I said."

"Your Honor, may I approach the witness?" asked Strobel.

"Yes," said Ichabod without looking up.

Strobel began making his way toward Dr. Rydell, waving two papers, one in each hand.

"I have here two actual gas chromatographs, one that is of this compound you mentioned, methylecgonidine, and one that represents an entirely different compound. I'd like to show them to you and see if you can even tell me which is which."

Brad jumped to his feet to object, but before he could talk, the witness was answering.

"Don't bother," said Rydell. "I wouldn't have the foggiest idea. I would rely on the toxicologist to interpret those for me."

Although he conceded the point, he did it in such a nonassuming manner that it appeared he had not conceded a thing. This aggravated Strobel, who was not about to let the point die a quiet death. He stood just a few feet from the witness box and jabbed the air with the gas chromatographs.

"In fact, everything you have testified about today you gained from talking to others or reading research papers, because you are not a trained toxicologist. Until you talked to someone else, you had no idea what this substance even was, did you?"

"It's correct that everything I know about methylecgonidine I learned from others in the last few months. But the reason I researched the issue was because I watched the videotaped depositions of those witnesses that you took in Saudi Arabia. You know, the former members of the church—the ones who claim that the Reeds used cocaine. As you know, Sarah Reed claims that her husband must have been injected with the drug, but your witnesses claim—"

"Just answer the question that you've been asked, Doctor, and save the speeches," Strobel demanded. His face was red, and he emphasized each word in a staccato style: "Did you or did you not learn everything you know about methylecgonidine from talking with others or from reading research papers in the last few months?"

"Yes, I did."

"Then isn't it true, Doctor, that you would defer to those with specialized training and experience as toxicologists?" Strobel's voice was gaining volume.

"Yes, I would defer," said Rydell matter-of-factly.

"And if they had different opinions about the absence of this compound in the urine, then you would defer to the opinions of those specialists. Correct?"

"I suppose that would depend on the reasons, but generally, yes." Rydell obviously saw no harm in conceding the obvious.

Strobel then turned to Ichabod to make his case. "Then, Your Honor, in light of the witness's own admissions, I would ask that all testimony from this witness, with regard to whether the cocaine in Dr. Reed's system was snorted, smoked, or injected, should be struck as outside the realm of his expertise."

"I agree," said Ichabod as Brad was opening his mouth to respond. Ichabod turned to the jury. She left Brad standing speechless at counsel table, his face showing his disgust.

"You will disregard any and all testimony by Dr. Rydell about whether Dr. Reed had been injected with cocaine. In that regard, you should also ignore all testimony about this compound...uh, what's it called, Doctor?"

"Methylecgonidine, Your Honor," Rydell pronounced the name of the metabolite slowly and distinctly so that the jury could remember.

"Yes. You will disregard all testimony about that substance. You may not base any aspects of your deliberations on such testimony. For all practical purposes, you must simply eliminate that testimony from your mind and give it no credibility in this case. Now, is that understood?"

The jurors nodded and assured Ichabod they would wipe their thoughts clean of this enticing information. But the genie was out of the bottle and could not be put back. Most all of the jurors appeared to like Rydell. It was obvious. And Brad suspected the questions on the jurors' minds were no longer about whether Dr. Reed had been injected with cocaine, but how and why. And by whom?

Brad continued to look disgusted as he walked behind the podium to resume his examination of Rydell. He pouted through the next few questions, just to emphasize to the jury how unfair Ichabod had actually been.

Inside, he was smiling.

■ ■ ■

Rydell's testimony would have been the perfect way to end the first week of trial if Ichabod had not decided to weigh in with some preliminary opinions after she dismissed the jury for the day.

"Don't forget, Mr. Carson, that the jury only decides the case against Mr. Aberijan, but I must decide the case against the nation of Saudi Arabia. And I must say that I'm very disappointed that we've completed our first week of testimony and I have yet to hear any evidence that would implicate the nation of Saudi Arabia."

She paused, sighed, and glanced around the courtroom, as if searching for some shred of evidence that might impress her. She turned back to Brad.

"Even if I had not struck the testimony of Dr. Rydell, the most you would have is a client whose husband had been injected with cocaine. Now let's assume, although you have put no evidence into the record showing this to be true, that Mr. Aberijan himself injected Dr. Reed with cocaine. Does that mean that the nation of Saudi Arabia has to answer for everything Mr. Aberijan did? I think not."

The words, the tone, the matter-of-fact dismissal of some of his strongest evidence chiseled away at Brad's confidence and enthusiasm. Though he knew the rest of his team, including Sarah, would take their cues from him at this critical moment, he still couldn't help but lower his eyes and sag a little deeper in his chair.

"It seems clear to me that if Mr. Aberijan did any of these terrible things you have accused him of doing, he would have been exceeding his authority as an agent of the nation of Saudi Arabia, and therefore Saudi Arabia would no longer be responsible for his actions. I am therefore assuming you have some direct evidence that the nation of Saudi Arabia, through its official representatives, either authorized beforehand or ratified after the fact the alleged actions of Mr. Aberijan." She raised her eyebrows to emphasize her point. "Without that evidence, you cannot win this case."

Brad vehemently disagreed with the court's reading of the legal standard required to sustain a verdict against Saudi Arabia, but he also knew that five o'clock on a Friday afternoon was no time to start that argument. The eyes of Ichabod, his own team, and the rest of the courtroom were now on him.

He rose from his seat and stood straight, meeting the judge's steady gaze, and buttoning his top suit-coat buttons.

"We have clear and convincing evidence on just that point, Your Honor," promised Brad.

And at that very moment, he and everyone else in the courtroom wondered what in the world it could possibly be.

32

B rad had been waiting for this night for a long time and was deter-mined to make it special. He raced home after court to get out of his navy-blue, pinstriped suit and yellow power tie and throw on a com-fortable pair of jeans and a golf shirt. He was tired of dressing up and being on display. Tonight would be laid-back and casual. He would relax with a vengeance. He also threw on a pair of penny loafers with no socks. It was the Virginia Beach way.

He had offered Leslie a chance to change at his house, but she had declined. Instead, he would pick her up at the office. She wanted to cram in a few more minutes of work before taking the night off. Brad had never seen anyone obsess over a case like she did.

The rain had stopped, but it was still brisk. Brad grabbed a Wind-breaker and the keys to the Viper he kept nestled in the garage. His Cherokee would have to sit this one out. The Jeep was his workhorse, and it was littered with transcripts, trial notes, soda cans, and coffee cups. It was in no shape for a date.

But the Viper was another story. He bought it three years ago as his reward for a surprisingly big verdict in a notoriously tough case. Now it was in danger of becoming a collector's item. It had not been out of his garage for months, because he saved it for those leisurely drives that he never found time to take or those special occasions that somehow never came. But tonight qualified. This night would be special. And Prince Charming intended to show up in his jet-black, albeit dusty, Dodge Viper. Cinderella would love it.

The drive from his house to the office generally took twenty minutes without traffic, with an additional twenty minutes in rush hour. Tonight, anxious to see Leslie and driving the Viper opposite the homeward-bound traffic, he made the trip, portal to portal, in just over fifteen.

Brad parked in the fire lane outside his office building, bounced into the lobby, and waited impatiently for the elevators. Just for good measure, he punched the "up" button several times before the elevator finally arrived, an action that only seemed to slow things down. An interminable two minutes later, he stepped off at the fifth floor and entered the office of Carson & Associates.

He found her sitting in the war room, hunched over a deposition transcript, chewing on the top of her pen. She looked up when he entered and broke into a bright smile that accentuated her beautiful white teeth, high cheekbones, and sparkling blue eyes. Leslie was gorgeous. Her auburn hair was pulled back and clipped and fell softly against her white cotton blouse. She had caught the spirit of the night and wore blue jeans and white docksiders sans socks to honor the culture of the beach. Brad stared, awestruck for a moment at her natural beauty—the graceful lines of her face—then caught himself feeling embarrassed to be gawking like a teenager.

"You look great," he managed when all his glib trial skills failed him. "Its nice to see you looking so relaxed."

"Thanks, boss," she replied with a bounce in her voice, "I've been looking forward to tonight."

"Me too," said Brad, cursing himself for not being able to think of anything more clever and for not being able to take his eyes off her. "You ready?"

"I've been ready." She came over, took his hand, and gave him a quick kiss on the cheek. "And I'm starving. Where're we headed?"

Her soft touch electrified him, an invigorating surge that brought every nerve alive. Just holding her hand energized his body and paralyzed his brain. He couldn't speak, couldn't force himself to let go, couldn't alter the intensity of his gaze into her eyes.

She must have felt it too. Her eyes conveyed a depth of emotion that had never been spoken.

How can someone I've been spending so much time with suddenly make me so tongue-tied? Brad wondered. He didn't want to leave the office; he would just hold her and kiss her on the spot. He wanted to draw her to him and tell her eloquently and passionately everything he felt. She made him complete. She made him alive. She made him dizzy with emotion. Weak-kneed.

But in this defining moment, his greatest asset failed him. The tongue wouldn't work. He could think of no words to express the depths of his emotions. He was mute. Incapacitated. He would tell her later. For now he would chicken out.

"It's a surprise," he said gamely. "You'll have to trust me."

He took her hand, led her down to the Viper, and started another tour of his favorite spots in Tidewater.

"Rule number 1," Brad insisted, "is that we do not discuss work tonight."

Leslie looked at the list of questions she had jotted down on an index card, pursed her lips, then stuffed it into her pocket. "Okay," she said grudgingly, "but I'll bet Strobel's not taking the night off."

"You're incorrigible," complained Brad.

"And you love it," teased Leslie, reaching over and rubbing the back of his neck.

Indeed he did!

This was not a night to discuss the case. It was a night for wisecracks and laughing, for deep conversations, for building on the explosive chemistry between them. It was a night for holding hands and acting crazy. It was a night to become soul mates.

The couple began with a relaxed dinner at the Boulevard Café, an out-of-the-way place featuring exotic food and indoor-outdoor dining. They chose to sit under the stars and enjoy the cool evening breeze of the perfect autumn night. Much to Brad's delight, the breeze and night-time air combined to chill Leslie, causing her to move closer to him after the main course. He wrapped his arm around her and kept her warm while they nursed some hot chocolate.

For dessert Brad took her to a Tidewater icon—Doumar's Drive-In. This quaint Norfolk restaurant claimed to be the original home of the ice-cream cone and remained the undisputed ice-cream champ in the Tidewater area. Here the couple shared a banana split the old-fashioned way, as waitresses on roller skates delivered dessert to the Viper, though Brad insisted they not hook a tray on the driver's window. For tonight, and tonight only, Brad would violate one of his hard and fast rules that strictly forbade any eating in his beloved automobile. After all, rules were made to be broken.

From Doumar's, they went to MacArthur Mall for a movie. Not just any movie, but a romantic chick flick that would require no thinking, only feeling. But as the plot dragged on and the adrenaline wore off, the exhausting week in court caught up with the two of them. Leslie dozed first, then Brad succumbed, and together they slept through the second half of the film.

They laughed as they exited the mall into the parking garage and were greeted again by the cool night air. Brad told himself that he had stalled long enough. It was time to tell Leslie the depth of his feelings toward her, how much she really meant to him. The night had been perfect, and soon it would be time for a perfect ending.

"Do you remember what level we parked on?" he asked. The little things in life had never commanded much of his attention. He clicked the remote lock button on his key chain, listening for the telltale beep from his faithful Viper.

"I could have sworn we were in 3A,"said Leslie, tucked under Brad's arm.

"Oh well, it's a beautiful night for a walk," he muttered.

And walk they did. They scoured all levels of the parking garage, middle to top and back again, before they reached the only reasonable conclusion.

"It's stolen," Leslie surmised. "I know we parked on level three. We should call the police."

"I can't believe this," fumed Brad. It would be hard to pour out his feelings without the Viper. The back of a cab just didn't have the same ambiance. "It's the only mall in America that charges you to park, and they don't even patrol the garage? These rent-a-cop guards at the mall are a joke. With all the money they're making off parking fees, you'd think they could afford—"

It hit him in midsentence. A scenario worse than a stolen car. This couldn't be happening. *Couldn't be.* Not tonight.

Only one person would know. He needed to call her, but he had left his cell phone in the Viper. "Can I borrow your phone?" Brad asked.

A few minutes later he was on the phone with a groggy Bella.

"I'm sure they repossessed it, Brad. I've been stalling your banker all week. I made a few payments on the Jeep, but I knew you never used the Viper. Frankly, your banker said he had to do something to make it look like he's being aggressive. I told him not to touch the Jeep or the house. I guess he took that as a green light to go after the Viper. I'm sorry, Brad. I figured it wouldn't see the light of day until the case was over."

"Don't worry about it, Bella. You're doing the best you can. We'll just catch a taxi."

"No you won't, Brad Carson. I wouldn't hear of it. You just sit tight."

Shrugging off Brad's protests, Bella showed up at the parking garage ten minutes later. She was wearing her bathrobe.

"Hop in," Bella said cheerily—and entirely out of character. "I'll chauffeur you guys to your destinations."

Brad opened the back door of the Honda Accord and choked slightly on the smell of cigarette smoke. He moved a few empty fast-food bags and their matching cups. Carefully avoiding the stale fries on the floor, he slid over next to the dry cleaning, and Leslie gingerly joined him.

For the next twenty minutes, they listened politely, and sometimes even responded, to Bella's endless banter about the case and Ichabod. Bella insisted on using the rearview mirror to maintain eye contact as she talked, a habit that only exacerbated her horrid driving skills. After a few minutes of foolishly trying to survive Bella's chauffeuring without seat belts, Brad and Leslie pulled the begrimed belts from between the seat cushions, dusted off the crumbs, and put them to good use.

They were greatly relieved when Bella pulled next to Leslie's car in the parking lot at the office.

"Thanks so much, Bella," said Brad as he and Leslie climbed out of the car. "Leslie can give me a ride home from here."

"Nonsense," replied Bella. "She's got to drive all the way to Williamsburg. I'll take you home. I've got nothing else to do. And Leslie, you can stay at my place tonight if you want to."

"Thanks Bella," said Leslie without a moment's hesitation. "But I really do need to get home tonight. I've got lots of errands to run first thing in the morning."

"Suit yourself," Bella shrugged her shoulders and took out a cigarette. "Brad, this will give us a chance to talk about the financial picture and any personal items you had in that Viper. Besides, I've got some news on my mother you'll love to hear."

"Okay," said Brad, looking at Bella and winking. "Just give me a minute."

He was determined not to let this opportunity pass. He walked Leslie to her car and helped her in. She rolled down her window, and he leaned down to talk out of Bella's hearing.

"Sorry about the way this ended," he said. "It wasn't exactly how I planned it."

"But it was still perfect," she said. "Because I got to spend time with you."

Leslie placed her hand behind Brad's head and gently pulled him toward her. They closed their eyes and savored the moment, lost in the gentle passion of the kiss, the warm rush of emotion, oblivious to the missing Viper, Bella, or anyone else in the world.

It was, Brad thought, the perfect ending to the perfect night.

■ ■ ■

Hanif completed his sermon with a flourish and closed his Bible. He lowered his voice a few notches and stopped his pacing. Now was not the time for motivation but for a straightforward family chat.

He looked into the eyes of the upturned faces of the church members. They occupied every inch of the living room and spilled into the kitchen.

"Two things can bring this church down," he began in an earnest tone, "and both have to do with controlling the tongue. Remember the words of James, 'The tongue is a little member and boasts great things. See how great a forest a little fire kindles!'

"There are some among us who cannot keep the secrets and confidences of this church. I have reason to believe that in the days ahead the persecution of the church will intensify, and the efforts of the Muttawa to hunt us down and destroy us will increase. If you are not ready to endure for the cause of Christ, then you should leave now."

Hanif paused and surveyed the room. He saw little fear. His tone remained calm and reassuring. "If you leave, this church will understand, and you will not be held in contempt. We will not speak or think badly of you. The narrow path is not for everyone."

He waited again. Nobody moved. Most scarcely breathed.

"If you stay, we must demand utmost secrecy in the days ahead and your complete allegiance. Remember, 'God has not given us a spirit of fear, but of power and of love and of a sound mind.'"

The amens floated upward.

"There is one other matter of the tongue," Hanif continued. "It has to do with spreading rumors about one another."

He again paused and looked around, intentionally catching the eyes of the most likely offenders. "One rumor in particular has to do with one of the founders of this church, my brother, Rasheed, and his wife, Mobara. I have heard it rumored that Rasheed sold out this church, gave testimony in the American legal system against the matriarch of the church, Madame Sarah Reed, and then turned his back on the faith."

He had their attention. The rumors had indeed been flying. And it didn't help matters that Rasheed and Mobara had been absent for months from the meetings of the very church they had helped establish.

"I know personally that these rumors are not true. I know things I cannot tell you. On this, you must trust me. But I can tell you that my brother and his wife have never turned their backs on this precious faith. They no longer attend this church because they are being watched closely and followed by the authorities. They love this church too much to thrust it into danger. They have banished themselves from meeting with you. But they asked me to express their love and prayers."

Hanif paused, and silence engulfed the small room. "It is true that Rasheed gave testimony in the American case involving Madame Sarah Reed. Again, there are things I cannot tell you about that testimony. But this I can say: Mr. Ahmed Aberijan has not heard the last from Rasheed Berjein."

Hanif looked around the room. Heads were nodding. Those who knew Rasheed seemed glad to see the rumors put to rest.

"I wish I could tell you more, but I may have already said too much. At the right time, not so long from now, you will understand completely. 'Now we see in a mirror, dimly, but then face to face.' Until then, hold all these things in strictest confidence. Now let us pray."

As Hanif closed his eyes to lead in prayer, he wondered if he had done the right thing. "Tell the truth and trust the people," Rasheed once told him. But maybe there were some things better left unsaid.

■ ■ ■

Nikki's peaceful Sunday morning faded a bit more with each click of the remote. Coverage of the trial was everywhere. Judge Cynthia Baker-Kline's intemperate remarks at the close of court on Friday sent a shock wave of urgency into the public relations war. The Christian Right sensed another betrayal coming from the leftist and elitist judiciary. Conservative talk-show hosts and firebrand preachers took up the cause and filled the airwaves with dire predictions and sky-is-falling rhetoric.

In the other corner, the radical Muslim groups used Baker-Kline's comments to paint the picture of a case built on evidence so flimsy that not even a judge biased against their cause would buy it. What a travesty, they suggested, if such a spurious case went to this prejudiced jury who would then find against them based solely on Arab and Muslim stereotypes.

Nikki poured herself another Diet Coke, energized by the caffeine and the controversy.

The renewed intensity of the debate sparked threats of protests and civil disobedience from various antiestablishment groups. The leftist fringe groups, from hard-core environmentalists to libertarians, took the opportunity to rail against a corrupt American judicial system and to promise all sorts of trouble for the overworked police. The right-wing militias could not sit idly by as their counterparts on the left took up arms. The militias railed against the corrupt American judicial system and threatened to take matters into their own hands if the police couldn't handle the nuts on the left.

National networks and cable news channels, loving the hailstorm of controversy, spent their time interviewing the most colorful and outspoken proponents of the various causes and reminding the public of upcoming special coverage. Even the president got into the act. He called for cool heads and peaceful protests and, together with the governor of the Commonwealth, ordered the Virginia National Guard to be on standby with full riot gear when the courtroom opened on Monday morning.

"I can hardly wait," Nikki muttered and turned to MTV.

■ ■ ■

"I don't know why you're so stubborn about when Shelhorse is going to testify," Leslie huffed, her arms folded in exasperation. Friday night seemed distant. The happy couple had morphed into two strong-willed, disagreeing attorneys by Sunday afternoon.

"I told you, we've got to finish strong," insisted Brad. "We already have one dynamite rebuttal witness. If we save Shelhorse for rebuttal as well, then we'll finish with a very strong one-two punch before the case goes to the jury."

"We may not even get it to the jury if we don't put on our best witnesses when we have the chance," argued Nikki. "Shelhorse is strong. She may help turn Ichabod before it's too late."

Brad had cleared a path for pacing around his side of the large conference room table. He gnawed on his glasses.

"But if we put her on before Strobel's case, before Strobel shows the videotaped testimony from those former church members, her testimony will lose its impact. If we wait, she'll make it plain that Khartoum is a liar. Putting her on first will just cause Strobel to withdraw the testimony of Khartoum and not show the videotape."

"He can't do that," said Leslie. "He's already showed portions of those videotapes in his opening statement."

"And you think that will stop him?" Brad asked, his voice rising.

They had debated this for thirty minutes, and Leslie sensed that any further argument would fall on deaf ears. She instead tried to convince Brad with stony silence, pursing her lips and pinning her eyes to the table. When all else failed, especially with a guy who's nuts for you...pout.

Nikki joined her in this quiet conspiracy.

"Look," Brad said finally, "I know you don't agree with this strategy, and if Bella were here it would probably be three against one, but my gut tells me this is the way to go. We put Aberijan on the stand as a hostile witness for cross-examination on Monday. Then we put our police-brutality expert and our other docs and nurses on the stand Tuesday and Wednesday. We end our case with the kids on Thursday.

"Then we hunker down for Strobel's case. He'll play the videotapes and put about ten experts on the stand to contradict everything we've said. That will take two weeks. Then we call our rebuttal witnesses—including Shelhorse—and leave their compelling testimony ringing in the ears of the jury just before closing arguments. Do you really think that's such a bad plan?"

"Yeah," Nikki shrugged.

Leslie still had her arms folded and lips pursed. "Does it matter?" she asked sarcastically.

"Not really," said Brad. "Let's get busy."

"You're such a chauvinist." Leslie could not let it go.

"Don't give me that," Brad said. "This has nothing to do with what sex you are; it has everything to do with who's financing the case and who has twenty years of experience, and who's ultimately responsible for calling the shots. I highly respect you and Nikki and your opinions. But on this one, I've got to go with my gut."

"That's what I'm saying," Leslie retorted. "This 'go with your gut' thing, this 'make the tough call on your own' mentality even if everybody else thinks it's a bad idea—it's all such a macho deal to you."

To Brad's credit he stood his ground in silence for a full minute as the women stared at him.

"I've got to make this call, and my gut tells me this is the way to go," he said finally, almost to himself.

Leslie and Nikki looked at each other and shook their heads. "He's a chauvinist," they said in unison.

■ ■ ■

Bella had dreaded it all weekend. But she absolutely knew she needed to speak to Nikki. She had tried on Friday night, but the timing wasn't right. Saturday and Sunday had been major workdays, and now it was already Sunday night.

Bella decided to have one more cigarette first, just to calm her nerves. She shuffled down to the kitchen, feeling more guilty than ever about her cigarette breaks. One more nail in her coffin, as Nikki would say. She was definitely going to quit. She was dead serious about it. Since becoming a Christian, she had started praying that God would take this habit away. If He didn't do it by the end of the *Reed* case, then she would take matters into her own hands.

One way or the other, she was going to quit. Definitely.

She lit the cigarette and inhaled deeply, the very rhythm of it calming her down. She craved her smokes more than ever these days. Just knowing that she would soon quit had her thinking about it all the time. She sucked on the thin white stick again, a long and smooth breath, and sent smoke rings toward the ceiling.

How would Nikki react? Would she scream and cuss? Faint? Just stand there stunned?

Another drag, this time not as hard. She wanted to make this one last. Afterward, with no excuses, she would march straight into Nikki's office and confront the matter. No sense rushing that moment.

Quicker than she would have liked, her cigarette was gone. She snuffed it out, thought about another, and talked herself out of it. She would come back after her talk with Nikki. She would certainly be entitled by then.

She walked slowly down the hallway, her head down. Against all of her rationalizations, she walked straight to Nikki's office, defeating one by one each of the excuses her brain was throwing at her. The door was open, and she walked in.

To her great surprise, and even greater relief...the place was empty. Nikki had already left.

It must not be God's will to do this, thought Bella. *At least not tonight.*

She had tried. God knew she had tried.

She sighed and headed back toward the kitchen. She covered the same ground more quickly this time, and her lighter was in her hand before she made it through the kitchen door.

33

Monday morning, after a few hours of last-minute cramming, the trial team from Carson & Associates piled into Brad's Jeep for the morning commute. Bella stayed behind to call witnesses and tend to other office matters. Leslie drove so that Brad could spend a few more minutes going over the planned cross-examination of Aberijan.

"You ready?" she asked.

"I don't really know. You tell me at lunch whether I was ready. I ought to be done by then."

"I expect him to break down on the stand and start crying, Perry Mason style," said Nikki from the backseat. Brad immediately thought about Sarah's performance as a witness, and an awkward silence followed.

The point appeared to be lost on Nikki. "Hey, can you turn that up?" she asked. The radio station was playing one of her favorites.

"Actually, could you turn that off for a few minutes?" asked Brad. "I need to go over this one more time, and it's hard to concentrate."

"Tomorrow, I drive my own car," declared Nikki. "You can't get ready for trial without tunes."

Leslie killed the radio, and the crew drove on in relative silence. While Nikki hummed, Brad looked through the contents of his briefcase one more time, reviewing the tools of his cross-examination.

He glanced over the marked and indexed deposition transcript of Aberijan. If the man tried to deviate from the deposition in the slightest way, Brad was prepared to beat him up with the prior testimony. He double-checked the exhibits he would be using as well: medical records for

Charles and Sarah Reed, the police report from that fateful night, and the court records of the former church members who testified against Sarah.

Brad's briefcase nearly overflowed with weapons for cross-examination. Aberijan didn't know it was coming. He would never guess Brad would call him to the stand as an adverse witness in the middle of the plaintiff's case. Brad couldn't wait to see the look on his face.

There was nothing Brad liked better than trial by ambush.

■　■　■

As Brad and his team walked around the corner and onto Granby Street, they got an up-close look at the chaos outside the federal courthouse. The huge block-and-mortar special, built during the public works projects of the Depression years, spanned the entire block. The sidewalk in front was cordoned off by police tape and a human wall of law-enforcement officers and National Guardsmen, working valiantly to keep the sidewalk open for court personnel and others with official business.

Demonstrators pressed against the line of officers and spilled out into Granby Street, blocking traffic. As usual, the camps squared off against each other in the roadway.

As Brad walked toward the volcanic mass of humanity, he had a feeling that something didn't seem quite right, something other than the magnitude of the crowd was different today. In the next instant, he realized what it was. For some reason, possibly having to do with who arrived first at the courthouse that morning, the demonstrators had switched sides. Today, the people who were sympathetic to Saudi Arabia and the various leftist causes stood between Brad's team and the courthouse.

There would be no high-fives this morning. Instead, Brad and the team would have to run the gauntlet of a hostile crowd.

Brad instinctively picked up the pace and moved in front of the women on the sidewalk. He pulled Sarah close to his right side. Nikki fell in step behind Brad, Leslie behind Sarah. Brad missed Bella.

"It's Carson and Reed," yelled a cameraman.

As if on cue, a wave of demonstrators pivoted in the team's direction and hurled themselves forward in fits and surges. The police line held, their shields and arms forming a barrier for Brad and his team. Brad stared ahead and set a faster pace, concerned about the uncontrollable sea of wild-haired radicals, some with signs and others with that possessed look in their eyes, pressing in on the police officers. The crowd lunged again, and the officers hoisted riot shields and started pushing against the crowd, holding them back.

Who started what, Brad had no idea, but screams and the sound of breaking bottles filled the air. The mob panicked.

"Run!" Brad yelled.

He and the women sprinted for the courthouse steps. He reached out to grab Sarah's arm and glanced over his shoulder just in time to see a protester with a leather vest and orange hair break through the police lines and grab Nikki. Brad turned and swung his briefcase with all his might, catching the demonstrator on the shoulder and neck, knocking him to the ground. Nikki's blouse ripped, but she pulled free, kicked off her heels, and raced toward the steps.

The police instantly subdued the demonstrator, but by breaking ranks they allowed another wave onto the sidewalk. Bent on revenge, the angry group grabbed Brad and mauled him.

He landed on the ground with what seemed like two tons of humanity on top of him. Pain shot through his right knee and hip. He tried to catch himself, but his arm buckled and his elbow bounced on the hard surface. He tried swinging his arms and kicking his legs against this suffocating mass. A fist caught him in the right eye. He tried desperately to get up, but his arms and legs were pinned beneath the mass of bodies, the piles of beefy flesh on top of him.

He heard somebody yell "tear gas," and he closed his eyes and held his breath. In the next moment, he felt the bodies rising off of him. He struggled free, squinting to see. A huge mountain of a man helped him to his feet. The man propped Brad up, wrapped a thick arm around his slender shoulders, and shielded the attorney as they walked toward the courthouse. Brad coughed and hacked, his eyes watering. He saw at least two bottles bounce off the man's shoulder as they advanced together toward the steps.

The man opened the door and nearly threw Brad inside, then he followed and pulled the door shut behind him. Leslie and Sarah, who had each somehow avoided the clutches of the mob, embraced Brad. Nikki sat in the hallway in her stocking feet. She looked stunned. Brad's benefactor and new friend helped her to her feet. He wore a federal marshal's uniform. The man's massive back muscles heaved as he caught his breath.

"You okay?" he asked.

"Yeah, I'm great," Nikki answered. She had apparently conquered her initial fear and now looked thirsty for revenge. Fire blazed in her eyes. "Let me borrow your piece, and I'll go out there and calm things down."

The man laughed deep and loud, then turned to look at Brad. "You okay?" he asked.

"I guess," said Brad, letting out a huge sigh as he let go of Sarah and Leslie. He extended his sore right arm to shake the man's hand.

"Clarence!" Brad suddenly exclaimed.

He threw his arms open and gave Clarence a huge hug. "Where would I be without you, man?"

"I reckon you'd still be a human punching bag outside," Clarence drawled. "Where's that beefy secretary of yours when you really need her?"

Brad laughed—it felt good to laugh—and then he began taking stock. He had lost his briefcase in the struggle, and his arm ached where his elbow had hit the pavement. His ribs hurt, his right eye throbbed, and both eyes stung from the tear gas. He wondered if the right eye would bruise and make him look like a raccoon. His knee and hip, however, hurt the most. He noticed a small tear on the knee of his pants and a slight trickle of blood. He was beat and bruised, but worse, he couldn't remember landing a single good punch.

As the adrenaline began to wear off and pain surfaced in its place, the voices in the hallway became distant. Clarence and the others swirled around him. Nausea. Vertigo. Brad looked down at his trembling hands, tried to steady himself, and decided to find the men's room. He staggered down the hallway, refusing assistance, one hand steadying him along the wall. He made it into one of the stalls, bent over the toilet, and hurled his breakfast.

A few minutes later, he heard the door open and the sound of heavy steps on the tile floor.

"The ladies sent me in to check on ya. How're ya doin'?" Clarence asked.

"Never better," Brad gasped between heaves.

■ ■ ■

Ichabod stared impassively at Brad Carson in her chambers as he recounted his ordeal.

"I need a one-day continuance, Your Honor. After what happened this morning, I just need a little time. Look," he said as he showed Ichabod his ripped pants. "Plus they took my briefcase, which has my notes for my examination of the next witness."

Ichabod removed her glasses and rubbed her eyes. She was suddenly weary. *This can't be happening. What is it with this guy? Always the martyr.* She would have to tread carefully here.

"I'm sorry you were assaulted," she began. Her face betrayed no emotion. "If you need medical help, let's get you to the hospital." She paused for a beat and sucked in a huge breath. "But if not, I'm not inclined to delay the trial. They'll just be back in greater force tomorrow if they know they can disrupt these proceedings, and we've already got the jury here. We can't let the protesters run our trial schedule."

Brad Carson stared at his feet and shook his head.

She could feel the sympathy in the room. Even Strobel didn't look happy. Silence descended on her chambers.

Leslie finally broke the quiet. "You've got to be kidding," she said incredulously. "This man almost got killed outside, the police had to use tear gas to control the mob, and you're not going to give us one lousy day to get his notes back together?"

Just what I need. Brad Carson in a skirt.

"Don't take this out on me, young lady," Ichabod scolded, now standing behind her desk. "I'm sorry you went through a gauntlet out there, but maybe if the lawyers in this room would keep their mouths shut"— she realized her voice had crescendoed, and she stopped to catch her breath and soften her tone—"if they would not be so vitriolic when the media start asking questions, we wouldn't have such a circus out there."

"This is ridiculous," Leslie muttered under her breath.

"Do you have something to say?" Ichabod shot back.

"Not to you."

"Then you'd better keep your mouth shut, or you'll be reading about this case from jail." Ichabod stared Leslie down for a moment as the words echoed in her chambers. Leslie stared back, refusing to divert her eyes and give Ichabod a psychological victory. Finally, the judge looked at Brad, released a huge sigh, and sat back down in her chair. She took a few deep breaths, and some of the tension seeped from the room.

"Look, I know this is not easy for anyone," she said at last. "So here's what I'm going to do. I'll give you the morning off to get checked out and to get a change of clothes. We'll reconvene at 1 P.M. I'll keep the jury waiting in the jury room until then. I don't want to send them out past that mob." She paused and took a reading of the lawyers in the room. "Is that acceptable, Mr. Carson?"

"If we can't get a full day's continuance, then I'd rather start this morning," Brad said stubbornly.

Ichabod snorted. *Whatever!* "All right then. Have it your way. Court will reconvene in fifteen minutes. Let the record reflect that I offered Mr. Carson a continuance until this afternoon and he refused."

"And let the record reflect that I object," Brad added.

Ichabod bolted up out of her chair and surveyed the room. "You are dismissed," she said. She leaned forward, unsmiling and impassive, on her desk as Brad, Leslie, the court reporter, and Strobel filed out of her chambers.

It was not easy being a federal court judge. But even in chaotic times like this morning, some principles were intransigent, unchanging, and sure.

Justice delayed is justice denied, she reminded herself as she slipped on her black robe and prepared to enter her fiefdom. Things in the street might border on anarchy, but in Courtroom Number 1, Judge Cynthia Baker-Kline maintained order with an iron fist.

■ ■ ■

If he was surprised, he didn't show it. When he heard his name called as the next witness, Ahmed Aberijan stood up tall and straight and absolutely sauntered to the witness stand. He proudly took his seat and glared out at Brad with cold, dark eyes. A translator stood next to him.

"Raise your right hand and repeat after me," said the court clerk. The translator spoke. Ahmed did not move his hand. He spoke back to the translator in Arabic.

"He cannot take the oath," the translator said, "for religious reasons."

Ichabod seemed irritated, but she had undoubtedly confronted this before. "Just ask him if he promises to tell the truth," she instructed the translator. "Tell him it's not an oath. But also tell him that if he does not tell the truth, he will be guilty of perjury and face a possible fine or jail time."

After speaking to Ahmed, the translator turned back to Ichabod. "He understands," he assured the judge. "And he wishes me to thank this court for not forcing an oath."

Brad rolled his eyes and took his place behind the podium, shielding the small tear in his slacks. Nikki had told him there was a dark shadow forming around his right eye and suggested he turn a little more to the left so the jury would notice it. Brad ignored her advice and stood squarely facing Ahmed. He had no notes or papers at the podium with him. He felt vulnerable and exposed, nearly naked, the weapons of his cross-examination lost somewhere on Granby Street.

He began his questions more confidently than he felt. "We can dispense with the pretense that you don't understand English, can't we, Mr. Aberijan? Isn't it true that you speak English very well?" Brad asked sharply.

The translator did his work and issued his reply. "This is not true. I do not understand more than a few words of your language."

"Do you remember when you were personally served with this lawsuit by my paralegal, Ms. Moreno, at the law firm of Kilgore & Strobel."

"Yes, I remember very well," came back the translated reply.

"And isn't it a fact, Mr. Aberijan, that you threatened her in English? That you said to her, after she served you with the suit papers: 'You will pay?'"

After the translator finished, Ahmed looked perplexed. He gave a lengthy reply that the translator interpreted in segments.

"No, this is not a fact. Your paralegal, this Miss Moreno, she comes running at me at the law firm like she will attack me. Mr. Strobel is running behind her because she has entered his offices illegally. I think maybe she carries a gun. She throws the papers at me and is arrested for her unlawful conduct. I speak to her in Arabic saying, 'What is the meaning of this?' I do not give her any threats or say anything in English."

As Ahmed answered, Brad kicked himself. *Never ask a question that allows the witness to give a narrative response. Never ask a question you don't know the answer to. Establish rhythm. Keep him off balance. C'mon, Carson. It's Lawyering 101.* He took a deep breath.

"I noticed you refused to take an oath because of religious reasons. True?"

"This is true," said the translator after an exchange with Ahmed.

"And you believe this court should not require you to take an oath. Correct?"

"This is also true," the translator affirmed.

"In fact, if the court had tried to make you take an oath on the Christian Bible, you would have refused to do that because of religious reasons. Correct?"

"Objection," said Strobel, standing. "This is irrelevant."

"I will link it up if the court allows me a few more questions," promised Brad.

"You're on a short leash, counselor," Ichabod warned. "Go ahead."

The translator spoke to Ahmed. "Yes, that is right."

"And the basis on which a person like you can refuse to take an oath in an American court, if the oath violates your religious beliefs, is because we have freedom of religion based on the U.S. Constitution and the UN Declaration of Human Rights. Correct?"

"How can he possibly know that?" Strobel jumped up and asked. "He's not a lawyer."

"Is that an objection?" asked Ichabod.

"Yes."

"Sustained."

Though the words had not been translated, the smug look on Aberijan's face deepened. Brad's goal in this examination was to wipe it off.

"Well, Mr. Aberijan," continued Brad, "you are an officer of the law and of the courts in Saudi Arabia. Correct?"

"Yes, that is true," the translator answered.

"And in Saudi Arabia, the court procedures and laws are based on Islamic law, and no one can refuse to follow them even if they have different religious beliefs. Is that true?"

The question and answer were translated.

"Yes, Mr. Carson. Our people are an Islamic people. Our laws and our procedures follow the Koran and honor Allah. When foreign citizens like Mrs. Reed come to our country, they know that they must follow our customs and our laws to live in our country."

"Is your country a member of the United Nations?" asked Brad. It was hard to get a rhythm with this guy. The translator interpreted the questions and answers slowly, giving Ahmed plenty of time to phrase his answers.

"Yes."

"And your country has signed the UN Charter and the UN Universal Declaration of Human Rights. Correct?"

"Yes, we have."

"Are you aware that Article 18 of the Declaration states as follows," Brad reached down and took a copy of the exhibit from Leslie. Fortunately, Leslie had kept a copy of this one critical document in her briefcase. "'Everyone has freedom of thought, conscience and religion; this right includes freedom to change his religion or belief, and freedom, either alone or in community with others and in public or private, to manifest his religion or belief in teaching, practice, worship and observance?'"

The article was translated in bits and pieces to Ahmed. He thought for a moment, recognizing the precariousness of his position, and apparently decided that ignorance would be bliss.

"I am not aware of the exact language, no."

Brad looked incredulous. He hoped the jury was watching.

"You mean to tell me that you are the head of the Muttawa, the religious police in Saudi Arabia responsible for enforcing laws that govern religious activities and worship in your country, and you are not familiar with the language from the UN Charter that your country signed?"

The heads on the jury swung from Brad to Ahmed during the translation. Their faces were skeptical.

"This Charter is not what governs my work in our country. Our laws require our citizens to follow Islamic law and practice. The United Nations is not sovereign in my country; the government of the Kingdom of Saudi Arabia is sovereign."

"In Saudi Arabia, does a Muslim have the freedom mentioned in Article 18 to change his religious beliefs and become a Christian?"

"No," was the translated reply.

"Does a Christian in Saudi Arabia have the freedom mentioned in Article 18 to practice his religious beliefs, if that practice includes seeking converts?"

"No."

"And isn't it true that if someone tries to convert from Islam to Christianity in your country, they can be punished with death?" Brad picked up the volume, the pace, and the intensity of his words.

"Objection," inserted Strobel. Brad knew the old warrior was just trying to disrupt his rhythm.

"Based on what?" asked Ichabod.

"Relevancy," explained Strobel. A typical answer when lawyers don't know what else to say.

Ichabod smirked. "Nonsense. Overruled. Mr. Carson is asking about the very law Mr. Aberijan enforces."

Brad was surprised and energized by her ruling. Could it be that Ichabod was finally starting to support his cause? He would push it and find out, but first he waited for Aberijan's reply.

"Yes," Aberijan admitted through his translator. "We are an Islamic country founded on Islamic laws. Conversion to another religion is blasphemous of Allah and punishable with death."

"And you yourself, Mr. Aberijan, have presided over numerous public beheadings of those whose only crime was to follow another religion. True?" Brad rocked forward as he spoke, his tone and face registering his total condemnation, his disgust for the man sitting before him. The man with the smug little smile.

"Objection," said Strobel. "This is ridiculous. Prior actions of this man are not relevant. We are here today only with regard to what happened between Mr. Aberijan and the Reeds, not with regard to the alleged punishment of others who violated Saudi law in the past."

"I agree," snarled Ichabod. "Mr. Carson, that question is improper. Ladies and gentlemen of the jury, you will ignore the question and any implications associated with it. You must completely erase it from your mind. Whatever Mr. Aberijan did or did not do in the past is not relevant here. You are to judge only his conduct on the night in question."

So much for Ichabod's changing her mind.

The jurors nodded their agreement with Ichabod's instructions, but their eyes betrayed a growing distrust for Ahmed. Brad decided to drive the point home.

"And it's the job of your agency, the Muttawa, to enforce these laws that require death for any Muslim converting to Judaism or Christianity or Buddhism or—"

"Objection!"

"Mr. Carson," interrupted Ichabod, almost simultaneously with Strobel's objection, "move away from this line of questioning and get to the facts of this case *now*." Her telltale vein became noticeable.

"Judge, I believe we have a right to show that the laws of this man's country permit executions for religious reasons, and that this man has himself executed offenders in the past and would not hesitate to do so with regard to Dr. Reed, even without the formality of a trial and conviction."

Brad had lit the fuse, and the Ichabod bomb responded. "Dismiss the jury," she ordered.

The jury stood and filed out. Some members quietly glanced over their shoulders at Brad, offering support with their eyes. It was all the encouragement Brad needed to face the fuming Ichabod.

For the next five minutes, Brad endured a tongue-lashing that made him wish someone would throw him back to the demonstrators. Ichabod's adjectives for his conduct included everything from *unethical* to *childish*. Her threats ranged from contempt to reporting his conduct to the state bar to ensuring that he would never practice law in federal court again. Her speech was punctuated with "yes ma'ams" from Brad and an occasional "sorry, Your Honor." He sounded contrite and fell all over himself to apologize. He took his licks, content in the knowledge that while Ichabod screamed, the jury sat in the conference room and contemplated the likelihood that, as part of his job, Ahmed had killed previously in the name of religion and would probably do so again.

The Ichabod storm eventually fizzled out with no major damage to Brad's wallet and no jail sentence. Brad considered himself a lucky man. Ichabod called the jury back into the courtroom.

■   ■   ■

The drama created by Ichabod's wrath and the showdown between Brad and Ahmed caused all eyes to focus on these actors at center stage of the theater of the courtroom. For that reason, no one but Leslie seemed to notice when two well-dressed, middle-aged men with thin briefcases entered through the back door and squeezed into the seats on the first row just behind the barefooted Nikki.

Nikki whispered something to the men, but Leslie could not hear her words. One shook his head. "Not yet," Leslie saw him mouth to Nikki, who turned back with a frown. Leslie could not catch her eye.

The men turned their attention to Brad's cross-examination. Leslie pretended to be equally focused, but she kept watch on the men—and Nikki.

■ ■ ■

Brad shifted his weight, wincing at the pain that stabbed his knee, and reached for his reading glasses from his suit-coat pocket. Gone. Lost in the ruckus that morning. With or without his glasses to gnaw on, he decided to attack the issue of whether Ahmed had been acting as an agent of the government of Saudi Arabia when he visited the Reeds' apartment.

"Who was paying your salary on the night in question?"

"The government of Saudi Arabia." Brad could see the wheels turning in Ahmed's head as he tried to anticipate where Brad was going.

"And who paid the salary of the other members of the Muttawa?"

"The government of Saudi Arabia."

"And who owned the squad cars that transported you to the scene?"

"The government of Saudi Arabia."

A light of recognition dawned in Ahmed's eyes. That smug, tight-lipped smile, however, never changed.

"You do admit, do you not, that a stun gun was used that night on Dr. Reed?"

"Yes, a stun gun was necessary to subdue him. He was violent and out of control, probably because of the drugs he had taken."

"Who owned the stun gun?"

"One of my officers."

"No. I mean, who provided all the equipment—the handcuffs, the stun guns—all the things you used as an officer of the law."

Ahmed hesitated after the translation. "They are provided by the government of Saudi Arabia."

"You, sir, were there to enforce a law of the Kingdom of Saudi Arabia in your capacity as head of the Muttawa, the religious police of Saudi Arabia. You were paid by Saudi Arabia, equipped by Saudi Arabia, and authorized by Saudi Arabia. Isn't it true you were acting as an agent of Saudi Arabia at the time of this arrest?"

For Brad and, he hoped, for the jurors, the answer was obvious. He didn't really care what Ahmed said in response. The power was in asking the question.

Still Ahmed appeared unfazed.

"I was acting as an agent of Saudi Arabia to enforce its laws," the translator explained. "And as long as I and the other officers acted lawfully, we were within our authority. And we did nothing wrong. But if any officers had done what your client suggests, if any officers had tortured the Reeds or planted drugs or killed Dr. Reed or Mrs. Reed, those officers would have been outside their authority and no longer acting lawfully on behalf of the Kingdom. Our highest-ranking officials have made it clear that they will not tolerate any kind of police misconduct."

"Did anyone from Saudi Arabia ever investigate your conduct on the night in question?"

"Of course," was the reply. "We were investigated by many."

"Did any government official ever discipline you, reprimand you, or in any way tell you that they disapproved of your conduct?"

"No, because we did nothing wrong."

"Charles Reed died!" Brad blurted out. "And you have the audacity to say you did nothing wrong?" Brad was livid at Ahmed's cool and calculating manner on the stand. The smug little act of this unflappable sadist was getting under his skin.

The translator gave Brad a puzzled look. "Could you use a different word than 'audacity'?" he asked innocently. "I do not think I can translate that word."

Juror number 4 snickered.

"Withdraw the question," Brad snapped. "Why did you raid the Reed's apartment on a Friday evening?"

"We were informed they would be having a meeting of their church and drug operation at that time."

"Were they?"

"No, the other members of the drug ring were not present. We believe someone inside the church found out about our plans."

"And therefore when you arrived on Friday night, the only persons home were the Reeds. Correct?"

"Yes."

"Then answer me this," said Brad. "If someone informed the Reeds that you were coming, and they cancelled a meeting of the church, why would the Reeds inject cocaine before you came, knowing that they would just be arrested and thrown into jail?"

"Objection," announced Strobel. "He can't possibly answer that question without being a mind reader."

"That's precisely the problem," answered Brad before Ichabod could rule. "Nobody could possibly answer that question, because no logical answer exists. I'll withdraw the question at this time."

It was one of many unanswered questions from Brad's seven-hour cross-examination of Ahmed Aberijan that would later haunt the jury.

At 5 P.M., Ahmed dodged his last question, and Ichabod dismissed court for the day. The two well-dressed gentlemen and Nikki exchanged some notes and a handshake. Clarence reappeared at Brad's elbow and escorted all the lawyers and litigants out a well-concealed side exit, away from the volatile demonstrators on Granby Street.

■ ■ ■

Brad had been practicing law for twelve years and had never endured a day remotely like this. He had been roughed up by demonstrators, chewed out by the judge, and forced to conduct the biggest cross-examination of his life while wearing torn clothes and without the benefit of his notes or his beloved reading glasses. As Leslie drove back to the office and the sun inched lower in the sky, Brad felt the adrenaline and energy leave his body. The boisterous voices of the women, who were making fun of Ahmed's evasive answers, faded into the background and morphed into Brad's dreams. By the time they reached the parking lot, he was fast asleep.

They didn't move him or wake him as they softly closed the car doors and cracked the windows. Leslie would handle the medical doctors and nurses who would testify tomorrow. The least they could do was allow Brad a few hours of well-earned sleep. So, while the rest of the team prepared for court on Tuesday, and while commentators around the world critiqued the day's events, the man who had been at the vortex snored soundly, sprawled out in the front seat of his Jeep in a Virginia Beach parking lot. For an hour and a half, he enjoyed dreams of captivated jurors and endured nightmares of outraged judges. And for an hour and a half, the world turned without the help of Brad Carson.

34

Tuesday provided a much-needed respite in the trial's intensity level. The demonstrators discovered that the National Guard and Norfolk's finest were serious about arresting anyone who disturbed the peace again, a fact that had a calming effect on all but the most radical elements. Ichabod had no more to say about the paucity of Brad's evidence, giving the demonstrators one less reason to get their blood in a boil. All in all, Tuesday was just another day in court.

Leslie handled the witnesses while Brad sat at the counsel table and nursed his shiner. The doctors at the base hospital who treated Charles Reed marched to the stand and swore under oath that the stress, the cocaine, and a weak heart combined to take the missionary's life. They testified that Reed exhibited none of the classic signs of habitual cocaine use. On cross-examination, they endured attacks on their integrity, consistency, and credibility. They left the stand bowed but unbroken, tarnished by Strobel's subtle implication that the doctors sought someone else to blame for their own failed medical treatment.

■ ■ ■

That evening, Barnes chewed on the stub of a fine Cuban cigar while he waited for Strobel to invite him into the firm's luxurious conference room. He decided not to light the cigar at this particular moment. He had other ways of knocking the socks off these prissy big-firm lawyers without destroying the uneasy peace he now shared with Strobel.

"This is Mr. Frederick Barnes," explained Strobel, introducing Barnes to the three men sprawled around the conference room table. "He is an eminently qualified private investigator and consultant hired by Mr.

Aberijan. At our last meeting, Win suggested we engage someone to tail each juror. I hired Mr. Barnes to conduct the surveillance, and well, I'll let him tell you what he found."

Barnes took a seat, tucked the cigar stub into a corner of his mouth, and cleared his throat. He looked into the expectant faces around him and savored his moment in the spotlight.

"We found some of the usual stuff you might expect on a case of this magnitude. Jurors reading the newspaper when they think no one else sees them, that type of thing. One juror even went to a Barnes & Noble and bought a book on Saudi Arabia. But none of this provided much to hang our hat on until we got a break with juror number 4, Zeke Stein."

The faces around the table remained blank, but Barnes knew he had them. Lawyers liked nothing better than a little intrigue on the jury.

"Mr. Stein met with an unidentified man on three separate occasions in three different public places during the first few weeks of trial. At the third meeting, Stein accepted an envelope from this guy. We had a hunch that maybe Stein was getting paid off, so my men conducted a thorough search of his house the next day. We found the envelope in the bottom of a sock drawer. There was ten thousand in cash stuffed in it. If we check his bank account, we're liable to find a lot more."

Barnes could read the worry and delight that mingled on the faces. An illegal search! A corrupt juror! Bribery! Blackmail! These men were silk-stocking lawyers, not used to playing at this level of corruption.

Barnes reached into his pocket and threw a series of photos on the table. Zeke Stein sat on a park bench shoulder-to-shoulder with a man. Barnes' favorite shot showed Stein accepting an envelope, clearly visible, from the other man.

"So what's our next step?" Strobel asked his partners. "How do we play this out?"

"We go straight to the court," answered Teddy without delay. "You get your mistrial, and this juror serves time. I don't see anything to discuss."

From the looks on the other faces, it was clear that they thought there were several matters to discuss. But nobody wanted to be the first to tell Teddy.

Finally, when it was obvious the others would just sit there, Barnes spoke up. "What do you plan to tell the judge?" he asked Teddy. "That you hired a P.I. who saw two men meet and then broke into the house of a juror and found a bunch of money stashed in an envelope? Assuming my guys would be willing to say that and risk going to jail, which they wouldn't, there's still one small problem. We don't have the money, and it would be our word against Stein's."

"How do you explain the fact that you're surveilling the jurors?" queried Melvin Phillips.

"And how do you know Ichabod won't just dismiss Stein and replace him with one of the alternates?" asked Win.

Barnes kept an eye on Strobel as the questions flew.

"Wait a minute," said Mack, with the kind of authority that demanded everyone's attention. "Juror number 4 is the one juror who's giving us all kinds of positive body language. If there's one guy on the panel who we've got, it's him. How do we know that one of Ahmed's own men is not paying him?"

The carefully phrased question shielded a more pointed question that Mack had decided not to ask his partners. Barnes and Mack were the only ones in the room who had been part of the jury selection process in the courtroom, the only ones who knew juror 4 was only on the panel because Ahmed had insisted they select him.

Mack's eyes narrowed and caught Barnes' as he waited for the answer. They were accusatory eyes, and they were telling Barnes that Mack wanted no part of this sinister plot.

"We don't know who's paying Stein," Barnes said with a straight face, "but I think the court will assume that if you're the ones bringing this to the court's attention, then you must not be the ones doing the bribing."

"What are you suggesting?" asked Strobel.

"I say we wait until deliberations begin," schemed Barnes. "That way the judge will have to declare a mistrial because a tainted juror has participated in the deliberative process."

Strobel looked at Mackenzie and raised an eyebrow.

"In a few more days, I'll provide you with an anonymous tip, complete with photographs, alleging that Stein is getting paid off," Barnes continued. "That will give me time to check his bank accounts." He notice surprised looks. "Don't ask how. You take the photos to the court and ask her to authorize a search of Stein's house and a subpoena for his bank records. You'll have your mistrial, and this guy will be on his way to the pen."

Strobel was shaking his head. "I don't like sitting on this information. This ought to be brought to the court's attention immediately."

"We can't prove anything yet," Barnes insisted. "We don't have any legally permissible evidence to show this guy accepted any money. We've got to have a little time to build the case, and coincidentally, I'll deliver my evidence to you a few hours after the deliberations begin."

Teddy had been making faces that grew more contorted as the conversation progressed. Finally, he said, "I don't like it, but I really don't see that we've got any choice. Mack, you know my style; I would never advocate hiding anything from the court. But we've got to have something more solid before we go to Judge Baker-Kline."

"I don't like it either," grumbled Strobel. "It's one thing to follow the jurors around and obtain evidence to justify a mistrial. It's another thing altogether to engineer a mistrial ourselves."

"Relax," Barnes snorted. "You aren't engineering anything. We'll just follow our boy Stein around and see what we come up with. Look, we're not the ones giving or receiving bribes. We're just trying to catch this man in a way that benefits our case." He chewed on his cigar and spat a small piece on the conference room floor. "What're you guys feeling so guilty about?"

Barnes had presented them with a storybook ending. He was sure they would accept it, even if it meant they had to get their hands a little dirty.

"All right," Strobel said as he broke the long silence. "But as soon as you get solid evidence you bring it to me—whether the jury has begun deliberating or not. Now, let's get back to work."

Barnes allowed himself a cocky grin, cigar and all. He was buoyed not by what Strobel said, but by what Strobel didn't say. For whatever reason, Strobel had apparently decided to keep to himself the fact that Ahmed had demanded juror number 4 stay on the jury. This implicit pact of silence was all that Barnes could ask for.

"Why do I always feel like I need to shower after I meet with you?" Mack asked in a whisper as he showed Barnes to the door.

■ ■ ■

In less than a week, Hanif's promise that his brother would have the last word with Ahmed had evolved into a widespread rumor that Rasheed himself was plotting an assassination attempt. The news reached Ahmed on Tuesday night.

"Increase surveillance on Berjein," the director of the Muttawa ordered. "Wire his phones and follow him day and night. If he makes any attempts to contact Carson or any of his associates, including Sa'id el Khamin, let me know immediately. I will personally fly back to Riyadh and deal with him. If he makes any attempt to leave the country, terminate him."

■ ■ ■

On Wednesday, Brad ended his case with a whimper. Dr. Calvin Drake, an economist, testified about the value of Charles Reed's life. He talked about the lost income and the lost services to Sarah and the kids. He tried to put a dollar value on the emotional suffering, but Ichabod wouldn't let him. The jury was as well qualified to decide that issue as the distinguished economist, Ichabod said, and therefore did not need his expert help. Brad kept Drake on the stand for less than an hour as he talked about the loss of earnings potential, present value calculations, and inflationary factors.

Although the eyes of most jurors glazed over after only a few minutes, Brad felt they would generally believe Drake because he sounded like he knew so much about the Byzantine world of economics and because he had an elaborate graph to support every one of his opinions. The bottom line, according to Drake, was that the missionary pastor could have earned a nice round one million dollars over the rest of his working years if his life had not been cut short by the events of this case.

Strobel's associate performed a nifty cross-examination of Drake, poking holes in both his math and underlying assumptions. None of the jurors appeared interested. The situation was helped neither by the economist's monotone and soothing voice nor by the fact that the courtroom seemed noticeably warmer than usual. Brad managed to stay awake by analyzing the body language of the jurors with Leslie. Nikki stayed alert by sending e-mails via her PDA, which she had managed to sneak into the courtroom. Bella made lists of things she should be doing at the office, although she had insisted on coming to court this morning so she could be there when Brad concluded the case.

By the end of Drake's testimony, three of the jurors had fallen asleep, their heads bobbing erratically on rubberized necks. This sideshow was sufficiently interesting to keep the other jurors awake and snickering at their compatriots. The end result was that Drake's cross-examination was heard in its entirety by only four of seven jurors and by both alternates, although Brad doubted any could have passed a pop quiz on a single thing that Drake had said.

After Drake stepped down, Brad stayed true to his earlier determination to save his expert toxicologist, Nancy Shelhorse, for a rebuttal witness. When Dr. Drake's uninspiring testimony was complete, Brad shocked the world and awakened the three slumbering jurors by proudly announcing, "Plaintiff rests, Your Honor."

"You what?" asked Ichabod, making no effort to hide her surprise.

"The plaintiff rests," he repeated.

Strobel stood immediately.

"Then I have a motion to make, Your Honor," he announced, loud enough for everyone in the courtroom to hear it, "and it may take a fair amount of time to argue it."

Brad knew Strobel was referring to a motion for a directed verdict. He would ask the court to throw out the case based on insufficient evidence. It was a routine motion, typically made by a defendant whenever the plaintiff rested her case. In most cases, it would be routinely denied.

But Ichabod sat up straight, apparently energized by the thought.

Out of the corner of his eye, Brad caught Leslie's "I told you so" look.

"I believe Mr. Strobel's motion merits serious consideration," Judge Baker-Kline said. "Accordingly, we will take a ten-minute recess and then use the rest of the morning to argue the motion. The jury will be reconvened, if necessary, after lunch."

With that short speech, Ichabod turned the dull events of the morning into high drama. As soon as she left the bench, the courtroom erupted. Reporters used their cell phones, spectators chattered, and the lawyers headed to the hallway to plot strategy.

■ ■ ■

As she walked down the aisle with the rest of Brad's team, she noticed that Ahmed Aberijan lingered behind at his own counsel table, engrossed in writing a note. She had been looking for this type of opportunity all morning, so she headed back to her own counsel table and wrote a quick note of her own, anxious to deliver the message before the chance passed. She would have to hurry before the team missed her.

She finished the short message, folded the paper, and placed it under a deposition transcript. As she turned to walk out of the courtroom, she dropped the folded paper onto the table directly in front of Ahmed. Before he could unfold it, she was halfway down the aisle heading out the back door.

■ ■ ■

Ahmed looked around to see if anyone had seen the subtle exchange. He opened the paper and quickly read it.

"Our case is finished, and Shelhorse did not testify. It's time to pay. I'll expect the money and the signed trust agreement by the end of the day tomorrow. The price for the verdict is still two million."

Ahmed jammed the note into his pocket and stroked his beard. He thought for a few minutes, then took out a fresh sheet of paper and scribbled his reply. He needed to make the words vague so they would not be incriminatory if they ended up in the wrong hands, but the message must be clear. He settled on two simple sentences: *I choose to wait until the pending motion is resolved and rebuttal witnesses are called. If necessary, we will proceed at that time.*

■ ■ ■

Ten minutes later she followed the rest of Brad's team back down the aisle and toward the counsel table. Her mind raced with thoughts of the upcoming argument, her note to Ahmed, the implied threat from Ichabod to dismiss the case. Where would her little scheme be then?

For his part, Ahmed was already seated at the defense counsel table, looking away from her and talking to the interpreter. He acted like he didn't have a care in the world.

Halfway down the aisle, she felt a tug at her elbow. She turned and encountered the squat face of a man who had been with Ahmed every day of the trial, either a bodyguard or some type of private investigator.

"You dropped this," he said, stooping to retrieve an envelope from the floor.

As he handed it to her, she was too stunned to think or talk or do anything except take the envelope, fire off a reproving look, and hustle to her seat.

They had contacted her in the middle of the courtroom! In broad daylight! Within spitting distance of Brad Carson and within plain sight of her colleagues.

She slumped in her chair and stared at Ahmed's back, willing him to look so she could scold him with her eyes. When he didn't, she sat up and hunched over a document, slipping the envelope open in front of her. Ahmed's cryptic note was not the answer she expected. Things were spinning out of control.

Until she had the escrow agreement with a hundred million tucked away in a Swiss bank account, the only thing keeping her alive was the promise that she could keep Shelhorse from testifying and sway juror number 6 in the deliberations. These were no small matters, but she was also smart enough to realize that if Ichabod granted the motion for a directed verdict, Ahmed would no longer need her services. She would be expendable. A liability. She reviewed again the plans she had made for such a contingency and waited for Ichabod to return to the bench.

She took one last look at Ahmed, who suddenly turned and stared back. Narrow eyes. Lasers drilling through her. The smirk was gone.

Ahmed was all business.

■　■　■

When court resumed, Strobel was ready. Before starting his argument, he handed the judge and Brad a copy of a forty-five-page brief setting forth the reasons why Ichabod should dismiss the jury and enter a directed verdict for the defendant.

For nearly an hour he argued his case, referring the court to the appropriate passages in his brief and supplementing his written submission with a passionate oral plea.

Ichabod listened intently and asked no questions.

Brad sank in his seat. He had not expected the motion to be taken so seriously. The blow could be fatal. So much for his chauvinistic gut. He could not look either Leslie or Nikki in the eye.

Brad and Leslie took turns responding to Strobel's undeniably strong submission. Unlike Strobel, they had no written brief to give the court. Unlike Strobel, they did not experience Ichabod's silence. She peppered them with questions, interruptions, and sneers. She thought out loud about every reason that would justify dismissing the case and sending everyone home.

But at the end of their argument, Ichabod simply postponed her decision.

"Counsel," she announced, "this motion has strong merit, and the cases cited in Mr. Strobel's brief appear to be on point. Nevertheless, I want to act cautiously as I make my decision. Accordingly, we will recess for the rest of the day so that I can do my own research. Mr. Carson, I would have been better prepared for this motion, but I didn't realize your case would end quite so abruptly. I will be prepared to announce my decision tomorrow morning."

Ichabod stood to leave the courtroom. "All rise," demanded the court clerk.

■ ■ ■

Before leaving, Judge Baker-Kline stole a quick glance at a worried Brad Carson, who looked pale, tired, and beaten. *This will teach him,* she said to herself.

35

I chabod enjoyed the theater of the courtroom, particularly when she took center stage. On Thursday, she entered her packed court with her robe flowing behind her and a legal pad tucked under her arm. All eyes followed her as she took her seat and prepared to announce her ruling. She paused to look over the top of her glasses at Brad Carson and his team. His eyes were sad and bloodshot, deep wrinkles creasing his forehead. She had made him sweat it out; now she would do what she had intended to do all along.

"I have before me a defense motion for a directed verdict. By his motion, Mr. Strobel is requesting that I dismiss the jury and direct a verdict in favor of both the individual defendant, Mr. Aberijan, and the codefendant, the nation of Saudi Arabia. In considering this motion, the standard is clear. To grant the motion I must find that no reasonable jury could find in favor of the plaintiff on this evidence."

She hesitated for effect. And she looked down at the lawyers, who held their collective breath. She locked on to Win Mackenzie, seated directly behind Ahmed. He was ready for the payoff. She could see it in his eyes.

"I am *not* prepared to say that a reasonable jury could not find in favor of Sarah Reed against Mr. Aberijan. On the contrary, a jury could easily find the testimony of Sarah Reed, Dr. Rydell, and other plaintiff's witnesses to be credible testimony in providing evidence that Mr. Aberijan at the very least injected both Sarah Reed and her husband with cocaine in order to justify an arrest. A reasonable jury could very well conclude that an overdose of cocaine was a contributing factor in the death of Charles Reed. A reasonable jury could believe Sarah Reed when she testified that Mr. Aberijan, in essence, ordered his men to rape her. And a reasonable jury could believe that the only reason the rape did not happen is because Sarah Reed resisted so violently that she was knocked unconscious before this heinous act could occur. In short, counsel, I am denying the motion insofar as it pertains to Mr. Aberijan."

Sarah, Brad, Leslie, and Nikki let out a collective sigh of relief. The sad, long face of Brad broke into a small smile.

Ichabod, however, was not finished. "With regard to the codefendant, the nation of Saudi Arabia, I find this to be a much more difficult call. Frankly, I have listened to day after day of testimony and have yet to hear anything that convinces me that the nation of Saudi Arabia authorized Mr. Aberijan's conduct either before or after the night in question. I still have some doubts as to whether Mr. Aberijan even did the awful things he is accused of doing. But I have no doubt that if higher-ups in the Saudi government were aware of such conduct, they would have ended it immediately."

She glanced up from her papers again, catching a hopeful look from Mackenzie.

"Nevertheless, the appellate courts caution us against granting directed-verdict motions without hearing the entire case. I am not sure if anything would change my mind on this matter, but I will reserve my judgment until I hear all the evidence from both sides. I am therefore denying Mr. Strobel's motion at this time, but I am also issuing a very strong warning to plaintiff's counsel that I am not yet convinced that the plaintiff should recover even one dollar from Saudi Arabia.

"You may bring the jury into the courtroom, and we will hear Mr. Strobel's case."

■ ■ ■

Carson and his associates had dodged a bullet. He and Leslie smiled broadly. He took her hand under the table and squeezed it.

Nikki, who was sitting at the far end of the table, couldn't resist responding more verbally. "Yes!" she whispered loud enough for everyone in the first three rows to hear. Sarah looked toward the ceiling and mouthed a silent thank-you.

The celebration was short-lived. Within minutes, Strobel called his first witness, and it was time for Sarah and her lawyers to face the best defense that money could buy.

■ ■ ■

For the first two days of his case, Strobel trotted out character witnesses who vouched for Ahmed Aberijan's credibility. These witnesses seemed to come out of the woodwork, and all swore that Ahmed was a devout Muslim who would rather die than lie. Each was prepared to give specific examples of his fairness and truthfulness, but each was prohibited by the federal rules and Judge Baker-Kline from doing so. Although the process was cumbersome and the testimony became bogged down in translation, the cumulative effect was still strong.

Friday afternoon, just before court adjourned for the weekend, Strobel dimmed the lights and played the videotaped testimony of the former church members.

The jury leaned forward and listened raptly as Tariq Abdul testified that he and his wife had been members of the Reed's drug operation. They heard Tariq describe the volatile temper of Charles Reed and the strong-arm tactics the Reeds used to get Muslim children to convert to Christianity. They heard Tariq describe the drug use by the Reeds and other members of the church. And they saw the token cross-examination conducted by the timid Sa'id el Khamin.

All afternoon the jurors kept their eyes glued to the portable television screen. And during the fifth videotaped deposition, the jury seemed especially intrigued by the cross-examination conducted by Brad Carson. Some jurors even wrote down the final few questions and answers.

"Did you ever smoke crack cocaine, or did you ever see the Reeds smoke crack cocaine?"

"Sometimes."

"Sometimes what? Sometimes you smoked crack, or sometimes the Reeds did, or both?"

"Sometimes the Reeds did. They tried to get me to do it, but I wouldn't."

"Explain the process of how they would prepare the crack and then smoke it."

There was a long pause and a slow, calculated answer. "Because I wouldn't join them in smoking crack, I never actually saw them do it. I know they did smoke crack because I saw them heating the cocaine and preparing the crack."

"How did they heat it? How hot?"

Another pause was followed by another evasive answer. "It is a complicated process that I cannot describe. I believe temperatures would be very hot—more than 250 degrees."

"One final question. When you snorted cocaine, how long did it take before you felt the rush, and how long did it last?"

"I would get a huge rush right away, and I wouldn't come down for hours."

"That's exactly what I thought. No further questions," said Brad as the tape faded to black.

Strobel was apparently not content to let the jury think about the cross-examination of Omar Khartoum all weekend. He asked if they could at least begin the videotape of Rasheed Berjein.

"How long is his testimony?" Ichabod asked.

"Less than two hours," promised Strobel.

Ichabod deliberated for a moment. Her reputation as a no-nonsense, workaholic judge was on the line. In a high-profile case like this one, her work habits could reach legendary status if she played her cards right.

"Mr. Strobel, I will not only let you start his videotaped testimony tonight, but I will also require that you play that testimony in its entirety. This type of firsthand testimony is too important to break up."

Several jurors crossed their arms and scowled. Before long, however, the testimony of Rasheed transfixed them.

The jury watched unblinking as Rasheed handled every question Brad threw at him. You could almost feel the momentum in the case shifting ever so slightly with every condemning word Rasheed spoke. After a fast-paced ninety minutes, the screen again faded to black.

Ichabod decided to punish the jurors for their sulking about the late working hours and at the same time impress the world with the speed of the "rocket docket." And so, at 6:30 on Friday night, she announced that court would begin Monday promptly at 8 A.M. and conclude no earlier than 6 P.M. In fact, said Ichabod, the entire week would proceed in that fashion, and she expected Strobel to rest his case by the next weekend. She saw no reason why they could not have closing arguments a week from Monday, thus allowing the jury to begin deliberations later that same day.

It was not a matter open for debate, and it was a good thing. Many of the jurors looked like they were ready to revolt at the first opportunity. By judicial fiat, Ichabod had kept everyone late and thrown day-care arrangements and other weekend plans into chaos, thus imposing a great burden on the only people in the courtroom who were not being well paid for showing up.

36

The weekend flew by, leaving Brad and Leslie no time to focus on each other. Instead, they worked with Nikki and Bella around the clock to prepare for a full week of Strobel's hired guns—the expert witnesses. They knew that Strobel would not disappoint.

Mack Strobel started bright and early Monday morning with the medical experts. His first witness, who was sworn in promptly at 8 A.M., was a world-class toxicologist. For two hours he wowed the jury with charts and videos, educated them about the effects of cocaine use, and described the toxicological testing for the drug. In a polite way, the witness said that Dr. Jeffrey Rydell was either lying or misinformed about his toxicological analysis. There was no way, according to this expert witness, to tell from the lab data whether the cocaine in the blood had been injected, snorted, or smoked.

Brad and Leslie had already decided on the theme for their cross-examination, and Leslie wasted no time in getting to the point.

"Doctor, what is your hourly rate for this testimony?"

"I am not charging for my testimony. But I do bill my services as an expert at $350 per hour."

Leslie looked at the jury and saw eyes popping out. They each received twenty dollars a day in jury pay.

"And you also charge a premium when you testify, don't you, Doctor? Tell the jury what that number is."

"Four hundred per hour."

Leslie thought she heard one of the jurors let out a soft whistle.

"And you also have a minimum charge per day, don't you? In other words, whether you work five hours a day or not, if you pick up the file and travel on a case, your client pays you two thousand dollars for that day. Correct?"

"Yes, that's right."

Leslie shook her head almost imperceptibly, emitted a nearly silent "wow," then started in on the rest of the expert's testimony. For the next hour or so, she chipped away at his foundation, bit by bit, piece by piece. She concluded by asking for an estimate of the total amount he had billed Kilgore & Strobel to date.

"About twenty-three thousand dollars," the expert replied.

"And one last thing, Doctor," said Leslie as she returned to her counsel table and turned around. It was a move she had seen Brad do many times. "You never actually treated either Charles or Sarah Reed, like Dr. Jeffrey Rydell did. Correct? I mean, your opinions are based on a cold and impersonal review of the records."

"That's right," the expert responded.

Leslie harrumphed and sat down. She stared impassively ahead as the expert stepped down. Under the table she softly slapped Brad's palm.

Strobel followed his toxicologist with a well-paid and well-known cardiovascular surgeon. This expert testified in detail about all the weaknesses of Charles Reed's heart caused by advanced hardening of the arteries. He told the jury that other issues probably impacted Charles Reed's poor health, including extended use of cocaine. He further opined that Charles Reed would have died on the night in question from a heart attack, with or without the cocaine in his body. In laymen's terms, it was a bad heart, not cocaine, that killed Charles Reed.

To nobody's surprise, the cardiologist hauled down more for his testimony than the toxicologist. And to nobody's surprise, Brad Carson explored all the details of his compensation on cross-examination. This expert actually charged five hundred dollars per hour for his time, and he reminded Brad that he could make more if he stayed in surgery and didn't mess with the lawyers. Brad got the man to admit that he had billed Strobel a total of forty-five thousand dollars to date and, like the toxicologist, charged a minimum per-day fee. Brad acted surprised to discover that the cardiologist did not bill a premium for time spent in court. Just before returning to his seat, Brad suggested that the witness might want to add that little trick for his next case. The jury laughed, and from the looks on their faces, they did not appreciate Ichabod's prompt and stern lecture on courtroom decorum.

The parade of highly paid experts continued for two days. An expert in international human rights praised the Saudis' continuing improvement in the area of religious freedom. He charged only $250 per hour and clearly had a thing or two to learn from the doctors.

An expert in police tactics testified that Ahmed and his gang did everything by the book in dealing with the drug-crazed conduct of Charles and Sarah Reed. He was Strobel's best bargain, charging only $150 per hour, but he made up in volume what he lacked in price. Even Leslie was stunned to learn that he had managed to bill Strobel more than fifty thousand dollars for services to date.

Experts in intergovernmental relationships testified that the Saudis had already been held accountable for their conduct as a result of the scathing report issued by the Senate Foreign Affairs Committee. These experts were in the middle range, billing around $250 per hour. By the time their cross-examinations were completed, however, it was clear that if Strobel gave them a dime, he gave them too much.

■ ■ ■

While Brad and Leslie grilled the expert witnesses, Nikki was en route to Saudi Arabia. If successful, she would help Rasheed and Mobara gain political asylum through the U.S. Embassy, and she would have Rasheed prepared to take the stand as a rebuttal witness the following Monday. Brad believed Strobel might finish his case on Friday morning. Brad's own toxicologist, Dr. Nancy Shelhorse, would be called as a rebuttal witness and take the remainder of the day on Friday. It was critical, Brad told Nikki, that Rasheed and Mobara not arrive in the United States any earlier than necessary in order to maximize the element of surprise and thwart any attempts by Ahmed to intimidate or coerce the Berjeins.

Brad and Nikki carefully prepared the documents requesting political asylum, explaining the circumstances of the *Reed* case and documenting the threats against Rasheed and Mobara if they testified truthfully. Upon her arrival in Saudi Arabia, Nikki would also obtain, from Sa'id el Khamin, a videotape through which Sa'id outlined the circumstances of the case and the reasons why political asylum would be appropriate for the young couple.

Nikki flew out of Washington late Wednesday evening. She would meet Sa'id Thursday to prepare the final details of the application and take Rasheed and Mobara to the embassy late on Friday afternoon. If all went according to plan, Nikki and the Berjeins would leave Riyadh together late Friday night and be on American soil by early Saturday morning.

■ ■ ■

The Moreno girl has left the country.

Ahmed read Barnes' note during the experts' testimony. Within twelve hours, he was headed for Saudi Arabia in his private jet. Something was afoot with the Berjeins. If they attempted to help the plaintiffs, Ahmed would personally preside over their executions, even if it meant he had to miss two days of expert witness testimony to do it.

■ ■ ■

Nikki's first meeting with Sa'id transpired right on schedule. By late Thursday morning, Riyadh time, they had finalized the asylum petition. Rasheed and Mobara would join them at Sa'id's office the next day at five o'clock, and they would all head to the Embassy together. Sa'id was confident the petition would be granted.

Late Thursday night, Nikki went to a pay phone in the hotel lobby and phoned Bella to inquire about the trial.

"Brad told you not to use the phones," Bella chided her. "O'Malley says they might be tapped."

"Don't worry about it."

"Well, use your Blackberry next time. O'Malley tells me those doohickeys are as good as a phone, even over there. They're safer anyway."

"Takes too long," Nikki said. "And besides, I can't get reception here."

"Is everything all right with Rasheed and Mobara?" Nikki heard concern in Bella's voice. An unauthorized phone call usually didn't portend good news.

"Everything's on schedule," Nikki assured her. "How's the trial going?"

"I ate lunch with Brad and Sarah, but I've been at the office since. They said it was more of the same. One high-paid expert after another. Strobel apparently told Ichabod that he would finish tomorrow morning. We'll put Shelhorse on as a rebuttal witness tomorrow afternoon and then Rasheed on Monday."

"Any chance that Ichabod will hold court on Saturday?"

"She hasn't mentioned it, and I think she would make a lot of jurors upset if she did. We're safe betting on Monday."

"With Ichabod you never know. Is Brad sure he can stretch Shelhorse out through the entire afternoon on Friday? I mean, if he gets done early, we would have to rest our case without putting on Rasheed."

"Don't worry, Nikki. Brad said he's got six hours of questions for Shelhorse if he needs 'em." Bella was starting to sound defensive.

Nikki had what she needed. "Give my best to Brad and Leslie," she said.

"Okay. Be careful, Nikki."

"Right. Careful's my middle name."

Nikki hung up and looked at her watch. It was now 10:30 on Thursday night in Riyadh. She was eight hours ahead of Norfolk time. She checked her notes and phone numbers. The timing would be critical. And the timing would be tight. Everything would have to work just as she had planned.

■ ■ ■

O'Malley had planted his own bugs in the phones at Carson & Associates on Wednesday night while he supposedly swept the office for bugs. He monitored the calls all day Thursday. He took his cue from the phone call between Nikki and Bella.

He stopped by Carson & Associates a few minutes later. He greeted Bella and began his rounds, letting her know he would be checking each phone. When he was finished, he declared the office clean and told Bella that he had a few hours to kill. He talked her into going to court with him to watch some of the afternoon testimony. Anything she had to do at the office, he assured her, could wait.

They rode to court together, and for a few minutes they enjoyed watching Brad get after another one of Strobel's expert witnesses. But suddenly O'Malley remembered that he was running late for an appointment. Bella assured him she could get a ride back to the office with the trial team at the end of the day.

■ ■ ■

Dr. Nancy Shelhorse enjoyed her work as an expert witness. Toxicology, her daily work, could be dry stuff. The same could not be said of serving as an expert in a high-profile case. And the pay wasn't bad, either.

Shelhorse had once heard a lawyer describe a perfect expert witness as a glib person with a résumé and a suitcase. She qualified on all three counts. Shelhorse was a natural teacher, serving as an adjunct at the University of Richmond Medical School and teaching clinical courses to residents. She also had the credentials. She was experienced and board certified, and she had published enough peer-reviewed articles to bring down several trees. And in this case, like so many others, she was testifying outside the Richmond area where she lived and practiced medicine. For some strange reason, lawyers and juries seemed to believe that nobody could be an expert unless they traveled great distances to testify or at the very least were not one of the "locals."

She was not just qualified; she was also prepared. The prior night she had driven two hours to Norfolk so she could spend another night rehearsing her testimony with Brad and Leslie. They had run through several mock cross-examinations, but the lawyers couldn't put a dent in her testimony. Brad finally declared her bulletproof and sent her back to Richmond. She planned to return again tomorrow—Friday morning—and wait in the hallway outside the courtroom until she was called to testify. She was looking forward to it; she had so much to say.

For that reason, the message she received at the hospital at 3:30 on Thursday afternoon was both a disappointment and a surprise. Her assistant said someone from Brad Carson's office had called and indicated they might not need her to testify after all. According to the caller, she should check her e-mail as soon as possible, where she would find a full explanation.

Anxious to know what was happening, and knowing it would take thirty minutes to get from the hospital to her office, Shelhorse asked her assistant to log on and retrieve any messages from Carson & Associates.

"Here's what it says, Doctor: 'We are truly sorry for the short notice and the change in plans, but the trial has taken some interesting twists this afternoon. As a result, we will not need your testimony. In fact, we believe the defendants will try to contact you and somehow subpoena you and force you to testify. This would be very damaging to our case.

"'You have done nothing wrong. But this is a complicated and unexpected occurrence that could greatly work to our advantage so long as you cannot be found or forced to take the stand. Accordingly, we will pay for your full day tomorrow at your customary hourly rate, but we would ask that you find a secluded place for all of tomorrow and Saturday, do not tell ANYONE where you are going, and do not communicate with anyone until Saturday night.

"'We can assure you that there is no subpoena for you to testify as a witness at this time. But please do not attempt to contact us after you receive this message. If Mr. Strobel is granted a court subpoena for your appearance, and you call us, we would be forced to disclose your whereabouts. I know that this is an extraordinary request, and we would not make it if it were not absolutely necessary. Thanks for your understanding. We will be in a position to explain fully our strategic reason for doing this when we call you on Sunday.'

"And then at the bottom, there's a note that says 'From the Hand-held Blackberry Device of Nikki Moreno, Legal Assistant, Carson & Associates.'"

Shelhorse was shocked. It took her a minute to gather her thoughts.

"Are you still there?" her assistant asked.

"Does this make sense to you?" Shelhorse responded.

"Not really. But I don't understand how trials work very well, either."

"When was the message received?"

"The header says 2:47 this afternoon."

Shelhorse thought about the implications. She was insulted to think that the defendants somehow thought they could now turn her testimony to their own advantage. She saw her moment in the spotlight slipping away, her escape from monotony closing off, her expected career boost imploding.

"I can't believe Strobel would have issued a subpoena for my appearance already. I'm calling Carson."

Shelhorse pushed the "end call" button on her cell phone and dialed the number for Carson & Associates. She heard the recorded and dreary voice of Bella give her the extensions of the various staff members. Shelhorse pushed the numbers for Brad Carson. His voice mail told her how important her call was to him and asked if she would leave a message.

"Brad, this is Nancy Shelhorse. What in the world is going on with regard to my testimony tomorrow? Call me back on my cell as soon as you get a chance. If I don't hear from you, I'll just assume Strobel has issued a subpoena for my appearance, and I'll lie low as you suggested on Friday and Saturday."

Shelhorse hung up the phone and shook her head in disgust. "Lawyers," she mumbled with heartfelt disdain.

■ ■ ■

O'Malley's appointment took him straight back to the offices of Carson & Associates. He parked himself at the receptionist's desk and patiently monitored the phone numbers that registered on the switchboard every time an outside call came in. He also periodically checked everyone's e-mail and voicemail.

At 3:38 the phone rang. The receptionist's screen reflected a Richmond originating number. O'Malley listened intently as he heard Brad Carson's phone ring on an internal line. The call had been transferred.

He waited a few minutes, then logged on to Brad's voicemail using the passwords Bella had provided him weeks ago. He listened to the message from Shelhorse, deleted it, and left the offices of Carson & Associates, locking the door behind him.

37

Nikki Moreno's wake-up call came bright and early, just a few minutes before noon. She mumbled her thanks to the operator without enthusiasm and slid lower under the sheets. Slowly, Room 703 came into focus, and she began to review the challenges of the next twelve hours. She forced herself out of bed, one leg at a time, and shuffled over to the sliding-glass door that led to her balcony.

Her head throbbed, and her stomach was in knots. Her mouth was dry as cotton, her nose stuffed up—she basically felt like scum. She looked down at the dresser and cursed last night's bottle of scotch that was the source of this morning's pain. She had been lonely and wired last night, unable to sleep. To comfort and calm herself, she had allowed herself a few too many shots from the bottle that had made the transatlantic trip in her garment bag. If her first trip to Saudi Arabia had taught her anything, it was that she would have to bring her own booze to this parched country or go without.

This morning—or was it this afternoon already?—she wished she had gone without.

Nikki took her time showering and primping, as if slow movements would calm her stomach and stop the pounding in her head. Today she would be as inconspicuous as a tattooed Latino could be in Saudi Arabia. She wore no makeup and threw on the hated abayya that Sa'id had given her on the first trip. She could not possibly wear the head covering in the heat, but she would try her best not to be noticed. She would not carry a briefcase. She would not look men in the eye when she talked. In fact, she would avoid talking whenever possible. She would focus on her plan and nothing else.

■ ■ ■

At 9 A.M. in Norfolk, Bella hit the panic button.

Shelhorse was nowhere to be found.

She was supposed to meet them in the hallway outside the court-room at 7:30. But she was late. Experts were always late. That part irritated Bella but did not panic her. But now Shelhorse was beyond late. Something serious was wrong. And Bella was frantic.

Brad had been at it for more than an hour and was running out of cross-examination questions for Strobel's last witness. While pretending to listen to an answer, he scribbled a note and handed it to Bella. "I can make this last till ten, no more. Go find Shelhorse."

Bella hustled into the hallway and repeated her earlier series of phone calls. She called Shelhorse's office and left her third urgent message of the morning. She called Shelhorse's cell phone. Another recording. Another message. No answer at the home phone. No response to the page. Bella was going crazy.

It was now 9:15. Bella stared at the pay phone. Another minute ticked by. *The firm's voicemail.* Maybe Shelhorse had an accident or some other unexpected occurrence and had left a message. Bella turned in her Daytimer to the page containing the passwords she had given O'Malley.

She started with her own phone, then Brad's, and then Leslie's. She heard plenty of messages, including a sweet one from Leslie to Brad, but nothing pertaining to Shelhorse.

Nikki's messages, of which there were many, proved far more interesting. Bella listened with sordid amusement to the personal calls from the various men who didn't seem to know that each other existed. But it was a business call that riveted her attention. She played it back several times and wrote it down word for word.

"Ms. Moreno, this is Chad Hamilton again. We've been playing some serious telephone tag lately. And rather than continuing to trade calls, let me just give you the bottom line. One point five million. Take it or leave it."

Bella raced back into the courtroom. Brad was still methodically questioning the witness and taking increased heat from Ichabod to move his cross-examination along. When Brad saw Bella plop back down in her seat at counsel table, he gave her an expectant look. Bella frowned and shook her head no. Brad returned to his questioning, rehashing some turf he had already covered.

"No message from Dr. Shelhorse anyplace, and she doesn't answer any of her phones," Bella whispered to Leslie. "It's like the woman just dropped off the face of the earth. So I called our office to check voicemail messages. Look at this note. It was a message left on Nikki's voicemail."

"Did you go into my voicemail too?" Leslie whispered before looking at the note.

"Just read the note," said Bella, louder than she intended. Ichabod glared at her. Bella mouthed a silent sorry.

"Don't you ever go into my voicemail," Leslie warned.

"Just read the note."

As Leslie read it, she furrowed her brow. "What do you make of this?" she whispered.

"I thought you might know."

Leslie didn't. She gave Bella a blank shrug, then retreated to her thoughts while the witness droned on.

"Here's what I want you to do," Leslie whispered at last. "Go back to the office. On the way, call O'Malley and have him meet you there. Keep calling Shelhorse. If you find out anything, buzz my Blackberry. When you get to the office, you and O'Malley go through everyone's e-mail and see if that helps. I'm not accusing Nikki of anything, but we've got a missing witness and a strange phone message."

"Okay," said Bella, frowning. "I knew we couldn't trust her."

■ ■ ■

Nikki arrived late because she couldn't communicate with the cab driver and he didn't have the foggiest idea where he was going. Sa'id's office was not exactly center city with the top-tier firms. Nor was it in an industrial or office park where the second-tier firms were located. Instead, the one-story law office was on an out-of-the-way side street flanked on one side by a small Laundromat and on the other side by a cramped restaurant that also sold groceries in bulk—the Riyadh equivalent of a deli.

Narrow alleys separated the three bland, stucco commercial buildings. All needed repair, Sa'id's especially. The numbers on his building had long since disappeared, exacerbating the problem for the already confused cab driver.

When Nikki finally arrived at 5:20, Sa'id greeted her warmly at the front door.

■ ■ ■

He pulled the nondescript black sedan over and parked a block away from the building. He immediately radioed the others.

"She just entered the lawyer's office," he reported. "Can't tell if she's armed."

"You may be getting some more company soon," came the reply. "Wait there."

■ ■ ■

Once Nikki was inside, Sa'id introduced her to Hanif. Immediately, Nikki noticed his striking resemblance to Rasheed. Sa'id explained that Hanif wanted to ride to the embassy with them to see his brother off. Hanif, all smiles, shook Nikki's hand with unbridled enthusiasm.

Sa'id shared his building with three other tenants, all with small offices adjoined by a common hallway. Sa'id took Nikki and Hanif to his cramped office to view the videotape Sa'id had made. His prior shoddy work aside, the man had done a good job with this. Hanif split his attention between the tape and the front window of the office, where he separated the blinds with his fingers at eye level to watch for his brother.

On camera Sa'id was passionate and earnest, clearly presenting the case against his own government. Nikki was impressed that a devout Muslim would put his reputation on the line to gain religious and political freedom for a Christian couple he did not even know. Sure, so it wasn't much of a reputation. But still…

Despite Sa'id's roly-poly build, unkempt and gnarly beard, annoying habits, and awkward attempts at flirtation, Nikki liked the little guy. He seemed to have no God-given talents or graces, that is, aside from a sunny disposition and a huge heart. Even those traits probably weren't worth the sixteen hundred Saudi riyals per hour he was hauling down. But in the grand scheme of things, he had exceeded her expectations.

Nikki thanked Sa'id for the excellent work on the tape and watched him beam. She then tucked it inside her loathsome abayya and joined Hanif as he kept watch at the window.

■ ■ ■

The Berjeins did not arrive until nearly six.

"How could you be so late?" Nikki fumed. "We're supposed to be at the embassy in ten minutes."

Sa'id tried to translate Nikki's tone as well as her words. The Berjeins looked crestfallen.

"We were being followed," Rasheed said. "We tried to lose them but couldn't. We think they are still outside."

This chilling news caused Hanif to dart back to the window for another look. Nikki leaned over his shoulder. A black sedan contained two men, who were both looking at the building. The one nearest the building was slender and evil-looking, with beady, dark eyes and a signature scar that graced his left cheek and disappeared into his beard. The other agent towered over the first and barely fit in the passenger car seat.

The Berjeins had indeed been followed. And the men out front didn't seem to care if the Berjeins knew.

They stepped away from the window, and everyone but Nikki began speaking in Arabic at once. She tried desperately to think despite the noise and confusion. She could finally stand it no more and simultaneously stamped her foot hard on the floor and screamed.

"Stop! Just shut up for a minute!" All gave her their undivided attention.

"I'll call the embassy and get the meeting postponed for a half-hour," she said. She waited for Sa'id to translate.

Then she looked at Sa'id. "How far away is your house and in what direction?"

"North of the city. Forty minutes by car."

"That'll never work," she said, then paused. "Okay, here's what we're going to do."

She looked from one brother to the other and smiled at her good fortune. Rasheed, the older brother, was taller by about two inches, and about ten pounds heavier. But their similarities swallowed their differences. Same athletic builds, same prominent noses, same huge deep-set eyes underlined by large circles. The male genes in the Berjein stock were strong and distinctive.

Nikki tried to imagine Hanif with a haircut and no beard.

She looked at Rasheed then back to Hanif one more time. "It's time to use a little misdirection," she said, "which happens to be my specialty. Sa'id, do you have a pair of scissors and a razor?"

"I have scissors, of course. We could buy a razor next door."

"Good. Hanif will shave his beard and cut his hair to look as much like Rasheed as possible. They will also change clothes. I am about the same size as Mobara. We will change clothes, and I will wear her abayya and face shawl. Hanif and I will leave the building first, disguised as Rasheed and Mobara, and drive to my hotel. Sa'id, you will leave next, taking a different route, then meet us at the hotel."

She paused again. More translation. More skeptical looks. She decided to sound more animated, act more enthusiastic. Maybe they would buy it. After all, it was the only plan she had.

"We will both watch our mirrors. Hopefully these men will follow Hanif, Sa'id, and me to the hotel. If my plan doesn't work and they don't follow us, then Rasheed and Mobara should stay put until we come back here. Sa'id, is there a rear exit in this place?"

Sa'id nodded.

"Call a cab to pick up Rasheed and Mobara back there. Tell them they should watch and see if the men out front follow us. If they do, tell Rasheed and Mobara to take the back exit and grab the cab to the embassy. Give them the videotape. Have them wait for us there."

Sa'id translated Nikki's impromptu plan for the sake of the others. They argued briefly in Arabic.

"They said it will never work," reported Sa'id.

Nikki threw her hands in the air. "Then tell them to come up with something better," she snapped.

Two minutes later, Sa'id headed next door to buy a razor.

■ ■ ■

Nikki, dressed in Mobara's abayya, stood and admired the new clean-cut Hanif. She had him stand next to his brother. She looked from one to the other and back again. A smug smile graced her face.

"You're the spittin' image of your brother," she said to Hanif.

He gave her a puzzled look.

"Never mind," she said and turned to Sa'id.

The little guy looked more excited than ever, his eyes practically glowing with the enthusiasm of the moment. At once, Nikki felt a wave of gratitude for the man and a wave of guilt for putting his life in such danger. "You don't have to do this, you know," she found herself saying.

"I know," he replied, looking more determined than ever. "But I've never been a part of something like this before...something this important," he waved his hand in an arch, "people this committed."

Nikki nodded her thanks and patted him on the side of his arm. "Give Hanif directions to the hotel, and ask if he's ready."

Sa'id explained the route to Hanif and told Nikki that he was indeed ready. Hanif turned and faced his brother. They blinked back the tears. They both seemed at a loss for words.

After a few beats of respectful silence, the brothers exchanged some solemn sentences in Arabic while the others looked on. Then Hanif gave his older brother a bear hug, and tears welled up in both men's eyes. They ended their embrace, and Rasheed patted Hanif on the shoulder, nodding his head with pride and looking steadfast into his brother's glistening eyes.

Without a word, Hanif turned toward Nikki, grabbed her hand, and headed out the front door.

Sa'id followed a step behind.

38

The two men in the black sedan took notice as the couple left the building and hustled into their automobile. The lawyer followed on their heels and went to his car.

"Follow him," the slender man instructed his partner. "I'll call for backup to come keep an eye on Moreno."

The mountain man climbed out of the sedan and raced to another car, bent over to avoid attention, keeping one eye on Sa'id.

The other man followed Hanif and Nikki and called in the situation. "Moreno is still inside. She came in a cab and should be alone now. If she leaves, call me."

Then he put a call in to Ahmed, who had been on his way to Sa'id's office. The strike would take place elsewhere now, and the best they could do was follow the prime suspects and figure out where.

■ ■ ■

Nikki slouched low in the seat, resisting the urge to look at herself in the visor mirror. She wanted to tell Hanif he was doing great, but he wouldn't understand. She congratulated herself on the fine job she had done in cutting his hair, given the time constraints. In fact, Hanif looked handsome, in a rugged kind of way. She liked his style.

"You look good with your new 'do," she said.

Hanif glanced sideways at her, nodded his head in acknowledgment, and smiled.

"You don't speak English, do you?"

Hanif nodded his head again and gave her the same smile. Nikki breathed a sigh of relief.

She could see the black sedan in the sideview mirror. The driver appeared to be alone, and she hoped the other man followed Sa'id. By now, Rasheed and Mobara should have left unnoticed out the back door, followed the alley to a side street, and hopped in a cab to the embassy. She hoped they had escaped safely. She didn't allow herself to dwell on the alternatives. Instead, she turned her thoughts toward what she and Hanif must do when they reached the hotel.

At present, she had no clue.

＊　＊　＊

By 10:05, Brad had exhausted his delay tactics and put Ichabod in a foul mood.

After the witness stepped down, Strobel proudly stood to his feet and announced: "The defense rests." He renewed his motion for a directed verdict, and the court again took it under advisement.

"Mr. Carson, do you have any rebuttal witnesses?" Ichabod asked without looking up from her writing. "And as I mentioned before, keep it brief."

Brad stood and glanced around the courtroom one more time, hoping that maybe Nancy Shelhorse had slipped in unnoticed. "Your Honor, we have two brief rebuttal witness. One is an expert witness, our toxicologist, and the other is a fact witness. Unfortunately, with Mr. Strobel's case concluding so unexpectedly, our witnesses are not yet here. Would it be possible for us to break now for the weekend and then briefly put those witnesses on the stand first thing Monday morning?"

You could tell from the looks on their faces that the jurors thought it would be a good idea. It was the first time they had had any life in their eyes all morning.

"Mr. Carson, you know the rules of this court. If your next witness is not ready, you rest your case. Madame Reporter," Ichabod said, turning to the court reporter, "let the record reflect that Mr. Carson will be calling no rebuttal witnesses."

"Wait, Your Honor," Brad blurted out, "that's not true. We do have rebuttal witnesses."

"Then where are they?" demanded Judge Baker-Kline.

"They're on their way," Brad insisted.

"And the check's in the mail," said Ichabod sarcastically. "Here's what we'll do, counsel, and let me warn you that this is more than I usually do. It goes against my better judgment here, but I'll do it anyway. We'll take a fifteen-minute break, and if your witnesses show up, fine. If not, we'll proceed to closing statements."

"All rise," announced the court clerk, "this court stands in recess for fifteen minutes."

■ ■ ■

"I'll kill her, Leslie. I swear. If I get my hands on her, I'll kill her."

"Bella, calm down." Leslie lifted the pay-phone receiver a few inches away from her ear. "What did you find?"

"Nikki sent a message from her handheld last night telling Shelhorse not to come! Can you believe this!"

"How can you even know this, Bella, if she sent it from the handheld?"

"Because these newfangled Blackberries automatically transmit a copy via satellite to your desk unit whenever your desk unit is hooked up to the Internet. It's there plain as day on Nikki's desk."

"There's got to be an explanation—"

"Why does everyone insist on defending this woman? First the voicemail. Some guy no one knows offers to pay her a million five. Now the e-mail deep-sixing our main expert witness. I think we've got enough to go to the cops."

"Bella, think for a minute. What if it's a setup?"

"Leslie!" Bella was screaming so loud that the reporters on the other pay phones could hear. "How can you get any more proof than a recorded voicemail and an e-mail? C'mon..."

"All right. But the first thing we have to do is find Shelhorse. She can confirm whether Nikki really sent her the e-mail. We've got fifteen minutes, Bella. " Leslie's mind raced. She had to keep Bella calm. She had to break the news to Brad. She had to keep this fragile case from spinning out of control. "In the meantime, we can't let Nikki know we're onto her."

Leslie forced herself to speak slowly and calmly. She covered the phone and her mouth with a cupped hand so as not to be overheard. "I'll tell Brad about Nikki. And I'll call Saudi Arabia and warn both Sa'id and Rasheed not to trust her. If we're right about this, she'll just deliver them into the hands of Aberijan."

"Okay. And I'll keep trying to reach Shelhorse. But tell Brad that if I'm the first to see Nikki when she gets back into this country, he's gonna have a murder case to defend."

"Let's leave that stuff to Ahmed," Leslie forced a laugh, trying to lighten things up a little.

She received only a dial tone in response.

■ ■ ■

Sarah watched and listened as Leslie rushed back to the courtroom to inform Brad.

"Why is Ichabod so insistent on starting closing arguments *today?*" Leslie sputtered. "You aren't ready, are you? I mean, is her beloved rocket docket so important that justice just gets steamrolled in the process?"

Brad listened without comment. "We just can't get a break," he said in resignation.

"This is so ridiculous," Leslie continued. "When the icewoman comes back on the bench, let me argue for a continuance. She can't make us start closing arguments today! She's at least got to give us the weekend to get Rasheed here…doesn't she?"

If Leslie's looking for encouragement from Brad right now, she's looking in the wrong place, thought Sarah.

"She's the judge. She can do whatever she wants," Brad said.

For the first time in the case, Sarah noticed a sagging of Brad's shoulders and a hanging of his head that told her the fight had gone out of him. He sat heavy in his chair, leaned back, and rubbed his face. It was the posture of confusion and defeat.

"You guys have been great," Sarah said with a soft tone of encouragement. "This will work out. You'll think of something."

"Thanks," Brad said. But his downcast face never changed expression.

"I'll get on the phones," Leslie said. She glanced down at Brad as she was leaving. "You okay?"

He nodded and slumped lower in his chair as she left the courtroom again.

Not knowing what else to do, Sarah sat beside him in his silence. He had been a great encourager throughout the case, had done more than any other lawyer could have done. He had fought the good fight. Now, if he needed someone to just sit beside him silently and watch the precious minutes tick away, that was the least she could do. She sensed that this was not a time for words.

The minutes passed, and the courtroom started filling back up. Brad sat up straighter in his chair and folded his hands on the table in front of him. He stared straight ahead, not breaking his silence. Ten minutes were gone. In five more, Ichabod would be back on the bench, demanding that they put up or shut up.

It was Clarence who finally got Brad to speak. The big marshal sauntered over to Brad and sat part of his haunches on the table. The oak squealed in protest.

"You don't need no rebuttal witnesses, Brad Carson. You've already opened a can of whuppin' on 'em just as it is. I'd jest dazzle 'em with one of yer fired-up closin' arguments and wait fer the money. Brad, I'm tellin' ya, them jurors is eatin' out of yer hand. Now git yer chin up before they file back in."

The simple and complete optimism of the man seemed to make an impact. After Clarence had finished, Brad looked up at the mountain sitting in front of him, forced a grin, and finally spoke.

"Thanks, Clarence. I might just do that."

Clarence gave Brad a playful punch on the arm, and Sarah noticed Brad wince. It would probably bruise. Sarah was glad the big man was on their side.

As the marshal walked away, a look of epiphany swept Brad's face. His eyes lit up, and his lips curled into an unforced smile.

"Wait a second, big guy," Brad called. "You got any big-time cocaine dealers in that jail of yours?"

■ ■ ■

Ichabod glowered at him from her high bench. Brad needed another five minutes or so before Clarence would return with an inmate in tow. Getting those minutes would not be easy with the impatient Ichabod.

"Call your next witness," she demanded.

"Let me handle this," Brad whispered to Leslie. Her phone calls had been futile.

He rose and walked slowly to the podium. Very slowly. "Your Honor, may I explain the situation with my two rebuttal witnesses?" He inquired politely and deferentially.

Ichabod seemed pleased with his attitude but still emanated a "show-me" look. She leaned back in her chair, folded her arms, and sighted Brad over the end of her nose. "You may explain, Mr. Carson, so long as you don't hold out any hope that this court will entertain any excuses for witnesses being late. But if you just want to put your explanation in the record, feel free."

"Yes ma'am," Brad replied. "I know the court wants to begin closing arguments on Monday. I would like to propose we have a brief session tomorrow, on Saturday, like we did last weekend, in order to accommodate some unavoidable problems with these two witnesses."

"I'm not inclined to make everyone in this courtroom come in on Saturday just because you couldn't get your witnesses here on time, Mr. Carson." Ichabod paused and shook her head, as if she couldn't believe she was actually going to ask this. "Who are these witnesses, and what are their problems?"

Brad had his opening.

"The first is Dr. Nancy Shelhorse, an expert in toxicology from the University of Richmond Medical School. She will offer testimony about the toxicology results for Charles Reed and will also rebut the testimony of the former church members regarding the issues of cocaine usage. She was supposed to meet us this morning. We've been trying to contact her through cell phones, office numbers, beepers, and who knows what else. We are afraid that something serious must have happened to her on the way to court, and we request a day to investigate."

Brad didn't like the idea of announcing in open court his next rebuttal witness. But at this point Brad didn't have much choice.

"Our second witness is Rasheed Berjein, the same man who earlier testified in Mr. Strobel's case by videotaped deposition. Mr. Berjein is prepared to renounce his earlier testimony and state under oath that the only reason he gave such testimony is because he had been threatened by Mr. Aberijan. Mr. Berjein will further testify that there is no truth whatsoever to the allegations that Charles or Sarah Reed, or anyone else in their church, sold or used drugs."

"And why isn't he here?" asked Ichabod. Her eyes were still narrow, her arms still folded. The queen of cynicism.

"My paralegal is at this minute in Saudi Arabia helping him to obtain political asylum. We thought Dr. Shelhorse would be testifying this afternoon and Mr. Berjein would not be needed until Monday."

"Well, apparently you thought wrong," said Ichabod. "Mr. Carson, neither of these excuses is sufficient. Dr. Shelhorse should have come into town last night, and Mr. Berjein should have been brought to this country earlier. But I'm going to bend over backward to be fair to you without jeopardizing our trial schedule."

Ichabod thought for a moment, and Brad held his breath.

"I really don't have much sympathy with regard to Dr. Shelhorse," Ichabod continued. "She is a local witness and should have been managed properly. But with respect to Mr. Berjein, I can understand that political asylum can be an unpredictable process, and I'm willing to give you one more day to get him here. We will reconvene tomorrow morning at 8 A.M. If Mr. Berjein is not here by then, he will not testify. Closing arguments will commence as scheduled on Monday morning."

"Thank you, Your Honor," said Brad.

"Note my objection, Your Honor," said Strobel.

"Very well," said Ichabod. "Anything else for today?"

Leslie handed Brad a note. His eyes lit up, and he turned to see Clarence at the back door of the courtroom, squeezing the arm of a ratty-looking man in an orange jumpsuit.

"Yes, Your Honor," said Brad. "In light of the fact that Dr. Shelhorse will not be testifying, I do have one brief rebuttal witness to take her place today."

"And who is that?" asked Ichabod.

Brad turned and pointed to Clarence and his prisoner. "That man standing back there in the orange jumpsuit," Brad announced.

■ ■ ■

Nikki barely had time to change out of the smelly abayya when she heard the knock on her hotel-room door and went to the peephole. She kept the chain lock in place just in case. While she checked, Hanif hid inside a closet, ready to pounce on any intruder that might barge into the room.

She exhaled deeply when she saw the distorted and balding head of Sa'id. She unhooked the chain lock, cracked the door open, and yanked him inside.

Hanif slid back the closet door and jumped out. Sa'id grabbed his heart. His mouth was open, but no words came out. He finally managed to stammer out something in Arabic that made Hanif laugh. Still clutching his heart, Sa'id stumbled over to the king-size bed and flopped down, lying on his back.

"Were you followed?" Nikki asked, as she slid the chain lock back in place.

"Yes, but I lost him," said Sa'id. "They don't know the back streets in this city like I do."

"Good," Nikki said, encouraged by this rare piece of good news. "By now Rasheed and Mobara ought to be at the embassy. I'm going to pack my stuff up and join them." She looked around the room; her clothes and makeup were scattered everywhere.

Sa'id glanced around curiously at the mess in the room.

Nikki shrugged. "I thought I'd have some time to come back after we processed Rasheed and Mobara," she said. "Sa'id, can you give me a ride to the embassy and let Hanif know that he can go now? Tell him thanks for everything."

As Sa'id opened his mouth to reply, a blast in the hallway blew the door partway open. Only the chain lock kept it from opening completely.

"I thought you weren't followed!" Nikki yelled.

"I didn't think I was," Sa'id retorted, staring at the door in disbelief.

While Sa'id stared, Hanif reacted. He grabbed Nikki by the arm and lunged for the sliding-glass door that led to the balcony on the opposite side of the room. He yanked it open and flung her out onto the concrete balcony. Another blast hit the hotel-room door. This time the chain lock broke, and the door banged open against the wall.

A large concrete pillar on each side of the balcony separated it from those belonging to the adjoining rooms. A waist-high, cast-iron railing kept anyone from falling seven floors to the hard pavement of the parking lot below. In the split second available to decide, Hanif apparently decided to take an escape route that headed down.

He grabbed Nikki under both her arms and swung her over the railing. She was petrified and didn't dare move. Hanif let his strong hands slide up her arms as he lowered her quickly toward the deck of the balcony below. His hands gripped tightly around her forearms, then he swung her body slightly out away from the building and let the momentum carry her back toward the deck of the balcony. At the last second, he released her and Nikki landed shaken but unhurt on the balcony below. Hanif then swung over the railing himself, hung down as far as possible while grabbing the lowest part of the railing, and swung and jumped onto the deck next to Nikki.

After regaining his balance, he reared back and kicked with all his might, landing the heel of his shoe squarely against the sliding glass door of Room 602. The door shattered, and in a heartbeat he unlocked the door and pulled Nikki inside the room. She heard a thud behind them, signaling the arrival of one of Ahmed's men on the balcony just a few steps away.

Hanif and Nikki sprinted into the hallway, slamming the door behind them. To their left, just a few short feet away, a large metal doorway led to a stairwell. To the right a long hallway led to elevators and another stairwell. Hanif pushed Nikki to the left and yelled, "I pick you up out back," as he sprinted down the hallway. Nikki stared for a split-second after him, wondering if she would ever see him again.

Stunned, she turned and ran through the door directly in front of her and into the stairwell. The metal door slammed, and she immediately felt claustrophobic, surrounded by masonry walls with no windows, trapped in a narrow stairwell with only one way out. She instinctively grabbed the handrail and took a few steps down. Then she heard it. The sound of heavy breathing in the stairwell below her, accompanied by hurried footsteps coming in her direction. The footsteps of a man, huffing as he climbed. Probably the mountain man she had seen outside Sa'id's office.

She could not go back through the steel door and into the hallway, because she might encounter the man on the sixth floor. She couldn't go down, or she would run smack into the arms of the mountain man. And so she started climbing as fast as her legs would carry her.

She went up six flights and started slowing, her legs heavy, her chest tight and heaving. The relentless sounds of the footsteps below were still coming, but they were farther away. Those hours on the StairMaster had paid off. The prey gained a few seconds on the predator.

She closed her eyes, took her chance, and ducked into the hallway of the twelfth floor. She ran halfway down the carpeted corridor, glancing over her shoulder and noticing that most of the doors on her right were open. She looked into one room as she was sprinting by and saw a maid with a cart of cleaning supplies. Nikki ran a few steps past the room, turned quickly around, and darted back into the room where the startled maid was making the bed.

"Do you speak English?" Nikki asked breathlessly, bent over with her hands on her knees, sucking wind.

The maid just lifted her hands, palms turned upward.

Nikki put her fingers to her lips, signaling the maid should be quiet. She then pulled a wad of riyals from her pocket and put them in the maid's hand. Without saying another word, Nikki climbed into the large cloth bag on the maid's cleaning cart, curled up in the bottom of the bag, and covered herself with used room linens. The maid apparently understood. Nikki could hear her humming and tucking in the sheets on the bed.

Nikki had never been so scared in her life. She lay perfectly still. The maid's humming was drowned out by the sound of Nikki's own ragged breathing and the pounding of her heart. She felt hot beads of sweat dripping down her back. She was helpless, totally at the mercy of a woman she didn't know, banking on that woman's willingness to help a stranger escape detection.

Ahmed's men could enter the room at any time, and the maid needed only to nod toward the laundry bag. It would be over before Nikki even knew what had happened.

She thought about her life, all the things left undone. Her back to the wall now, all her cleverness, confidence, and guile were of no use. She didn't know what else to do as she lay there, curled up and trembling.

So she prayed.

Dear God, if You're out there, if You are as real as Sarah says You are, please help me! I know I don't deserve it, but I'm desperate, and Sarah needs me alive. Please blind these men looking for me.

Nikki thought for a moment about this next line. She had heard Sarah pray this way before, but it seemed to limit the type of God she was praying to. If the Hindus or Muslims were right, she was about to make a big mistake. But then again, if the Muslims were right, why would God rescue her anyway? After all, she was trying to help a Christian missionary.

In the name of Jesus, amen.

A few seconds later, Nikki heard a breathless male address the maid in Arabic. The woman responded, and a short discussion followed. Nikki braced herself for the sound of a gunshot, the feel of bullets ripping into her flesh.

But only silence ensued—no talking, no humming, no noise at all. Nikki thought about coming out from under the laundry. But just before she could make her move, she felt a strong hand reach through the sheets and pull her up by her arm.

Busted.

It was the smiling maid.

She was chattering in Arabic and pointing wildly in the direction she had just sent the Muttawa officer. Nikki climbed out of the laundry bag, but before she headed off in the opposite direction, she gave the maid a spontaneous hug. The maid seemed entirely unimpressed, and when Nikki released her, the maid held out her open hand for a more tangible reward. Nikki gave her another fistful of riyals, thanked her again, then headed out of the room and away from the stairwell— toward the elevators.

Nikki wondered how many members of the Muttawa still roamed the Hyatt. With any luck, only a few.

Where would I look if I were in their shoes? They last saw me climbing the stairs, heading up. They would be looking for me to escape using the stairs or climbing from balcony to balcony. No person in her right mind, fleeing for her life, would ever allow herself to be trapped in the elevators…so, that's exactly what I'll do. Take the elevator down to the second floor. Get below them. Then sprint down a flight of steps and into the parking lot.

Nikki's recklessness surprised even herself. She waited at the elevator door, glancing left and right, left and right, for an interminable two minutes. The car going down was empty. She jumped in and prayed some more. Amazingly, the elevator didn't stop until the second floor. When the elevator door opened, Nikki stuck her head out and quickly looked both ways. Then she ran down the hall and sprinted down the stairs, surprised not to see any of the Muttawa along the way. She slipped out the side door and into the parking lot.

As soon as she exited the building, she heard an engine turn over and, seconds later, saw a car swerving toward her. Hanif! She jumped in, glancing behind her. He gunned the engine and squealed the tires as he exited the parking lot.

"Thanks," Nikki gasped as they sped away.

"Any time. You still like my 'do?" he asked in stilted English.

"I thought you didn't speak English," she said sheepishly. "But the answer is yes."

She leaned her throbbing head back against the headrest and counted her blessings. They would soon be at the embassy, hopefully without further incident. "Thanks, God," she said under her breath.

She wondered what happened to Sa'id.

■ ■ ■

Sa'id looked pathetic as Ahmed and the mountain man rejoined a dark-eyed Muttawa officer who kept watch in Room 703. The trembling Saudi lawyer lay on the floor next to the king-size bed, his hands cuffed behind his back. The officer kicked Sa'id and commanded him to stand when Ahmed entered the room. He obeyed immediately but kept his gaze downward, not daring to look Ahmed in the eye.

"Take the handcuffs off," demanded Ahmed.

The man with the dark eyes and scar removed the slender manacles.

Ahmed walked over to Sa'id, towering over him. Sa'id, only five-nine when he stood straight, hunched forward in humility. Ahmed, nearly six inches taller to begin with, grabbed Sa'id's right hand and pushed the hand down toward the right forearm, nearly bending Sa'id's pudgy wrist in half.

Sa'id whimpered at first, then let out a bloodcurdling scream.

"What do you want?" he cried in Arabic as Ahmed increased the pressure.

"Where did Rasheed and Mobara go? What happened to the American?" Ahmed hissed. He pushed harder on the wrist, forcing Sa'id to kneel in pain.

This was his moment of truth, left at the mercy of a man who showed no mercy. Whether he lied or told the truth, Sa'id sensed he was drawing his last few breaths. Rasheed, Mobara, and Nikki would need all the time possible to make the embassy, gain asylum, and leave the country. Every minute could be the difference between their survival or their capture. The truth might cost them dearly. But a lie would betray his country and his god. He had but a moment to think.

Like Nikki had done a few minutes earlier, Sa'id prayed quickly and silently. Another desperate prayer, but this one asked Allah for forgiveness.

"They are driving to Dhahran," Sa'id gasped, struggling for breath in spite of the pain. "Rasheed and Mobara…just left." His voice quickened, sharp words through the pain as the pressure on his wrist increased. "They are heading back to my office to pick up Moreno and will drive to Dhahran. They knew you would go to the Riyadh airport… They will leave through Dhahran… They already have visas."

■ ■ ■

Ahmed squeezed on the wrist with all his might until he heard the pleasing sound of breaking bone. He released it, and the wrist hung limp. Sa'id whelped and collapsed on the floor, holding his broken wrist gingerly with his other hand. As Sa'id moaned, Ahmed withdrew his gun and pointed it at the attorney's forehead.

"Beg, you dog," he ordered. Sa'id was of no further use.

"In the name of Allah, please! I will help you catch them! Please, sir! Spare my life!" Sa'id struggled to his knees, holding his wrist in his left palm, begging for mercy and looking desperately at Ahmed.

"I said beg!" yelled Ahmed.

Sa'id fell on his face at Ahmed's feet, groveling and pleading for his life. When he had heard enough, Ahmed reached down and grabbed Sa'id under his chin. He pulled the man's head upward so he could enjoy the terror in Sa'id's eyes. With his free hand, Ahmed calmly placed his gun against the small man's forehead, smiled, and pulled the trigger.

"Clean this place up and write a report. Make it self-defense." Ahmed said to the man with the scar and the dark eyes. "I want the Dhahran airport crawling with officers. And send a few to Riyadh just in case, though I don't think this worm had the guts to lie."

Ahmed turned to leave the hotel room, but first stopped in the bathroom to wash the blood from his hands.

39

The prisoner in the orange jumpsuit took his time getting to the stand. He moved slowly because his ankles were chained together, and he clanged when he walked. Though manacled, the young man still managed to swagger. He strutted his youth, his dreadlocks, his multiple tattoos, and a five-day growth of curly stubble.

When he finally took the stand, he slouched in his seat, put his chin in his hand, and scowled.

"State your name for the record," said Brad as he took his place behind the podium, giving the convict a wary look. He was beginning to wonder if this was such a good idea.

"Othello Biggs," came the muffled reply. "They call me Shakespeare."

Brad couldn't tell whether the man was kidding, so he played it straight.

"Mr. Biggs, do you know why you're here?"

"Huh-uh."

"Mr. Biggs, this is a civil case. My client is Sarah Reed, this lady seated at counsel table to my right." Brad motioned toward Sarah, but Shakespeare didn't bother to look.

"So what?" he glowered.

"We have sued the defendants because we say the police in Saudi Arabia wrongfully arrested Mrs. Reed and her husband. We say they tortured the Reeds and ultimately killed Mr. Reed. So basically, this is a case where we are trying to prove police misconduct."

Shakespeare scowled at the defense lawyers. He had probably been the victim of police misconduct a few times himself. Brad could sense a little softening as Shakespeare turned back to him.

"The police say the Reeds were actually running a drug ring and selling cocaine and marijuana," Brad continued. "We say the Reeds were missionaries, just having a little church."

Shakespeare laughed out loud at that one.

"Very creative," he scoffed.

Strobel rose. "Does Mr. Carson have any *questions* for this witness, or does he plan to tell him about this case for the rest of the day?"

"I'm providing some context, Your Honor," Brad explained. "It won't take much longer."

"It better not," Judge Baker-Kline warned. Brad took that as a cue to continue.

"We've heard testimony about the use of cocaine, a subject that I understand you might know something about. I want to show you some of that testimony and see if what they said is true."

As Brad spoke, Leslie prepared to cue the tape of Omar Khartoum's testimony.

"But first, I've got to establish your experience in this area. Mr. Biggs, how many times have you been arrested for drug use?"

"State or federal?" he asked proudly.

"Both," Brad clarified.

"I been arrested 'bout ten, twenty times. I only done time three times, 'cludin' this one."

"Mr. Biggs, you'll have to sit up straight and speak into the microphone," Ichabod scolded.

Biggs didn't move.

"How many of those were cocaine arrests?" asked Brad.

"Most of 'em."

"Have you ever been convicted of selling cocaine?"

"I said I did time. Somethin' 'bout that you don't understand?" Biggs' scowl told Brad they had spent enough time on his arrest record.

"Just a few more questions about experience," said Brad, treading lightly. "For how many years have you been involved with cocaine use?"

"Since I was thirteen," he said.

"And how old are you now?"

"Twenty-two."

"Do you have experience with smoking crack cocaine as well as snorting cocaine?"

Shakespeare snorted as if that were the dumbest question he'd ever heard. "'Course."

Brad signaled Leslie to begin the tape, and everyone watched a few minutes of the cross-examination. Khartoum was shown tasting the cocaine. Then Brad asked Khartoum, "How did you know it was fake from tasting it? How is this substance different from the real cocaine you've tasted?"

"The substance is sweeter," was the translated reply on the tape.

"Is that how you tell whether a substance is cocaine? You see how sweet it is?" Brad asked on the tape.

"Yes," was Khartoum's reply.

Brad hit the pause button. "Is he right about the way cocaine tastes?" asked Brad.

"That fool's lyin'," said Shakespeare disdainfully, apparently happy to catch another witness in a lie. "He ain't never tasted rock, man. You know it's real cause it bites. Man, it numbs yo' whole tongue and the whole inside yo' mouth if it's pure stuff. Ain't nothin' 'bout it that's sweet." He furrowed his eyes at Brad, daring the attorney to question his judgment on this matter.

Brad rolled some more tape. Khartoum demonstrated how he would snort a large pile of cocaine.

"What do you think of that?" Brad asked.

"I said he's a fool," said Shakespeare, "or he's trippin'. You use a rolled-up bill, man. You don't jus dump it on the table and snort." Shakespeare chuckled derisively. "And man, if you snorted that much snow, you'd be dead like that." He snapped his fingers for emphasis.

Brad rolled some more tape. Khartoum described how they would cook the cocaine to make crack, at temperatures in excess of 250 degrees. This time, when Brad shut off the tape, he didn't have time to ask a question.

"If that boy heated coke at two-fifty, he's an even bigger fool than I thought."

Strobel shot to his feet again. "Your Honor, I object to the way this witness characterizes Mr. Khartoum. This is not testifying to facts. It's character assassination."

"I agree," said Ichabod. "Sir, please limit your testimony to your own factual knowledge. Do not evaluate the testimony of Mr. Khartoum."

Shakespeare just shook his head. "He still don't know what he's talking about," he said defiantly. "I know for a fact you don't make crack by cookin' it at like two-fifty. You get it that hot, you destroy the cocaine, it turns into vapor. I done it before, man. I know."

"One more question," said Brad. "Let me show you one more segment of this tape and ask if the testimony is accurate based on your own personal experience."

Brad rolled the testimony of Khartoum as he described the rush he got from snorting cocaine. "I would get a huge rush right away," Khartoum asserted, "and I wouldn't come down for hours."

"That fool's so full of it," interrupted Shakespeare.

"Objection," shouted Strobel.

"Sit down and shut up, baldy," snapped Shakespeare.

"You close your mouth, Mr. Biggs, or I'll hold you in contempt," shouted Ichabod.

"And what?" asked Shakespeare, in a mocking tone. "Throw me in jail? Now I'm *scared*."

Ichabod chose to ignore this last comment. She could no doubt tell he was not the least bit intimidated by her judicial powers.

"Objection sustained," she ruled. "And if the witness makes one more remark like the last one, I will dismiss him from the stand and strike his testimony."

Brad worked hard to keep from smiling. The marshals were probably loving this guy. Shakespeare might get a private cell tonight.

"Is it true," Brad asked quickly, "that you get a sudden rush from snorting cocaine and that the rush lasts for several hours?"

"No way," said Shakespeare, with the authority of a man who had been there a few times. "That's why you smoke crack. Snortin' don't give you no rush for a long time, and the high don't last that long once it comes. Maybe a half-hour, maybe an hour…max. But smoking crack, man, that's a different game. It's like"—and now Shakespeare leaned back and brushed both arms up over his body—"this incredible rush hits you right away, man." He smiled, as if reliving a high right there on the stand. Then he turned serious. "But you don't get nothin' like that jus' from snorting cocaine. Nope. I don't care what this judge and baldy are saying, that man on the tape don't know what he's talking about."

■ ■ ■

On mile four of his run Friday evening, Brad still couldn't make sense of anything. He couldn't believe that Nikki had sold him out. The e-mail from her computer to Shelhorse bothered him most. Why would someone as savvy as Nikki leave such obvious evidence of being a traitor? It only made sense if she had already cut her deal and decided to stay outside the country. If that were the case, Brad knew he would never see Rasheed take the witness stand the next day. In fact, the man was probably already dead.

But if Nikki had already cut her deal, then why was this man named Hamilton calling and offering her one and a half million? Was Nikki somehow double-crossing Ahmed and getting paid off by some third party? But why would this Hamilton leave such an incriminating message in such a nonchalant manner on Nikki's voicemail?

Every question yielded ten more. Where was Ahmed? Could someone have broken into Nikki's office and sent a message to Shelhorse over her computer? But how would you explain the other leaks, such as the inside information about Worthington that knocked him out of the case? Could there be another traitor on the inside, a person who saw an opportunity to set up Nikki while she was out of the country? And who could that possibly be? Bella? Leslie? Sarah? O'Malley? He could not make himself believe, even for a passing moment, that any of these would betray him.

Time would sort out the mystery. If Nikki returned on schedule early Saturday morning, it would be hard for him to believe that she was involved. If she did not, he would know she was rich and Rasheed was dead. But who was Chad Hamilton? And why would Nikki betray Brad and Sarah?

He ran farther and faster, but he could not clear his mind this evening. He could not exorcise the demons of doubt.

40

T his is stupid," Bella whispered to nobody in particular. "She isn't coming. Let's just face it." Brad ignored her. He could do without her negative thoughts right now.

The jury gathered in the jury room, and the lawyers sat at their respective counsel tables. Few protesters met in front of the courthouse this morning; a few seats stood empty in the gallery for the first time in days. The early morning newscasts had speculated that today Brad would announce he was resting his case. Brad noticed that Ahmed was back in the courtroom, bearing his normal scowl. 8 A.M.

Nikki and Rasheed *could* show. It was still possible. If they had gotten out of Saudi Arabia late Friday evening, they would have just enough time to make it to Norfolk by early Saturday morning. But Brad had still not heard from them, and even the eternal optimist in him had to admit that he was out of options.

"All rise!" commanded the court clerk, hushing the crowd. "Silence is now commanded while court is in session. The Honorable Judge Cynthia Baker-Kline presiding. God save this honorable court."

God save me, thought Brad.

"Please, take your seats," Ichabod said in businesslike fashion. Brad remained standing in order to address the court and request additional time. He was not relishing the task.

"Call your next witness, Mr. Carson," ordered the judge.

"Your Honor," began Brad, "our next witness was to be Rasheed Berjein. As you know, as recently as yesterday, we were trying to gain political asylum for Mr. Berjein so that he could leave Saudi Arabia and testify in this trial. He's a critical rebuttal witness. Absolutely critical. He has already testified by videotape, but he is now prepared to correct that testimony in person. We have tried unsuccessfully in the last twenty-four hours to reach either Mr. Berjein or my paralegal who went to help him in this process. Accordingly, we would respectfully ask that his testimony be postponed until Monday."

"Request denied," Ichabod said firmly. Brad slumped his shoulders and pursed his lips. The fabricated testimony of Rasheed on videotape would stand.

"But I will grant a half-hour recess, Mr. Carson. A few minutes ago, in my chambers, I received a telephone call from your paralegal. She said she had been trying to reach you by phone but could not reach you, presumably because you could not bring your cell phone into court. She said that she had just received a number of e-mail messages on some kind of handheld computer device, now that she's back in the country and within range of the cells where it works, informing her about court this morning. Ms. Moreno said she would be at the courthouse in about ten minutes. I decided to be generous and give you half an hour."

The thought crossed Brad's mind that if Ichabod truly wanted to be generous, she would have told him about this development when she first took the bench, but he was not about to complain. Nikki *was* coming. And she *was* bringing Rasheed.

"Court stands in recess for half an hour," the clerk announced. Ichabod left the bench, and all eyes turned to the doors at the back of the courtroom.

None watched more intently than Ahmed.

■ ■ ■

Twenty minutes later Nikki burst through the doors with Rasheed in tow. Neither had slept for nearly forty-eight hours, except for a few fitful hours on the plane. Cognizant that all eyes were on her, Nikki self-consciously took inventory of her haggard appearance. She wore a pair of skintight faded jeans, an untucked blouse, and no makeup. Her normally pampered hair was oily and unkempt. She couldn't remember when she'd last brushed it. At least her Oakleys hid her bloodshot eyes—assuming Ichabod didn't make her take them off. But when she saw Brad, she forgot all about that.

Nikki ran down the aisle and threw her arms around her boss. "I love this country," she whispered. "Hope I'm not too late."

"You're right on time," he assured her.

She turned to see Rasheed and Sarah embrace. Then Sarah tilted her head back, looked Rasheed over, said a few words of Arabic, and the two embraced again. Rasheed smiled widely with a kind of stupefied grin.

Bella stood a few feet away, left out of the original round of hugs. Nikki felt so good to be back on American soil, even if it was Ichabod's courtroom, that she took a step toward Bella to embrace.

But Bella's sour expression never changed. As Nikki stepped forward, Bella brought her two arms up like pistons, landed them hard against Nikki's shoulders, and jarred Nikki backward. "You traitor," sneered Bella. "How dare you come waltzing—"

Stunned by the reaction, Nikki stood frozen for a split second. But she wasn't about to take a blow from the whale woman without retaliating. She regained her balance and lunged at Bella, fingernails searching for skin, insults flying from her lips. Brad jumped between them, grabbing Nikki before she could land any blows. Facing her, he held her back as she hurled invectives at Bella.

He eventually talked Nikki into taking a seat at the end of the counsel table farthest from Bella. She did so only after promising she would rip Bella's lungs out, one at a time, as soon as court was over.

"This is the thanks I get?" Nikki asked. "For risking my life?" She stared at Bella, as if calling her out with her gaze.

Bella, now seated, stared stoically ahead and ignored her nemesis. Leslie sat next to Nikki, strategically placing herself in the way of Nikki's challenging stare. Sarah sat next to Bella.

Brad turned and addressed the curious reporters. "Just a little family feud," he said nonchalantly.

She's history, Nikki thought, plotting her revenge. *It's just a matter of time.* Bella didn't know who she was messing with. She didn't know the half of it.

"All rise," the court clerk commanded, and everyone scampered to their seats. In the next moment Ichabod dashed into the courtroom, looking furious as ever. She stared at Nikki, who stared back from behind her shades. They were not coming off without a fight.

Ichabod apparently decided not to push the point. "Is Mr. Berjein prepared to testify?" she asked.

"Yes, Your Honor," Brad announced wearily.

And at long last, Rasheed Berjein walked proudly to the front of this American courtroom, raised his hand, took the oath, and climbed into the witness box to testify against his tormentor—Ahmed Aberijan—in the U.S. District Court for the Eastern District of Virginia.

■ ■ ■

Sarah listened intently to Rasheed's testimony, affirming him with her eyes. Even with the necessity of translation, his testimony was spellbinding. He spoke from his heart about the history of the small Riyadh church. He testified that, on the same night that Charles Reed died, Rasheed and his wife were arrested by the Muttawa on trumped-up drug charges as well. The Muttawa threatened them and beat them, made them recant their Christian conversion, then released them.

Rasheed described the sleepless nights after denying his Christian faith, his search for forgiveness, and the rebirth of the church. Without divulging the names of any church members, he detailed the tumultuous growth of the small church and the persecution it suffered. Sarah swelled with pride at the way the church had reestablished itself and carried on. She marveled at how the Lord had preserved some seeds from the church that was persecuted and nurtured them into a whole new church reaching the lost and preaching the gospel.

The thriving church was nothing short of a miracle, and it was marvelous in her eyes.

She glanced at Bella out of the corner of her eye. Rasheed's testimony had obviously not captivated the still-seething legal secretary. Sarah picked up her pen and carefully wrote on the yellow legal pad in front of her. She slid it in front of Bella.

I don't think Nikki did it, read the note. *Why would she have come back with Rasheed if she was a mole for the Muttawa? This testimony is too damaging.*

Bella read the note and scribbled something in response. She slid it back to Sarah. *Then how do you explain the e-mail from Nikki to Shelhorse, and the voice mail offering Nikki $1.5 mil?*

Sarah thought for a moment, looking at Rasheed but not really listening. A lot of things didn't make sense. She wrote a response and slid the note back to her right, even as she looked at the witness. She felt like a schoolgirl passing notes in class.

Why would Nikki write the e-mail to Shelhorse from her own computer? the note asked. *Nikki knew we would eventually speak to Shelhorse and that Shelhorse would tell us where the message came from. Why would Nikki set herself up like that?*

Out of the corner of her eye, Sarah watched Bella read the note and shrug. She didn't pick up her pen to draft a response.

Sarah sensed that Bella was softening. She grabbed the paper again and decided to appeal to Bella's new spiritual side.

The Bible tells us not to judge one another, Sarah wrote. *Especially motivations. I think you owe Nikki an apology. How will Nikki ever be drawn to Christ if she doesn't notice a change in you?*

She said a quick little prayer and slid the paper down the table again. Bella read it and hung her head. A certain sadness crept into her eyes. She stared down at the table and eventually wrote a one-word response.

Okay.

Sarah gave her a small smile and a quick squeeze of the hand. Bella didn't squeeze back, and Sarah decided not to push her luck.

■ ■ ■

"Did there come a time," Brad asked, "when you were approached by Ms. Moreno from my firm about the possibility of testifying in this case?"

"Yes, I remember the day well," the translator replied.

"Tell me about it," said Brad.

"Ms. Moreno and a Saudi Arabian attorney, a man named Sa'id el Khamin, told me what happened to Pastor Reed and Sarah." As he talked, Rasheed frequently looked over at Sarah, seemingly drawing strength from the brave missionary.

"I talked with your Ms. Moreno and agreed to give testimony in this case," the translator continued as Rasheed spoke. "We met in their car because Ms. Moreno believed my apartment was, how to say, others were listening to my phones. Your Ms. Moreno said I should be ready for a visit from the Muttawa as soon as Ms. Moreno and Mr. el Khamin leave. So we agree on a plan."

"What was that plan?"

"That day, I give your Ms. Moreno a written statement, how do you say it… I swear is true—"

"An affidavit?" offered Brad.

"Yes, that is it," came back the translated reply. "Then Ms. Moreno says I will be asked to give my story before the trial in something called—" Rasheed could not find the word, the translator waited.

"A deposition?" Brad volunteered.

"Yes. So Ms. Moreno and myself agreed that I would say whatever the Muttawa wanted me to say in the deposition. They had my wife—"

The translator waited on the visibly shaken Rasheed. The memory of his wife's life hanging on his every word seemed to unnerve him anew. He shook on the stand, his lip quivering, staring at his hands, unable to speak.

The silence became uncomfortable, and Ichabod intervened. "Would the witness like to take a break?" she asked the translator.

The offer was translated, but Rasheed shook his head. "He just wants to get it over," said the translator.

After another awkward pause and a glance at Sarah for reassurance, Rasheed continued.

"They, the Muttawa, were listening to the deposition in another room with my wife—"

"Objection," called out Strobel, causing the witness to start and lean back in his chair, wide-eyed. "This is classic hearsay."

"Sustained," said Ichabod without enthusiasm. "Tell him to state only what happened, and not what he heard from others," she instructed the translator.

Seeing the look of confusion on the translator's face, Brad intervened.

"Did you tell the truth in your deposition?" Brad asked through the interpreter.

"No."

"Why not?"

"Because I had been threatened—"

"Objection...hearsay," said an exasperated Strobel.

"It's not offered for the truth of the matter asserted, Your Honor," Brad explained. "It's offered only to show motivation."

This bit of verbal hocus-pocus seemed to satisfy Ichabod. "I'll allow it," she ruled. "But ladies and gentlemen of the jury, the alleged threats made against Rasheed should be considered only for the purpose of deciding whether he had a motivation to lie in his deposition. You should not concern yourself as to whether the threats were in fact true. Do you understand?"

Of course they didn't. But the jurors nodded their heads as if they understood perfectly, anxious to hear all about these threats.

"I was told that if I did not testify and say that Pastor and Sarah Reed, and even myself, used drugs, I would never again see my wife alive. But Ms. Moreno and myself, even in our first meeting, had already thought about this possibility and agreed on two signals. The first signal was for this jury." Rasheed turned and faced the members of the jury. "We agreed that Mr. Carson would ask a question a certain way and I would answer a certain way in order to show you, as the jury, that I was lying just to survive."

The slightest smile creased Rasheed's face, a smile of pride as he explained his clever little plot. Strobel rose to object but could apparently think of nothing to say. Without uttering a word, he sat back down.

"What was the question and answer?" asked Brad.

"You asked me to look you in the eye and tell you that I had not been threatened by the Muttawa. I was to answer but stare down at the table, to show the jury that I could not look you in the eye and say my testimony was true. This is universal language, Mr. Carson. Can you look someone in the eyes and tell them it is the truth? If not, it is a lie. This was my signal to this jury. I was telling them, by that signal, my deposition testimony was a lie."

Brad was sure the jurors had not forgotten the last question of Rasheed's deposition. The camera had focused on the top of his head as the picture faded to black.

"And what was the second signal?" Brad asked.

"The next day after the deposition, I was to go to a pay telephone and call Ms. Moreno. If I was still ready to give up my homeland, my church, my family, and my friends, if I was still ready to seek political safety in the United States and testify in this trial, then I was to tell Ms. Moreno 'everything is fine' in Arabic. I taught her that phrase during her first visit because we knew we would have no interpreter. If I was not willing to be involved any further, I was to tell her 'I must stay' in Arabic."

"Did you call Ms. Moreno, and, if so, what did you say?"

"I am here," replied Rasheed, "and it has not been easy. I called her and told her 'everything is fine.'"

_____

41

Leslie listened to Rasheed's testimony and, out of the corner of her eye, watched Nikki. Nikki was leaning forward, hanging on every word that came out of the witness's mouth, looking every inch a supporter of the witness. She did not bear the posture of a woman who had tried to sell out her own trial team.

Leslie leaned to her left, put an arm around the back of Nikki's chair, and whispered in her ear.

"Who is Chad Hamilton?" she whispered.

"Who wants to know?" whispered Nikki, shaded eyes still on the witness.

"I do," said Leslie, her mouth close to Nikki's ear. "Bella found a voicemail message on your office phone where this guy Chad Hamilton offered you one point five million."

"Bella's a pig," Nikki said with conviction, louder than a whisper, still looking straight ahead.

"Nikki, there's the voicemail message from Chad Hamilton, and there's also an e-mail message sent from your Blackberry telling Dr. Shelhorse not to come and testify. And Shelhorse didn't show." Nikki took off her sunglasses and gave Leslie a dumbfounded look. "Who is Chad Hamilton?" Leslie asked again.

"Is that why Bella attacked me?" Nikki whispered through gritted teeth. "Does Bella think I'm some kind of spy for Aberijan?"

Leslie nodded her head.

"I barely escaped from Aberijan with my life." The color was rising on the back of Nikki's neck, and she shot a wicked glance at Bella.

"So who is Chad Hamilton?" whispered Leslie. It still made no sense.

"He's the insurance adjuster for the Johnson case," Nikki said. "Brad doesn't know it, but I'm negotiating an awesome settlement for Mr. Johnson. Brad and Bella—heck, even the client—told me to settle for $550,000. I ignored 'em. And now it sounds like I'm going to get almost three times that. We'll make half a million in legal fees."

This bit of news rocked Leslie back in her chair. "Then who wrote the e-mail message on your computer to Dr. Shelhorse?" asked Leslie.

"Probably Bella," said Nikki, making no effort to whisper.

"Shhh," whispered Leslie.

"Probably Bella. Who else is in our office during the day while you and Brad are in court?"

Leslie did not respond. There was so much to process. Most of what Nikki said made perfect sense, except for one small item.

How did Nikki know the e-mail to Shelhorse had been sent while court was in session?

■ ■ ■

While the ladies whispered and wondered, Rasheed concluded his testimony. "Please answer any questions Mr. Strobel might have," Brad said as he returned to his seat.

Strobel shot out of his seat and started firing questions even before he made it to the podium. Everything about his demeanor and tone of voice conveyed one message: He was on the attack.

"So let me get this straight," he boomed. "Your sworn videotaped testimony was just a bunch of lies. Is that right?"

"Yes," Rasheed admitted through his translator.

"And not only did you lie in that sworn testimony, but you and Ms. Moreno planned ahead of time that you would lie to this court and this jury. Right?" Strobel was livid, his face dark with anger.

"Yes," both Rasheed and the translator said meekly.

"And you say that you lied because you were afraid that Mr. Aberijan would harm your wife?"

"Yes, his men were with my wife during my deposition and would have harmed her if I told the truth."

"But today you're telling the truth because you have gained political asylum and are no longer afraid of Mr. Aberijan?"

"Yes, this is true."

"Then why didn't you seek political asylum before you ever gave your deposition so that you would not have to mislead this judge and jury?"

"I do not know, except that was not the plan."

"Who came up with this wonderful plan?"

"It was Ms. Moreno's plan."

"And did Ms. Moreno tell you that you could get political asylum and get a chance to live in the United States if you were willing to testify for Mrs. Reed?"

"Yes and no. She told me we could get, as you call it…political asylum, if I agreed to tell the truth."

"And did she promise to help you find work in America?"

"Ms. Moreno says she and Mr. Carson will try to help me."

"Are you glad you gained political asylum and now have a chance to live in America?"

"I look forward with hope to life in this country."

"In America you get a clean start, but in Saudi Arabia, Mr. Berjein, you were a convicted drug dealer, right?"

"I was forced to plead guilty, but I did not use drugs."

"Isn't it true that you did in fact use drugs, that your earlier testimony was true, but that you saw a chance to get a new start in the wealthiest nation on earth—the United States—and all you had to do was give a little false testimony to make it happen?"

"I object," said Brad, "that's argumentative and improper."

"I'll withdraw the question," said Strobel before Ichabod could rule.

For a full hour, Strobel attacked the witness. He painted Rasheed as an opportunist, ready to jump at a chance to come to the United States.

He reviewed all of Rasheed's videotaped admissions about his drug use and pointed out that Rasheed knew a lot of details about cocaine for someone who now claimed he had never tried the stuff. It was a crafty cross-examination and a reminder that Strobel was well worth the four hundred dollars per hour that he charged his clients to dismantle witnesses like Rasheed.

But Rasheed survived the onslaught and nearly sprinted from the stand when Ichabod told him he could step down.

"This court will take a ten-minute recess," Ichabod declared and left the bench.

■ ■ ■

Brad and his team breathed a collective sigh of relief as Rasheed rejoined them. Brad shook the man's hand, patted him on the back, then watched with satisfaction as Rasheed gently embraced Sarah, kissing her on both cheeks. The others gathered around as well, slapping Rasheed's back or putting an encouraging hand on his shoulder.

As the team gathered around the table, Brad noticed Bella take a tentative step toward Nikki. He tensed, ready to spring between the two women who were now locking eyes.

"I'm sorry," Bella said, extending her hand. "What I did was stupid."

Nikki looked at Bella's hand, hesitated long enough to teach her a lesson, then accepted.

"Don't worry about it," Nikki replied. Her voice was still sullen.

Brad felt some of the tension in the air dissipate.

"The voicemail from Chad Hamilton was about the Johnson case," said Leslie helpfully. "He's an insurance adjuster."

Brad looked straight at Nikki, who shot Leslie a "button it up" glance. "I thought we settled that case weeks ago," he said.

Bella, now standing with her arms folded across her chest, looked at Brad and nodded. *I told you so,* she said with her eyes.

Nikki twisted her lips into a sheepish grin and watched Brad for a hint of a reprieve. "It's a long story…"

"Make it short."

"Okay… I settled for almost three times the amount you told me to accept several weeks ago."

"You mean you ignored my instructions—the client's instructions."

"Look, if you don't want the extra money, I'll keep it," Nikki sighed and slumped her shoulders, playing the role of the persecuted. "I just knew I could get more money…a lot more money…if they could see us in action." She looked at Brad, whose expression had not softened. "So I invited Hamilton and his boss to the trial. I arranged it so they were here during the cross-examination of Ahmed Aberijan. They saw all the fireworks: Brad threatened with contempt, the works. They knew we'd do whatever it takes to win a case. I told them our bottom line was one-point-seven million, take it or leave it, by the end of this case. They've now offered one-point-five."

"Talk to the client," Brad said, but his voice contained no enthusiasm. "If he agrees, take the money." He looked down, searching for just the right words, "But Nikki…"

"I know."

"You pull a stunt like this again and deliberately disregard my instructions—you're fired."

Nikki snorted. "You're welcome," she muttered, just loud enough for the others to hear.

"What about the e-mail to Shelhorse?" asked Bella. It was time to pile on.

Nikki shrugged. "The only thing I know about that is what Leslie told me while Rasheed was testifying. I couldn't have sent that e-mail from Saudi Arabia even if I wanted to— I couldn't get any reception for my Blackberry."

Bella gave her a raised eyebrow.

"Check it out," Nikki said, holding the device in her hand. "I didn't send anything until I hit American soil. Somebody who had access to the office computers," she looked straight at Bella, "sent the e-mail and made it look like it came from my Blackberry."

This spawned a round of furious speculation about the e-mail to Shelhorse. Bella recalled that O'Malley had come by the office about an hour before the e-mail was sent and accompanied Bella to court for a few hours to watch the trial. Someone, she surmised, must have seen Bella and Patrick leave the office, then broken in and sent the e-mail. It was an outside job, no doubt about it.

Everyone but Brad nodded in agreement.

■ ■ ■

"All rise," cried the bailiff, "this court is now in session, the Honorable Judge Cynthia Baker-Kline presiding."

In a few minutes everyone had scrambled to their seats, the courtroom was quiet, and the jury was seated in their box.

"I assume that the plaintiff now rests. Is that correct, Mr. Carson?" Ichabod asked.

"Yes, Your Honor."

Strobel was up. "We'd like to call one surrebuttal witness, Your Honor—Mrs. Sarah Reed."

Brad bolted from his chair and jerked his head toward Strobel. In the commotion of the last few days, he had forgotten all about Strobel's plans to recall Sarah and force a mistrial by asking her to disclose the name of her informant.

"If Mr. Strobel is recalling Mrs. Reed solely to ask the name of her informant, we would like to renew our objection," Brad said, addressing the court. "Not only does such a question unfairly require Mrs. Reed to jeopardize the life of this person, which she is not willing to do, but it also serves no useful purpose at this stage of the proceedings. It's not like Mr. Strobel now has time to subpoena this person and put him on the stand in this case. By waiting until the very last minute of the trial, Mr. Strobel has shown that the only reason he asks this question is to harass my client and force a mistrial."

"Your Honor," drawled Strobel, "we waited because we thought the information might come out by some other means and we could spare Mrs. Reed this question. But it did not, and so we are back where we started. The court ruled before that we were entitled to have this question answered. We are simply following through on that ruling now."

Judge Baker-Kline shook her head! Brad's heart raced. It was the first time in the trial Ichabod had shown any hint of being swayed by Sarah's case.

"You had your chance, Mr. Strobel. I would have made Mrs. Reed answer this same question earlier in the trial. But now, having just heard the testimony of Mr. Berjein, I am concerned about the safety of the informant. And I am also concerned about your timing, sir. If you really wanted this question answered, you should not have withdrawn it earlier. The objection is sustained. Mrs. Reed will not take the stand for surrebuttal."

As usual, Strobel's poker face did not show a hint of disappointment. "Then the defense rests," he announced to the jury, standing ramrod straight and looking them directly in the eye.

Brad had never felt better about his case.

"Thank you, Mr. Strobel," Ichabod said. "We will start closing arguments Monday promptly at 9 A.M. And Mr. Carson?"

"Yes, Your Honor."

"I have yet to hear any evidence, not even one shred, that leads me to believe the nation of Saudi Arabia ratified this alleged misconduct. Keep that in mind as you prepare your closing. You may be able to change my mind. But right now, I just don't see it."

"Yes, Your Honor," Brad mumbled reflexively, as Ichabod burst the bubble formed by her own prior ruling.

What in the world does she want, Brad wondered, *an engraved letter from the crown prince?*

The irreverent sound of juror number 4's snickering broke the courtroom's silence.

■ ■ ■

It's amazing what you can do with a telephoto lens, thought Frederick Barnes. He'd caught the juror dead in the act on Kodak film—400 millimeter. Incontrovertible proof. Earlier today, he'd slipped the photos into a small white envelope with gloved hands.

His gloved hands placed two-sided tape on the outside of the envelope, and he now waited patiently for his chance to make a clean pass of the photos. Barnes was a careful man. He would wait for the perfect opportunity, or he would not do it at all.

The moment came right after Ichabod dismissed the jury, the moment that juror number 4 snickered.

Brad Carson had left a copy of Rasheed's deposition on the podium. One hundred pages of transcribed testimony bound with a soft plastic cover on the front and back. It was better than jumping on the elevator with them and trying to drop the photos in a briefcase. It was so natural. It was perfect.

Barnes slid out of his seat in the first row and walked nonchalantly to the podium. He glanced around, then picked up the deposition and taped the photos inside the back cover. He discreetly removed the latex gloves and stuffed them in his pocket.

He turned toward plaintiff's counsel table and tapped her on the shoulder.

When she turned, he caught the flash of anger in her eyes. A "how dare you come over here, to our side, and talk to me in open court" look. She seemed to catch herself, and wariness replaced the anger in the beautiful dark eyes.

"Mr. Carson left this deposition and these two exhibits on the podium," explained Barnes. "I didn't want them to get mixed up with our stuff as we packed."

She took the deposition, but her dark eyes never left his.

"Thanks," said Nikki Moreno.

42

B arnes responded immediately to the summons on his cell phone. Within minutes he joined Ahmed in his hotel suite.

"She wants to meet tonight at nine," said Ahmed. "She wants to meet in the bar downstairs, corner table, on the pool-room level. She gave me the usual nonsense about coming alone."

"I'll personally cover you," Barnes said. He walked over to the floor-to-ceiling windows that overlooked the harbor and stared at the driving rain pelting the glass. A ragged bolt of lightning electrified the sky, and the rumbling from the thunder rattled the two-inch-thick pane. "What's the plan?" he asked, turning to face Ahmed.

Ahmed sat down on the sofa, grabbed the remote, and clicked off the television. Barnes hated it when Ahmed did this—took his sweet time answering—just to show who was in control. "Do we need juror 6, or can we get a mistrial without him?" he finally asked.

"I don't know yet. The plan's in place to bump Stein. But if the timing's not right, if Strobel has him dismissed before the jury begins deliberating, then the judge might say that the jury pool was not contaminated. She might just dismiss Stein and still not declare a mistrial. If she does that, then we'll need the vote of this other juror. Juror 6 is our insurance policy."

The Saudi looked up and stared at Barnes, looked right through him, and the silence became almost intolerable. But Barnes never considered breaking it or even moving until he had Ahmed's implicit permission to do so.

"How sure are we that our friend can deliver juror 6?" Ahmed asked.

"She's delivered everything else."

Ahmed sneered at the thought. "We have come too far to take any chances now. We may need juror 6. You talk to Strobel and make sure he waits until the jury begins deliberations to ask for a mistrial. I'll meet our friend tonight. When I do, I want you to wire her car...and her cell phone if she leaves it behind. I'll give her the trust agreement she's demanding, carrying the signature of the minister of public safety. We'll monitor her after our meeting. If she checks out, she'll find a hundred million in her little trust account on Monday morning."

The Muttawa leader slammed the jury consultant's notebook down on the glass coffee table. He stood and stretched his massive pecs and broad shoulders. He rotated his thick neck and rubbed vigorously at the base of his skull. This was not a man used to having things out of his control.

"We will play this game," he snarled, "and buy our verdict." He paused and looked at Barnes through cold gray eyes. "As soon as the jury returns its verdict, she dies."

"And let a hundred mil pass to Sarah Reed and her family?" Barnes asked incredulously.

Ahmed scoffed. "I said the trust agreement had the signature of the minister of public safety. I did not say the signature was genuine."

"What good does a forgery do? The money's still held in trust."

"If the signature is a forgery, then the terms of the trust agreement fail, and the money in the account reverts back to its original owner—Saudi Arabia." Ahmed paused. "Our friend is not as clever as she thinks."

He walked over to the small wet bar in his room, poured himself another soda, and took a long swig.

"Nobody blackmails Ahmed Aberijan and lives."

"What's your plan for taking her out?" There was a slight tremor in Barnes' voice. He was trying to act tough, like this was all in a day's work, but he had never been an accomplice to murder before.

"Not *my* plan," laughed Ahmed. It was a hollow and mirthless laugh. "I'm leaving the country as soon as the jury starts deliberating. How she dies, that's up to you. It's why you get paid so handsomely."

Ahmed pretended to ignore the stunned look of silent protest on the face of Barnes. In truth, he had no intention of leaving such an important and rewarding matter in the hands of a hired henchman. But the look on Barnes' face told him everything he needed to know. When push came to shove, the investigator could not be trusted. He simply didn't have the guts to kill, or worse, he had determined that it was not in his best interest to do so.

Either way, Ahmed would be forced to take matters into his own hands. And with that issue settled, Ahmed receded back into his own little world, deep in thought. He stared out the window for several minutes, soaking in the storm, and did not blink as Barnes left the room, softly shutting the door behind him.

■ ■ ■

Barnes arrived fifteen minutes late for his meeting with the brain trust, an unlit stogie tucked firmly in the corner of his mouth. The greetings were cool and guarded, and Barnes got right down to business. He stood at the end of the conference table, his large girth nearly resting on the table itself. The group's mood matched the weather, and they frowned disapprovingly at this man whom fate had chosen to be their ally.

"Here are some more photographs," he said, slapping a folder down on the table. "I'll have the man who took the photos ready to testify in court tomorrow."

Strobel grabbed the folder and ripped it open. The photos showed the face of juror number 4 and the back of another man. There were two sets of photos from two different restaurants.

"They have met at least three times in the last few weeks," said Barnes. "In one of the restaurants, my man was seated close enough to overhear some of their conversation. Stein has promised his vote for one hundred thousand cash, fifty now, fifty later. If you check his bank account at the Bank of Tidewater, you'll see that fifty has already been deposited. He's definitely working for Brad Carson."

"How do you know that?" asked Teddy.

"I can't say," answered Barnes smugly. "But I'll stake my reputation on it." Barnes paused for a moment and eyed the lawyers, daring any of them to challenge this information.

"Why would a juror take this incredible chance for a mere hundred thousand?" asked Win. "It almost destroys your faith in the system."

"A hundred thousand is still a lot of money to some people," replied Barnes. His voice reproached these big-firm lawyers. He looked from one to the next with disdain. He took a small bite of the cigar, spitting the piece to the side. "But that's beside the point," he continued. "Our old buddy Zeke Stein happens to be cheating on his wife. So the deal is not just his vote for a hundred thou; it's his vote for a hundred thou and the silence of the plaintiff's investigator.

"Here are the pictures to confirm the affair, if you're interested," said Barnes, tossing another folder onto the table. Unlike the other folder, nobody snatched this one up. All four men stared at the folder, resisting the urge to grab it, tear it open, and gawk at the contents. Their dignity and status in life required no less…at least for now.

"How did you find out about the affair?" Win asked.

"You mean juror 4's affair?" Barnes asked, as he tossed an accusatory look toward Win.

"Of course."

Barnes smirked. "My man will testify that he heard juror 4 and Carson's lackey, the man whose back you see in the pictures, talking about it at the restaurant. That man confronted juror 4 with pictures of the affair.

"And after the conversation in the restaurant, my man followed Mr. Stein around for a while and…*voila*…we've got our own photo gallery of him and his little mistress. It seems our man just can't stand to be away from his Internet sweetheart. He's probably with her right now."

Win couldn't seem to take his eyes off the folder, obviously riveted by the thought of what it might contain.

"I'm assuming that you're planning to take this information to the judge first thing tomorrow morning?" Teddy said to Mack.

It was not so much a question as a command. But Barnes harbored no respect for the old guy and did not realize that Teddy's suggestions should be treated like they came down from the mount.

"I would still recommend holding it until the jury actually starts deliberating," Barnes suggested before Mack could reply. "That way you've got a surefire mistrial because, by then, this juror will have poisoned the deliberations. If you unveil this stuff first thing Monday morning, the judge could just dismiss juror 4 and allow the other jurors and substitute alternate to begin deliberations." Barnes paused, chomping down hard on his cigar. "And fellas, I don't want to be the one to break it to you, but you don't have the most appealing jury case."

Teddy Kilgore clenched his jaw and stood slowly, using the table to help himself up. He extended a long, bony, trembling finger toward Barnes. "Listen here, sir, you will not come waltzing into these offices and tell us how to try this case. Your suggestions are both unwise and offensive." His voice was rising, nearly cracking with anger.

"You suggest that this firm should lie to the court for strategic reasons? Sacrifice the integrity of this firm and the trust of the bench, which has taken decades to build, just to get a mistrial? If we wait until after the jury begins deliberations to put your man on the stand, the judge will rightfully ask why we didn't bring this to her earlier. And either your man lies, and he says we just found out about it, or we look like complete fools. Am I right?"

Barnes knew better than to answer the question.

"Then what you are actually suggesting is that your man perjure himself on the stand and that Mr. Strobel should knowingly present perjured testimony to the court," Teddy continued, the long knobby finger pointing at Barnes' stubby nose.

It was exactly what Barnes was suggesting, although he may have phrased it somewhat more delicately.

"You obviously do not know this firm very well," Teddy huffed. He sat down, but his gaze did not leave Barnes. "You'll have your man in the courtroom, ready to testify, first thing tomorrow morning. Mr. Strobel will keep the photos of the meeting between juror 4 and Carson's gopher for evidence. You may take your other sleazy photographs and get out!" With this, Teddy waved his hand in a long arch, dismissing Barnes, the photos, and a guaranteed plan for a mistrial.

Out of the corner of his eye, Barnes saw Win, ever so subtly, cock his head to the side and look at Mack. *Do something,* the look screamed.

But Mack ignored him. Teddy still had a towering presence and great influence in this firm. And it was obvious that he had just levied a nonnegotiable edict.

Even Barnes knew better than to take on the man in this setting. Instead, he stuffed the folder back into his briefcase and stalked out the conference room, cursing Teddy Kilgore under his breath.

His plans for a mistrial had been dealt an unexpected blow. But for something this important, Barnes believed in redundancy planning. Exploiting juror number 4 was now a bit more challenging, but Barnes still had a way. And securing the vote of juror 6 was no longer a luxury. The informant would have to deliver.

He flicked some ashes on the Persian rug as he headed for the elevator.

■ ■ ■

She drove like lightning through the downpour. At ten minutes until nine, she was still twenty minutes from downtown Norfolk. Brad had kept everyone late while he reviewed his closing argument. They had videotaped him, then spent several hours critiquing his closing. Listening and critiquing. Listening and critiquing. Afterward, he still wanted to practice it several more times.

As far as she knew, Brad was still pacing around the conference table, cajoling the empty chairs, choreographing every inflection and gesture. And here she was, about to meet with Ahmed Aberijan one last time and render that closing argument moot.

The rain continued to fall in sheets against the windshield, the lines on the interstate becoming a blur. At least the thunder and lightning had stopped. Her wipers beat furiously, but they were no match for this flood from heaven. She hit a pool of standing water, and the car pulled hard to the right, almost ending in a spin. Her heart pumped harder as she realized she had almost lost it. She strained her eyes for more dark pools of water. Her speedometer said eighty-five.

The cell phone rang, and she jumped. She slowed slightly and took one hand off the wheel.

"Hello," she said tentatively.

"Man, girl, you are bookin'. Slow down a little. Ahmed ain't goin' nowhere." It was O'Malley. She had lost his headlights in her rearview mirror a few minutes earlier.

"Are you sure this'll work?"

"Look baby, you're totally wired. First sign of trouble, I'll be there," he promised.

"What if he pulls a gun?"

"I'll be right outside. Ten seconds, max. You've got to relax, hon. Aberijan can smell fear."

"Easy for you to say." She hydroplaned on another pool of standing water. "I've got to go... Thanks for being here, Patrick."

"Don't mention it."

She made it safely to the hotel but was ten minutes late. She pulled up under the overhang in the front of the building and gave the valet her keys. She walked through the large revolving doors and into the luxurious lobby. She took a deep breath and turned left down the hallway toward the combination deli restaurant and bar. A waiter greeted her with a smile.

"May I help you?" he asked.

"No, thanks. I'm just looking for someone."

She walked a few feet into the restaurant and took stock. Immediately in front of her, a few patrons enjoyed a late dinner and watched a large television. To her right, a few corporate road warriors sat in the sunken bar and talked to the bartender. A flight of stairs to her right led to a dimly lit area with a pool table and a few private dining tables. It overlooked the remainder of the restaurant and was bounded by a black iron railing. Two patrons played pool, but otherwise the upstairs room looked empty.

She headed up and wondered why she had chosen this place. The *Reed* case had received so much publicity that she could no longer meet with Ahmed in public. *But why here?* She had eaten here before—many times. But tonight it felt different. Darker. Musty. She could *feel* the evil.

She walked past the pool players and nodded at them. Then she saw him. Sitting in a booth in the far corner, not even visible from the main floor of the restaurant. He saw her too, and he locked on to her. She could not meet the gaze of his emotionless gray eyes.

She sat down at the booth without a word of greeting. She knew he could sense her fear, but there was nothing she could do about it.

"Did you come alone?" she asked.

"No," he said firmly. He was obviously done playing games.

She nodded in question toward the men at the pool table.

"No." He did not take his shrouded eyes off her; it seemed he did not even blink. She began glancing around the room.

"Give me the wire," Ahmed demanded.

"I don't know what you're talking about," she lied.

"You're wearing a wire. Either give it to me or this meeting is over."

Slowly, she reached under the table, under her fleece and sweater, and pulled out the small microphone, wire, and transmitter. She laid it on the table.

Ahmed picked it up carefully and studied the equipment. "The lady is signing off now," he said into the mike. Then he placed the equipment gently on the floor and stomped hard, crushing the pieces with his heel.

"Now we can talk," he said.

■ ■ ■

Barnes watched the valet park the car in the first floor of the parking garage, then jog out of the garage to fetch the next one. He had been watching the young man for nearly twenty minutes, and calculated it would take several minutes for the valet to return. Plenty of time to get the job done.

He pulled out a small black bag of high-tech gadgets and strolled toward her car. He popped the lock with a slim-jim and was inside in seconds. With a small screwdriver, a sharp knife, and practiced fingers, he unhooked the dome light, stripped the hot wire, and connected a small microphone to this energy source. No batteries necessary. It would record indefinitely.

He hid the mike inside the plastic covering of the dome light, clipped the cover back in place, and went straight for the cell phone. Nokia—perfect. Quickly, efficiently, he removed the plastic cover, planted the bug, then wired the bug to the cell phone's internal antenna. As he snapped the cover back on, he heard the muffled sound of a car engine. He softly closed the driver's-side door, slid down in the seat, and watched through the side mirror as the valet drove by. Barnes listened as the car engine shut off and the door closed. He sat still for another two minutes—enough time for the valet to be out of the garage.

Barnes slowly lifted his head, checked every direction, then opened the door and got out of her car. His task complete, he strolled calmly out of the garage and headed around the corner to the front door of the Marriott.

■ ■ ■

"I came through on Shelhorse."

"And I came through on the money," Ahmed hissed.

She was very much alone. Terrified. Though her voice would probably tremble, she needed to stay on the offensive. "The Shelhorse money was nothing. I want the rest on deposit by tomorrow morning, 9 A.M., or we pull back our friend on the jury."

Ahmed laughed. It was a bitter, forced laugh. A mocking laugh. "Someone as smart as you proposes a plan like this? Let's see, I wire a million into one account—let's call it the 'verdict account.' And then a hundred million into another account—let's call it the 'trust account.' And then you say 'thank you very much,' leave the country, and are never seen or heard from again. You double-cross me, the jury returns a huge verdict against me, and I...do what? Go to the police? 'Officer,' I say. 'This lady did not uphold her end of a jury bribery scheme.'"

"The hundred million will be protected by the trust agreement."

"I'm not worried about the trust account," snapped Ahmed. "That money will be there before the jury begins its deliberation. But the verdict account—that million dollars is protected by what? Your *promise* that I'll get a verdict?"

"First, the price is two million, not one," she swallowed hard. "And second—"

At the edge of her peripheral vision, she saw a man just behind her shoulder. She flinched, ducking to the side and turning.

"Can I get you anything to drink?" the waiter asked.

It was impossible to respond immediately, her heart was in her throat. Ahmed flashed the same smug smile he had worn when he testified. She took a deep breath and ordered a Diet Coke so the waiter would be forced to return soon.

Ahmed ordered nothing. He did not even look at the waiter. His eyes remained glued on her, and she subconsciously slid to the end of the booth.

"Do you have the signed trust agreement?" she asked after the waiter left. She wanted to make this as quick as possible, to get out of a trap that she sensed would spring soon.

Ahmed took an envelope from the seat beside him and placed it on the table. He did not let go with his hand, and she did not try to take it.

"How do I know you will deliver juror 6?" he asked.

"So you need him now?"

"How do I know...you will deliver?"

It was time to feign indignation. She scowled and spoke in an intense whisper, meeting Ahmed's fixed gaze with an unblinking stare of her own. "You don't trust me? I'm shocked."

"I love it when you talk tough," Ahmed mocked. "But I need something more than your word to justify this rather substantial investment. Tell you what. You deliver the verdict first, then I'll pay. You have *my* word for that."

That smirk was driving her nuts. *What did he know? What was about to happen?*

She withdrew a two-page document from her pocket and unfolded it, trying hard to control the trembling of her hands. "Here are the wire *and investment* instructions for the Swiss bank account where you wire the two million dollars. You can check this one out too. As soon as the money hits the account, it gets invested in put options on U.S. oil companies. There's also a caveat that these investment instructions cannot be changed for two weeks."

Ahmed gave her a puzzled look, and her confidence grew. "These put options are basically a bet that the stock prices of these companies will go down. If the stock prices stay the same, the put options will lose a little value, though not much. But we both know that a verdict against Saudi Arabia would destabilize relationships with the United States," she continued, "and cast a cloud over foreign oil supplies. If that happens, the stock prices for U.S. oil companies will go through the roof."

She slid her paper next to the envelope Ahmed was holding. "If the stock prices of U.S. oil companies go up, the put options that will be purchased with this account become essentially worthless. In other words, if there's a verdict against Saudi Arabia, the money in this account will disappear."

She looked dead into his eyes. "In addition to that, you have my word," she said sarcastically.

"Clever," said Ahmed. The detestable smirk was back. He took her paper and slid his envelope toward her. She carefully peeled it open. It appeared to be the same trust agreement that she had drafted, but she still read every word—forced herself to concentrate in spite of her fears—to ensure he hadn't changed the language. She saw the verified signature at the bottom of the last page, a signature belonging to the minister of the department of public safety. Two others had signed as witnesses. One of them was Ahmed. The signatures had been notarized.

She placed the agreement back in the envelope. "I'll have someone checking the accounts tomorrow morning," she promised. "If the money's in the trust account, and they confirm it's being held subject to this trust agreement...*and* if the verdict account contains two million dollars," she paused, "you can start celebrating your verdict."

"Let's talk about the price of that verdict," said Ahmed. "I don't think we ever agreed."

She sensed that Ahmed was trying to keep her there for some reason, and she wasn't about to find out why. Out of the corner of her eye, she saw the waiter coming with her drink. It would be a good time to make her move. Perhaps her only time. She rose as the waiter approached the table. "My friend here will be getting the bill," she said crisply. She looked straight at Ahmed. "Two bucks," she said.

The waiter gave her a curious look.

"I've only got a buck fifty," Ahmed replied.

"Okay," she replied, slapping a dollar down on the table. "You pay a buck fifty, I'll cover the rest."

Then she turned and hurried down the steps.

She rushed outside the hotel and stood under the overhang, waiting for the valet to bring her car. The rain was still coming in sheets, blown sideways by the wind, and spraying her despite the protection of the overhang. She was thinking about Ahmed, wondering what was taking so long, when she felt a hand on her shoulder. She jumped and turned, her heart pounding madly against her chest. She faced a short, stocky man chewing on the stub of a cigar, the same man who sat behind Ahmed every day of the trial.

She jerked her shoulder away.

"Let me give you some free advice," he whispered, although there was nobody else around. "Don't mess with that man in there. Do exactly what you promised. And if you want to survive, your man on the jury better be able to deliver. Get the defense verdict, and get out of town. And that agreement in the envelope? It isn't worth the paper it's written on."

She eyed him warily. *Was this a setup? Was he here at Ahmed's instructions?* "What are you talking about?"

The stocky man didn't answer. He pulled his hood up on his Windbreaker and headed down the sidewalk, disappearing into the night.

This was getting too weird. She felt lightheaded and vulnerable. She wanted to sit, but there was no seat near her. She waited in the biting wind for what seemed like an eternity before the valet arrived with her car and helped her in the driver's door. He handed her a piece of paper, then waited, expecting a tip, but she was too preoccupied to catch his hints. When he reluctantly shut the door, she wasted no time in hitting the gas and putting some distance between her and the Marriott.

She turned on the dome light and read the note as she drove. One eye on the road, one eye on the disconcerting note in her trembling right hand.

The rain continued to come in torrents as she headed west on I-264. The wind was so strong she could feel it pushing her car sideways. This time, she was in no hurry. She flicked off the light in order to concentrate on the road and think her thoughts in darkness. As she drove, she wiggled out of her fleece and turned up the heater. At least her jeans and pullover wool sweater were still partially dry. The radio blared, but she didn't hear it. She stayed in the right lane, doing no more than the speed limit, and still she had a hard time seeing the lines on the road. The wipers, beating furiously, mesmerized her.

She shuddered from either the cold or the thought of Ahmed, filled with bile, staring her down. She now had a bounty on her head. One hundred million dollars. Her death grip on the steering wheel turned her knuckles white. *Relax,* she told herself. *The worst is over.*

Then why am I shaking? Why am I starting to cry?

C'mon girl, get a grip! She willed herself to relax, to take one hand off the wheel, to stop grinding her teeth. With her free hand, as an act of studied nonchalance, she flipped her wet hair out of her face and over her shoulder.

The headlights from the vehicle behind reflected off the mirror and illuminated her silhouette—a model's face and a long thin neck— framed by the sheen of her windblown and rain-soaked long auburn hair.

———

43

L eslie didn't know how long the vehicle had been there, but she suddenly realized she was being followed. The headlights were elevated—
it must be a truck or SUV of some sort. She slowed to give the tailgater a
chance to pass. The lights, however, grew closer. She began to panic.

She put both hands back on the steering wheel, resumed her iron
grip, and started gradually increasing her speed to see if the tailgater
would drop off. But the tailgater maintained the distance, as if attached
to her car by a tow bar. The interstate suddenly seemed deserted, and she
sensed real danger. She picked up more speed. The tailgater followed
suit. She hydroplaned and regained control. The vehicle behind her was
still there.

The tailgater flashed his headlights and laid on the horn. Leslie's
hands were frozen on the wheel. She was in the left lane, passing what
few vehicles were braving the night. Still the tailgater stayed glued to her
bumper. She glanced down quickly at the odometer. Eighty-four miles
per hour in the pouring rain. *Where are the police when you need them?*

Her cell phone rang, and her heart raced. *Who's calling me now?*
Who's chasing me? Should I answer? Her thoughts became jumbled, and
her fears fed on themselves. *Must settle down. Maybe it's O'Malley. If they*
wanted to kill me, they wouldn't have waited for me to get on the interstate.

Answer the phone!

"Hello," she managed, in a feeble voice.

"It's me. Brad. Behind you," he shouted into his phone. "Slow down
and pull over."

Relief surged through her body, like a death-row inmate with an
eleventh-hour reprieve.

"Okay," she said and hung up.

Thank God. She slowed the vehicle and started looking for a shoulder. And then a new anxiety attack started. *How did he get there? What does he know?*

What will I tell him?

She found a good spot, the best that could be hoped for in the driving rain, and pulled over. Her car came to a skidding halt in a wet, grassy spot several feet off the road. She stayed in the driver's seat with the door locked, staring back into the headlights of the vehicle behind her.

It looked like Brad's Jeep, but she couldn't be sure. She could make out only the shadow of a driver. There was no one visible on the passenger side.

She saw a figure open the driver's door and step out into the wind and rain. She put the car in gear, ready to leave in a hurry. Cars flew by, casting long shadows off the silhouette moving toward her. The walk, the build, the posture, the way he carried himself—it was all Brad!

She exhaled and pried her hands off the wheel. She hadn't realized she'd been holding her breath. She put the car in park and jumped out, without even putting on her fleece, and started toward him. They met between the two vehicles, with the glare of the headlights in her eyes, the sound of cars rushing by on the interstate, the rain pelting them, and the wind blasting them. They stood there for a split second, her hair dripping wet and hanging in her face, her sweater quickly soaking through. She watched the rain pouring off his chin and onto his Windbreaker.

He was the most beautiful sight she had ever seen.

She had rehearsed in her mind over and over what she would say if she ever got caught. How she would act. How he would respond. But now that the moment was here, all those strategies seemed useless, lost deep in the gaze of his confused and hurting pale-blue eyes.

■ ■ ■

He was angry, bitterly disappointed, and drenched.

"Brad, I'm so glad it's you." She started toward him, but he took a step back.

He shook his head. Slowly at first, then with more determination. He held up a palm to stop her approach.

"It was you, wasn't it?" he shouted over the sound of the storm and the traffic. "It was you all along. Sleeping with the enemy. I saw you outside the Marriott tonight…meeting with Ahmed's investigator!" He was yelling now, emphasizing every syllable, hands gesturing wildly in frustration. He gave her no chance to answer. "You sold us out! *Sold…*us out."

"No!" she yelled in response. "What're you talking about? Let me explain…" She reached out to grab Brad by the shoulders to calm him down and get his attention. Her eyes were pleading for a chance to be heard.

Brad brushed her arm aside and continued his tirade. "I *have* listened to you. I've listened to you through this whole case." He paused, stuttering for the right words, "You…Leslie… I saw you with my own eyes…*my own eyes!* There's no explaining that."

"What were you doing there?" she looked astonished. Then, "Brad, you've got to…to trust me—" she began inching slowly toward him as he backed up to the hood of his car, shaking his head. He thrust his hands deep into his pockets. He didn't dare reach out for her, knowing that the magic of her touch would melt his defenses and transform his anger to forgiveness.

"You want to talk about trust!" he yelled. "Let's talk about trust. I trusted you with everything…my feelings, my case… And what happened to that trust?" Now they were face to face, his muscles tensed, the rain pouring down his face.

"Brad, I can explain everything… Just give me a chance," she pleaded.

Brad wanted desperately to reach out and hold her, to draw her to himself and tell her that it would be okay. But he couldn't let himself do it. He shook his head as words betrayed him. She was looking at him now, beckoning with her eyes. He could barely meet her gaze, but he forced himself to look into those sad blue eyes, beautiful even with the mascara streaking down her cheeks, the eyelashes matted together. And despite everything she had done—all the lies and deceptions—at this moment, he felt nothing but pity.

He allowed her to take another step toward him, then another, to wrap her arms around his neck, to put her head on his shoulder. Slowly, almost uncontrollably, he pulled his hands from his pockets and squeezed Leslie to himself. And he wondered what in the world he was doing.

"O'Malley and I ate dinner together at the Marriott," Leslie said. "If you don't believe me, just call him. We were going on a hunch…wanted to see if anybody we knew would be stopping by Ahmed's hotel tonight. When I left…this guy you saw—the one who's with Ahmed—came up to me and basically threatened me…"

He wanted to believe the fairy tale; the death of his dream was just so painful. But the same instincts and suspicions that caused him—literally propelled him—to follow her in the first place, would not allow him to believe her now. He had waited out in front of the Marriott, parked down the street, and watched the front door. She had been inside for no more than ten or fifteen minutes, certainly not long enough for dinner. And Brad had never seen O'Malley, either coming or going.

"I'm sorry for being so paranoid, Leslie," he said calmly as he stared into the distance. "I guess the pressure of this case is just starting to get to me." He gave her a reassuring squeeze.

He would definitely call O'Malley. As soon as he pried himself loose from this woman he could no longer trust.

■　■　■

Leslie dialed O'Malley's number the moment she pulled away from her roadside rendezvous.

"Hello, beautiful," O'Malley answered.

"I just had a close call with Brad," she said, then explained that she would need O'Malley to back her story about dinner at the Marriott.

"No problem, Leslie. Now tell me about the meeting with Ahmed."

For the next few minutes, she recounted every detail of her meeting with Ahmed. But she decided not to say anything about her brief encounter with Ahmed's investigator.

"Perfect," responded O'Malley. "So the money hits the accounts sometime tomorrow morning?"

"So he says."

"Once I confirm, I'll pass the word to our juror. You sure we shouldn't have held out for two mil?"

She paused. He sounded disappointed. "I don't know. I guess I just got a little spooked."

"Don't sweat it, babe. A million and a half is still a lot of money."

There was a small beep on the phone. "Brad's calling," O'Malley said. "Gotta run. See you tomorrow."

"Okay," she said. "Don't forget the tickets."

※　※　※

Barnes watched Ahmed digest the words of Leslie's phone call, then turn toward him. "Wire a million five to this account tomorrow at 8 A.M." He handed Barnes a sheet of wiring instructions. "But I've got a bad feeling about this other trust account; there's something we're missing…"

Ahmed stopped in midsentence; his eyes focused on something a world away. "We never technically agreed on a time deadline for the trust account, as long as it's there before the jury starts deliberating. Don't wire the money until after closing arguments are completed. If everything still looks good at that point, then follow these instructions." He gave Barnes the second sheet with wiring instructions for a hundred million dollars.

"You might not need to wire the money at all," Barnes suggested.

Ahmed raised an eyebrow. "Why's that?"

"I haven't played out my full hand on juror 4 yet. You know we've had our man paying juror 4, pretending to be working for Carson…"

"Of course. It's why he's been sending them such negative body language. Mr. Stein doesn't like getting blackmailed."

"Well," explained Barnes, barely containing his enthusiasm, "yesterday in court, I planted some compromising photos of Stein in the back of a deposition transcript that Carson's paralegal left sitting around. They cart those things to court every day and religiously unload them on their counsel table. I'm sure they'll have them for the closing arguments."

Barnes looked straight at Ahmed, studying the man for even the smallest sign of approval. "When Strobel introduces the photos of juror 4 in the restaurant being bribed, I'm going to go put my arm around one of those marshals and tell him that I just saw the Moreno woman stuff something like photos in the back of one of their deposition transcripts. When the marshals check, if Ichabod lets them, they'll have proof that it was Moreno and Carson bribing juror 4. And then…well, the fireworks should be interesting."

Ahmed thought about this for a moment, then his lips slowly curled into a wicked little smile. "Moreno, huh."

"Moreno."

"Perfect."

Barnes returned the smile, watched Ahmed turn serious again, and endured a long silence, the only sound coming from the speaker in the middle of the table as it captured the music from Leslie's car radio.

"One more thing," said Ahmed, "Find out where Connors and O'Malley plan on going tomorrow. Under the present circumstances, I think it would be best if I terminated them myself."

Barnes tried to take this news as calmly as possible, cognizant of the fact that Ahmed was watching him for any hint of a reaction.

■ ■ ■

Pastor Jacob Bailey and the faithful members of Chesapeake Community Church filed out of Sarah's house and headed home. They had prayed for Brad and his closing argument. They had prayed for wisdom for the jury and the judge. They had prayed for safety for the Riyadh church. And they had prayed for patience and strength for Sarah.

At Sarah's suggestion, they even prayed for Ahmed, Mack Strobel, and the rest of the defense trial team. They specifically asked that Sarah might be a testimony to those men, causing them to accept Christ as their Savior.

Bella had joined the prayer meeting and lifted up some passionate prayers of her own, though she couldn't quite bring herself to pray for Ahmed or Strobel. The others enjoyed listening to Bella pray, since she didn't use the platitudes and Christianese everyone else seemed to fall into. Instead, Bella prayed the street-savvy prayer of a Brooklyn girl—direct, bold, and to the point. She didn't hesitate to share everything on her heart. She was a breath of fresh air to the others, who sometimes prayed to God but cared more about the Christians who were listening than the audience of one in heaven.

After an appropriate season of prayer, the church members had enjoyed sharing a potluck dinner. Everyone had brought a favorite recipe, at least half of which fell into the category of sweet desserts. Bella especially liked this part; clearly she was born to be a church member. She would probably have her rough edges from here to eternity, but God was hard at work on her temper and judgmental tendencies. What a difference a prayer made!

By 10:30 the last prayer warriors left, and Sarah began getting ready for bed. When she heard the doorbell ring, she assumed somebody had left behind a dish, a Bible, or some other item of value. She was already in her baggy flannel pajamas and anxious to get into bed; tomorrow was a big day. She hoped it was not someone with a confidential crisis, circling back after the other church members had all left.

She was too tired tonight to bear even one more burden. She padded to the door hoping she could dispose of this caller quickly and feeling a little guilty for even thinking that way.

She opened the door and stood there...blinked twice... *Who in the world?*

She was staring at the drenched and frowning face of a middle-aged woman she had never met before.

"I'm assistant district attorney Angela Bennett," the woman said, flashing an ID. "And I think we'd better talk."

44

B rad dragged himself out of bed at 5:30 Monday morning and decided to skip his morning run. He still had some major work to do on the most important closing argument he had ever delivered. And he had no energy.

He had spent the night trying to sort out his feelings. He stared at the ceiling and watched infomercials on television. He was on the raw emotional edge all night—too tired to get out of bed and work on his closing but too heartbroken to sleep.

O'Malley had confirmed Leslie's story, but Brad still had his suspicions. *Is O'Malley in on this too?*

It was all impossible to believe.

He shuffled to the kitchen, fixed some coffee, and set up shop at the kitchen table. He scribbled some notes, reviewed some trial court transcripts, and thought some more about Leslie. The night's events had drained all his energy and destroyed his enthusiasm for the case. The whole thing was like a hall of mirrors. *Who's working for whom?*

Brad resisted the urge to crawl back into bed, pull the sheets over his head, and let the world turn without him. Despite his misgivings, today he would be on center stage in the wild and unpredictable drama of the *Reed* case, and the whole world would be watching.

■ ■ ■

It seemed that the whole world had indeed shown up and set up camp outside the courthouse on Granby Street. The prior night's storm had left a brisk and sunny fall day in its wake. The weathercasters predicted a high of nearly sixty under clear skies. And the protesters, attention-seekers, rabble-rousers, and hangers-on were taking full advantage of the good weather and the armada of reporters in order to shine a national spotlight on their favorite cause.

Just as the man in the yellow chicken suit predicted, the scene outside the courthouse resembled a cross between a sidewalk bizarre, a political rally, and a church picnic. There were T-shirts, coffee cups, and other trinkets for sale, all containing cute slogans commemorating the latest trial of the century. If you were a supporter of Sarah Reed, you could get a shirt that said "Pray for the Persecuted" or a shirt listing the great martyrs of the faith, including the name of Charles Reed. If you supported the defendants, there were shirts reading "Reed Versus Aberijan: The Witch Hunt Continues" or "The Inquisition: It Isn't Just for Europeans Anymore."

Since the man in the chicken suit was a natural enemy of fundamentalist Christians, he had favored the defendants at the start of the trial. But as the days wore on, his allegiance had gradually shifted to Sarah Reed. He was impressed by the simplicity of Sarah and her trial team. In the early days of trial, they walked through the protesters, carrying their own briefcases and exhibits, while the defense team showed up in limos and didn't get their hands dirty.

The man in the chicken suit had witnessed Brad dump his box of documents on the courthouse steps and handle it graciously. The man had also witnessed in horror the attack on Brad and Nikki and their close escape. As the days passed, he had grown tired of the smug looks on the faces of Ahmed, Mack Strobel, and the others on the defense team as they exited their fancy vehicles surrounded by security guards. It was no single thing, but all of these events taken together, at least in the mind of the chicken man, created this unnatural alliance between this protester and the team representing Sarah Reed. If the opportunity arose on this last day of trial, he would prove his new allegiance.

■ ■ ■

At precisely 8:55, having traveled directly from home, Brad entered the packed courtroom. He was wearing his closing argument suit, a black

Armani number with a subtle windowpane pattern, custom made for Brad—at a cost of more than seven hundred bucks—after a big verdict a few years back. The suit only saw the light of day for closing arguments, and in the last two years, the suit had only lost twice.

Both those losses, of course, occurred before Brad purchased the lucky Bruno Magli shoes and monogrammed shirt with gold cufflinks—fourteen karat—as well as the iridescent silk tie that mesmerized juries with its dark hues of purple, navy blue, and mauve that subtly changed colors as it reflected light. The combination of suit, shirt, shoes, and tie had proven unbeatable. In every other case, when he had put on these threads, he felt empowered—ready to argue the stars down.

But this morning, the clothes could not make the man. The suit hung on him like a scarecrow's would. His lean body had shed nearly ten pounds during the hectic weeks of the trial. His chiseled face looked drawn and gaunt. Dark circles surrounded his eyes. He looked, in the words of Bella, "like death on a bad day."

He walked down the aisle feeling tired, confused, and alone. His head was here—his argument might even be compelling—but he had left his heart by the side of the road last night. Betrayal did that to a person. He could muster no *passion*. He was on automatic, and Sarah's case would rise or fall on the mechanical closing argument of a lawyer who felt like a robot.

To Brad's relief, Leslie was not seated at counsel table. He glanced quickly around the courtroom—there was no sign of her anywhere. But Nikki, Bella, and Sarah were all huddled together as he approached, anxiety etched on their faces.

"Where have you been?" asked Sarah.

"We've got to talk for a moment," said Brad.

"I know," Sarah responded. She pulled Brad aside, away from Nikki and Bella.

For the next few minutes, she talked and Brad listened. She first apologized for what she was about to do, then reminded Brad that she held the trump card. Either Brad would carry out the strategies she was suggesting or she would ask him to step down as counsel and she would do it herself. She was dead serious and unwavering. She was a different Sarah from the one Brad had grown to admire.

First, she demanded that Brad argue for the chance to present one more witness based on newly discovered evidence. In fact, Sarah had a typed copy of the argument she wanted Brad to make, and he was to deliver it word for word. He just stared at her, not even looking down at the paper, as if she had lost her mind. Second, she wanted Brad to inform the court that Leslie had agreed to withdraw as co-counsel effective immediately. This one Brad had no trouble accepting. Third, if the court accepted Brad's argument and allowed him to call a final witness, Sarah would provide a written proffer of the testimony that had been drafted by assistant district attorney Angela Bennett. Sarah turned and nodded toward a woman seated in the second row. Bennett rose and started walking toward them.

Brad had heard enough. "Sarah, this is crazy. There're things you don't know…"

"All rise," commanded the court clerk as Judge Cynthia Baker-Kline stormed onto the bench.

"Do it," whispered Sarah. "Please."

Brad looked at the paper in his hand, then at Sarah's pleading eyes. By now Bennett was next to them, and she shoved another paper into Brad's hands.

"Read it," she said.

"Counsel," said Ichabod sharply. "You might want to take your seat."

Brad hustled to his seat and quickly skimmed Sarah's instructions.

"Good morning, ladies and gentlemen," Ichabod said to the crowded courtroom. "Before we bring the jury in for closing arguments, are there any matters that merit our attention?"

"I have one," announced Strobel.

Brad rose, still uncertain as to whether he should do this. He was only halfway through the written argument he was supposed to deliver. A glance at Sarah convinced him, and he declared, "I have one as well."

Ichabod blew out a quick and irritated breath. "Then let's start with counsel for plaintiff. But let me tell you gentlemen right now, I'm not inclined to delay these closing arguments for one minute. We've got a jury waiting. So this better be good."

Brad walked slowly, tentatively, to the podium, carrying Sarah's typed document with him. He placed it on the podium, stared at the paper, then looked over his shoulder one last time at Sarah. She waved her hand in small, discreet circles, egging him on. He shook his head in resignation.

"First, Your Honor, I need to inform the court that Ms. Leslie Connors has withdrawn as co-counsel of record, effective immediately."

Ichabod let out a sigh. "On what grounds?"

"I'm not at liberty to say, Judge."

Judge Baker-Kline made a perturbed face. "Okay, what else."

Brad began reading the argument in front of him, his voice flat and emotionless. "Your Honor, during our case I promised the court that we would present compelling evidence implicating Saudi Arabia in the conduct of Mr. Aberijan and the Muttawa. I realize that this is the eleventh hour. But this weekend, we became aware of new evidence that this court must hear before deciding this case, if the court is truly interested in a search for truth. We ask for leave of the court to call one additional witness and present approximately one hour of testimony from that witness."

The lines on Ichabod's face deepened in disapproval. The gallery, who had come to hear the drama of the closing arguments, began to murmur its disapproval.

Nevertheless, Brad continued. "Knowing that this is an extraordinary request, and that the testimony would have to be extraordinary in nature to merit this court's indulgence, we have a one-page summary of the testimony we would like to submit to the court as a proffer." Brad held up Angela Bennett's proffer. He had only been able to skim the first few lines.

Ichabod sat there, chin on her hand, sending every signal possible that she was not the least bit impressed with this melodramatic last-minute request. "No way, counsel. I told you last week that we would start closing arguments this morning. Now you want to try some type of desperate 'Hail Mary' maneuver?" She leaned forward on the bench and practically spit the words out. "Not in my court, counsel."

Brad's heart wasn't in this request, but Ichabod's cavalier dismissal angered him. She had treated him with such utter disdain through the whole trial, and he was at the end of his emotional rope. *Didn't this request at least merit some consideration? What would it hurt to take five minutes and read the proffer?* His competitive juices were engaged, and he couldn't resist taking a few swings on the way down.

"Does the court intend to dismiss my request without even reviewing the proffer?" Brad asked. "Is keeping to the court's sacred schedule more important than a witness who can shed light on the search for truth?"

"Counsel, you're treading on very thin ice here," Ichabod replied impatiently. "I have ruled."

He glanced again over his shoulder, this time locking eyes with Bennett, seated in the first row, immediately behind the counsel table. She nodded her head ever so slightly, and Brad turned to face the judge.

"I don't understand why the court insists on punishing my client because of a personality conflict between the court and me," he said fuming. "I don't understand why the court, after a three-week trial, will not take five minutes to read a summary of what might be the most important evidence in the case. Is the court interested in truth, or is the court interested in revenge?"

Strobel was on his feet now, looking perplexed and agitated. "I object. The plaintiff rested her case on Saturday. This is *highly* irregular and *highly* improper. I've been practicing law for thirty-eight years and have never seen such an unethical and desperate move by—"

"Don't lecture me on ethics," Brad shot back.

"Counsel, I don't interrupt you when you're talking—" Strobel countered.

"That's because I don't make hypocritical accusations—"

"Order!" Ichabod barked as she banged her gavel. The courtroom fell silent. Brad stared straight ahead. Strobel stared at Brad. "You two sound like children," she lectured. "And I'm tired of these outbursts in my court!"

"I apologize, Your Honor," said Brad.

"As do I," echoed Strobel.

■ ■ ■

Ichabod paused. She wanted to slap Brad Carson down for making such a scene. She wanted to rip up his one-page proffer into tiny little pieces without even reading it. She wanted to hold him in contempt. She wanted to make him suffer.

But she was no fool. She remembered the last time he was about to lose a case in her court. She remembered how he had goaded her into losing her temper and sending him to jail. She remembered the embarrassing appeal he planned to file based on her alleged bias and failure to maintain decorum. Even though she had forced Carson's client to accept a plea bargain, he had tarnished her reputation in the process. She would not allow it to happen again.

If everything went according to plan, she was on her way to the Fourth Circuit Court of Appeals. She could not let an arrogant con man like Brad Carson stand in her way.

It was time for a little reverse psychology.

She was sure the testimony he wanted to present was of minimal importance. He was probably banking on the fact that she would not consider the proffer. Then he could argue judicial bias on appeal.

Not this time, she decided. *I refuse to throw you into that briar patch.*

"Counsel," she said in measured tones. "Present Mr. Strobel with your one-page proffer and hand the original to the court. We will stand in recess for five minutes while I consider whether I should allow this witness to testify." She banged her gavel, accepted the one-page summary of the proposed testimony, and left the bench.

■ ■ ■

The courtroom broke into bedlam as soon as Judge Baker-Kline made her exit. Dozens of reporters surrounded Brad and fired questions about the proffered testimony. Sarah bowed her head to say a word of thanks.

Strobel and his legal team huddled around the document. After a few minutes, Strobel slid the photographs and evidence gathered on juror number 4 into his briefcase.

Just a brief glance at the document convinced Strobel that he would no longer be needing those photos. The trial of the century had just taken a sudden and irrevocable turn.

■ ■ ■

Things were not going at all according to the perfectly laid plans of Frederick Barnes. All the hours of research and planning, of painstaking investigative work, of operatives following precise orders and carrying out detailed stings and counterstings—all for naught. Barnes felt sick.

He glanced at the document handed to Strobel and had the sinking feeling that the photos of juror 4 would never see the light of day. It was such a pity; it would have been the perfect plan.

What fun, what sheer genius it would have been to dupe the street-savvy paralegal who had already caused so much trouble. But now Barnes' cleverly planned fireworks would never explode. With this proffered testimony, everything had changed. Juror 4 was the least of their worries.

There was only one thing left to do.

■ ■ ■

In the turmoil, only Nikki noticed that Ahmed Aberijan leaned over the rail separating defense counsel from the gallery and said a few words into the ear of the short and stocky investigator who had handed her the deposition at the close of court Saturday. Ahmed then joined the man as the pair headed for the back door of the courtroom.

Nikki glanced over Brad's shoulder as he looked through the proffer. She let out a soft, low whistle and said to nobody in particular, "No wonder he left."

She grabbed Bella, whispered a few things in her ear, then ran out the back doors of the courtroom to follow Ahmed. Bella in turn found Rasheed Berjein in the second row of the spectator section. She pulled on his arm, and he followed Bella out of the courtroom, just a few seconds behind Nikki.

■   ■   ■

In the downstairs lobby, Frederick Barnes and Ahmed Aberijan impatiently waited to retrieve their firearms from the marshals who manned the metal detectors. As was their daily habit, the marshals had taken the guns, tagged them, and placed them in a locker to be reclaimed at the end of the day.

But now, as Ahmed and Barnes tried to leave the court building, the marshals were busy checking a long line of persons entering the court through the metal detectors. So the two men waited. And waited. And waited.

Nikki stepped off the elevator and made herself inconspicuous on the other side of the lobby, keeping a close eye on Barnes and Ahmed.

"Gentlemen," said an exasperated Barnes, "we are severely pressed for time. Here are our tags. You've got our weapons in your lockers, and we need them as we leave."

"Sir," said one of the harried marshals, "we'll be with you as soon as we can. Can't you see we've got a lot of people to process?"

"I don't care how many people are lined up to get into this place," Barnes said. "We're entitled to get out." He gritted his teeth. "Now, *get us our guns.*"

"That attitude just earned you an extra five minutes," replied the marshal. "We give the orders, not you."

Barnes looked at Ahmed and shook his head in disgust. "You wait here for the guns," Barnes said. "I'll get the car and bring it out front."

Barnes left the courthouse, cut through the protesters, and headed north on Granby Street to where he had parked. Nikki exited a few seconds later, cut through the protesters, and headed south on Granby Street two blocks to get her car. She looked over her shoulder and saw the stocky man break into a jog. Nikki kicked off her heels and broke into a run of her own.

The timing was perfect. Ahmed received his Glock from the marshal just as Barnes pulled in front of the courthouse in his black Lincoln Continental. The marshal refused to turn loose Barnes' Smith and Wesson unless Barnes himself presented the claim slip. Ahmed gave the marshal some severe grief, in nearly flawless English, then decided it wasn't worth the hassle. Barnes could get his weapon later.

The police cleared a path through the demonstrators as Ahmed exited the courthouse and entered the backseat of the Lincoln. His presence on Granby Street created quite a furor, as some of the protesters broke out in cheers and others hurled insults.

As Ahmed climbed into the vehicle, the man in the yellow chicken suit saw his chance for glory. He ditched his sign, slipped through the police lines, jumped up onto the hood of the Continental, and started shouting incoherently. In his mind's eye, it was a heroic move akin to Boris Yeltsin's mounting the Russian tank during the Moscow coup.

To the police, he was just another fruitcake who needed to be arrested.

Barnes blew his horn furiously, but the chicken kept jumping around on the hood. The police mounted the fenders, grabbed the man by the feathers, and pulled him, sliding, onto the pavement. They cuffed him, read him his rights, and dragged him kicking and screaming into a nearby squad car. They finally cleared a lane, and the Continental sped south on Granby, free at last from the circus in front of the courthouse.

The delay in the Continental's departure had allowed Nikki to reach her Sebring and position her car one block south of the mob that had delayed Barnes. As the Continental flew by in the opposite direction,

Nikki pulled a quick three-point turn, holding up traffic and setting off a chorus of horns, then headed out in pursuit of Barnes.

Barnes had already placed several hundred feet and more than a few cars between his vehicle and Nikki's. But Nikki was determined and kept him in sight. The pursuit carried them through the busy side streets of Norfolk and then racing out of the city on I-264. As she drove, Nikki wondered where Barnes was headed and what in the world she would do if she actually caught him. But, as always, she would take it one step at a time, and for now her only goal was to keep him in sight and not let him get away.

■ ■ ■

Barnes called his firm in D.C. from his cell phone. "Lease a private jet immediately," he ordered. He thought for a moment. If he guessed right, the Norfolk airport would be crawling with federal agents within the hour. He would try a private municipal airport in Hampton. Nobody would expect that. "Lease it from the Hampton Municipal Airport. We'll be there in thirty minutes. File a flight plan for touchdown at Reagan National and then on to Riyadh, Saudi Arabia. We must take off immediately. We'll work out clearances for the other end once we're in the air. Two passengers. I don't care what it costs."

He ended his first call and immediately made a second. "Cancel the money wire," he said. "Everything's changed."

He had about thirty miles of interstate to cover to get to the airport, including a trip through the Hampton Roads Bridge Tunnel. It was risky. But he knew the attorneys would be squabbling in court for at least thirty minutes before Ichabod even knew what was happening. It would be another hour before she could order any type of bench warrant. By then, Aberijan would be in the air and on his way outside the jurisdictional limits of the United States, far away from the reach of Ichabod and her federal-court marshals.

But first Barnes had to shake Brad Carson's pesky paralegal. He kept the accelerator against the floor, intent on burying the speedometer needle, and flew by the other vehicles on the interstate. He would simply outrun Moreno. And if that didn't work, he would pull over and let her catch up. He would drag her into their vehicle, and Ahmed would put a gun to her head and end it. He knew that nothing would give the Saudi more pleasure than to extinguish the life of a woman who had already caused him so much grief.

45

J udge Cynthia Baker-Kline took her perch on the bench in the hushed courtroom. She held the one-page proffer in her left hand and peered down over her long nose and reading glasses at Brad Carson.

"Mr. Carson, there are very serious accusations contained in this document. The court does not take these allegations lightly."

The proposed testimony had stunned Brad just as much as it had Ichabod. He was just now getting his bearings and thinking straight. He still didn't understand all the implications. But he was in too far to turn back now.

"And we do not make them lightly," he answered.

"I'm going to allow the testimony, Mr. Carson," Ichabod ruled, her face wrinkled into sternness. "But if these accusations turn out to be unfounded, if this is just another gimmick, then I will personally petition the state bar to revoke your license. Is that clear?"

"Crystal clear, Your Honor."

Brad waited for the jury to return to their seats. He stood tall and straight, facing the rear of the courtroom. He looked down at Sarah one last time.

"She cares about you," Sarah whispered. "Trust her."

"The plaintiff calls Leslie Connors as our next witness," Brad announced.

A marshal disappeared into the hallway and a few seconds later opened the rear door of the courtroom. Leslie walked elegantly down the aisle, her head held high, her perfect lines gracing the courtroom. She avoided looking at Brad as she walked past him and stopped in the well of the court, raised her hand, and took the oath. She was dressed in a conservative white blouse, a black pinstriped skirt that hovered just above the knees, and a matching vest. Her auburn hair was pulled back and braided. Dark-blue makeup accentuated her deep-set sky-blue eyes.

How could the men on the jury not listen to *her?*

She took the stand with an unmistakable air of dignity. Only the redness of her eyes and the slight puffiness surrounding them betrayed the fact that this witness had probably not slept much the prior night.

"Please state your name for the record."

"Leslie Connors."

"Were you formerly co-counsel for the plaintiff in this case?"

"Yes."

"When did you withdraw from that role?"

"This morning."

Brad felt like he was in a dream; this moment was so surreal. He was starting the examination of his own co-counsel, a woman he had dated, and he didn't have the foggiest idea where this was ultimately headed. He was no longer in control, but at the mercy of a woman who had double-crossed him just last night. Still, the situation felt right.

There had been a flicker of hope in his subconscious the night before, a thought he didn't dare acknowledge, a spark that had now become a flame. Despite what he saw, could he still trust her?

At present, he had no choice.

"Are you testifying today under a grant of immunity?" Brad asked. He had picked up that much from reading the proffer.

"Yes."

"Will you tell the court how that came about?"

"Would you like me to start at the beginning?" asked Leslie.

"Please," said Brad. It was one of the best ideas he had heard in days.

■　■　■

Nikki flew down the interstate, trying her best to keep pace with Barnes but dropping farther behind every minute. He was still barely in sight, now headed west on I-64 toward the Norfolk airport. She hoped the police would see the speeding vehicles and pull them over. She slowed ever so slightly and took one hand off the wheel to reach for her cell phone. She used the speed dial to reach Bella.

"Aberijan is heading west on 64. The airport's the next exit. I've barely got him in sight."

"We're not too far behind you," said Bella. "I'm pushing my Honda as fast as it'll go. Rasheed is with me, and the old boy looks like he's in shock."

"Look out!" Nikki heard Bella scream, apparently to some other driver. Nikki envisioned poor Rasheed, white knuckles clutching the dashboard, wondering what he had gotten himself into.

"Why don't you call the police?" Nikki heard Bella yell into the car phone.

"And tell them what?!" asked Nikki. "That they should pick up this visiting foreign dignitary for speeding? What about diplomatic immunity? The police won't get involved."

"Then why are *we* chasing him?" Bella asked. "What are *we* going to do?"

"I'm not sure," admitted Nikki, "I just know that if he leaves the country, we'll never see him again, but if...Bella! He went by the airport exit! He's heading for the tunnel!"

"Wha—" then Nikki heard the sound of Bella's cell phone hitting the floor. She heard muffled shouts from Bella and Rasheed, but she heard no squealing of tires or crunching of metal.

She hit the "end call" button and focused on the traffic she was flying by.

Then why are we chasing him? Bella had asked. *What are we going to do?*

In truth, Nikki had no idea what she would do if she caught Ahmed, but in the deepest depths of her subconscious, she knew exactly *why* she was chasing him. And now, for a fleeting moment, as the cars on I-64 became a blur, she allowed those subconscious thoughts to bubble to the surface—she allowed herself to admit it, to own the reason she was doing this. And she knew in that same instant that there could be no turning back.

Ahmed was no different than her father. Abusers prey on the innocent until they meet resistance, then they flee. Nikki had never tried to withstand her father when he beat on her mom...couldn't have stopped him if she tried...so she just turned up the volume of the music in her bedroom to drown him out. Then one day he up and left. Just like that. And she let him go...happy to rid their family of the beast.

But she had never confronted him, and nobody had ever held him accountable for the scars he had created. Sure, she ignored him; she never spoke to him again. That would hurt him, she told herself, that would pay him back.

Who was she kidding?

Years of abuse, and he just walked away! And right now he's probably doing it again to someone else. Years of hating myself because I never took him on.

Abusers prey on the innocent, then they run. Gone forever. Scott free.

Not this time, she told herself.

The Sebring was now doing ninety-eight. She was gaining on them.

◼ ◼ ◼

"It all began this past summer," Leslie recounted, "when I returned from Europe to work full-time on this case. The first thing I learned was that I had missed a deadline for objecting to interrogatories—written questions that Sarah Reed had to answer under oath—and that Mr. Strobel was trying to use that mistake to win the case on a technicality."

"How was he trying to do that?" Brad asked. He remembered full well the tactics of Strobel, but he wanted to make sure the jury understood.

"Well, one of the interrogatories they sent to us asked Sarah to identify all the members of the churches in Saudi Arabia whom she ever worshiped with. Sarah knew that if she did that, they would be in danger—"

"Objection, she can't testify about what Sarah Reed knew or didn't know," said Strobel.

"Sustained," ruled Ichabod.

"Anyway," continued Leslie, without flinching, "I knew that we would not provide those names under any circumstances for fear of what might happen to those persons. So when we missed the deadline for objecting to the interrogatory, Mr. Strobel filed a motion asking this court to either make us answer that question or dismiss the case against us."

Brad was amazed at Leslie's apparent composure. Her voice and gaze were steady, hardly betraying the incredible pressure she was under. But she could not entirely fool Brad. He noticed the small red blotches on her neck, a sure sign she had scratched nervously in the hallway before she took the stand.

"How did that lead to a meeting with Mr. Aberijan?"

"It was at that point that I realized the defendants were not interested in justice, only about winning this case, and they would do anything to make it happen." She turned to the jury.

"Objection," shouted Strobel. "She's got no right to mischaracterize our conduct like that."

"Mr. Strobel, sit down and let the witness testify," Ichabod said curtly. "You can cross-examine her later."

Strobel sat down hard and dropped his pen noisily on the table. Ichabod shot him a look but said nothing.

"At that point," continued Leslie, unflustered by the distraction, "I decided that two could play this game. I couldn't bear to lose this case knowing that Mr. Aberijan had killed Sarah Reed's husband. I lost my own husband not so long ago to cancer, and I guess I became personally involved in Sarah's quest for justice. And I began to believe the system could not deliver justice on its own; it needed help. To Mr. Strobel, it seemed that justice was just a game, and I was not about to let him beat us at the game and deny my client the justice she deserved."

Strobel stood to object.

"Overruled," said Ichabod before he could speak.

"So I set up my own little sting operation," said Leslie. "I knew Aberijan would deny what he did until the end, so I decided to set a trap and obtain a confession."

"Why didn't you tell me?" asked Brad.

For the first time Leslie diverted her gaze from Brad and the jury. A pained expression crossed her face, her shoulders slumped, and she compressed her lips. When she spoke, her words came out softly, in the manner of a confessional.

"Because I knew you played so much by the book that you would never have allowed it. And by the time I was ready to come to you…wanted to come to you…I was prohibited by my immunity deal from doing that. There was so much at stake…this case, my future, everything really…"

It was starting to make sense to Brad, but the sting of her betrayal lingered. Maybe she wasn't working *against* him on the case, but she was still going behind his back. She didn't trust him; it was as simple as that.

He could barely bring himself to ask the next question. It was of no legal significance, but he simply had to know. "Would you do it the same way again?"

Leslie hesitated and seemed to shrink back from the question. "Never," she said in a barely audible tone. "Your unshakeable faith in the system and Sarah's unshakeable faith in doing the right thing have impacted me in ways you'll never know. I eventually realized that the only thing that separates the good guys from the bad guys is that we're not willing to bend the rules to obtain justice."

Brad let out an audible sigh.

Brad now had a million other questions swirling through his mind. But first he needed to nail down the basics. Leslie was testifying under a grant of immunity. A good lawyer always put the details of those deals on the table first.

"Did you eventually negotiate with the authorities?" he asked.

"I approached Angela Bennett in the U.S. attorney's office," Leslie said. "She agreed to grant me immunity and agreed I could testify in this case before any arrests would be made." At this critical moment in her testimony, Leslie paused ever so slightly to let the tension build. She turned to face the jury squarely. "In return, I agreed not to talk to anyone else about this plan, except for a gentleman named Patrick O'Malley, who already knew, and I agreed to help obtain substantive evidence against Mr. Aberijan for obstruction of justice, witness intimidation, jury tampering, and conspiracy to commit murder."

This shocking list of accusations set off a wave of activity in the courtroom, ranging from gasps to a general buzz of excitement. Mack Strobel stood and asked to approach the bench. Even Brad rocked back on his heels in disbelief.

■ ■ ■

"Approach," Ichabod said.

Ichabod had a feeling during Leslie's testimony that something in the courtroom was different; something was out of place. Now, as she quickly surveyed the courtroom, her eyes came to rest on the first row of the spectator section, and she realized what it was. There, for the first time the entire trial, sat ADA Angela Bennett. And on the defendants' side of the courtroom, though the lawyers were all sitting in their proper places—mouths now hanging open—Ahmed Aberijan had vanished.

"Ms. Bennett, you too," Ichabod commanded.

"Mr. Strobel," Ichabod said as she glowered at the defense lawyer over her wire rims, "I'm sure you've got a hundred and two objections, and we'll deal with those later. Right now, I need to know why Mr. Aberijan is not with us in court."

Mack Strobel looked at her and clenched his jaw. "I do not know where Mr. Aberijan is or why he is not here," he said tersely. "Further, even if I did know where he was, I would not be at liberty to say since he is my client and any information I have about his whereabouts would be protected by the attorney-client privilege."

Ichabod turned from Strobel to Bennett. "Is this true—this testimony about a deal to obtain evidence against Aberijan?"

"Yes."

"Jury tampering? Obstruction of justice?"

"Yes."

"Conspiracy to commit murder?"

"Yes."

"Thank you," said Ichabod. "You may return to your seats." She waited calmly for the lawyers to take their places. "We will continue with testimony from Ms. Connors. But before we do, there is another urgent matter that we should tend to. Based on a sidebar with counsel of record and Ms. Bennett, I am hereby issuing a bench warrant for Mr. Aberijan to be brought into this courtroom to answer potential contempt charges along with other matters."

She turned to the marshals. "I want him brought before this court immediately, and I want you to begin by contacting the Norfolk airport and alerting officials there to check all outgoing international flights— including private charter flights."

The judge then turned to Brad, who had taken his place behind the podium. "You may now resume your examination," she said in the calmest tone imaginable.

■ ■ ■

Clarence lumbered from the courtroom and went straight for the pay phones. The other marshals could call the Norfolk airport. He would call Bella Harper.

46

The object of the U.S. marshals' manhunt cursed the traffic as his vehicle approached the Hampton Roads Bridge Tunnel. Barnes kept his expletives to himself. They had entered the span of the bridge that snaked out over the Elizabeth River inlet of the Chesapeake Bay separating Norfolk from Hampton. The cars, SUVs and trucks lined up bumper-to-bumper, barely inching along, as far as Barnes could see.

The bridge accommodated two lanes in each direction, with separate spans for the northbound and southbound traffic. There were small shoulders between the outside edges of the two lanes heading northbound and the three-foot-high, two-foot-wide concrete abutments on each side of the bridge. The span hovered about thirty feet above the water when the river was at high tide, and it was undergirded at regular intervals by bundles of huge concrete pillars that supported the road surface and ran deep into the river bottom below. The bridge spanned about two miles of the river, then disappeared into a tunnel that took it below the river's surface. If Barnes and Ahmed could make it to the other side of the tunnel, they would be in Hampton and well on their way to the waiting jet.

"Do something, you fool!" the Saudi shouted from the backseat of the Lincoln. "We're losing valuable time."

Spurred by Ahmed's anger, Barnes turned on his flashers and rolled down his window. He moved from the left lane partially onto the left shoulder, but the big Lincoln could not maneuver past the car ahead, and so it straddled the yellow line marking the outside of the left lane. He pulled the vehicle as close to the concrete abutments as he dared, yelled out his window, and blew his horn. Slowly the drivers in front of him pulled partly into the right lane, allowing him to pass on the shoulder of the roadway.

■ ■ ■

Less than a half-mile back, Nikki mimicked Barnes' driving strategy and gained the right shoulder of the roadway. The narrow frame on her Sebring made it much easier to get by, and she had a good alibi. She stuffed a pair of sweatpants and a T-shirt from her gym bag inside her blouse. She then hit the flashers, leaned on the horn, and yelled that she was on her way to the hospital.

"My water broke!… Thank you!… I've got to get to the hospital!… Baby!… Thanks!" The cars parted like the Red Sea, as she advanced up the right-hand shoulder.

Her phone rang. "What?" she yelled. This was no time for a call. She had Barnes in sight no more than fifteen car lengths ahead.

"Ichabod issued a bench warrant for Ahmed," yelled Bella into the phone. "Don't let him get away."

"I won't, he's within sight… Excuse me, sir—got to get to the hospital! Thanks, so much… How far back are you…? Hey! Get out of the way! I'm going to the hospital… Hurry up, Bella…"

Nikki needed a break and found one just a few hundred yards from the tunnel. Barnes was wedged behind a pickup truck, and the two bubbas inside looked like they had no intention of letting him by. Barnes leaned out the driver's window and yelled at them over his hood, commanding them to move out of the way because he was on official government business.

The bubbas gestured and moved farther onto the shoulder to block the path of the Lincoln. The bigger of the bubbas even got out of the truck, stood on the shoulder, and asked Barnes if he wanted a piece of that action. Barnes continued to yell at the man but stayed in his car.

On the opposite shoulder, Nikki glided past the Lincoln and the pickup.

Suddenly the traffic began to pick up speed. Nikki glanced over her shoulder to see that the pickup was moving and that the Lincoln was cruising along behind. Traffic was only rolling at about fifteen miles an hour, but Nikki knew the fickle nature of the tunnel snarls and estimated that in no time the vehicles could be moving at close to normal speeds.

If Barnes and Ahmed made it to the other side of the tunnel, they could not be contained. Several quick exits led to hundreds of roads, and Nikki was sure she would never see them again. They had to be stopped now.

She pulled her Sebring squarely into the right lane of traffic. There traffic moved at about twenty miles an hour. She was about four car lengths in front of the pickup and the Lincoln, which were moving slightly faster in the left-hand lane. Nikki said a quick prayer for forgiveness, then made her move.

She cranked the wheel hard left, broadsiding the car next to her and wedging him at an angle into the concrete abutment at the left-hand edge of the road surface. Then she swerved hard to her right, forcing her car perpendicular to the traffic, turning straight toward the concrete abutment on the right side of the road. She slammed on her brakes.

In the very next instant, a millisecond of time, she felt the jolt of her own sudden stop, her head jerked about like a rag doll. She heard the sound of crunching metal and broken headlights, the squeal of tires, and the blaring of horns. She braced herself to be hit broadside. The second collision, however, never came. The cars behind her miraculously came to a stop just short of her Sebring.

Nikki jumped out of the car and surveyed the damage she had caused. The car she had forced into the abutment had been hit in the rear by another at a low speed. That fender bender, coupled with her car angled across the right shoulder and right lane, brought traffic to a complete stop. There was no room for even one lane to get through. The occupants of the other cars appeared to be fine. For a split second, Nikki flushed with pride at her accomplishment.

Her pride quickly gave way to fear. Barnes and Ahmed came sprinting toward her, Ahmed wielding a large black pistol. Other drivers also alighted from their cars and were now yelling at Nikki. In the chaos, Ahmed ran ever closer…then crouched.

Nikki moved toward the concrete abutment behind her Sebring. She pointed at Barnes and Ahmed. "They're trying to kill me!" She yelled as she backed toward the edge of the bridge.

As Ahmed crouched, he extended both arms, steadily taking aim. He was no more than fifty feet away. The barrel of the gun looked huge. She could dive behind her vehicle, but if she hit the ground, Barnes would be on top of her in a second.

She felt the concrete behind her, turned, placed both her hands on the abutment. She heard Barnes yell "Stop!" as he closed on her.

Nikki glanced in fright at the choppy water below, then thought about the gun. She took a deep breath and swung her legs out to the side, jumping over the top of the abutment and pushing off with both hands. She brought her legs together so that she would knife into the water.

She held her breath and prepared herself to plummet through thirty-three feet of air. As she closed her eyes, she heard the pop of Ahmed's gun.

■ ■ ■

"Let's go back to the beginning," suggested Brad. "Why don't you explain the circumstances leading to your first contact with Mr. Aberijan on this case."

Leslie looked out at the back wall, collecting her thoughts, then turned to Brad. "The day that I learned Mr. Strobel was trying to have this case dismissed on a technicality, I had a long talk with Sarah. I remember that I was filled with anger about what the defendants were doing, but she was so forgiving and accepting. She told me that she harbored no hatred toward either Mr. Aberijan or Mr. Strobel. She said that hate only consumes the person who hates."

She looked admiringly toward Sarah and continued. "The night after we had that conversation, I couldn't sleep and could only think about losing my own husband and about Sarah's loss. That night I decided to take matters into my own hands."

"What did you do?"

"I had been working on a document called 'Preliminary Game Plan for *Reed v. Saudi Arabia.*' It had lists of witnesses, exhibits...those types of things. Frankly, it was all the kind of stuff that the defendants would be entitled to obtain through the normal discovery processes, but I knew that Mr. Aberijan wouldn't know that. So I took that document and edited out any confidential stuff I didn't want the other side to see, like the fact that we would be calling Rasheed Berjein as a witness, and I mailed a sanitized version to Mr. Aberijan along with a letter demanding fifty-thousand U.S. dollars and containing wiring instructions for a Cayman Island bank account."

"Did Mr. Aberijan know who you were at this time?"

"I don't think so. The letter was anonymous."

"Okay," said a curious Brad. "When did you contact Mr. Aberijan a second time?"

"The second time was after I met with and prepared a potential expert witness for us named Alfred Lloyd Worthington—"

"I should have known," mumbled Brad.

"What was that, counsel?" asked Ichabod. She was leaning forward now, her scribble pad sitting untouched in front of her.

"Nothing, Your Honor."

Leslie continued. "Mr. Worthington was a Washington lobbyist and former congressman who served on the House Foreign Relations Committee. He was going to testify about how the nation of Saudi Arabia sanctioned the actions of their religious police, the Muttawa."

"Your Honor, this is ridiculous," interjected Strobel. "They did not call Worthington to testify. They should not be allowed to put in his testimony by proxy through this witness."

"I agree," said Ichabod. "Ms. Connors, refrain from discussing the proposed testimony of Mr. Worthington."

"Yes, Your Honor," said Leslie, without missing a beat. "In the course of preparing him for his testimony, I learned that Mr. Worthington had pled 'no contest' to a misdemeanor charge that resulted from beating his wife. I was not about to put a wife beater on the stand as an expert in a case alleging police abuse by Mr. Aberijan. I also believed that the defendants would uncover this information too, so I decided to use Mr. Worthington's testimony as my second piece of bait."

"Then how did you think we were going to make that part of our case?" Brad's frustration was beginning to show. He didn't like hearing his expert witnesses referred to as "bait."

"I knew," said Leslie, "that if this sting worked, we wouldn't need Worthington. And if it didn't work, all the Worthingtons in the world couldn't help us. I knew it was a huge gamble, but it seemed like a chance I had to take."

No it wasn't, he wanted to say. *You didn't need to resort to this to win this case.* But he would admonish her later.

"How did you use Worthington's testimony as bait?" Brad asked, getting back on track.

"I sent a second anonymous letter that explained that Worthington had an Achilles heel that could be exploited. I basically told Mr. Aberijan about the no-contest plea of Worthington in Alexandria General District Court. I told him that information would cost one hundred thousand dollars."

Brad could feel the heat rising on his neck. It was a wonder he had any case left at all. "What happened at Worthington's deposition?" he asked.

"Mr. Strobel asked him a few questions about whether he had ever abused his wife, and Worthington withdrew as an expert," Leslie summarized.

Judge Baker-Kline eyeballed Strobel. She was not content to let this go. "Do you have any information to suggest that Mr. Strobel was part of this conspiracy?" she asked Leslie.

Leslie looked hard at Strobel and then furrowed her brow as she considered her answer. The man's reputation hung in the balance, and Brad could sense that Leslie was wavering. If the shoe were on the other foot, Strobel would hang them out to dry in a heartbeat. *What did Leslie know? And what would she tell?*

"No, none at all," she said at last.

Other than a slight relaxation of his shoulders, there was no visible reaction from Mack Strobel.

"What happened next?" A safe question to ask, as Brad had no idea where the witness was heading.

"I decided it was time to bring Mr. Aberijan to the trap," answered Leslie coldly.

"How did you do that?"

"Well, I figured the best place to meet a man as dangerous as Mr. Aberijan would be a public place with lots of police officers. So I picked General District Court in Norfolk. I sent him a letter and told him to meet me there alone on a certain date. I told him to bring some transmitters so I could bug our office."

"You did what?" asked an astonished Brad, eyebrows raised in disbelief.

"You'll remember that after the Worthington incident, we were all paranoid and decided we would not use our office phones for any confidential communications. We hired a private investigator, Patrick O'Malley, to check for listening devices. He would come by the office and do that every morning. I believed that I needed something to cement Mr. Aberijan's trust so that he wouldn't think he was being set up. I knew that if I placed some bugs on our office phone lines, he wouldn't hear anything more than harmless information. I also knew that he would no longer have any suspicions about a setup. And finally, I knew that I could simply reattach the transmitters every morning after O'Malley left and take them off every night."

"I thought you said O'Malley already knew."

"Now you're getting ahead of the story."

"Then tell us what happened at this meeting."

"We had a very short conversation. When I invited Mr. Aberijan to the meeting, I told him that I had a plan for knocking out our best remaining expert, Dr. Nancy Shelhorse. I told him the price would be one hundred thousand dollars. At the meeting, he delivered three short-wave radio transmitters. He told me he actually thought it was a bad idea. I think his words were something like, 'Do you really think these are necessary?' But I assured him I knew what I was doing, then left."

Brad was having a hard time believing what he was hearing. From the moment he saw Leslie at the Marriott the prior night, he assumed that she had been responsible for keeping Shelhorse out of the case. But he allowed himself to hope otherwise. Now the reality of it was sinking in, and he was numb.

"But you still didn't talk to me about this."

"I started getting nervous, realizing I was in way over my head. I was playing an awkward game of espionage with a cold-blooded killer. A part of me desperately wanted to tell you everything that was happening, but it was more important for me to protect you and keep you out of this nightmare I had created." Leslie bit her lower lip and paused. "I didn't want to lose you."

Brad looked down at the podium. He felt uncomfortable discussing such a private matter in open court. He admonished himself to stick to the facts, make it easier on Leslie.

"What happened next?"

"I needed more proof before I could go to the authorities," she said, regaining the cool professionalism that had characterized her testimony thus far. "But my plans started to unravel on the third day of trial."

"What do you mean?"

"Mr. Aberijan approached me in the elevator and handed me a note. In it, he demanded details about my plan to deal with Shelhorse. He also demanded a meeting for that Friday at 8:30 A.M. in Norfolk General District Court. He also wanted the transmitters back.

"His boldness scared me, but the note gave me what I needed to go to the district attorney. The problem was that I needed to get back to the office before everyone else after court that day in order to retrieve the transmitters.

"When I returned to the office, Patrick O'Malley was there. Instead of his customary inspection that morning, he had conducted his search just a few minutes prior to my arrival that afternoon. Of course, he had found the three devices I was using."

"What did you do?" asked Brad. He was still having a hard time believing his old friend O'Malley was in on this.

"I took Mr. O'Malley into the conference room and told him everything. He agreed to hold it in confidence and help me if I promised to go to the authorities the next day. He became a partner in my sting operation."

"Did you go to the authorities?"

"Yes. The next day, Mr. O'Malley and I went to see Ms. Bennett. She agreed to grant me immunity and let me testify in this case before she had Mr. Aberijan arrested. But it was conditioned on catching Mr. Aberijan with some hard evidence and also on not talking about this operation with anybody else." Leslie paused and gave Bennett a look, then she turned back to Brad. "Including you."

Brad was not surprised. Bennett had never liked him much.

"What happened when you met Mr. Aberijan this second time?"

"I went to the meeting with Mr. Aberijan," explained Leslie, "knowing that he was somehow scanning me for bugs. But I also knew that I would be returning the three transmitters he had originally given me. Mr. O'Malley found a way to tap into the frequency of Mr. Aberijan's shortwave transmitters. So Mr. O'Malley stationed himself outside the courthouse, listened to our conversation, and taped every word."

"What happened?"

"Mr. Aberijan accused me of wearing a wire. I simply gave him the three transmitters. He was very rough with me. He grabbed my arm and jerked me around. He demanded to know the plan for waylaying Shelhorse."

"What did you tell him?"

Leslie paused. There was not the slightest stirring in the courtroom. "I told him I could buy one of the jurors," she said.

Brad looked to the jury box in time to see juror 4 turn ashen.

"And what was his response?" asked Brad reluctantly. He was no longer sure he wanted to know. Things were growing more bizarre by the minute.

"He wanted to know which juror," said Leslie. "He said that they already owned one."

"I object," Strobel announced, no longer able to contain himself. "This is blatant hearsay."

"No it's not," countered Brad. "It's an admission of a party opponent. Besides, it's all on tape. I'll have some equipment brought in here and play the tape if I have to."

"There's no need for that at this point," said Ichabod. She seemed anxious to hear the rest of this testimony. "We'll play the tape later. But this witness is entitled to testify from memory about this conversation and the resulting admissions of a party opponent. Objection overruled."

"May I continue?" asked Leslie.

"Proceed," granted the judge.

It seemed to Brad that Ichabod was displaying the slightest hint of a growing respect for this witness. Maybe she liked her bold search for the truth. Maybe she liked the fact that Leslie had done all this behind Brad's back. Maybe she just liked the scenario of a resourceful young woman outfoxing an experienced and powerful man. But whatever was causing her change in mood, Ichabod was plainly fascinated with this testimony.

"Mr. Aberijan told me that they already owned a juror. So he asked me which one I was dealing with to make sure it wasn't the same one."

"To make sure the record is clear," said Brad. "Had you actually talked to any jurors up to this point in time or have you talked to any jurors since?" He held his breath.

"No," said Leslie.

Brad exhaled. "What did you say to Mr. Aberijan?"

"I knew I had to make a quick guess." Leslie turned slightly in her seat and faced the jury head-on. Most of the jurors crossed their arms and gave her a stern look. "Based on blatant body language during the trial, I assumed that juror number 4 was firmly on their side. So I would not name him. Frankly, I assumed that he was the one Ahmed already 'owned.'" She leveled an accusatory gaze at the pale face of Zeke Stein. He had his arms crossed and stared right back.

"The one juror that had been impossible to read throughout the trial—the one who just sat stoically and impassively through everything—was juror number 6. I concluded that if I had noticed, Mr. Aberijan must have noticed too. So it would be believable if I picked juror number 6, so long as he wasn't actually on the take already. That's what I guessed. And Ahmed accepted it." She turned directly to juror number 6. "I'm sorry, sir," she said.

Juror 6 nodded his head ever so slightly, his expression never changing.

Strobel rocketed to his feet. "Objection," he roared. "That is highly improper, and I move for a mistrial."

"Objection sustained," said Ichabod. "Please disregard Ms. Connors' apology. As for the mistrial, I can see why you would want one, but you're not entitled to one."

Something suddenly dawned on Brad.

"Ms. Connors, how did you communicate with Mr. Aberijan on these occasions? I am under the impression that he does not understand a word of English?"

Leslie smiled for the first time since taking the stand. "I thought you'd never ask," she said. "The man speaks almost perfect English. You'll hear it yourself on the tape."

"What else will we hear on the tape?" asked Brad.

"Two other things of importance," noted Leslie calmly. "The first is my reference to a trust document for an account in a Swiss bank. I called this my life insurance policy, but it was really a means to show that Mr. Aberijan was not acting alone. I asked that one hundred million be deposited in a Swiss bank account subject to the terms of a trust agreement that was to be signed by a high-ranking Saudi official other than Mr. Aberijan. The trust document would state that if I died, the executor appointed in my will would investigate my death. If he concluded that I was murdered, the one hundred million would go to Sarah Reed and her children. If he concluded that I died of natural causes, the one hundred million would revert to the nation of Saudi Arabia."

"Amazing," said Brad without thinking. *It truly was a brilliant idea.* "And was this trust agreement ever signed?" he asked.

"Yes. It was delivered to me at the last meeting that I had with Mr. Aberijan, which occurred just last night. Mr. O'Malley should be bringing a copy of it to court in a few minutes. He'll also have a fax showing the balance of the Swiss account with a deposit this morning of one hundred million dollars."

Brad allowed a small smile to crease his lips. *This girl thinks of everything.*

"And the second item of interest?"

"After I left the meeting, Mr. Aberijan had possession of the transmitters, and they were, of course, still transmitting. After he left the courtroom, he called another gentleman and ordered this gentleman to find out who the executor of my will was." She tilted her head sideways as she looked at Brad. *Are you ready for this?* she asked with her eyes. He nodded.

"You will hear Ahmed Aberijan order the murder of both me and my executor within one day after this jury returns a verdict."

A collective gasp filled the courtroom. Reporters, no longer able to contain themselves, scurried for the doors. The remaining spectators all talked at once, and Ichabod had trouble restoring order as she furiously banged her gavel.

"We need some equipment in here to listen to that tape," she barked to her bailiff. *"Now!"*

■ ■ ■

In the excitement swirling around him, Mack Strobel was largely ignored. All of his years of experience had never prepared him for this. He had rapidly absorbed one shocking revelation after another. And now he was about to listen to his client admit to jury tampering and order two murders, all on tape. Any other lawyer would have been packing his bags. But not Mack Strobel. His expression never changed.

"This old dog still has one more trick," he mumbled to himself.

But it would be hard to argue with a tape.

47

N ikki Moreno heard the shot but felt nothing except the exhilaration of her free fall. She had no time to be thankful. In the next instant, she was knifing through the murky depths of the Elizabeth River. The icy water stabbed at her like a million needles and sucked her breath away.

She descended into the depths for what seemed like an eternity, then she gained the presence of mind to flail her arms and legs to reach the surface. She kicked and pulled, kicked and pulled, but still the water overhead was black. Her breath was gone, but she kicked and climbed some more.

Finally...the surface.

She sprang out of the waters gasping for breath, constricted by the cold. She quickly looked up, just in time to see Barnes leaning over the concrete abutment. He was joined by Ahmed, whose gun was pointed at her. She filled her lungs and dove under the water.

The bullet made a short hissing sound as it entered the water. It must have been inches from her head. She had not had a chance to collect much air in her lungs, but she forced herself deeper and began frog kicking toward the concrete pillars just under the bridge. If she could just get to the pillars and slide to the side opposite the men, perhaps she would live.

Her lungs gave out before she felt the pillars. Nikki surfaced quickly, gagging on the salt water, and looked up. Ahmed was almost directly overhead and had anticipated her move. He aimed his gun straight at her head and flashed a wicked smile.

■ ■ ■

Rasheed and Bella were caught in the snarl of the traffic jam. Like the others, they had tried to sneak forward on the shoulders of the roadway, but they had not had much success. Bella began pounding on the steering wheel in frustration. Rasheed looked at her, peered ahead at the traffic, pointed to himself, then pointed ahead on the bridge. He jumped out of the car and sprinted past the stopped traffic.

Bella called after him, but Rasheed never turned around. She almost cursed, and bit her tongue instead. She said a quick prayer, turned on her flashers, grabbed her pistol from her purse, rolled out of the vehicle, and lumbered after Rasheed.

■ ■ ■

Rasheed heard the horns blowing as he ran. He heard shouts in the distance between Barnes and the men in the pickup truck. A few seconds later, he heard the smashing of metal and the breaking of glass. He saw the havoc caused by Nikki's kamikaze maneuver. As he approached the scene, he witnessed Barnes and Ahmed getting out of their car and running toward Nikki. He saw Barnes run ahead and Ahmed crouch. Then he saw Nikki jump.

When they saw Ahmed fire, gawking motorists ducked in their vehicles or jumped behind them for cover. Ahmed ran to the edge of the bridge and leaned over the concrete wall. Barnes stood next to him, also looking over the edge and searching the waters. As he ran, Rasheed saw Ahmed aim and fire a shot at the water below.

A few more steps and Rasheed was rounding the back of Nikki's car, just a few feet from Barnes and Ahmed. The director of the Muttawa raised his gun again and took aim. Rasheed launched himself into a flying tackle, landing his shoulder squarely against Ahmed's broad back. Rasheed's body slammed against the bigger man, jarring lose the gun, sending it tumbling toward Nikki in the river below. The blow also jolted Ahmed and hammered his body against the concrete abutment. Both men fell hard, in a pile, onto the pavement with arms, legs, and torsos intertwined.

■ ■ ■

Ahmed shook Rasheed loose and staggered to his feet. Rasheed got halfway up, still bent at the waist, one hand on his knee. Ahmed stepped toward the smaller man and pounded a vicious forearm into Rasheed's face, knocking him onto his back. Ahmed spit at Rasheed, then turned around to look back over the edge of the bridge.

Nikki was nowhere in sight.

He stared at the water, waiting for her to surface. But there was no sign of her in the water.

Ahmed turned back to Rasheed, who was lying on his back on the pavement, trying to rise, and shaking his head to clear the dizziness. Ahmed stepped forward, practically frothing at the mouth. A powerful kick squarely on Rasheed's jaw would snap the man's neck like a twig.

Other motorists still kept their distance. Barnes stood back as well. He knew there was no way to stop the Right Hand of Mohammed.

"Beg," sneered Ahmed, as he towered over Rasheed. He repeated the command in Arabic.

He waited as Rasheed looked up at him. But this time, there was no fear in Rasheed's eyes. Only contempt.

"Never," Rasheed replied softly in Arabic.

"Beg!" screamed Ahmed, determined to smell the fear before he killed. "Beg like a dog!"

Rasheed stared back in determined silence.

Ahmed flexed every muscle and drew back his powerful leg.

■ ■ ■

"Don't move!" Bella yelled in a shrill, breathless voice. She was still several feet away, huffing and puffing, but she clutched the small Beretta pistol in her hand and pointed it squarely at Ahmed. In all her excitement, she couldn't remember if she had correctly released the safety.

Ahmed relaxed his leg and turned a contemptuous look on Bella. He stared for a second, sizing up the woman, and began to walk slowly toward her. Her hands shook as she tried to remember the shooting lessons she had taken so long ago.

"One more step and I'll blow you away!" she screamed. It was meant to sound tough, but it came out more as a squeal than a command.

Ahmed continued to advance.

"I mean it!" she yelled.

He was less than twenty feet away. A few more steps and he could lunge at her.

She decided to scare him by firing at his feet. Show him that she meant business. She aimed, closed her eyes, and squeezed the trigger.

She also jerked her arm up at the last second.

Bella heard the smack of the bullet, the tearing of flesh, the cracking of bone, and a full-throated yell. She opened her eyes to see Ahmed's right knee buckle. She watched in horror as blood poured through his pant leg and flowed onto the pavement.

She swung the gun toward Barnes, who took a few giant steps back and never took his eyes off Bella. Then her hands began shaking uncontrollably, and she dropped the gun. She collapsed into a heap and sobbed.

■ ■ ■

Rasheed was still woozy but had the presence of mind to grab Bella's gun. He motioned with it for Barnes to stand next to his wounded partner. Then, with the small but lethal Beretta still aimed at the two men, Rasheed slowly circled around them and shuffled over to the edge of the bridge.

While watching his new prisoners, Rasheed leaned slightly out over the concrete abutment and yelled down to the water below.

"Everything is fine!" he screamed in Arabic.

■ ■ ■

In the next second, Nikki poked her head out from behind one of the concrete pillars.

"Everything is fine!" she yelled back in Arabic as she looked in disbelief at the smiling face of Rasheed above. Her lips were going numb as she shivered in the water, but she could hold on for a while longer. She now had hope.

And she could hear the beautiful sound of sirens wailing in the distance.

■ ■ ■

Ichabod and the jurors barely moved as they listened to Ahmed boast on tape, in perfect English, about the juror he "owned." They heard him discuss the terms of payment for knocking Nancy Shelhorse out of the case and for buying a defense verdict. And they stared at the tape player in disbelief, straining to hear Ahmed, as he ordered the murders of Leslie and her executor. It was hard to make out all the words, but a discriminating listener could clearly hear Ahmed pronounce the death sentences.

Ichabod had Brad rewind the tape and replay it three times. The recording changed many things for Brad. He could hear the trembling in Leslie's voice as she tried to act brave in front of Ahmed. He could hear the business-as-usual tone of Ahmed as he ordered the murders. It drove home to him, for the first time, how much Leslie had risked. His thoughts were no longer about *himself*—why didn't she tell *me?* Why did she lie to *me?* His thoughts turned to *her*—the danger *she* was in. The pressure *she* was under. The brilliance of *her* plan.

When he finished playing it the third time, Brad moved the tape into evidence, and Exhibit Number 63 became an official part of the case.

Leslie explained how she and O'Malley prevented Shelhorse's testimony. It was O'Malley, she said, who sent the e-mail from Nikki's computer. And it was O'Malley who deleted a telephone message left by Shelhorse later that day.

With the jury still intently focused on his witness, Brad directed her attention to the prior night and her meeting with Ahmed. He had Leslie describe the meeting and how she had finally obtained the trust agreement signed by the Saudi minister of public safety. Leslie told the jury about her bizarre encounter with Frederick Barnes outside the Marriott.

"What happened after Mr. Barnes left?"

"The valet brought my car around. He slipped me a note when he opened my door."

"From whom?"

"Mr. O'Malley. The note said that listening devices had been placed inside my car and cell phone while I was meeting with Ahmed. The note said to be careful about what I said." She paused, her lips forming a thin and worried line. The events of last night seemed to pain her the most. "When I talked to Mr. O'Malley later that night on the phone, we both made it seem like we were really going to buy a defense verdict, then leave town."

Brad paused for a moment and pondered his next question. Part of him wanted to drag her through last night's confrontation again, ask her to explain one more time why she lied to him, make her realize how much it had hurt him. But another part of him, the part that saw her nervousness under the mask of cool, the part that noticed the red blotches on her neck, the part that *loved* her, wanted to spare her any more pain. She had been through enough. She had done it for him, for the case.

It was no contest.

"Let me direct your attention away from the events of last night," Brad resumed, "and to the issue of the trust agreement."

He carefully studied Leslie's reaction, but instead of relief washing over her face as Brad expected, he watched her countenance fall, the blood instantly draining from her face. It was the same look Brad had seen on the first day of trial, when Leslie told him they had drawn Ichabod as their judge.

■ ■ ■

Leslie happened to be looking toward the back of the courtroom when O'Malley entered. A quick shake of his head told her everything she needed to know. It was O'Malley's job to get a faxed copy of the Swiss account showing the hundred-million-dollar deposit. His dejected look, one Leslie had never seen on his face before, made it obvious that he had failed.

All this work down the tubes. The planning. The risk. Jeopardizing my relationship with Brad. All for naught if I can't prove the money is in the account. What will prevent Strobel from arguing that Ahmed forged the signature and acted alone? The nation of Saudi Arabia will be off the hook.

God, cut me a break. Just once. For Sarah's sake.

O'Malley walked down the aisle, whispered a few words in Brad's ear, then handed Brad two documents. As she watched, the private investigator glumly took a seat in the front row.

Brad placed exhibit stickers on the documents, then looked up at Leslie. She expected panic on his face but saw none. Not even a hint of disappointment. Leslie had seen this look before—the moot court tournament. *Trust me,* he was saying. *Gladly,* she smiled back.

"I'd like to hand you two documents marked for identification," Brad said. "The first is a signed trust agreement, the second is a faxed bank statement showing the balance in a Swiss bank account subject to the trust agreement."

Mack Strobel jumped to his feet. Brad's eyes twinkled. "Objection," he roared, "how can this witness possibly authenticate these documents that were just now handed to Mr. Carson. He hasn't even established if she's seen them before."

Brad spread his palms in protest. "That's because I haven't had a chance."

Judge Baker-Kline looked over her glasses at Leslie. "Didn't you say Mr. Aberijan gave you the signed trust agreement last night?"

"Yes ma'am."

"And this account balance, have you ever seen that before?"

Leslie paused and sighed. For effect. "No, Your Honor," she replied gloomily. "I haven't."

"Then I'll sustain the objection as to the account balance statement and overrule the objection on the signed trust agreement."

"But, Your Honor—" Brad protested.

Has he lost his mind? Leslie wondered.

"Mr. Carson," Ichabod cut him off. "I've ruled."

Brad frowned. "Yes, Your Honor. After the introduction of this exhibit, I'll pass the witness."

■ ■ ■

Brad handed the signed trust agreement to the court clerk. He took his seat and placed the bank account statement, showing that not a dime had reached the Swiss trust account, onto the table in front of him. He casually placed a legal pad on top of it.

Mack Strobel, always the consummate showman, rose slowly and furrowed his brow. He took on a pained expression, as if he had a grave announcement to make about a matter that troubled him greatly.

"Before I begin my cross-examination, I have a motion to make." He shuffled some papers, then looked up at Ichabod. "From the outset of the case, I have doubted whether I could fairly represent both Mr. Aberijan personally and the nation of Saudi Arabia without generating a serious conflict of interest. I warned Mr. Aberijan about this at our very first meeting."

He paused for effect, and Brad rolled his eyes, hoping one of the jurors was watching.

"It has now become clear that I can no longer represent both defendants. I therefore request leave of the court to withdraw as counsel of record for Mr. Aberijan because of an unavoidable conflict of interest. From this point on, I can represent only the nation of Saudi Arabia."

"I can understand why you would want to withdraw as counsel for

Mr. Aberijan," Ichabod commented. "And since he is not here to object, your motion is granted. But it does not mean that this trial will be delayed even one minute so that he can get a new lawyer. Is that clear, Mr. Strobel?"

"Yes, Your Honor, and thank you for your indulgence," Strobel responded. Then he took his place behind the podium and turned to Leslie.

"Did you ever speak with the Saudi Arabian minister of public safety about this case?"

"No."

"Or anyone else from Saudi Arabia for that matter, other than Mr. Aberijan?"

"Yes, I spoke to Mr. el Khamin."

"Anyone other than Mr. el Khamin? What I mean is, did you ever speak with officials from the Saudi Arabian government?"

"No."

"And have you even seen an authentic signature of the minister of public safety, to compare with the purported signature on the document provided by Mr. Aberijan?"

"No."

Strobel nodded solemnly, as if he had just elicited a stunning admission.

"Then isn't it possible that the same Ahmed Aberijan whom we just heard on the tape casually order the deaths of two people and talk about bribing jurors, isn't it just possible that this deceitful man might have forged the signature of the minister of public safety? Couldn't this all just be a fraud perpetrated by Mr. Aberijan himself, with absolutely no authority or sanction from the Saudi government?"

It doesn't take Strobel long to turn on a former client, Brad thought.

"No, I don't believe that's possible." Leslie said confidently.

"Not even *possible?*" asked Strobel, emphasizing the last word and raising his eyebrows. "Why not?"

"Because I didn't believe then, and I don't believe now," answered Leslie coolly, "that Mr. Aberijan had access to a hundred million dollars of his own. I believe that Mr. Aberijan's higher-ups are very much aware of what he did to Charles Reed and very much involved in this case. Where else could money for this trust account come from? Your client, the nation of Saudi Arabia, is every bit as much to blame as Mr. Aberijan."

"But you have no proof that any money is sitting in that Swiss account. Do you Ms. Connors?"

Brad couldn't help but flinch. He noticed Leslie quickly scratch at the base of her neck. Then calmly, precisely, she steadied her gaze. "Mr. O'Malley is sitting right there in the first row, sir. Why don't you call him to the stand and ask him?"

Beautiful.

Brad glanced at Strobel and, for the first time in the case, saw something other than confidence in the man's eyes. Strobel had been hit with so much, so fast, that he never saw that answer coming. It was a rookie error, asking a question like that. Now Brad could tell that Strobel was instantly recalculating the case, assessing the danger of this witness, forming the desire to get done with this cross-examination quickly and gracefully—before more damage could be done.

"And even though you never talked to anyone, never met anyone, and never communicated with anyone from the nation of Saudi Arabia about this case, except for Mr. Aberijan himself, you somehow think that the nation of Saudi Arabia is responsible for Mr. Aberijan's conduct?"

"That's absolutely right," said Leslie.

"Then if *that's* plaintiff's case," Strobel noted derisively, "I renew my motion for a directed verdict on behalf of the nation of Saudi Arabia. The plaintiff has no proof whatsoever that Mr. Aberijan did not simply forge the signature of a Saudi official and embezzle the money for the trust account himself."

Before Brad could speak in opposition, Ichabod responded. "Isn't that a motion that should be more properly considered outside the presence of the jury?"

"Absolutely, Your Honor," Strobel replied.

"Then the witness may step down. Bailiff, please excuse the jury for a few moments so I can announce my ruling," she ordered.

Leslie breathed a huge sigh of relief, held her head high, and stepped down from the witness box. As she walked past the counsel table, most eyes in the courtroom were on the jury members, particularly juror number 4, as they shuffled out of the box. Brad took advantage of this momentary distraction and grabbed Leslie's hand as she passed. He pulled her next to him and whispered in her ear.

"Does the witness have plans for this evening?" he asked.

Leslie placed a hand on his shoulder and whispered. "Spending time with my former co-counsel, if he'll let me."

She pulled back, but her look lingered. He winked, and she nodded, then thrust her chin out and walked elegantly down the aisle, taking a seat in the back of the courtroom.

■ ■ ■

Within minutes, the jury had exited, and all eyes turned to Judge Cynthia Baker-Kline.

"Do you have any evidence of your own, Mr. Strobel, any live witnesses or documentary evidence that would suggest this trust agreement signature is a fraud?" she asked.

"Not at this time," answered Strobel. "But if we could have a twenty-four hour continuance—"

"Nonsense," interrupted Ichabod. "We've been doing nothing but continuing and delaying this case since we started. Either put up or shut up." She knew her comment was rude, almost childish. But she had heard enough about continuances and delays. She glanced toward Brad Carson, who had folded his arms and leaned back in his chair, apparently enjoying the sight of somebody else getting chewed out for a change.

"Mr. Carson," Ichabod snarled. Brad practically jumped out of his seat. "Do you have a motion to make?"

"Um, yes, Your Honor," he stuttered, obviously unaware of what she meant. Then a look of recognition gleamed in his eyes, followed by a look of skepticism and a look of hope. It was almost as if he didn't trust her, or couldn't believe what he thought he was hearing.

Finally, he cleared his throat. "We also move for a directed verdict, but in favor of the plaintiff, not the defendant."

"Thank you, counsel," Ichabod said. "You may both be seated."

The judge intended to savor this moment of high drama in the courtroom as she considered her ruling. She jotted a few notes down on her legal pad —"2% milk, English muffins, laundry detergent, chips" —keenly aware that every eye was watching every scratch of her pen.

She thought about Win Mackenzie, smugly perched in the front row, convinced that she would never do anything to jeopardize her chances for an appellate court nomination. She allowed herself to dwell just briefly on the years of hard work—the drug cases, the asbestos cases, the pure junk that marched through her courtroom every day. How sweet it would be to sit on the court of appeals and hear only the interesting cases being argued by top-flight lawyers. One step below the Supremes!

She glanced up from her scribbling and looked straight into the eyes of Win Mackenzie. Confident eyes. Presumptuous eyes. He knew how badly she wanted it.

"Gentlemen, I have never, in all my years on the bench, seen a case where both sides showed such little respect for the judicial system." She knew vintage scolding was her strong suit. "Plaintiff's counsel has tried every trick in the book to goad me into losing my composure so he can have a mistrial. At the same time, his co-counsel has breached the professional rules of responsibility for lawyers and tape-recorded a conversation with an adverse party in the case. Her conduct was clever, and her plan was bold, but it hardly comported with model conduct for an officer of the court."

Ichabod glared at Brad. She looked for Leslie and spotted her in the back. Leslie's face was bright red.

"On the other hand, her plan did shine much light on some of the most reprehensible conduct I have ever witnessed in all my years on the bench. Suffice it to say there is clear and convincing evidence that the defendant will do whatever it takes to win, including bribing jurors and intimidating witnesses."

Ichabod paused again for effect and watched as Leslie's face regained some of its natural color.

"After what I have heard today, I can only conclude that this jury panel is so tainted, including at least one member who has been bribed, and possibly more, that the panel itself is of no further use in this case. If I allowed this jury to decide the case, their verdict would surely get reversed on appeal, and we would all be right back here all over again.

"But fortunately, we have available a procedural mechanism called a directed verdict. Any trial judge may dismiss a jury and decide the case herself if she is convinced that no reasonable jury could ever render a verdict different from the one she is prepared to render. After hearing the testimony of Ms. Connors, whom I find to be very credible"— another glance at Leslie, this time accompanied by the slightest hint of a smile—"and after hearing the recording of Mr. Aberijan, and after considering the signed trust agreement introduced into evidence, I have concluded that a reasonable jury could only decide this case one way."

Ichabod stared sternly at Brad Carson through the glasses perched on the end of her long nose. She knew she was about to make him a multimillionaire, and she hated every second of it. But she also thought about Sarah Reed and her children. And she thought about her own immense and growing disdain for Ahmed Aberijan. And she knew in her heart that justice demanded this verdict.

She shifted her gaze to Winsted Mackenzie. Her one satisfaction would be watching the look on his face as she forfeited her career for the sake of justice.

"Accordingly, I am hereby *denying* defendant's motion for a directed verdict and *granting* plaintiff's motion for a directed verdict against both Mr. Aberijan *and* the nation of Saudi Arabia."

Mackenzie's head shot back, his eyes wide.

"I am setting the damages at nine hundred thousand dollars for compensatory damages and *fifty million* in punitive damages."

■   ■   ■

Brad could not breathe; the ruling sucked the air right out of him. He was not alone. For a fleeting moment, the courtroom was dead silent, *stunned* by a judge who had taken justice into her own hands, dispensed with closing arguments and jury deliberations, and brought this case to a swift and merciful close. The words sunk in. Brad caught his breath.

And pandemonium broke lose.

Sarah reached over and hugged Brad's neck. Reporters rushed for the exit. Excited spectators raised a clamor, struggling to be heard. And the defense team slumped back in their chairs, unable even to scribble the enormous number on their legal pads. All the while, as the noise crescendoed, Ichabod furiously banged her gavel.

After a few minutes, the noise abated on its own. The judge took advantage of the lull to issue her last speech.

"I have issued a bench warrant for Mr. Aberijan. When he is found, assuming that he has not escaped this country's jurisdiction, I want him brought back into *my court* to personally answer to *me*. I expect the assistant district attorney will also be issuing indictments against him. Because those indictments arise out of this trial, I am assigning Mr. Aberijan's criminal case to my docket so that I can preside over that matter as well. Is that clear, Ms. Bennett?"

Bennett stood and assured the court that she understood.

"Good," said Ichabod. "And one more thing, Ms. Bennett."

"Yes, Your Honor?"

"I had better have indictments on my docket within a week for any jury members who accepted a bribe or violated their oath in any way. Is that also clear?"

"We've already issued subpoenas for every juror's bank records, Your Honor."

"Very well."

It was a well-known tradition in the Eastern District of Virginia federal court for the judges to conclude cases by telling the lawyers, in front of their clients, what kind of service they had provided to their clients. Even Ichabod was duty bound by this tradition. She turned first to Mack Strobel.

"Mr. Strobel, as usual, you have tried an exemplary case. I have no reason to believe that you were engaged in or responsible for any of your former client's misconduct. You were thrown some curves in this case that no one could have foreseen, and you handled them with tact and diplomacy. If, God forbid, I am ever in need of legal services for a high-stakes trial, I think I would give you a call."

"Thank you, Your Honor," replied a pale Mack Strobel. Brad could barely hear his baritone voice.

"And Mr. Carson," she said, turning to Brad. "While I do not sanction your occasional theatrics and unorthodox conduct in the courtroom, I will say that you are an effective advocate and a tenacious trial lawyer. Congratulations."

It was a backhanded compliment, and Brad knew it was the best he could ever hope for from her. It didn't bother him. He knew it was unprofessional, but he couldn't wipe a silly grin off his face. He had been wearing it since Ichabod announced her verdict.

"Thank you, Your Honor," he said sincerely. Fifty million could change his mind about someone in a hurry. "And I want to thank the court for handling this difficult case fairly and evenhandedly in the midst of some very tense moments."

Ichabod looked down again at Brad, one last time, over her annoying wire-rimmed glasses. She gave him the familiar scowl.

"That's kind of you, Mr. Carson, but also easy to say when you've just won a big case. I would love to hear that same kind of comment from you sometime after you have just lost a case in my court."

Brad's grin disappeared.

He wanted to respond in the worst kind of way. Her comment was unfair and untrue. He got along with fair-minded judges, he would tell her, but not with tyrants. She needed to learn how to take a compliment, he would tell her, because with her personality, they would be few and far between. He had a million things to tell her, but he bit his tongue and said nothing. After all, this was federal court, and Brad knew the unwritten rules. One of them was that a federal court judge always has the last word.

"Case adjourned," said Ichabod, striking her gavel.

Epilogue

Brad's team members accomplished little in the days immediately following the directed verdict. They were too busy granting interviews, basking in the limelight, and dreaming about ways to spend their money. Not until Friday of that week did the office return to any semblance of normalcy. Even Bella, always the workhorse, found it hard to get motivated.

She arrived at the office at 9:15 and was not surprised to be the first one there. She turned on the lights, made some coffee, and resisted the urge to grab a smoke. It was her third day of trying to quit. The prior two had ended in glorious flame-outs right after lunch.

She settled in at the front desk and let the phone ring while she finished an intriguing novel about a dreamy hunk named Brandon. She didn't feel the least bit guilty. Brad had told everyone to take the week off.

At 10:30, Nikki waltzed through the door and acted surprised to see Bella.

"Couldn't stay away," she shrugged.

"Me either," said Bella. She held up a check. "The Johnson money came in today."

"Better check to make sure it doesn't have an extra million bucks," Nikki said on her way through the reception area. "I'd get fired for sure then."

Bella felt the heat rising in her cheeks. Typical Nikki. You try to be nice; you get rewarded with sarcasm. She would tell Nikki a thing or two. She stood, scowled…then sat back down and started counting. She made it to ten, then twenty…fifty…a hundred. She could feel herself calming down.

She needed a Camel.

She stood again, her body screaming for a quick trip to the kitchen. *It would calm my nerves. I could finish the book. Nikki wasn't going anywhere.*

Instead, she turned down the hallway and headed for Nikki's office. She stood in the doorway and waited for her to look up.

"Um…" Bella rubbed her hands together. She had practiced this speech so many times. *How did it start again?*

"What's up?" Nikki asked. It was more of a "why don't you hurry up and say what's on your mind" tone than it was a question.

"Well," Bella said, looking at her hands, "I've tried t-to…um, come down and say this about a hundred times in the last few weeks, b-but I… I dunno…"

Nikki put down her pen and gave Bella her undivided attention. "Tried to say what?"

Okay. There's no easy way to do this. Just blurt it out. "I'm sorry, Nikki." She looked up and saw the blank look on Nikki's face. "That's it… I've just been meaning to apologize for the way…for the way I've treated you…" She paused and shrugged. *This was really starting to seem like a dumb idea, even if it was Sarah's.* "From day one."

That was it. Her whole speech. She glanced again at Nikki, expecting…well, truthfully, she didn't know what to expect.

"Don't worry about it," shrugged Nikki.

That's all! No "Gee, I'm sorry too." No "Man, that's really big of you, Bella." No "Great, let's be friends now." Just a simple "Don't worry about it" and a blank stare. After all I put myself through, that's the best she can offer?

A crestfallen Bella turned to walk out the door. There was no sense pushing this any further. She had tried, given it her best. Some things just weren't meant to be. She would tell Sarah that confession and reconciliation were highly overrated.

"Wait," called Nikki. Bella turned back around and saw Nikki coming out from behind her desk. "Can you give me a hand for a minute?"

"Huh?"

Nikki pointed to the pictures hanging on her wall. "You know...getting rid of these things. It's starting to feel like an aquarium in here."

■ ■ ■

It was Brad's idea to celebrate at the Lynnhaven Mariner. He would never forget the first time he and Leslie came to this place. It seemed like an eternity ago. She had charmed him with her beauty and poise. He had regaled her with his stories of the law. And this was the spot where the *Reed* case was born, where Brad and Leslie decided to make new law.

But that was months earlier, and their naive idealism about the case had been shattered by the emotional scars of battle. The beautiful spring day on which they had launched their plan had yielded to this cold and drizzly November day that forced them to enjoy lunch inside rather than on the deck.

It was Sunday afternoon, six days after the directed verdict. The fickle media attention, so white-hot intense in the days immediately following the latest trial of the century, had moved on to more important matters.

Ahmed and Barnes were in custody. Leslie was preparing to go back to school in January and finish her degree. Brad and Sarah were now household names.

Brad had grabbed the brass ring, won his case of national import, and realized that there was no lasting satisfaction in such an accomplishment. One week later, the interviews were over, and the ecstasy was gone. Only the relationships remained. From Leslie, he was learning each day to treasure a woman who understood him and accepted him for who he was. From Sarah, he had witnessed the strength of a personal relationship with God, through his Son Jesus Christ. Brad wasn't ready to jump yet; all of this religious stuff was still very new to him. But he could not deny the comfort and contentment that both Sarah and Bella had found in their faith. He had heard Bella speak of her conversion experience. He had seen her change. And now he wondered if it could happen to him.

It was, to Brad's way of thinking, an intensely private matter, and one he was not yet ready to discuss even with Leslie. Right now, as they finished their seafood feast, he had things of a more immediate concern on his agenda.

"So what are your plans now?" He was playing with the cheesecake Leslie had forced him to order. She seemed determined to make him regain ten pounds in one week. But, as usual, she had skipped dessert herself and was nursing a cappuccino.

"I guess going back to school will seem pretty tame after this," she said, playing with her drink. "But it'd be nice to actually have a law license if I intend to practice law."

"What's our future, Leslie?" he asked bluntly, embarrassed at himself even as the question crossed his lips. "What about us?"

Leslie paused before responding, and Brad looked down at his plate, pushing his cheesecake around with a fork. He loved her so much he was afraid to hear the answer.

"I could use a good tutor, if that's what you mean," Leslie quipped. "Especially in my legal ethics class. As you know, that's not exactly my strong suit."

Brad put down his fork and looked into her beautiful blue eyes. He reached out his hand without speaking, and she placed hers in it.

"I'm serious, Leslie," he was almost pleading. "We've been great together, but was it all the result of the pressure and the case, or is there something special between us? Something we can build on?"

He hesitated. *Was it too much too fast? Would he scare her away and ruin the only part of his life that really mattered?* His instincts told him to go for it. Now was the time. He would never forgive himself if he didn't.

"I love you, Leslie Connors," he said softly. "And I'll move heaven and earth to make it work for us." He squeezed her hand, held his breath, and waited.

She stared at their hands. "I promised myself after Bill died that I would never again love another man like I loved him. I thought it would be disloyal," she stopped, blinked a few times, then continued, "and it hurt so much when I lost him." She looked up at Brad with glistening eyes. The world around them came to a stop.

"Then you came along and had the audacity to sweep me off my feet." A small smile. "I fought it as hard as I could, for as long as I could. But something about you and about this case—"

"Sir," said their smiling young waitress with the bleached-blond hair, oblivious to the moment she was destroying, "I have some good news for you."

Brad didn't take his eyes from Leslie. He totally ignored the waitress, pretending she didn't exist. But Leslie cut her gaze away from Brad and up at the perky intruder.

"That's great," Leslie said, flashing her easy, sparkling smile. She brushed a tear from her eye with her free hand. "We're always in the market for some good news."

"That man in the corner has taken care of your bill," the proud waitress said and, to Brad's surprise, pointed to a smiling Mack Strobel, who sat with some men Brad did not recognize. He gave them a quick wave.

"That man?" said Leslie incredulously. "Are you sure?"

"Yes ma'am," said the blond. "He said to tell you it was the least he could do."

"Wow," said Leslie. She and Brad unclasped their hands, and both nodded back at their nemesis.

"Did he take care of your tip too?" Brad asked the waitress, who was still conspicuously hanging around.

"Oh, yes sir," she replied enthusiastically. "He sure did."

Brad felt the need to thank Strobel. Leslie followed at his shoulder.

Mack stood and offered his hand. His eyes were glazed, and he had a smile pasted on his lips.

"Bradley!" he said warmly and loudly.

Brad winced but was determined to be gracious. "Thanks for lunch, Mack. You didn't have to do that."

Strobel released Brad's hand and extended the same courtesy to Leslie.

"As I told your waitress, it's the least I can do," Mack said smiling. "You've already helped me have one of my best billable years ever, and I haven't even started on my appeal yet."

Strobel was talking loud enough so that several of the patrons stopped eating and began staring.

"You can chase those old rabbits by my door anytime you want," continued Mack. "In fact, you keep bringing me juicy cases like that one, I might have my firm take out keyman insurance on you. It's plaintiff's lawyers like you who keep old hacks like me in business."

Brad grinned and tilted his head. He didn't quite know what to make of the old man.

"You tried a great case," said Brad.

"As did you, young man," Strobel said loudly. "I just try to give my clients their money's worth."

"They got every penny's worth from you," Brad replied earnestly.

Strobel turned to Leslie. "And as for you, when you get out of William and Mary and want to start a real international law practice, I've got an office right next to mine with your name on it."

Leslie narrowed her eyes, and Brad sensed that she was ready to tell him what she thought of that offer. But Strobel didn't pause long enough to give her the chance.

"I know the fringe benefits might not be as good as Carson & Associates," he continued with a wink, "but at least you wouldn't have to worry about any antinepotism policy."

He slapped Brad on the back. Brad wondered how many drinks Strobel had knocked down at lunch.

"I'll keep that in mind," Leslie said without conviction.

"Do that," Strobel grinned. He was rocking back and forth, barely maintaining his balance.

"Well," Brad said as he started to move away, realizing how little he had in common with Mack, "gotta run. Take care of yourself. And much as it helps your billable hours, I hope I don't see you in court again any time soon. There are much easier defense lawyers out there."

"I'll take that as a compliment," grinned Strobel. "And you probably won't be seeing me in court for a while anyway. I'll be spending the next few months jousting with the district attorney. Can you believe, after everything that happened, Aberijan retained me to handle his criminal case?"

"And you took it?" cried Leslie, wide-eyed in utter disbelief.

"It was all part of the master plan," Strobel said, grabbing the back of the chair and steadying himself. "All in a day's work. He pays the retainer. I take the case. And I think we've got a pretty good argument on entrapment."

Brad noticed the blood rising in Leslie's face. He grabbed her gently by the arm and steered her away.

"And we wonder why lawyers have a bad name," Leslie murmured under her breath as they headed toward the coat rack.

Brad enjoyed helping her into her overcoat and kept his arm around her shoulder as they walked toward the door. Like a refined gentleman, he held the door open for her and for another couple on their way in. The cold November wind blasted his face as he stepped outside. He used it as an excuse to pull Leslie close.

They walked around the corner of the building to where Brad had parked his jeep. Leslie seemed agitated by Strobel's comments.

"Entrapment?" she asked.

"Fat chance," replied Brad confidently. "Entrapment only works if the government entices you into doing something you wouldn't otherwise do. And since Aberijan had already bribed a juror before you ever dealt with him, how could he make that argument? Plus, nobody enticed Aberijan to order a hit on you and O'Malley. He did that entirely on his own."

"What about the appeal of the civil case?" Leslie asked. "Does he stand a chance?"

"I don't think so," Brad replied without hesitation. "You were a pretty convincing witness with some pretty damaging evidence. He may delay it for a while, but he'll pay. And we can afford to wait now that we have the settlement check from Johnson. In the meantime, the phones are ringing off the hook with new clients. It's nice being famous."

Leslie put her arm around his waist. Brad's confidence seemed to reassure her and put her mind at ease.

But his mind was not, and it had nothing to do with the case. It had taken all his nerve, but he had said it. He had shared his feelings, told her that he loved her, and waited to hear her say it in return. Then the moment was lost to Mack Strobel, almost as if Strobel had planned the whole frustrating thing.

"Brad!" she yelled and pointed toward his Jeep. He jerked his head up just in time to see it on the business end of a tow truck heading out of the parking lot and onto the highway.

Brad sprinted across the parking lot to catch the driver before he made the turn.

"Hey!" he yelled and ran faster. The tow truck was waiting for a break in traffic, and Brad had about fifty yards to go. "Hey! That's my car! It's a mistake! I'm a lawyer! I'll sue!"

Brad caught the eyes of the tow-truck driver as he looked in his mirror then back to the highway. Brad was sprinting hard, closing on the truck. Ten yards to go…a small break in traffic…a spinning of truck tires on loose gravel…rocks and sand kicking up toward Brad…and the tow truck was on his way.

Another day, another repo.

"Ugh!" Brad threw up his hands, then leaned forward on his knees, catching his breath.

"This stinks!" he yelled in frustration. He kicked at the gravel. He had been looking forward to spending the day with Leslie: a romantic drive across the Chesapeake Bay Bridge Tunnel and some time together on the secluded eastern shore. *And now this.* Stuck in a parking lot with no wheels, and a hard northeastern wind blowing in a storm.

Leslie walked toward him, smiling. "Maybe we should call Bella," she teased.

"I'm calling a cab," he said. He started walking around Leslie, who had stationed herself between him and the restaurant. "And since my cell phone's in the Jeep, I've got to do it from a lousy pay phone."

As a frustrated Brad walked by, Leslie grabbed his arm, pulled him toward her, stood on her toes, and attacked him with a kiss. He closed his eyes and forgot about the weather, the Jeep, Strobel, and the pay phone. For the first time since they met, he could now focus entirely on Leslie, freed from the pressures of the case, untold secrets, and unspoken feelings. Freed from wondering whether she felt the same way he did.

And when their lips finally parted, they still embraced, her head on his shoulder, his arms gently and tenderly holding her close. They stood there in silence for a moment, then she turned her head and whispered softly and confidently in his ear.

"I love you too, Brad Carson."